EARTHBLOOD
& OTHER STORIES

KEITH LAUMER
AND
ROSEL GEORGE BROWN

EDITED BY
ERIC FLINT

D1012789

EARTHBLOOD & OTHER STORIES

Acknowledgments
Earthblood was first published as a serialized story in If, April-July, 1966.
It was subsequently reissued as a novel by Doubleday in 1966.
"The Long Remembered Thunder" was first published in *Worlds of Tomorrow* in April, 1963.
"The Other Sky" was first published in Worlds of Tomorrow in April, 1963.
"The Soul Buyer" was first published under the title "The Further Sky" in *Amazing* in December, 1964.
"Save Your Confederate Money, Boys" was first published in Fantastic Universe in November, 1959.
"Flower Arrangement" was first published in Galaxy in December, 1959.
"Fruiting Body" was first published in *The Magazine of Fantasy* and *Science Fiction* in August, 1962.
"Visiting Professor" was first published in *Fantastic* in February, 1961.
"Car Pool" was first published in If in July, 1959.
"And a Tooth" was first published in *Fantastic* in August, 1962.

A Baen Book

Baen Publishing Enterprises
P.O. Box 1403
Riverdale, NY 10471
www.baen.com

ISBN: 978-1-4516-3820-2

Cover art by Bob Eggleton

First Baen paperback printing, February 2012

Distributed by Simon & Schuster
1230 Avenue of the Americas
New York, NY 10020

Library of Congress Cataloging-in-Publication Data: 2007038971

Printed in the United States of America

10 9 8 7 6 5 4 3 2 1

⚹ WHEN IN DOUBT—ATTACK ⚹

"Blast us out of here, fast," a heavy voice growled. Roan shook himself, forced his eyes to focus on the lifeboat's control panel. As in a dream, his hands went out, threw levers, punched keys. The screens glowed into life. Against the black of space, the long shape of the immense Niss war vessel glowed, the enemy ship's bulk blotting out the stars as Roan thrust home the main drive control.

Roan slumped in the padded seat, let his hands fall from the controls. "We're clear of the ship," he said. Behind him, the crew members began arguing about the next move. Scuffling started, was choked off by the sheer cramping of the confining space of the little boat.

Roan stood, turned on the men. "All right," he roared—an astonishing shout that cut through the hubbub like a whiplash through cotton cloth. "You can belay all this gab about who's in charge! I am! If you boneheads can stop squabbling long enough to let a few facts into your skull, you'll realize we're in trouble—bad trouble! There are forty of us, crowded into a boat designed for thirty! We've got enough food for a few months, maybe, but our air and water recyclers are going to be overloaded. And you can forget about getting to the nearest planet; it's nine months away."

"We'll die aboard this can," a shrill cry came.

"We can't make planetfall," Roan's voice blanketed the others. "But we've got our firepower intact. And there's food, water, fuel, and air just a few miles away . . ." He stepped aside, pointed to the forward screen, where the Niss ship swelled now to giant size.

"What do you mean?" a one-eyed crewman growled. "You're asking—"

"I'm asking nothing," Roan said harshly. "I'm telling you we're going in to attack the Niss ship."

Baen Books by Keith Laumer

*

edited by Eric Flint:

Retief!
Odyssey
Keith Laumer: The Lighter Side
A Plague of Demons & Other Stories
Future Imperfect
Legions of Space
Imperium
The Universe Twister
Earthblood & Other Stories (with Rosel George Brown)

*

The Bolo Series

The Compleat Bolo by Keith Laumer

*

Created by Keith Laumer:

Honor of the Regiment
The Triumphant by David Weber & Linda Evans
The Unconquerable
Last Stand
Old Guard
Cold Steel
Bolo Brigade by William H. Keith, Jr.
Bolo Rising by William H. Keith, Jr.
Bolo Strike by William H. Keith, Jr.
Bolo! by David Weber
The Road to Damascus by John Ringo & Linda Evans
Old Soldiers by David Weber
The Best of the Bolos: Their Finest Hour

To purchase these and all other Baen Book titles in e-book format,
please go to www.baen.com.

EARTHBLOOD
& OTHER STORIES

TABLE OF CONTENTS

✳PART I✳
EARTHBLOOD

KEITH LAUMER
AND
ROSEL GEORGE BROWN

PROLOGUE

The sign scabbed to the dog-yellow wall read:

**FOR SALE—VIABLE HUMAN EMBRYOS
GENUINE TERRESTRIAL STRAIN**

"This is the place, Bella," Raff Cornay said. "By God, we're a long way from home."

Bella smiled up at him and bit at her dyed lips. Having them dyed hadn't really made her look twenty years younger—or even a year younger. She moved closer to his side, put lean, grayish fingers on his thick, brown arm, looking up the dark ravine of the stairway.

"Raff, it's so…" she started, and then left it, because when you've been married twenty years all those words aren't necessary.

Raff hitched at the harness that crossed his heavy, rounded shoulders, brushed with a finger the comforting bulge of the short-barreled power pistol.

"We'll be all right, Bella." He patted her thin hand, moved ahead of her to the high, narrow steps, worn into hollows pocketing oily puddles. The heat and sounds of the plaza faded as they climbed through layered odors of

3

decay and alien cookery, passed a landing railed with twisted iron, reached a towering, narrow doorway hung with a dirt-glazed beaded arras that clashed softly as Raff held it aside.

There was a leathery rustle, a heavy thump, the clack of clawed feet. An enormously tall, stooped figure in ornately decorated straps and bangles minced forward from yellowish gloom, ruffling molting plumage. It settled itself on a tall stool, clattering stiff, flightless feathers, blinking translucent eyelids from Raff to Bella.

"What do you want?" the Rheops chirped. "There is no charity here."

"There's a lady here'd like to sit down too, maybe," Raff said sharply.

"Then sit."

Raff looked around. There was no other chair. He looked at the proprietor, eyeing the red, leathery neck, the tarnished beak.

"I never knew one like you before," he said. "What are you, you don't know how to treat a human lady?"

"Human?" The alien clacked its beak contemptuously, staring at Bella's gray Yill skin.

"Don't, Raff." Bella put her hand on his arm. "We don't care nothing about him. All we want's the baby." Through the ill-fitting youth suit he had bought for the trip, she could feel him forcing himself not to care. Maybe he was too old for the legal adoption agency, but he was as good as any man a hundred years younger.

"We've got money," Raff said tightly. "We're here on business."

The big eyes blinked at him. "How much money?"

"Well—almost five hundred credits."

The tall creature on the stool closed its eyes, opened them again. "I can offer you something in a sturdy mute, guaranteed I.Q. of 40 . . ."

"No," Raff and Bella said together. "No defective stock," Raff went on. "Your sign down on the square said Genuine Terry Strain."

"Too much intellect in a slave is undesirable. Now, this line of stock . . ."

"You think we'd make a slave of a human child?" Raff snapped. "Can't you see we're Terries—Terry stock, anyway," he added, as the round eyes flicked over him, then Bella. She stirred and wrapped her cloak closer.

The dealer clacked its beak contemptuously. "Five hundred credits—and for this, I should produce perhaps a conquistador, complete with Sc.D. certificate?"

"Just an ordinary boy," Raff said. "Just so he's normal. Earth normal. We don't mind if he's maybe color blind—"

The dealer cocked its head, eyed Raff. "What kind of citizenship do you have?"

"What? Why, we're Freeholders, from Granfont."

"You have papers?"

"Sure. Otherwise we'd never . . ."

The dealer half turned, raised its voice in a sharp cry. A small slave in trailing rags came in from a side room.

"Bring benches for my valued customers—and brandy. The Fleon, '49." It turned back to Raff, its hooded eyes sharp and interested now. "A happy blending of rain, sun, sulphur, and fungi . . ."

"We don't need the buildup," Raff said. "We didn't

come here to socialize . . ." He stopped. It wasn't a thing you could put words to. *We came to buy a human child . . . to buy a son . . .*

"Ah, but I like people with resources. I confide in them." The dealer was beaming owlishly now. "You wish an heir. I understand. You have come at a fortunate time. I can offer a most exceptional embryo—a son fit for an emperor."

"We're not emperors," Raff said. "Just plain folks. We want a plain Terry boy . . . "

"So." The dealer ruffled limp shoulder plumes indifferently, its expression abruptly cold again. "If you want to rear inferior stock, I can sell you something cheap—"

"Good. How much?" Raff rose, resting his hand on his credit coder.

"Wait!" Bella cried. "I want to know what he means. What's the . . . the other kind you was talking about?" She pulled Raff back into his chair as the slave returned with a tray bearing a clay pot and bell-shaped glasses.

The dealer placed spidery, plucked-chicken fingers together, waiting while the slave poured and withdrew. It cocked an eye at Bella.

"As it happens, I am in a position to offer top price for freehold citizenships—"

"Are you crazy?" Raff started. "How'd we ever get back—"

Bella picked up a glass and said, "Wait, Raff." She made a great thing of sipping the brandy, making it a compliment.

"Sell our citizenships!" Raff snorted. "It takes us for ignorant rubes, Bella."

The Rheops hunched on its stool, fragile feathers raised in a halo around its head, eyes on Bella now.

"I happen, at this moment, to have in my tanks," it said with impressive gravity, "a prime-quality fetus intended for the personal service of—a most high official. A magnificent blastophere, large, vigorous, and of a superior intellectual potentiality."

"What's wrong with it, this high official didn't take delivery?" Raff asked bluntly.

The round eyes blinked. "Alas, the Shah is . . . er . . . dead—together with his heirs and assigns. One of these annoying uprisings of the rabble. By great good luck, an agent of mine— But no matter. I lost two valuable servants in the acquisition of this prize, which now, frankly, must be transferred soon to a suitable artificial placenta, or be lost. I confide this in you, you see."

"This is just sales talk, Bella," Raff said. "To build up the price."

"A rustic's shrewdness is the merchant's joy," the dealer quoted sharply. It raised its head and shrilled for the slave again, chirped instructions. Raff and Bella waited. The slave returned, toiling under a small, glittering, stone-encrusted box. At a sign from the dealer, it handed the casket to Raff. He took it; his hands sagged under the unexpected weight.

"This golden incubator, set with diamonds, awaited the favored tot; now heavy-footed bucolics haggle for his destiny. The price is two thousand credits—or two freehold citizenships."

"That's twice the going black-market price," Raff said weakly, overwhelmed by the box and what was in it.

"You're not bargaining for black-market goods now. I'm a legitimate trader, licensed by the Sodomate!"

"I'll give you one citizenship," Raff said. "Mine. I can earn another with a few years' work."

The dealer snapped horny lips together. "I'd decant this jewel among lads into the hive sewers before I'd cut my price a demi-chit! The descendant of kings deserves no less."

"Raff . . . " Bella said, appeal in her voice.

"How do we know he's telling the truth, Bella?"

"I have a license to protect, outlander," the tall creature said. "You think I'd risk my reputation for your paltry custom? The Shah paid fifty thousand Galactic credits—in rhodium ingots—"

"But if you don't sell it quick—"

"I've told you my price. Take it or leave it—and then get out!"

"Well . . . " Raff hesitated.

"We'll take it," Bella said.

They moved through the noise of the plaza, Raff leading the way among hawkers' stalls, Bella clutching a two-inch glass cylinder to her lean chest. Yellow dust swirled, stirred by a fitful desert wind. The second sun was low in a bronze-black sky.

"We shouldn't have spent all that credit," Raff said. "How're we going to get back, Bella?"

"We'll find a way," Bella said. "But first, we got to find a Man doctor."

Raff halted. "Bella—you ain't coming down sick?"

"We got to have the baby implanted—right away, Raff."

"Bella, you know we can't afford that now. We'll wait till we're back on Granfont, like we planned—"

"We thought we'd have time, Raff—but we don't. He'd never have sold so cheap if time hadn't been short—awful short."

"But we were going to use Len's stock brooder. Where'd we ever find a mammal brooder here? And we'd have to stay nine months—"

"We won't have to stay, Raff. I'll have the baby implanted—in me."

Raff stared at her. "Bella—you sure? I mean, could you . . . could it . . . ?"

She nodded. "I asked Doctor about it once—a long time ago. He said—first he took a lot of tests—and then he said I could."

"But, Bella, you're . . . you're not . . . "

"He said I could—even if I'm not human." Her vertical-slitted eyes were bright in her still piquant face. "I'll be the mother of our son, Raff. He'll be our human boy, born to me . . . "

Beside Bella, Raff raised his head suddenly. He moved closer to Bella, put a protective arm around her.

"What is it, Raff?"

"Bella—somebody's following us."

"Following . . . why?"

"I don't know. Give me the boy. And stay close."

They turned into a canyon hung with harsh lights, pushing through the jostling crowd. Alien hands plucked at their sleeves, alien eyes stared, alien voices implored, cursed, begged, threatened. The dust rose, hot and corrosive.

"Down here," Raff gasped. In the shelter of a narrow way they clung together, coughing.

"We shouldn't have left the main plaza," Bella said. "Tourists don't come here . . . "

"Come on." Raff led the way, thirty feet back, where the twisted path ended between high walls in a cul-de-sac. They turned—

Two figures, one squat, one tall, both wrapped in heavy, dun-colored togas, waited at the alley mouth.

"Stay behind me." Raff tucked the cylinder in a harness pouch, put his hand inside his tunic to rest on the pistol butt, started forward; the short creature came to meet him, waddling on thick, bowed legs. Ten feet apart, they halted. Raff looked down into dead eyes like black opals in a face of bleached and pocked wood.

"We are stronger than you," the alien grated. "Give us the royal slave and go in peace."

Raff brought the gun into view. There was blue stain across his throat where the cheap dye of the youth suit had dissolved in sweat.

"Get out of our way." His dry mouth made his voice rasp.

There was a moment of silence. Then:

"We will pay," the alien said. "How much?"

"I'll sell you nothing. Just clear out of my way." Raff licked sweat from his upper lip.

The tall alien had moved up behind his dwarf companion. Beyond, a heavy, lizard-bodied cuspoid with a scaled hide painted in garish colors moved into view; and behind him were others.

Raff took a step forward. The gun was almost touching the dusty folds of the other's toga. "Out of my way or I'll shoot sure as hell—"

A stumpy arm whipped out; Raff fired—a momentary flare of blue; then the gun was flying as the weight of the alien slammed against him, and he reeled back, grappling for a hold on horny hide. He caught a sinewy arm, twisted with all his strength, heard gristle creak, snap. He hurled the alien from him, leaped past him, swung at the tall one, missed as he leaned aside. The gun lay two yards away; he dived for it—and a vast weight slammed against him, driving out his breath in an explosive grunt. He was aware of the roughness of the cobbles against his face, a fiery pain that rolled in waves from his shoulder. Far away, Bella's voice wailed.

Raff rolled over, came to his knees; a wide foot in a ragged sandal smashed at his face. He caught at it, held on, dragged a kicking, fighting body down, hearing himself cry out at the agony in his shoulder; and then he found a grip on yielding flesh and clung, crushing, feeling cartilage crackle under his thumbs. He grunted, hunching his shoulders as talons raked his face once, twice, then scrabbled and fell away. Hard hands hauled at him, threw him on his back. He struck out blindly, rolling over to protect the cylinder with his body. A red-hot vise closed on his leg. He tried to crawl toward the gun, but a boulder, falling from an immense height, had crushed his body and his lungs were charred pits in his chest. His arms and legs moved, though he had forgotten now why he must crawl . . .

A last, brilliant light flared and died into bottomless

darkness, and Raff felt himself fading, fading, winking out . . .

He lay on his back, hearing their voices.

"This one fought like a scalded dire-beast!"

" . . . cartilage like rods of granite!"

"Break them . . . "

The blows were remote, like distant thunder. The beating went on for a long time. Raff didn't notice when it stopped; he floated in a silence like a sea of molten lead. But voices penetrated the silence. There was the deep rumble of one who demanded, and a thin cry . . .

Bella.

Raff moved an arm, groped over his face, wiped blood from his eyes, feeling broken flesh under his fingers. He blinked, and through a red blur saw Bella, held pinned against a wall by a cloaked figure. Its arm rose and fell, rose and fell again . . .

Raff reached, groping. His hand fell on the power pistol. He tried to sit up, coiled away from agony like a worm on a hook. He dragged the gun around, leveled it on the yellow cloak, and fired. The cloak crumpled. Another caught at Bella, whirled her around as a shield.

"You will kill your woman," a thin voice said flatly. "Give us what we seek and go your way. We are stronger than you."

Raff was watching Bella. She hung in the grip of the alien, small, limp. He saw her hand move—

"Why do you struggle so, foolish one?" the alien grated.

Bella's hand was at her girdle. Light glinted on steel. Raff saw the thin arm grope, finding the vulnerable spot between plates of scale-armor . . . and then sudden movement—

There was a grunt from the creature who held Bella. He leaned, fell stiffly, the handle of Bella's rattail poniard against his side. Behind her, a dark shape moved. Raff fired, a near miss. But the alien halted, called out in a strange tongue. Raff blinked gummed eyes, aiming . . .

"Wait, Raff," Bella called. She spoke rapidly, incomprehensibly. The alien answered. Raff held the gun aimed at the voice.

Bella was beside him. "Raff, this one's a Yill—like me. He gave me his parole."

"Parole, hell!" Raff croaked.

"Raff, if we spare his life, he'll be our slave. It's true, Raff. It's the Yill law. And we need him . . . "

The gun fell from Raff's hand. He tried to reach for it, to curse the weakness, but only a thin moan came.

There was a babble of alien talk, Bella's voice a thin thread against the rumble of the other. Raff tried again.

" . . . Bella . . . "

"Yes, Raff. It'll be all right now. T'hoy hoy will take us to a place . . . "

"Use the gun," Raff gasped out. "Make sure of the rest of 'em—all of 'em."

"Raff—if we just go now—"

"No good, Bella. No law in this place. Taking no chances. There'll be no wounded devils tracking us . . . "

Afterward, there was a confused memory of strong arms that carried him, and pain like a blanket of fire, and the bite of the night wind, suddenly cold; and later, voices, the clink of keys, and at last a nest of moldering furs, and Bella's hands, and her warm breath against his face.

"Raff . . . poor Raff . . ."

He tried to speak, gasped, tried again. "Our boy," he said. It was important to explain it to Bella, so she'd see how it was. "Our boy: bought with money and bought with blood. He's our boy now, Bella . . ."

Leaning heavily on his cane, Raff looked down at his wife and his newborn son while the slave T'hoy hoy washed out rags in the tin tub by the door.

"This ain't the way I meant it to be," Raff said. "Here in this fallen-down shack in the ghetto. Gee, Bella . . ."

"When you get more able you can paint it. Pretty and white. And it's on the other side of Tambool from the bazaar. They won't look for him here. Roan."

"My son," Raff said, touching one tiny, curled fist. "In fifty years, maybe, he'll be a full-grown human Man."

CHAPTER ✴ ONE

Roan was bored watching his mother wash dishes.

"No," she said. "I can't take you outside now. After I do the dishes I got to grind the grits and then shell some snails and clean your daddy's brushes so's he can do some spring painting when he gets back from that job in town. And then . . . stop that!" Bella cried.

Roan tried to stick the paper back on the wall but it wouldn't stay.

"Daddy fix," he said. His nose was running and he wiped it on the end of the curtain.

"*Not* on the curtain," Bella said. "I just washed them and I didn't make no more soap yet."

Roan reached for the salt cup. Salt was a nice thing to taste, a little at a time. Only it all came over on him.

"The *salt!*" Bella screeched. "Now that's the end! Raff worked all day one day just to get that salt for you and there it's all over the floor and how'm I going to wash salt?"

Roan began to wail again. Everything he did was bad.

"All right," Bella said. "All right. I guess maybe you

could go out in the back. You stay right near the house. And don't get into no trouble, and leave them chunck flowers alone. That juice don't wash out."

Roan ran out into the sunshine with a whoop of joy. He could taste the sun all over him except where his clothes were.

Oh, what lovely chunck flowers! Purpler than purple-fruit, redder than blood, greener than grass.

Mustn't pick the chunck flowers.

He wandered to the other side of the yard where it trailed off into a dusty lot beyond the careful picket fence that Daddy was going to paint again soon. Roan liked to pick the flakes of old paint off it, but today something more interesting was there.

On the other side of the fence were a bunch of wiry, leathery little gracyl children, and oh, what fun they were having!

"Hello!" Roan called. "Hey! Hi! Come play!"

Some of them looked up.

"You're not a gracyl three," one of them said.

"*Here* is where the three years gracyls dig, not *there*."

"I can help," Roan said. "Help dig."

He began to clamber over the fence. It was hard work and he tore a long strip off his shirt on the top of a picket.

Then, once over, he was suddenly shy and stood and watched the gracyl threes burrowing into the ground, their sharp claws working quickly.

"Me, too!" he cried then, and started in on a gracyl's burrow. The gracyl kicked him disinterestedly and kept on burrowing, and Roan burst into tears and went to help another, and got kicked again.

"Dig your own burrow," one of them finally said, not unkindly. Roan could see he was a little different from the others. One embryonic wing had failed to develop.

"You don't got a wing bone," Roan said. "Where's you wing bone?"

The gracyl stretched out his one good wing into an infant fan. "They grow later," he said. "You don't have *any* wings."

Roan tried to feel beneath his arms but he couldn't find anything.

"I'm going to grow my wings later," he said excitedly. "Then I'll fly. I'm Roan."

"I'm Clanth," his new friend said, and then noticed the others had already burrowed ahead of him. "Shut up and dig."

Roan began to dig and found out almost immediately it wasn't as easy as it looked. The dirt at the top was loose, and came right out, but underneath the ground got damp and harder.

"Mama cutted my fingernails," Roan said bitterly. He *knew* she shouldn't have cut his fingernails and now look—he couldn't dig like everybody else.

Roan went and found a sharp stick and began to do a little better. He hit hard with it and suddenly a hole opened up all by itself. A nice, big hole and Roan crawled into it and a gracyl came up and punched him and said, "Dig your own burrow, you freak."

Roan took his stick and began digging down some more.

"You're doing it wrong," the gracyl said, and went on lengthening his burrow.

But as Roan gouged at the earth, it fell in again, and he was in another burrow and it was quite dark and a little cold, but Roan crawled further along into the burrow and then he ran into something furry that he couldn't see in the dark.

"That's funny," Roan said aloud and laughed, because something was tickling the inside of his mind.

"Here it is lovely and cool and dark and no winds blow. Here live we Seez and who are you?"

"I'm Roan," Roan said aloud.

The See put out a soft claw and felt Roan. *"You do not feel like you look in your mind,"* it said. *"There are no wings and no digging claws. Tell me again what you are."*

"I'm Roan," Roan said, and laughed again. And then there was a silence in Roan's mind while the creature felt around in it, and he waited, feeling the strange sensation.

"There's something amiss with you," the See said. Roan felt him backing off. *"You can't tell me who you are. And some terrible power lurks there in your mind. And such enormous puzzles, and things that are strange . . ."*

Roan could feel a shudder from the creature's mind and then it was gone and he was alone. Alone in the dark cold, with all those strange things the See said were in his mind. And the ground smelled dead and damp and wormy and there might be Charons crawling through the burrows to eat dead things and suppose they thought he was dead?

Roan started to back out and found he was scared and all he wanted was Daddy or Mama and his own bed. He sat down and opened his mouth and howled.

The tears poured out of his eyes and he felt dirt in his

mouth and he screamed with all of his body and he was wet, now, too, and that made everything worse.

Then he felt Raff's strong hands on him and even though he knew it was Raff he had to go on screaming to show how scared he had been.

"Boy," Raff said when he got him out and the screams quieted to sobs. "Boy, I been looking all over for you." Daddy sounded funny. Daddy was scared, too.

"And I'm going to do something I never done before. I'm going to give you a good lickin'."

And he turned Roan over his knee, but Roan didn't mind the licking. By the time it was over he'd stopped crying altogether and he got up and looked solemnly at his father and Bella, who was hysterical and hollering for Raff to bring Roan in for a bath.

Roan wiped his nose on the back of his hand and said, "What am I?"

"You," Raff said, "are a human boy. And some day you'll be a human Man. Pure Terran you are, boy."

"But I got funny ears," Roan said, feeling one ear, because suddenly it seemed as though it was mostly his ears, his funny, rounded ears on the side of his head, that might be causing all the trouble.

"What's Terran?" Roan asked T'hoy hoy, as the Yill slave carefully washed him in a big wooden tub of hot water, while Bella hovered, checking.

"Terran?" T'hoy hoy echoed. "Well, a Terran is from Terra."

"Unca T'hoy hoy know a song about Terra?" Roan asked hopefully. Roan knew from his voice that he did.

T'hoy hoy had a special way of pronouncing things he knew stories about. Sort of singsong, like he said the stories, speaking the ancient, melodic language of the Yill.

"Yes. And if you stand still while I wash you and then eat all your dinner and go right to bed, I'll be telling you the story."

"Oh yes!" Roan said. "Yes and yes and yes and yes!" And he made a big splash in the water, but then he really was still and T'hoy hoy began his story.

"Once upon a time, longer ago than the oldest creature in the oldest world can remember now, there was a world called Terra."

"Is it still there?"

"We'll get to that later. A long time ago, and so far away you can't even see its sun in the sky from Tambool, there lived people on the world named Terra, and these people all looked just like you."

"Like me!" Roan's eyes grew wide, and he stood even stiller than he needed to. "With funny ears?"

"Your ears aren't funny," T'hoy hoy said. "Not to a Terry. Now, one day these Terrans built the first space-ships that ever were. A whole new kind of thing that had never been built before. Only Terrans could do that. Then the Terrans went to other worlds in their spaceships and after thousands of years, creatures all over the universe learned that those twinkles in the sky were stars with worlds around them. Because previously each world had thought it was the only one. And each thought it had the only God, whereas there are actually nine Gods.

"And Terrans learned to live on those many worlds,

but some of them changed, and on many worlds they met other beings, not human, but not too different, so that they could think some of the things Terrans think, but not all of the things."

Roan sat down in the warm bath because he was getting goose bumps standing in the cold air. "You not a Terran," he said, touching T'hoy hoy's Yill ear.

"No, I'm all Yill, as far as I know. But these people began to build things of their own and do many Terran things. And since these worlds sold things to one another, and visited each other, pretty soon they also began to have wars, because each wanted to be the strongest. So the men of Terra decided to rule the universe and keep the peace."

"I got soap in my mouth," Roan said. "Tase's terrible."

T'hoy hoy carefully wiped the inside of Roan's mouth with a damp cloth.

"Then something very unhappy happened. Strange people came, from far away—on the other side of the Galaxy—or maybe even from another Galaxy—and their weapons were strange but powerful and they challenged Terra for the overlordship of the universe. And they fought a great war that lasted for a thousand years."

"Naughty," Roan said. He could tell from the tone of Uncle T'hoy hoy's voice. "*Very* naughty."

"Yes, indeed," T'hoy hoy said. "These bad people were called the Niss, and such was their power that even great Terra couldn't defeat them."

"Did they kill the Terran dead?"

"No. They put a circle of armed Niss spaceships around the planet Terra. And after that no one could get to Terra and the Terrans couldn't go anywhere. So nobody has been to Terra in five thousand years."

"What's five thousand years?" Roan asked, jumping from the tub into the drying cloth T'hoy hoy held for him. Roan loved to be dried off in the lovely, warm cloth and he liked to wear it wrapped around him while T'hoy hoy got his clothes together.

"A long, long time. I'm not even sure how long. But the story says five thousand years, so that's what I say."

At dinner Roan crammed food into his mouth with both hands and Raff and Bella were too exhausted to make him try to use his spoon.

"This how *Terrans* eat," Roan said, to excuse himself. "Terrans do this." And he filled his mouth so full his cheeks bulged out.

"Terrans do *not* do that," Raff said. "And beginning tomorrow night you'll always eat like a Terran."

And T'hoy hoy began to tell Roan how Terrans eat and what Terrans eat, but Roan was asleep before T'hoy hoy could get past the hors d'oeuvres.

CHAPTER ✳ TWO

Roan's turn came.

The others were already across. Except the gracyl who'd fallen, and was probably dead by now.

Everybody's wings had worked, the young, pink membranes fanning out along their torsos, along under their arms—all but Clanth's. He hadn't even tried. He had looked down into the ravine and then gone home alone.

They were all laughing, on the other side of the ravine. First at themselves, because it was so much fun, and then at Roan, because he was hesitating.

It had been easy. They were proud of their wings, amused because that one gracyl had managed his wings badly and fallen. *He* hadn't been clever. Now they watched Roan, the only one not over.

"Roan is the dumbbell of the sevens," they began to chant, flapping their wings at him. "Roan is stoo-oo-pid."

"I'm going to do it," he called. "Just watch me."

But still he hesitated. He didn't *have* any wings.

The idea was to take the rope vine, which was just long

enough to swing three-fourths of the way across Endless Ravine, and swing out into the dizzy air, and then sail the rest of the way across on your own power.

Roan tested the rope vine, swinging softly on it, looking up to where it hung from high, high in the purplefruit tree, and then looking across Endless Ravine, across the impossible distance to where the other seven yearers stood.

Roan's pink face was drenched with perspiration, his tunic pasted to his childish body, his whole being drenched with fear.

He clung to the swaying rope and thought of how it would be if he just let go and ran home. Ma would say, "What did you do today?" and he'd say, "Nothing," and the day would end, just like any other day.

"Stoopid!" they called. "Roan is a dumbbell."

They'd said that before, that way, about other things, and Roan had decided it wasn't going to happen again. No—he'd show them, show them, show them—and some day there's be something *he* could do that they couldn't do.

Roan made himself relax, muscle by muscle, as Ma had taught him to do when he was angry and couldn't go to sleep. All I think about is getting to the other side, he said to himself, and didn't mention the ravine. He measured the distance with his eyes and gauged the swing of the rope vine with his whole body.

With luck, he'd make it.

Roan ran back with the rope vine, as far as it would go. Then he clung, feeling himself part of the arc of the swinging, willing the swing to be far enough, forcing himself to know when the top of the arc came, to let go at just the right moment.

The air was in his ears and the mouth of the ravine opened to swallow him, but his eye was on the soft pasture grass of the other side, and he let go at the apogee of the swing. Then, not knowing whether he would land or not, he relaxed himself for the landing, feeling the whistle of the air . . .

He struck, rolled freely to lessen the impact of the earth on his soft human body, hardly feeling as his foot caught briefly, then rolled free with him.

He laughed up at the group of empty faces. Somewhere inside of him something was pumping him in and out, as if he were a pair of bellows.

"Yah, I did it better than any of you," he said, and jumped up to walk off and show it hadn't been anything, to jump over a ditch.

"Yah," he said.

And fell down and went black.

He awakened slowly, into red and green flashes of pain, and he couldn't see anything but glaring sunlight. The other children had gone. They'd figured he was just dead.

If this was what death was, somebody ought to care.

Ma and Dad would care.

Roan started pulling himself along by his hands and his right knee. His left foot pulsed with pain that flared up his leg and into his groin. He had to peer through the brilliant sunshine as though it were a fog, to see which way home was. He would have to crawl to the swinging bridge over Endless Ravine, and across it, and then across more countryside to home.

Up the hillock and down, his dead, screaming foot dragging uselessly behind him. Roan wanted to die at home. Or not die, if Dad could fix him. But he wasn't going to lie and die where he was, as the gracyls did.

His foot bumped over a sharp stone, caught in a prickle bush. The prickle bush uprooted and clung to the dragging foot like a great insect. Like the Charons that cleaned the flesh off gracyl bodies.

That gracyl at the bottom of Endless Ravine. He'd be thick with them.

Roan stopped to retch, and he thought of removing the prickle bush from his foot but it was too much to do anything else except crawl toward home.

He came to the swinging bridge and here the crawling was worse, infinitely worse, because his hands slipped on the smooth, worn boards, and it was possible that he'd slip off, between the ropes along the sides, and always the bridge swayed nauseously.

The wood smelled dry and hot and burned his arms and hands and the prickle bush made an arid, insistent rustle, scraping along with the dead foot.

He crawled forever through the hot, bright fog, his whole leg burning like a torch. He reached home and crawled up on the stoop and called, "Ma! Dad!" and went black again, still calling through the infinite dark corridors of his unconsciousness.

Ma was saying, "Drink this," and he drank it.

"Raff!" she called. "He's awake."

Dad was there, his big, broken body looming in the doorway. You knew he was big, but he stood shorter than Ma.

"Stop that sniffling, Bella," he said. "I'll do it good."

Roan was gladder of Dad. Ma was so old. Like curled leaves. Like things the winds toss up.

Raff sat down heavily, arranged himself on the chair, his bent legs awkwardly set back and his twisted torso facing to one side so that his face was over Roan's, his good eye bright and blue.

"Don't worry, boy," he said. "It's all right."

"I'm broken, Dad," Roan said, and realized something suddenly. "Like you." And began to cry.

"Oooh!" Ma said, almost whistling it. "Oooh."

"Get out of the room, woman," Dad said, looming over to pat Roan's shoulder. "I'll fix you, boy. Shut up, Bella. My hands are good. I don't have anything else left, but I've got that."

Raff felt softly of Roan's foot. Roan screamed.

"The drink'll help some, boy," Dad said. "But this is going to hurt. There's no help for it. Let it hurt."

Roan was shaking all over and Ma was sobbing and saying, "Stop, Raff, stop, I can't stand it." And Dad was doing something to his foot and Roan shuddered and shuddered and finally thought, I'm going to die. Dad is killing me. Dad is killing me because I'm broken.

The first day that Roan was outside exercising his foot the gracyl sevens came by. Roan was carefully limping. Putting even a little weight on the foot hurt.

"He's *alive!*" one of them said, and they all stood still

and gaped at him, and came close and then edged back a little.

"Go ahead, *walk*," Dad said to Roan.

Roan limped painfully.

"Put your weight on it. It doesn't matter how much it hurts. *Use* it. Show 'em."

"He ain't natural," a gracyl child said.

"He was dead," another added.

"His father ain't natural, either. Look at 'em. They're both dead people walking around alive, that's what they are."

The children edged back some more, flapping their skinny arms excitedly, showing the pink membranes of their developing wings.

One of them picked a bright orange chunck-flower pod from the front garden. It missed Roan and made a garish stain on the little house Raff so carefully whitened every spring.

Another child threw a brown one and Roan ducked and a green one hit him over his right eyebrow and hurt and the acrid juice dripped into his eye and stung.

Dad started after the gracyl and the child laughed and spread its wings and flew off in little jumps. Raff swore at his twisted bones and useless muscles and tried to catch the children, and, forgetting himself, fell and lay there futilely trying to twist himself over like a turtle.

"Roan's old man is broken," they chanted. "Roan's a freak, and he's broken, too . . . " They howled with glee and tossed the chunck-flower pods as fast as they could pick them, and when the pods began to run out they used gobs of mud.

Bella came to the front door and screamed.

Roan forgot his foot. He didn't even know it hurt. He ran to the nearest gracyl and wrested the pod from his hand and smeared the juice in his eyes. Then he grabbed the next one and did the same thing.

They were all upon him, but they didn't fight together. They didn't have one hold him while another hit; Roan fought them one at a time. He kicked one gracyl and caught another around the neck with his hands, and bit a third that fell against him.

Finally those who hadn't gotten hurt bounded off, in their half-flights, and the rest lay there to see whether they were going to die or not.

That evening before dinner Roan took off his tunic and looked at himself in the mirror, examining himself carefully all over. He felt of his hair and poked at his teeth. He twisted around and examined his back minutely and then moved his arms and poked his wing bones in and out, seeing the sharp edges move beneath the thin skin.

He went down to dinner, but he didn't look at the food on the table; he looked at Ma and Dad. And he asked, "What am I?" He always asked, but he never understood.

"You," said Dad, "are a human being. And don't you forget it." That's what he always said.

Roan looked at the steaming plate Ma put before him and didn't want it. "Then that's why I'm so stoopid. Why I can't do anything the gracyls can do."

Raff and Bella exchanged glances.

"That's why you can do everything the gracyls can't do," Raff said. "Or that anybody can't do."

"You cost two thousand Galactic credits," Bella said proudly.

"I cost that much!"

"You were special," Bella said. "Very special."

Roan thought of the insignificant white body he'd just examined, and how it got so easily hurt and broken and how he didn't have any wings and how he'd had to learn how to burrow and swim instead of just knowing as the gracyls did, and how he couldn't just let himself die when he was broken but had to cause everybody a lot of trouble . . .

"You got gypped, didn't you?" Roan said, and ran to his room to cry alone.

But when he'd finished crying he was hungry and he went down and ate and Raff talked to him about what a great thing it was to be a human—and of the original Terry strain. Roan kept trying to believe all the things Raff told him.

Raff was enjoying this talk with his son, and thinking how more and more his son would be a companion to him, and how it had been worth the trouble and the expense of adopting Roan and seeing him through the difficult years of babyhood—and hadn't the boy grown fast!

"You weren't born to be a slave. The Shah could have those a dime a dozen. Or for a common soldier because those were easy come by, too. You were something special . . ."

"But when will my wings grow?" Roan asked, watching Raff's wide, brown face.

Raff shook his heavy head. "You don't need wings,

boy. You've got something better: you've got your humanness—"

"Oh, don't try to explain him all that, him only seven years old, even if he is big for his age," Bella said, coming in with another hot dish.

"He's old enough to understand he's a Terry—a real Terry, genuine Terrestrial strain," Raff said. "Not mutated, like me . . ." He nodded proudly at the boy. "And not just humanoid, like your ma." He leaned toward Roan. "Some day you'll know what that means. Real Terry—the breed that settled the whole universe—that built the empire, long ago."

"I thought they were all stuck on Terry," Roan said. "That's what T'hoy hoy says."

Raff looked confused. "Yes, but . . . you were a special case."

"And if I'm a real Terry, why do we have to live in the ghetto with a bunch of old gracyls, and—"

"Here, don't go worrying your mind about all that," Raff cut in. "You're genuine, all right. I can tell. I've seen pictures. Look at you: pale skin, like skim-ice, and hair the color of wineberries, and—"

"But how did I get here, and where are the other real Terries, and—"

"Raff, I told you it wasn't good for the boy to get talking about all those things."

"Some day when you're older," Raff said. "Now just eat your dinner, and take my word for it: you can hold your head up anyplace in the Galaxy and be proud. You're a Terry. Nobody can take that away from you."

T'hoy hoy had come in to put Roan to bed. "I didn't

mean to upset the boy," he told Raff, "telling him about the Terran blockade and all the old Terran legends."

"Tell him the legends," Raff said. "I want him to know. Tell him your stories, T'hoy hoy."

"Then, Roan, tonight I tell you the song of Silver Shane the warrior, who defeated a Niss dreadnought single-handed by crawling up through the waste ejector and holding a fusion bomb while it exploded."

It was winter and the incontinent rains of Tambool swept across the hills and found out a hole in the ceiling of the Cornay's house and Roan heard it drip, drip and it was the last straw, to try to read with that drip, drip happening and the frowsy house smelling of age and poverty, the house they could have because nobody else wanted it.

"It's nasty outside," Bella said.

"It's nastier inside," Roan said, and flung his book across the room. "I'm through."

"You haven't even started," Raff said. "Sit back down."

Roan stood at bay before his parents. Bella set her bone-white lips and began picking irritably at the shedding skin on her thin arm, and Raff tried to work up a temper over the boy, but he couldn't. He's beautiful, Raff thought. No other word for it. Beautiful. Standing there tall for his ten years and glowing in his anger and with the dark red curls tumbling over his forehead.

"Everything," Roan shouted. "I have to do everything the hard way. I'm tired of it. *They* don't study, study, study. They know how to read just looking at the graffiti."

"They're only gracyls," Raff said. "Charons know how to build mud houses without learning. It's the same thing."

"I want to do whatever it is humans know how to do without learning. A two thousand credit Man ought to be able to do *something*."

Raff pounded his right fist into his left hand and wished he could flex words the way he could flex his hands. "I've tried to make you understand. I don't know how to say it so's you'll see. Humans are superior, but that doesn't mean everything's easy for you. But you can do things no gracyl can do—"

"One thing humans don't do is read," Roan interrupted. "I hate reading."

"But you can read *good*," Bella said. "You read better than me. Better than Raff. And you can read Gracyl and Universal and those Terran books we kept for you."

"I know he can read good," Raff cut in. "I want him to read better. Good isn't enough."

"Humans *aren't* superior," Roan said. "They're—"

"That's enough, boy," Raff said sharply. He rocked in his chair, watching Roan sliding his foot in a puddle of rainwater on the floor. Bella went to the crockery shelf and took down a bowl to put under the leak in the roof. "Suppose you can't read for Studies? You'll get sent away from home with the Junior Apprentices."

Raff frowned, watching her mop up the floor with the dish towel. "Of course he can read good enough for Studies. If only he don't trip up on a word we haven't come across in the gracyl graffiti yet. Even so, a gracyl that develops seventy per cent literacy goes for Studies. Roan's reached that by now."

Bella straightened painfully from the floor and rubbed at her shedding skin with the dish towel. She looked at

Roan and bit at her lip, an old gesture that had once even been cute.

"He's been working so hard, Raff. Maybe we ought to let up on him some."

Roan went to the door.

"Here! Where you going, Son?"

Roan looked defiantly at Raff. "I'm going to do what humans can do and gracyls can't. And it isn't reading and it's not flying." And he was out of the door into the rain.

"Raff, stop him!"

"Don't worry. He's human. He knows what to do even if he doesn't know he knows."

They both sat by the strip of cloudy plastiflex window and watched the rain on the garbage dump, waiting. They didn't reach for each other any more. Only for the boy.

The ten yearers were hilarious with the game of swoop ball in the rain when Roan came over the hill in sight of them. It was a simple game. The idea was to keep hold of the ball. They played in a grove of scattered trees, and whoever decided to take the ball would swoop down on whoever had it and take it away and then another would swoop down and take it from the second one, if possible in mid-air. And when you took the ball, you also knocked the gracyl out of the air, which was easy, and if possible into the yard-deep ditch of muddy water that ran along the edge of the little grove.

Roan leaped lightly across the muddy ditch.

The gracyls were delighted to see him. The gracyl with the ball tossed it to him and then four of them swooped straight at him and their momentum shoved him back, straight down into the mud of the ditch.

"OK," Roan said, climbing out of the oozy mud. "OK. I just wanted to be sure I was in the game."

One of the trees was a young purplefruit tree, and Roan found a straight rope vine and cut off a good length from it, several times longer than he was tall. He tied a slip knot in one end and then coiled the rope and slung it in his belt. At the edge of the grove by the ditch, he picked a quarter-grown sapling and climbed up its straight trunk, hanging by his hands when it began to bend, and edging along the length of the young, springy tree until the top of it bent down to the ground. Then carefully, using his full strength, he bent the tree all the way back on itself and used a length of rope to tie the top to the lower part of the thin trunk. He still had plenty of rope left.

The gracyls gathered around and jeered. "That's a silly game," they said. "Who ever played that?"

"It's part of swoop ball," Roan said. "You just watch."

"Yah, yah," said the gracyl who had the ball at the moment. He was up in a nearby tree and he swooped to a lower branch. Then another gracyl swooped the ball away from him and Roan was twirling his rope as the last gracyl was flying across the grove with the ball.

He caught the gracyl around the leg in a beautiful loop and drew him in squawking.

Roan calmly took the ball away and threw it to another gracyl to start the game again, and trussed the lassoed gracyl to the sapling and slipped the rope, so the gracyl went sailing away over the ditch.

Roan climbed up the sapling and bent it again. It no longer stood straight but there was plenty of spring left in it. He looped his lasso again and caught the next gracyl that came sailing by.

"I seem to keep winning," Roan said, trussing the next gracyl to the tree and slipping the rope again. This one landed right in the ditch and scrambled out and made for home.

The gracyls could have played swoop ball higher up in the trees, where Roan's lasso couldn't reach them. Or they could have moved the game. But they didn't; *this* was where gracyls played swoop ball.

Roan took care of two more gracyls. "Give up?" he asked the rest.

"Yah, you can't even fly," they said, and kept on playing exactly the same way. No one tried to take his rope away. No one tried to keep him from bending the sapling.

Pretty soon there were no more gracyls. The last one went sailing over the ditch and hopped off home, whining.

All except Clanth, of course, with his one undeveloped wing. He'd learned to sit and watch games.

"That was fun," Clanth said.

Roan tossed the rope into the muddy ditch and leaped across it and turned back to watch the deserted spot where the swoop ball game had been. He rubbed the mud off his hands down the sides of his trousers.

"I won," he said, and grinned, and went home to practice his reading.

CHAPTER ✷ THREE

Roan sat on the stoop of his house with a large book spread in his lap. It was entitled *Heroes of Old Terra*, and it was packed with shiny tri-D pictures of men and ships and great towering cities. It was a very old book, and some of the pages were missing, but the pictures were still bright.

"Hey, c'mon," someone said. Roan's mind swam out from the book. Clanth, who was the nearest thing Roan had to a friend, stood waiting.

"Where?" Roan asked.

"Where!" Clanth flapped his one, useless wing. His black, leathery gracyl face was alight with excitement, the round amber eyes asparkle. "It's the spring pre-mating. Out in the grove."

Roan's fair cheeks flushed, back to the roots of his deep red hair. "Don't be ridiculous," he said. "But . . . good flying," he added, so as not to offend his friend. It might have been an offensive phrase to Clanth, because of his disability, but Roan had found that Clanth preferred for him not to be sensitive about it.

"I . . . Oh, I'm not like the others, either." But Clanth was handsome, gracyl handsome, and well developed for fourteen, and you noticed that before you noticed about his wing. And since he was in Studies, not Labor, it didn't make so much difference about the wing. "C'mon, Roan . . . "

"What would I do there?" Roan asked. "Provided I could get a female up a tree to begin with?"

"Well . . . wings aren't really necessary. At least I hope not. Look at me." And he raised his wingless right arm.

"I'd rather not try." Roan pictured the black, screeching little gracyl females. He was glad he didn't want one, because she'd laugh at him if he did. Sneer at him. Flap her wings at him.

"But gee, here you are fourteen years old," Clanth persisted. "What are you going to *do?*"

"I'll wait," said Roan.

"For what?" Clanth asked, and didn't wait for an answer, for a gaggle of fourteens went by and Clanth ran off to join them.

Roan watched them go, then sat with the book in his lap, gazing at the clouds and trying to picture a human female. The portraits in his books, the descriptions he'd read; he tried to put all his knowledge together, but it wouldn't add up to a definite picture. Every time he thought he had it, it slipped away from him.

Day wore into evening and still Roan sat, and he thought about human women and then about human men, and the old heroes of his book, who left human women to go out and find new worlds, and died showing there were places besides earth where human men could bring human women.

Human women were not like Ma. They were . . . Roan couldn't find the thought. He didn't know.

The gracyls had finished going by. The crowds of young males had gone out, and the crowds of ripening females. The first moon was still white in the sky, but it was brightening and soon the sickle anti-moon would come up and the ceremonies would begin and Roan wished Clanth well and hoped his female would not laugh too much at his poor wingless arm.

Another group of youths was coming along; there was a low mutter of talk and laughter among them—and they were not gracyls.

"Supper!" Ma called. And came to the door. "What are you doing reading in that light?"

Roan peered through the gloom to see who was coming. The Veed. What were they doing out of their ornately decorated quarters in the heart of the town?

"Has there been a Veed murder or something?" Roan asked, because Ma always managed to know, without talking to anybody, what was going on in the adult world.

"If there has I don't want to know about it and neither do you," said Ma, retreating further behind the front door. "You come on in. You don't want to tempt that trash to stop here."

But Roan waited to watch them go by, the young Veed, their scalesuits glittering faintly even in the tarnished twilight. They walked upright, looking almost human, talking their Veed talk.

"They're children," Roan said, and went in finally. "About my age."

"About fifty years old," Ma said, spooning stewed

limpid seeds onto the grits on his plate. "That would be about half mature, for them."

"One of them was an aristocrat. I saw the iridion quadrant on his cheek." What magic lives they must lead, Roan thought, those Veed, with their painted porches and their gardens and their endless games of slots and colored beads, and their lives that stretched on forever.

"When will I die?" Roan asked, and Dad dropped his knife with a helping of purplefruit balanced on it.

"What made you ask that?"

"Nothing. I just wondered. I mean the Veed take forever to grow up and gracyls die if they get broken badly, but what about me?"

"You," Dad said. "Well, I've always answered you straight. You'll live a long time yet. Take me. I'm a hundred and eighty, and still got lots of years ahead. You'll live longer yet. You're prime Terry stock, boy."

"Even if I don't get broken or something? That's all I'll live? I'll just die?"

"There's a story," Raff said, picking up his knife and scraping the dirtied fruit off on the side of his wooden plate, "an old, old story that at the beginning of time the nine Gods called all the species of intelligent beings together and asked them which they preferred, a long life or a glorious one. Only Man chose the glorious life. And he's always been proud of it."

There was another sibilance of Veed going by outside and Roan scurried to the dark front window and saw a second group, headed the same way, toward the gracyl mating grove, the grove of trees by the ditch, where long ago Roan had used his lasso to win a game of swoop ball.

The sapling was a tree with spread limbs now, and maybe Clanth would be waiting in it to drop down and catch his female.

The moonlight shown yellowish pink now, and the garbage dump outside the window was jeweled with it. It was Veed garbage, Roan thought, and for some reason this made him love the gracyls and hate the Veed.

"There's going to be trouble tonight," Roan said, and finished his dinner thoughtfully.

Raff silently got down his big hammer and nailed a panel and a bar of wood across each plastiflex window.

"No," said Roan, when Raff started to nail the door bolt from the inside. He wiped the last of the grits off his knife and stuck it through his rope vine belt. He pulled his tunic up short, so that it draped over his belt and left his legs free for running. Raff looked at him.

"Clanth's out there," Roan said. "I'll be back after a while."

"Now, boy," Raff started. But Roan was already gone, out into the moonlight and the warm spring night.

"Why did you tell him that silly story?" Bella asked, sitting in the darkened house and miserable at the thought of the long, dark hours before Roan might come home.

"Because," Raff said, "I think it's true."

Roan knew something the Veed didn't know. He knew every shack and rock and ditch and garbage pile in the slum. As he came out of the house he sensed another group approaching, and he ducked into a tunnel through the heaped garbage.

They were speaking Veed, their hushed, hissed tongue, so Roan could not tell all of what they were saying, though they passed so close he could have spit on them. But he did catch "gracyl" and "moon," which were the same in all their languages.

If it were only the children out, that meant it was a lark, not a hunt in retribution for some crime or suspected crime. "Ten half-breeds for one Veed," was their rule. Half-breeds included anybody that wasn't Veed.

But this. This was children playing. Or practicing.

Roan gave the Veed a good head start.

He went through the back yard of the funny old voiceless couple that kept mud-swine, and around another garbage heap, and through a series of gullies, and then crept up the knoll that overlooked the ditch and the grove of trees where the gracyl were sporting.

In the grove, where the moonlight could pick them out through the trees, Roan could see the running gracyl, and hear their high, shrill calls. They had no thought for anything but each other. He even thought he could make out Clanth, flapping grotesquely in the tree that Roan had known as a sapling. And he thought he saw something else, very strange. It looked like a white figure, high in one of the trees, looking on very still.

Around the grove, in the ditch, the Veed boys were gathered in full force, a ditch full of glittering Veed, swaying silently in unison. They must be almost ready for the attack.

Roan leaped to the top of the knoll and filled his lungs. "Danger!" he screamed, and the gracyl began running about in the grove in confusion and making for the treetops.

The Veed attacked immediately and furiously. No one seemed to have noticed that the scream had not come from within the grove. Roan was through the ditch and at the grove in seconds.

The Veed filled the grove now, furious, slashing about with their razor-sharp wrist talons. They had planned to catch the gracyls on the ground. With the gracyls in the branches of the dark trees it was going to be harder, and less fun.

Roan crept forward and into and up the side of the dry ditch.

And got caught by a Veed as he started up the purple-fruit tree on the edge of the grove. He'd thought it was a tree that brought him luck.

The Veed's raking hands curled around his thighs and he felt the blood spring out into a thin line of pain and he jerked the knife free of his belt and slashed the coarse Veed flesh and felt the hands recoil instantly.

In the brief moment this gave him, Roan was scrambling up, swinging on a rope vine to the next tree. Around him gracyls fluttered and squawked. The cry of the wounded Veed had brought his fellows to his side; and there were indignant conferences and hisses of outrage. No gracyl had ever dared to use a weapon against a Veed.

Roan listened, catching a word here and there. They were out without permission, because young Veed were always carefully protected. So they couldn't complain to their elders about the wounded Veed. This meant they had to take their vengeance on the spot.

But they couldn't get up into the trees because their bodies were too awkward for climbing and they couldn't throw things up into the trees without hitting each other.

Several of the Veed went over to one of the slenderest of the trees, where three gracyls hung in the branches like clumps of moss, and began pushing the trunk back and forth. The gracyls screeched, clinging tighter in their panic, and as the tree gained momentum, one of them fell to the ground, too panicked to try to fly.

The Veed were gleeful. It was like shaking the purple-fruit off a tree.

Several Veed grabbed the gracyl and Roan carefully didn't watch what they did with him.

"Fly to the next tree," Roan called to the other two gracyls. "All you have to do is stay calm."

But they couldn't. They could only cling and screech, the way gracyls always did when they were frightened. They couldn't change, even to save their lives.

Another gracyl fell.

Other Veed were starting on other trees.

"Make for the thickest trees," Roan called. "They can't shake the thickest ones."

But no gracyl moved. Roan burned with the frustration of it all, the helplessness of the gracyls and the blunt cruelty of the Veed. Where was Clanth? Perhaps he was already safe in a broad-trunked tree.

"Clanth!" he called, but there was no answer. Perhaps Clanth couldn't hear him, or perhaps he was clinging to a tree, squawking with terror, like the other gracyls. But he had always been a little different; surely he would save himself. Then Roan remembered. Clanth couldn't fly.

Roan's tree began to sway.

He looked around for a rope vine, to make it to the broader trees toward the center of the grove, but there was no rope vine. He cursed himself for not having cut one and looped it through his belt when he was in the first tree. But it was too late.

Well, it would be easy enough for him to hang on. He stood on one branch and held on to the next, watching the gleeful Veed below, their teeth gleaming as they smiled their crocodile smiles, their crests swaying contentedly.

Something dropped past Roan and fell into the waiting arms of a Veed. They gasped to see it and so did Roan. It was all white and for a moment Roan thought it must be a human child.

That was the moment he leaped.

He leaped for the back of the Veed holding the screaming white creature and he drove his knife deep into the Veed's right eye, through to the brain, and the Veed died beneath him.

Roan pulled the knife out and stood on the dead Veed, the white creature clinging to his neck, and stood to meet the slashing blows of the other Veed.

But they backed away from him.

They were in awe and fear of him, that he had wounded one Veed and killed another. They had seen many a gracyl die, and that was funny. But they had never seen a Veed die before; they hadn't thought anybody could kill a Veed.

They fled to take revenge on more gracyls. It was safer.

Roan pulled the white creature from his neck and looked at it.

She was a white gracyl.

"I'm not dead," she said wonderingly. Gracyl fear didn't last long when the danger was over. "I knew I was going to be broken and I prepared to die and . . . now I feel as though I must have died and here I am still alive."

"You're a half-breed?" he asked. "Or a mutation?"

"I'm an albino," she said. "You saved my life, didn't you? You did that on purpose."

Then they were silent a moment, looking at each other in the little moonlight. Caught in the brief bond of savior and saved, they tried to meet minds across the deeps and dimensions that separated their alienesses.

"I belong to you now," she said, and clung to him, and he held her close and felt her whiteness and kissed her strange, cold mouth and it was all a part of the swaying darkness and the hissing Veed and the dying gracyl and the death that Roan had made. The dead Veed and the victory.

Roan had lost the threads that bound him to himself and all that was left was the white gracyl woman under his hands in the sickle moonlight.

Across the grove, the gracyls were screaming as they fell but Roan was not thinking of them dying, only of the distant music of their voices.

"That one was Clanth," she said dreamily. "I was going to be his female and now . . ."

"Clanth!" Roan cried, and came to himself.

"Yes. Only Clanth. After all, I just took him because nobody else wanted me and now it doesn't matter."

"Doesn't matter!" He yanked her savagely to her feet. "Show me which way the scream came from! Show me where Clanth is!" He had not been listening. He had been not caring. He had been as bad as a gracyl. Worse, because they couldn't help it and he could.

He saw the Veed beginning to leave the grove as they made their way through the trees. Either they had had all their fun or it was time for them to get back before their parents discovered they were gone.

"There he is," said the white gracyl female. "What do you want with him?"

One last Veed, seeing Roan, gave Clanth a parting slash and moved sinuously off. Roan knelt by the dying gracyl. "Clanth, I couldn't find you. I couldn't help." But he hadn't looked.

"I'm broken," Clanth said. "But, Roan, I had a female."

"I brought her to you," Roan said. He stood and put his knife at the white female's back until she came over to Clanth. "You can die in her arms."

"That was silly," she said when Clanth had died.

The gracyls, those that were left, were coming down from the trees now and incredibly starting their mating ceremonies again.

Roan walked away through the grove, and out into the white moonlight. He climbed to the top of the tallest garbage heap and sat, looking down on the ghetto, not listening to the happy gracyl sounds, thinking about what a human woman might be like.

CHAPTER✴FOUR

Here on the high ledge, the wind was sharp with sand particles, buffeting angrily like a gracyl when you held him upside down to show him that even if you didn't have wings, you weren't something to throw chunk flowers at. Roan got to his feet, holding on tightly to the tiny finger-holds of the wind-worn carving, feeling with his toes for a firm grip. He was high enough now: over the tops of the purplefruit trees, he could see the glare panels strung out across the arena gate, spelling out:

GRAND VORPLISCH EXTRAVAGANZOO!!!
Renowned Throughout the Eastern Arm!!
Entrepreneur Gom Bulj Presents:
Fabulous Feathered Flyers!
Superb Scaled Swimmers!
Horrific Hairy Hurlers!
A Stupefying Spectacle of Leaping Life-forms,
Battling Boneless Beasts, Wingless Wizards of Wit,
Frightful Fanged Fighters!
See Iron Robert, Strongest Living Creature—

Stellaraire, the Galaxy's loveliest creation!
Snarleron, Ugliest in the Universe!
ADMISSION, G. CR. .10, plus tax.

Roan's hand twitched, wanting to go to his credit
coder to check once more; but he restrained it. He knew
what it would show. The balance gauge would barely
glow. Even the five demi-chits he'd earned stacking
bread-logs for the Store was gone, spent for dye-wood
billets for carving. He'd have to be satisfied with what he
could see from here—not that that would be much. He
could hear the noisemakers faintly, but the dusty grounds
of the arena were mostly obscured by the trees and the
high wall, crumbling along its top like all the Old Things,
but still high enough to shield the marvels from his view.

But on the other side, there, where the great white-
boled Never-never tree grew . . .

It was beyond the Soetti Quarter, where Dad had told
him never to put a foot—but it spread wide, almost to the
rubble-littered top of the wall, where it dipped down in a
sort of notch.

He wouldn't really be going into the Soetti Quarter—
just passing through . . .

Ten minutes later, Roan perched in an arched
opening, just above the lower gates, breathing a little fast
from the quick climb down. He checked to be sure no
heavy old gracyl mares were stretching their atrophied
wings on nearby balconies; then he jumped, caught at
ancient green-scaled tiles, scrambled up to a position
astride the steep gable of the first house. From the
balconies below, he heard a clatter of food troughs, a few

shouts, a lazy pad of feet, the slam of a door; the oldsters' early-evening siesta was under way and everyone else was at the Extravaganzoo. Roan rose, ran lightly along the ridge tiles, jumped the gap to the next house. There were carved devils at ten foot intervals here; he had to drop flat at each one, work his way under, then up again. At the end, he swung down under the eave, dropped to a shed below, then swarmed up the carved gable end of the next house; but then it was easy; a series of wind-god altars, like stepping-stones, led to the end of the last house before the high, black-glazed Barrier. He jumped for a drain ledge, worked his way along to a down gutter, held on with his fingers, and slid quickly to the yellow dust of the path. Roan grinned to himself. All those years of playing with gracyls had almost taught him how to fly.

The burrow under the Barrier was almost choked with rubble and blown prickle bushes; it had been a long time since he and Yopp, a Fustian eggling, had last explored it. Maybe he was too big now; he grew so fast—like a Soetti, Raff had said once, grumbling at having to cobble new shoes so soon after the last ones . . .

But it was all right; once the last prickle bush was dragged clear, Roan went in head first, pulling himself along with his hands until he came to the straight-up part; then he stood, put his back against one wall and his feet against the other, and walked up.

The iodine smell of the Soetti was strong, even before he reached the top and pulled himself out into the hazy, late orange sunlight, filtered dark by the great, sagging, patched nets the Soetti used to hold in their kind of air. Roan lay flat, breathing close to the ground; when he had his lungs full—even though they burned a little, from the bad Soetti air—he jumped up, ran for the high fences barely visible in the gloom at the far side of the quarter.

He was halfway there when a big Soetti—almost five feet high—in greaves, a flared helmet with black eye shields, and a heavy cloak, popped out of a hut in his path, blocking his way, heavy pincers ready. Roan slid to a stop, watching the violet-freckled claws. They looked too massive for the short, spindly Soetti arms, but Roan knew they could cut through quarter-inch chromalloy plate.

From burrows all around, bright Soetti eyes winked, ducking back as he looked their way. The warrior advanced a step, snapping his claws like pistol shots, pow! pow! Roan stooped, picked up a four-foot stick of springy booloo wood. He waved it at the Soetti; it hissed, its arms twitching in instinctive response to the movement. It saw what Roan was trying to do, and backed quickly; but Roan moved in, flicked the stick almost under the Soetti's faceted eyes; the pincers flashed, locked on the wand, as involuntarily as a wink; and Roan jerked the stick, hard, throwing the warrior off balance. He dropped the stick and sprang past the creature, sprinting for the board wall, laughing as he ran.

The Never-never tree was three yards thick at the base, rising like a column of buttressed white stone set with daggers of crystalline lime. It wasn't hard to climb, as long as he just held on with his knees and elbows and didn't touch the spines; and the branch, the one that reached out to the wall—it wasn't very big, but it would probably hold all right—even with the weight of a sixteen-year-old Man on it.

Roan started up; the first fifty feet was simple enough, the spines were as big as Roan's wrist, set well apart; he could even use them as footholds.

He reached for a higher grip—and a spine broke under his foot. His hand snapped out to seize a razor-edged spine while his knees gripped the narrowing buttress between them. Pain tore through his hand and snaked down his arm, red pain and blood. Roan hated the dumb way his hand had grabbed, like the Soetti's claws, at whatever came near. The Soetti's claws couldn't learn but maybe Roan's hand could, if it hurt enough. And it did hurt enough and now it was slippery as well.

Pain was a taste of death in Roan's mouth, like the time he'd broken his foot. But something else Roan could do was force himself to forget things. He ignored the hand and went on.

The branch that stretched over the wall had patches of peeling bark adhering to it. Roan brushed them away before stepping out on it; he couldn't take a chance on losing his footing; with his slippery hand, he might not be able to hold on if he fell. He wiped his hand again on his tunic, then clenched it to hold in the pain and the blood. The branch moved gently underfoot as he walked out on it, swaying to the gusty wind, and dipping now under his weight. Raff was right; he did grow too fast. He was heavier than an old gracyl brood master. The tip of the branch was level with the top of the wall now; and now it dipped lower, the shiny blue leaves at its tip clattering softly against the weathered masonry. But he was close now; the whine and thump of the noisemakers were loud above the chirp and bellow of the crowd beyond the walls, and he could see the blue-white disks of the polyarcs glaring on the dusty midway.

The last few yards were hard going. The tiny spines were close together here—and sharp enough to stab through his bos-hide shoes. If the slender bough sank much lower under his weight, he wouldn't be able to reach the wall. But he knew. He knew from the gracyl games how much weight a tree limb could hold.

Balancing carefully, Roan started the branch swaying, down, up, in a slow sweep, down, heavily, then shuddering up . . .

On the third upward swing, Roan jumped, caught the edge of the wall, raked at loose rubble, then pulled himself up and lay flat on the dust-powdered surface, still hot from the day's sun. He opened his hand and looked at it. The blood had formed a blackish cake with the dust. That was good; now maybe it would stop running all over things and spoiling his fun. He patted it in the dust some more, then crawled to the edge of the wall and looked over into the glare of the grounds—

Sound struck him in the face like a thrown chunck-flower: the massed roar of voices, the shrill clangor of the noisemakers, the rustle of scaled and leathered bodies, the grating of feet—shod, horned, clawed, hooved. The cries of shills and hucksters . . .

It was dark now. Twenty feet below Roan, the heads of the crowd stretched in a heaving sea of motion, surging around the pooled light of the midways, alive with color and movement. There, a jeweled harness sparkled on tandem hitched bull-devils; there a great horned body, chained by one leg, pranced in an intricate dance; and beyond, caged dire-beasts paced, double jaws gaping.

Roan forgot to breathe, watching as a procession of scarlet-robed creatures with golden hides strode into view from a spotlighted arch, fanned out to form a circle, dropped the red cloaks, and rushed together, cresting up into a living pyramid, then dropping back to split and come together like a wave breaking against a wall, and then . . .

He had to get closer. He raised his head and looked along the broken wall, following its great arc to the far side where it loomed black against the luminous amber twilight. He could jump down easily enough, but not without landing on a bad-tempered gracyl or a wide-jawed Yill.

He rose and moved off, stepping carefully among the rubble. It was almost full dark now. Ahead, he made out the heavy sagging line of an anchor cable, its end secured to a massive iron capstan set in the stone coping. He clambered up, followed the cable with his eye as it dipped, then rose up to meet a slender tower. This was almost too easy: the base of the tower was hidden in shadow behind a cluster of polyarcs. No one would notice if he walked across and slipped down there . . .

He stepped out on the taut cable; it was much easier than the branch had been; it was only as big as his finger, but it was steady. No one looked up from below; he was above the polyarcs, invisible against their glare.

He walked out across the crowd, reached the tower, swung quickly down—

A hand like an iron clamp locked on his ankle. He

looked down. A face like a worn-out shoe blinked up at him. Gill flaps at either side of the wide head quivered.

"Come down, come down," a curious double voice said. "Caught you—ought—you good—ood."

Roan held on and pulled; it was like trying to uproot an anvil tree.

"Let go," he said, trying to make his voice sound as though it were used to being obeyed by beings with old-shoe faces and hands like ship grapples.

"You're—re—going to see—ee the boss-oss." The iron hand—which was bright green, Roan noticed, and had three fingers—tugged, just gently, and Roan felt his joints creak. He held on.

"Want me—ant me to pull—ull your leg—eg off—off?" the hollow voice echoed.

"All right," Roan said. He lowered himself carefully until his other foot was on a level with his captor's hand. Then he swung his free leg back and kicked the creature in the eye.

The grip was gone from his ankle, and he leaped clear, landed in dust, turned to duck away—

And slammed against a wide, armored body that gathered him in with arms like the roots of the grizzly-wood tree.

It was dark inside the big tent, and hot, and there were odors of seaweed and smoke. Roan stood straight, trying not to think about the way his hands were numb from the grip on his wrists. Beside him, the shoe-faced creature flapped its gills, blinking its swollen eye. "Ow—ow," it said, over and over. "Ow—ow."

The being behind the big, scarred, black-brown desk blinked large brown eyes at him from points eight inches apart in a head the size of a washtub mounted on a body like a hundred gallon bag of water. Immense hands with too many fingers reached for a box, extracted a thick brown cigar, peeled it carefully, thrust it into a gaping mouth that opened unexpectedly just above the brown eyes.

"Some kind of Terry, aren't you?" a bass voice said from somewhere near the floor.

Roan swallowed. "Terry stock," he said, trying to sound as though he were proud of it. "Genuine Terrestrial strain," he added.

The big head waggled. "I saw you on the wire. Never saw a Terry walk a wire like that before." The voice seemed to come from under the desk. Roan peered, caught a glimpse of coiled purplish tentacles. He looked up to catch a brown eye upon him; the other was rolled toward the gilled creature.

"You shouldn't have hurt Ithc," the deep voice rumbled. "Be quiet, Ithc." The wandering eye turned back to Roan. "Take off your tunic."

"Why?"

"I want to see what kind of wings you've got."

"I don't have any wings," Roan said, sounding as though he didn't care. "Terries don't have wings; not real original Terrestrial stock, anyway."

"Let's see your hands."

"He's holding them."

"Let him go, Ithc." The brown eyes looked at Roan's hands as he opened and closed them to get the blood going again.

"The feet," the basso voice said. Roan kicked off a shoe and put his foot up on the desk. He wriggled his toes, then put his foot back on the floor.

"You walked the wire with *those* feet?"

Roan didn't answer.

"What were you doing up there?"

"I was getting in without a ticket," Roan said. "I almost made it, too."

"You like my little show, hey?"

"I haven't seen it—yet."

"You know who I am, young Terry?"

Roan shook his head.

"I'm Gom Bulj, Entrepreneur Second Class." One of the broad hands waved the cigar. "I'm owner of the Extravaganzoo. Now—" the heavy body hitched forward in the wide chair. "I'll tell you something, young Terry. I haven't seen a lot of Terries before, but I've always been a sort of admirer of theirs. Like back in ancient times, the wars and all that. Real spectacles." Gom Bulj thumped his desk. "This desk—it's made of Terry wood—*woolnoot*, I think they call it. Over six thousand years old; came out of an old Terry liner, a derelict on—" He cut off.

"Never mind that. Another story. What I'm getting at is—how would you like to join my group, young Terry? Become a part of the Grand Vorplisch Extravaganzoo! Travel, see the worlds, exhibit your unusual skills to appreciative audiences of discerning beings all over the Western Arm?"

Roan couldn't help it: he gasped.

"Not much pay at first," Gom Bulj said quickly. He

paused, one eye on Roan. "In fact, no pay—until you learn the business."

Roan took a deep breath. Then he shook his head. Gom Bulj was still looking at him expectantly.

"No," he said. "Not until I ask Dad . . . " Suddenly Roan was remembering Ma, waiting, with his dinner ready now, and Raff . . . Raff would be worried, wondering where he was . . .

"I've got to go now," he said, and wondered why he had such a strange, sinking feeling.

Gom Bulj drummed his tentacles under the desk. He sucked on a stony-looking tooth, eyeing Roan thoughtfully.

"No need to trouble old Dad, young Terry. You're big enough to leave the burrow, no doubt. Probably he'll never miss you, new litters coming along—"

"Terries don't have litters; only one. And Ma only had me."

"You'll write," Gom Bulj said. "First planetfall, you'll write, tell them what a mark you're making. A featured sideshow attraction in the finest 'zoo in this part of the Galaxy—"

"I'll have to ask Dad's permission first," Roan said firmly.

Gom Bulj signaled with a finger. "You'll surprise him; come back some day, dressed in spangles and glare-jewels—"

Ithc's reaching hand grazed Roan's arm as he ducked, whirled, darted for the tent flap. Something small, with bright red eyes, sprang in front of him; he bowled it over, ran for the tower, darting between the customers milling in the way between the bright colored tents under the polyarcs. He veered around a cage inside which a long-legged creature moaned, jumped stretched tent ropes, sprinted the last few yards—

A hulking, gilled figure—a twin to Ithc—bounded into his path; he spun aside, plunged under an open tent flap, plowed through massed gracyls who hissed and struck out with knobbed wing bones. A vast gray creature with long white horns growing from its mouth teetered on a tiny stand; it trumpeted nervously and swung a blow with a heavy gray head-tentacle as Roan darted past; then Roan was under the edge of the tent, up and running for the wall. Behind him, an electric voice crackled, deep tones that rattled in a strange tongue.

He saw the gate rising up, light festooned, above the surging pack. To one side, another of the gilled creatures worked its way toward him, knocking the crowd aside with sweeps of its three-pronged hands. Roan threw himself at the mass before him, forcing passage. Another few yards—

"Roan!" an agonized voice roared. By the gate, Raff's massive white-maned head loomed over the crowd. "This way, boy . . . !"

"Dad!" Roan lowered his head, threw himself against the slow-moving bodies in his way. The gill thing was close now—and there was another—

And then he was at the gate, and Raff's hand was stretched out to him above the crutch—

The gilled creature thrust itself before Roan, arms spread wide. Roan whirled—and saw the other—and beyond, a third, coming up fast. He feinted, dived between the two nearest—

The steel grip caught his arm; he looked up into the old-shoe face, swung his doubled fist—

Both hands were caught now. He kicked, but only bruised his toes against the horny shins.

And then Raff was there, his brown face twisted, his mouth open. Over the mob roar, Roan couldn't hear what he was shouting. He saw Raff's thick arms swing up, and the crutch came down in a crashing arc on the gilled head, and for an instant the grip loosened, and Roan pulled a hand free—

And then a gray-green figure loomed behind Raff, and a three-fingered hand struck, and now Raff's face was twisted in a different way, and he was falling, going down, and the white head was flushed suddenly crimson, and he lay in the yellow dust on his face, and Roan felt his throat screaming—

His hand was free, and he struck, felt something yield, and he ripped at it, feeling his jaws open, teeth hungry for the enemy, and then both hands were free, and he smashed at the old-leather face, seeing it reel back, and then the other was at him with three-taloned hands clutching, and Roan seized two long fingers in his two hands and tore at them and felt them break and rip—

And then he was falling, falling, and somewhere voices called, but they were far away, too far, and they faded, and were gone . . .

And he was alone and very small in the dark.

CHAPTER ✳ FIVE

Gom Bulj's diamond stickpin glittered like his eyes, and he smoked his cigar as though he had tasted and wearied of all other cigars in the universe.

"You're a wild one, Terry," he said, both eyes staring at Roan. "What was the idea of crippling up Ithc? You should see his hand. Terrible!"

"I hope he's ruined," Roan said, not crying, not thinking about the ache that made the side of his head feel as big as Gom Bulj's. "I wish I'd been able to kill him. I *will* kill him the first chance I get . . . " He had to stop talking then, remembering Dad, trying to help, then falling . . . and the dust on his face . . .

"There was no need for the dramatics; no need at all. If you'd come along quietly, you'd have found life in the Extravaganzoo most rewarding—and I'd still have the use of Ithc. Did you know you nearly tore his finger off?"

"He killed Dad," Roan said, and now there were tears; his face tried to twist and he felt dried blood crack on his skin; but he stood as straight as the Ythcan's grip on his arms would let him and looked Gom Bulj in one eye, the other being busy now with some papers spread on the desk.

"I know everything you're going to say," the entrepreneur said, "so don't bother to say it. Just let me indicate to you that you are a very lucky Terry, Terry. If you weren't a valuable Freak, I'd put you out the nearest lock for the trouble you've caused me. But I'm a businessman. You'll start in as a scraper-punk and double in green-face." He jerked his huge head at the three-fingered guard. "Take him along to a cubicle on number two menagerie deck with the other Freaks—and see there's a stout lock on the door."

Green arms like cargo cranes turned Roan and propelled him into the corridor. The vibration of the engines and the stink of ozone were more noticeable here than in the deep-carpeted office of the 'zoo owner. For a moment Roan felt a surge of excitement, remembering that he was aboard a ship, in deep space. He wanted to ask where they were bound, how long the voyage would last, but he wouldn't ask the Ythcan. He might be one of the ones who'd helped to kill Raff. Roan couldn't tell them apart. But there was one he would recognize . . .

Roan sat in the limp hay that was his bed. The metal-walled cell smelled of animals and old air. He was sore all over but his mind was clear, and he listened to the sound that had awakened him with a feeling of suspense that was almost pleasurable. Something was working at the latch to his door, and he looked about for a weapon, but there was nothing. Nothing but four stark walls and the used hay. Not even clothes: they had taken his tunic away;

and he thought, I'll have to fight with my hands and teeth, and he crouched, ready.

But the door didn't open; instead, a metal panel swung back and suddenly Roan was looking through bars into ocher eyes in an oval face with skin as pale and smooth as a Tay-tay leaf, and a cloud of soft hair the color of early sunshine.

She laughed, a sound like soft night rain, and Roan stared at the tender red mouth, the white teeth, the tip of a pink tongue.

"You're . . . " Roan said, "you're a human woman . . . "

She laughed again, and he saw a delicate purple vein that throbbed faintly in her white throat. "No," she said in a voice that seemed to Roan like the murmur of evening wind in the crystalline leaves of the Never-never tree. "I'm a mule."

Roan came close to the barred window. He looked at her: the slender neck, the shapes of yielding roundness under the silver clothes, the tiny waist, the long, slim lines of her thighs.

"I've seen pictures," Roan said. His voice seemed to catch in his throat. "But I never, ever saw . . . "

"You still haven't. But Pa said I could pass for Pure Strain in a bad light." She put her hands on the bars, and they were small and smooth, and Roan put out a hand and touched her.

"A mule's a cross between two human strains that never should have got mixed up together in the first place," she said carelessly. "Mules are sterile." She looked at him.

"You've cut your head. And you've been crying."

"Will you—" Roan started, and swallowed "—will you take your tunic off?"

The girl looked at him, still smiling, and then the pale cheeks quite suddenly were pink. She laughed, but it was a different laugh.

"What did you say?"

"Please—take off your tunic."

For a long moment the ocher eyes looked into Roan's blue ones. Then she stepped back from the door, her soft hand slipping from under Roan's for a moment. She did things to the silver garment and it fell away, and she stood for a moment poised and straight, and then she turned slowly, all the way around.

Roan's breath came hard through the turmoil in his chest.

"I never dreamed anything could be so beautiful," he said.

The girl drew a quick breath, then bent, snatched up her garment, and was gone. Roan pressed his face to the bars, caught a glimpse of her as she darted past a lumbering, bald humanoid who turned and stared after her, then came clumping up to the cell door. He looked angrily at Roan.

"What the hell's wrong with Stel?" he barked. He looked down, clattering keys. "All right, Terry, the vacation's over. I'm Nugg. You work for me. I can use some help, the devil knows . . . "

The door clanked open. Roan stepped out, measured the alien's seven foot height. The creature raised a fist like a stone club.

"Don't get ideas, runt. Just do your work and you'll get

along. You'll need some shoes, I suppose. And a tunic. Around this place clothes are the only way to tell the Freaks from the animals."

"Who was she?" Roan said. "Where did she go?"

Nugg glared at him. "Keep your mind off Stel; Stellaraire, to you. She dances. She's got no time for Freaks and scrapers. I know about you; you're a mean one. You watch your step, Terry, and tend to your scraping—and your greenface. Now come on."

Roan followed the hulking humanoid along the echoing corridor, noisy with the rumble of ventilators, the clamor of voices, the thump of feet, to a dingy room of shelves heaped with equipment. Nugg hauled a large duffel bag of used clothing from a locker, dumped it out onto the floor.

Roan discarded a bra affair that might have fitted a midget Stellaraire, a zippered tube that seemed to be made of human skin, a hexagonal wired corset, and a gauze veil before he came up with a simple buttoned tunic only a few sizes too large. But he found a marvelous belt made of flexible metal links that fitted itself perfectly to his slim waist. He also found a pair of heavy hide sandals.

Nugg grunted. "Get down to C deck. One of the boys will tell you what to do." He gave Roan directions. "And stay out of trouble!" he added.

Roan rode down the lift, stepped out into a sour reek of stables, a vast, steel room echoing with grunts, squeals, and the shuffle and clatter of hooves and the pad of horny feet. Through bars he saw shaggy pelts of black and pink and tan, glistening hides, scaled, knobbed, smooth, the flash of light on horns, tusks, fangs, the curl of sinuous tails, the reach of taloned limbs, and tentacles that groped restlessly.

"You—oo son of a bitch—itch," an echoing voice said. Roan turned. On the other side of a massive grill a seven-foot Ythcan glowered, one three-fingered green hand thrust through the bars, the thick fingers closing futilely an inch from Roan's tunic. The other hand was a round knob of dirty bandages.

Roan stepped back and looked around for a weapon. Ithc raised his maimed hand and shook it. "It wa—as my skilled—illed hand—and. You—oo've ruined it for life—ife."

"Good," Roan said. "I'm going to ruin the other one too."

"You—oo wait there—ere," Ithc said, moving along the grill. "I'm—mm coming to kill—ill you—oo."

There was a long-handled pitchfork against the bulk-head with straw and dung matted in the tines. Roan clanged it against the steel wall and ran to meet Ithc. A wide gate at the end of the grilled wall stood open. The Ythcan halted just beyond it and Roan stepped through, the pitchfork raised.

Ithc made a sudden motion and the heavy, motor-driven grill slammed against Roan, knocked him off his feet, pinning him in the opening. The Ythcan planted a horny, three-toed foot against Roan's chest and with his good hand drew a knife from behind him. He clicked a catch and the blade guard dropped off the knife and what was left was a glistening razor that made Roan bite his teeth to look at.

"I'll—ll cut your wrist tendons first—irst," Ithc said.

He leaned close, just out of reach of Roan's hands. His gill flaps rippled, flushed pink. "Then—en I'll do—oo your eyes—ss . . . " He held his bandaged hand before him for balance, weaving the blade to and fro.

Roan was watching the dagger. Every time it moved, he had his hands ready to grab. With a sudden, unexpected motion the Ythcan jabbed for his shoulder; Roan struck out—and the Ythcan jumped back, holding his bandaged hand. A red stain grew on it. Roan's hand tingled from the blow he had struck.

"Ow—ow," Ithc keened. "Ow—ow." He stepped back, holding the dagger by the point now and lining it up with Roan's left eye. Roan got ready to dodge, then realized that was what he was supposed to do. The Ythcan would throw for some other spot.

There was the clank of a door, then the sound of running feet along the corridor.

Stellaraire's woman-voice rang. "Ithc, you smelly animal! Get away from that gate. Let him up!" She was standing over Roan, long, slim legs planted astride him, fists on rounded hips. Ithc held up his bloodstained bandage.

"Because of him—im I lost—ost my job—ob. Now I'm just a dirty scraper—rr."

"You'll be worse than that if I tell Gom Bulj about this!" She pushed at the heavy gate.

"He hurt me—ee," Ithc said. "Ow—ow." But he let the gate come open. Roan rolled over and sat up. He looked at the pitchfork, and the girl followed his look.

"Terry, you've got to promise me you won't start it again . . . "

"I'm going to kill him . . . " It was hard for Roan to breathe. His ribs hurt.

"He would have killed you if I hadn't made him let you up. Now call it square!"

Roan looked at her. "Maybe he would and maybe he wouldn't. He doesn't move very fast."

"Look, you've got to forget what happened. He's too dumb to hate."

"Hey—ey," Ithc started.

"You shut up," Stellaraire snapped. "Now go on, get out!"

Roan watched Ithc move off, holding his bad hand in his good one. "All right," he said. "I'll leave him alone—until the first time he bothers me." He lay back against the cold metal floor, wanting to moan, but not wanting the girl to see how much pain hurt him.

Stellaraire's hand was cool on his forehead. "You take it easy a minute, honey . . . "

"I have to get to work."

"You're a *real* sucker for punishment! You stay where you are, till you get your breath."

"He's still walking. So can I."

"You don't have to tell me, sugar. You're a tough one. I saw the fight when they caught you. The Ythcans don't have much brains, but they're awfully strong. I saw Ithc's hand before they bandaged it. It's ruined for life. I've never seen anybody fight like that before, and believe me, I've seen a lot of fights in my carny days. What made you so mad?"

Roan sat up, remembering, feeling the hot tears ready behind his eyes. "My father," he said. "They killed my old man."

"Ah, sweetie, that was a lousy thing to do . . . " She was kneeling, cradling his head in her arms. "Go ahead; it feels better if you cry. But you fixed that Ithc good. He can't be on Security any more; not with that hand. Gom Bulj has already sent him down here as a scraper."

"He didn't have to kill Dad," Roan said. "My father was a cripple. He was crippled defending me before I was born."

"How much real Terry strain do you have?" Stellaraire asked. "Your mother?"

"I'm all Terry," Roan said. "Raff was only my foster father. Ma wasn't really human. They lived all their lives in a garbage dump on account of me and Dad got killed on account of me. And Ithc walks around with nothing but a bad hand."

"My folks were a funny pair," Stellaraire said. "Pa was a water miner on Archo Four. He came of one of the Ganny crosses; real short-like, and he could go fifteen minutes without taking a breath—and o'course real coarse skin. Mother came from Tyree's World; she was dark, with light hair, and real slender. I've got her eyes, but outside of that, I'm kind of a throwback, I guess."

"You're beautiful," Roan said. "I love your eyes. If . . . if it wasn't for Dad, I'd be glad they kidnapped me."

"That's right." Stellaraire smiled. "Just think about the good part."

"I've never had a friend before," Roan said. "A real friend."

"Gee," said the girl, and her eyes grew round like a child's. "Gee, I could make you a list ten miles long of all the things men have called me since I've been with the 'zoo, but this is the first time it was 'friend.'" Her hands moved gently over his chest and arms. "There are the oddest things about you. This fuzz; what's it for?" She touched his cheek. "And your face is prickly."

"That's my beard. I have to shave nearly every day."

"I like it. It gives me nice shivers to get scraped with it. But I wonder what kind of adaptation it was supposed to be for. Open your mouth." The girl looked at Roan's teeth.

"You have such nice, white teeth—but so many of them . . . " She counted. "Gosh, thirty-two." She looked thoughtful, moving her tongue around inside her mouth. "I only have twenty-six."

"The better to eat you with, my dear—"

The grilled door slammed open. A thick, boneless gray arm with a mouth at the end of it reached in, groped over Stellaraire, then curled around her and pulled her to the door.

"Stellaraire!" Roan gasped, and jumped to his feet, grappling the arm.

But Stellaraire was laughing, perched in the curve of the massive tentacle. Beyond the doorway, Roan saw a vast creature like a mountain of gray rock. The girl put a foot on a great curving tusk, stepped up to the enormous head.

"It's just Jumbo. He knows how to work the lift and sometimes he gets loose." Jumbo reached his mouthed arm into a bin and came out with a wad of hay, which he stuffed into the other mouth, under his single tentacle.

"Stel!" a rasping voice called. "Get that damned bull back down where he belongs." The bald humanoid Nugg came stamping up. He looked angrily at Roan.

"Stel, this Terry's dangerous. You stay away from him—"

"You're not talking to your scraping crew now, Nugg," Stellaraire said sharply. "Don't go giving me orders. And you'd better keep an eye on Ithc. He started trouble with the kid here."

Nugg looked angrily at Roan. "All right, you. Get to work. I told you—"

"He's not working today. He might have busted ribs; that damned Ythcan goon slammed the door on him. I'm taking him to the vet."

"Look here, Stel—"

"Tell it to Gom Bulj. Come on, Terry."

Roan looked at the elephant, then up at Stellaraire. He put out a hand and touched the gray hide, then stepped into the curve of the trunk and was lifted up beside the girl.

"This is the strangest-looking creature I ever saw," he said, trying to sound casual. "And you don't have to call me Terry. My name's Roan."

He held on as the bull turned ponderously, swayed off along the corridor.

"And I don't need to go to any vet," he added. "I'm all right."

"Suits me. I'll take you to my room and clean you up. You smell like a scraper already. And I want to see to that cut on your face."

Roan's eyes opened wide when he saw Stellaraire's quarters. The single room, three yards by four, had a low ceiling which shed a soft light on three walls decorated with patterns of flowers and a fourth which was a panel of greenish glass behind which small vivid fish waved feathery fronds, moving with dreamlike slowness through an eerie miniature landscape. There was a low couch by one wall, a table of polished black wood, a carpet of soft gray into which Roan's feet seemed to sink ankle-deep.

He drew a breath, wrinkling his nose. "It smells— pretty," he said. "I never smelled a pretty smell before."

"It's just perfume, silly. Sit down—over there on the bed. I'll get some medicine."

Roan waited quietly while the girl cleaned the deep scratch on his cheek, painted it with a purple fluid that burned like cold fire, and sprayed a bandage in place.

"There. I'm as good a vet as Grall any day. I ought to be—I've done enough of it. Now go in there"—she pointed—"and take a bath."

Roan went to the door and looked in. There was a large basin in the floor, with glittering knobs and spouts around it.

"I don't see any water . . . "

Stellaraire laughed. "You're such a baby—except when you're mad. Here, just turn this . . . " Water churned into the tub.

"Now take off your tunic and get in. You *do* know how to rub yourself, I hope."

Roan stepped into the warm water. "This is strange," he said. "Taking a bath—inside a room. I always used to go to the river."

"You mean right outside—with fish and things bumping into you? And mud? How could you ever do it?"

"It was nice. And fish don't bump into you. I could swim right out across the water to the other side, and lie on the bank and look up at the sky. But this is nice, too," he added.

"Here, I'll do your back. That Nugg, putting you in that dirty pen where they used to keep the mud-pig until he died! I'm going to tell Gom Bulj a thing or two. You'll have a room right by mine. You're a valuable Freak, Roan. What's your act?"

"Walking a wire. Gom Bulj said Terries aren't supposed to be able to, but I don't have any trouble."

Stellaraire shuddered. "I'm afraid of heights. But you said you grew up among those flying things—grapples or whatever they are—I guess that makes a difference. What's he paying you?"

"I don't know. Nothing, I guess, until I learn the business."

"Ha! We'll see about that. Why, you're the only real Terry in the show. Don't say anything to Gom Bulj about the extra teeth and he'll never know the difference."

"I don't want anything from him. I'm going to get away as soon as I can, and go . . . go . . . "

"Yeah, sweetie, go where? You'd have to earn passage money back to Tambool—and believe me, it costs plenty. You'd better stick with the show at least until you've saved some money—and I'll see that you're paid what you're worth."

"I don't want you to get in trouble."

"Don't worry about Gom Bulj. He's really a kind of a nice old cuss, after you get used to that tough talk. He's so used to these tough Geeks he thinks he has to talk that way to everybody—but he doesn't try it with me."

Roan dried on a huge soft towel that smelled as sweet

as the room and dressed in a clean tunic that Stellaraire took from a locker filled with bright clothes.

"Come on," she said. "I'll show you around the ship. It's over five thousand years old . . . "

For an hour Roan followed the girl along endless corridors filled with hurrying creatures, sounds, colors, odors, through vast, echoing halls which Stellaraire said had once been ballrooms and dining areas, up wide staircases and down narrow companionways, to a broad, curved room with a wall of ink-black glass set close with brilliant points of colored light.

"You mean . . . that's the sky?" Roan said, and watched the fantastic array of slowly proceeding lights, realizing for the first time what it meant, to be in space. So much nothingness there. He looked around the rest of the room—a vast array of instruments and dials and a door with a red glare that said BATTLE CONTROL— AUTHORIZED PERSONNEL ONLY.

"What's all that?" he asked. "And who does the controlling in that room?"

"All that's not anybody's business. Nobody goes in that room and nobody knows what all that's for. It's separate from the guidance system. This was originally a Terran warship and all that's for fighting. Gom Bulj says it works automatically if we run into another warship. But that isn't likely. The thing to remember is not to touch any buttons or switches and not to go into that little room."

Roan went over to look at the instrumentation closely. *His* people had built this ship and old heroes had flown them, fought in them.

"I've got something a lot more interesting than that to

show you," Stellaraire said. "Come on. I want to show you Iron Robert."

"Who's Iron Robert?"

Stellaraire laughed and shuddered at the same time. "Wait and see."

They rode a lift, passed along a hall which vibrated with the thunder of the idling main drive, went through a high-domed room where several dozen ill-assorted beings sat in a group, puffing and thumping strange implements. Roan winced at the din of squealing flutes, blatting horns, clacking tambourines, whining strings.

"What's all this noise for?" he called over the cacophony.

"Oh, a band is traditional with a 'zoo. It goes back to Empire days. The Old Terrans always used to have noise-makers with social events. Some of our instruments even date from then."

"It's terrible!" Roan watched a short, many-armed being in yellow silks puffing away at a great brass horn. "It's like some kind of battle."

"Gom Bulj says the Terry noisemakers used some kind of charts, so they all made the same noises together, but our fellows don't know how to read the charts. They just make any old noise."

"Let's get out of here!"

Nine decks below, in an armor-plated hold where heavy cargo had once been stored, Stellaraire took Roan's arm, nodded toward a wide aisle which led back into gloom.

"It's along here," she said. "He has the whole last bay."

"Why are you whispering?" Roan was looking around

at the battered bulkheads. "I didn't know anything could make dents in Terry metal. What happened?"

"This is where Iron Robert exercises for his fights; and who's whispering? Come on . . . " She led the way along the unlit passage, stopped before an open bay which was a cave of deeper gloom.

"He's in here," she whispered. She was still holding Roan's arm, tighter than before. He went closer, wrinkling his nose at a faint odor of sulphur, peering into the darkness. He could see dim walls, an object like an over-sized anvil in the center of the floor, and near one wall an immense lumpy shape that loomed up like an incomplete statue in gray stone.

"He's not here," Roan said. "There's nothing here but an old boulder."

"Shhh—" Stellaraire started.

The boulder moved in the shadows. It leaned forward, and Roan saw two bright-faceted jewels near the top, which caught the light and threw back a green glint. There was a low rumble that seemed to come from the bottom of a volcano.

"Why you wake Iron Robert up?"

"Hello, Iron Robert," Stellaraire said in a squeaky voice. "I . . . I wanted our new Freak to . . . to meet you . . . He's a Terry, sort of, and he's going to do a wire-walking act and double in greenface . . . " Her voice trailed off. Her fingers were digging into Roan's arm now. He wanted to take a step back, but she was half behind him, and he would have to push her out of the way, so he stood his ground and looked into the green eyes like chips of jade in an ancient idol hewn from lava.

"You mean new Freak want to look at old Freak. Go'head, Terry, take good look. Iron Robert strongest living creature. Fight any being, anytime, anyplace." The giant's voice was a roll of chained thunder.

Stellaraire tugged at Roan's arm.

"We . . . uh . . . didn't mean to bother you, Iron Robert," she said breathlessly. She tugged again, harder. But Roan didn't move.

"Don't you have any lights in this place?"

The dark shape stirred, rose up in the shadows, nine feet tall, massive as a mountain.

"Iron Robert like dark. Sit in dark and think of old battles, old days." He took a step and the deck boomed and trembled under Roan's feet. "You come meet Iron Robert? OK, you shake hand that can tear leg off bull-devil!" He thrust out a vast, blunt-fingered, grayish-brown paw. Roan looked at it.

"What's matter, Terry, you 'fraid Iron Robert tear arm off you?"

Roan reached up, put his hand in the stone one before him. It was rough and hard and warm, like rock in the sun, and it made him feel as soft and weak as a jelly-toad. Iron Robert flexed his fingers, and Roan felt the grating slide of the interlocking crystals of the incredible hide.

"You small, pale being," Iron Robert rumbled. "You really Terran?"

Roan tried to stand up straighter, remembering that once Terrans had ruled the Galaxy.

"That's right," he said. He looked up at the rough-hewn face above him and swallowed. "Why do they call you Iron Robert instead of Rock Robert?" He hoped his voice sounded bold.

Iron Robert laughed, a deep, gutsy laugh. "I come of royal ferrous stock, Terry. See oxidation?" He turned his arm so that Roan could see the flakes of rusted iron in the silicon of his skin.

"You look as though you'd last forever," Roan said. He was thinking suddenly of mountains, and how they weathered and endured, and of his own soft, inadequate flesh and the maybe two hundred years he had left.

"Why not?" the giant said, and he took his hand away and turned and went back to the cast-iron slab that was his bed. Roan's eyes were accommodating to the dim light now, and he saw a wall plaque over the bunk, a carved design of growing flowers. One of the blossoms, half-blown, leaned, dropped a petal that fell with a gritty crunch, crumbling into dust.

"Petals all gone soon," Iron Robert said. "Then last remembrance of home gone. Flower getting old, Iron Robert old, too, Terry. Last long time, maybe, but not forever."

"Well, 'by, Iron Robert," Stellaraire said, and this time when she tugged at Roan's arm, he went with her.

That night Stellaraire made Roan a pallet in a small room near her own. She dressed the scratch on his face again, and the other, deeper one on his thigh, adjusted the blanket under his chin, did something nice to his mouth with hers, then went away and left him alone in the silence and the dark. For a while he thought of the strangeness of it, and suddenly the loneliness was almost choking him, like the bad air in the Soetti Quarter. Then he thought of Stellaraire, and of suddenly having a friend, something he had almost forgotten since Clanth had died so long ago.

Then he slept, and his sleep was tortured with vivid, dying images of Dad . . . of Dad's sad corpse, crying for blood.

CHAPTER ✳ SIX

Roan awoke with a foot digging into his side.

"So here you are," Nugg growled down at him. "Let me tell you I got better things to do than look all over the ship for you, Terry! Here!" He dropped a box on the floor by Roan.

"Chow's been over for an hour. What do you think this is, a vacation cruise?"

Roan sat up, rubbed his eyes, feeling the cold, early-morning feeling, even here in a ship in space, far from any sun, with a temperature controlled by machines so that it never varied, year in and year out . . .

He picked up the box Nugg had tossed to him, got the lid off. Inside were two lumpy-shelled eggs, a slab of coarse, gray bread, a fruit that looked like a small purple-fruit; there was also a lump of raw, greenish meat and a red, coagulated pudding that almost turned his stomach in spite of the sudden hollow hunger feeling.

"Thanks, Nugg—" Roan started. But Nugg cut him off with a snort.

"If you don't eat you'll be too weak to work. Hurry it

up." While Roan ate, Nugg went on grumbling about dangerous Freaks, malingerers, and interference with discipline by privileged characters. Roan finished, then pulled on his tunic, feeling the pain as he stretched his wounded flank. It hurt more than a deeper wound might have, and it reminded him of Ithc. The feeling of hatred warmed him. It made his heart thump and his body ache. He hated Ithc worse than he loved Stellaraire—

Love, he thought loudly. That's what love is.

He stood, doing up buttons and thinking of the slender mule, and how it felt to love a girl who was human, or almost human—

"I'm taking you off scraping. You'll work in Stores. It's only a short hop to Chlora, and there's inventory to take."

Roan buckled on his belt. It made him feel strong, the hard embrace of the belt, and he wondered if this were why there were so many stories of magic belts, like the ones Uncle T'hoy hoy used to tell him.

"If I have to work all the time," he asked as he followed Nugg out into the corridor, "when do I practice my wire-walking act?"

"Practice? What's that?"

"I need to get ready for the show. Gom Bulj said—"

"You're supposed to be a Terry who can walk a wire like a vine-rat; that's why Gom Bulj took you on. You either can or you can't. Practice! Hah!"

Roan followed Nugg through the din of the Freak Quarter, past the bumps, hisses, shouts, the dragging of boxes, and the commotion of people doing things in a hurry. He stared at furred and scaled and feathered faces, massive bodies that clumped on short legs, and lean ones that jittered on limbs with too many joints, tiny things that scuttled, and here and there the bald, clumsy-looking shape of a Minid or a Chronid, or some other creature with some faint claim to a trace of natural Terran or humanoid blood.

He looked around for Stellaraire but there were only strangers everywhere, all hurrying and shouting to each other, their faces hot and busy-looking. He passed Gom Bulj at the center of a crowd, snapping out orders and smoking two cigars at once. The entrepreneur saw him, waved a nine-fingered hand, and called out something Roan couldn't hear.

They went down, down, into smellier and less crowded levels. In a vast, noisy storeroom, Nugg pointed out a skinny, scruffy being like an oversized and wingless gracyl.

"He's foreman of the shift. Do what he tells you. And stay out of trouble." He walked off and left Roan standing alone.

The foreman had been watching from the corner of a moist eye. He stalked over to Roan, looked at him, then gave a shrill cry. The workers who had been crawling over the heaped goods stopped what they were doing and gathered around. Others appeared from aisles. Altogether there were fifteen or twenty of them, no two alike. They all stared at Roan.

"What are you?" the foreman whistled. "Never saw one like you before."

"I'm a Terran," Roan said.

Somebody hissed.

The foreman clacked his shoulder blades together and ruffled out a fringe along the side of his neck. "I'm Rik-rik and I'm the boss here," he whistled. "Now, you're new. Your job will be to carry out the slop jars. And some of the boys don't have sphincters; you'll take care of the diapers. And o' course, some of the gang are messy eaters, regurgers, you know. *That* has to be cleaned up. And—"

"No," Roan said.

The circle around him moved in closer. Something plucked at Roan's tunic from behind.

"I'm boss here, Terry," Rik-rik shrilled. "You'll do what I tell you, right, fellas?"

The tug came again, and Roan whirled, grabbed at a snaky tentacle that was wiping something slimy on him. The being who owned the member yanked angrily, but Roan hauled it close, then suddenly shoved it back. It fell. The others made excited noises. Roan faced Rik-rik.

"I didn't ask to be here," he said, "but I'm here anyway. I'll work, but I won't carry slop. Your men can clean up their own messes."

"You're the newest one," Rik-rik squeaked. "You're supposed to carry the slop. The newest one always does . . ."

"Not me," Roan said. "Leave me alone and I'll work as hard as anybody. But don't think you can pick on me." He looked at the being who was shifting from one of its eight or nine feet to another and snorting softly through its trunklike tentacles. "And if *you* ever touch me again, I'll tie a knot in that arm of yours."

"Spoilsport," someone grumbled.

Rik-rik stared at Roan angrily. "You're a troublemaker, I can see that. Probably you'll want off three or four hours in a cycle to hibernate; most of you would-be Terries do."

"I sleep eight hours a day," Roan said, "in a bed."

"And you'll want food every day, too—"

"Three times a day."

"Maybe it'd like to join our sex circle," a bulbous being suggested. "We have a vacancy in—"

"No, thanks," Roan said. "We Terries prefer our own kind for that."

"Chauvinist," a gluey voice said.

"Hah," someone else commented. "Thinks he's something special, I guess."

"All right," Rik-rik said sharply, taking charge again. "Back to work all of you. And as for you . . ." he gave Roan a threatening look. "I'll have my eye on you."

"That's all right," Roan said. "As long as you keep your hands off."

For the next eight days Roan worked sixteen hours at a stretch among the stacks of supplies, lifting heavier weights than he had ever lifted before, climbing long, wobbly ladders, counting, tallying, arranging boxes and cans and jars in even rows which the issue clerks promptly disarranged. When he left the storeroom to go to the mess hall or to his room, he looked for Stellaraire along the corridors and in the rooms he passed, but he never saw her. She's forgotten all about me, he thought miserably. She fixed up my cuts like you'd try to help a scratched gracyl who was lying on the ground expecting to die. Now she was busy with other things—and other people.

On the ninth day Nugg came to the warehouse, signaled to Roan.

"We're coming into Chlora; planetfall in a few minutes. Plenty to do: tents to set up, midway to lay out, rigging to stretch . . . " Roan followed while Nugg talked in his usual grumbling way.

"I need to know more about what I'm supposed to do, if I'm going to put on a wire-walking act tomorrow," Roan interrupted.

"Tonight," Nugg corrected. "What do you need to know? Does a Flather need someone to tell it how to fly? You're a Terry wire-walker; so walk the wire . . . "

There was a sharp change in the ship's gravitation, and Roan caught at a handrail to keep from falling. His feet were like lead, suddenly, and his breakfast was heavy in his stomach.

"What's the matter?" Nugg called. "Never felt high-G before?"

"N-no," Roan said. He swallowed hard, twice.

"You'll get used to it," Nugg said carelessly.

The gravity pulled and the deck trembled and vibrated. There were noises and sudden tiltings underfoot. A roaring whistle started up, went on and on. There was a final, violent shudder, and the ship was abruptly still. The gravity was worse now, if anything.

"We're down," Nugg said. He stopped at a door, unlocked it with a big electrokey, motioned Roan into a dingy storeroom. He hauled a heavy wooden mallet and a vast bundle of plastic stakes from a shelf, shoved them at Roan.

"Go ashore and help stake-out. There'll be Mag to show you what to do. You do your job and stay out of Ithc's way, see? When you finish, go to tent three, cell

103, and get ready for your stunt." He walked off, and Roan shouldered his load and went looking for the debarkation deck.

A stream of circus creatures were pushing into an elevator, each carrying a box or piece of equipment and Roan, caught in the press, went into the elevator with them, and along the long central corridor of the ship and down the ramp, out into the strange smell of another world.

He started sweating almost immediately. The heaviness felt worse outside, in the heat, and Roan didn't like not knowing where he was supposed to go and having only a vague idea what he was supposed to do.

He was walking across a landing field. Not an official, well-groomed one, but more like an abandoned launching pad; just a flat, cracked concrete ramp. Beyond, a garbage dump of a neighborhood crawled up a hillside. It reminded Roan depressingly of home.

Beyond the garbage dump neighborhood reared a blue metal city, flashing harshly in the merciless sunshine. A flat, shining sky loomed overhead.

The crowd from the circus ship thinned out, everyone hurrying to an appointed task.

Miraculously, the incredible, monstrous tents began to go up. Roan walked toward them. A diminutive red-eyed creature scurried up to him, pulling a heavy cart that bumped over the cracks in the concrete. It stopped in front of Roan and jumped up and down, chattering, waving a stick overhead. "Mag! Mag!" Its voice was like fingernails on dry wood.

"I guess you're Mag," Roan said. "Where do I go?"

Mag started off with the cart again and Roan followed him across the field where the garbage was being cleared off as the tents went up.

Mag pointed with his stick to a spot marked with powdered chalk and Roan pounded the first stake in. The hammer felt like a tree trunk and he brought his whole body down with it when he struck.

After the first stake, he wanted to throw the mallet down and sit on the ground and catch his breath, but Mag chattered and waved his stick and danced toward the next chalk mark, and Roan followed. There were other stake drivers at work, big, thick-armed humanoids mostly. They swung their mallets with effortless ease, knocking a stake into the hard soil with two or three easy-looking blows and moving on to the next. Roan struggled with the heavy mallet, raising it and letting it fall. Sometimes he missed the stake completely. After each stake, he promised himself he would rest—but the others never paused, and somehow, he didn't want to be the first to stop work. His aim got worse and worse. He broke one stake with a glancing blow, and Mag jumped up and down and his screeching went up into the supersonic. Roan leaned on his mallet and breathed dust, then started in again.

For hours in the blinding sun, Roan drove stakes. All around, the magic tents rose, cables arcing to their high peaks, pennants breaking out to flutter against the steely sky. Zoo people came and went carrying props, equipment, tools. Processions of ambling animals with caked dung on their flanks went by, driven by cursing menagerie keepers; a few curious locals wandered along the now dusty paths between the canvas tops, ogling the show people. Once Roan looked up to see Ithc standing twenty yards away, eyeing him, fingering the butt of a nerve gun strapped to his birdlike hip. His injured hand behind him, the tall alien came closer, his gill flaps working nervously.

"I'll—ll be watching—ing tonight when you walk the high wire—ire," he said. "Maybe—aybe you'll fall—all . . . "

Roan made his face smile. "Some day I'll catch you alone, without a weapon, Ithc," he said, trying not to breathe hard from the stake-pounding. "Then I'll kill you."

Ithc showed a gristly ridge where teeth should have been and walked away with his queer, gliding walk that reminded Roan of the Veed and the smell of alien hate and cruelty. Ithc wants revenge, Roan thought, watching him go. But he doesn't really know what wanting means.

The stakes were all driven at last, and Mag squeaked and took his cart away, without even looking back.

Roan found tent three, and in room 103 he found two Freaks. Two other Freaks, he thought wryly. One was a transparent post, and it wasn't until it moved that Roan saw it was a creature at all. The other was a thing with a hide like a skinned tree, covered with orange polka dots, and with a double-faced head set on one shoulder. Its modesty section was apparently approximately at the left knee, for it was carefully covering it with a little patch of black plastiflex. As far as Roan could tell, all it was covering was an orange polka dot exactly like all the others.

Roan settled for arranging his tunic into a skirt, pulling it around his belt.

A bell rang—they seemed to ring every few minutes—and he followed the first creature out into the dust and heat of the midway. The creature ambled stiffly over to a row of cages, got in one, and reached a flipper around to close the big, fake lock, which was supposed to indicate that the Freaks were dangerous. It motioned Roan to the next cage.

Roan looked curiously at the sign on the bars. PRIMITIVE MAN, it said in Panterran, the fifth legend in a long row, all in different scripts. He climbed in and clanged the door shut and sat on a wooden bench. This part of the job was easy enough. It felt good just to sit and rest.

Roan sat in his cage for two hours. The ponderous creatures of Chlora crowded past, pointing and making noises. One Chloran stood in front of Roan's cage for a long time, making sketches and taking notes in a curious script. Once a child prodded him with a long stick. But they didn't seem to find Roan very spectacular. Most of the Freaks were much larger and more colorful.

Roan hardly noticed the Chlorans filing past because he had fallen to musing about himself again. Some day I'll find out, he thought. I have to know who I really am, who my parents were, where my people are—my home.

Home. Somewhere was home for him, and it wasn't Tambool.

I'll take Stellaraire with me and there's where we'll live. Among our own kind. Surely Stellaraire was near enough human so it wouldn't matter.

Another bell rang. Dusk had fallen, Roan noticed. The days were short here on Chlora. The Freak exhibit was now empty of spectators, a garish and lonely place under the polyarcs glaring far above.

Roan got stiffly out of his cage. He'd sat too long and his thigh had stiffened a bit again.

Mag was there waiting for him, the little red eyes catching a glitter from the arc lights; he chattered and hopped on his spidery legs, clutching his stick, and Roan followed him through the huge, billowing tents. It was much cooler now that evening had come. Almost cold when the wind blew, ballooning out the tents and flapping against the poles.

Roan walked through the dizzying flickers of colored lights and blasts of noise from the noisemakers and the twirling of weird creatures.

At the base of a vast mast as big around as Roan, Gom Bulj appeared from the crowd, his walking tentacles rippling as he hurried over.

"Ah, there you are, young Terry! You're on! Now, I'm expecting great things of you! See that you perform in a style worthy of the Extravaganzoo!"

"What am I supposed to do?" Roan asked. "I don't know anything about being in a 'zoo. Don't I wear a costume?"

"Do? Costume?" Gom Bulj popped his huge eyes at Roan and drummed on his wide torso with his thick fingers. "You're the first Freak I've had who wanted freaking lessons. You have expensive ideas, young Terry!" He plucked a cigar from the flowered weskit that stretched across his chest, stuck it in his mouth.

"Later on, we'll see; for the present, you're on probation. Oh, it's a gamble, taking on new talent! Never know how the public will receive 'em." He drew a tremendous breath that made the cigar burn bright yellow, letting the ash fall with the insouciance of those who never have to clean up after themselves.

"It wasn't my idea for you to kidnap me," Roan said.

"Tush, tush! I'm going to forget you said that, young Terry." Gom Bulj flung his red-lined cloak about him and rippled his legs. "Good luck—and if you *should* fall, do it nicely, as though it were part of the act." He loosed a vast cloud of smoke from his air-discharge orifice and hurried off.

Mag pointed with his stick to the rungs set in the pole. Roan looked up. He couldn't see it, but somewhere up there, in the backwash of the cacophony of circus sounds and colored lights, there was a tightrope . . .

Ithc strolled up, tall and alien, his gills moving in and out, his greenish face shadowed sharply black in the harsh light. He was still wearing the nerve gun.

"Go—oh up—up," he said. "All—ll the way—ay up—up."

"I'll go up," Roan said. "You couldn't do it, but *I* can. I'm a Terran." A short life and a glorious one, he thought, looking up the swaying pole. Stellaraire would be here somewhere; maybe she'd be watching him. He'd have to throw off the tiredness now, and forget the stiffness in his leg. He wanted to do his act smoothly, just as though he'd been with a 'zoo all his life. He wanted her to be proud of him.

He stopped to rest halfway up. He didn't want to be tired or breathless. It was going to be hard, walking the rope with that gravity pulling at him. And he already felt hot and dizzy and his leg ached.

Roan looked down. Ithc was still there at the bottom of the ladder, a toy Ithc, far off, looking up. If he shot Roan with the nerve gun, everyone would assume Roan had merely fallen.

Roan climbed slowly now. He was safer on the high wire. Ithc's gun couldn't reach him that high up. But he felt eyes on him and looked back again. A bright spotlight was on him and so were a million eyes. A voice was booming over the loudspeaker, in Chloran, and Roan knew it was announcing him. He heard the word "Terran."

There was noise for him, loud and insistent.

He forgot the eyes and the noise and kept climbing. The metal of the ladder was cold, from the wind blowing on it, and slippery in his sweaty hands.

He reached the platform at the top. A few feet above him the top of the tent billowed and flapped. The noise of drums rose to him, commanding him on, and the spotlight felt like a ray of heat. Everything seemed to spin slowly, and he held onto the flimsy rail for support.

There was nothing to catch him if he fell.

Roan put a foot on the wire and inadvertently looked down. The world fell away endlessly at his feet. He pulled his foot back and felt his stomach sweating coldly inside, and the fear reaching to hold his body rigid.

He held on to the bars around the edge of the platform and shook. He was afraid even to stand there on the little platform. I'm a coward, he thought with horror.

But he couldn't do anything about it. All he could do was hold on for dear life and wonder how he was going to get down—and knew that Ithc was waiting below with the nerve gun in case he tried to back down, hoping he'd fall . . .

Roan wanted to die—but not by falling. Just to die now, without effort.

"Roan!" a voice called, faint and clear from the middle of the air. Roan looked. Stellaraire was on the platform at the distant, other end of the tightrope. She was dressed in gold skintights now, from head to toe, and she called, "If you don't come here, Terry, I'm going to come there."

Roan held on and looked at her. He remembered how she had shuddered when he told her what his specialty was. But she had climbed up here to the crow's nest to watch him. She had known he might need her.

He let go of the rail. Falling wasn't anything. He would just die—like Dad. But to fail, and have to go on being alive . . .

He went to the taut, black cable, stepped out on it, stood balanced on the wire that swooped down and up again to the blob of light and the golden figure. Then he was laughing aloud, with relief that he wasn't a coward, and with love for his woman, with the deep joy of life.

He walked right across the tightrope, stopping in the middle to wave to the invisible faces below; he was master of the crowd now, tuned to the strong noise of the drums.

Then he was at the other end and Stellaraire caught his hand and pulled him close, looking up at him, and there were tiny flecks of gold dust in her hair.

❊ ❊ ❊ ❊

Would you have done it?" he asked her afterward, when they were back on the sawdusted ground among the black shadows from the high, hazy polyarcs.

"I would have tried," she said. "Now it's time for my dances." She squeezed his hand and slipped away in the crowd. As Roan turned to follow, he saw Ithc's yellow eyes watching from the shadow of a ticket booth.

Stellaraire's act was terrific. It was an erotic dance in five cultures, and the Chloran part must have been crude enough for the crowd to understand, because they roared with enjoyment.

But part of the dance was for Roan alone, out of the thousands. He liked it; he liked her being his woman, when everybody else wanted her.

"Even I," said a bald, purplish Gloon standing by, "even I can find her attractive. She can dance in such a way as to seem a regal bitch of Gloon. She can be anything you want her to be. Anything you pay her to be. A tramp of rare talent."

Roan whirled with his fists clenched, but the Gloon was already moving off, not even noticing Roan.

He watched the dance to the end, not enjoying it now. There had been other men for Stellaraire, he knew that—even creatures not men. But one other thing he knew: she wasn't any tramp. And there weren't going to be any more men except Roan.

After the dances he watched to see which way she went, but she disappeared through the crowd along one of the aisles.

✴ ✴ ✴ ✴

Half an hour later he was still looking for her, along corridors of smelly canvas and rope, among sagging, faded banners and garish lights and the shouting of hucksters and the blare of noisemakers and the clamor of the crowd that seemed to be everywhere now, flowing among the tents and stalls and poles like a rising flood of dirty water. A grossly fat being in a curly silver wig directed him to Stellaraire's dressing room, after he had asked and been ignored or insulted a dozen times.

But Stellaraire wasn't in her pink, tawdry tent room. Roan stood there undecided, feeling an uneasy sensation washing up inside of him. He wanted her—the reassurance of her. He recalled that she smelled of young trees.

"Where did she go?" he asked Chela, one of the girls who shared the dressing room. "Did you see her?"

Chela was a tiny, graceful saurian, faintly humanoid, with long, heavily made-up eyes. She flapped her artificial lashes at Roan and showed her little teeth.

"Ithc came and got her. He wanted her for something." She looked demurely at the floor and by some trick of musculature curled her eyelashes back.

"There's always me," she added.

"Wanted her for what?"

"Reely!"

"Where did they go? Did you see?"

"No. But Ithc lodges in Quadrant C." She was putting purple paint on her lip scales now, bored with Roan's questions.

He made his way through the rings where shows were going on, pushed through the crowds on the other side.

Once, he saw Nugg's heavy, ugly face, and heard him call. "Here, where you think you're going . . . ?" but he ignored him, pushed on through the crowd.

There was a taste in his mouth that was part fear and part something else, he didn't know what. The uneasy feeling was like a sick weight inside him.

A clown was shot from a cannon and the smell of gunpowder spread through the tent. Lights went off and on, and colored spots were a kaleidoscope of dancing patterns. Roan went through a slit in the back of the huge tent into cold night air, crossed a path, and went into a smaller one where most of the roustabouts quartered.

"Where's Stellaraire?" he asked of a wrinkled olive-colored being who was sitting on an upturned keg, nursing a vast clay mug with both hands.

The oldster let out a long breath. "Working," he said, and winked.

"Where?"

"In private."

There was a sound—a kind of animal moan—from the adjoining room. Roan flapped through two stiff partitions, came into a dim, cluttered room with a mud-colored rug, beaded hangings on the walls, the reek of a strange incense. Ithc stood across the room, the nerve gun gripped awkwardly in his good hand, his gills working convulsively. Stellaraire stood before him, her golden costume torn off one shoulder. One arm seemed to hang limp.

"Dance—ance," Ithc commanded, and aimed the gun at her as though he would shoot. The double voice issuing from his gills seemed to send a shudder through the girl. There were several circus people ranged along the far wall: an underdirector whom Roan recognized, a pair of Ythcan laborers, some minor creatures in second-string clown costume. One with a dope stick blew a cloud of smoke at Stellaraire.

"Come on, dance," he urged carelessly.

Stellaraire took a step back.

"Come—umm here—ere," Ithc said.

She turned to run, and Ithc's finger tightened on the firing stud of the nerve gun, and as Stellaraire fell Roan heard the animal noises again.

Roan's body hurt with hers, but he held himself rigid, hidden in shadows. This wasn't a time for gestures. Whatever he did now had to count. He stepped softly back, whirled, ran across the tent where the old being hiccupped into his beer, out into the dark. There were tent stakes stacked there, somewhere. They were pointed at one end and knobbed at the other, and heavy. He groped, stumbling among tent ropes, feeling over damp ground, lumpy refuse, hitting things in the dark. His hand fell on a bundle, and he ripped the twine away, caught up a yard-long, wrist-thick bar of dense plastic.

He ran around the tent to the side that opened on the alley, lifted the heavy flap, stepped into the smell of snakes and Ythcan dope smoke. A small clown in colored rags was just in front of him; beyond, Ithc stood, tall, lean, slope-shouldered, long-necked. He was holding his bandaged hand close to his side, and the other with the nerve gun was held awkwardly out. That was the first danger. Against the gun Roan would have no chance at all. There was no question of fair play; it was simply necessary to save Stellaraire from what was happening to her, in any way possible. And he would have to do everything right, because he wouldn't have another chance.

He gripped the club carefully, stepped quickly past the ragged clown, set himself, and brought the club down on Ithc's gun hand. He had decided on the hand instead of the obvious target, the head, because he wasn't sure where Ithc's brains were; hitting him on the head might not bother him much.

It was surprising how slowly the gun fell. Ithc was still standing, holding his hand out—but now the hand was oozing fluid, and the gun was bouncing off the dusty rug and falling onto a pile of dirty clothing, and Ithc was bringing his hand in and starting to turn. Roan brought the club up again—how heavy it seemed—and aimed a second blow at the back of Ithc's neck; but Ithc was turning and ducking aside, and the blow struck him on the shoulder and the club glanced off and jarred from Roan's hands, and then he was facing the tall, pale-green, mad-eyed Ythcan, seeing the dirty yellow of the gill fringes as they flapped, smelling the penetrating chemical odor of Ithc's blood.

"Owww—owww," Ithc moaned, and brought a foot up in a vicious kick, but Roan leaned aside, caught the long-toed member, and threw all his strength into twisting it back and around, driving with his feet to topple Ithc. They fell together, Roan on top, Ithc's sinewy body buckled under him, and his knobbed knees battered against Roan's chest. But he held on, twisting the foot, feeling the cartilage crackle and break, remembering Dad, and the sounds Stellaraire had made, and he twisted harder, harder . . .

Ithc roared a vibrating double roar, fighting now to escape, but Roan reached after him, caught the other foot, tore at it, twisting, tearing, while the now helpless creature fought to crawl away. Then Roan was on Ithc's back, his arm locked around the other's throat, crushing until Ithc collapsed, fell on his face, his legs twitching.

Roan got to his feet. He was only dimly aware of the faces watching, of Stellaraire still moving on the floor beyond her fallen tormentor, of the stink of alien blood and burning dope. He looked around for the club, saw it tangled among unwashed garments on an unkempt heap of bedding by the sagging canvas wall. He caught it up, turned back to Ithc. The alien lay half on his side, his broken feet grotesquely twisted, his gills gaping convulsively. A deep, reedy vibration of agony came from him. Roan brought the club up, and paused, not hesitating, but picking the best spot—the spot most likely to kill.

The yellow eyes opened. "Hurry—urry," Ithc said.

Roan brought the club down with all his strength, noting with satisfaction that the Ythcan's limbs all jumped at once. He hit him twice more, just to be sure Ithc would never bother him again. The last blow was like pounding a side of meat hanging in a kitchen. He tossed the club aside, picked up a dirty blanket and wiped the spattered yellowish blood from his face and hands. He looked around at the circus people who watched. Two of the small clowns were edging forward, looking Ithc over, a little saliva visible at the corners of their beaklike mouths.

"Nobody helped Stellaraire," he said. "Nobody helped me. Anybody on Ithc's side can fight me, if they want to." He glanced toward the club, flexing his hands. He was breathing hard, but he felt good, very good, and he was almost hoping the other Ythcan would step forward, because it had been a wonderful feeling, killing Ithc, and he felt as though he could beat anybody, or all of them together.

But no one moved toward him. The one with the dope stick ground the smoke out on a horny palm, tucked it in a pocket of its black polyon blouse.

"It's your fight. Gom Bulj won't like it; Ithc was a valuable piece of livestock. But who'll tell him? He may not even notice. Who cares?"

"We'll take care of the remains," the small clowns said, clustering around the body.

The others were leaving, wandering off now because the fun was over. Roan went to Stellaraire and lifted her in his arms. He was surprised at how light she was, how fragile for all her sumptuous curving flesh; and how sharp was his need to take care of her.

She smiled up at him. "He . . . must have gone . . . crazy."

"He won't bother you any more, Stellaraire."

Out in the cold night, the blaze of stars, the rise and fall of the mob noise, Stellaraire's arm went around his neck. Her face was against his, and her mouth opened hungrily against his.

"Take me . . . to my tent . . . " she breathed against his throat, and he turned and walked along the shadowy way, aware only of the perfume and the poetry and the wonder of the girl.

CHAPTER ✳ SEVEN

In the gray light of Chlora's dawn, Roan worked with the others, dismantling the tents, folding the vast canvasses, coiling the miles of rope, stacking and bundling stakes, striking sets, and packing props and costumes. The wagons puffed and smoked, and hauled everything back up the ramps into the ship, and then they lowered their scraping blades and pushed all the garbage back into the circus grounds where it belonged, with the stripped yellow bones of Ithc at the bottom.

Later, in Stellaraire's room, she poured Roan a glass of wine and sat on his lap.

"I never knew how much I loved you, until you fought Ithc for me," she said.

"Nobody's said anything about him," Roan said. "Aren't they going to investigate his death?"

"Why should anyone bother? He wasn't much use with a ruined hand, anyway."

"But what about his friends . . . "

"You're talking like a Terry," Stellaraire said, and sipped her wine appreciatively. Roan tasted it, too. It was a blossom-pink Dorée from Aphela and it tasted like laughter.

Algol II was a wonderful pale green gold-edged mountain that filled half the immense view screen in the dusty old room that had once been the grand observation salon.

"I've got an idea," Roan said, standing with his arm around Stellaraire's slim waist. "I've been thinking about what you said, about there being a lot of mutant Terrans here, and about the climate being like Terra. Why don't we stay here? When the show pulls up, we'll disappear. Gom Bulj wouldn't go to the expense of coming back after us—"

"Why?" the girl asked, raising her violet-penciled eyebrows. "What would we do on Algol II?"

"We wouldn't stay—just until we made enough credit to leave. I have to get back ho—back to Tambool. Ma's still there, all alone now."

"But the 'zoo is my home! I've never been any other place, since I was ten years old. It's safe here; and we can be together."

"And besides," Roan went on, "Ma will know all about where I came from; maybe who my blood father and mother are. I have to find out. Then I'm going to Terra—"

"Roan—Terra's just a mythical place! You can't—"

"Yes, I can," he said. "Terra's a real place. I know it is. I can feel inside that it's real. And it's not like other worlds. On Terra everything is the way things should be. Not all this hate, and not caring, and dirt, and dying for nothing. I've never been there, but I know it as though I'd spent all my life there. It's where I belong."

Stellaraire took his hand, leaned against him. "Ah, sweetie, for your sake I hope it's really there—somewhere. And if it is," she added, "I know someday you'll find it."

The 'zoo went well on Algol II. Roan was surefooted and nimble on the high wire in the light gravity, only three-fourths ship-normal, and Stellaraire's dance was an immense success with the mutant Terrans, who were odd-looking dwarfs with bushy muttonchop whiskers and bowed legs and immense bellies and no visible difference between the sexes; but they appreciated the erotic qualities of her performance so well that a number of the locals occupying ringside boxes began solemnly coupling with their mates before she had even finished.

Afterward, Roan found Stellaraire by the arena barrier, watching Iron Robert in his preliminary warm-up bout.

"I've planned a route for us," he said softly. "As soon as—"

"Shhh . . . " she said, and put a hand on his arm, her eyes on the spotlit ring, where the stone giant was strangling a great armored creature with insane, bulging eyes. It was already quite dead, and he was mauling it for the amusement of the crowd, which had no way of knowing the beast had died minutes before.

"Listen," Roan insisted. "I have clothes and food in a bundle; are you ready to go?"

She turned to look up at him. "You really mean it? Now? Just like that, just walk off and . . . "

"What other way is there? This is as good a time as any."

"Roan, it's crazy! But if you're going, I'm going with you. But listen. Wait until after Iron Robert's act. We can slip away while the tops are going down. Somebody might notice if we tried it now—and whatever we do, we don't want to get caught. Gom Bulj has some pretty drastic ideas about what to do with deserters."

"All right. As soon as the fight's over and the noise-makers come on, we'll mingle with the marks and go out gate nineteen. There's a patch of big plants growing over on that side, and we can duck in there and work our way to the town."

There was scattered applause as Iron Robert tossed his victim aside and raised his huge, square hands in his victory sign. He came over to where Roan and Stellaraire stood, accepted a towel tossed to him by Mag or his twin brother. He wiped pale pink blood from his face and hands, then took a scraper from his belt pouch and began to clean himself, frowning as he worked. He was very neat and meticulous and it made a tooth-cracking noise.

"How you like fight, Terry?" he asked suddenly, scraping his arm with long strokes.

"I didn't really see it," Roan answered. "When I got here it was already over."

Iron Robert chuckled, a sound like a boulder rolling downhill. "Fans like see plenty action," he said. "Iron Robert kill too quick, have to ham up act little, give every-body money's worth." He finished his toilet and put the scraper away.

"Next fight different maybe," he said. "Parlagon easy.

Tear up whole parlagon with bare hands. Chinazell next. Never see chinazell before. Chinazell pretty tough, some say. What is chinazell? Who care? Tear him up, too."

"I guess you can beat just about anything they put in against you," Roan commented, looking around to see if Gom Bulj was in sight. It wouldn't do to have him watching when they made their try.

"So far, Terry," the giant said. He looked at Roan with an unreadable expression in his green-glass eyes. "Iron Robert meet all comers. Some day meet being too tough to kill." He waved a hand at the stands. "That what all come, hope for. Some day they see. Maybe today. Maybe next year. Maybe hundred years. Meantime, fight to win. Iron Robert born to fight. Fight until die."

A horn blew long, nerve-shredding blasts. Crews were hauling sections of heavy fencing into the cleared arena. The PA system boomed out a description of the coming battle. Iron Robert took a gallon-sized swig from a bottle, tossed it aside, stalked out into the center of the ring under the glare of the lights. Jumbo appeared, hauling a vast, iron-barred cage. Its sides trembled as something inside slammed against the bars. The crowd fell suddenly silent. An immensely tall, thin being dressed in green silks that flapped about its long shins pulled a rope and the end of the cage fell aside.

A triangular, scaled head poked out, swaying inquiringly on its serpentine neck. Then the chinazell bounded from the cage and shook the ground when it landed. It was an incredibly monstrous creature, a primitive world dinosaur type with bony plates along its high-arched spine. But the fearsome thing about it was the gleam of intelligence in the small, glittering eyes. It paused a moment, surveying the sea of faces behind the barriers, and gauging Iron Robert, half its size, who stood watching it and gauging it back.

Roan heard Stellaraire's quick intake of breath. "No wonder the betting was so high," she said. "Gom Bulj said a syndicate was importing something special from Algol III, just for the fight. It's a high-G planet, and that monster's used to weighing twice as much as he does now. Look at him! I don't think I want to watch this . . . "

"You're not really worried, are you?" Roan asked. "I mean, it's fixed, isn't it?"

Stellaraire whirled on Roan. "I've known Iron Robert ever since I was a little girl," she said. "I've seen him go up against the awfullest fighters and the cruelest killers on a hundred worlds, and he's always won. He wins with his strength and his courage. Nothing else. Nobody helps him—any more than they helped me—or you!" She looked back toward the arena, where the chinazell had seen Iron Robert now. It gathered its legs under it, watching him standing with his back to his opponent, his arms raised to the crowd in the ancient salute of the gladiator.

"I'm afraid, Roan," Stellaraire said. "He's never fought anything like this before!"

The chinazell moved suddenly; it rose up on its hind legs and charged like a huge, ungainly bird straight toward Iron Robert's exposed back. Stellaraire's fingers dug deep into Roan's arm.

"Why doesn't he turn . . . !"

At the last possible moment, Iron Robert pivoted with

a speed that seemed unbelievable in anything so massive, leaned aside from the chinazell's charge, and struck out with a clublike arm. The blow resounded against the beast's armored hide like a cannonball striking masonry; it staggered, broke stride, sent up a spray of dust as it caught itself, wheeled and pounced. The vicious triangular head whipped down with open jaws that clashed against Iron Robert's stony hide, dragged him from his feet—

His arms encircled the scaled neck, hugging the monster close. In sudden alarm, it braced its feet and backed, and Iron Robert held on, twisting the broad head sideways, his fingers locked in the corners of the clamped mouth. The heavy reptilian tail slammed the ground in a roil of dust; sparks flew where the bright talons of the creature's short arms raked Iron Robert's invulnerable chest and shoulders. Then it opened its jaws, whipped its neck, flung Iron Robert aside. He rolled in the dust, and before he could come to his feet, the chinazell sprang to him, brought an immense hind foot down in an earth-shaking kick.

Roan coughed as dust floated across from the scene of the battle.

"I can't see . . . " Stellaraire wailed. "What's happening?"

Iron Robert was on his feet again, grappling a hind leg nearly as big as himself. The chinazell, its weight down on its stunted forelimbs, sidled awkwardly, trying to shake its attacker loose. Its head came around and down, striking at Iron Robert. He hunched his head closer to his shoulders and reached up for a higher grip.

"The thing's too big for him," Stellaraire gasped. "He can't reach a vulnerable spot . . . "

With a surge, the chinazell raised the trapped leg clear of the ground and dashed it down. Iron Robert slammed against the concrete-hard clay—but he kept his grip.

"He's hurt!" Stellaraire choked. "It's all he can do to hold on—and that isn't doing him any good. But if he lets go, it will kick him again—"

"At least its teeth aren't hurting him," Roan said. "He's all right. He'll hold on until he tires it, and then—"

"It won't tire—not in this light gravity . . ."

The chinazell stood, its ribby sides heaving, its head on its long neck twisted to look at Iron Robert, who shifted his grip suddenly, leaped, caught a bony boss that adorned the dino's withers, and hauled himself across the creature's back, his weight bearing it down. Its legs sprawled out, and it plunged violently, striking with its yard-wide jaws as dust rose up in a dense cloud . . .

The chinazell came out of the dust cloud, wheeled, and charged down on Iron Robert as he came to his feet. It bounded past him and struck with its immense tail, a blow like a falling tree. Iron Robert went down, and the dino galloped away, circled, and Roan saw that its tail was broken, the hide torn, blood washing down across the scales, caking the dust. The head writhed on the long neck as the voiceless creature shuddered its pain. It came to a halt, the broken tail dragging now. Its head whipped from side to side as though seeking some escape from its torment. Fifty yards away, Iron Robert came slowly to his hands and knees.

"He's hurt!" Stellaraire cried. "Oh, please, Iron Robert! Get up!"

The chinazell moved heavily, painfully. It walked to

Iron Robert, stood over him. It maneuvered into position, raised a leg like an ironwood log set with spikes, brought it down square on Iron Robert in a blow that shook the ground.

"Gom Bulj has got to stop it!" Stellaraire screamed. "It will kill him . . . !"

"Wait!" Roan caught her arm. "He's not finished yet! Look!"

The chinazell was moving awkwardly sideways, its head held low. Iron Robert's mighty arms circled the lean neck. As it dragged him, he freed one arm, raised it, drove his stony fist into one small, lizard eye. The chinazell bucked, tried to shake free, but Iron Robert held on, twisted, struck at the other eye. The dino reared and plunged desperately, and Iron Robert dropped away, lay on his back. He raised his bloody fists, let them fall back.

The blinded chinazell stopped, squatted; thick blood ran down the triangular face; the primitive mouth opened in voiceless agony. It rose, ran a few yards, dragging its dead tail, then squatted again, its small cunning gone with its eyes. A murmuring ran through the silent crowd, and someone started a hissing, and at the sound the chinazell leaped up, crashed aimlessly against the thick fence. People scrambled back in fright, screaming, and the panicked beast lunged, brought down a section of the barrier, then turned and blundered back, struck the fence again. There was a blare of noise from the PA system, and Gom Bulj appeared, a vivid, bloated figure in scarlet capes, carrying a heavy power gun. He took aim, blew the head off the maimed beast. It fell over sideways like a mountain, kicked out once, twice, then lay still. The headless neck twitched as blood pumped out to puddle in the dust like black oil.

Gom Bulj walked over to Iron Robert, stood looking at him, still holding the gun in his hand; he raised it . . .

"No!" Stellaraire was round the barrier, running toward the entrepreneur.

"You can't!" Roan heard her voice, almost drowned in the angry shouting of the crowd that had seen the two most deadly fighters in the Galaxy maim each other, and still felt cheated because there hadn't been more blood and agony.

As Roan came up, Gom Bulj was holding up a wide, many-fingered hand.

"As you wish, my dear," he was rumbling. "I merely thought—"

"Iron Robert's not just another wounded animal," Stellaraire flared.

"But of course he is," Gom Bulj boomed, lighting up a foot-long cigar. "What else would you call him? But no matter, say your farewells or whatever, and then back to work, eh?" He turned away.

"We'll have to get a crew over here," Roan said. "He's too heavy to lift—"

"Leave him where he is," Gom Bulj said. "Disposal is the locals' problem. And now I really must—"

"Aren't you even going to try to help?" Roan demanded, standing in front of the bulky businessman.

Gom Bulj waved his cigar, blinking at Roan. "Ah, you Terries," he chuckled. "So impractical . . . " He rippled quickly to one side and past Roan and the crowd of hurrying circus hands swallowed him up. The audience was melting away and almost before they were clear the seats were going down, and the crews had started on striking the top. Stellaraire was bending over Iron Robert.

"Good-by," she said sadly. "You fought awfully well, Iron Robert; he was just too big for you."

The stone giant opened his eyes. "Chinazell . . . tough fighter," he said in a gritty, labored voice. "Dirty . . . trick . . . gouge . . . eyes." His craggy face was contorted and his huge chest labored with the effort of his breathing.

"Do you think you could stand?" Roan asked. He gripped a massive arm and pulled, but it was like pulling on the trunk of a fallen tree. "We've got to get help," he said, looking over toward the ship that was visible now where the tent had been peeled back. A crew was folding up the arena partitions, and a group of busy locals were setting to work to skin out the chinazell. There was no one else near.

"No one will help," Stellaraire said. "They just . . . don't help. And anyway . . . " she paused, looking at Iron Robert as he lay sprawled out on his back.

"Anyway . . . no use," the giant growled. "Iron Robert bad hurt. Bone in back broken. Legs . . . not move. You go now, Gom Bulj not like you be late."

A bald, thick-necked humanoid came up, cradling Gom Bulj's power gun in his arm.

"Get moving, you two," he ordered. "There's work to be done. Gom Bulj said—"

"Don't you give me orders, Bulugg," Stellaraire snapped at him. "Anyway, we were just going—"

"I'm not leaving him here like this," Roan said. He

looked helplessly around. The skinners were lifting a sail-like flap of horny skin from the chinazell, exposing the bone-white flesh of the dino's flank. No one was paying any attention to Iron Robert's plight, Roan saw. No one cared. Beyond the busy throng folding canvas, the animals were moving up the aft gangplank into the ship. There was a holdup as a humped animal decided to sit crossways and someone yelled for the electric goad. Then Roan saw Jumbo heaving over the 'zoo grounds like a ship in a slow sea.

"Get Jumbo," he said to Stellaraire. "I'll find some rope . . . !"

"But, Roan—"

"Do as I tell you!" he snapped. He started away and the guard said, "Hey!" and brought the gun around.

"Shut up, Bulugg!" Stellaraire said. "And don't get any ideas with that gun. You're just supposed to hold it and scare people."

Roan looped the thick, oily plastic cable under Iron Robert's arms, tied it in a vast knot. Stellaraire was perched on Jumbo's head with her legs hanging down over his gray, furrowed forehead. The pachyderm moved his trunk restlessly as Roan tied the cable to his leather-and-chain harness. Looking toward the ship, Roan saw that the animals were almost all aboard now; the last of the yard wagons were puffing away toward the greenish blaze of the setting sun with their loads. A shrill whistle sounded from the ship.

"Hey, shake it up!" Bulugg called. "That's minus a quarter. Whatta, ya wanna get left?"

"Pull, Jumbo!" Stellaraire cried. "Hurry! Pull!"

The elephant took a step and jolted to a stop. He looked back over his shoulder, puzzled, and flapped his ears.

"Pull, Jumbo," Stellaraire called; and Jumbo leaned into his harness and pulled, sensing the necessity of something more than ordinary effort. Iron Robert budged, dragging a furrow in the ground and Jumbo strained, putting his back into it, placing his great feet and thrusting, hauling the dead weight of many tons across the dusty clay of the empty arena.

At the gangplank, Bulugg jumped at the sound of the shrill last-warning whistle. He waved the gun nervously. There were faces at the port above, looking down curiously.

"Five minutes to the Seal Ship bell," he blustered. "You can leave that hunk of rock right here and get aboard . . . !"

Jumbo put a foot on the wide gangway, started up. A loudspeaker was chanting checklist orders. Gom Bulj appeared above, looking out from the cavernous hold.

"Here, here, what's this?" he bellowed. He waved his arms, staring around as if outraged. Iron Robert's vast inert weight dragged in the dust like a broken monument, reached the end of the gangplank—and jammed. Jumbo heaved, the harness taut across his chest. A rivet popped from it and clattered against the hull. Roan ran to the fallen giant, caught up a long pole, levered at the stony shoulder. Jumbo rocked twice, then heaved again—and Iron Robert bumped up on the gangway, grinding along the incline with a noise like a wrecked ship being hauled off a launch pad.

Then they were in the hold and Gom Bulj was rippling his walking tentacles, muttering loudly, and the others were staring and then walking away, bored quickly with Terry foolishness. Stellaraire's lavender powder was caked with sweat and two of her gold-painted, so-carefully tended fingernails were broken off, but Roan looked at her and found her beautiful, with dust in her ocher eyes and streaks down her face, and her gold tights plastered against her body. The port clanged shut, and the ship's lights came on, and they stood and looked down at the great body they had salvaged.

"Well, there went your chance to run away from the 'zoo," Stellaraire sighed. "What are you going to do now? Just leave him here?"

"We'll get the vet to look at him; he'll know how to fix him. You and I will bring him food and scrape him. After a while he'll be all right again."

The girl looked into Roan's face curiously. "Why?" she asked. "He was nothing special to you—you hardly knew him . . . "

"Nobody should be left alone to die just because they're hurt," Roan said shortly.

"You crazy, funny, Terry," Stellaraire said, and then she was crying, and he held her, wondering if it was because she was a mule and not a real Terran that she was so hard to understand at times.

For two months Iron Robert lay in the canvas-hung compartment Roan and Stellaraire had arranged for him in the cargo hold, with his lower body encased in massive concrete casts to remind him not to try to move. Every day Roan or the girl went over him with a scraper, and assured him he was as handsome as ever. Now and then Gom Bulj came down to stare at the huge invalid, rap his nine knuckles against the casts, and mutter about expense.

When the day came that the vet said the casts could come off, Nugg came down and helped Roan work carefully with a jack hammer, freeing him. When they finished, Iron Robert sat up, then got to his feet and stood, whole again.

"Terry customs strange," he rumbled, looking down at Roan. "Not call you Terry now. Call you Roan. Iron Robert your friend, Roan. Not understand Terry ways, but maybe good ways. Maybe better ways than Iron Robert ever know before."

Gom Bulj appeared, puffing two cigars. He looked Iron Robert over, shaking his head.

"A remarkable thing, young Terry. It appears you were right. A valuable property, and good as new—I hope. I'm a fair being, young Terry, and I have decided to reward you. Henceforth, you may consider the mule, Stellaraire, as your personal concubine, for your exclusive use—except when I have important Terry-type guests, of course—"

"She's not yours to give away," Roan said sharply.

"Eh? What's that, not mine?" Gom Bulj blinked at Roan. "Why I paid—"

"No one owns Stellaraire."

"See here, my lad, you'd best remember who it is you're addressing! Are you forgetting I could have you trussed up in leathers and flogged for a week?"

"No," Iron Robert rumbled. "No one lay hand on Roan, Gom Bulj. Iron Robert kill any being that try— even you."

"Here . . . !" Gom Bulj backpedaled, staring around wildly. "What's the cosmos coming to? Am I to be threatened by my own property?"

"Iron Robert not property," the giant rumbled. "Iron Robert of royal ferrous strain, and belong to no being. And Roan my friend. Tell all crew, Roan friend to Iron Robert."

"And since you can't give me away," Stellaraire put in, "Roan still has a reward coming. I think it's time you gave him full Freak status and started paying him. And he should be freed from all duties except his high-wire act. And he should eat in the Owner's Mess, with the other stars."

"Why, why . . . " Gom Bulj stuttered. But in the end he agreed and hurried away, still muttering to himself.

CHAPTER✶EIGHT

There had been a party celebrating Iron Robert's successful defense of his title against a Fire-saber from Deeb, and Roan had drunk too much and not left Stellaraire until almost ship-dawn, and now he struggled out of a dream in which he fought against iron arms that closed on him, hearing the beloved voice that called by the arena gate. His eyes were open now, and he could hear his own breath rasping in his throat, and the voice was the wailing of a siren, but the crushing weight still held him, flat on his back with the edge of the bunk cutting into his arm, and a wrinkle in the blanket under him like a sword on edge. Far away, bells clanged, and a tiny glow grew behind the black glass disk above the cabin door, swelling into a baleful red that flashed on, off, on . . .

Roan moved, dragged an arm like an ironwood log across his body, turned under the massive pressure and fell with stunning violence to the floor from the bunk.

Lying on his face, he felt the deep vibration through the deck plates. The engines were running—here in deep space, four parsecs from the nearest system! He rose to his feet, his bones creaking under the massive acceleration—three gravities at least. Far away, over the bellow of the engines, the clang of bells, the whine of the siren, he thought he heard the sound of Jumbo's trumpeting . . .

He made his way across the room, into the corridor, dragging feet like anchors, while the noise swelled, crimson lights screamed red alarm, faraway voices called. At the end of the corridor the lift door waited, open. Inside, he reached to the control panel, pressed the button for the menagerie deck. For a moment, magically, the weight went away and he drew a breath—then massive blackness clamped down while tiny red lights whirled . . .

He was lying on the floor of the car, smelling the salty sea smell of blood. Through the open door under the blue-white glare of the ceiling, he saw the long white corridor, the barred doors. Crawling again, he made his way along the passage, feeling the slickness underfoot, seeing how the pattern spread from under the doors, blackish red and harsh green mingling in a glistening film that trembled in a geometric resonance pattern.

All around him, over the mind-filling Niagara of the engines, there were bellows, groans, grunts of final agony. Roan went on, not looking into the cages as he passed them one by one, seeing the film of blood dance spreading.

The high, barred door of Jumbo's stall was bulged outward, one two-inch steel rod sprung from its socket. Behind it, the elephant lay, blinded, ribs broken, one tusk snapped off short. Blood flowed from the open mouth, from under the closed eyelids. Roan could see the animal's massive side rise in a tortured heave as it struggled to breathe.

"Jumbo!" he choked.

The heavy trunk groped toward him. The great legs stirred; a moan rumbled from the crushed chest.

Roan looked at the power rifle clamped in a bracket beside the stall door. He pulled it free, checked the charge, raised it against the relentless pull, aimed between the closed and bloody eyes, and pressed the firing stud . . .

Alarms jangled monotonously in the carpeted corridor outside the quarters of Gom Bulj. Roan dragged leaden feet past the fallen body of an Ythcan, lying with one three-fingered hand outstretched toward the door of the patron's apartment.

Inside, Gom Bulj lay sprawled, his body crushed against the floor, his eyes bulging from the pressure. He moved feebly as Roan came to him and went heavily down to hands and knees.

"Why are you . . . killing us all . . . Gom Bulj?" Roan asked, then stopped to breathe.

"No . . ." the entrepreneur's voice was a breathless wheeze. "Not me . . . at . . . all . . . young Terry." He drew a hoarse breath. "Old battle . . . reflex . . . circuits . . . triggered . . . somehow. Maximum acceleration . . . three . . . standard . . . G . . ."

"Why. . . ?"

"Ah, why indeed . . . young Terry . . ."

"What . . . can we do?"

"It's . . . too bad . . . too bad, young Terry. No help for

us. The time has come . . . to terminate . . . the biological processes . . ."

"You mean . . . die . . .?"

"When the . . . environment becomes . . . hostile . . . a quick demise . . . is greatly . . . to be desired . . ."

"I want to live. Tell . . . me what to do . . ."

Gom Bulj's massive head seemed to sink even deeper into the compressed bulk of his body. "Self-preservation . . . an interesting . . . concept. A pity . . . we won't have . . . the opportunity . . . to discuss . . . it . . ."

"What can I do, Gom Bulj?" Roan reached to the bulbous body, gripped a thick arm. "I have . . . to try . . ."

"I suggest . . . you suspend . . . respiration. Five minutes . . . should do the trick . . . As for me . . . I may thrash a bit . . . but pay . . . no attention . . ."

"I'll turn off the engines," Roan choked. "How . . .?"

"No use . . . young Terry. Too far . . . Even now . . . blood runs . . . from your nostrils . . ."

"Tell me what to do . . ."

"On the war deck . . ." Gom Bulj gasped. "Command . . . control panel. A lever—painted white . . . But . . . you can't . . ."

"I'll try," Roan said.

It was an interminable time later, and Roan's hands and knees left red marks against the gray decking as he pulled himself across the raised threshold of the door above which the red glare panel warned: BATTLE CONTROL—AUTHORIZED PERSONNEL ONLY.

Across the dusty room, the dead gray of the great screens had changed to vivid green-white on panels alive now with dancing jewel lights. A dark shape moved on the master screen; below, mass and proximity gauges trembled; numbers appeared and faded on the ground-glass dials. Roan pulled himself to the padded Fire Controller's seat, spelled out the symbols flashing in blue: IFF NEGATIVE.

A yellow light blinked suddenly in the center of the panel. Red letters appeared on the screen, spelling out words in archaic Universal:

MAIN BATTERIES ARMED

The words faded, changed:

MAIN BATTERIES FIRE,
TEN SECONDS ALERT. . .

The auxiliary panels blinked from yellow to red to white.

FIRE ALL, the panel spelled out. Through the seat, Roan felt a tremor run through the ship, briefly rattling a loose bolt in the panel. Before him, the banked controls sparkled row on row, telltale lights blinking insistently, gauges producing readings, relays closing, clicking, as the robot panel monitored the action. Roan's eyes blinked back haze, searching for the white-painted switch. . .

It was there, just to the right of the baleful crimson dial lettered MAIN RADAR—TRACKING. He reached out, forcing his heavy hand up, grasped the smooth lever, threw it from AUTO to MANUAL.

The war lights blinked off. He searched the

instruments before him, found a notched handle lettered
EMERGENCY ACCELERATION, threw it to ZERO.

A thousand noises growled down to silence. Roan
seemed to float upward from the chair as the pressure
dropped to the ship-normal half-G. In the stillness, metal
popped and groaned, readjusting to the reduced stresses.
Distantly, someone screamed, again and again.

Roan thought suddenly of Stellaraire, alone in her
cabin. . .

He ran, leaping down the companionways, along to
her door. It stood ajar. He pushed it wide—

With a sound like the clap of gigantic hands, the room
exploded in his face.

He was a dust mote, floating in a brassy sky.
Somewhere thunder rolled, remote and ominous.
Somewhere, a voice called to him, and he would have
answered, but his lungs were choked with smoke as thick
as syrup. He fought to clear them, and then his eyes were
open and he saw broken metal, the fragments of a flower
dish and of a yellow blossom, and a white hand, limp, the
fingers curled.

He was on his feet, choking in an acrid reek of burned
metal, throwing aside a shattered chair, heaving at a
fallen fragment of paneling, coughing as dust boiled up
from the rubble of insulation, charred cloth, smashed
glass and wood and plastic.

She lay on her back, her eyes closed, her face
unmarked, her platinum hair swirled across her forehead.

"Stellaraire . . . !" He knelt, feeling scorching heat
against his face, brushing away dust, splinters, paper—

The duralloy beam lay across her pelvis, pinning her tight. Roan felt his throat close as he gripped the cold metal, strained at it, felt its massive inertia. On his knees, he wrapped his arms around the metal section, heaved back until the room swam red. The odor of smoke was stronger now. Roan stood, hearing the ringing in his head, seeing the pale yellow flames that licked at scattered paper and torn cloth. Twisted wires and broken conduits sagged from the broken wall. Water trickled from a ruptured pipe, and beside it a stream of sharp-odored liquid poured down.

The little colored fish from the tank lay stiff on the floor.

Too late, Roan whirled, threw a quilt over the burning paper. With a whoosh! the coolant fluid ignited, and now red fire boiled black smoke, and a wave of heat struck Roan's face like a whip. He seized a blanket, thrust it against the broken waterline, then threw the wet cloth over Stellaraire's body. It hissed when it touched the floor beside her. He threw himself down, not noticing the searing pain against his back, braced his feet, set his shoulders against the beam, and pushed. It was like pushing at a granite cliff. The air he breathed burned in his throat.

There was a fallen length of duralloy channel under his hand. He thrust it under the beam, levering until the shirt split across his back. The channel buckled. When he tossed it aside, there were yellowish-white burns on his palms.

Stellaraire's hair was burning, the platinum-gold strands blackening and curling. Roan stumbled to the door, out into a smoke-blinded corridor. He would find Iron Robert, and together they would free Stellaraire. . .

In the thick-rugged chamber of Gom Bulj, the entrepreneur lay where Roan had left him, in a puddle of blood, heavy lids half closed over dull eyes.

"You succeeded, young Terry," he said, his voice a thin echo of its old rumble. "Too late for me, I fear. . ."

Roan swayed on his feet. "Where is Iron Robert, Gom Bulj . . . ?"

"Alas, I don't know." The dull eyes turned to Roan's hands, his blackened clothing.

"You are burned, poor lad. Now you will die, there's a clever boy. Too bad. I had great ambition for you, young Terry. One day . . . I would have billed you . . . as the Galaxy's greatest freak . . ."

"It's Stellaraire," Roan said, talking now through a black mist that closed over tighter, ever tighter. "I need Iron Robert . . ."

A wall annunciator crackled and a strange voice spoke: "Attention all hands! Assemble in the main dining hall at once! Bring no weapons! Disobedience is death!"

"What voice is that?" Gom Bulj said faintly. "Are we boarded then?"

Roan made his mind work. "I saw a ship," he said, "on the screens. We fired—and they fired back. I think they won."

"Yes," Gom Bulj blinked heavy lids. "I knew it. I felt the shocks. Alas, in her day *Belshazzar* was a mighty dreadnought of the Empire—but now she has fought her last action. . ." His voice faded to a whisper.

"What should I do, Gom Bulj?" Roan cried.

The heavy body stirred; a last hoarse breath sighed out.

Roan looked down at the still body.

"Gom Bulj is dead," he said aloud. "Jumbo is dead . . . and . . . and . . ." He whirled, ran into the corridor and toward the dining hall.

All around, sounds of destruction echoed along metal halls. A muffled blast shook the deck plates underfoot. Harsh odors of hot metal and things that burned caught at Roan's throat. He came to the arched entry over the two wide steps leading down to the broad dining room with its threadbare eternon carpets and blackened gilt fixtures, and stopped, seeing overturned tables, huddled bodies, and standing among them, legs braced wide, cradling weapons, five creatures in coats covered with tight-curled hair.

"Help me!" Roan called.

The nearest creature whirled, swung his weapon around in an easy gesture. There were horns on his head, and his eyes were black stones.

A big creature in a radiation mask stepped to the horned creature's side, knocked the weapon aside, then turned the power pistols gripped in his big fists on Roan, looked him over through the slits in the mask.

"Don't burn this one, Czack. Can't you see he's a Terry?"

"To the pit with Terries," the other snarled—but he lowered his gun.

"It's Stellaraire!" Roan said. "Help me!"

The tall creature holstered one pistol and took off the mask. Roan looked into wide gray eyes, saw the thin nose, the edge of white teeth between the thin lips . . .

Roan stared.

"You look like pretty pure stock, kid," the tall Man said. "Where you from?"

"You're a Terran," Roan said. "Help me. The fire—"

The horned creature stepped close, swung a wide hand against Roan's head. He staggered; the room rang . . .

"—hands off the kid," the Man said. Roan shook his head, blinking back a blurring film.

"But I asked you a question, kid. Henry Dread doesn't ask twice." The pistol was still centered on Roan's chest.

Roan turned, started back up the steps. A horned humanoid blocked his way, swinging a slow blow that Roan leaned aside from.

"Get out of my way," Roan said. "I have to find Iron Robert . . ."

"Hold it." Henry Dread had both guns in his hands now, and he turned to the arched doorway. A tall, green-skinned Ythcan stood at the top of the two steps. Beside Roan, Czack brought his power rifle up. There was a deafening ba-wam; and a flicker of blue light—and the Ythcan spun back, fell, kicked, and lay still.

"See if there's any more," Henry Dread snapped. A hair-coated creature with hunched shoulders and a bald skull moved past Roan, sprang up the steps. Beyond him, Roan saw a wide silhouette looming against the corridor's glare.

"Iron Robert!" Roan shouted. "Run!"

Facing Iron Robert, the bald creature fired at point-blank range. Roan saw the flicker of blue light that played for an instant against Iron Robert's broad chest, heard a deep grunt; then Iron Robert took two steps, plucked the bald one from the floor, whirled him high, and threw him against the wall. He rebounded, lay utterly still, his face oddly flattened, blood dribbling from his ear.

"Stand clear," Henry Dread barked. "My blasters will take him."

Roan struck with the edge of his hand at the horned one's arm, caught the power rifle as it fell, swiveled on Henry Dread.

"Don't shoot him!" Roan said.

Iron Robert stood, his eyes moving from one to another of the six weapons aimed at him. Beside Roan, the horned creature snarled.

"What are you waiting for? Kill him!"

Henry Dread looked at Roan. He turned slowly, bringing his guns around to aim at Roan's chest.

"Drop it, kid."

"No," Roan said.

The Man's mouth twitched. There was sweat on his forehead. "Don't try me, kid. I'm supposed to be fast—and you're covered. Now let the gun down nice."

"Roan," Iron Robert's deep voice rumbled. "I kill this one?" He took a step toward Henry Dread. Six guns tracked him.

"No, Iron Robert. Go to Stellaraire—quickly!"

"I kill him easy," Iron Robert said. "Have only two small guns."

"Help Stellaraire, Iron Robert!" Roan shouted. "Do as I tell you!"

Standing straight, Roan forced himself not to think about Stellaraire or about the burns on his hands and body, or about the smell of charred flesh, but only about holding the gun aimed at the pirate's chest. And Iron Robert understood and turned and went.

"Be smart, kid," Henry Dread said between gritted teeth. "Drop it, before I have to burn you . . ." He was tall and solid, with a scarred face and thick fingers. He stood, two guns aimed at Roan, tense and ready, and the sweat trickled down his face.

"Try it," Roan said.

Henry Dread's mouth twisted in a sort of smile. "Yeah, you're fast, kid. Nobody ever took a gun away from Czack like that before. I don't think he likes you for it—"

"Why don't you kill the muck-grub . . . !" The horned one stood in a half crouch, eyes on Roan.

"Go ahead, jump him, Czack. Even if I put two through the head, I'll bet you a keg he'd nail you on the way down. Want to risk it?"

The other answered in an incomprehensible language. Henry Dread barked an order. His creatures stirred; two of them filed carefully past Roan and out into the corridor.

"Don't let them try to hurt Iron Robert," Roan said. "If he doesn't come back, I'll shoot you."

The pirate licked his lips, his eyes on Roan's. "What's that walking Bolo to you, kid? You're human—"

"He's my friend."

"Friends with a Geek?" Henry Dread sneered.

"Why are you killing everyone?"

"This tub fired on me first—not that my screens can't handle museum pieces like you tossed at us." The Man's eyes narrowed. "Nobody lobs one into Henry Dread and gets away with it."

"You killed Jumbo—and Gom Bulj—and maybe . . ." his voice broke.

"Don't take it so hard, kid. With me it's business. I needed fuel and ammo . . ." the voice seemed to fade and swell. Roan held his eyes open, leaning against the wall just slightly, holding the gun steady.

". . . this tub happened along. That's life."

There was a movement in the corridor behind Henry Dread. Iron Robert stepped into view. Behind him, a hair-coated creature stepped from a door, brought up a gun—

Roan swiveled and fired, and was back covering Henry Dread's belt buckle in a movement quicker than the eye could follow. The gunner fell and lay still.

"Wait there, Iron Robert," Roan called.

The big Man lowered his pistols, tossed them aside. He looked shaken. "Holding these things is likely to be dangerous," he said. "Kid, you move like a fire lizard on Sunside. But you're burned pretty bad. You need to have my medic take a look at you. Now, just aim that blaster off side, so no accidents happen, and we'll talk this thing over."

Roan held the rifle steady, listening to the surging in his head. In the doorway, Iron Robert waited.

"Look, kid, you put the gun down, and I'll guarantee you safe conduct. You and the one-man task force, too. You can't hold the iron on me forever."

Roan looked at the Man's eyes. They were steady on his.

"Will you give me your word as a Man?" Roan asked.

The Man stared at him. "Sure, kid." He glanced at Czack and the others.

"You heard that," he said flatly.

Roan lowered the rifle. Czack moved in, snatched it away, brought it up and around—

Henry Dread took a step, slammed a gnarled fist against the horned head. Czack dropped the rifle and spun against the wall. Henry Dread massaged his fist. "The slob didn't think I meant it." He looked at Roan. "I guess us Men got to stick together, eh, kid?" He bent and scooped up a gun. Iron Robert came toward him, a blackish stain on his shoulder.

"Shall I kill this one now?" he rumbled.

"No . . . Iron Robert . . . Stellaraire . . ." Roan leaned against the wall, feeling the dizziness rising. Iron Robert caught him.

"No, Roan." The great ugly head shook slowly. "The Fair One is gone away, now. Now she dances for the Gods in their high place, above all sorrow . . ." The deep voice seemed to come from far away.

"Take Roan to your doctors, Man."

"Yeah—the kid's in bad shape. You better come too, big boy. You're a tough one. You took a blaster on half-charge at five paces, and you're still walking and ready to eat 'em alive. Maybe I can use a Geek like you at that . . ."

CHAPTER ✳ NINE

They were alien hands, gentle but impersonally insistent, and they poked and prodded with a feel of slick, scaly hide, too-thin fingers. There was no comfort in alien hands; they weren't like Stellaraire's hands, warm and soft and—human. Roan moved to thrust the hands away, and searing pain flashed through his body and he gasped, not at the bodily agony but at the sudden vivid remembrance of hands that would not touch him again, and white-gold hair, and smiling ocher eyes . . .

"He wakes," a reedy voice said. "A tenacious organism. Not like some of these beings, who seem almost eager to flee to the long darkness. I feel their souls tremble and shrink under my hands, and they are gone like a snuffed candle. But not this one . . ."

"Make Roan live, Man doctor," Iron Robert's basso rumbled. "Make Roan live strong."

"Yes, yes. Stay back, you great ugly lout. Now, the wounds are clean. And I have here . . ." There was a sound of rummaging . . . "Aha! Now, we'll see—"

Roan stiffened at a sensation like molten lead poured

131

across his chest. He was aware of white lights glaring through his eyelids. He moaned.

"Eh, he feels it now: Lie easily, Terran. It is only pain . . ."

"You make pain go away, Man doctor!"

"I've yearned for a proper patient for these medicines, ugly giant! A fabulous pharmacopoeia, all made for Terrans ages dead; long have I saved them. Henry Dread likes to fancy his rogues have human blood, but my knives know all their secrets. Half-castes, mutants, humanoid trash! Now, this lad's different. He's almost a textbook example of your pure Terry stock. A rare creature . . ."

The thin voice rambled on, and the hands probed and the fire touched, flamed, and faded into a dull numbness. Roan let out a long breath and felt drugged drowsiness creeping over him like warm water rising in a tub.

"This skin," the voice went on, far away now. "The texture! How nicely the blade slides through it! And the color. See, look at this illustration in my book . . ."

"Does he sleep, Man doctor? Or . . . ?"

"He only sleeps, monster. Faugh, I'm pleased I have no need to take a scalpel to that horny hide of yours . . . Now, get back. I've two hours of close work ahead, and no need of your rusty bulk to hinder me."

It was many hours later; Roan opened his eyes and by a faint light filtering through a barred transom saw the massive silhouette beside him.

"Iron Robert . . ." Roan's voice was a weak croak.

"You wake now, Roan. You sleep, good. Man doctor small foolish creature, but he fix you good, Roan."

"I should have shot him, Iron Robert . . ."

"No, Roan. He fix you."

"I mean the Man. He killed Stellaraire. I should have killed him. You should have smashed them, smashed their ship—"

"Then Roan and Iron Robert die, too, Roan. Too soon to die for you. Too many strange things to see yet, too many places still to go. Long life ahead for you still, Roan—"

"Not for me. I'm only a Terry Freak, and I'm almost dead already. Dad told me. Humans only have time to start living and they die. And living's no fun—not any more . . ."

"Sure, lots of fun still to come, Roan. Many great jugs to drink, and far suns to see; many females to take, and enemies to kill, and whole universes to see and smell and taste. Plenty time to be dead after."

"All my friends are dead. And Stellaraire . . ."

"I still alive, Roan." Iron Robert moved and Roan heard a soft metallic clash. "Iron Robert your friend, sure."

Roan raised up on one elbow, ignoring a tearing sensation in his bandaged arm, peering in the dim light. Massive chains lay across Iron Robert's knees, and his wrists were circled by shackles of finger-thick metal.

"Iron Robert—you're chained to the wall . . .!"

"Sure—Henry Dread scared of me, you bet. I let him put chains on me if he send Man doctor to you."

Roan pushed himself upright, ignoring the pulse that started up, drumming in his temples. He swung his feet heavily to the floor. A blackness filled with whirling lights swelled to fill the room and he gripped the edge of the bunk, waiting for it to go away.

"I'll make him take them off," he heard himself saying. "I'll make him. . . . It was a Man to Man agreement . . ."

"No, Roan, you lie down! Bad for you to move now . . ."

"I don't want to lie down. Call him. Call Henry Dread . . ."

"Roan! You got to do like Man doctor say, otherwise you get bad sick . . ."

Roan was on his feet, feeling the floor sway and tilt under him.

"Henry Dread," he called, hearing the words emerge as a croak.

"Wait, Roan. Somebody come . . ."

There were metallic sounds in the corridor; a splash of light glared suddenly; long shadows crouched away from the door that swung wide, and a tall, broad figure stood squinting into the room.

"You yelling for me, were you, boy? Hey—on your feet already—?"

"You chained Iron Robert. You didn't keep your word."

"Henry Dread always keeps his word, you . . . !" The Man's wide shape seemed to blur; Roan blinked hard, wavered, caught himself.

"Unchain him. He's my friend . . . !"

"You better crawl back in that bunk, boy; you're raving! I'm captain aboard this vessel; you're a slave of war. I let the sawbones patch you up, but don't let it go to your head . . ."

Roan advanced toward Henry Dread on uncertain feet.

"Unchain him, liar! Keep your word, murderer!"

Henry Dread's eyes narrowed. "Why, you lousy little—"

Roan lunged, and Henry Dread leaped back, jerked his pistol from his hip holster and aimed it. Iron Robert came to his feet in a clash of chain.

"I'm aiming this right between your eyes, Terry boy," Henry said between his teeth. "One more step, and so help me I burn you down."

"I don't care about that," Roan said, taking a step. "That isn't anything."

"No, Roan!" Iron Robert boomed. "You do like Henry Dread say now, Roan!"

Roan tried to take another step, but the floor tilted and he gritted his teeth, and willed himself not to fall, willed the blackness to retreat . . .

"I wear chains for you, Roan. You do this for me."

"Kid, you're crazy . . . !" Henry Dread's voice barked. "You'll kill yourself!"

"You wait, Roan," Iron Robert said. "Later, when you get well, then you have chance to kill this one."

Henry Dread laughed, a harsh snarl. "Yeah, listen to your sidekick, kid. You kill me when you feel better."

Then the shadows moved and the light narrowed down and was gone in a clang of metal, and Roan sank down, groped, found the bed, fell across it.

"He's a Man, Iron Robert. A Terry—almost like me. But he's not like Dad said the Terries were."

"Henry Dread might scared Man, Roan," Iron Robert rumbled softly. "And maybe he not such mean Man like he make out. He come plenty quick, first time you call.

Maybe Henry Dread wait outside, hope you call his name. Maybe Henry Dread plenty lonely Man, Roan . . ."

The bars welded across the doorframe of the warhead storage room were as thick as Roan's wrist and close together. He leaned on the mop and looked through the bars at Iron Robert, who sat on a duralloy slab that sagged under his weight, almost invisible in the shadows of the lightless cell.

"The Minid they call Snaggle-head is the worst," Roan said. "He's about seven feet tall and he smells like a Charon's mud-hive. Yesterday he tripped me and I almost fell down the aft companionway."

Iron Robert's chains clanked. Roan could see his small eyes gleam. "You be careful, Roan. You don't let riffraff get you mad. You do like I say; wait."

"I don't want to wait. Why should I wait? I—"

"You wait cause you got plenty bad burns, not healed up yet. You want to get crippled for life? You wait, don't pay mind to anybody teases you."

"I do mind, though. I know which ones I'm going to kill first, just as soon as—"

"Roan, you stop that fool talk, you remember how you promise to do like I say."

"I'll keep my promise. Just because Henry Dread's word is no good doesn't mean I'm a promise-breaker, too."

"You wait a minute, Roan, you too much angry against Henry Dread. He keep promise, all right. He say you and me, he won't kill us. Well—both of us alive, all right."

"I'm going to tell him if he doesn't free you, I'll steal a gun the first chance I get and kill him."

"You do that, you big fool, Roan. I don't mind sit here in dark, rest. Not much rest for me, long time. I sit and think about old days, back home, time Iron Robert young being, have plenty fun. I got pretty good eidetic recall, remember all smells, tastes, sounds, faces. Sure, I got plenty good memories, Roan. First time I got time really look at them good."

"You're stronger than any of them—" Roan took a breath and made his voice angry to cover up the break. "You let them chain you, you big dumb hunk of scrap-iron—"

Iron Robert rumbled a laugh. "Plenty easy sit here with chains on. Tough for you, Roan, have to stay outside and let Snaggle-head push you round. But you show you got brains, Roan. You stay quiet, you wait. One day you heal up good, then maybe we see."

Roan looked along the corridor. A hatch clanged as three Minid crewmen emerged from a cargo hold.

"Well, you'll get a chance to see how they operate now, Iron Robert." Roan felt his throat turn dry. "You'll see how much good ignoring them does."

"OK, Roan, you go now, quick, don't have to wait for herd of mud-pigs—"

"I'll take it without hitting back," Roan said between his teeth. "But I won't run from them, I don't care what you say." He began working the mop, eyes on the floor.

The leading crewman hooked his thumbs in his sagging pistol belt and started toward Roan, laying a trail of oily sandal prints across the shiny expanse of freshly scrubbed floor. He had thick bowed legs and a hairless skull and there were wide gaps in the row of spade-shaped bluish teeth he was showing in what might have been a grin. Three loops of rough-cut yellow jewels hung against a grimy gold-braided tunic. He stopped two yards from Roan, plucked a dope stick from a breast pocket, bit off the cap and spat it on the floor, sniffed it appreciatively with wide nostrils, and said:

"Hey, boys, looky what's here . . ." He pointed with the dope stick, his wide mouth forming a loose-lipped O of mock amazement. "What is it, a itty bitty baby boy playin' like a growed-up Geek?"

"Naw, it's a cute little pansy-pants, talking to its sweety through the bars," a second crewman offered. "It thinks that rusted-out Freak is mighty sexy—"

"Hey, don't talk dirty in front of it," another said. "It might learn a dirty word and use it in front of its mama and get 'panked.'"

"Always thought old Henry wasn't as tough as some thought," Snaggle-head stated. "Now he's got hisself a play-dolly." He chuckled, a sound like gas escaping from a sewer. "Next thing, Old Cap'n'll get hisself a little Terry bitch and start in breedin' 'em." He haw-hawed, hawked, spat on the floor at Roan's feet. Roan stopped mopping, stood looking at the wide mural on the lounge wall, with its audio-vision of a rolling seascape. In the silence the crash and hiss of breakers was loud. Snaggle-head chuckled again, took a final puff, and dropped the dope stick on the floor.

". . . but I notice he still don't trust him far; not since he held that gun on his belt buckle. I think his little pet plumb scared him that time—"

Casually, Roan slapped the wet mop across

Snaggle-head's sandal; the big crewman jumped back with a yell, stamping his wet foot against the deck. The grin had vanished from the loose mouth; the other crewmen watched with bright, interested eyes. Snaggle-head drew his massive head down close to his burly shoulders. His mouth was open, his brow creased in a black frown.

Ignoring him, Roan thrust the wet end of the mop into the filter unit, watched the rollers close and open, went on with his mopping.

Snaggle-head stepped in front of him; his grimy finger prodded Roan's chest. Roan looked into the oversized face, spotted here and there with coarse hairs sprouting from inflamed warty blemishes.

"What you think you're lookin' at, punk?"

"It looks like the hind end of a crundle-beast," Roan said clearly, "only hairier."

The coarse face tightened; the finger jabbed again, hard. "You take a lot of chances, softie—"

"Whatever it is, I'll remember it," Roan continued. "Some day I'll put my foot in it."

Snaggle-head's eyes narrowed. "It's a mean-talking one," he said softly. "Too bad it ain't got the guts to back up the talk." The heavy hand swung in a short arc, slammed Roan's head against the metal bulkhead. He staggered, caught himself with the unbandaged arm, shook his head to clear it.

"Is that . . . the best you can do?" he asked blurrily. "I guess you're scared to get too rough; there's only three of you . . ."

The crewman shook clawed hands, palms up, under Roan's nose.

"One of these days, pansy, I'll put the thumbs in, where it counts. I'll put 'em in till the blood squirts—"

Roan looked into the pale eyes. "You will, eh? You think Henry Dread will let you?"

The wide mouth dropped open. The pasty face turned a dull pink. "Whatta I care about Henry Dread? As soon as I get ready to croak you, rube, you'll know it—and to the Nine Hells with Henry Dread."

"Careful," Roan said, nodding toward the others, "they're listening."

"Huh?" The heavy head swiveled quickly to look at the two crewmen. They looked at the ceiling.

"All right, you slobs. Let's get moving. We ain't got all day to gab with sissy-britches here." The two filed past in silence.

"I'll get to you later, cull," the lead crewman grated.

"Roan," Iron Robert's voice rumbled from the cell. "You got to learn keep mouth shut sometimes. That space rat hurt you much?"

"He didn't hurt me." Roan's face was white in the gloom.

"You not be so dumb, you not talk back, you don't get hit."

"It's worth it."

"Maybe some day he get really mad, hit too hard."

"He hasn't got much of a punch."

"Maybe he got better punch than you think. Maybe what you said not so far off true."

"What do you mean?"

"Maybe Henry Dread better friend than you think, Roan. I think he tell all Gooks and Geeks, hands off human boy. I think he have plans in mind for you, Roan."

CHAPTER ✳ TEN

The surgeon clicked his lipless mandibles, peeling off the protective film under which the burns on Roan's shoulder and arm had been healing for many weeks.

"Eh, pretty, very pretty! Pink and new as a fresh-hatched suckling! There'll be no scars to mar that smooth hide!"

"Ouch!" Roan said. "That hurts."

"Ignore it, youngling," the surgeon said absently, working Roan's elbow joint. He nodded to himself, tried the wrist, then the fingers.

"All limber enough; now rise your limb here." He indicated shoulder level. Roan lifted his arm, wincing. The surgeon's horny fingers went to the shoulder joint, prodding and kneading.

"No loss of tone there," the surgeon muttered. "Bend over, stretch your back . . ."

Roan bent, twisted, working the shoulder, stretching the newly healed burns. Sweat popped out on his forehead.

"At first it may feel as though the skin is tearing open," the surgeon said. "But it's nothing."

Roan straightened. "I'll try to remember that."

The surgeon was nodding, closing his instrument case. "You'll soon regain full use of the limb. Meanwhile, the hide is tender, and there'll be a certain stiffness in the joints—"

"Can I—ah—do heavy work now?"

"In moderation. But take care: I've no wish to see my prize exhibit damaged." The surgeon rubbed his hard hands together with a chirruping sound. "Wait until Henry Dread sees this," he cackled. "Calls me a Geek, does he? Threatens to put me out the air lock, eh? But where would he ever find another surgeon of my skill?" He darted a final, sharp glance of approval at Roan and was gone. Roan pulled his tunic over his head, buckled his belt in place, and stretched his arms gingerly. There was a wide header over the doorway. He went to it, grasped it, and pulled himself up carefully. The sensation reminded him of a Charon he had seen stripping hide from a dead gracyl . . . but the injured arm held his weight.

He dropped back and went out into the corridor. There was a broken packing case in a reclamation bin in the corner. Roan wrenched a three-foot length of tough, blackish inch-thick wood from it. He looked toward the bright-lit intersection of the main concourse. A steward in soiled whites waddled past on bowed legs, holding a tray up on a stumpy arm. Henry Dread and his officers would be drinking in the wardroom now. It was as good a time as any . . .

Roan turned and followed the dull red indicator lights toward the lower decks.

He was in a narrow corridor ill lit by grimed-over glare

panels. Voices yammered nearby: shouts, snarls, a drunken song, a bellow of anger; the third watch break hour was underway in the crew quarters. Roan hefted the skrilwood club. It was satisfactorily heavy.

Feet clumped in the cross-corridor ten feet away. Roan ducked into a side passage, flattened himself, watched two round-backed barrel-chested humanoids high-step past on unshod three-toed feet, bells tied to their leg lacings jingling at each step. When they had passed, he emerged, following the tiny green numbers that glowed over doors, found one larger than the others. Roan listened at the door; there was a dull mumble of voices. He slid the panel aside, stepped in; it was a barracks, and he wrinkled his nose at the thick fudgy odor of unwashed bedding, alien bodies, spilled wine, decay. A narrow, littered passage led between high bunks. A dull-eyed Chronid looked up at him from an unkempt bed. Roan went past, stepped over scattered boots, empty bottles, a pair of six-toed feet in tattered socks sprawling from a rump-sprung canvas chair. Halfway along the room, four large Minids crouched on facing benches, bald heads together. They looked up. One of them was Snaggle-head.

He gaped; then his wide lips stretched in a cold grin. He thrust aside a leather wine mug, wiped his mouth with the back of a thick, square hand, got to his feet. He reached behind his back, brought out a knife with an eighteen-inch blade, whetted it across his bare forearm.

"Well, looky what's got loose from its string—" he started.

"Don't talk," Roan said. "Fight." He stepped in and

feinted with the club and Snaggle-head stepped heavily back, snorting laughter.

"Hey, looks like baby face got hold of some strong sugar-mush." He looked around at the watchers. "What'll we do with him, fellers—"

But Roan's club was whistling and Snaggle-head jerked back with a yell as the wood smacked solidly against his ribs. He brandished the knife, leaped across a fallen bench; Roan whirled aside, slammed the club hard against the Minid's head. The crewman stumbled, roaring, rounded on Roan, a line of thick blackish blood inching down his leathery neck. He lunged again and Roan stepped back and brought the club down square across the top of the bald skull. Snaggle-head wheeled, kicked the bench aside, took up a stance with his feet wide, back bent, arms spread, the blade held across his body. He dashed blood away from his eyes.

"Poundin' my head with that macaroni stick won't buy you nothin', Terry," he grated. His mouth was set in a blue-toothed grin. "I'm comin' to get you now . . ."

He charged, and Roan watched the blade swing toward him in a sweeping slash and at the last moment he leaned aside, pivoted, and struck down at the Minid's collarbone; the skrilwood club hit with a sound like an oak branch breaking. Snaggle-head yowled and grabbed for his shoulder, spinning away from Roan; his face twisted as he brought the knife up, transferred it with a toss to his left hand.

"Now I kill you, Terry!"

"You'd better," Roan said, breathing hard. "Because if you don't, I'm going to kill you." Roan moved in, aware of a layer of blue smoke in the muggy air, wide eyes in big Minid faces, the flat shine of Chronid features, the distant putter of a ventilator fan, a puddle of spilled beer under the fallen bench, a smear of dark blood across Snaggle-head's cheek. The Minid stood his ground, the knife held before him, its point toward Roan. Roan circled, struck with the club at the knife. The Minid was slow: the blade clattered from the skinned hand, and Roan brought the heavy bludgeon up—

His foot skidded in spilled beer, and he was down, and Snaggle-head was over him, his wide face twisting in a grimace of triumph; the big hands seemed to descend almost casually and Roan threw himself aside, but there were feet and a fallen bench, and the hands clamped on him, biting like grapple hooks, gathering him into a strangling embrace.

He kicked, futile blows against a leg like a tree trunk, hearing the Minid's breath rasp, smelling the chemical reek of Minid blood and Minid hide, and then the arms, thick as Roan's thigh, tightened, and Roan's breath went out in a gasp and the smoke and the faces blurred . . .

". . . let him breathe a little," Snaggle-head was saying. "Then we'll see how good his eyeballs is hooked on. Then maybe we'll do a little knife work—"

Roan twisted, and the arms constricted.

"Ha, still alive and kicking." Roan felt a big hand grope, find a purchase on his shoulder. He was being held clear of the floor, clamped against the Minid's chest. The Minid's free hand rammed under Roan's chin, forced his head back. A blunt finger bruised his eye.

"Let's start with this one—"

Roan wrenched his head aside, groped with open jaws, found the edge of a hand like a hog-hide glove between his teeth, and bit down with all the force of his jaws. The Minid roared, and Roan braced his neck and clung, tasting acrid blood, feeling a bone snap before the hand was torn violently from his grip—

And he struck again, buried his teeth in Snaggle-head's shoulder, grinding a mass of leather-tough muscle, feeling the skin tear as the Minid fell backward.

They were on the floor, Snaggle-head bellowing and striking ineffectually at Roan's back, throwing himself against the scrambling legs of spectators, kicking wildly at nothing. Roan rolled free, came to his knees spitting Minid blood.

"What in the name of the Nine Devils is going on here?" a voice bellowed. Henry Dread pushed his way through the crewmen, stood glaring down at Roan. His eyes went to the groveling crewman.

"What happened to him?" he demanded.

Roan drew breath into his tortured chest. "I'm killing him," he said.

"Killing him, eh?" Henry Dread stared at Roan's white face, the damp red-black hair, the bloody mouth. He nodded, then smiled broadly.

"I guess maybe you're real Terry stock at that, boy. You've got the instinct, all right." He stooped, picked up Snaggle-head's knife, offered it to Roan. "Here. Finish him off."

Roan looked at the Minid. The cuts on the bald scalp had bled freely, and more blood from the torn shoulder had spread across the chest. Snaggle-head sat, legs drawn up, cradling his bitten hand, moaning. Tears cut pale paths through the blood on his coarse face.

"No," Roan said.

"What do you mean, no?"

"I don't want to kill him now. I'm finished with him."

Henry Dread held the knife toward Roan. "I said kill him," he grated.

"Get the vet," Roan said. "Sew him up."

Henry stared at Roan. Then he laughed. "No guts to finish what you started, hey?" He tossed the knife to a hulking Chronid, nodded toward Snaggle-head.

"Get the vet!" Roan looked at the Chronid. "Touch him and I'll kill you," he said, trying not to show how much it hurt to breathe.

In the profound silence, Snaggle-head sobbed.

"Maybe you're right," Henry Dread said. "Alive, he'll be a walking reminder to the rest of the boys. Ok, Hulan, get the doc down here." He looked around at the other crewmen.

"I'm promoting the kid to full crew status. Any objections?"

Roan listened, swallowing against a sickness rising up inside him. He walked past Henry Dread, went along the dim way between the high bunks, pushed out into the corridor.

"Hey, kid," Henry Dread said behind him. "You're shaking like a Groac in molting time. Where the hell are your bandages?"

"I've got to get back to my mop," Roan said. He drew a painful breath.

"To hell with the mop. Listen, kid—"

"That's how I earn my food, isn't it? I don't want any charity from you."

"You'd better come along with me, kid," Henry Dread said. "It's time you and me had a little talk."

In his paneled, book-lined cabin, Henry Dread motioned Roan to a deep chair, poured out two glasses of red-brown liquid.

"I wondered how long you'd take the pushing around before you showed you were a Man. But you'll still have to watch yourself. Some of the boys might take it into their heads to gang up on you when they think I'm not looking."

"*I'll* be looking," Roan said. "Why do they want to kill me?"

"You've got a lot to learn, lad. Most of the boys are humanoids; I've even got a couple that call themselves Terries; I guess they've got some Terry blood, but it's pretty badly mutated stock. They don't like having us damn near purebreds around. It makes 'em look like what they are: Gooks." He took a swallow from his glass, blew air over his teeth.

"I don't like to work around Gooks, but what the hell; it's better'n living with Geeks."

"What's the difference between a Gook and a Geek?"

"I stretch a point: if a being's humanoid, like a Minid or a Chronid, OK, give him the benefit of the doubt. Maybe he's descended from mutated human stock. You got to make allowances for Gooks. But a life-form that's strictly non-human—that's a Geek."

"Why do you hate Geeks?"

"I don't really hate 'em—but it's them or us."

Roan tried his drink, coughed, put the glass down. "What's that? It tastes terrible."

"Whiskey; you'll learn to like it, boy. It helps you forget what you want to forget."

Roan took another swallow of the whiskey, made a face.

"It doesn't work," he said. "I still remember."

"Give it time," Henry Dread growled. He stood and paced the room.

"How much do you know about Terry history, boy?"

"Not much, I guess. Dad used to tell me that once Terries ruled the whole Galaxy, but then something happened, and now they're scattered, what there is left of them—"

"Not 'them,' boy. 'Us.' I'm a Terry. You're a Terry. And there are lots more of us. Sure, we're scattered, and in lots of places the stock has mutated—or been bred out of the true line—but we're still Terries; still human. And it's still our Galaxy. The Gooks and Geeks have had a long holiday, but Man's on the comeback trail now—and every Man has to play his part."

"You mean murdering people like—Stellaraire and Gom Bulj—"

"Look, that's over and done. To me a Geek's a Geek. I'm sorry about the girl, but what the hell: you said she was only a mule—"

Roan got to his feet; Henry Dread held up a hand. "OK. No offense. I thought we had a deal? Let's lay off this squabbling. We're Terries: that's what counts."

"Why should I hate Geeks?" Roan finished his drink,

shuddered, put the glass on the table. "I've got reason to hate you, but I was raised with Geeks. They weren't any worse than your Gooks. Some of them were my friends. The only human I ever knew was my father—and I guess maybe he wasn't all human. He was shorter than you, and wide through the shoulders, and his arms were almost as thick as a Minid's. And he had dark brown skin. I guess that couldn't be real Terry human stock."

"Hard to say. Seems like I read somewhere that back in prehistoric times, Men came in all kinds of colors: black, red, yellow, purple—maybe green, I don't know. But later on they interbred and the pure color strains disappeared. But maybe your old man was a throwback—or even descended from real old stock."

"Does anybody know what a real Terry looks like?" Roan took a lock of his thick dark red hair between his fingers, rolling his eyes up to look at it. "Did you ever see hair that color before?"

"Nope; but don't let it worry you. Everybody's got a few little flaws; Hell, Men have been wandering around the Galaxy for over thirty thousand years now; they've had to adapt to conditions on all kinds of worlds; they've picked up everything from mutagenic viruses to cosmic radiation to uranium burns; no wonder we've varied a lot from the pure strain. But pure or not, us humans have got to stick together."

Roan was looking at the empty glass. Henry filled it and Roan took another drink.

"He wasn't really my father," he said. "He and Ma bought me in the Thieves' Market on Tambool. Paid two thousand credits for me, too."

"Tambool; hmmm; hell of a place for a Terry lad to wind up. That where you were raised?"

Roan nodded.

"Who were your real parents? Why did they sell you?"

"I don't know. I was only a fertilized ovum at the time."

"Where'd those Geeks get hold of Terry stock?"

"I don't know. Dad and Ma would never talk much about it. And Uncle T'hoy hoy either. I think Ma told him not to."

"Well, it doesn't matter. You're the closest thing to pure Old Terry stock I've seen. I've made you a member of my crew—"

"I don't want to be a member of your crew. I want to go back home. I don't know if Ma's still alive, even, with Dad not there to look after her. I miss Dad. I miss Stellaraire, too. I even miss Gom Bulj—"

"Don't cry into your beer, kid. What the hell, I've taken a liking to you. You play your cards right and you'll do OK. You'll live well, eat well, see the Galaxy, get your share of loot, and some day—when I'm ready—you may be in on the first step toward something big—bigger than you ever dreamed of."

"I don't want loot. I just want my own people. I don't want to destroy. I want to build something."

"Sure, you've got a dream, kid. Every Man has. But if you don't fight for that dream, somebody else's dream will win."

"It's a big Galaxy. Why isn't there room for everybody's dream?"

"Boy, you've got a lot to learn about your own kind.

We've got the drive to rule—to conquer or die. Some day we'll make this Galaxy into our own image of Paradise—nobody else's. That's the way Men are."

"There's billions of Geeks," Roan said. "But you're the only Man I've ever seen."

"There are Terries all over the Galaxy—wherever the Empire had an outpost. I mean to find them—one at a time, if I have to. You think I'm just in this for the swag? Not on your life, boy. I could have settled down in luxury twenty years ago—but I've got a job to do."

"Why do you want me? I'm not going to kill Geeks for you."

"Listen, kid, goon squads are cheap; I can hire all I want for the price of a good dinner at Marparli's on Buna II. But you're human—and I need every Man I can get."

"I still haven't forgotten," Roan said. "That whiskey's a fake. So are you. You killed my friends and now you think I'm going to help you kill some more."

Henry gripped Roan's shoulder with a hard hand. "Listen, boy: a Man's got to live. I started off in the Terry ghetto on Borglu, kicked around, spit on, worked like a tun-lizard in the wood mines. There wasn't a day they let me forget I was a Man—and that all I'd ever get was a Man's share—the scraps, and the kicks, and the curses. I hung around back doors and ate garbage, sure. A Man's got a drive to live—no matter how. And I listened and learned a few things. They used to call me in and laugh at me; they'd tell me how once the Terry Empire had stretched across half a Galaxy, and how Terries had been the cock of the walk in every town on ten million worlds, master of everything. And how I was a slave now, and just about good enough, maybe, to wash their dirty clothes and run their errands and maybe some day, if I was a good worker, they'd get me a half-breed wench and let me father a litter of mules to slave for them after I was gone.

"Well, I listened—and I got the message—but not the one they had in mind. They didn't know Terries, boy. Every time they'd show me a book with a picture of a Terran battle officer in full dress, and tell me how the Niss had wiped out the fleet—or hand me an old Terran pistol and tell me how their great grandpap had taken it off a starving Man—it didn't make me feel like a slave. It made me feel like a conqueror. One day one of them made a mistake. He let me handle a Mark XXX hand blaster. I'd read a book or two by then. I'd studied up on Terran weapons. I knew something about a Mark XXX. I got the safety off and burned old Croog and two bystanders down and then melted off the leg band . . ." Henry Dread stooped, pulled his boot off, peeled back his sock. Roan stared at the deep, livid scar that ringed the ankle.

"I made it to the port; there was a Terry scout boat there, dozed offside, buried in the weeds. I'd played around it as a kid. I had a hunch maybe I could open it. There was a system of safety locks—

"To make it short, I got clear. I've stayed free ever since. I've had to use whatever gutter scrapings I could find to build my crew, but I've managed. I've got a base now—never mind where—and there's more battlewagons ready for commissioning—as soon as I get reliable captains. After that—

"Well, I've got plans, boy. Big plans. And they don't include Geeks running the Galaxy."

"Iron Robert's a Geek—and he's my friend. He's a better friend than any of those Gooks of yours—"

"That's right, boy. Stick up for your friends. But when the chips are down—will he stick by you?"

"He already has."

Henry Dread nodded. "I have to give him credit. I admire loyalty in a being—even a Geek. Maybe old iron pants is OK. But don't confuse the issue. A good, solid hate is a powerful weapon. Don't go putting any chinks in it."

"Iron Robert is a good being," Roan said. "He's better than me—and better than you, too . . ." Roan stopped talking and swallowed. "I feel kind of sick," he said.

Henry laughed. "Go sleep it off, kid. You'll be OK. Take the stateroom down the hall from mine here. A Terry crew member doesn't have to sleep with Gooks any more."

"I've got some rags in the corridor outside Iron Robert's cell. I'll sleep there."

"No, you won't, kid. I can't have a Terry losing face with Gooks—for the sake of a Geek."

Roan went to the door, walking unsteadily. "You've got a gun," he said. "You can kill me if you want to. But I'm going to stay with Iron Robert—until you let him out."

"That animated iron mine stays where he is!"

"Then I sleep in the corridor."

"Make your choice, boy," Henry Dread's voice was hard. "Learn to take orders, and you live a soft life. Act stubborn, and it'll be rags and scraps for you."

"I don't mind the rags. Iron Robert and I talk."

"I'm *asking* you, kid. Move in next door. Forget the Geek."

"Your whiskey's no good. I haven't forgotten anything."

"What's the matter with you, you young squirt? Haven't I tried to treat you right? I could send you below decks in lead underwear right now to swab out a hot chamber!"

"Why don't you?"

"Get out!" Henry Dread grated. "You had a big credit with me, kid—because you looked like a Man. Until you learn to act like one, keep out of my way!"

Outside in the corridor, Roan leaned against the wall, waiting for the dizziness to go away. Once he thought he heard a sound—as though someone had started to turn the door latch—but the door stayed shut.

After a while he made his way down to Iron Robert's cell and went to sleep.

CHAPTER✻ELEVEN

Iron Robert shook the bars. "You big fool, Roan, go on raid with riff-raff, maybe get killed. What for? You stay safe on ship—"

"I'm tired of being aboard ship, Iron Robert. This is the first time Henry Dread has said I could go along. I'll be all right—"

"What kind gun Henry Dread give you, Roan?"

"I won't need a gun. I won't be in the fighting."

"Henry Dread still 'fraid give you gun, eh? He big fool too, let you go in combat with no gun. You small, weak being, Roan—not like Iron Robert. You stay on ship like always!"

"There's a city on this world—Aldo Cerise—that was built by Terrans, over ten thousand years ago. Nobody lives there now but savages, so there won't be much of a fight—and I want to see the city—"

"Extravaganzoo play on Aldo Cerise, once, long time 'go. Plenty natives, plenty tough. Have spears, bows, few guns too. And not fools."

Roan leaned against the bars. "I can't just stay on the

ship. I have to get out and see things, and listen and learn, and maybe some day—"

"Maybe some day you learn stay out of trouble—"

A wall annunciator hummed and spoke: "Attention all hands. This is Captain Dread. All right, you swabs, now's your chance to earn some prize money! We're entering our parking orbit in five minutes. Crews stand by to load assault craft in nine minutes from now. Blast off in forty-two minutes . . ." Roan and Iron Robert listened as Henry Dread read the order of battle, feeling the deck move underfoot as the vessel adjusted its velocity to take up its orbit four hundred miles above the planet.

"I've got to go now," Roan said. "I'm in boat number one, the command boat."

"Anyway Henry Dread keep you by him," Iron Robert rumbled. "Good. You stay close, keep head down when shooting start. Henry Dread not let you get hurt, maybe."

"He wants me on his boat so he can keep an eye on me. He thinks I'll try to run away, but I won't—not until you can go, too."

Boots clanged at the far end of the corridor. Henry Dread, tall in close-fitting leather fighting garb, swaggered up. He wore an ornate pistol at each lean hip and carried a power rifle in his hands.

"I figured I'd find you here," he grated. "Didn't you hear my orders?"

"I heard," Roan said. "I was just saying good-by."

"Yeah. Very touching. Now if you can tear yourself away, we've got an action to fight. You stay close to me. Watch what I do and follow suit. I don't expect much static from the natives, but you never know—"

"Roan should have gun, too," Iron Robert rumbled.

"Never mind that, Iron Man. I'm running this operation."

"You nervous as caged dire-beast, Man. If everything so easy, what you afraid of?"

Henry narrowed his eyes at the giant.

"All right, I'm edgy; who wouldn't be? I'm hitting what used to be the capital of one of the greatest kingdoms in the Empire—and me with a seven-thousand-year-old hulk and a crew of half-breed space-scrapings. Who wouldn't be a little nervous?"

"Give Roan gun; or does lad make you nervous too?"

"Never mind, Iron Robert," Roan said. "I'm not asking him for anything."

Henry Dread's jaw muscles worked. He jerked the power rifle. "Come on, boy. Get down to the boat deck before I change my mind and give you a job swabbing the tube linings!"

"You bring Roan back safe, Henry Dread," Iron Robert called. "Or better not come back at all."

"If I don't, you'll have a long wait," the pirate growled.

In the cramped command compartment of the assault boat, Henry Dread barked into the panel mike: "Now hear this, you space scum! We're dropping in fast, slick and silent! I'm giving you a forty-second countdown after contact, then out you go. I want all four Bolos to hit the ramp at the same time, and I want to see those treads smoke getting into position! Gunnery crews, sight in on targets and hold your fire for my command! Heli crews . . ." The pirate captain gave his orders as the boats dropped

toward the gray world swelling on the forward repeater
screen. The deck plates rumbled as the retro-rockets fired
long bursts, correcting velocity. Atmosphere shrieked
around the boat now. Roan saw the curve of the world
swing up to become a horizon; a drab jungle continent
swept under them, then an expanse of sparkling sea, and
a white-surfed shoreline. There was a moment of vertigo
as the vessel canted, coming in low over green hills; it
righted sluggishly, and now the towers of a fantastic city
came into view, sparkling beyond the distant forest-clad
hills.

"Remind me to shoot that gyro maintenance chief,"
Henry growled. Roan watched as treetops whipped past
beneath the hurtling ship. Then it was past the wooded
slopes, and the city was close, looming up, up, until the
highest spires were hazy in the airy distances overhead.
The ship braked, slowed, settled in heavily. A ponderous
jar ran through the vessel. The torrent of sound washed
away to utter silence. From below, a turbine started up,
ran sputteringly, smoothed out. Henry looked at the panel
chronometer.

"If one of those slobs jumps the gun . . ."

A light blinked to life on the panel.

"Ramp doors open," Henry murmured. "Thirty-eight,
thirty-nine, forty!" He whirled on Roan.

"Here we go, kid! With a little luck we'll be drinking
old Terry wine out of Terry crystal before the star goes
behind those hills."

Roan stood with Henry Dread at the foot of the ramp,
looking out across a pitted and crumbling expanse of

ancient pavement. Far across the field, four massive tracked vehicles aimed black gun muzzles at the silent administrative sheds. Nothing moved.

"Empty emplacements," Henry said. "Missile racks corroded out. It's a walkover . . ."

"Iron Robert said the 'zoo played here once," Roan said. "He said the natives have guns and bows, and know how to use them."

"The carny was here, eh? Who'd it play to, the rock lizards?"

"People," Roan said. "And they wouldn't have to be very smart to be smart enough to stay out of sight when they see a shipload of scavengers coming."

"Corsairs," Henry barked. "We don't scavenge, boy! We fight for what we take. Nothing's free in this universe!" He thumbed his command mike angrily.

"Czack! Wheel that tin can of yours over here!" He turned to Roan. "We'll go take a look at the city." He waved his rifle toward the towers beyond the port. "This was one of the last Terry capitals, five thousand years ago. Men built the place, boy—our kind of Man, back when we owned half the Galaxy. Come along, and I'll show you what kind of people we came from."

There was a high golden gate before the city and at the top, worked in filigree, was the Terran Imperial symbol, a bird with a branch in its mouth, and a TER. IMP. above it.

"I've seen it a million times, in my books back on Tambool," Roan said. "That bird and the TER. IMP. above it. Why a bird, anyhow?"

"Peace," Henry Dread said. "Czack!" he barked into his command mike. "Bring that pile of tin up here and put it in High." Then he turned back to Roan. "TER. IMP. means Terra ran the show. And any bird that didn't keep the peace got his guts ripped out. That's how Men operate, see?"

Peace, Roan thought, turning it in his mind, trying to smooth off the sandpapery edge Henry Dread gave to the word, watching the massive combat unit rumbling up beside him.

"Take it slow. Put it in Maximum now," Henry Dread said to Czack. "That fence is made of Terralloy and nothing'll tear it down but a Terry Bolo."

"But it's stood like this for five thousand years and nobody can put up another one," Roan said, wanting the TER. IMP. and the bird to stay there another five thousand years. "Why tear it down? Couldn't you just blast the lock?"

"Maybe. But this impresses the Geeks more, if they're watching. OK. Take it, Czack."

The gate screamed like a torn female, bent slowly, and finally went over with a horrible clang, and the Bolo, a crease along its top turret now, went on through and Czack traversed his guns, looking for natives.

The quick silence from the fallen gate and the dead city was eerie. Czack appeared at the upper hatch and swore at the gate and the Bolo and Aldo Cerise in general. He spotted the dent in the Bolo turret and swore worse.

"Maybe we'll find more Bolos in the city," Henry Dread said. "Never seen an Imperial city without 'em and this was a great one. Get you a nice, new Bolo and some nice, new guns. Now get back in the tin can and keep us covered while we do some ground reconnoiter. Shoot anybody you see."

Henry Dread tucked the mike under his tunic. His heavy boots rang on the mosaic of the walkway they took beside the road, and he gestured with his gun as they went along.

"Those buildings," he said. "Ever see anything that high for beings that don't have wings?"

The Terran buildings climbed into the sunlight, incredibly straight and solid. From here it all looked perfect. But at Roan's feet the tiles of the intricate mosaic were broken and missing in spots, and Henry Dread kicked at the loose ones as he walked along.

Roan paused to watch a fountain throwing rainbows into the air, spinning shifting patterns of water and light.

"They *built* things in those days," Henry Dread said. "That fountain's been running five thousand years. More, probably. Anything mechanical breaks in this city, fixes itself."

Roan was looking at the house beyond the fountain, with the TER. IMP. symbol on the door, and he gaped up at row on row of floors, windowed and balconied.

"It looks as though that door might open," Roan said. "People might walk out. My people." He paused, wondering how he would feel if this were home. "But it's all so perfect. So wonderful. If they could build like this, how could anyone beat them?"

"The Lost War," Henry Dread said, coming up to the fountain and drinking from a side jet. He wiped his mouth on his sleeve. "They call it the Lost War but we didn't lose it. Terra never lost a war. A stalemate, maybe—we didn't win it, either. Anybody can see that. But we broke the power of the Niss. The Niss don't rule the universe. There's supposed to be the Niss blockade of Terra, and they say there's still a few Niss cruisers operating at the far side of the Galaxy. But that's probably just superstition. I've never run into a Niss. And never met anybody that did—Man, Gook, or Geek."

Henry Dread got out his microphone. The men had come in through the ruined gate and were scrambling over the Bolo, perching on its armored flanks and hanging off the sides.

"Fan out in skirmish order," he barked. "Shoot anything that moves."

Roan followed Henry Dread. "Empty," Roan said. "I don't see anything that looks like natives might be living here. I wonder why not? With all this . . ."

"Superstition. They're afraid of it." Henry Dread's eyes were darting in all directions. "But that doesn't mean there might not be a few natives inside the fence. And they may be right to be afraid of the city. Look over there."

There was a deep hole, blackened at the edges.

"Booby-trapped," Henry Dread said. "Don't know how many might be around the city, or where. So watch out."

They came to a high wall, set with clay tiles, and between the tiles grew tiny, exquisite flowers.

"Park," said Henry Dread. "Full-blown memento of Terran luxury. Maybe have time for it later."

"Tank here!" one of the men called from behind a nearby building. "Bolo Mark IX, factory fresh—"

"Don't *touch* her, you slat-headed ape!" Czack's voice crackled from his Bolo. "I don't want nobody's filthy hands on her until I see her."

Henry Dread laughed. "It's not a woman, you rack-skull. And it's *my* freaking tank and *I'll* see it first."

"Look, I'm going into that park," Roan said. "Call me when you want me."

Henry Dread stopped, looked back at Roan, frowning.

"I won't desert," Roan said. "Not as long as you've got Iron Robert back there in the hold."

"Maybe," Henry Dread said. "Maybe if you go in that park you'll find out the difference between Geeks and Men. Maybe you'll see what I'm after."

"Boss!" Czack called. "Take a gander at this. Full fuel tanks and magazines and . . ."

"Don't touch anything!" Henry Dread called. "These damned Gooks have scrambled eggs for brains," he added.

"OK," Roan said, starting to climb up a gnarled old tree that looked over the garden wall. "Fire three shots when you want me to come out."

"Watch out, boy," Henry Dread said, and stopped again. He took out his Mark XXX blaster and handed it over to Roan.

"You'll come back," he said. "And you'll know more than you do now."

Roan balanced the gun in his hand, sitting on a lower limb of the old tree. He felt the solid metal of it, the waiting, repressed power, the cold steel with the flaming soul. He looked briefly at Henry Dread, who laughed, knowing what Roan felt with the gun.

Then Henry Dread was striding away across the plaza and Roan clambered up the tree, thinking as he climbed of the gracyls and how he'd climbed to follow their flights, and of the circus and the tree he'd climbed to see it, the Never-never tree, little thinking it was his last day on Tambool. And at the height of the wall he thought of Stellaraire and the tightrope and his eyes stung, but then he looked over the wall toward the park.

And there was no room for thought of the past. Here lay the Terran civilization that Henry Dread talked of rebuilding.

Within the park green grass spread and flowers bloomed and Roan could see small automatic weeders moving along the paths where fountains rose and splashed untouched by time.

And across the manicured precision of the lawn, a fallen statue lay—a vast statue with a tunic draped around its hips. It lay face up, one arm raised, an arm that had once pointed at the skies.

It was a Terran. Pure Terran.

And made just like Roan.

Roan leaped down from the wall onto a bank of springy grass, and ran to the statue. Feature for feature—eyes, ears, nose, the connections of muscles—this was Roan. Terran.

Did my father look like this? Roan wondered. Who was this Man? Where did he come from? He walked around to the base of the statue. TER. IMP., it said, with the dove and the branch. And then:

ECCE HOMO, July 28, 12780

"Ecce," Roan said to the statue, touching it, wondering how the name was really supposed to be pronounced.

Then he became aware of sound scenting the air; the sound and scent seemed the same, both swirling faintly through the still air and he followed the melody. The scent was not the heavy perfume Stellaraire used, nor were the sounds the coarse sounds of the circus noisemakers. It was all something else. Something that stirred memories— hints, odors of memories—far in the deeps of Roan's mind.

Sunlight he'd never drowsed in, winds he'd never felt, peace he'd never known.

Peace, he thought, knowing Henry Dread had said it wrong.

The razored, spring-green turf came down to the edges of the pebbled path and ran between gardens of jewel-bright flowers. A wide-petaled blue blossom, with black markings like a scream in its throat, opened and closed rhythmically.

The music stopped briefly and then changed, as though drawing out things in Roan's mind. In the small pause, Roan heard the play of a fountain, the silver sound of music.

Then, more silver still, came the faint call of horns rising and loudening and loosening old locks in Roan's mind. A smokelike drift of stringed music floated into the horn motif, countering it softly, and then running away and coming back a little differently, so that the horn challenged it and took up the string song itself and then a further, tinkling sound joined the horn and strings and built an infinite, convolute structure in Roan's mind that spread through his whole being and finally broke into a thousand crystals, leaving Roan almost in tears for the old, old things that are lost and the beautiful, infinitely beautiful things that never existed.

A fat bee droned past, bumbled inefficiently into a flower, and hunted nearsightedly for a drop of honey. The flower folded a maternal petal over the bee and he emerged covered with yellow pollen and bumbled away looking triumphant and ridiculous.

Roan laughed, his nostalgia broken.

The music laughed, too. A little flute giggling and teasing and running away.

Roan went after the sound.

The park went on and on and the flower scents changed and interwove like their colors. Roan came to a still, blue lake, floated with flowers and enormous, long-necked birds that swam like boats and drifted up to him inquiringly when he came to the edge of the lake.

Roan turned from the lake into a wood where the vines made bowers—thorned vines heavy with sweet berries—slim, curled vines bright with wide-faced flowers. He walked through sunny slopes where tall grasses rolled like water in the wind, and deep groves where the moss grew close and green in the still shade of warm-barked trees. Then the grove narrowed to a dark, arching tunnel of branches that ended suddenly in sunlight.

Ahead of Roan was a wide, white flagstone walk that curved between fountains of flying water and led finally to a colonnaded terrace. From the terrace rose a fretted cliff of airy masonry. A house the wind blew through.

Roan, thirsty now, scooped up a handful of smooth, cool water. It had a taste of bubbles, a smell of sunshine.

But the water had not been put there for any purpose, even to drink. It showered into the air merely to fall back into the pool. It pleased Roan somehow to think that the mighty Terrans made the water go up just so they could watch it coming down.

He went up the wide, shallow steps, into the airy building that up close seemed as solid and lasting as time itself. The marble floor within was an intricate design of reds and blues that moved into purple and led the eye straight to a ramp slanting up to a gallery on the left.

Roan listened for a moment to the ringing stillness, then started up the sloping way.

The house was a maze of rooms within rooms, all neatly kept. The air filters whispered noiselessly, doors opened silently to his presence, lamps glowed on to greet him, off to bid him good-by. On polished tables were set objects of curious design, of wood and metal and glass. Roan picked each up and tried to imagine its use. One, of green jade, grew warm as he held it, but it did nothing else and there were no buttons to press. So he carefully replaced it and went on.

Then Roan noticed the pictures. He stood in the middle of a room and his eye was caught by a picture in sinuosities of blue, as interwoven and complex as the music he'd heard. Every time he looked at the picture the lines caught his eye a different way, led them along a different trail, and he looked at the picture so long the blue disappeared and then the picture itself until finally he was left following tortuous convolutions in his own mind, and it was a shaft of late afternoon sun, burning through a high window, that brought him to himself and made him blink hard to get the sun glimmers from his eyes.

Some of the pictures were like the Blue; others seemed to project out from the walls, or were sheer patterns of light hanging in empty air. And some—as Roan looked and noticed—some were pictures of Terran places and houses and . . . people? The figures were so tiny and distant. Hunt though he did, he couldn't find any close-ups of Terran people. It didn't really matter. But it was what he most wanted to see.

Roan went on, walking right through a misty Light Picture in the middle of one of the rooms. All this. What was it for? Just to look at? Just to enjoy?

It seemed a human way to be. A Terran way to do things. Roan felt a kinship with all this. He knew how to look at the paintings, how to enjoy the music.

Then Roan walked into a room wide with windows, so that the sunshine shimmered clearly in it. Marble benches stood beneath the low windows and green plants hung over a scoop-shaped sunken pool. As Roan went over to stand on the edge of the empty pool there was a soft click! and water began foaming into the pool.

Roan laughed with pleasure. It was a bath! An enormously magnified version of the one Stellaraire had had in her quarters with the 'zoo. He stripped off his shabby, ill-fitting tunic, realizing suddenly how dirty he was.

He stood by a jet of soapy foam and scrubbed himself thoroughly. The pool carried off his dirt and dead skin cells in eddies of black and whirled in renewed, clean water. Roan luxuriated in the bath for an hour, watching the chasing clouds and blue sky through the windows, and wondering at the delicate veining of the Terran plants that nodded over the water.

And thought wistfully of Stellaraire and how if she were here they'd splash water at each other and be foolish and afterward walk in the garden and make love with timeless joy in the deep grasses. And live here forever in this enchanted place where there was no violence, no raspy, alien voices, no ugly, misshapen faces, no one hating or despising or envying Roan his Terran ancestry, his Terran inheritance.

But there was no Stellaraire. Only a memory that overfilled him now and then, like a bud with no room to open into a flower.

Behind a colored glass panel Roan found simply designed but beautiful clothes, of some close-woven material that sprang to fit him as he put it on. There were silver tights that fitted from his ankles to his waist and were cool to the touch. Then a short, silk-lined scarlet jacket, soft to the skin but stiff outside with gold and jewel embroidery. He found boots that fitted softly like gloves, and protected his feet without heavy soles or heels. All this he put on, though there were other things. Thin white shorts and singlets and short cloth boots that were too thin to be used for walking.

The only other thing Roan took was a magnificent, massive jewel, engraved TER. IMP. It hung around his neck from a gold chain and where it rested against his bare chest, between the edges of his scarlet jacket, it warmed him, almost seeming to throb like a beating heart.

I look the way a Terran ought to look, Roan thought, looking at himself in the enormous mirror that backed the door to the bathing room. The jewel glowed on his browned chest and his freshly washed hair clustered in dark red curls over his forehead.

Roan wondered if a Terran would think him handsome. A Terran woman. Oh Gods, how long since he'd had a woman!

Roan buckled back on his old link metal belt. He wondered why he thought it brought him luck, because it didn't really. Then he reluctantly picked up the Mark XXX blaster. Here, it didn't seem right. But he shoved it into the belt, which stretched to hold it.

Roan retraced his steps through still corridors, down to the echoing concourse, out onto the broad terrace.

Far in the sky the lowering sun flashed orange from the towers of the city—where Henry Dread was searching for loot now with his vicious crew of cutthroats. It was soiled, grubby—all of the universe—but here it didn't exist. He didn't want to call it into being again.

Roan took a new path, beyond the house, walking quickly because he didn't have much time left. Night was coming. He'd seen, perhaps, most of what there was to see, and one more quick turn—

Roan drew up short.

Because reflected in a round mirror pool, among fragile violet flowers, was a human woman.

She was flushed pink in the sunset, pouring water from a long-necked jar. The water, sparkling pink, too, in the light, rippled over her slim neck, between her lifted breasts and around her softly bent body over her flanks, and finally ran murmuring into the mirror pool making no splash or ripple.

"Oh. Please," Roan said, not meaning to speak, and went up to the woman. But it was a statue, smiling its dreamy, carved smile, thinking the secret thoughts of stone.

Roan reached out and touched the soft curve of the hard, marble cheek.

And far away came the violent stutter of guns. Then a single shot—a power rifle.

Perhaps it was the anger against life that filled him or perhaps it was a premonition of what was really happening, but Roan was running. Along the curved paths and then straight across the middle of the park where there was a wide concourse and through a small grove where night had already come, and up the fence, holding to the nearest heavy vine, and slowing to be quiet now, along the fence to the tree.

A gun rattled, paused, fired again. A voice shouted.

Roan looked from the top of the wall. The streets were violet shadows now, the towers bright-edged silhouettes against the orange and purple sky. There was a faint movement in the gloom below the tree and a face, a white blob in the darkness, looked up toward Roan, the glint of a knife in the teeth.

There was a sharp hiss. Something chipped at the tiles and then another hiss and whoever it was starting up the tree fell back and slumped to the ground.

Roan hefted the gun out of his belt. His Mark XXX that he'd all but forgotten in the park. Well, that dream of peace was over now.

Roan waited, heard a few shots, distant now, saw nothing moving. He dropped softly from the tree, squatted, turned the body on its back. The coarse, slack features of a bald Minid stared past him with dead, surprised eyes. The stump of a broken-off wooden shaft poked from the Minid's chest just below the edge of the sheepskin vest.

One of the crew. A mean, dirty creature, but somehow one of *his* . . . Roan stood, trying to see through the dark streets; the firing was becoming steadier now, coming from locations to the north and east. A cold evening wind blew up, and one brilliant orange star came out. Probably the next planet of the sun Aldo.

Roan crossed the street, started up one of the dark avenues toward the north. Lights came on suddenly to illuminate the city; mists of light that seemed to hang in the air like clouds.

There was a sharp hiss. Something struck the doorway of the house near Roan and clattered on the steps. Roan dropped, rolled, brought his gun around and fired at a figure bounding from the shadowed doorway across the street. The figure fell, under the misting streetlight.

Roan retreated to crouch in the angle between the steps and the Terran house. Three long-legged, round-shouldered creatures emerged from the side street. He saw the thick, recurving bows in their hands, the lank hair that dangled beside their oddly flat faces, the heavy quivers slung at their backs. They paused, fanning out. One saw the dead bowman, made a hoarse noise. At once, the three whirled, angled off quickly in different directions. One was leaping toward Roan. He brought his gun up, fired, swung and fired on a second savage as the first slammed to the curb of the mosaic sidewalk, almost at his feet. The second bowman reeled, stumbled, went down. Roan swung to the third and it dived for the black shadow of the building at the corner as his shot sent blue sparks from the door of the Terran house.

Roan was up instantly, dashing for the corner, rounding it as a heavy arrow touched his shoulder, skipped high, flashed off into darkness. Roan skidded to a stop, stepped back to the corner, dropped flat, thrust himself out. The native was charging from cover. Roan's shot caught him full in the chest and he fell with a tremendous heavy slam, an impact of utter finality. Roan let his breath out in a long sigh, slumped against the pavement, listening. There were no sounds, no moving feet, no stealthy breathing, only the intermittent rasp and crackle of guns, nearer now but still, he guessed, a street or two away.

He got to his feet, moved off quickly, following a side street that would bring him to the scene of the action by a roundabout route.

From a low balcony which he had reached by clambering up the shadowed carved front of a peach-colored tower, Roan watched as a party of a dozen or so bowmen assembled almost directly below him in a narrow way. The sounds of firing came closer from along the wide avenue. Roan could see the blue flashes of power guns now, the yellow stabs of pellet throwers. Below, the leader of the ambushing party spoke, and his bowmen set arrows, crouching silent and ready. Down the avenue, Roan made out Henry Dread's tall figure among a huddle of humanoids. There were not more than fifty in the party, he estimated—out of over eighty who had landed; a straggling band of cursing, frightened raiders, caught off guard, retreating under a rain of arrows that flew from the darkness without flash or sound. A bald Minid screeched, spun, fell kicking. The others passed him by, firing at random into the shadows, coming closer to the ambush.

Below Roan, the bowmen gathered themselves; there was a single, grunted syllable from the leader. He stepped forward—

Roan shot him, swept the gun across the others as they sprang back gaping; three more fell, and the rest dashed for the deep shadows, disappeared between close walls. No one in the retiring ship's party seemed to have noticed the byplay. They were formed up into a defensive ring, watching each side street as they passed. Henry Dread held up a hand, halted the group fifty feet from Roan's vantage point. Lying on the balcony, he had a clear view of the pirates, and the empty streets all around.

"Belay firing!" Roan heard Henry Dread's voice. "They've pulled back for now."

There were snarls and mutters from the crewmen. They shifted uneasily, watching the dark mouths of side streets. A gun winked blue, a harsh buzz against silence.

"I said belay that!" Henry Dread grated. "We'll hold up here for ten minutes to give stragglers a chance to join us."

"To the Pit with stragglers," the crewman who had fired his gun cut in. "We should stay here and let these local slobs surround us? We're moving on—fast."

"Shut up, Snorgu," Henry Dread snapped. "Maybe you've forgotten I busted you out of a Yill jail after you were dumb enough to get caught flat-footed strangling an old female for her nose ruby. And now *you're* going to do the thinking for my crew—"

"*Your* crew my hind leg, you lousy Terry. We've taken enough orders from your kind. What about it, boys?" Snorgu glanced around at the watching pirates. Henry stepped up to the heavy-shouldered crewman. "Hand over your gun, Snorgu!"

Snorgu faced Henry, the gun in his fist aimed at the pirate leader. He laughed.

"I'm keeping my gun. And I'm firing when I feel like it . . ."

A crewman beside Henry moved suddenly, caught the pirate captain's arms from behind; another struck out, knocked Henry's gun from his hand. A third stooped, came up with it.

"Here's where we get a new captain," Snorgu growled. "Lead us into an ambush, hah? Some captain you are. I guess us Gooks have got just about a gutful of fancy Terry ways."

"I seem to remember giving some orders about looting parties posting sentries," Henry drawled. "And about skeleton crews on the Bolos—"

Snorgu snarled and jammed the gun hard against Henry's chest. "Never mind all that. Hand over the keys to the chart room and the strong box in your office."

Henry laughed, a hard sound like ice breaking. "You're out of luck. You think I carry a bunch of keys around for stupid deck-apes like you to lift the first time you see a chance? They're combination locks. Kill me and you'll never get 'em open."

"You'll open 'em," someone barked. "A couple of needle-burns through the gut, and a couple of days for the rot to set in, and you'll be screaming for somebody to listen to you sing, and all you'll ask is a fast knife in the neck before your belly explodes."

"Meanwhile, how do you plan to get back to the ship?" Henry Dread cut in. "There might be a few natives between here and there that don't want to see you run off after such a short stay."

"Gun him down," someone suggested. "We've got enough on our hands without we got to watch this Terry."

"Sure. We can beam them locks open."

"Suits me." Snorgu grinned, showing large, widely spaced teeth in a loose-lipped mouth wide enough to put a hand in sideways. He stepped back a pace, angled the gun down at Henry's belt buckle—

Roan took careful aim, shot Snorgu through the head. The pirate's gun flew into the air as his hand jerked up; he stumbled back and fell, and Henry stepped forward, caught the falling gun out of the air, held it aimed from the hip. The crewmen gaped.

"Anybody else care to nominate himself captain?" Henry's sharp voice cut across the silence. The men were craning their necks, looking for the source of the shot. Roan saw one ease a gun around, aim it at Henry Dread; he shot him through the chest. As he fell, another brought a gun up, and Henry, whirling, beamed him down.

"Next?" he said pleasantly. No one moved. The crewmen stood stiffly now, cowed, worried. Henry laughed shortly, lowered his gun.

"All right, spread out in a skirmish line and let's get

moving." He motioned them past with his pistol. Roan lowered himself over the balustrade and climbed quickly down. Henry Dread watched him come. His narrowed eyes were on the gun at Roan's hip.

"Found out how to use it, eh?"

"Comes in handy," Roan said casually, imitating Henry Dread's manner. He stood with his thumbs hooked in his belt, looking at the older man. Henry's eyes went from Roan's scarlet vest down the length of the silvery trousers, back up. His eyes locked with Roan's.

"You had a good chance to shoot me then," he said. "But when it got right down to it, you sided me." His face broke slowly into a smile. "I knew you'd figure out which side you were on, boy. You picked a good time. Something you learned in that park?"

"I found a garden," Roan said. "It was perfect; the most perfect place I ever saw. I wanted to stay there. There was everything you could ever need. And then I saw a statue, and I touched it, and all of a sudden I saw that it was all dead, frozen, just a fossil of something that was alive once. Something that could live again, maybe. I decided then. I want to make it live, Henry. I want to do whatever I have to do to make it come to life again. I want that stone girl to turn to living flesh and walk in that garden with me."

Henry's hand thrust out. Roan took it. "We'll do it, Roan," the pirate said. "Together, we'll do it."

Smiling, Roan said, "Want the gun back?"

Henry Dread's smile was grim. "Keep it," he said. "From now on, you walk behind me. Keep the gun on your hip, and your right hand loose."

He turned and followed the huddle of pirates, and Roan trailed him, walking with his head up, liking the feel of the heavy gun in his belt.

CHAPTER ✳ TWELVE

"These past two years have been good, Roan," Henry Dread said, refilling his heavy wine mug. "Seven raids, all successful. Enough new men recruited to more than cover our losses; and our fuel and ammo reserves are at the best level in years—"

Roan looked at his half-full glass sullenly. "And we're still no closer to starting a new Terra than we ever were. We haven't found even one more Man to add to the roster. There's still just you and me; two Terries, two Freaks, talking about what we'll do some day—"

"Look here, Roan, we've followed every rumor of a Terry we've run across. Is it my fault if they didn't pan out? We'll find a colony of Terries yet; and when we do—"

"Meanwhile Iron Robert's still chained. I want you to release him, Henry."

The pirate's hand came down to slam the table. "Damn it, are we going to start into that again? Haven't I explained to you that that man-eater's a symbol aboard this vessel? My cutthroats saw him stand up to a blaster; they heard him threaten to pitch me through the side of my own ship! And I let him live! As long as he's chained to the wall his talk is just talk; maybe a blaster can't touch him—but Henry Dread has him under lock and key! But turn him loose—let him stamp around this ship a free Geek—well, you get the picture!"

"I get the picture," Roan said. "For over two years now I've been living off the fat of the land while my friend sits in the dark with half a ton of steel welded to his leg—"

"Hell, let's be realistic, boy! He doesn't mind it—not like you or I would! He says so himself; he sits and goes off into some kind of trance; doesn't even eat for days at a time. He's not human, Roan! By the Gods, with Man's Galaxy at stake, you worry about one damned Geek!"

"Set him free; he won't cause any trouble; I'll be responsible for him—"

"That's not the point," Henry said in a hard voice. "You'd better settle for having him alive. He's the first Geek I ever let live aboard my ship!"

"That's what your grand dream really boils down to, isn't it, Henry? Killing Geeks . . ."

Henry swiveled to stare into the view screen that curved above the command console. "Somewhere out there, there's a Niss warship," he said quietly. "We're closing the gap, Roan; the stories we've picked up these last couple of months all tell the same tale: The Niss ship is real, and it's not far off. We'll pick it up on our long-range screens any day now—"

"More Geeks to kill. That's all it is. It isn't a war; the Niss were beaten—at least as much as the Empire. They're no threat to us—or to anybody. They haven't attacked anyone—"

Henry swung back. "Haven't they? What about the Mandevoy patrol boat they vaporized last year—at a range of twelve thousand miles—"

"The Mandevoy went out looking for trouble. They admitted that. The Niss haven't attacked a planet, or any ship that stayed clear of them. Let's forget the Niss. It's Terra we're interested in. Let's look for Terra—"

"Terra!" Henry snorted. "Don't you know that's just a name, Roan? A mythical wonderland for the yokels to tell stories about! The Terran Empire isn't some two-bit world somewhere at the far side of the Galaxy; it's humanity—organized, armed, and in charge!"

"There *is* a Terra," Roan said. "And some day I'll find it. If you've given up on it, I'll find it alone—"

"Given up!" Henry Dread roared, coming to his feet. "Henry Dread never gave up on anything he set out to do! I'm not chasing rainbows! I'm fighting a live enemy! I'm facing reality! Maybe it's time you grew up and did the same!"

Roan nodded. "You're right. Just set me down on the next inhabited world with my share of the spoils. I'll leave your grand scheme to you; I've got a better one of my own."

Henry's eyes were fierce fires blazing in a face purple with fury.

"By the Nine Gods, I've got a good mind to take you at your word! I picked you out of a damned 'zoo, a Freak in a cage, and made you my second-in-command—and tried to make you my friend! And now—"

"I've never asked you for anything, Henry," Roan cut in, his blue eyes holding the pirate's. They stood face to face, two big, powerfully built Men, one with gray hair and a face of lined leather, the other with a mane of dark red curls hacked short, the clean features of youth, a flawless complexion marred only by a welted scar along his right cheek where Ithc's talons had raked him, long ago.

"But you've taken plenty!"

"I was content with the 'zoo. I had friends there, a girl, too—"

Henry Dread snarled. "You'll befriend any lousy Gook or Geek that gives you the time of day; but me, a commander in the Imperial Terran Navy—I'm not good enough for your friendship!"

Roan's expression changed. He frowned.

"You said—the Imperial Terran Navy . . ."

Henry Dread's eyes held steady. "That's what I said," he grated.

"I thought," Roan said carefully, watching Henry Dread's eyes, "that the ITN was wiped out, thousands of years ago . . ."

"You did, eh?" Henry was smiling a tight, hard smile. He looked at Roan bright-eyed, enjoying the moment. "What if I told you it wasn't wiped out? What if I said there were intact units scattered all over the Eastern Arm when the shooting stopped? What if I said Rim Headquarters had taken over command control, reorganized the survivors, and held the Navy together—waiting for the day a counterattack could be launched?"

"*Are* you saying that?" Roan tried to hold his voice level and calm, but it broke on the last word.

"Hell, boy, that's what I called you up here to talk

about, before you started in on your pet Geek!" Henry clapped Roan's shoulder. "I've watched you close, these last years. You've done all right, Roan—better than all right. It's time I let you in on what you're doing here— what we're doing. You thought I was just a pirate, raiding and looting just for the hell of it, getting fat off the leavings of Geeks and Gooks—and you thought my talk about getting the Galaxy back for Man was just talk. I know . . ." He laughed, with his hands on his hips and his head thrown back.

"I can't say I blame you. Sure, I've got a hold full of heavy metal and gem crystals and old Terry cloth and spices and even a few cases of Old Imperial Credit tokens. But that's not all I've got tucked away. Come here."

He turned, walked across the broad command deck of the ancient battlewagon, tapped keys on the panel. An armored door swung open, and Henry stepped inside, ducking his head, came out with a wide, flat box. He lifted the lid with a flourish, held up a garment of close-woven polyon, shook it out. Roan gaped.

"My uniform," Henry Dread said. "As a commander in the Imperial Terran Navy. I'm assigned to recruiting and fund-raising duty. I've done all right as far as funds are concerned. But this is my first recruitment . . ."

Roan's hungry eyes held on the rich cloth, the glitter of ancient insignia. He swallowed, opened his mouth to speak—

Henry Dread stepped back into the vault, came out holding a second box in his hands. He tucked it under one arm.

"Raise your right hand, Lieutenant Cornay," he said . . .

✳✳✳✳

Roan stared into the mirror. The narrow-cut, silver-corded black trousers fitted without a wrinkle into the brightly polished ship boots. Over the white silk shirt, the short tunic was a swirl of braid, a gleam of silver buttons against royal blue. A bright-plated ebony-gripped ceremonial side arm winked at each hip against the broad, woven-silver belt with the big, square buckle adorned by the carved TER. IMP. and bird symbol.

He turned to Henry Dread. "I've got about a milliard questions, Henry. You know what they are . . ."

Henry Dread laughed again. "Sure, I know." He eyed a mike, snapped out an order for a bottle and glasses. "Sit down, Lieutenant. I think you can forget about Geeks for a few minutes now while I tell you a few things . . ."

Iron Robert stirred as Roan called to him. His heavy feet scraped the rusted deck plates; chains clashed in the gloom and his green eyes winked open.

"What you want, Roan," the heavy voice growled. "You wake Iron Robert from dream of youth and females and hot sun of home-world . . ."

"I . . . just came to see how you are," Roan said. "I've been busy lately; I guess I haven't gotten down to see you as often as I'd like. Is there anything you need?"

"Just need to know you well and happy, Roan. I think now you and Henry Dread friends, you have good time, not be so sad like before."

Roan gripped the two-inch chromalloy bars of Iron Robert's cell. "It's not just a good time, Iron Robert. I'm doing something: I'm helping to put the Terran Empire back together. I know, it's not much—just one ship, cruising space, looking for Terrans, or rumors of Terrans, and collecting funds for the Navy, gathering intelligence to use when we're ready to launch our counterattack—"

"Counterattack against who, Roan? You already attack all Gooks and Geeks you find, take all guns and fuel and money—"

"You have to understand, Iron Robert! We're not just looting. We need those things! We're cruising according to official Navy orders, hitting every world in our assigned sector. Captain Dread's already been out twelve years. Two more years, and we finish the sweep, and report back to Rim Headquarters—"

"Just so you happy, Roan; have good time, live to full, eat good, drink good, have plenty fight, plenty women."

"Damn it, is that all living means to you? Don't you understand what it is to try to build something bigger than you are, something worth giving everything that's in you for?"

"Sure, Roan. Iron Robert understand big dreams of youth. All beings young once—"

"This isn't just a dream! The Terran Empire ruled this Galaxy once and could rule it again! Haven't you seen enough suffering and torture and death and indifference and ruins and greed and hate and hopelessness to understand how it is to want to change all that? The Empire will bring back peace and order. If we left it to the damned Geeks it would go on like this forever, only worse!"

"Maybe true, Roan." Iron Robert's voice was a soft rumble. "Fine thing, build towers up into sunlight, squirt water, make pretty sounds—"

"Don't make fun of my garden! I shouldn't have told you about it! I might have known a Geek couldn't understand!"

"Hard thing for Geek to understand, Roan. What place Geeks have in Terry Empire? Geeks get to walk in pretty garden, too?"

"The Geeks will have their own worlds," Roan said sullenly. "They'll have their own gardens."

"Iron Robert have garden once too, Roan. Fine black stones, and pools of soft mud to lie in, and hot, stinky water come up out of ground. But I think Roan not like my garden. I think hard thing for Roan and Iron Robert to walk in garden together, talk over old times. Maybe better have no garden, just be together, friends."

Roan leaned his head against the cold bars. "Iron Robert, I didn't mean—I mean . . . We'll always be friends, no matter what! I know you're locked in here because of me. Listen, Iron Robert, I'm going to tell Henry Dread—"

"Roan not tell Henry Dread anything! Iron Robert made deal with pirate; Geek keep word as good as Man—"

"I didn't mean it when I called you a Geek, Iron Robert—"

"Just word, Roan. Iron Robert and Roan friends, few angry words nothing. Iron Robert not 'shamed to be a Geek. Fine thing to be royal ferrous strain and have friend like Roan. Human flame burn short but burn hot, warm old stone heart of being like Iron Robert."

"I'm going to get you out of there—"

"No, Roan. Where else I go? Not like Terry cabin, too

small, too weak chair. And only cause trouble. Henry Dread right. Crew not like see Iron Robert free being. Better wait here, be near Roan, and some day maybe we make planetfall together. Meantime, you got destiny to work out with Henry Dread. You go ahead, chase dream of ancient glories. Iron Robert be here by and by."

"We'll be at Rim HQ soon—in a year or two. I'll make them give me a ship of my own then—and you'll be my second-in-command!"

"Sure, Roan. Good plan. Till then, Iron Robert wait patient—and Roan not worry."

Roan stood up, stretched, rubbed his eyes, drained the mug of bitter brown coffee, clattered the empty cup down on the chart table.

"I'm tired, Henry. Over thirty-six hours we've been hanging over the screens, and we've seen nothing. Let's admit it's another wild-goose chase and turn in."

"They're close, Roan," Henry snapped. His face was grayish and hollow in the lights of the panel. "I've chased the Niss for forty years; another forty minutes and maybe I'll see them in my sights."

"Or another forty days—or forty years, or a thousand, for all we know. Those clodhoppers back on Ebar probably just gave us the story to get rid of us before the boys got bored and started shooting the town up again."

"They're out there. We'll close with them this time."

"And if they are—what about it? We're on a recruiting and fund-raising mission, aren't we? What's that got to do with launching one-man attacks against Niss warships—if there is any ship, and it really is Niss."

"They're there, I said! And we're a fleet boat of the Navy! It's always our job to seek out and destroy the enemy!"

"Henry, give it up. We don't know their capabilities. I know we've got special long-range indetectable radar gear, but they may still blast us out of space like they did that Mandevoy scout a few years ago, before we even get close—"

Henry Dread whirled, stared up at Roan from his seat. "Scared, Lieutenant?"

Roan's tired face smiled humorlessly. "Sure, I'm scared, if that's what you want to hear. Or maybe I've just got common sense enough not to want to see all you've worked for—all *we've* worked for—destroyed just because you've got the itch to fire those big batteries you've been keeping primed all these years."

Henry Dread came to his feet. "That's enough out of you, Mister! I'm still in charge aboard this tub! Now get on that screen until I give the order to leave your post!"

"Slow down, Henry—"

"Commander Dread to you, Mister!" Henry's face was close to Roan's, his square jaw, marred by a slight sagging of the jowls, thrust out. Roan straightened, settled his gun belt on his hips. He was an inch taller than Dread now, and almost as heavy through the shoulders. He looked the older man steadily in the eye.

"We're just nine months out of Rim Headquarters, Henry. Let's see if we can't get there in one piece—both of us . . ."

Henry Dread's hand went to his gun. He half drew it, looking into Roan's eyes, his teeth set in a snarl.

"I gave you an order!"

"You're a big enough man to take an order back, when you see it's a mistake," Roan said flatly. "We both need rest. I know a couple of crewmen who'd like to see the pair of us out on our feet." He turned away. Henry Dread's gun cleared the holster.

"Stop right there, Mister—"

A clanging alarm shattered the stillness into jagged fragments. Roan spun; his eyes leaped to the long-range screen. A bright point of blue light glowed near the lower left corner. He jumped to the panel, twisted knobs; the image centered. He read figures from a ground-glass plate.

"Mass, five point seven million standard tons; velocity, point oh-nine light, absolute; nine-eighty MPH relative!"

"By the Nine Devils, that's it!" Henry Dread's voice choked. He stared across at Roan, then grabbed up the command mike, bawled into it:

"All hands, battle stations! Secure for action! All batteries, full-arm and countdown! Power section, stand by for maximum drain!"

A startled voice acknowledged as he tossed the mike aside, looked across at Roan. His eyes were wide, bright.

"This is it, Roan! That's a Niss ship of the line, as sure as I'm Henry Dread!" His eyes went on the screen. "Look at him! Look at the size of that devil! But we'll take him out! We'll take him out!" He holstered his gun, drew a breath, turned to Roan.

"For the first time in five thousand years, a ship of the Imperial Navy is engaging the enemy! This is the hour I've lived for, Roan! We'll smash them like a ripe fruit . . . !" He raised his clenched fist. ". . . and then nothing will stop us! Are you with me, boy?"

Roan's eyes held the long shape growing on the screen. "Let's break it off, Henry. We've established that we can get in range, and we have them located. When we reach Rim Headquarters, we can . . ."

"DAMN Rim Headquarters!" Henry Dread roared. "This is MY action! I tracked that filthy blot on the human sky halfway across the Eastern Arm, and now I'm going to burn it clean—"

"You're out of your mind, Henry," Roan snapped. "The damned thing outweighs us a hundred to one—"

"Crazy, am I? I'll show you how a crazy Man deals with the scum that challenged Terran power at its peak—"

Roan gripped Henry's shoulders, eyes on the screen. "It's not just you and me, Henry! We've got eighty crewmen below! They trust in you—"

"To hell with those Gooks! This is what I was born for—" He broke off. A tremor rattled the coffee mug on the table. There was a sudden sense of pressure, of impending violence—

The deck rose up and struck Roan a mighty blow. Instrument faces burst from the panel, screens exploded in smoke and white light. He had a glimpse of Henry Dread, spinning past him. A thunderous blast rolled endlessly, and then it drained away and Roan was whirling in echoing silence.

He was on the floor, looking up at a soot-smeared figure in rags, bleeding from a hundred cuts, hunched in the command chair, square fists clamped on the fire-control levers. Roan coughed, raised himself on one elbow, got to his hands and knees. The walls spun dizzily.

"How bad are we hit?" he choked.

"Filthy, sneaking Niss," Henry Dread chanted. "Let 'em have another broadside! Burn the devils out of the sky . . . !"

Roan's eyes swept over the shattered panel, the smashed instruments, fixed on the controls in Henry Dread's hands. They hung slack and useless from broken mountings.

"Henry—let's get out of here—the lifeboats . . ."

"Maximum beam," Henry Dread shouted. "Forward batteries, fire! Fire, damn you!"

"We've got to get out," Roan staggered to his feet, grasped Henry's shoulder, pulling him away from the devastated control console. "Give the order—"

Wild eyes in a white face stared up at him. "Are you a fighting man of the Empire or a dirty Geek-loving spy?" Henry tore himself free, lunged for the command mike, dangling from its socket.

"All hands! We're closing with the enemy! Prepare to board—"

Roan tore the mike from Henry's hands.

"Abandon ship!" he shouted—and threw the dead mike from him as Henry yelled, swung a wild blow. He leaned aside, caught the other's wrists.

"Listen to me, Henry! We've got to get to the boats! We can survive to fight again!"

Henry stared into Roan's eyes, breathing hard. Swelling blisters puffed the left side of his face. His hair was singed to curled stubble. There was blood at the corner of his mouth. Quite suddenly, the wildness went out of his eyes. His arms relaxed; he staggered, caught himself.

"Two boats," he mumbled. "I've fitted 'em out as raiders; armor, an infinite repeater each, two torpedoes . . ." He pulled free of Roan's grip, pushed past him toward the lift doors, stumbling over the debris littering the deck.

"We're not beaten yet," he was shouting again. "Slip through their screens—hit 'em in close . . ." Smoke swirled from the lift as the doors clashed open. Henry Dread lurched inside, and Roan followed.

On the boat deck, a dense-packed mob of shouting, struggling crewmen fought for position at the two escape locks.

"It's Captain Dread!" someone yelled.

"Here's the Terry swine now!"

"Open up!"

"Get the boats clear!"

Henry slammed his way through the press, gun in hand. He smashed it down over the skull of a horned bruiser in blackened sheepskin, whirled to face the mob. Behind them, the glare of raging fires danced against the bulkhead visible at the end of the long corridor.

"Listen to me, you swabs," Henry roared. "There's room in the two boats for every gutter-spawned rascal here—but by the nine tails of the fire devil, you'll form up and board in a shipshape fashion or fry where you are! You there! Gungle! Let him be! Get back there! Askor!

Take number one port!" The pirate chief bellowed his orders, and the frantic crewmen broke off their struggles, moved back, taking places in two ragged lines.

Roan pushed through them, coughing, blinking through the smoke.

"Here, where do you think you're going!" Henry Dread bellowed after him. But Roan was clear of the press, into the transverse corridor now; the smoke was less here. He ran, bounded down a companionway, leaped the crumpled form of a Minid with a short knife standing in his back; someone's grudge settled, Roan thought as he dashed along the cargo level way.

He skidded to a halt at Iron Robert's cell. Through the layered smoke, he made out the massive figure, seated stolidly on the steel-slab bench.

"Iron Robert! I'll get you out! The keys are in Henry's cabin—"

"Just minute, Roan," the rumbling voice said calmly. "What happen? Iron Robert wake, hear engines dead, plenty smoke in room—"

"We tried to attack a Niss warship! It hit us before we even got close, smashed our screens, burned out our circuitry; we're a hulk, on fire. We're abandoning ship!"

"You want Iron Robert go free out of cell? Don't need key, Roan. Easy . . ." The giant stood, brought his massive arms forward, and snapped the chains as easily as loops of wet paper. He stooped, tore the ankle chains from the wall, then peeled the massive welded collars from his ankles.

"Stand back, Roan . . ." He stepped to the grating, gripped the wrist-thick bars, ripped them aside with a screech of metal, forced his nine-foot bulk through the opening like a man brushing aside a beaded hanging, and stood in the corridor, looking down at Roan.

"You could have broken them—any time," Roan stuttered. "You stayed there—in chains—for five years—on my account . . ."

"Good place as any to sit, think. Now fire grow hot; time to go, Roan."

Roan whirled, led the way along the smoke-fogged corridor, up the companionway, along to the boat deck. Half the crew had entered the lifeboats now. Two dead men lay on the deck, blasted at short range by Henry Dread's guns. The grizzled Terran caught sight of Roan.

"You're taking number two boat! Where in the Nine Hells have you been—" Iron Robert lumbered from the smoke behind Roan.

"So! I should have figured!" The gun swiveled to cover the giant. "Get aboard, Roan! We're running out of time!"

"I'll load when my crew's loaded." Roan walked past Henry, ignoring the gun, to the gangway where burly humanoids pushed, crowded through the port.

"I said get aboard!" Henry bellowed.

There were half a dozen more crewmen. They pushed, shouting; answering shouts came from inside the sixty-foot boat, cradled in its massive davits in the echoing, smoke-filled hold. A broad-faced Minid thrust his head from the lock of number one boat.

"We got a full load!" he roared. "You load any more in here, they'll be standin' on each others' shoulders!"

Henry's gun swung. "I don't care if you have to stack 'em like cordwood! Get 'em in, Askor!" He spun back to face Roan. "What the hell are you waiting for, boy? Get aboard that boat—now! Can't you feel that heat? This tub will blow any second—"

"Iron Robert," Roan called past him. "Go aboard—"

"There's no room for that hulk!" Henry shouted. "That was an order, Mister!"

Three frantic crewmen struggled at the port of number two boat.

"No more room!" a hoarse voice bellowed from inside the lock. A broad foot swung out, kicked at one of the men. He fell from the gangway, and the two behind leaped forward. A fight developed in the lock. Henry Dread took a step, aimed, fired once, twice, a third time. Two dead crewmen fell, rolled off onto the hot deck plates. A third was lifted, tossed from inside.

"Fight your way in there, Roan," Henry yelled. "Shoot as many as you have to!"

"Iron Robert—"

"I said he's not going aboard!"

Roan and Henry Dread faced each other, ten feet apart across the blood-spattered deck. The pirate captain's gun was aimed unwaveringly at Roan's chest.

"He goes or I stay," Roan yelled above the clamor.

"For the last time—follow your orders!" Henry bellowed.

"Iron Robert, go aboard—" Roan started.

"Roan—" Iron Robert took a step, and Henry Dread wheeled, and blue fire lanced, splashed harmlessly from Iron Robert's chest.

"You board boat, like Henry Dread say, Roan," the giant rumbled.

Henry took a step backward, his gun covering Roan again.

"Listen to Iron Man," Henry grated. "He's telling you—"

"Let him board, Henry!" Roan said.

"Over my dead body," Henry grated. "Not even you can—"

"Roan, no—!" Iron Robert cried—

In a motion too quick to follow, Roan's hand had flashed to his gun, brought it up, fired, and the pirate leader was staggering back, his knees folding, the gun dropping from his hand. He seemed to fall slowly, like an ancient tree, and he struck, rolled over, lay on his back with his eyes and mouth open, smoke rising from a charred wound centered on his chest.

"Roan! You big fool! No room on boat for Iron Robert! Now you kill Henry Dread, true Man who love you like son!"

Roan tossed the gun aside, went to the fallen pirate, knelt beside him. "Henry . . ." His voice caught in his throat. "I thought—"

"You wrong, Roan," Iron Robert's voice rumbled. "Henry Dread not shoot you in a million years. Try save your life, foolish Roan. You go now, quick, before ship explode—"

Henry Dread's open eyes flickered. They moved to Roan's face.

"You . . . in command . . . now," he gasped. "Maybe. . . right . . . Iron Man . . . OK. . . ." He drew a ragged breath and coughed, tried to speak, coughed again. "Roan," he managed. "Terra . . ." The light died from his eyes like a mirror steaming over.

"Henry!" Roan shouted. Two mighty hands clamped on his arms, lifted him, thrust him toward the port.

"You go now, Roan, live long life, do, see many things. Think sometime of Iron Robert, and not be sad, be happy, remember many good times together—"

"No, Iron Robert! You're coming—"

"No room; Iron Robert too big, not squeeze through port." Roan felt himself propelled through the narrow opening into the noise and animal stink of the crowded lifeboat. He fought to regain his feet, turned to see the wide figure of Iron Robert silhouetted against the blazing corridor. He lunged for the port, and a dozen pairs of horny hands caught at him, held him as he kicked and fought.

"You got to navigate this tub, Terry," someone yelled.

"Dog down that port," another shouted. Roan had a last glimpse of Iron Robert as hands hauled him back. The heavy port swung shut. Then he was thrust forward, passed from one to another, and then he was stumbling into the command compartment. Rough hands shoved him into the navigator's chair. The cold muzzle of a gun rammed against his cheek.

"Blast us out of here, fast," a heavy voice growled. Roan shook himself, forced his eyes to focus on the panel. As in a dream, his hands went out, threw levers, punched keys. The screens glowed into life. Against the black of space, the long shape of the immense Niss war vessel glowed no more than a thousand miles distant, its unlighted bulk blotting out the stars.

Roan gathered himself, sat upright. His teeth were set in a grim caricature of a smile. He twirled dials, centered the image in the screen, read numerals from an instrument, punched a code into the master navigator panel, then with a decisive gesture thrust home the main drive control.

CHAPTER ✳ THIRTEEN

Roan slumped in the padded seat, let his hands fall from the controls.

"We're clear," he said dully. "I don't think the other boat got away. I don't see it on our screens—"

A clay-faced creature with the overlong arms and the tufted bristles of a Zorgian pushed through the crew packed like salted fish in the bare, functional shell of the lifeboat.

"Listen to me, you muckworms," he hooted in the queer, resonant voice that rose from his barrel chest. "If we wanta make planetfall, we got to organize this scow—"

"Who asked you?" a gap-toothed, olive-skinned crewman demanded. "I been thinking, and—"

"I'm senior Gook here," a bald, wrinkled Minid barked. "Now we're clear, we got to find the nearest world—"

Other voices cut him off. There were the sounds of blows, curses. Scuffling started, was choked off by the sheer cramping of the confining space.

"I don't, we don't wanta all die," a hoarse voice yelled. "We got to pick a new cap'n!"

"I won't have no lousy Minid telling me—"

"Button yer gill slits, you throwback to a mudfish—"

Roan stood, turned on the men. "All right," he roared—an astonishing shout that cut through the hubbub like a whiplash through cotton cloth.

"You can belay all this gab about who's in charge! I am! If you boneheads can stop squabbling long enough to let a few facts into your skulls, you'll realize we're in trouble—bad trouble! There are forty of us, crowded into a boat designed for an emergency cargo of thirty! We've got enough food for a few months, maybe, but our air and water recyclers are going to be overloaded; that means tight rationing. And you can forget about the nearest planet; it's nine months away at fleet-cruise acceleration—and we've got less than ten per cent of that capacity—"

The Zorgian bellied up to Roan. "Listen, you Terry milksop—"

Roan hit the humanoid with a gut punch, straightened him out with an upward slam of a hard fist, pushed him back among the crewmen.

"We've got no discharge lock," he grated, "so if anybody gets himself killed, the rest of us will have to live with the remains; think that over before you start any trouble." Roan planted his fists on his hips. He was as tall as the tallest of the cutthroat crew, a head taller than the average. His black-red hair was vivid in the harsh light of the glare strip that lit the crowded compartment. Coarse faces, slack with fright, stared at him.

"How many of you have guns?" he demanded. There was muttering and shuffling. Roan counted hands.

"Sixteen. How many knives?" There was another show of hands, gripping blades that ranged from a broad, edge-nicked machete to a cruel, razor-edged hook less than six inches long.

"Where are we going?" someone called.

"We'll die aboard this can," a shrill cry came.

"We can't make planetfall." Roan's voice blanketed the others. "We're a long way from home, without fuel reserves or supplies . . ." The crew were silent now, waiting. "But we've got our firepower intact. There are two thousand-megaton torps slung below decks and we mount a ten mm infinite repeater forward. And there's food, water, fuel, and air just a few miles away . . ." He stepped aside, pointed to the forward screen, where the Niss ship swelled now to giant size.

"We're inside her defenses now," he said. "They won't be expecting any visitors in a hundred ton dinghy—"

"What do you mean?" a one-eyed crewman growled. "You're asking—"

"I'm asking nothing," Roan said harshly. "I'm telling you we're going in to attack the Niss ship."

At five miles, the Niss dreadnought filled the screens like a dark moon.

"They don't know we're here," Roan said. "Their screens aren't designed to notice anything this small. We'll close with her, locate an entry lock, and burn our way in. With luck, we'll be in control of the COC before they know they've been boarded."

"And what if we don't have luck?"

"Then we won't be any worse off than we would be

eating each other and dying of foul air aboard this tub."

"Four miles, rate of closure twenty meters per second," called a crewman assigned to the navigation panel.

"Slack her off there," Roan ordered. "I want you to touch down on her as soft and easy as if you were lifting a purse back on Croanie."

The crewman showed a quick, nervous smile. "Sure. I don't want to wake nobody up."

"What's these Niss like, Terry—"

Roan turned and slashed his forearm across the mouth of the speaker.

"That's 'Captain' to you, sailor! I don't know what the Niss are like, and I don't give a damn. They've got what we need and we're taking it."

"The size of that scow—there must be a million of 'em aboard . . ."

"Don't worry—just kill them one at a time."

They watched the screens in silence.

"Two miles," the navigator hissed. "No alarm yet . . ."

The lifeboat drifted closer to the swelling curve of the miles-long warship. The scrawl of great alien characters was blazoned across the dull black of the hull. Complex housings set at random caught the faint glint of starlight. Roan selected a small disk scribed on the metal plain below.

"Match us up to that, Noag," he ordered. "The rest of you suit up."

He hauled a stiff vacuum suit from the wall locker, settled the helmet in place, flipped switches. Stale air wafted across his face from the suit blower.

The lifeboat's engines nudged her, positioning the lock directly over the hatch of the Niss ship. Roan stood by, watching the maneuvering on a small repeater screen.

"Quiet now, all of you," he said. "Any noise we make will be transmitted through the hull."

The two vessels touched with a barely perceptible rasp of metal on metal.

"Nice work, Noag. You're learning," Roan said. "Hold her right there and magnetic-lock." He listened. Through his deck boots he could feel the vibration of the engine; nothing more.

"Cycle her open," he ordered.

"Hey, what kinda air these Niss use?" someone called. "My tanks are low."

"What's the matter, you gonna stay here if it ain't to your liking?" another came back.

Air hissed as the lock cycled. Roan's suit plucked at him as the pressure dropped. Through the opening the iodine-black curve of the alien hull blocked their way.

"Cut into her, Askor," Roan commanded. The crewman pushed into the opening, set a blaster on narrow beam, pressed the firing stud. The dark metal reddened, turned a glaring white, went bluish, then puddled, blowing away, driven by the pressure of released gasses. The soft spot bulged, blew out under the pressure of the Niss ship's internal atmosphere. Askor worked on, widened the opening, cut out a ragged hole a foot in diameter.

"Shut down." Roan stepped past him, reached through, found a release, tripped it. The Niss lock rotated up and away, exposing the lightless interior of the empty ship; icy air gusted into the lifeboat, bringing a faint, foul taint. Frost formed on the metal where it touched.

"Let's go." Blaster in hand, Roan stepped through the opening; the beam of his hand light lanced ahead, picked out curving walls, complex shapes fitted to what should be the floor. Festoons of odd-sized tubing looped across the room. There was a scattering of heavy dust over everything.

Silently, the boarders followed through the broached hull, gathered in a huddle around Roan. Their breath made frosty puffs before their faces.

"Where do we go from here?" Noag muttered.

Roan threw his light on a narrow vertical slit in the wall. "That might be a door," he said. "We'll try it."

The corridors of the Niss ship were high, narrow, lit by dim strips that had glowed to reluctant life in the minutes after the invaders had boarded. The walls seemed to press in on Roan. It was hard to breathe, and there was sweat on his forehead, in spite of the chill that cut at his exposed hands and face like skinning knifes.

"She's pulling a half-G," Askor said. "There's power on somewheres . . ."

"I don't like this," Noag muttered behind Roan. "If they jump us now, we're stuck like mud-pigs in a deadfall . . ."

"Shut up," Roan said. His heart was pounding high up under his ribs, and what Noag was saying made it worse. He strode on, careless of sound now, emerged from the constricting passage into a wide chamber walled with honeycombed storage racks. The crewmen gathered, staring around. One went to the nearest niche, drew out a heavy bundle wrapped in stiff, waxy cloth. He plucked at the bindings, tore the covering away, blinked at a grotesquely shaped metal casting, peppered over with tiny fittings. The others craned, took the object as the finder passed it around.

"What th' Nine Hells is that . . . ?"

"Hey, how about the next rack—"

"Can't you slobs even wait until after the fight to start looting?" Roan snapped. "Put that back where you got it—and cut out the chatter." The men fell silent, listening for the enemy they had, incredibly, forgotten for the moment.

"Come on." Roan led the way out of the storeroom along another narrow way that stretched into darkness.

"These passages," a crewman whispered hoarsely. "There's miles of 'em. What if we get lost in here . . . ?"

"That's easy," another offered. "We just pound on the walls until the Niss come to see what's the matter."

"Where they hiding, anyways?" Noag shifted his power gun from his right fist to his left. "We been prowling this tub for an hour . . ."

The corridor ended at a blank wall ahead. Roan raised a hand.

"Hold it up," he said. He indicated the passage along which they had just come. "I've been counting paces. We've come about half a mile along here. That puts us on the opposite side of the ship from the hatch we came in by. All we've seen is cargo, supply, and utilities space. We're going back to the big corridor we crossed and move forward. I'm guessing we'll find the personnel areas in that direction. We're going to string out now, and keep our eyes open. The first man that talks without something important to say will get a mouthful of pistol butt. Let's go."

Roan led the way back a hundred yards, turned left into a wider passage, like the others, gray, featureless, faintly lit by a feeble glare strip set in the ceiling, stretching on and on into remote distance.

"I'm freezin'," a crewman whined. "I ain't gonna be able to fire my gun, my fingers is so stiff."

"Holster your guns and get your hands warm," Roan said quietly. He went to a narrow door set in the wall, pushed at its edges. It yielded at the center, swung inward in two panels. He looked into a square room with papers scattered across the floor, a slanted table attached to one wall. There was a saddlelike seat mounted on a four-foot stand before the table. Roan picked up one of the paper scraps; it crumbled in his fingers. There were strange characters printed on the fragment he held.

He stepped back out of the room, continued along the wide passage.

In an immense, dim-lit hall, Roan looked at ranked hundreds of saddlelike perches arranged in endless rows on either side of foot-wide counters that ran the length of the vast room. A hint of a vile odor hung in the still air. Dust stirred underfoot as the nervous-eyed men stared around, fingering guns.

"This is an eating room, I think," Roan said. "We're getting closer."

"Closer to what?" a voice grumbled.

"We'll take the next ramp up. The crew quarters will be somewhere near the mess—"

"Hey—what's that . . . ?" A short-necked, round-backed crewman pointed a blunt finger. Roan walked over to look. What looked like handfuls of fish bones were scattered in a mound seven feet long, inches wide, half-buried in dust. The crewman dug a toe in, uncovered a dull metal object like a strap buckle. He kicked again, and a curious double-bladed knife with a knobby grip at the center skidded across the floor. The finder exclaimed, jumped after it, picked it up.

"Neat!" he stated. He gripped the weapon, one stubby blade protruding on either side of his rocklike fist. "Ya get 'em goin' and comin'—"

"Cripes," another grunted, eyeing the heaped dust and the fish bones, "that's one of 'em; what's left of a Niss . . ."

Roan looked around the broad room, saw other mounds here and there.

"Let's get moving," he said. "I want to see what's up above."

They were in a long, narrow, high-ceilinged room lined with saddles before racks and dusty screens interspersed with panels of tiny glasslike buttons. One screen glowed faintly, showing a greenish image of stars against space, and a tiny oblong that drifted, turning on its short axis. Above the screen, scattered beads of light glowed. On the floor below the panel lay two of the long dust heaps that had been Niss. The crewmen were busy picking ornate metal objects from among the fish bones.

"This guy must of been a big shot," Noag rasped. "Look at this knickknack!" He held up a star burst done in untarnished yellow metal with a giant jewel at its center.

"Chief, this must be the command deck, right?" Askor muttered. He was a hulking hybrid of mixed Minid and Zorgian blood, with the stiff, tufted hair of the latter scattered incongruously across the typical broad Minid skull.

"I think so," Roan said. "And that's *Warlock* on the screen there."

"I don't get it . . ." Askor looked around the long room. "Where are they? What are they waiting for?"

Roan stood, staring at the screen. As he watched, the blip that had been Henry Dread's ship expanded suddenly into a vivid sphere that swelled, spreading out in ragged streamers . . .

"She blew," Askor stated. "It's kind of a funny feeling. I lived aboard her for thirty years . . ."

"In reply to your question," Roan said in a harsh voice, tearing his eyes from the screen, "they're all around us. We've seen forty or fifty of them in the past three hours."

"Yeah, but them was just bones. I'm talkin' about—"

"You're talking about the Niss—the crew of this vessel," Roan cut in. He pointed to the scattered remains on the floor. "There they are. Meet the captain and the mate."

Askor furrowed his heavy brow. "Somebody fired that broadside that knocked out *Warlock*," he growled.

Roan jerked a thumb at the glowing lights. "The automatics took care of that," he said. "They were set to blast anything that came in range. I'd guess the power piles are nearly drained. That's why her bombardment didn't annihilate us completely."

"You mean—they're all dead?" Askor looked down at the dust and fine bones. His face spread into a broad grin. He chuckled, then put his wide hands to his chest and laughed, a booming guffaw.

"That's rich, hey, Chief? Us pussyfooting around like that—"

"Chee," a bystander commented. "Think a' that! How long's this tub been floating around like this?"

Roan kicked the bones aside, hoisted himself into the saddle before the command panel, began punching keys at random.

"I don't know," he said. "But I think it's a fair guess she's been cruising for the best part of five thousand years, with a full complement of corpses aboard."

In a cramped, metal-walled chamber lost far aft of the immense engines, Askor looked sideways at Roan.

"Looks like the Niss had a few captives aboard, eh, Cap'n?"

Roan looked down at the scattered bones of men, and the smaller bones of women, and in the far corner, two small skeletons of children—human bones; Terry bones, moldering among chains.

"Gather up the identity disks," he said emotionlessly. There was a clump of feet in the corridor. The horned head of Gungle appeared in the doorway, his eyes wide with excitement.

"Cap'n, we found something! A slick thousand tonner,

a Navy job, banged up a little but spaceworthy! She's
slung in the boat deck . . . !"

Roan followed the man along dark ways littered with
discards from the looting parties ransacking the ancient
vessel, now and again passed the scattered remains of a
long-dead crewman.

"Wonder what killed 'em all, Cap'n?" Askor kicked a
mound, sent foul dust flying.

"Disease, starvation, suicide. What does it matter?
Dead's dead."

Askor cast a quick glance at his grim-faced captain,
said nothing.

On the boat deck, Roan studied the businesslike lines
of the sleek vessel poised in a makeshift cradle between
malformed Niss scout boats, the numerals printed across
her bows, the ITN crest.

"Looks like she took a hit aft." Noag pointed out areas
of fused metal beside flaring discharge nozzles. "But they
made repairs. Musta been getting her ready for some kind
of sneak job . . ."

Roan mounted the access ladder, shouldered through
the narrow port. There was an odor of mildew and dust.
He flicked on lights, went forward, climbed a companionway to the surprisingly spacious command deck, stood
looking around at the familiar Terran screens, instruments,
fittings. He threw open a wall locker, choked at the dust
that flew, hauled out a ship suit. He thumbed the
tarnished TER. IMP. affixed above the pocket, read the
name stenciled below.

ENDOR.

"Hey," Askor said from behind him. "That's the same

as it says on one o' them ID's we took off them bones . . ." He sorted through the bright metal disks, handed one over.

"I didn't know you could read Terran." Roan eyed the half-breed.

"I can't exactly read, Cap'n—but I'm good at rememberin'. They look like the same marks to me."

"So the captain died in chains." Roan tossed the disk back. "I think his suit will fit me."

"How about it, Cap'n?" Noag called from the entry. "How's she look?"

"Check her out," Roan said. "If everything works, load her up and figure out how to get those hull doors open."

Askor rubbed calloused palms together with a sound like a rasp on rough wood.

"She's a sweet tub, Cap'n. Not as big as *Warlock*, but we never needed all that tonnage anyways. I'll bet she's fast. We can hit and get out before the dirt-huggers know what hit 'em—"

"We're through raiding for a while," Roan said. "There's more loot aboard this hulk than we can haul— enough to make every man aboard rich."

"Not gonna raid . . . ?" Askor scratched at his bristled scalp. "Where we goin' then, Cap'n?"

"Set your course for a world called Tambool. It'll be listed in the manual." Roan indicated the glowing face of the index set in the navigator's panel.

"Tambool? What's there?"

"My past—maybe," Roan said, and turned away to pore over the ancient star maps on the chart table.

CHAPTER ✳ FOURTEEN

Askor sat beside Roan, staring into the wide, curved panoramic screen that filled the wardroom wall. He sipped his Terran coffee—a drink that it had taken many months to develop a habit for—then cleared his throat self-consciously.

"It's been a long cruise, Cap'n," he said.

Roan didn't answer.

"A few more hours," Askor went on. "We'll be touching down at Tambool. Not much of a place, but there'll be a few kicks—"

"I'll distribute a few kicks myself if you don't shut up," Roan said.

Across the table, a crewman named Poion laid down his ever present stylus, closed his pad; he flickered his translucent eyelids down over his bulging eyes, fingering a wineglass delicately.

"Gee, Chief," Askor tried again. "It's been nine months now since the fight with the Niss ship and all. You been snappish as a gracyl in molting season ever since you took over as captain. You didn't used to be this way, back when you was Cap'n Dread's Number Two—"

"I'm not anybody's Number Two now," Roan said. "I'm Number One, and don't ever forget it." He drained his glass, refilled it.

"What do you seek on the minor world Tambool, Captain?" Poion asked in his soft, breathy voice. "Henry Dread's mission was not there . . ."

Roan looked at the Beloian curiously. Poion seldom started conversations, and never personal ones.

"I thought you could read minds."

"I read emotions. I compose with emotions. It is the art of my people. I am now scoring a composition for ten minds and a dozen experimental animals—"

"Let's hear you read my emotions," Roan cut him off abruptly.

Poion shook his head as though to dislodge a troublesome thought. "I cannot. That's why I asked you the question. I haven't the talent for Terran emotions. They're not like the others. They're in a different . . . mode. More powerful, more brutal, more . . . primitive."

Roan snorted. "So you can't tell anything from my mind?"

"Oh, a little," Poion said. "You are engaged in a *noston*, a return home. But your nostalgia is not the nostalgia of any other creature in the universe." He sipped his wine, watching Roan. "Because you have no home."

On the screen Tambool rose on the left and the ship turned on its gyros and an arrow swung. Roan gripped his glass, watching the world swell on the screen.

"Perhaps," he said, at last.

The vibrations of landing stopped and Roan rose and

walked back through the crew compartments. He found
Askor by the exit port, rattling a gun nervously against his
belt.

"I told you this wasn't like other ports," Roan said
sharply. "You'll keep the men under control. They're to
pay for what they take. And no shooting."

Askor muttered but Roan ignored him. The port
cycled open; Askor ducked his head and peered out at the
puddle field, the drab row of sheds, the dismal town
straggling up the hillside.

"Cripes, Chief, what's this crummy dump got that's so
hot?"

"Not much; but such as it is, I don't want anybody
bleeding all over it." The other men had crowded around
now, decked out in their shore-going clothes, guns and
knives in belts, anticipatory grins in place.

"My business won't take but a few hours," Roan said.
"While we're here, forget looting. There's not much you'd
want anyway."

The men muttered and shuffled their feet, but no one
said anything loud enough to take exception to.

"No reception party," Sidis commented as the men
followed Roan down the ramp. "At least not in sight . . ."
He licked his lips and watched the windows of the sheds
and peered at every shelter that might house an ambush.

"Anybody that wants to land here can land," Roan
said. "Nobody cares, and you shift for yourself. It's not
rich enough to loot and it's useless as a base. It's a place
for outcasts to come and lose themselves."

Poion glanced sideways at Roan. Roan saw the glance.
He was talking too much—more than the men expected

of their taciturn captain. It was a sign of nervousness, and it made the men nervous too.

He walked on in silence, heading for the jumble of shacks behind the port. Had it been this derelict—this dirty and depressing when he'd left it as a boy?

It didn't matter. He was returning as a Man, and he'd come for a purpose, and let anyone who got in his way look out . . .

Roan marched the men past the tented Soetti Quarter, under the walls and towers of the Veed section, into the gracyl slums. He almost marched past his old house without recognizing it. Everything seemed smaller, dirtier than he remembered. A group of unwashed gracyl infants dug morosely in their instinctive way in the dust of the yard, and Roan thought fleetingly how strangely each gracyl reenacted his race's evolution from a primitive burrowing rodent. The flower garden was gone and no one had whitewashed the house for years. A suspicious gracyl mare peered from the window where Bella had once flapped a towel to call Roan to meals.

He swallowed a nostalgia that he hadn't expected to have and marched the men on past the garbage dump, now bigger than ever. No one knew, or asked, why he took that route. He walked confidently, head up, his guns strapped to his hips, his boots kicking up decisive splatters of mud as though he knew where he was going.

He had no friends to look for, no hint as to how to find Bella. But Uncle T'hoy hoy had had a favorite haunt—a tumbledown bar where he had been wont to huddle with other hard-bitten slaves, sipping at vile Yill drinks and muttering unknowable Yill secrets. It would be a starting place.

Roan turned a corner, and the men behind him murmured, and he could picture the grins spreading. This looked more like it, the pirate's part of his mind noted automatically. Ahead a carefully trimmed wine vine made an enclosure, and beyond could be seen the spangled tops of rich houses. A small party of Veed petty nobles was coming through the gate; some had iridion clasps on their pleated skirts and one had a diamond class badge attached to his neck. The only weapons they carried were daggers and whetted talons, and their slithering gait had the native insolence of those who think daggers are enough. Roan felt the men slow behind him, watching the Veed; he turned and gave them the look of ferocity that came so easily now.

"All right, you hull-scrapings, I've warned you! The first man that gets out of line gets a bullet in the guts."

"These Geeks friends of yours?" Noag inquired loudly, watching the Veed move past. Noag was a Gook and he had no use for Geeks.

"I have no friends," Roan said. "If you think I'm kidding, try me."

The Veed had paused and now two of them swaggered over.

"Get you gone from the places of the noble Veed," one said in flat, badly accented Interlingua.

"And take these mud-swine of half-caste Terries with you," the other added. They stood with their hands resting on their knives and they looked as though they hoped someone would give them some slight cause to draw them.

"OK if I kill these two?" Sidis asked hopefully. He was grinning and his polished teeth shone like silver.

"No killing," Roan said. The other men moved up and began to ring in the two Veed; they moved together, suddenly nervous, realizing that these were not local outcasts.

"Begone," Roan said in the faultless Yill Bella had taught him. "My slaves scent easy blood."

The two Veed took their hands from their knives and made inscrutable Veed faces. "Take your vile scent with you," one said, but he moved back.

"Before you go," Roan said, "give me news of T'hoy hoy, the Yill bard and teller of tales." He put his hands on his guns to show that it was no idle inquiry.

"It is said the one you name can be found over his cups in any pothouse so undiscerning as to accept his custom," the Veed snapped the answer.

Roan grunted and turned on toward the gate. He remembered that once the Veed Quarters had been sacred and taboo, and that he hadn't been good enough to be allowed there except when he ran messages or delivered merchant's goods. But now he was Roan the Man and he went where he liked. He strode through the gate, and Veed faces turned, ready to hiss their anger; but a silence fell over them as the small party tramped past. There were a few halfhearted catcalls, but no one moved to intercept them. The Veed had seen the byplay at the gate with the two dagger men, and understood that it was a time for discretion.

On the far side of the Veed Quarter, in the swarming

artisan's section of the city, Roan halted the men at a tavern under the battered red, green, and purple symbol of an all-blood establishment.

"You wait out here," Roan said. "I'll send out a round. And keep your hands off your guns and other people's belongings."

There was a Yill inside; he wasn't Uncle T'hoy hoy but he was the Twix caste, one of those inconspicuous ones who were always to be found in public places sitting unobtrusively in a corner to pick up information, compose their strange Yill poems, and be available in case there were messages to be sent.

Roan slid into the cracked seat across from the Yill, ordered Bacchus wine for himself and Fauve for the old Yill, then took out an oblong coin and put it on the table.

The Yill winked his eyes at Roan and let the coin lie there. There were many things a Yill would do for money and other things nothing could make them do, and the Yill was waiting to find out which kind of things Roan had in mind.

"First," Roan said, coming directly to business in the Yill fashion, "I want to find my mother, Bella Cornay. Then I want to find T'hoy hoy, my foster uncle."

The Yill took the coin with pointed fingers from which the fighting talons had fallen long ago, deposited it under his tongue, and watched while the clumsy, frizzle-haired waiter brought the wine. He smelled the Fauve, looked keenly at Roan, and said, "I am L'pu, the Chanter of Verses. I know you: the flame-colored Terran boy who filled the empty life of the faded beauty Bella. You were a small, wild flame of a youngling, and you have lived to become a fire of a man. Your mother's heart would have leaped for your beauty, which is that of all great beasts of prey."

"Mother is . . . dead?" Roan felt a slow sadness. He had never loved his mother enough, and it had not been fair. All he'd ever thought about was Raff.

"She is no longer alive," the Yill said. He was being precise about something. Roan waited to see if he would say more, but he didn't and it was no use to ask.

"Uncle T'hoy hoy?"

"At this moment, T'hoy hoy listens at the house of the autocrat of the noisome Soetti. Would you have me fetch him?" Roan nodded and the Yill drank off his wine and slipped away. Roan sat and waited in the small, dank tavern; the room smelled of a hundred liquors, poison to each other, and of alien sweats. Outside the flaps of the cellophase windows the men were bored, talking too loudly and throwing knives carelessly at each others' feet. Rain started up and drummed on the tin roof. It reminded Roan suddenly, overwhelmingly, of Bella. But he thrust the emotions back under a gulp of strong wine. Home was gone, had never been. Tambool was a place like any other and in a few hours he'd be on his way. He had another drink and waited. Bella was no longer alive, L'pu had said. What did that mean?

Finally he heard the men jibing at someone outside, and the tavern lighted with an opening door and feet shuffled. It was Uncle T'hoy hoy. He had gotten old, so old, and his gray face was like shriveled clay, but it rose into smiles for Roan.

"My boy," he said. "Oh, my boy." And Roan saw that if a Yill could cry, Uncle T'hoy hoy would have cried.

Roan embraced the old slave and ordered two more Fauves.

"I guess I've changed," he said. "Would you have known me?"

"You have changed but I would have known you, Roan. But tell me the story of your years. Have you killed and have you loved and have you hated?"

"All that and more," Roan said. "I'll give you my story for your collection. But my mother. What happened to Bella?"

Uncle T'hoy hoy reached under his belt, inside his tunic, brought out a thick gold coin and offered it to Roan. "Your inheritance," he said. "All that remains of a once-fair flower of Yill . . ." Uncle T'hoy hoy was a storyteller and he couldn't help being poetic, Roan told himself, suppressing his impatience.

"Where did Bella get gold?" Roan fingered the coin. It was an ancient Imperial stater, and represented a lot of money in the ghettos of Tambool.

"She had nothing for which to live, with Raff dead and you stolen. She sold herself to the Experimental College for vivisection. This was her pay, and she left it for you in case you should ever return."

"And . . . she left no message?"

"The deed speaks all that need be said, Roan."

"Yes . . ." Roan shook his head. "But I don't want to think about that now. I have to hurry, Uncle T'hoy hoy. My men are itchy for action and loot and if anybody even looks at them sideways they're going to cut loose. I came here to find out who I am. I know Dad and Ma bought me at a Thieves' Market here on Tambool, but I don't know which one. Did they ever give you a clue?"

"No clue was needed, Roan. I was there."

"You?"

"I came here, all the way from a far world, to kidnap you," T'hoy hoy said, remembering an old irony and smiling his strange Yill smile at it.

"You!" Roan was grinning too at the unlikely image of the old Yill as a hired adventurer.

"Ah!" T'hoy hoy said. He shook his head. "Better it were perhaps if all this were left untroubled under the mantle of time—"

"I want to know who I am, Uncle. I *have* to know. I'm supposed to be of Terran blood—Pure Strain. But who were my parents? How did the dealer get me?"

Uncle T'hoy hoy nodded, his old eyes remembering the events of long ago.

"I can tell you my story, Roan. Your story you must find out for yourself."

"I've shot my way in and out of a lot of places," Roan said. "But you can't shoot your way into the past. You're my only lead."

"We came here," T'hoy hoy said, "following orders. We were minutes late at the bazaar—but the dealer talked a little. We trailed the purchasers, and they went to earth in a closed place where tourists never venture. When we saw them, we laughed at how easy it would be; a frail Yill woman and an old hybrid Terran in an ill-fitting suit . . ."

"Raff was never old."

"So we discovered. It was incredible. He fought like a fiend from the Ninth Pit, and even after his body bones were broken, he fought on, and killed all the others, and he would have killed me, but the lady Bella saw that I was Yill, like her, and that I would yield; and she needed me, so my life was spared. Then by my oath I was forever bound to her, and to Raff. And to you."

Outside, the men had begun a game of rolling the tankards their drinks had been served in, and shooting at them. Inside there were only Roan and T'hoy hoy, and the bartender frowning worriedly over his pewters, and casting glances toward the door.

"Send out a refill," Roan called. He poured his and T'hoy hoy's glasses full.

"Dad used to say I was Pure Strain; but whenever I asked him what made me any more valuable than any other more or less pure Terran, all he said was that I was something special. What did he mean, T'hoy hoy?"

"Special you were, Roan, for many men died for the owning of you. But how, I cannot say."

"This market where I was bought, tell me where it is; maybe the dealer who sold me knows something."

"As to the bazaar, tell you I will, but as for the dealer . . . alas, he died of a throat ailment."

"A throat ailment?"

"There was a knife in it," T'hoy hoy said a little guiltily. "Ah, I admit, Roan, I was not so even-tempered then as now." T'hoy hoy told Roan the location of the Thieves' Market on the far side of Tambool. "But let me advise you to stay clear of the place, Roan. It was a evil haunt of the scum of the Galaxy twenty-five years ago, and the neighborhood has since deteriorated . . ."

Roan was watching through the window as a large company of Veed gentry went by outside; his crewmen stood silent, watching, but everything in their stance suggested disrespect. Sidis was tossing his knife in the air and catching it without looking, and grinning his steel-toothed grin.

"They're like children," Roan started, and broke off. A lone Veed had hurried past, trailing the group, and the diamond at his throat had glinted like a small sun, and from the corner of his eye Roan caught a sudden movement and now he heard an almost silent thud.

He was out in the street in a moment, in time to see Noag's short cloak flutter at an alley mouth. Roan sprang after him and whirled the lumbering Minid around, but it was too late. The young Veed noble's head dangled at a fatal angle. An angry buzzing was growing among the gathering bystanders. They didn't like Veed nobles, but strangers killing them in the public street was too much.

"Come on, you brainless slobs!" Roan yelled. "Form up and let's get moving." He looked at Noag, and the Minid fingered his knife and looked back.

"You can stay here with your Veed and his diamond," Roan grated, and passed him by.

"Huh?" Noag looked puzzled. "You can't do that! It'd be murder," he roared, starting after Roan. "I got no Tamboolian money! I don't know the language! I won't last a hour!"

"Tough," Roan said. "Cover him, Askor, and shoot him if he tries to follow us."

T'hoy hoy was trotting beside Roan, looking back worriedly. "Cleverly done," he puffed. "The sacrifice will satisfy them for the moment, but you'd best not tarry.

Farewell, Roan. Send word to me, for I would know how your saga ends."

"I will, Uncle," Roan said. He pressed a heavy Imperial Thousand credit token into the old Yill's hand and hurried after his men. At the gate he looked back; Noag was squatting at the alley mouth. Tears were streaming down his face but he was cutting the diamond off the dead Veed.

CHAPTER ✻ FIFTEEN

It was a steaming, screaming color blaze of a bazaar, and the dust was like yellow poison, and as Roan marched his men through the narrow, twisting ways between stalls, no one gave them a second look. No one gave anything a second look in the Thieves' Market unless it was something he wanted to steal.

They came out into an open plaza and wended their way across it among sagging stalls with sun-faded awnings. Merchants too poor to rent booths squatted by heaps of tawdry merchandise and gold and green death-flies buzzed everywhere, and the air reeked of opulent perfumes and long-rotted vegetables and sweat and age and forbidden drugs. They passed a scarlet and blue display of Tirulean silks that were worth fabulous amounts and a spread of painted esoterica that was worth nothing at all and came up to a crumbling wall cut from the chalky ocher rock face that towered over the square. A hand-painted sign beside a dark stair said YARG & YARG, LIVE STOCK. Under the first sign, another hung by one rusted pin. It said FOR SALE—VIABLE

HUMAN EMBRYOS. Something had been painted beneath the words, but the letters had been scratched out.

Roan turned to the men. "Go shopping," he said, and they stood and looked amazed.

"Go shopping. Spread out so you don't look like an army; and don't start anything."

"Where you going, Boss?" Askor inquired.

"I'm going to see how easy it is to become a father."

Roan climbed the narrow, hollowed steps, pushed past the remnant of a beaded hanging into a dark and smelly room lit by a crack in the ceiling. From behind a desk, a mangily feathered Geek in tarnished bangles looked at him with utter insolence.

Roan kicked a broken chair aside and leaned on the desk.

"What do you want?" the creature rasped in a scratchy, irritable voice. "Who referred you here? We deal wholesale only, to selected customers—"

"I don't go through channels," Roan interrupted. "I came to inquire about buying an embryo: a human one, like you advertise outside."

"We have thousands of satisfied customers," the dealer said automatically, but in a tone that indicated that it had no need of another. It was looking Roan over distastefully. "How much are you prepared to pay—if I should happen to have something in stock?"

"Money doesn't matter—just so it's the real thing."

"Your approach appeals to me." The dealer fluffed out its molted face ruff and sat up a little straighter. "But you have to have at least one wife. Sodomate law. The Feds would get me."

"Let me worry about that. What have you got?"

"Well, I could offer you a good buy in a variety of FA bloodlines—"

"What does FA mean?"

"Functionally adapted. Webbed digits, heavy-gravity types, lightly furred—that sort of thing. Very nice. Guaranteed choice, selected—"

"I want genuine Terry type."

"What about our number 973? Features the cyclopic maternal gene, rudimentary telepathic abilities that could be coaxed along—"

"I said Terry type, the original variety."

"Nonsense. You know better than that. It doesn't exist—"

"Doesn't exist, eh?" He bent close to the dealer. "Take a look. A *good* look."

The dealer clacked its tarnished beak and looked at Roan worriedly. Its large round Rheops eyes were watery.

"My goodness," it said. Then: "The feet. You'd be surprised how often it's the feet."

Roan stepped back and pulled a boot off and planted his bare foot on the massive old desk.

The dealer gasped. "*Five* digits! One might almost think—" It looked up into Roan's face with a sudden alarm. It slid off its stool and hopped back.

"You're not—oh, no—"

"Sure I am," Roan said. "I came from right here. Twenty-five years ago. And now I want to know all about the circumstances surrounding my presence on your shelves."

"Go away! I can't help you! I wasn't here then! I know nothing!"

"For your sake," Roan said, "you'd better know something." He took a gun out of his belt and hefted it on his palm.

"My . . . my uncle. Uncle Targ. He might—but he left word he wasn't to be disturbed . . . !"

"Disturb him," Roan said ominously.

The dealer's eyes went to a corner of the room, flicked back.

"Tomorrow. Come back tomorrow. I'll check the files, and—"

Roan came around the desk and headed for the corner the Rheops had glanced at. There was the tiny glint of an oculus from a shadowy niche. The feathery alien skittered across to intercept Roan.

"Uncle Targ isn't active in the business any more! He's not a well being! If you'd just—"

"But I see he still retains an active interest." Roan swept the dealer aside and raised the gun and fired a low-power blast at the wall. Plaster shattered all around the Eye, exposing wires which led down toward a circular hairline crack in the fused-sand floor. Roan brought the gun up and fired at the crack. The dealer jumped at him and hauled at his arm, squawking. Abruptly, the trapdoor flew up and a tiny, old voice screeched in five languages: "Stop, cease, desist, have done, give over!" A naked ancient head popped up from the opening, its three remaining feathers in disarray. "Break off, check, stay, hold, cut short! Chuck it, I say!" it shrilled. "Terminate—"

"I've already stopped," Roan said. "Uncle Targ, I presume?" He tossed the dealer aside, stepped to the opening. Spidery stairs led down. He holstered the gun and descended into the heavy reek of sulphur dioxide. Uncle Targ danced on skinny, scaled legs, screaming curses in at least four tongues it hadn't used before.

"You swear with great authority," Roan said when the oldster paused for breath. "Why all the flummery?"

The creature skittered to the wall and plugged a wire dangling from its wrist into a socket.

"I should have let you rot! I should have decanted you at the first sight of that accursed box with its crests and jewels and its stink of trouble! Because of you, my very own pouch-brother was hacked to spareribs in the flower of his dealership! But instead, I maintained you at the required ninety-eight degrees Fahrenheit for days, and this is the thanks I get!" It stopped and breathed heavily for a moment. Then:

"Go away," it piped in a calmer tone. "I'm an old being."

"You're an old windbag, but that's your problem," Roan said carelessly. "All I want to know is who am I?"

"All that shooting! You could have shorted my metabolic booster unit!"

Roan looked around at the dim-lit room. There were no windows, but the walls were paneled in pure gold and somebody kept it polished. There was a chandelier hung with diamonds and a burl desk that must have cost a couple of thousand Imperial to import from Jazeel. The creature's flimsy old body was swathed in yards of silver damask, and in one side of its beak it wore a ruby that looked like the heart of a rare red wine.

"You've got a right nice sickroom," Roan said. "And it's a matter of no moment to me whether you're evading the Feds or the tax collectors or if you just like to be alone. But I'm still waiting for an answer." He tossed the gun impatiently and motioned with his free hand at Uncle Targ's wires. "I can either plug you," he said, "or unplug you."

Uncle Targ squeaked around in the back of its throat as though it were pulling out rusty file drawers in its head.

"I'll have to get your records." It hesitated. "Don't look, now." It sounded as though it had them in its lace bra.

Roan went on looking, but Uncle Targ played a tune with its fingers on a solid piece of wall and a drawer slid out. A card flipped up.

Roan reached over Uncle Targ's shoulder and grabbed the card. Somehow, he'd expected to see names on it: his father's name, or his mother's. Or a country.

Instead, it said, *Pure Terran, Beta. ITN Experimental Station, Alpha Centauri. (special source d.g.)*

"What does 'Beta' mean?" Roan asked.

"Beta is you. Alpha was somebody else. And then there was Gamma, and the others."

"Others. Pure Terran . . ."

"They weren't viable."

"Were they my brothers?"

Uncle Targ shrugged. "Alien biologies have never been a hobby of mine."

"But what else do you know?"

"What's the difference? Why do you care? You're you and it seems to me you're pretty lucky. Suppose you were me, getting older and older and all the money I've got won't buy even a minute of the pleasures you can get free." The screech was a whine now.

"Why I care is my business. Telling me is your business."

Tremulously, the old creature unplugged itself, teetered across to its stool, perched, and lit up a dope stick. It was obvious from the way it caressed it that it wasn't allowed to have them very often.

"So long ago," it murmured, looking at the ceiling.

"Did you know I was stolen?" Roan asked.

"You *are* crude," Uncle Targ said distastefully. It pushed a button and the trapdoor slammed shut in its nephew's face peering from above.

"I'm waiting," Roan reminded it.

"I, ah," Uncle Targ said. "That is, so many of one's usual sources had withered away—you understand—"

"What made me so valuable?"

"You? Valuable? You retailed for a miserable two thousand, if I recall correctly."

"Still, there *was* your brother. And someone went to considerable trouble to come after me."

Uncle Targ blew smoke from orifices in the sides of its head. "Who knows? You do seem to be a more or less classic specimen of Man, if anyone has an interest in such matters." It sighed. "I envy anyone who cares that much about anything at all. With me it was money, but even that palls now."

"The card said I came from Alpha Centauri; can't you tell me any more than that?"

Uncle Targ rolled one beady eye at Roan. "On the flask," it said, "there was a name: Admiral Starbird, and the notation 'Command Interest.' I have no idea what that might mean."

"Are there Terrans on Alpha?"

"I know nothing whatever of this Alpha place," Uncle Targ piped. "And I do not care to know. But there are no Terrans living there—or anywhere else, for that matter. The Pure Terran is a myth. Oh, ten, fifteen thousand years ago, certainly. They kept to themselves, lords of the universe, practiced all sorts of racial purity measures—except for the specially mutated slaves they bred. But then they had the poor judgment to lose a war. Since then the natural tendency toward environmental adaptation has had free rein. And with the social barriers down, the various induced mutations inbred freely with the Pure Strain. Today you're lucky if you can pick up what we in the trade call an Eighty X; a reasonable superficial resemblance to the ancient type."

"What about me?"

"Umm. If I were to cut into you, I daresay I'd encounter all sorts of anomalies. How many hearts do you have?"

"I don't know. I thought you said alien biology wasn't a hobby of yours."

"One can't help picking up a few—"

There was a loud thud from above and plaster fell down on the burl desk. Uncle Targ screeched and jumped for the trapdoor button. The lid sprang open and a solid slug wanged off the gold wall by Roan's ear and the ancient being's profanity cut off in mid-curse. Roan yanked out his gun and flattened himself against the wall; through the trapdoor he could see Askor holding Uncle Targ's nephew by the neck and slamming the feathered head against the desk. A small ragged slave was scrabbling frantically for the beaded hanging, but Sidis' unsheathed claws held him pinned by a trailing cloak. Roan fired a shot into the ventilator grill. It made an echo like eternity bursting.

"All right, boys, break it up," he called, and clambered up into the shop. Sidis looked at him, grinning his metallic grin, and the slave broke free and bolted from the room. Askor waved the dealer in a wide gesture as though he had forgotten he was holding him.

"Poion seen you come in here and we thought we heard some shots and then we couldn't find you."

"So all you rowdies could think of was to shoot the place up. I told you to go shopping."

"*Pay* for stuff?" Askor tossed the dealer aside; it struck with a clatter of beak and claws and bangles and crept to a neutral corner. "We figured you was kidding."

Roan glanced down into Uncle Targ's private retreat. The ancient Rheops lay on its back, glazed eyes wide, with its mouth full of blood.

"Come on," Roan said. "Let's get out of here."

Back in the plaza the bazaar had died as though a sudden storm had slammed it shut. Roan could feel the eyes staring at him from behind blind shutters and past barely parted hangings at narrow windows and through cracks in sagging facades. Askor glanced around, strutting.

"I guess they know we been to town, hey, Chief?"

"Shut up and march," Roan said.

This is what I always leave behind me, he thought. Fear . . .

"I don't get it, Chief," Askor grumbled, sitting beside Roan in the eerie light of the central panel. "For better'n a year and a half now—ever since we lost *Warlock*—we been bypassing dandy targets, blasting balls to bulkheads from one two-bit world to another. And when we get there—no shooting, you say. Go shopping, you say. The boys are getting kinda fed up—"

"We stopped and took on supplies once or twice," Roan said. "But I suppose that wasn't enough to satisfy your sporting instincts."

"Huh? Aw, that was peanuts; just grocery shopping, like."

"With a few good-natured killings thrown in, just to keep your hand in. Well, you can tell the crew there'll be plenty of action from now on."

"Yeah? Say, that's great, Cap'n! What you got in mind? A run through the Spider Cluster, maybe, and knock off a few of them market towns that ain't been hit for a hundred years—"

"Nothing so pedestrian. Set your course for Galactic East . . ."

Askor scratched at his hairless skull. "East? Why do we want to head out that way, Chief? That's rough territory. Damn few worlds to hit, and them poor ones."

"There'll be plenty of worlds; and after the first couple years' travel, we'll be in a part of space no one's visited for a few thousand years—"

"A couple years' run out the Arm? Cripes, Cap'n, that'll put us in No-man's-space. The ghostships—"

"I don't believe in ghostships. We may run into Niss, though. That's where the last big engagements were fought—"

"Look, Chief," Askor said quickly. "What about if we talk this over, huh? I mean, what the hell, there's plenty good worlds right here in this sector to keep us eating good for the next two hundred years. What I say is, why look for trouble?"

"You're afraid, Askor? That surprises me."

"Now wait a minute, Cap'n! I didn't say I was scared. I just . . ." His voice trailed off. "What I'm getting at is, what the hell's out there? Why leave good hunting grounds for nothing?"

"Alpha Centauri's out there," Roan said.

"Alpha . . . That's the place you said the ITN was. Cripes, Chief, I thought you said we was through with that chasing around—"

Roan came to his feet. "What do you think this is, a ladies' discussion circle? I gave you an order, and by the Nine Hells, you'll carry it out!"

Askor looked at him. "You sound more like old Cap'n Dread all the time," he said. "I'll follow your orders, Cap'n. I always have. I know I need somebody with brains to tell me what to do. I just made the mistake of thinking we could talk about it—"

"We've talked enough," Roan cut him off. "You plot your course to raid every second-rate planet between here and Alpha, if that's what it takes to make you happy. Just don't forget where we're headed."

Askor was grinning again. "That's more like it, Chief," he said. "This is what the boys been waiting for. Boy, what a cruise! It'll be a ten-year run, cutting into new territory all the way!"

"And no more talk about ghostships—or live Niss either."

"OK, Cap'n. But with some good targets in sight, it'll take more than a shipload of spooks to scare the boys off."

After Askor left the bridge, Roan sat for a long time staring into the main view screen, with its spreading pattern of glittering stars.

So much for the next ten years, he thought. After that . . .

But there'd be time enough to plan that when the sun called Alpha Centauri filled the screens.

CHAPTER✳SIXTEEN

Roan sprawled in his favorite deep-leather chair in the genuine wood-paneled officer's lounge of the heavy cruiser *Archaeopteryx*, which had served the free-booters as home for seven years now, since a stray missile had uncovered the underground depot in which the retreating ITN had concealed it, fifty-seven hundred years before. Sidis sat across from him, his grin ragged now with the absence of five front teeth, carried away by a shell fragment in an engagement off Rastoum the previous year. Poion perched in his special seat, fitted up to ease the stump of his left leg, toying with a massive silver wine goblet. Askor was tilted back with a boot on the mahogany tabletop, paring chunks from a wedge of black cheese and forcing them into his capacious mouth.

"I called you here," Roan said, "to tell you the cruise is nearly over. The story that last batch of prisoners told fits in. The sun ahead is Alpha."

"Not many of the old bunch still around, hey, Cap'n?" Sidis observed. "Bolu, Honest Max, Yack—all gone."

"Whaddaya expect?" Askor inquired with his mouth

full. He lifted his alabaster chalice and washed the cheese down with green Bacchus wine, then belched heartily. "We been on, lessee, twenty-one raids in the last eleven years, and fought three deep-space engagements with wise-guy local patrols—"

"You can reminisce later," Roan said. "I expect the ITN to pick us up on their screens any day now. I don't like that, but it can't be helped. If they let us alone, however, I'm making planetfall on the fourth world of the system. According to the records, ITN Headquarters is on the second."

"From the stories we been hearing, I got my doubts the ITN has a cheery welcome for nosy strangers," Askor said. "What you want with them Terries anyway, Chief?"

"I'm a Terry myself," Roan said. "I've got business with the ITN."

"In his origins a being finds hints of his destiny," Poion murmured. "Alas, our captain knows his not . . ."

"You'll wait for me on Planet Four," Roan went on, "and stay under cover. If I'm not back in ten days—you're on your own."

"Hey, you mean . . . ?" Sidis' grin was sagging, hooked up on the bad side by twisted scar tissue. He looked from Roan to Askor to Poion. "You're talking about letting the captain walk in there alone? And where does that leave the rest of us—"

"You'll be all right," Roan said. "You'll be happy; you can raid back down through the Eastern Arm and shoot up everything in sight, without me to nag you."

"Just like that, huh? Thirteen years together, and then, srrikk!" he made a cutting motion across his throat.

"I didn't take you to raise," Roan growled. "I remember you, the day we met: you were pounding some Ythcan's brains out against the bulkhead. You were doing all right."

"Back out through the Ghost Fleet, alone?" Sidis' grin was a grimace now. "To the Ninth Hell with that! I'm going with you, Cap'n!"

"I'm going alone," Roan said flatly.

"Then you'll have to shoot me, Cap'n," Sidis said distinctly.

Roan nodded quietly. "That could be arranged."

"And me too," Askor said. "Count me in."

"And I," Poion said. "I shall go or die, as my captain wills."

Roan looked from one to another. He lifted his glass and took a long draft, put it back on the table.

"You're *that* scared of the ghosts of departed Terries?"

Nobody spoke.

"You Gooks amaze me," Roan said. "All right, we four: But no more."

Sidis' grin was back in place. Askor grunted and carved off another slab of cheese. Poion nodded.

"It is well," he said. "We four."

"Gungle," Roan asked, "you think you can navigate *Archaeopteryx* now?"

"Yeah, Chief," Gungle said, grinning his snaggle-toothed grin. "Yeah, I think. You show me what to feed in, I feed it in."

"Suppose you were captain now. What course would you set?"

"No offense, Chief, but I'd plug in a straight line back

outa East Sector. Me and the boys, we heard back on Leeto about the Terry Ghost Fleets, and there ain't no civilization for parsecs. Just these dead worlds like Centaurus Four here, without even no air."

"What are your coordinates for the nearest all blood joy city?"

Gungle grinned wider, flicked a chart of the Eastern Sector on the navigation screen, and punched out a course to Leeto.

"OK," said Roan. "You're captain in full charge until I get back."

"Huh?"

"I'm taking Poion, Askor, and Sidis with me to Centaurus Two."

Gungle gaped. Roan took the heavy gem he'd worn on his chest since Aldo Cerise and tossed it to the newly appointed captain, who hung it around his neck and threw his shoulders back and stood proud, the grin turning into a stern look of dignity.

"Now pipe the crew up," Roan told him.

"Men," he said, when they had all assembled, "I'm going to leave you for a while—" and raised a hand to still the muttering that started up. "Meanwhile Gungle's captain and he'll do any gut-splitting that's necessary. And anybody that's got any ideas about anybody else being captain had better think twice. That's my Terran magic jewel Gungle's wearing. As long as he wears it nothing can touch him."

The men rolled their eyes at Gungle and made magical signs in twenty-four different religions, but no one raised any objection.

✻ ✻ ✻ ✻

"That thing really magic?" Sidis asked, as the scout boat nosed on toward the brilliant star that was Centaurus Two, with *Archaeopteryx* four days astern, outward bound for Leeto.

"It created magic in the heart of Gungle," Poion answered. "He is now a man and a leader. It created magic in the hearts of the crew as well. They fear him. All this I could feel very plainly."

"Yeah, but that's not what I mean," Sidis started—

"Look!" Roan was pointing at the forward view screen.

"A ship," Askor said. "Heavy stuff, too . . ."

"It didn't take 'em long to spot us," Sidis said. "Somebody's awake in these parts."

"We'll hold our course steady as she goes," Roan said. "Leave the first move up to them."

"What if the first move is a fifty megatonner amidships?" Sidis inquired.

"That'll be a sure sign we ain't wanted," Askor grunted.

Roan tuned the all-wave receiver, picked up star static, a faint murmur of distant planetary communications. Then the drone of a powerful carrier came through.

"Inbound boat, heave to and identify yourself," a voice barked in a peculiarly intoned Panterran.

"Survivors from the merchant vessel *Archaeopteryx*," Roan transmitted. "On course for the second planet. Who are you?"

"This is the Imperial Terran Navy talking. Ye're in Navy space. Stand by to receive a boarding party and no tricks or we'll blow ye to kingdom come."

"Are we glad to see *you*," Roan transmitted. "Any hot coffee aboard?"

But there was no answer and the four ex-pirates watched the Terran vessel growing in their tiny view screen.

"Ah, Captain," Poion observed sadly, "again the Terran Navy is a disappointment. You look for home and there is no home."

"Your emotion receiver's working overtime," Roan said. "But I admit our welcome lacked a certain something."

"Me, I feel like a fly that's about to get swatted," Sidis said. "Why don't you ever read my emotions, Poion?"

"You're too stupid to have emotions," Askor said. "We shoulda brought *Trixie* in; she could handle that Terry tub."

The ITN vessel came in, paced the tiny scout boat at a distance of fifty miles and then came alongside, looming like a dull-metal planetoid. There was a heavy shock as its magnetic grapples embraced the boat.

"Open up there," the harsh but strangely cultivated-sounding voice said from the communicator.

Roan nodded to Askor. He operated the control and the four pairs of eyes watched the lock cycle open. Hot, dense air wooshed into the boat from the higher-pressure interior of the naval vessel, bringing odors of food and tobacco and a pervading animal stink.

Askor snorted. "Terries! I can smell 'em!"

Boots clanged against metal decking. A tall, lean Man wearing an open blue tunic over a bare chest ducked through the lock. He had a lined, triangular face and there was sweat glittering across his forehead and chest and his pale eyes were restless. He gripped a power rifle with both hands and looked at the three massive humanoids and then past them at Roan.

"Who are ye?" he demanded of Roan, ignoring the others.

"Roan Cornay, master of *Archaeopteryx*."

"Who're these beasties?" he jerked his chin at the three Gooks, not looking at them.

"My crew. We were all that got out, and—"

"You go aboard," the Man said to Roan, keeping the power rifle pointed at him. "These others stay here."

Roan hesitated a moment. Poion caught his feeling and nodded imperceptibly at Askor. Then Roan stepped accommodatingly toward the port behind the Man, and as he passed he half turned quickly, slammed the gun from the Terran's hands with a lightning blow. Askor caught it, flipped it up, and let it point casually at its former owner.

"I prefer to keep my crew with me," Roan said calmly.

The Man had flattened his back against a bulkhead and his mouth was open. "Ye're stark, raving mad," he said. "I'm Navy. One yell . . ."

". . . and I'll have your guts plastered on the ceiling," Askor said, grinning. "Whattaya say, Cap'n. Let him have it?"

"Oh, I don't know," Roan said, watching a rivulet of sweat that was crawling along the Man's neck. "Maybe he's going to be nice after all. Maybe he'll decide to extend the hospitality of his ship to all of us. How about it, Terry?"

And Roan smiled an ironic grin at himself. This was

the first time he'd called anybody else Terry. And it came out like a dirty word.

Askor nodded. "He'll need to point his popgun at us." Askor pushed a thumb against the firing stud of the Man's power rifle and bent it out of line. He tossed it back to the Man. "Don't worry," he said. "We won't tell nobody it don't shoot."

Roan walked close behind the Man as they went through the port into the Navy ship. "No need to be nervous," Roan told the Terran. "Just say all the right things when you see your buddies."

A small, roundly built Man with a high, pale forehead stood waiting for them in the hold. He wore the tarnished silver leaf of an ITN commander on the shoulder of his uniform and he was flanked by four armed Men. He had small, dim eyes and they squinted at Roan and his companions, as though the brilliant lighting of the hold blinded him.

"Some reason why ye didn't dump 'em back out into space, Draco?"

Draco cleared his throat. "Distressed spacemen, Commander Hullwright."

Commander Hullwright frowned, still looking hard at Roan. "Aren't they all. But I see. This one seems . . ."

"Yes, sir," Draco said quickly. "He's Terran, but I don't think he even knows it. That's why I brought him in to you."

Hullwright grunted, but to Draco's obvious relief he was looking at Roan and ignoring the others.

"Ye speak a little Panterran?" the commander asked Roan.

"Yes, I recognized your voice."

"Then why didn't ye answer me hail?"

"I did."

"Hmmmph. Blasted receiver's prob'ly out again. Draco, see to it." Draco drifted back, eyeing Askor and Sidis nervously, and Commander Hullwright forgot about him again.

"Don't know you're Terran, eh lad?" Hullwright asked Roan. "Ye must be pretty overwhelmed with all this," indicating with a wave the Navy ship and himself and his officers.

"I've seen ships before," Roan said.

"Um. Got an ugly tongue in your mouth. No doubt ye're a dirty spy from Rim HQ. Blan send ye?"

"No."

"Fat chance ye'd tell me if ye *were* a spy. What's your story? What are ye supposed to be doing in ITN space?"

"My merchant man *Archaeopteryx* blew up a couple of parsecs back. I was outbound for Leeto for shore leave. We had a brush with pirates off Young and I guess they mined us. We four escaped in the boat; I was afraid we'd drift forever."

"Left ye'r ship and crew to fend for themselves, eh?" Hullwright's lip curled. "All right. I'll give ye a berth and ye can start in the Navy, swabbing decks. Maybe ye can work up to something. Maybe ye can't. Take care of him, Draco . . ." He shot a look at Askor and Sidis. "And put the animals back on their boat."

"Wait a minute," Roan said. "These are my men and they're hungry and thirsty. And I don't swab decks. I'm a master."

"Right now you're the most insignificant swab in the

Imperial Terran Navy, you puppy," Hullwright barked. "And as for your 'men,' they'll have to find their own animal feed in space. Put 'em back and cast 'em loose, Draco."

Draco shuffled his feet unhappily. "Uh, Commander. They claim to be distressed spacemen . . ."

"What's this—pretty sentiments about distressed Gooks? What's going on, anyhow? Are ye in on this mutiny I keep hearing rumors about? What . . ."

The four armed men with Hullwright had tightened up their ranks and one drew the gun from his holster. "Drop that power rifle, Draco," he said.

Draco dropped it. Sweat dripped from the end of his nose. "Listen, Commander," he said hoarsely, "they made me—" Roan took a quick step while attention was centered on Draco; his right hand made an expert chop across the throat of the man with the unholstered gun. Askor leaped like a cork from a bottle, seized two of the Men in his vast hands, slammed their heads together in his favorite tactic. Sidis caught the last of the four as he was bringing up his gun, yanked the weapon from the Terran with such force that the Man skidded across the hold and slammed against the bulkhead screeching, clutching a bloody hand.

"Hey look," Sidis said cheerfully, holding the gun up, "his finger's still stuck in the guard!" Sidis dislodged the amputated member and tossed the gun up. "What do we do with these nancies, Chief?"

"Poke them in the ship's lazaret. Commander Hullwright's coming with us for a little pleasant conversation, aren't you, sir? We'll go to the bridge where we can talk in privacy and comfort."

Askor gathered up the guns, gave the best one to Roan, handed the others to Poion and Sidis.

Commander Hullwright's ineffectual little eyes were frightened. "What," he began, "what are you . . ."

"Now, now, be calm, Commander," Roan said. "If you play it cleverly, you may even live through this."

Roan sat in the captain's padded chair, gnawing a roasted leg of fowl and studying the charts of the Space Traffic Control Area surrounding Nyurth, the second planet out from Centaurus, and other charts showing the layout of the vast headquarters complex.

"You know, Commander," Roan said, "I'm impressed with the Imperial Terran Navy after all. I'll just want a few details from you so I can be even more impressed. Care for another piece of bird?"

Hullwright snarled. Sidis cracked him across the shins with the power rifle.

"Answer nice when the cap'n speaks to you," he admonished.

"No, I don't want a piece o' bird, you pirate!" he roared.

"Tell me about the defenses, Commander," Roan said.

"I'll tell ye nothing, ye murdering mutinous crossbreed Geeks!"

"Our captain objects to adjectives," Poion said mildly, giving Hullwright a gentle but telling twist of the ear. "And I find your emotional radiation both primitive and appalling. Answer the captain correctly and succinctly."

"I'd eat me own tongue first!"

Roan tossed the chicken leg aside and began peeling a

banana. "Umm. Now, about these charts. How many of
the emplacements are operative and which ones?" He
held the chart for Hullwright to see.

Hullwright was silent. Sidis jabbed him roughly with
the end of the gun.

"Ye think I'd betray me uniform, ye scum?"
Hullwright snarled.

"That's right," Roan said. "Unless you'd rather die—
one piece at a time."

"Ye wouldn't dare lay a hand on me, ye filth! I'm an
officer of the Imperial Terran Navy!"

"I killed a captain once," Roan said. "It's just as easy as
killing a Gook."

Hullwright tried to keep his defiant look in place, but
the spirit had wilted from him.

"Damn ye'r eyes," he said, "ye won't get through
anyway. Untie me right hand and I'll point them out to ye
on the chart."

Hullwright sagged in the chair. His little eyes were
closed and he rubbed his sparse eyebrows with his right
hand. Empty glasses and plates littered the plotting board
and chart table, the remains of meals brought up from the
galley at the commander's reluctant request, and passed
in through the service slot.

"I've told ye all I know," Hullwright said hoarsely.
"Ye've sucked me brain dry as a mummy's tongue."

"You've done very well, Commander," Roan said.
"Askor, what's the plot for Planet Three?"

"Twenty-seven million miles abaft our port beam,
Cap'n."

"Fine. Now, Commander, I've got just one more little favor to ask, and you've been so nice. Pass the word to your second officer to assemble the crew on the boat deck in fatigues for calisthenics in exactly ten minutes."

"Hah? Whazzat?"

Askor applied the butt of the rifle. "Jump, Terry!"

After two more prods of increasing severity, Hullwright complied. With the cold muzzle of Askor's rifle against his left temple, his ragged voice sounded through the vessel.

"And now, good-by, Commander," Roan said. "Askor, you and Sidis take the commander to join his men; they'll be in their skivvies and unarmed, so you shouldn't have to kill many of them. Dump all but two kilotons of reaction mass from our lifeboat; then load the commander and his men aboard and cast them off."

"That's cold-blooded murder, ye swine . . ." A crack across bloody shins cut Hullwright off.

"You'll have enough fuel aboard to reach Centaurus Three. According to your charts, it has a breathable atmosphere. There are forty-three of you and the supplies and water should last you a couple of months, if you're not careless. And if I find you've been honest with me about the information you gave me, I'll see that you're picked up in good time."

"Wait a minute," Hullwright said blurrily. "I just remembered. About that picket line, the outer one . . ." The commander corrected a few errors he had made. Then Askor took him away, followed by Sidis with his toothy grin.

* * * *

Alone, Roan said in the bridge and knew he was a fool. He could have gone on looting the universe, or set himself up for life on some pleasant planet, with never another care in the world. Instead, here he was alone with three Gooks, going in to face the Imperial Terran Navy. And why?

I'm still looking for Terra, Roan thought. Poion says I'm looking for home and I have no home to find. Man has no home. Perhaps there is no Terra. But that's something Poion wouldn't know—and the Imperial Terran Navy might. They might know the truth of the story of the ancient Niss blockade of Terra. Roan thought of the dead Niss ship firing its last volley, and that made him think of Henry Dread, and even now he couldn't remember Henry Dread without pain. He had had blood on his hands before, but Henry's was the only blood that stained.

Poion came in with his silent tread. "Let that memory die, my Captain," he said, "and gird yourself for the future."

Roan felt the boat lurch slightly. That would be the lifeboat kicking free. Askor and Sidis came back into the control deck in high good humor. Their laughter was like a cannonball rolling over an iron grill.

"That was cute, Chief," Sidis said. "The tub's all yours. What are you going to do with it?"

"First we're going to scuttle her," Roan said, smiling grimly at three astonished expressions. "Then we're going to ride what's left into ITN HQ on Nyurth."

"And after that?" Askor asked.

"After that we start taking chances."

CHAPTER ✷ SEVENTEEN

It took nine hours to burn a carefully aligned series of holes through the bulkheads of the ITN destroyer, so arranged as to destroy food and water supplies and smash unimportant portions of the control system, while leaving intact the vital minimum of instruments and fuel reserves. The final punctures through the outer hull plates were bored by Sidis, cramped in a too-small ITN regulation vacuum suit, at points marked by tiny pilot holes cut from within. When the job was complete, crude patches were rigged and the foursome gathered in the now sealed-off control deck, surrounded by heaps of supplies placed there before the work was begun.

"Get the story straight," Roan said. "We're from an ITN detachment on Carolis. That's far enough away they won't know any better. We found this tub derelict, beyond the fourth from Centaurus, driving out-system at a half-G. We boarded her and sealed off the leaks, restored atmosphere to the conn deck, and headed her for her home station for salvage."

"What were we doing nosing around this sector?"

Askor asked, levering the cap from a can of compressed quagle eggs.

"We were lost," Roan said. "And next time you get a yen for quagle eggs go in the john. They smell like a corpse's armpit." There were a few things the Minids ate that Roan could never get used to. "We left our scout ship in orbit around fourth from Centaurus. We were out of supplies and almost out of fuel. When we first saw the Navy ship we thought we were being rescued. Then we found out it was a ghostship. We're distressed spacers—nothing more."

"We'll be more distressed yet, when the ITN gets hold of us," Askor said.

"I get distressed every time you open your ugly mouth," Sidis said. "Why don't you shut up and let the cap'n do the worrying?"

"It's a good forty hour run into the Planetary Control Area," Roan said. "We'll stand watch two on and four off. Every half hour we transmit our Mayday signal. We'll keep our receivers open; I doubt that we'll pick up anything, but if we do, ignore it."

"What if we hear an order to heave to?"

"Our receivers are out. We keep going."

Roan keyed the transmitter to the ITN distress channel.

"ITN vessel *Rage of Heaven*, under salvage crew, calling ITN HQ at Nyurth," he called. "We're headed in-system on course for Nyurth; our position is . . ."

At the center of a box of four heavy destroyers which paced the damaged vessel at a distance of one hundred miles, Roan steered the scuttled and patched *Rage of Heaven* in past the tiny outer moon of Nyurth, crossed the orbit of the massive inner moon, descended, braking now, into the turbulent upper reaches of the deep atmosphere. The escort moved in to fifty miles, then ten. On the screens, the telltales winked with the incoming pulses of long-range sensors aimed from the planetary surface nine hundred miles below.

"They're tracking us like we was a missile volley from a hostile super-D," Sidis growled through his carefully polished teeth. He was sharpening a new toothpick with a steel file, and sweat beaded his low forehead.

"At least they've laid off hailing us," Askor pointed out. "I thought maybe the bastards meant it when they gave us that final warning."

"Their emotions when we emerge from the ship should be fascinating," Poion said, delicately whetting an even finer edge on his already razor-sharp stiletto.

Sidis eyed the business end of his power gun and blew any possible dust out of it. Then he took out his whetstone and started honing his double-bladed Niss knife.

"You know, Cap'n," Askor said, "I dunno if it was a good idea, tricking us out in these Terry suits. A Gook ain't a Terry, no matter how you slick him up."

"You're honorary Terries," Roan said. "Now shut up and follow my lead."

The ship grounded clumsily at the extreme edge of the vast port complex. Roan watched on the screens as two of his escort settled in nearby, gun ports open and energy projectors aimed. The other hovered a mile or two above.

"They must think we got a army in here," Askor said.

The three crewmen looked at Roan. "Do we walk out there—just like that?"

"You know a better way?" Roan adjusted the set of the collar of his ITN uniform, hitched his gun belt to center the buckle.

"No weapons out," he said. "We can't buck the whole Imperial Terran Navy. Right now all we've got is my brains. So keep your traps shut."

"Well," Askor said, eyeing the bright sky, "it's as good a day as any to take a swig from the Hellhorn."

"I began to sense their emotions," Poion said. "Not death lust, but a mixture of curiosity and excitement and violence restrained. Something's afoot, Captain. Walk carefully among these Terries."

Roan led the way down the landing ramp, squinting at bright sunshine, sniffing the alien scent of fresh air. Across the field, an official, uniformed contingent of the Imperial Terran Navy was drawn up in a rank to greet him. Their shoulder insignia glittered in the sun, and their metal belts shone. Striding at the head of his hulking companions, Roan snapped over his shoulder:

"If one of you thugs disgraces me, I'll have his guts an inch at a time." The ranked Terrans stood rigidly waiting, and Roan admired their precise formation, their disciplined silence and stillness. And briefly he hated himself because he wished he were one of them, a Man among Men, and not a Terry Freak surrounded by bloodthirsty Gooks.

Then he was closer, and he saw they were not all the same height, as they had appeared to be, but were artfully arranged in graduated rows with the tallest on the right and the near-midgets at the far end. His step almost faltered, but he went on, seeing the alien faces now, the wrong-colored eyes under the regulation helmets, the queer-colored skin of wrists showing above six-fingered and four-fingered gloves, the slashes in polished boots to ease wide, webbed feet, the misshapen bodies that bulged under the uniforms of glory.

At twenty feet, he barked the order to halt. A heavy body bumped him from behind. He whirled, bellowed at the trio who were spreading out, gaping at the strangers.

"Back in line there, you bone-skulled sons of one-legged joy-girls!"

He turned again, saluted stiffly as a short, pink-faced Terran came up, casually returning Roan's greeting with a wave of a soft hand. He was wearing the insignia of a lieutenant commander, and he tucked a short swagger stick under his arm, glanced past Roan at his crew, wiped his nose with a forefinger.

"Commodore Quex would like to welcome you and your men and requests the honor of your presence at Imperial Naval Headquarters at your earliest convenience," he said in a high, melodious voice. A civilized voice.

Roan nodded, staring at the strange Terran's face. Except for Henry Dread, this was the first Terran face he'd ever seen. There were two heavy-lidded eyes—pale blue, Roan noted, with a small lift of excitement—a blob of a nose, a puckered mouth, folds of fat under the small chin. For some reason it reminded Roan of a baby Fustian, before its shell grew. It didn't look like the kind of face Roan had pictured conquering a Galaxy. But he concealed his disappointment and motioned his crew to follow him as the Terran led the way across the field.

"What do you get from them up close, Poion?" Roan asked softly as they marched behind the Terran officer, flanked by a squad of Men.

"Some sort of fear, oddly enough," Poion said.

"Fear? Of four ragged spacemen?"

"Not exactly of us. But that is the emotion I read."

The Headquarters of the ITN was a craggy many-towered palace built ages before by a long-dead prince of a vanished dynasty. It loomed like a colossus over the tumbled mud houses of the village. A vast green window like a cyclopean eye cast back brilliant viridian reflections as Roan and his crew marched in under the crumbling walls along a wide marble walkway, went up wide steps flanked by immaculate conical trees of dark green set among plants with tiny violet blossoms. It was faintly, sadly reminiscent of the garden on Aldo Cerise.

Inside, the sun glowed in long rectangles along the echoing floor of a wide, high room. Terries in fitted tunics of navy blue stood at rigid attention by elongated doors at the sides of the room. Above, a vaulted ceiling arched up into shadows where gold and blue mosaics caught occasional sun gleams among masses of hanging brass carvings, all polished, which dangled like earrings from a hundred peaked corners, clanging as the wind moved them. They went under a vast arch of enameled brass, across a wide floor of gleaming brass plates; far up among dark rafters, echoes of more brass clashed softly.

As the men marched by, Geek slaves prostrated

themselves. They were lean, ribby, deep-eyed creatures, with vestigial scales across high shoulders, long, finger-toed feet, and draggled manes of lank hair along their prominent spines. They wore only loin cloths in spite of the chill, and some of them trembled violently as Roan looked at them, from cold, or fear.

The small Terran officer trotted ahead, disappeared through high doors with a sign for Roan to wait. His men clustered close behind him, drawn together and suddenly alert, almost disciplined.

"We could jump 'em now," Askor growled. "I get jumpy just waiting."

"There is a certain pleasure in the experience of mortal suspense," Poion said. "In such moments the current of life runs deep and swift."

"You'll actually enjoy dying, you poetic bastard," Askor grunted.

Roan hissed at his men as they began to mutter. Waiting came hard to them. But there was no need to worry about them. They could smell danger at half a parsec—and it was an odor they were fond of . . .

Roan's guide reappeared and beckoned to him.

"Wait here," Roan said to his men, "and don't shoot anybody before I get back!" He followed through the bossed, agate-studded door into a shadowed, high-vaulted room in which ancient magnificence hung like rotted velvet drapes. A spider-lean, white-haired man in a rank-encrusted uniform rose from behind a desk like a beached freighter, offered a bony hand. Roan took it, and felt the stitching along the fingers where the webbing had been removed. He had a wide mouth and a strange, small chin; his ears were odd, and at close range Roan could see that they were edged with pink scar tissue.

"I am Commodore Quex," the man said in a soft, almost feminine voice. He was slight, delicately boned, but the cruelty in the slits of his too widely set eyes was that of a wolf, not of the cat.

Behind Roan, the Terran saluted and went out and the door closed behind him.

"I'm Roan Cornay," Roan said. "Lieutenant Cornay," he added.

"Ah, yes. From Carolis. What a pleasure to welcome you, ah, Lieutenant." A finger like a parchment-wrapped bone brushed at a red-edged eye. At close range, Roan could see a whitish crust at the corners of the puckered mouth. An unpleasant odor hung about the Man. He settled back into his chair, snapped his fingers. Something moved in the shadows, and Roan saw that it was a slave, face down on the thick, moldy carpet. It rose and scuttled to swing a heavy chair around for Roan to sit in.

The commodore glanced at a paper before him, then looked at Roan, his hand hovering near his eye. "Your ship, ah, Navy 39643-G4. Our records . . ."

"I captured her. After *Warlock* was lost."

"Ah, yes. So you said. Hmmm. *Warlock* was a valuable vessel. I don't believe your reports made it clear precisely *how* she was lost . . . ?"

"In action—" Roan paused, thinking of what he had been about to say about the Niss ship, and deciding quite suddenly not to say it. He let the sentence hang.

Quex was looking thoughtful. "Surprising . . . and

fortunate that you were able to obtain a replacement. And you say Captain Dread was lost as well?" The old voice was a purr. Roan felt tension creep along the back of his neck. He shifted in his chair so as to keep the door in view. "That's right," he said.

"And before his, ah, death, he tendered you your appointment?" The red eye peered past the finger at Roan.

"That's right."

"Ummm. And how did you happen to enter into your, ah, association with Dread?"

"He took me from a ship he captured."

Quex sucked in his dry lips. "Another naval unit?" he asked sharply.

"No; it was a traveling show. I was one of the Freaks— I—"

"You were a captive of non-humans?" Quex was digging at his ear now, angrily.

"Not really. I was, at first, but—"

Quex leaned forward. "You lived among them willingly?" There was an edge on his voice like a meat saw.

"They treated me well enough; I had good quarters and plenty of food—"

"Beware of Geeks bearing gifts," Quex said flatly. He leaned back, his thin fingers on the edge of the table.

"And what is your ancestry, Cornay? If you don't mind my asking." His voice indicated that he didn't care whether Roan minded or not.

Roan opened his mouth to say that he was genuine Terrestrial strain, but he heard himself saying, "I'm not sure. I was adopted. My folks didn't talk about it much."

"Mmmm. To be sure," Quex murmured meaninglessly. He poked at the papers on his desk.

"I want to get back in space as soon as possible," Roan said. "Who do I see about a new ship, and provisioning?"

Quex's mouth was open, showing inflamed gums and the tip of a white tongue.

"Provisioning? For what?"

"For my next cruise; my new assignment."

"Ah, of course." Quex showed the false face again. His finger was back at his eye. "But we can discuss these details later. I've laid on a dinner in your honor tonight. You'll want to prepare. Real Terran fare again, eh?"

"I take it most of the fleet it out on space duty now?" Roan said.

"Why do you say that?" Quex shot Roan a darting look.

"I only saw half a dozen ships at the port. Some of them seemed to be half dismantled. How big a force does Alpha command?"

Quex lifted the paper from his desk and dropped it again. "Ah, an extensive force, Cornay. Quite extensive. Rather extensive . . ."

"You have other bases here on-world?"

"Oh, ah, assuredly, Lieutenant. Why," Quex waved a hand toward the draped window, "you didn't imagine these few rusting hulks were our entire fleet?" He curved his puckered lips in a smile that crinkled the cruelty lines around his eyes. "Most amusing. Most. But . . ." He rose. "I suggest we allow these matters to wait until after our celebration of your happy return—"

Roan stood. "Certainly, sir. But I'd like to ask when the

counterattack is planned. I want to know how to set up
my cruise—"

"Counterattack?" Quex gaped.

"The massive offensive in force against the Niss. How
many of them are there? Where have they set up their
headquarters? What—"

The commodore held up two quivering hands. "Cornay,
need I remind you that all this is highly classified?" He shot
a look at the nearest slave, crouched against the floor.

"Oh." Roan glanced at the slave. "I didn't think . . ."

Quex rounded the desk. "Not that we have any trouble with our slaves. They know their place, don't they, old
one?" He kicked the slave hard in the ribs; it grunted and
glanced up with an almost human smile, then stared at
the floor again.

"Still, I shall have to dispose of this fellow now. Pity in
a way. He's been with me for twenty years and is well
trained. But getting old. Ah, well . . ." Quex took Roan's
elbow, guided him toward the door. "Until tonight, then?"

"What about my crew?"

"Your crew. Of course. Do bring them along. Yes.
Capital idea. Your entire crew, mind you. How many did
you say there were?"

"Just the four of us," Roan said.

"At second moonrise then, Cornay. Don't be late."

"We'll be there," Roan said.

Vast grins broke across battered faces as Roan
rejoined his crew.

"Glad to see you, Boss," Askor said. "We was about to
come in after you."

"Relax. I'll call the plays," Roan said.

A small, neat Terry with an elegant walk flicked ashes from a dope stick, came toward Roan and his men. The guard officer came to attention.

"That will do, Putertek," the newcomer said gently. He looked Roan over, smiling faintly, glanced at the others.

"But, sir. . ." the guard protested.

"And your watchdogs, too," the dandy said. He was carefully dressed in immaculate blue polyon with silver-corded shoulder boards bearing the winged insignia of a captain. His blond, rigidly waved hair shone with oil and he touched it with polished fingernails. His perfume reminded Roan distantly of Stellaraire.

"My name is Trishinist," he said with a small flourish of one manicured hand. "Sorry about the reception. These commissioned peasants—no finesse. Perhaps you'd like a bite to eat and then we can have a little chat?"

"My men are hungry, too," Roan said. "They never seem to get invited anywhere."

"The enlisted men's mess is . . ."

"They're officers."

"My apologies. Of course." Captain Trishinist led the way along a side corridor, chatting easily about the weather, the servant problem, the inadequacies of the mess cuisine.

The dining room was quiet with deep rugs and moss green drapes and immense, intricate chandeliers. Waiters sprang forward to draw out chairs at a long, white-linen table.

Askor and Sidis sat down awkwardly, then relaxed and grinned at each other.

Trishinist murmured an order to a servitor, waited and turned contentedly to the table as the waiter brought a loaded tray.

"Champagne and honeydew," Trishinist said as Roan's men eyed the frosted bottle and the breakable-looking glasses. "I hope you find it adequate."

Askor reached half a melon from the tray as the waiter passed, took a vast bite.

"Hey," he said, chewing juicily, "pretty good. But the skin's kinda tough."

"Wipe your chin," Roan said.

Askor used his sleeve. "Sorry," he muttered. Sidis had plucked the bottle from the tray and rapped it on the edge of the table to knock the top off. He jumped to his feet as the wine foamed out.

"Uh-oh," he said. "This one's went to the bad."

A waiter rescued the bottle with an impassive face, mopped up the wine. Poion took the bottle, sniffed it, then took a swig from the broken neck.

"An interesting drink," he said. "Effervescent, like the human mind. And worth a brief sonnet."

"What's the matter with you?" Roan snapped. "Offer the captain a drink."

Poion blushed and pushed the bottle along to Trishinist, who waved it away with a smile.

Roan picked up his melon and took a bite. "Good," he said around a mouthful of melon.

Trishinist's hand hovered over a spoon. Then he picked up his melon with delicate fingertips and nibbled its edge. "So glad you enjoy it," he said.

✻ ✻ ✻ ✻

Waiters cleared away the last of the dishes and filled glasses with mysterious-smelling brandy. Sidis slapped his belly and belched.

"A great feed," he said.

Askor plied a fingernail on a back tooth. "First real Terry chow I ever had," he commented. "Unless you want to count—"

"Thank you, Captain," Roan cut him off hurriedly. "It was a good breakfast."

Trishinist offered dope sticks all around and lit up as the waiters cleared the last of the dishes.

"Now, about *Rage of Heaven*," Trishinist said. "You say you found her abandoned. May I ask how it happened that you were cruising in this area?"

"We heard there were inhabited worlds in this area," Roan said carefully. "My ship was blasted by a time mine and we were drifting when we spotted the cruiser."

"You knew this was ITN controlled space?"

"Yes." Roan was watching Trishinist's face carefully. He wished Poion could tell him what Trishinist was feeling. It would help.

"And you encountered the derelict—where?"

Roan repeated the coordinates of the imaginary rendezvous beyond fourth Centaurus.

Trishinist glanced around; the doors were closed now and the waiters gone. He leaned across the table and his languid expression was gone. So were thousands of years of culture. It was as though suddenly all the waves went out of his hair.

"You're early," he hissed. "Four months ahead of schedule."

✳ ✳ ✳ ✳

Roan sat perfectly still, holding the interested smile in place.

"As it happens, we're ready here," Trishinist went on, licking his lips. "But I dislike Blan's imprecision. If we're going to be working together—"

"Hey, Chief," Sidis began.

"Hush," Poion murmured.

Trishinist squinted at the three crewmen and took out his pistol from its holster. "What about these?" he asked Roan.

"They do what I say," Roan said.

Poion smiled. "It is true," he said.

Trishinist frowned. "I had expected rather more . . . ah . . . representative individuals."

"They're as representative as I need them to be," Roan said.

"You have your identification?"

Roan reached inside his tunic, brought out an ITN identification disk on a chain, handed it across. Trishinist looked at it carefully.

"Endor," he murmured. "Blan's never mentioned your name to me, Captain."

"No doubt," Roan said.

"Blan is proposing no changes in the scheme at this date, I trust?" Trishinist said sharply. "I've fulfilled my part of the arrangement. I assume he's done as well."

"You see me here," Roan said.

"Where are his squadrons now?"

"They're in position," Roan improvised.

"Is he prepared to move at once?"

Roan frowned. "That depends on you," he said.

"On *me!*"

"Of course. We're early. You say you're ready, Captain. Just what do you mean by that? In detail."

Trishinist's jaw muscles were tensed up. "I told you, I've complied with our agreement in every respect."

"I can't work with you if you refuse to tell me anything. I want to know just *how* ready you are."

Trishinist relaxed his jaw muscles with a visible effort. "The organization among the rank and file is now over the eighty per cent figure. Sixty-four of the ninety-eight senior officers are aligned with us. Over ninety per cent of the junior corps. Our men control communications and three of the five major supply depots . . ."

Roan listened, taking occasional sips from his glass. Askor and Sidis sat, mouths slightly open, listening. Poion was smiling behind his hand. But Roan didn't kick him because it took some practice before a stranger could tell Poion was smiling.

"The units on maneuvers are, of course, those including high concentrations of unreliables," Trishinist concluded. "The base garrison has been carefully selected over the past three years and can be counted on absolutely. Now, what of your group?"

"We're ready," Roan said.

"At full strength?"

"I have triple the number of volunteers I expected."

"Excellent!" Trishinist pursed his lips. "How soon can you be in jump-off position?"

"We're already *in* position."

"You mean . . . you mean that literally?" The captain moved uneasily in his chair.

"Absolutely."

"Certainly you don't mean—today . . . ?"

Roan put both hands palms down on the table. "Now," he said, because all this was having such an extraordinary effect on Trishinist.

Trishinist's face seemed to fall apart as a look of comprehension and shock came over it. Sweat popped out on his forehead and his eyes went to Sidis, who was polishing his teeth, and Askor, who was just sitting, and Poion, who all of a sudden began to look as though there was something important about him.

"Oh, I see now," Trishinist said. "I see why you brought *them*. I . . ." A sick expression passed over his eyes. "You really think it's necessary to go that far?"

"What's the alternative?" Roan asked steadily.

"You're right, of course. Still . . . he *is* Pure Strain."

Roan stood up. "We've spent enough time talking about it. I'd like to meet him now."

"Meet . . . ?" Trishinist looked almost wild for a moment. "Oh . . ." He relaxed. "Just to . . . ah . . . assess him, of course."

"Of course."

"Very well." Trishinist rose. "Things are moving a trifle rapidly for me. But you're right. There's no need to delay."

At the door he hesitated, glancing at Askor, Sidis, and Poion.

"Ah . . . which one . . . ?"

Sidis grinned his jagged grin; Trishinist shuddered and went on out into the hall.

CHAPTER ✳ EIGHTEEN

Guards in bright-plated helmets snapped to attention as Captain Trishinist halted Roan and his men at a massive carved door.

"I'll introduce you as a new arrival from one of the Outer Towns," he said to Roan. "He likes to meet the new recruits. There are so few these days. The others will wait, of course."

Askor looked at Roan; Roan nodded. "Stay here," he said. "Don't wander off looking for liquor."

"Gee, Boss," Sidis said.

Trishinist opened the door; Roan followed him into an ivory-walled anteroom ornamented with a pale blue floral cornice. A harried-looking staff lieutenant came in from the room beyond, exchanged quick words with the captain, then motioned them through the arched way.

The room was wide, silent, deep-carpeted in dusty blue, with light curtains filtering the yellow light from tall windows. There were deep chairs, cabinets and book-shelves of rich polished wood, and a vast desk behind which an ancient Man with snow-white hair sat, his gnarled hands gripping the arms of his massive chair.

"Good morning, Admiral Starbird," Trishinist said. "I've brought a caller. . . ."

Starbird waved Trishinist and the aid from the room, indicated a chair, sat studying Roan's face in silence.

"Have I not met you somewhere, once, young Man?" His voice was the rumble of subterranean waters.

"I don't think so, sir," Roan said. He was staring at the other's lined face. He had never seen an old Man before, and he was remembering Henry Dread and the expression, at once that of the hunter and the hunted, that Henry had worn and that the old Man had too.

"That fellow," Starbird jerked his head toward the door through which Trishinist had gone. "He a friend of yours?"

"I just met him today."

"Vicious little ferret," Starbird said. "He's up to something. Thinks I don't know. Has his picked men all over my headquarters. But it doesn't matter. No guts. That's his trouble. Oh, yes, he'll plan; he'll talk. But there's no steel in the man." The admiral's eyes were on Roan's face, as though searching for a clue to something.

"From the Outer Towns, eh? What were your parents like?"

"I don't know, sir. I was raised by foster parents."

"And you want to fight the enemies of Imperial Terra."

"I've thought about it."

"If I were young again," Starbird said with sudden vigor. His fingers twitched on the chair arms. "I remember *my* first day. Ah, those were great times, young Man! There was something in the air, a feeling of things to be done, goals to strive for . . ." He sat, looking beyond Roan into the past.

"My father was on fleet duty then," he went on, talking to himself now, communing with the dead. "He commanded a five million tonner, gunned out of space by the Niss. Three hundred years ago that must be now. I was just a lad, then, on border duty in the north. I was to have been with him on his next sweep. He was a bold one; too bold. Who else would penetrate all the way to Sol? Nobody!" Starbird pounded his chair arm and looked at Roan. "Now look at the trash you see disgracing the uniform today! They're a cruel lot, young Man! And gutless . . ."

Roan sat silently, waiting.

"Revenge," Starbird said. "I swore I'd have it! But no suicide run, by God! Plenty of smirks and snickers thrown my way. All talk, they said. Talk! But I wasn't jumping off half-ready. I needed the rank first. Then reorganization, weeding out the corruption, the twisted element that was choking the service! Measure a man's genes instead of his guts, that was their way! Damn his genes! It's the dream that makes a Man, not the number of his toes!"

Starbird fell silent, his face twitching with the pain of old memories.

"I had my star at last," he said suddenly. "I put my plan before the general staff. The plan I'd worked out over all those years. Five hundred ships of the line, a million picked Men. We were to move in two echelons, blast our way past the Niss picket lines beyond Pluto, strike with our full power all the way in past the Neptune and Jupiter orbits—then—when they massed to meet us—split! Our probes had given us plenty of information on the Niss defensive patterns. I analyzed their data and saw the answer: We'd split beyond Mars, break up into two hundred and fifty pairs, and carry a running fight right in past Luna—then regroup in a beautiful maneuver I'd worked out as carefully as a ballet—and hit the Niss blockade with a spearhead that could blast its way through the walls of Hell!" The old Man's eyes blazed with a fierce light; then he let out a long breath and leaned back. He raised his hands, let them fall.

"They laughed at me," he said flatly. "We weren't ready, they said. The Niss were too powerful, we didn't have the firepower to stand against them. Wait, they said. Wait!" He sighed. "That was almost two hundred years ago. We're still waiting. And four lights away, the Niss blockade of Terra still stands!"

Roan was sitting bolt upright. "Terra?" he said.

"Ah, the name still has magic for you, does it, lad?"

"Only four lights from here?"

Starbird nodded. "Sol's her sun; the third planet, the double world, Terra the Fair. Locked up behind a wall of Niss!" Starbird's fist slammed the desk. "I'll never live now to see my plan used! We waited too long; somehow, the fire that we carried died while we talked—and the dream dies with it."

Roan sat forward in his chair. "Admiral, you said you weren't worried about Trishinist. What if he had outside help?"

Starbird's eyes narrowed. "What outside help?"

"A man named Blan."

"Blan? That warped imp out of Hades? Is he still alive?"

"His forces are due here in four months."

Starbird was sitting erect now, the force back in his voice. "How do you know this, lad?"

"Trishinist mistook me for Blan's emissary. He's ready to make his move now; today. He thinks one of my crew is assigned to assassinate you. I'm here now to size you up for the killer."

Starbird rose and walked across to the door. He was a tall, once-powerful man with square, bony shoulders and lean hips. He flipped a lock, threw a wall switch that snicked locks on outer doors. He came back and sat behind the desk.

"All right, young fellow: Maybe you'd better tell me all you know about this plot."

"That's as much as I was able to get out of him," Roan said. "With half the men backing him, he's in a strong position, even without Blan's reinforcements."

Starbird stroked the side of his jaw thoughtfully. "That timetable suits me very well. Let Trishinist go ahead with his plans; when he discovers his allies are missing, he'll collapse."

"I can't stay much longer, sir." Roan got to his feet. "Trishinist will begin to suspect something. What do you want me to do?"

Admiral Starbird thumbed his chin. "When's the assassination scheduled?"

"Tonight, after the banquet."

"Make it late; I'll be ready; just follow my lead. In the meantime, arm yourself. How many men do you have with you that you can trust?"

"Three."

Starbird nodded. A smile was growing on his seamed face. His hand slammed the table. "Young fellow—what was your name again?"

"Roan. Roan Cornay."

Starbird was cackling. "Terra excites you, does it?" The old Man turned to a wall safe, punched keys with trembling fingers. The door swung open and he took out a sheaf of many-times-folded papers.

"My attack plan," he said. "The ships are ready—over four hundred of them, in concealed docks on the other side of the planet. I've kept them ready, hoping. I needed a leader, Mr. Cornay. Trishinist has supplied the men. Let him try his coup! Let him send his killer to me! Then, when he comes along a little later to see for himself, I'll be sitting here, laughing at him! And the orders will be waiting! I have a few loyal officers; they'll command the five squadrons of the flotilla. And you, lad! You'll take command as acting Admiral of the Fleet!"

"You'd trust me, Admiral? You don't even know me—"

"I've known many Men in my years, boy. I can judge a fighting Man when I see one. Will you do it?"

"That's what I came here for," Roan said softly. "That's what I've lived the last eleven years of my life for."

Roan's thugs clustered about him in the windy bronze-and-mosaic hallway outside the grand dining chamber. They were splendid in new clothes of bright-colored silky cloth spangled over with beads and ornaments of glass and polished copper, and they smelled incongruously of flowers.

"Keep your guns out of sight," Roan ordered. "Keep your hands off the females and don't kick the slaves; that's a privilege we'll leave to our hosts. No rough stuff unless *I* give the word, no matter what happens. And any man that drinks so much he can't shoot straight will deserve whatever he gets." He settled his palm-sized power gun against his stomach under the wide scarlet cummerbund that had been wound around him by his assigned slaves in the dust-covered splendor of his quarters.

"Let's go," he said and pushed through the high mother-of-pearl inlaid doors. The clang and thump of noisemakers burst out; dancing girls sprang into motion, whirled forward strewing flower petals. A thousand tiny colored lights gleamed from chandeliers and winked from tiny fountains that sparkled on long tables spread with dazzling white cloths almost hidden under gleaming plates, polished eating tools, slender glasses as fragile as first love. There were hundreds of Terrans seated at the tables, and they rose, clapping their hands. Commodore Quex came forward, his eyes, set at the extreme edges of his face, flicking over Roan and past him at his crew. He took Roan's arm and tugged himself toward the nearest table. "You'll sit with me at the head table, of course . . ."

Roan held back without seeming to. "What about my men?"

"Oh, they'll be well taken care of." When Quex smiled, he kept his upper lip pulled down to cover his teeth, but Roan caught a glimpse of widely spaced points. A crowd of humanoid females with slender bodies and immense eyes and huge bare breasts were crowding around the men, taking their arms possessively, giggling up into surprised Gook faces that broke into vast, bristly, snaggle-toothed smiles.

"Belay that," Roan snapped. "You men will sit with me—or I'll sit with them," he amended, turning back to Quex. "I have to keep an eye on them," he explained.

"Ah, but, yes, as you wish, Lieutenant." Quex dithered for a moment, then signaled, and crouching slaves darted in, shuffled chairs and place settings about. Roan took the deep armchair Quex waved him to and looked around. Strange faces stared at him curiously.

"Where's the admiral?"

"He is unfortunately indisposed." Quex toed a slave aside and took the chair opposite Roan. "Chavigney '85 or Beel Vat?" he inquired brightly.

"Chavigney '85," Roan said, because he'd heard of it. "Indisposed how?"

"Admiral Starbird is getting on. He can't stand much . . . excitement." Quex showed his pointed teeth again and watched the slave pour ruby liquid into glasses. He picked his up and flicked a libation on the marble floor and nosed it. Roan drained his and thrust it out for a refill. No doubt the Chavigney '85 had a magnificent bouquet, but at the moment he didn't care.

Quex was staring at him; he remembered his smile when Roan looked at him. "I don't believe I've ever seen hair just like yours before," he said. "Quite . . . ah . . . striking."

"We all have our little peculiarities," Roan said shortly, and let his eyes rest on Quex's. They seemed to sit at the corners of his head and bulge.

"No offense," Quex said. "One sees a new face so seldom . . ."

"How many Terrans are there here at HQ?" Roan asked, glancing at the obvious Gooks along the table.

Something touched his shoulder and his hand went to his gun and then there was a choking cloud of perfume and a lithe, blue-trimmed girl was sitting on his lap. She had soft, round breasts with blue-dyed tips that poked through her beads, and she squirmed up against Roan's chest and nudged his wineglass against his lips. She looked a little like Stellaraire, and for an instant Roan felt a lost emotion clutch at him, but he took the glass and put it firmly on the table and palmed the female gently from him.

"Stand over there," he said sternly. "If I need anything, I'll call you."

The girl looked stricken, and then she looked at Quex and shrank back. The commodore slapped his hands sharply together, and the girl turned and was gone.

"I don't want her to get in any trouble," Roan started. "It was just—"

Quex hissed. The points of his teeth showed plainly now. "We do our best with our Gooks," he said. "But they are so abysmally stupid."

Slaves came with the food then. It was marvelous, and Roan forgot his problems for the moment, savoring the fabulous Terran cooking. The wine was good too, and Roan had to force himself to sip it carefully. Along the table, his men spooned in the delicacies, and then when they grew impatient with the small bites, used their hands. Their girls kept up a constant shrill giggling, slopping wine against big alien teeth, spilling it down across stubbled jaws. Beside Quex, Askor took a glass from his neighbor's girl's hand and poured the contents down his girl's throat. She choked and sputtered, and Askor caught Roan's eye and winked.

The noisemakers kept up their cacophony. Roan watched them, behind a screen of bushy potted plants, sawing and pumping and puffing at the gleaming, complicated noisemakers.

"You like music?" Quex asked, leaning across the table. There were purple, juicy stains at the corners of his mouth and his eyes bugged more than ever. He had loosened his collar, and Roan saw red scars down the sides of his neck where something had been surgically removed.

"I don't know," Roan said, because he had never heard the word before. "Is it something to eat?"

"The sounds," Quex said. He waved a hand at the orchestra, bleating and shrilling in the corner behind their screen of foliage.

"It's all right, I suppose," Roan said. "Back in the 'zoo, they were louder."

"You want it louder?"

"I remember a sound I heard once," Roan said, thinking quite suddenly of the deserted park in the Terran city on Aldo Cerise. "Real Terran sounds. Pretty sounds." He was feeling the wine, he realized. He took a deep breath and sat up straighter, and felt for his gun with his fingertips.

"Terry music?" Quex clapped his hands and a slave popped up and leaned close to get Quex's instructions, then slipped away. Roan glanced at his men. They were still chewing with their mouths open, reaching across each other's plates for juicy gobbets almost out of reach, wiping thick fingers on now-greasy silks. Henry Dread had picked his Gooks for size, not beauty, he was thinking, when he became aware of a sound penetrating the bellowed talk and laughter. It was an elfin horn, picking its way lightly above the uproar, and then it was joined by other sounds, deep and commanding, like the tramp of marching armies, and now the horns darted and flickered above like the lightnings of a coming storm while a bugle called demon troops to the attack. Roan pushed his glass aside, listening, searching for the source, and his eyes fell on the noisemakers behind the flower boxes.

"Are *they* doing that?"

"A clever group, eh, Lieutenant? Oh, they know any number of tricks: they can make a sound like a wounded dire-beast charging—"

"Shut up," Roan said, not even noticing he'd said it. "Listen . . ." Now a lonely horn picked out a forlorn melody of things beautiful and forgotten, and Roan remembered the glimpse he'd almost had, once, of how life must have been in the days of the Empire. The music faded to silence, and the players mopped at their faces with soiled handkerchiefs and reached for clay mugs. They looked tired and hot and ill tempered and frightened, all at once.

"How could a crew of ugly Geeks make sounds like that?" he wondered aloud.

"You like it?" Quex said coldly. He was fingering the braid on his sleeve rather pointedly.

"I'm sorry, Commodore," Roan said. "I was quite carried away."

Quex managed a sour smile. "It's some ancient thing

about a Prince called Igor," he said. "Would you like to hear another? They do a rather clever thing called *Jivin' Granny*—"

"No," Roan shook his head to clear away the vision.

Quex chose an attenuated cheroot from a blue-and-orange inlaid box a cringing slave offered him. The slave lit it, and when the lighted match fell on the floor from the creature's trembling hand, Quex planted a solid kick in its side. It grunted and crawled over to Roan and he took a cigar and watched the slave crawl away. When it thought it was out of sight, it patted its injured side and wept silently.

"Now, Lieutenant . . ." Quex blew out smoke impatiently, as though he enjoyed knowing he was smoking a rare weed, but was annoyed with the actual process. "You've just reported in from a long cruise. You deserve to relax—"

"I don't want to relax," Roan said. "I'd like to know about the Niss. What kind of fleet can they put in space?"

"Surely all that can wait," Quex said blandly. He waved his glass and wine slopped on the floor and a slave scrambled to lick it up. There were other slaves under the table, eating scraps, and still more crowded in, offering finger bowls. Another girl had gotten into his lap somehow, and she was breathing erotica into his ear. Roan was aware that he was dizzier than he should be, and he pushed the slaves away and forced his eyes to focus.

"I've waited long enough," he said. He could feel the thickness of his tongue, and he worked on getting angry enough for his temper to boil the lethargy away.

A slave shoved a vast plate of foamy stuff in front of Roan. Quex was clapping his hands again and there was a stir, and two immense dull-faced troopers were hauling someone small and struggling into the open space at the center of the square of tables.

"Sorry if I seemed to have been dilatory in handling this matter," Quex was saying, "but I always think executions go better with the dessert. . ."

Roan blinked while the two troopers held the girl down on a short bench with her head over one end. He recognized her as the one who had first gotten into his lap. Her gold-dusted hair was in disarray now, and her thin pantaloons stuck to her legs. One of the men holding her down got out a knife with a foot-long blade and casually thrust it into the side of her neck. She screamed once, and then she was slack, and the trooper was sawing away, holding the head by the hair. He got it free and held it up. There was blood on his hands to the elbow, and more was spreading out on the floor. Roan got to his feet, and his girl pulled him back, laughing.

"Clumsy oxes," Quex said. He picked up his cigar and drew on it, and then tossed it into the soup tureen. "You'd think they were butchering swine. Try your ice cream. It's rather good, considering."

Roan's men were staring at the body of the girl. They were used to bloodshed, but they'd never seen anything like this. The executioners trooped off, one with the head and the other with the body, and a slave came with a bucket of water and a nauseous-looking rag. It was a female slave, and her row of teats dragged along the floor as she scrubbed.

"What—what—" Roan stuttered.

Quex raised his plucked eyebrows. "The creature annoyed you. That's something we Terrans don't tolerate in slaves. . ."

Roan got to his feet, and the girl on his lap squalled and slid off onto the floor.

"All right, men! Up!" he bawled. "The party's over! Let's march!"

In the sudden silence, Sidis laughed foolishly. The ITN personnel stirred at their places, glancing toward Quex. Roan went along the table to Sidis and slapped him so hard it hurt at the other end of the room. He jerked him to his feet and turned, and Quex was holding a long-barreled nerve gun in his hand, aimed at Roan.

"Not so fast, Lieutenant—or whatever you are," the commodore said in a voice like chipped glass. "You made a poor choice of identities." The identity disk Roan had produced dangled from his finger. He tossed it to the floor. "Lieutenant Commander Endor was lost in action some six thousand years ago. You're under arrest for mutiny in Deep Space and the murder of Commander Henry Dread."

Roan looked along the table and caught Askor's yellow eye. The men were still in their places, waiting for the word. The garrison men were getting to their feet, gathering in clumps, watching. Some of them had guns out now.

Roan moved toward Quex and his gun, staggering a little more than was necessary.

"What do you want with me?" he said thickly.

"That's neither here nor there. Now, before we got any further, if you'll take off your jacket, please . . ."

Askor stirred, and Roan flickered an eyelid at him, and the half-breed settled back. Roan stripped off his braid-heavy jacket and tossed it on the floor. The Imperial Terran symbol over the pocket made a loud clink when it hit.

"To the skin, please," Quex insisted. Roan pulled off the silky white shirt, and the crowd staring at him drew in quick breaths. Quex got up and came around the end of the table, not bothering even to kick the crouching slave, and his eyes were round, taking in Roan's smooth, unscarred hide, the scattering of reddish hair across his chest.

"Your feet," he ordered. Roan pulled out a chair and sat down and pulled off his boots. The spurs clanked as he tossed them aside. Quex leaned close and stared.

"Unbelievable," he said. "You're a Terran. A *real* Terran. A textbook case." He looked into Roan's eyes with an expression almost of awe. "You might even be a Pure Strain . . ."

"Hurry up and shoot, if you're going to," Roan said. He picked up a glass and drained it. It would have been easy to toss it into Quex's face, but he wasn't ready for that yet.

"Where did you come from? Who were your parents?"

"My parents bought me as an embryo." Roan was watching Quex's face.

"Where?" Quex snapped.

"At the Thieves' Market on Tambool."

Quex raised a hand and brought it down in a meaningless gesture. "Of course. There is a certain fantastic inevitability to it! A Pure Terran, cast among Geeks; naturally, he would seek out his own—"

"What do you know about me?" Roan interrupted Quex's soliloquy.

Quex stepped back, signaled for a chair, sank down, watching Roan over the gun. He laughed shortly, a silly laugh. "I suppose I shall have to abandon the idea of shooting you. I'll make it up by planning something rather special for these animals of yours who've had the effrontery to plump themselves down at table with gentlefolk." And Quex tittered again, enjoying himself now. "In a way, I'm almost a sort of parent to you myself." He crossed his legs, swinging his foot.

"I was rather active in my younger days. The admiral honored me by dispatching me as his personal agent among the renegade pigs of the Gallian World. It was they who initiated the experiment. I took a chance—don't imagine I wasn't aware of the risks! I lifted the entire lot—the wealth of the Nine Gods, and you could hold it in your hand! The fools were careless, they practically invited me. And then I made my error. Trusting Geeks! I was an idiot!"

Roan saw Quex's finger tighten on the firing stud, and he tensed, ready to jump, but the commodore drew a shuddery breath and calmed himself.

"I was fool enough to divulge the nature of the consignment to the stinking animal who called himself captain of the Gallian vessel on which I had arranged passage. It was necessary, actually; I demanded refrigeration facilities, and one explanation led to another—

"He tricked me. At the end of a tedious run, I

discovered he had changed course for his own world. We landed and he turned me and my so carefully guarded prize over to his Shah. This heathen considered that it would be a tremendously impressive thing to parade a palace guard of Terrans—Pure Terrans, and all identical. Can you imagine it?" Quex held out his hand and a glass appeared in it, and was filled. He looked at Roan. "Am I boring you?"

Roan let out a breath. "Go on," he said.

"Alas," Quex continued. "At this crucial moment, a spontaneous popular uprising broke out. The Shah, his two hundred and thirty-four frightful little whelps, and anyone else who happened to be standing about were killed."

"Spontaneous?" Roan asked. He looked at the nearest slave, who crouched away, quivering.

"It was as spontaneous," Quex answered, smiling with his bright, cruel slits of eyes, "as the ITN could make it. My messages to Rim HQ had gone through before landing, of course; the forces arrived within a week to restore order. Of course, the natives were not so well domesticated then; they had a certain animal spirit which had to be curbed before they were made useful possessions. I was only one hundred and fifty-two at the time—some twenty-five years ago now, Terry reckoning—but I had a natural bent for such things." He waved a hand. "The rest is history."

"And how did I get to Tambool?" Roan cut in.

Quex frowned. "The discussion begins to tire me," he said. "You're a valuable though insolent property, and Admiral Starbird will be delighted when I report that I've recovered the breeding stock that slipped through our fingers all those years ago—"

"No, he won't," Roan said. "One of his spies has already slipped out by the side door to report on you—"

Quex jerked around to look where Roan had pointed and Roan's foot caught the gun, knocked it high in the air. With a bellow, Askor went into action in the same instant, and then Poion and Sidis were on their feet, reaching for the nearest ITN man. One aimed a gun at Askor and the giant half-breed dropped his first victim and charged for the man, knocked him spinning under the table, then whirled on a group of backpedaling dandies, cracked their heads together, tossed them aside, caught two more. Roan was holding Quex by the neck now, and drinking wine from the bottle with the other hand. The ITN men in the rear milled in loud confusion, unable to get a clear shot.

"You Gooks stand back, or we'll shoot!" A frightened-looking Navy man had climbed on a chair and was pointing a fancy power pistol wildly around the room. Sidis took aim, shot him in the head; he leaped back in a spatter of blood and fell among his fellows.

There were more shots now as the astonished hosts realized that their outnumbered victims intended to fight back. It was a mistake. Four pirate guns went into action, blasting wholesale into the screaming, panicked diners, who jammed into the corners and against the doors, making effective resistance by the few determined men among them impossible.

"Belay that!" Roan yelled over the din as a glass smashed beside him. He hauled Quex into a chair, shouted again. There were moans and howls from the wounded, bellowing from the enraged crew, the buzz and crackle of guns. Smoke poured up from smoldering hangings ignited by wild shots. There was a stink of blood and spilled wine in the air. Roan jumped on the table and shouted for order. By degrees the tumult abated.

"All right," Roan said. "They shot first and I don't blame you for getting annoyed, but I don't have any time to waste. I've got a few more questions to ask old rabbit-ears here." He stepped down from the table as the men began rifling the bodies and pulling fancy ornaments off the living. Quex stared at him with wide, shocked eyes.

"You can't—we outnumber you fifty to one—a hundred to one . . ." The commodore's voice rose. He started to his feet. "Attack them!" he screeched. Roan put a foot against his chest and slammed him back, then pulled a chair up and sat in it. There were two slaves mewling under the table; as they realized they were in view, they scuttled farther back. There was blood trickling down into Roan's right eye and around his face and onto his neck. It annoyed him, like an insect.

"Pardon this little interruption, Commodore," he said. "You had just come to the part where the ITN arrived to restore order. What did they do with the embryo—or should I say with 'me'?"

Quex babbled. Roan tossed a wine bottle to him, and it fell in his lap, bubbled down over his knees. He groped it up, drank, lowered the bottle with a sob.

"They . . . we . . . it wasn't there. It was gone . . . stolen . . ."

"It seems to have been remarkably hard property to hang on to. What made it so valuable?"

"A specimen of Pure Terran stock? Do you jest?"

"Sure—but there are some fairly pure Terries around, like Henry Dread. What made me different?"

"You *were* different. Oh, yes, different! You're Pure Strain; unbelievably pure strain—"

"All right. Who stole me?"

"One of my spies, the rotter! A creature I trusted!" Quex warmed to the memory. "He'd finished his work for me, and when I sent a couple of men with knives to advise him I had no more need of his services, he was nowhere to be found! He'd skipped out—and the special bejeweled incubator unit was gone with him! I searched— oh, how I searched! I tore the tongues from a hundred Men and five hundred Geeks, and then at last I got a hint—a word babbled by a former officer of the Shah's guard in his dying delirium: Tambool. I dispatched a crew at once—led by a sturdy Yill scoundrel. The best I could find among the rabble that follow the uniform of the Empire—but none of them ever returned. I heard tales, later, of how they were set upon by a horde of madmen— but the embryo was lost—"

"That horde of madmen was my dad, Raff Cornay," Roan said. "We'll drink to him." He raised his bottle and took a long swig.

"You're not drinking, Commodore," he said. "Drink!"

Quex took a halfhearted sip.

"Drink, damn you! Or do I have to pour it down your neck?"

Quex drank.

"Hey, this stuff is all junk, Cap'n!" Askor called, tramping over to where Roan sat with one foot on Quex's chair. He tossed a handful of brass jewelry on the table.

"Let's load up on Terry wine and shove off. And, uh, a couple of the boys was asking, OK if we take along a few broads too?"

The wounded were making a dismal sound from the heaps where they lay. Sidis went over and started shooting the noisiest ones. The rest became quieter.

"You know better than that," Roan said. "You louts would be cutting each other's throats in a week."

"Yeah." Askor scratched an armpit with a blunt finger. "It figures."

"Round the boys up now. I'll be through in a minute." Askor turned away with a roar of commands. Quex trembled so violently his seat bounced in the chair.

"What are y-you g-going to do with m-me?"

"Have another drink," Roan commanded. He watched while his victim complied.

"I—I'll be sick," Quex slobbered.

Roan got to his feet. He pulled his shirt and jacket back on, jammed his feet into his boots. There was a dead officer lying behind his chair. Roan paused long enough to take a handsome sheath-knife with the ancient Imperial Eagle from the body, clip it to his own belt.

"Askor, Poion; lock all the doors," he ordered.

Quex came to his feet. He pulled at the edge of his tunic, swaying. His eyes were like blood-red clams.

"You can't leave me here with them! Not after this!" He looked past Roan at the bright, staring eyes in the pale faces of his men. "They'll tear me to pieces . . . for permitting myself to be tricked!"

Askor and the others were by the main door now. They looked to Roan.

"Go ahead, open her up!" Roan called. He looked back at Quex. "Thanks for the dinner, Commodore. It was a nice party, and I enjoyed it—"

"Lieutenant!" Quex's voice had found a hint of a ring suddenly. He straightened himself, holding onto a chair back. "I'm not . . . Pure Strain . . . like yourself . . . but I have Terran blood . . ." He wavered, thrust himself upright again. "As a fellow officer . . . of the Imperial Navy . . . I ask you . . . for an honorable death . . ."

Roan looked at him. He shifted his pistol to his left hand, squared off and saluted Quex with his right, and shot him through the heart.

CHAPTER ✳ NINETEEN

Roan and his three men walked, guns in their hands, along the echoing corridor. No one challenged them.

"Why don't we pull out now, Chief?" Sidis demanded. "We can take our pick of the tubs on the ramp—"

"That isn't what I came for," Roan said. "I have unfinished business to take care of."

"Why bother knocking off any more of these Terries?" Askor queried. "Not much sport in it, if you ask me."

"I didn't!" Roan snapped. "Keep your mouth shut and your eyes open! We're not in the clear yet. Trishinist wasn't at the party—"

A thunderclap racketed along the corridor. Roan spun, went flat.

"Hold your fire!" he roared. Trishinist tittered, stepped out of the half-open door that had concealed him. There were at least a dozen more Men, emerging from the shelter of tattered drapes and chipped marble columns, peering down from a wrought-metal gallery, guns ready.

"I heard the, er, sounds of celebration," the Terran

confided. "It seemed wise to have a chat with you before you, ah, continue with what you're about."

"We've already talked," Roan snapped. "Tell your Terries to put their guns away before my men get nervous and shoot them out of their hands."

"Umm. Your Gooks *do* look efficient. Still, I daresay one or two of my chaps would live long enough to dispatch the four of you. So perhaps we'd best call a truce."

Roan got to his feet. His men stood, facing outward in a tight circle.

"I have an appointment with Admiral Starbird," Roan said. "Or have you forgotten?"

"I remember," Trishinist said quickly. "You haven't, um, changed your plans?"

"Why should I?"

"I thought perhaps—after all the excitement of the banquet—"

"You knew about Quex's plans for the evening?"

"I suspected something of the sort might take place. After all, strangers . . . ."

"Thanks for letting me know."

"Well, if you couldn't handle that situation, what good are you to me, ummm?"

"We're going on now," Roan said.

"Just so," Trishinist agreed. "But leave the guns."

Roan looked at Trishinist; there were small bubbles at the corners of his mouth.

"All right," he said. "Put 'em down, men."

"What for, Boss?" Askor inquired cheerfully. "Sidis still has his knife. That's all he needs."

Trishinist shuddered. Roan tossed his gun aside. The others followed suit.

"Now what, Chief?" Sidis asked.

"Now we get on with the job." Roan turned on his heel and started toward the apartment of Admiral Starbird.

It was silent in the corridor. The guards on the admiral's door were gone. Roan stopped, faced Trishinist.

"Send your Men away," he said. "You can stay. Keep your gun, if you feel like it."

Trishinist lifted his lip to show his pearly teeth. "You're giving *me* orders?" he said in a wondering tone.

"You want them to see it?"

Trishinist started. "I see," he murmured. He turned, gave crisp orders. All but four of the Men turned, formed up in a squad, marched away.

"They'll be waiting," Trishinist cooed. "Now—"

The door behind Roan clicked and swung in. Admiral Starbird stood in the opening, a gun in his hand—"'Ten-*shun*" he commanded.

Trishinist's men instinctively straightened and in the instant's pause, Askor, standing nearest them, swung and brought his hand down like an ax across the neck of one, caught his gun as it fell, swiveled on the next as he brought his gun around, and the two weapons fired as one. The guard spun, falling, his gun still firing, and a vivid scar raked the wall and doorjamb and caught Admiral Starbird full in the chest. The old man slammed back against the wall, fell slowly, sprawled full length in a growing stain of brilliant crimson.

Trishinist made a noise like repressed retching and stumbled back. Askor brought his gun around as the remaining two guards backed, white with shock but with guns leveled on Roan and his crew.

"You've killed him," Trishinist gasped. "The admiral is *dead!*"

"I can nail the pair of youse, easy," Askor grinned at the gunners. "Who's first?"

Roan knelt at Starbird's side, ignoring the confrontation of guns.

"Admiral . . ." He tried the pulse at the corded veins of the wrist, felt a faint flutter. "Get your doctors, Trishinist!"

"Yes . . . yes . . . Fetch Surgeon Splie, Linerman! Hurry!"

A man turned and darted away.

Starbird's eyes opened. He stared at the Men holding guns aimed at Roan. "At ease," he said, and died.

"You killed the admiral," Roan said slowly, looking up at Trishinist.

"Not I," Trishinist gasped, backing. "It was an accident. I won't have that on my conscience—it was them!" He pointed at the two guards. "Blunderers!" he croaked. "You've killed a Man of the True Blood!"

"Not me, Captain. Strigator was the one!" The guards looked shaken, still covering Roan and Poion while Askor covered them.

"Shall I kill 'em, Chief?" Askor inquired.

"Cover Trishinist." Askor's gun flicked to point at the small Man's chest. Poion licked his lips and eyed the gun on the floor.

"Don't try it," Askor rumbled.

"You have no chance," Trishinist said weakly, his eyes on the gun in Askor's hands. "Surrender and I'll deal leniently with you."

"Give us a ship," Roan said. "We'll go quietly."

"You with the gun," Trishinist addressed Askor. "Give up that weapon and you'll go free."

"What about the Cap'n and these two lunkheads?"

"*You'll* go free. Never mind about them."

Askor grinned, holding the gun steady.

"Very well, then. There's been enough bloodshed. You'll all go free."

"I'll keep the gun," Askor said. "But I won't use it unless I have to. How about that boat now?"

"Certainly." Trishinist licked his lips. "I'll give the orders. But only after you surrender the gun." Sweat was trickling down the small Man's face.

"What about it, Cap'n?"

"Do I have your word as a Man?" Roan asked. "A ship, and no pursuit—for all four of us?"

Trishinist nodded quickly. "Yes, of course, my word on it."

"All right, Askor," Roan said.

"Wait a minute, Boss—"

"Don't do it, Chief," Sidis barked. "Askor can get the both of 'em while they're shooting us! Then him and you can take fancy pants here fer a hostage—"

Roan shook his head. "Put the gun down."

Askor made a jabbing motion toward Trishinist, and the captain jumped back. Askor laughed and tossed the gun aside with a clatter. Roan faced Trishinist; the Man took out a handkerchief, mopped at his face.

"Very well," he said. He made a curt gesture to the two armed men. "Take these stupid pigs to D level."

With a bellow, Poion jumped, and the guard's gun shrieked and spouted blue lightning, and Poion whirled and fell, smoke churning from a gaping, blackened wound in his chest. He groaned and rolled on his back, and charred ribs showed before the blood welled out to hide the sight.

"Askor! Sidis!" Roan snapped. "Stand fast! That's an order!"

Roan looked at Trishinist, smiling. "You surprise me, Captain," he said. "I didn't think even a traitor like you would disgrace his Manhood in front of a couple of cross-bloods."

Trishinist tore his eyes from Roan's. "There's been enough killing. I'm ill with killing. Take them away—alive." He turned back to Roan. "I have every right to execute you—all of you—out of hand. I'm sparing your lives. Consider yourselves lucky. You'll be questioned, of course—later." He turned and stalked away.

"Poion," Roan called. "Are you . . . can you . . . ?"

"I have taken my death wound, Captain," Poion gasped. "How strange . . . that so many years of life . . . can end in such . . . a little moment . . . and the world go on . . . without me . . ."

"So long, Poion," Sidis said. "Take a pull at the Hellhorn for me."

"Nice try, old pal," Askor said hoarsely. "I think maybe you're the lucky one."

The man who had gone for the doctor came up with

a short fat Man in tow. He glanced at the admiral, shuddered, shook his head.

"What about him?" a guard pointed at Poion. The doctor pursed his lips at the wound. "No chance," he said and turned away.

"Surgeon—have you . . . no medicine to cure the pain of living . . ." Poion whispered.

"Hmmmph." The doctor opened a small case, took out a hypospray, pressed it briefly against Poion's laboring chest. A breath sighed out and then there was silence.

"Let's go," the guard said.

Askor reached up, gripped the chain that linked the manacle on his left wrist to a ring set high in the concrete wall, pulled himself up high enough to see through the foot-square barred opening in the cell wall. He grunted and dropped back.

"Nothing, Cap'n. Some kind of tunnel, I guess. We're fifty feet underground anyways."

Sidis squatted at the end of his tether near the door, angling the blade of his polished machete through the bars to catch the faint light from along the corridor.

"They's a guard post about thirty yards along," he said. "One Terry with a side arm."

"You shoulda let us jump 'em, Cap'n," Askor said. "It woulda been better'n this crummy joint. It stinks." He wrinkled his wide nose to dramatize the odor.

"I can smell it," Roan said. "And as long as we're alive to smell things we still have a chance."

Sidis was eyeing the barred door. "Them bars don't

look so tough," he said. "I bet I could bend 'em—if I could reach 'em."

"What do you figure'll happen, Chief?" Askor said.

"As soon as Trishinist recovers his stomach, he'll be along to find out who sent us and why."

Askor guffawed. "That'll be a laugh," he said. "He'll twist and slice us till he makes a mess a mud-pig would puke at, but we won't tell him nothing. We can't. We don't know nothing! That'll gravel him."

"If we was to bend them bars," Sidis said, "one of us could slide out and get to the joker with the blaster. Then he could come back and burn them chains off."

"Wise up," Askor said. "You got to get the chain off the first one first."

Sidis hefted his machete. "They left me this," he said thoughtfully. "Them crazy Terries. I guess they're so used to guns they forgot a knife's a weapon too."

"So what? It won't cut chromalloy."

Sidis backed from the wall until the six foot chain attached to his wrist came taut.

"How much time you think we got, Cap'n?" he asked.

"They'll be along soon."

Sidis licked his lips. "Then I better get moving." He brought the machete up and with one terrific stroke severed his left hand.

They stood in a dark room, amid a jumble of piping and tanks.

"Smells like a derelict's bilge," Askor snorted.

"Dead end," Sidis grunted. His stump was bound in rags torn from Askor's shirt and there was a tourniquet around his massive upper arm. His face looked pale and damp.

Roan went to the center of the room, studying the floor. "Maybe not," he said.

Askor came up. There was a three-foot metal disk set in the floor, with a ring near its edge.

Roan gripped the ring and lifted the lid, exposing a dark hole and the rungs of a corroded ladder. Water glistened at the bottom.

The voices outside were suddenly louder. Askor stepped to the door, looked out. "Oh-oh! They're right on our tail . . ."

"I hope they get here quick," Sidis said. "I don't want to miss nothing."

"Do you feel well enough to travel?"

Sidis nodded. "Never better, Chief." He took a step, staggered, then stood firm.

"Askor, you go first," Roan said quickly. "Sidis, you follow him."

"Too bad we had to burn the door; we could maybe have foxed 'em." Askor started down the ladder. "Come on, Sidis; shake it up."

"I'll stay here," he said. "They got to pass the door one at a time, and Gut-biter'll get all the action he wants."

"Down the hole," Roan snapped. "Fast!"

"Cap'n, I ain't—"

"That's an order!"

Sidis started down, awkwardly, one-handed.

"Hey, Chief, wonder where this thing leads to?" Askor's voice echoed from below.

Roan knelt at the manhole. "If you're lucky, it will take you out to a drainage ditch in the open."

Sidis turned his tattooed face up. "What's that mean, Boss? If *we're* lucky—"

"I'm covering you," Roan said. "I'll give you a ten minute start and then follow—"

Sidis started back up. Roan put out a hand. "If you get clear, wait for me ten minutes. Maybe they'll miss the door—"

Below, Askor was shouting: "Hey, what's that? What's Cap'n saying?"

"Shut up and get moving. If you get through, come back and get me. With our cruiser you can blow this place wide open—"

"We ain't going without you, Cap'n. You know better'n—"

"They won't kill me," Roan said. "I'm Pure Strain, remember? They'd burn you two down on sight—"

"We come this far, we ain't—"

"Did you ever hear of discipline?" Roan said harshly. "This is our only chance. If I've tried to teach you anything, it's how to follow orders like Men instead of behaving like a bunch of Geeks!"

Sidis looked at Roan. "If that's what you want, Cap'n . . . But we'll come back. You stay alive, Cap'n."

"I'll stay alive. Get going!"

When they were gone, Roan slid the manhole cover back in place and turned to face the door.

Captain Trishinist lounged behind the wide desk in the office recently vacated by Admiral Starbird.

"Why?" he repeated sourly. "Seventy-two hours, holed up in a filthy sewage pumping room, without food, drink, or sleep, aiming a gun at the door. Why? You must have known you'd be taken in the end."

Roan blinked at the fog before him. His head ached and his throat was like dried husks.

"Was it just for that precious pair of animals?" The captain's eyes seemed to glitter as he stared at Roan. "What hold had they on you?"

"Did they get clear?" Roan asked. His voice was blurry with fatigue.

"You're a fool," Trishinist said. "But you'll talk to me in time. There are methods for dealing with recalcitrants—effective methods."

"I'll bet they got through," Roan said. "Your kind couldn't stop them."

"Oh-hoh, you think to tempt me to angry disclosures!" The captain smirked. "How really quaint."

"You're so quaint you stink," Roan said. "But you can't touch me. You're afraid to. You'd gut your own grandmother and make bonfires out of children, but you can't kill a real Terry."

Trishinist glowered. "Don't press me too far, spy—"

Roan laughed aloud. "You're a poor half-breed with pretensions, Trishinist. You're pitiful. Even my poor Gooks got past you—"

Trishinist was on his feet, shaking with rage. "Your wretched creatures died in unspeakable agony an hour after you saw them last!"

"You're a liar," Roan said.

Trishinist spewed saliva and fury. "Dead!" he

screeched. "I took them and stripped the hide from them alive—"

"Prove it. Show me the bodies."

"I'll show you nothing! Slave! Treacher! Spy! What need have I to prove—"

Roan laughed in his face. "Good for Askor. I knew he'd get through. I hope he stole one of your better ships."

"Take him away!" Trishinist screamed. "Put him in the Hole! Let him rot there!"

The Man holding the rope looped around Roan's neck jerked it, and Roan stumbled and almost fell.

"And when you're ready to tell me your heart's secrets, beg, and perhaps! Perhaps! I'll find time to listen!"

Trishinist was still fulminating as Roan was led along the corridor. The rope urged him roughly through a small door into a paved court, across it and out onto dry hard-packed dirt. The air was cold here, and the sparse stars of the Rim gleamed through mist. Roan stumbled on, determined not to fall and be dragged.

The tugging at the rope stopped at last, and a rough hand shook him.

"Don't go to sleep standing up, you. Grab the rope—unless you want to hang!"

He took the slack rope on his hands, looping it around his forearms, and a blow on the back sent him reeling forward—and then he was falling, and his arms felt as though they had been torn from their sockets as he brought up short. He felt himself descending, the taut rope trembling in his grip. Above, the circle of dark-glowing sky dwindled. Down, down—

He slammed the mucky bottom with a force that knocked him flat. There was a whistling, and the coils of rope fell down about him. Far above, someone called:

"Trishinist won't kill ye, maybe, bucko! But if you die on your own, that's yer privilege!"

At first, Roan was hungry all the time. He was so hungry he chewed on the rope, and so thirsty he licked at the water that dripped everlastingly along the muddy circumference of the pit. And he tried, again and again, to climb the slimy sides of the hole. He scraped hand and footholds with his fingers, even after his nails had broken off, and always the crevices he made oozed away. And once, when he'd gotten several feet up, someone flashed a light in to watch him, and laughed when he fell. And Roan lay where he'd fallen, listening as the laughter echoed down the hollow hole.

One evening the old man threw down the bread and then something else, something alive and bristly that struck Roan on the arm and sprang away, and as it leaped across his hand, it bit him. It was hard to make out the shape of the thing in the dim twilight of the hole, but it had red eyes that glittered and it was bigger than Roan's foot.

Its frightened bite made a vicious, screaming kind of pain and Roan could feel the blood oozing from his hand. He found the bread and then sat in the dark, his back against the cold, wet mud of the wall that clotted in the tatters of his clothes, and ate. He no longer longed for a bath, just as he no longer felt hungry all the time. He watched the red eyes glitter in the dark, listened for the scrabble of its claws. It leaped at the walls again and again and fell back with a thud and a splash. Once in its panic it ran over Roan's lap and then leaped at the slime of the wall again.

Then, finally exhausted, it stopped, and crouched across the floor from Roan, panting horribly, loud as a man. The panting slowed, and Roan watched, his hands aching, thinking of ways to kill the thing—later, when he felt better. . .

Roan awoke with a start. The rodent had crept to his foot, attempted to gnaw his ankle. He kicked out, cursing. The rat retreated a few feet, sat watching him, sensing his weakness.

Roan felt the gashed skin of his ankle, the slippery blood. The bite on his hand ached, a swelling, throbbing ache. He was dizzy and hot now and, wiping his forehead, Roan realized it was dry, feverish. He shut out from his mind every thought except the need to survive. He wasn't going to be eaten alive by a rat at the bottom of a dark hole. Somehow, he was going to escape, and get to Terra. And if it was impossible, he'd do it anyway.

"Ye still alive, boy?" came the voice, and Roan, startled, came out of his sleep. He saw the head silhouetted against the dark sky above.

"Yes, curse you. I'm still alive and so is the rat. Double the rations."

The old man laughed. "Got no orders to double the ration."

The bread struck one side of the hole, bounced to the other, and the rat ran out, went for the crumbs that the bouncing had dislodged.

Roan stood, shakily, pulled off his heavy metal-link belt, tied his trousers in a knot at the top. They were inches too wide for him now, and the blades of his hips jutted out like knives. His dizziness turned to nausea whenever he moved. His strength had gone out of his body and into the earth . . .

Roan held the belt by one end, walked toward the rat, then swung with all his strength. He caught the rodent as it turned to dart away, and it screamed a woman's scream, kicking in the mud, filling the already fetid air with its smell of fear. Roan felt his knees going. He fell, lay in the mud, listening to the death struggle. Roan was afraid to believe it even when he could feel the death in it, so he strangled it again with his hands.

And knowing his weakness and starvation were probably going to kill him, feeling half insane but knowing he must have nourishment, he skinned the rat with the sharp edge of his belt buckle and ate it.

It was three days and nights before the fever went away; Roan tried to rebuilt his strength by pacing the circumference of the hole and swinging his arms, but he found it harder to exercise his mind, and sometimes all day would go by and it would seem like a minute, and other times a night would seem like centuries and the only time anything different happened was when it rained and the water rose knee-deep before it drained away. And time passed . . .

Then, one evening the old man didn't come with the bread. And Roan could do nothing but wait, wait eternities. The stars came and went and then the stars again, and

Roan, trapped for so long in the dark, slimy pit, wondered if indeed he had died and this was what death was—an aching and a waiting forever and all of the world a small hole and a circle of changing sky fifty feet above. Roan lay in one spot against the wall and ignored the pain in his stomach and tried to sleep, and perhaps dream of Stellaraire and of food. Stellaraire bringing him food, feeding him the delicacies of a hundred worlds washed down with ancient Terran wines, Stellaraire smiling . . . and fading. The food disappeared and Gom Bulj was yelling and Henry Dread was yelling and . . .

Someone *was* yelling, up above, a head silhouetted against dark sky. Roan saw the rope dangling in front of him. Was it real? For a long time it didn't seem worth the trouble of reaching up to find out. He had waited so long . . .

But he did reach up, almost without hope that it was a real rope, real people calling him to loop the rope around his waist. But he complied, and the rope pulled, lifting him, and it hurt, and he gripped the rope, thinking he would never reach the top. Probably there was no top.

Then hard hands were on him, lifting him up, and a broad, ugly face was bending over him, and he saw the glint of light on filed steel teeth.

"Gee, Boss," Sidis said. And Roan had the strange thought that it must be raining, because there was water running down the leathery face.

"You Gooks . . . took your time . . ." Roan said. And then Askor was there, grinning a meat-eating grin, and their faces were prettier than any faces Roan had ever seen, and he smiled, and smiling, he let it all go and whirled down into the bottomless soft night.

"Eat slowly," a testy voice said from somewhere; Roan's eyes were almost shut against the bright light. "And not too much."

Roan sipped a brothy soup, the bowl trembling in his hands. After the soup the doctor poked him, shone lights in his ears and mouth, and whistled. "I'm giving you a walloping shot of Vitastim," he said. "You'll feel human in about an hour. But don't overdo it. Unless, of course, you want to," he added.

Askor and Sidis hustled him into a hard shower, gave him a brush to scrub with. Then they let him sleep. By the time Roan had on a uniform which almost fit his bone-thin body, he'd come back to himself. The face that looked back at him from the mirror was a stranger's. A gaunt, old-looking, deep-eyed stranger. And the hair above his ears had silver streaks in it. But Roan grinned at the reflection.

"We're alive," he said. And behind him, Askor and Sidis smiled, too.

"Let's go, men," Roan said. "There's nothing more here for us."

Aboard the stolen light cruiser *Hell's Whore* and an hour's run in space, Roan relaxed in the big padded first officer's chair, studying the pattern of lights on the screen.

"I'm glad you two showed up when you did," he said. "But it was pretty stupid of the two of you to try it alone."

"We wasn't alone, Boss," Sidis corrected. "We had

their best bucket here. Tough we had to wait around out there on Four for three months to get a crack at her, but you know there wasn't much left of the old *Rage of Heaven*."

"Nice work, taking a cruiser with that hulk," Roan said. "Maybe you're learning after all."

"Nothing to it. They thought they was taking us."

"I wish I'd been there—instead of where I was."

"You didn't miss nothing." Sidis flashed his teeth and examined the tip of the steel toothpick with which he had been grooming them. "It was kind of pitiful, them bums pulling guns on us."

"And that's what they call the Imperial Terran Navy," Askor snickered. "Them nancies—"

"Those weren't real Terries," Roan said. "That was just some sort of ragtag gypsy outfit using the name. The real Terries are on Terra."

"I heard of it," Sidis said doubtfully. "But I thought— Hey, Captain, we ain't going *there*, are we?"

"Why shouldn't we go there?"

"I dunno. I figured maybe you was still working for the ITN, like Cap'n Dread—"

"I've seen enough of the ITN for now," Roan said shortly. He rose and picked up the folded garments of blue and silver polyon which he had replaced with the old familiar ship clothes, tossed them to Sidis.

"What'll I do with this stuff?" Sidis asked, holding the Terran uniform.

"Burn it," Roan said.

CHAPTER ✳ TWENTY

Sol was a brilliant jewel to starboard of *Hell's Whore* and now the tiny, faint points of light that were Sol's planets could be seen. Roan tried to pick out the one that might be Terra. But he couldn't be sure. It was a double planet, Starbird had said, but the faint companion, Luna, would be too dim to see at this distance.

There was the usual buzz of interstellar noise as he switched the receiver on, but nothing else. He took the microphone and began transmitting. "Imperial Terran Cruiser *Hell's Whore* calling Niss headquarters . . ."

"What makes you think they speak Panterran, Boss?" Sidis asked nervously. He had been nervous ever since they sighted the great, silent Niss ship.

"They did five thousand years ago," Roan said.

"How long's it been since anyone tried to run the blockade?" Askor inquired.

"Three hundred years," Roan said. "They didn't make it."

"Swell," Sidis muttered.

"We ought to be in detector range now," Roan said

calmly. He adjusted controls; a meteorite flashed around the repulsion field of the ship's hull. The image grew on the screens.

"She's a big baby," Sidis said.

"No bigger than the last one," Askor pointed out.

"Yeah—it was dead," Sidis conceded. "But what if this one ain't?"

"Then we'll get blasted into the Nine Hells. Why?"

"Just asking," Sidis said, and then they watched the screen in silence.

Up close, the Niss ship looked familiar, even to the characters scrawled across the dark curve of the hull; it was a twin to the dreadnought they had boarded after Henry Dread's death, so many years before—immense, ancient, dead. It took an hour with a cutting torch to force an opening. Dead air whistled, stilled. Inside, sealed in his atmosphere suit, Roan and his men walked along the narrow, empty, dim passageways, remembering the route, passing the little piles of dust and fish bones that had been Niss warriors.

In the control room there was an ancient, abandoned-looking uniform jacket hanging over the back of the pilot's chair—the first garment they had seen. Roan came closer to the control board.

"Terran!" an echoing voice said. "Stand where you are!"

Roan slipped his power pistol from its holster.

"Drop your weapon!" The voice was hollow, alien as not even a Geek's voice was alien, and filled with an inexpressible weariness.

Roan stopped breathing for a moment. Askor and Sidis stood behind him, silent.

"Never mind," the voice came again. "Keep your gun, Terran. I cannot keep this up; and I am dying, so there is no need to shoot me." The chair moved, swung around. In it was draped a creature that looked like a long, crushed polyon bag with something rotten in it. The part that moved, Roan decided, must be the mouth.

"My form shocks you," the voice said. "It is because my energy level is so low. But how did you come here? Where are my people?"

"I don't know," Roan made his voice sound. "You're the first Niss I've ever seen."

"I am over-great-one Thstt, Commander of Twelve Hordes; the alarm energized my far-traveler, and I came awake, here, in the stink of loneliness. I called, but none answers. Only you, Terran . . . ."

"I've waited years for this," Roan said. "I always thought it would be very satisfying to kill a Niss. But now I don't seem to care."

"Did the armies of Terra arise then and destroy us? I see our dreadnoughts, all in station, orbiting the enemy home-world. But no one answers my signals . . . and when I tried to call my home planet, I got only . . . listen."

The Niss floated out a portion of his polyoid body, threw a switch. "Listen!"

Roan could hear nothing. But out of the receiver came a swirl of purple smoke. No. Not purple. Some inconceivable color. It writhed into the room and disappeared without dispersing.

Thstt screamed, and his scream turned finally into a

smoke of the same color as that coming out of the receiver. The Niss's odd, formless body twisted and swelled, pulsating, and then shrank, slacker than before.

Roan stepped over, switched off the microphone. "I don't know what that means," he said in a shaken voice.

"It's the sound of desolation," Thstt said. "Don't you see? There is no one left but me. We had planned to seize your galaxy because our own was infected with a parasite that consumed Niss vital energies. But we have lost, and so we died—all but me, waiting here in alert stasis . . ."

"The Niss were never conquered," Roan said. "They just disappeared, as far as anyone knows. And the machinery has run down, over the eons."

"And so, I, too, die," said Thstt. "And with me the ancient and mighty dream that was the race of Niss. But do not shoot me, or I will implode and you, too, will die. There is no need to watch me. It is not pleasant. We Niss are strong, and strong is our hold on that mystery we know as life . . ."

But Roan did watch. The polyoid body first grew, expanding as high as the ceiling and half as wide as the room, exchanging an alien rush of terrifying colors within itself. Fascinated, Roan found himself hypnotized by the horror of the colors and by something else, as though the death agonies of this alien being were being breathed into his own nostrils, stuffed into his own ears, touching nerve endings . . .

Thstt began to shrink now, the colors becoming denser and slower and coagulating into painful scabs and Roan felt himself gasping painfully for breath and his mind reeled at the horror he felt—and then, suddenly, it was over. Roan let out his breath in a long sigh. He went to the crumpled polyon on the floor, and when he picked up the shrunken, pathetic thing, something clanked inside of it, like bones.

"Gee, Boss." Sidis spoke for the first time.

Askor wiped his face with a horny hand. "Let's get out of here, Chief."

Roan nodded silently and turned away, feeling a strange loneliness, as though a part of his life had died.

Even from a hundred miles up it was beautiful. At twenty miles the night side was misted with lights and the day side was a soft harmony of blue and green and russet. Roan could feel the leap of his heart, the shine in his eyes. Terra. Home. If only Henry Dread could have seen it like this.

Roan dropped deeper into atmosphere, and his men leaned close, scanning the scene on the high mag screen.

"Look, Boss," Sidis pointed. "They're coming up to meet us. Maybe we better arm a couple batteries."

Roan watched the atmosphere planes, flashing their wings in the sun, far below.

"They're coming to meet us, as you said," Roan pointed out. "Not to shoot at us."

A jet flyer barreled past, rolled like a playful fish, then shot away toward the west.

"Hey!" Askor was studying the charts and comparing them with the screens. "That there is Americanada. Only it's upside down."

Sidis keyed the communicator and called, for the

twentieth time. There was no answer. The jet was back, circling, than streaking away again.

"He wants us to follow," Roan said. He altered course, trailed the tiny ship. It led them over a dazzling blue and green coastline, across green hills, over a sprawling city, down to a wide paved field as white as beach sand. Roan lowered the ship carefully so as not to disturb the wide bands of colored plants massed beside the ramp. The ship grounded gently, and the rumble of the drive died.

Roan stood, feeling his mouth dry, his knees trembling slightly. It wasn't like fear; it was more like the feeling he'd had the first time he saw Stellaraire: Wanting her, and afraid that somehow he'd do some small thing wrong, and lose her . . .

Askor was buckling on his guns.

"Leave 'em here," Roan said. "This is home. You don't need your guns at home."

"Us Gooks got no home, Cap'n," Sidis said. "But maybe we can pretend."

Roan took a deep breath. "Maybe we'll all have to pretend a little," he said.

They descended from the ship into a world flashing with sunlight. Beyond the flower beds were trees that fluttered silver when the wind blew, and the air smelled of a thousand perfumes. It was so familiar to Roan's dreams that tears came to his eyes.

"Where's all the Terries?" Sidis wondered aloud.

Faint but pervasive, as though sounded by the motion of the air, came a gentle music.

"Come on." Roan led the way across the glass-white concrete, past Terran planes, blind and closed, past a row of empty, bright-colored buggies, used no doubt to convey passengers from the long-range planes to the building ahead where helicopters waited on the roof.

There was a wide, color-tiled walk between whispering, silver-leafed trees. Roan followed it and bumped into the door before he saw it. It was absolutely transparent glass, as was the wall. Only a faint line showed where the glass door joined the glass wall, and beyond it was a garden of thin-petaled flowers. Within he could see solid panels, walling off rooms, and more flowers and streams and fountains.

But no people.

Roan thought for a panicked moment of Aldo Cerise, of the beautiful, sad, dead city and the woman who was only a statue. But no. There were obviously people here. People? Could it be that the Niss had taken it over, that there were now only Niss?

He pushed at the door, but it didn't open and there wasn't a handle.

He heard running steps and through the trees came a child, a human child, and after the child a large white animal that Roan recognized as a dog, from the picture book he'd seen as a child.

"Paulikins! Paulikins!" called the dog, and then barked wildly, seeing them.

The child stopped before Roan, rocking a little after the run. He stared mercilessly, a beautiful pink and gold child with round blue eyes.

The dog ran up, panting, and cringed with his tail

between his legs. "It's only a child, sirs," he said and trembled all over. "A youngling. I don't know how he got . . ."

"It isn't old Niss," the child said. "It's just a funny man. Look at his funny hands. See, Talbot?"

"Of course we're not Niss," Roan said, and patted the child on the head. "We're human, like you."

Talbot was sniffing the air, and edged closer, trying to sniff at Roan without seeming to. His eyes rolled to take in Sidis and Askor, standing silently by.

"Is it a mama or a daddy?" Paulikins asked. "It smells funny, doesn't it, Talbot?"

"There's been a mistake, sir," Talbot said. He had lost his fear and sat on his haunches, looking serious. He was a big woolly white dog, spotlessly clean, and Roan could imagine that Paulikins rode on his back and afterward curled up on the grass and rested his head on his furry stomach.

"I see," Roan said. "We landed in a spaceship and naturally everyone would think we were Niss."

"If you could wait here a moment, sir, I'll inform the Culture Authorities. You see, they're fetching a Niss scholar; they didn't want anyone else to greet you."

"We'll wait," said Roan.

A helicopter hesitated and lighted easily as a fly on the roof. Askor and Sidis got up from where they had been sitting under a tree, smelling flowers they had picked. Roan was pacing under the trees, practicing Terran in his mind. The dog's accent had been smoother, much more precise than his own. Many of the words Roan had had to strain or guess at. Also, there was a rising inflection that Roan's language lacked.

The woolly dog was back and made a deferential noise in the back of his throat. "If you would come this way, sir, so that you can be properly received."

Roan turned to follow the dog and Askor and Sidis fell in beside him. He waved them back.

"You two wait here," he said. "I'll handle this."

"How come, Chief?" Askor frowned. "Up to now we always stuck together."

"I don't need a bodyguard here," Roan said. "And I don't want the sight of you two to scare anybody. Just stand by."

The glass door opened silently at a touch. Roan followed the dog into a paneled-off room which looked as transparent from the inside as the glass door had looked from the outside. The room was planted with a lush, green lawn that sprang softly under his feet. A breeze blew through the room, though there were no openings in the one-way glass.

A door slid open soundlessly across the spacious room, and a handsome young woman—no, a handsome young Man with bright brown hair that curled around his head like a cap stepped through and smiled. A dog followed, silent and watchful.

"I am Daryl Raim, the Niss expert," the Man said; his voice was low and controlled, as though he tuned each phrase before he spoke it. Roan felt his face looking angry.

"I'm no Niss," he said in a voice that sounded harsher than he intended. "I'm a Man."

"Of course; I see you are not Old Niss."

When Daryl smiled, a dimple broke in the smooth, white skin of his left cheek. Roan found himself for the first time a mixture of embarrassing emotions and to his horror, he blushed. There was something feminine and appealing about the dimple, and the smooth white skin glowed as though it wanted to be touched.

Daryl sat down gracefully, motioned Roan to a chair entwined with trumpet vines.

"I . . ." Roan didn't know how to begin. How to explain who he was. "I am a Terran," he said finally.

Daryl nodded, smiling encouragingly. Roan felt foolish. Always before, "I am a Terran," had been an impressive thing to say.

"Of course," Daryl said. "I assume you have some important message from Old Niss?"

Roan's mouth opened and closed. His face hardened. "No," he snapped. "I'm a Terran, coming home. The Niss are dead."

"Oh?" Daryl's voice was uncertain. "Dead? I'm sure this news will interest many people. But if you're not from Old Niss . . . ?"

"I was born on Tambool, out in the Eastern Arm," Roan said. "Out there Terra is a legend. I came here to see if it was real."

Daryl smiled apologetically. "Geography was never a hobby of mine . . ."

"Tambool is another world. It's half a lifetime away. Its sun is so far away you can't even see it in the sky from here."

Daryl smiled uneasily. "You've come from Beyond? You've really . . . returned from the dead?"

"Who said anything about the dead . . . ?"

"I can't believe it," Daryl seemed to be talking to himself now. "But you *do* look—and your ship is like— and—and I've seen your face before—somewhere!" He finished up with his voice almost on a note of fright. Roan thought he shuddered—but the smile never left Daryl's face. He held out his arm. "Look. Goosebumps!"

Roan got to his feet. The chair was too comfortable, the conversation too unreal. He looked around at the perfect lawn, the perfect invisibility of the walls, the perfumed and curled Man.

"Don't you realize what this means? The Niss blockade is over. Terra's an open world again!"

Daryl took out a thin golden cylinder, drew on it, blew out pink smoke through delicate nostrils. He rearranged his body with a subtle excitement.

"I haven't felt such a thrill in years," he said. "I half believe you really did come back from Beyond." He stood, a smooth, flowing motion. "I want you to come with me, talk to me. I promise you such a night as you've never experienced on either side of the grave. My equipage is waiting. Come along to my place . . ." He put a slender hand on Roan's arm. Roan knocked it away.

"Just tell me where to find your military leaders," he said harshly. He pushed past Daryl, who shrank back, his painted eyes wide. Roan groped, looking for the door. He slammed against the invisible wall, cursed, felt his way along it, banged his knee at an invisible corner. He whirled on Daryl.

"Get me out of here!" he roared. "Where in the Nine

Hells are the people who ought to be out here to hear what I have to tell them!"

Daryl huddled against his chair; Roan stared at him, feeling the anger drain away as suddenly as it had come.

"Listen—Daryl," he said, forcing his voice low. "I grew up among aliens, fought my way through aliens to come here. I've gotten what I've had out of life by force, by guile, by killing. Those are my methods—the way you survive on the worlds out there." Roan rammed spread fingers at the sky, accusing the worlds, accounting for himself. "I'm sorry if I hurt you," he finished.

Daryl smiled through glistening tears. He rose, all assurance again, touched his hair.

"You're quite wonderful," he said. "And of course you'll want to meet—oh, ever so many fascinating people."

"The place looks deserted," Roan said. "Where is everybody?"

"They're a little shy—you understand. We weren't just sure about Old Niss."

"You didn't seem to be afraid of me—at first," Roan said bluntly.

"Afraid? Oh, I see what you mean. No, of course I wasn't afraid. The restrainers are focused on you, of course."

"What's a restrainer?" Roan said in a tight voice.

Daryl giggled. "They're trained on your two— associates—too," he said. "Shall I give you a demonstration of what it does to them?"

"No!" Roan looked out across the flower beds beyond the glass. Askor and Sidis were standing together, squinting up at the strange blue sky of Terra.

"We need a place to stay," he said. He was looking around the room now, trying to pick out something that looked like a restrainer.

"Oh, you'll find many charming compositions to choose from," Daryl said. "But why don't you accept my invitation? It would be such a coup to have you all to myself this first evening."

"What about my friends?" Roan demanded.

Daryl arched his neck gracefully to look at them. "Such strange-looking, er, persons," he said. "If you don't mind my saying so."

"Why should I mind?" Roan snapped. "It's true enough, I guess. But there are a lot stranger, out there." He waved at the sky.

"They'll be quartered wherever you choose," Daryl said stiffly. "So long as you're sure they're not . . . Lowers . . ."

Roan rounded on him. "No, damn you! They're my friends!" And he hated the reluctance he felt in claiming them.

Daryl frowned. "Your manner is somewhat abrupt," he said stiffly.

"Too bad about my manners," Roan snapped.

"But I suppose you forget such things, Beyond." Daryl dimpled forgivingly, and led the way out through panels that opened before he touched them to the accompaniment of musical tones that shimmered in the air like soap bubbles. Outside, Roan beckoned Askor and Sidis over.

"This is Daryl," he said. "He's fixing us up with a place to stay—"

"Boss, did you say *he* . . . ?" Sidis grinned.

But Roan was staring at the heavy-maned, two-legged animals that pulled the open chariot. The chariot itself was a work of art—a composition of airy, fluted columns that supported a latticed roof. The columns were gold and the latticed roof seemed to be of glass or a plastic and changed color constantly, always glittering. The chariot had large wheels of gold, spoked with the same glittering lattice-work, whose convolutions suggested the forms of half-remembered dreams. And Roan would have stood puzzling over the lattice, except that his eyes kept going back to the heavy-maned draft animals . . .

"They're Men!" he cried suddenly, watching the dog adjusting their harness neatly. "Terrans, pulling your chariot!"

"Only Lowers," said Daryl. "You wouldn't have dogs do it? My charioteers are very well treated. Come, give them a sweet and see how happy they are." He smiled benignly, went over and took something from the pouch at his waist.

Roan watched, feeling something in his heart rip. Terrans! The magic that word had been, all across the universe. Askor and Sidis gaped, mouths open.

Daryl handed a square, white bit of food to one of the hairy Terrans. "Here, Lenny. Good boy."

Lenny took the candy and popped it into his mouth, then grinned happily. "Good master!" He almost jerked the chariot over as he got down to kiss Daryl's sandaled foot.

"Now, now, Lenny," Daryl reproved softly. "Such a good boy," he said, turning to Roan. "Would you like to give the other candy to Benny?"

"No, damn you!" Roan roared. "I'd . . ." and then stopped in shock when Benny—the other draft-human— burst into tears.

Daryl started to say something to Roan, sighed, and gave Benny the candy himself. "Roan is not familiar with our customs," he told Benny, patting him on the shoulder. "Good Benny. We all love Benny. Benny is pretty. Roan, *could* you tell Benny he's pretty?"

Roan bit his lip. Benny looked at him in agony, holding the sweet and too upset to eat it. Benny had wide, innocent eyes that went oddly with his square beard and intricately plaited mane.

"Benny is pretty," Roan choked out. Lenny was watching, looking confused and frightened.

"The slaves on Alpha Two at least hated being slaves," Roan said. "And they weren't even human."

"Hmmm," Daryl mused. "You feel that because Benny and Lenny have the same basic form as you that they should be in all ways the same as you? Whereas if they were a different shape . . .?"

"I don't know," Roan cut him off. He avoided the eyes of Askor and Sidis. "Come on, load up," he snapped.

"In this play-pretty?" Sidis growled.

"Unless you want to walk!"

"Yeah," Askor said. "We'll walk."

"I guess we can walk as fast as Benny," Sidis said.

"And Lenny," Askor added.

"Then walk."

The car moved off.

"You'll need a dog, of course; I'll see to it as soon as I have you situated. You'll have time for a bath and a nap."

Daryl gaily flicked the flower-decked reins over the broad tan backs. "And then—but you'll see for yourself—tonight!"

CHAPTER ✳ TWENTY-ONE

Roan woke in utter darkness, and his sleep had been so deep that it was still heavy on him, like a weight of blankets. For a moment he strained his ears for noise, hearing only silence that crowded his own heartbeat into his ears. Then he remembered; he was on Terra, in a room like a garden with flowers, high in a glassy tower. In the darkness, a breeze was blowing from somewhere and it smelled like a drowsy afternoon.

Then suddenly the darkness lightened and Roan looked up to see a large, short-haired brown dog, which nodded politely.

"Good Evening, Master. I am Sostelle. I am to be your dog—if you approve, sir."

Roan grunted, sat up. "My dog," he said. He had never owned a living creature before.

"I'm sorry to have disturbed you, Master—but Master Daryl was emphatic about the party—"

"That's all right. I'm hungry. Can you get me something to eat?"

Sostelle moved gracefully on his overlong hind legs,

trotted to the wall, pushed a button, and a tray of hot, glazed fruit came out. He pulled the legs down on the tray and rolled it over to Roan, pulling up a chair for Roan to sit on. He had hands like a Man's.

"Is this all there is?" Roan asked.

"It's usual," Sostelle said. "But I'll get you something else, if you wish."

"How about meat and eggs?"

"Dog food?" Sostelle looked as though he didn't know whether to frown or laugh.

"I can't live on candy," Roan said.

"I'll do my best, Master," Sostelle said. "Cutlets in Sun Wine and pheasant eggs Metropole?"

"OK," Roan said. "Anything."

"And shall I prepare a bath, Master?"

"I had one yesterday," Roan snapped.

"Still—it's customary . . ."

"All right." Roan looked at the dog. "I'm pretty ignorant, Sostelle. Thanks for trying to help me."

Sostelle's tongue came out in a canine smile. "I am sure that you will be a great master. I sense it. If you'll forgive a dog's foolish fancy, sir."

"Keep me from looking like an idiot in front of these pretty creatures and I'll forgive you anything."

The fete was held in a vast, silver-and-glass walled space where fragile columns as slender as reeds ran up to arch out and meet in a glitter of jeweled-glass panels high overhead. The floor was a polished expanse of pale violet glass, and the music was as stirring and as lovely as a flight of swans, as martial as the roar of lions, as gay as carnival.

To Roan's left and behind him, Sostelle stood in his stiff formal jacket, quite graceful on his hind legs, and whispered, "Hold your glass by the loop with one finger, Master, not with your whole hand."

Roan nodded, feeling awkward and almost naked, for Sostelle had depilated his face and dressed him in a silky, green and gold garment that folded and tied together and felt as though it might fall off if you moved too quickly in it. The guests carefully avoided staring at him and Sostelle pointed them out as they whirled past, their dance a dainty posturing in which neither partner touched even the fingertips of the other; Roan watched, overwhelmed by the blaze of light, of color, of movement across the vast expanse of multitiered transparent floor that made the throng of fancifully gowned men and women appear to be floating in the air. He finished the drink and another was there at once. Daryl appeared, transformed in a pink garment, silver-dyed hair, and feathery wings attached to his ankles.

"Roan—how marvelous you look . . ." He glanced at Sostelle.

"And Sostelle—an excellent son of a bitch. But didn't he offer you a choice of hair tints and scents? And what about decorative touches—"

"He offered them," Roan cut in. "I didn't want them. Look, Daryl; I can't afford to waste any more time. When will I meet your governmental leaders, your military men?"

A small crowd was gathering in Daryl's wake, watching Roan curiously. Someone tittered and discretely stopped.

"Waste time?" Daryl's nose got a pinched look.

"I seem to have offended everybody again," Roan said in the silence. "Didn't you warn them I'd forgotten my manners?"

A nervous laugh went through the group.

"Is that what it means to you?" he almost shouted. "Manners? Don't you care that Terra's a free world again—that the Galaxy is open to you?"

Daryl put a hand on his arm. "No one here is much on mythology, Roan. They—"

"Mythology, hell! I'm talking about a thousand worlds—a million of them—and once Terra ruled them all!"

A ripple of applause broke out.

Daryl joined in. "Charming," he said. "So spontaneous." He flicked his eyes at the others. "Roan's going to be wonderful," he said.

A girl was looking at Roan. If she had been done by a bad artist in brass, she would have looked like Stellaraire. She was the statue in the garden on Also Cerise, but her body was warm human flesh instead of cold stone, and her mouth by its very existence begged to be kissed. She had smiled when the others laughed. Her lips barely curved but her green eyes seemed to tilt up at the corners.

"I'm Desiranne," she said. "I don't understand what you've said—but it's exciting."

"Desiranne will entertain tonight," Daryl said. "It will be the high point of the evening." His eyes moved over her like a lecherous hand.

"Look," Roan said to the girl. "It's nice about the party and you're so beautiful a man almost can't endure it, but someone's got to listen to me. This is the biggest thing that's happened to Terra in five thousand years—but before long the ITN is going to realize the blockade is over. There's a fellow named Trishinist who'd give his hair to be the one to lead an invading force in here. They think of Terra as one big treasure house, ripe for looting—the richest prize of all."

Daryl laughed with a mouthful of smoke and ended up choking. Sostelle came immediately with a glass of water and a scented, gossamer tissue. People were turning away, already looking bored.

Daryl smiled knowingly, took out a cigarette. "I wouldn't," he said. "Not so soon. I'm sure you'll become a great favorite, but if you try to push yourself forward right away, people will resent it."

Roan growled and Daryl jumped. "Really," he said almost sharply. "You'll have to learn a few of the graces. And I'd also suggest you let your fingernails grow out a bit more gracefully and a few things like that which Sostelle will advise you about." He rose in a smooth balletlike movement.

"And now, I think Desiranne and I—"

"She'll dance with me," Roan said roughly. He finished his wine with a gulp, tossed the glass aside, walked past Daryl to the girl's side. She looked around, wide-eyed, as Roan took her in his arms. She was as light as a handful of moonbeams, Roan found himself thinking, suddenly struck dumb by her fragile loveliness.

But there was no need for talk. He was suddenly aware of the music, swelling louder now. There was a deep, booming throb that matched the cadence of the human heart, and a dazzling interplay of horns that repeated the rhythms of the human nervous system, and an intricate melody that echoed forgotten human dreams. Stellaraire had taught Roan how to dance, long ago; he had not forgotten. All around, the Terrans had drawn back, and now they stood, watching, as Roan responded with a lifetime's pent-up emotion to the call of the music and the girl and the strong wine of Terra.

And then the music ended on a fading susurration of cymbals and the high wail of brass. Roan swept Desiranne almost to the floor, and for a moment he held her there, looking into her perfect, half-frightened, half-enraptured face.

"I think I know now why I came here," he said. "I think I knew I'd find you. Now I don't think I'll ever let you go."

There were sudden tears in her eyes as Roan set her on her feet. "Roan," she whispered. "Why . . . why didn't you come sooner . . ." Then she turned and fled.

Suddenly, there was deafening applause. Shouts of bravo! and splendid! rang out. Everyone seemed to be staring at him with eyes that were bright with . . . fear? They came toward him almost cautiously, as though approaching a tame beast, led by a small, lithe brunette with long hair done into such a complex system of plaits and curls that her head looked too heavy for her small body. She had a sinuous, elongated walk, and her dress was the color of . . . . of air with sunshine in it.

"Mistress Alouicia," Sostelle whispered to Roan, "a dancer, and a very clever woman."

"Marvelous," she said. "Such a spectacle of primitive

savagery! For a moment I thought you were going to . . . to lose control and kill her, tear her throat out with those great strong teeth." She shuddered, showing Roan a smile that was just a little long in the tooth.

"I'd never understood ancient music before," a Man said. "Now I think I do . . ."

"The way he sprang at her," someone else offered. "And then putting his hands on her that way. It *was* intended to represent a tiger seizing his prey, wasn't it?"

"No, it was just a dance," Roan said; and turned to Sostelle and asked in a loud voice, "It's all right, isn't it, to say what you mean instead of making people guess?"

Sostelle, knowing this wasn't to be answered, kept a discreet silence and straightened the folds in Roan's chiton.

"Does everyone dance in that way in your homeland?" Alouicia asked, smiling a bit stiffly now.

"On every world there are different dances. Once I was with a circus and my girl did erotic dances in several different cultures."

"Erotic? How interesting . . ."

Roan was glad to have found a subject of interest. He was feeling the wine, wanting to put everyone at ease, and then go find Desiranne.

"It frequently led to public copulation," he added.

"To . . . to . . . what *did* you say?" Alouicia's eyes widened.

"What does it mean?" a high voice whispered loudly.

Someone tittered. "Like Dogs. Imagine!"

"Really! What sort of . . . animal . . . would perform such a dance?"

"She was beautiful," Roan said, remembering Stellaraire, and feeling that something should be said out of loyalty. "I loved her."

"He's not merely a savage," a voice said loudly behind him. "I do believe he's a Lower."

Roan turned. A tall, wide-shouldered Terran stood looking at him with an expression of distaste. He was deep-chested, well-muscled.

"Master Hugh, the famous athlete," Sostelle murmured.

"Hugh!" Alouicia said, her voice carrying the faintest edge of shrillness. "What an exciting confrontation: The strongest man on Terra, with your interest in the ancient athletic arts—and this . . . elemental man from—wherever he's from!"

"Please," Daryl said, putting a hand on Roan's arm. "I think—"

"Never mind," Roan said. "I'm not very good at remembering all the things that are too ugly for you pretty people to talk about. I'm a Man; I sweat and bleed and eat and excrete—"

"Roan!" Daryl said. Alouicia drew away with a small cry. Sostelle gasped.

"Go away," Hugh said. "I don't know who brought you here. You're not fit for the society of civilized people—"

"There's nothing civilized about the ITN," Roan said. "What would you do if *they* showed up? If they came storming across those pretty gardens and in through the pretty door; what would you do?"

"I'm sure that thirty thousand years of culture have prepared us to deal with whatever a barbarian might do," Daryl said uneasily.

Roan doubled a fist and held it before him. "Do you know what this is?"

Hugh eyed the doubled knuckles. His nose wrinkled. "Of course; the dawn-men—Romans, I think they were called—had a primitive sport in which they flailed one another with their hands held in that way. This was done in a coliseum called Madison Square Garden, and the winner was awarded a fig leaf, or something of the sort—"

Roan drew back his fist and hit Hugh square on the nose, taking care not to put too much power back of the blow. Hugh went down, blood streaming down across his lip and into his mouth. He cried out, dabbed at his face, stared at the crimsoned fingers. There were little shrieks all around.

"You—you *brute!*" Hugh said.

"All right," Roan heard himself shouting. "What do you do, with your thirty thousand years of culture?"

Hugh came to his feet; all around, people stared, eyes bright, lips parted. Roan stepped to Hugh and hit him solidly on the side of the jaw. Hugh fell down again, his mouth open and a look of utter amazement on his face.

"You're supposed to be an athlete," Roan said. "Get up and fight back."

Hugh got to his feet; he folded his fingers over his palms and held them in front of him; then he stepped up to Roan and struck out with an overhand blow; Roan casually brushed Hugh's arm aside and hit him in the stomach; as Hugh doubled over, Roan planted a left and right to the face. Hugh sprawled on the floor and began to cry.

Roan reached, caught his garment by the shoulder, hauled him half erect, slapped him across the cheek.

"It may surprise you," he said. "But members of an attacking army don't stop when you cry. They just laugh at you. And they don't fight nicely, like I do; if you're on the floor"—he let Hugh drop—"they kick you—like this." And he planted a solid blow in Hugh's ribs with his toe. Hugh scrambled back, tears streaming down his face; he was sobbing loudly.

"Get up!" Roan said. "Get mad! That's the only thing that will stop me!" He followed Hugh, dragged him to his feet, hit him in the eye, then, holding him up, punched him in the mouth. Hugh's face was a bloody mask now.

"Fight!" Roan said. "Hit back!"

Hugh broke away, stumbled back against the watching crowd. They thrust him back toward Roan. He saw their faces then, for the first time. They were like hungry Charons, waiting for an old gracyl to die.

"Kill him, savage!" a man called; saliva ran out of his mouth and down into his perfumed, pale blue beard. Alouicia held out her hands, the gold-enameled nails like raking claws. "Bite his throat!" she shrilled. "Drink his blood!"

Roan dropped his hands, feeling a thrill of horror. Hugh broke through the ring and ran, sobbing.

"Master," Sostelle said. "Oh, Master . . ."

"Let's go," Roan said. "Where's my crew?" He staggered, feeling the room tilt under his feet. Terran wine was made for Terran nervous systems; it hit hard.

"Master—I don't know. I heard—but—"

"Find them!" Roan shouted. People scattered before him. He was out in the wide entry hall now. The polished black floor threw back reflections of chandeliers and of the stars above the glass-domed ceiling. Sostelle hurried ahead, bounding on all fours. Two tall, wide shapes stepped from the shadow of a slender supporting rib ahead, stood silhouetted against the sweep of glass front.

"Askor," Roan called. "Sidis!"

"Yeah, Boss." They came toward him. They were dressed in their soiled ship clothes. Sidis wore a pistol openly at his hip.

"Thought I said . . . no guns," Roan said blurrily.

"I had a hunch you might change your mind," Sidis said; his teeth gleamed in the gloom.

"You did, eh?" Roan felt an unreasoning anger rising in him. It was almost like joy. "Since when did you start doing my thinking for me?" He took a step, swung what should have been a smashing blow to the Minid's head, but he missed, almost fell. Sidis hadn't moved.

"Gee, Chief," Askor said admiringly. "You're drunk!"

"I'm not drunk, damn you!" Roan planted his feet, breathing hard. "And what are you doing here in those rags? Why haven't you washed your ugly faces? I can smell you from three yards away . . . !" He could feel his tongue slurring over the words, and this made him angrier than ever. "You trying . . . 'sgrace me?" he roared. "Get out of here and don't come back . . . 'til you look like human beings!"

"That could be quite a while, Chief," Askor said. "Look, Cap'n, let's blow out of this place. It's creepy. And I can hardly keep my hands off these Terries of yours—"

"They're not mine," Roan yelled. "And I'll say when we leave—"

"He's right, Boss," Sidis cut in. "This world ain't good for us. Let's shove off, Cap'n. Just the three of us, like before—"

"I'm captain of the bloody menagerie," Roan yelled. "When I'm ready to lift ship, I'll tell you. Now get out of my sight! Get lost!"

"Master," Sostelle whispered.

"You, too, you Freak." Roan staggered, wiped a hand across his face. It was hot, feverish. Everything seemed to be spinning around him; his mind seemed to be floating free of his body, like a captive balloon. Then sky rockets came shooting up in a fiery shower and when they shimmered away into darkness there was nothing . . . .

Roan sat up and looked around. Noise roared in his ears. A face swam mistily before him.

"Ah, he's awake," someone called. Someone else thrust a thin-stemmed glass into his hand. He drank thirstily, let the glass fall. Daryl was there, looking at him eagerly with painted eyes.

"Roan! You looked so lovely sleeping, with your mouth open and sweat on your face . . ."

"Where's Desiranne?" Roan said. His head ached but he could speak clearly now.

"Eh? Why she's preparing for her performance, later in the evening—but—"

"I want to see her." Roan stood and the table fell over. "Where is she?"

"Now, Roan." Daryl was at his side, patting his arm.

"Just be patient. You'll see her." He laughed a high, tight laugh. "Oh, my, yes, you'll see her. You liked her, didn't you? You . . . you lusted after her?"

Roan took Daryl by the shoulder, lifted him from the floor. "Keep away from me," he snarled, and threw the Terran from him. His vision seemed cloudy, as though the room were full of mist. There were other people around him, but their faces weren't clear. Sostelle was there, his face worried and homely and familiar and dependable.

"Where is she, Sostelle?" Roan said. "Where did she go?"

"Master, I don't know. This is not a matter for dogs." His voice was almost a moan.

"Sure, I liked her," Roan said loudly. "I loved her!" He kicked a chair from his path, started across the floor. "She liked me, too, didn't she?" He rounded on the dog. "Well, didn't she?"

Sostelle's face assumed an unreadable canine expression. "Her interest in you was unmistakable, Master."

"You think so?"

"Certainly. She is a lovely lady, Master. Worthy of you." But there was something about his tone; something Roan didn't understand.

"I've got to find her. Can't leave this madhouse until I find her." He started on. The people before him flitted backward, just out of reach, just out of vision. The noise was like an avalanche of sound—a wild, screaming sort of music that seemed to tell of great birds of prey swooping to a feast.

"I will help you, Master," Sostelle said. "I will help all I can."

"You're a damned good dog, Sostelle. Hell, you're the only friend I've met here—"

"Sir!" Sostelle sounded shocked. "It's not done, sir, to call a dog a friend . . ."

Roan laughed harshly. "I guess I'll never learn the rules, Sostelle. I came too late—for all of us."

"Master—perhaps you should go now—and take me with you—"

"You, too? What is it, a conspiracy? I've told you, damn you, I'm not going until I find her!" There was a table in his path and he kicked it savagely aside.

"Roan, Roan," a quavering voice called. He stopped, steadied himself against a table, peered through the mist. Daryl darted up to him, his carefully coiffed hair awry. A smile flicked on and off like leaf shadows playing on water.

"It's Desiranne you want to see—and I promise you, you'll see her. Just wait. But now—come along with me. The party's just begun. We have wonderful things planned, and we *must* have you! It will be the greatest affair of the century—of a lifetime! And at the end of it— Desiranne!"

"Sostelle, is he lying?" Roan stared at the Terran, who was quivering with eagerness, like an Alphan slave awaiting a kick or the dregs of a wineglass, not knowing which it would be.

"Master," Sostelle whined, "Master Daryl speaks the truth . . ."

"Then I'll come."

"You'll be glad, Roan," Daryl gushed. "So glad. "And—"

"Never mind that. Where are we going?"

"First, we'll dine. After the dancing and the . . . excitement . . . we need to nourish ourselves, don't you think?" He giggled. "And then—but you'll see; there will be marvelous things—all the pleasures of Terra are waiting for you tonight!" He danced away, calling to others. Roan started after him, then turned back to Sostelle with a quick thought.

"Pleasure," he said, "is what you go after when there isn't anything else left."

CHAPTER ✳ TWENTY-TWO

The cold night air cleared Roan's head. He looked down from the open flyer in which he and Daryl and two women and their dogs sat on silken cushions, drinking from small, thin-necked bottles of spicy liquor. There were other airboats around them, darting in and out like a school of playful fish. Over the rush of air, thin cries of excitement mingled with the chatter of many voices talking at once.

The dog piloting the craft dropped it to the tip of a tall spire of glowing yellow glass. Roan followed the others through an entry that looked like solid glass, but parted before him with a tinkle of cold crystals. Flushed, bright-eyed faces swarmed around him, but none of them was Desiranne. A tall girl with heavy golden hair came up to Roan, her bare arms ivory-white. She looked at him with her eyes half shut, her lips parted, her pink tongue showing. Roan showed his teeth and reached for her, and she shuddered and shrank back. Roan laughed and pushed through to follow Daryl.

✳ ✳ ✳ ✳

He was trying hard to remember where the table was, how he had come there. He couldn't; there had been so many tables, so much noise, so many of the little bottles of spicy wine. He felt very sober, though, and his mind seemed to be working unusually clearly. Neatly dressed dogs were serving food. Roan ate with voracious appetite while his companions nibbled and watched. Roan hardly noticed them. Once he looked up to see the blond girl sitting across the table from him.

"You Terries know how to make food," he said. "This is better even than blood."

The girl—Phrygette, Roan remembered her name—looked sick and excited at the same time. She put out her hand as though to touch the hair on Roan's arm, then drew it back.

"You're strange," she whispered. "I wonder what you think about. You with your sixteen-thousand-year-old brain and your years of wandering the universe."

"I think about many things," Roan said carefully, wishing the hot feeling and the humming in his ears would go away. "I think about the Niss, and how Man destroyed himself fighting them, and how they died alone, then, and how their ghosts haunted the Galaxy for five thousand years."

"Old Niss," Phrygette said, boldly touching Roan's arm now. "I always thought he was a silly superstition."

"I did a terrible thing when I ran the Niss blockade," Roan said. "I didn't free Terra; I shattered the myth that had held the universe out for five thousand years. Now she's exposed to the sharks: Trishinist, and after him, others, until Terra is no different than Tambool."

Phrygette was looking around for her dog, Ylep, to come and fix her makeup.

"A new Navy, that's what you need," Roan said. "Trishinist can muster fifty thousand men, and he has the ships to transport them. You have ships, too—underground, waiting. You need to issue weapons and learn how to use them, prepare tactics to meet an enemy landing party."

Phrygette frowned at Roan. "Really, for someone from Beyond, you talk about the strangest things. Tell me how it feels to kill someone, Roan. Tell me how it feels to die—"

"You'll find out soon enough," Roan said roughly. Suddenly he felt very bad. His heart was trying to climb up his throat, and his head hurt terribly. He swallowed more wine, put his head down on the table. Phrygette got to her feet, wrinkling her nose.

"I'm afraid he's becoming a bore," she said to someone. "Let's go on to the Museum, Daryl. They've probably already started—without us!"

"They wouldn't dare!" Daryl said, sounding alarmed. "Not after *I* planned it!"

"They might—"

"Roan!" Daryl was shaking him. He raised his head and saw a crowd all around him, faces staring out of a blackish haze.

"Come on, Roan!" It was Daryl, catching at his hand. "You went to sleep again, you foolish boy, but now we're all ready to go to the Museum!"

"Go where?"

"To the Museum of the Glory of Man! Come on! Oh,

you'll be thrilled, Roan! It's an ancient, ancient place—just at the edge of the town. All sort of shuddery and dim—but marvelous, really! It's all there—all Terra's history. We've been saving it for a special occasion—and this is certainly the perfect night!"

"Funny place . . . for a party . . ." Roan said, but he got to his feet and followed the laughing, chattering crowd.

Out on the roof, the dogs jumped up, handing their masters and mistresses to their places in the waiting flyers, some of which hovered, waiting their turn. Roan felt as though he were moving in a dream imbued with a sense of terrible things impending. The dogs' eyes looked wide, afraid. Even Sostelle was awkward getting the flyer's door open. Roan's hand went to his belt, feeling for a gun that wasn't there.

"Askor," he said suddenly. "And Sidis. Where are they?" He half rose, sat down suddenly as the flyer jumped forward.

"They'll trouble you no more," Daryl said. "And now, Roan, just think! Objects that were held sacred by our ancestors, five thousand—ten thousand years ago—"

"What do you mean," Roan said, feeling a tightness in his chest. "Where are they?"

"Roan—don't you remember? You sent them away yourself . . ."

"Sostelle . . ." Roan felt a sudden weakness as he tried again to rise. Blackness whirled in, shot with fire.

"Master, it is true. You ordered them to leave you. They laid hands on you, to drag you with them, but you fought, and then . . . then Master Daryl was impelled to . . . to call for the Enforcers."

"What are they?" Roan heard his own hoarse voice as from a great distance.

"Specially trained dogs, Master," Sostelle said in a tight voice. "Led by Kotschai the Punisher."

"Are they—did they—?"

"Your companions fought mightily, Master. They killed many dogs. At last they were overwhelmed, and restrainers were focused on them. Then they were taken away."

"Then they're alive?" The blackness broke, flushed away.

"Of course, Master!" Sostelle sounded shocked.

Roan laughed harshly. "They're all right, then. They've been in jail before. I'll bail 'em out in the morning."

They had landed on the wide roof of an ancient palace. Roan tottered, felt Sostelle's hand under his elbow.

"I'm sick," he said. "I've never been so sick, since I was burned when Henry Dread shelled the Extravaganzoo. There was a Man doctor there; he cured me. He couldn't cure Stellaraire, though. She was crushed by a chromalloy beam, and then . . . burned . . ."

"Yes, Master," Sostelle soothed.

"Gom Bulj died from the acceleration. But I killed Ithc. And I killed Henry Dread, too. You didn't know that, did you, Sostelle? But Iron Robert—he died for me . . ."

They were inside now. The voices of the others were like birds, quarreling over a dung heap. Their faces were blurred, vague. All around, tall cases were ranged, faced with glass. Someone was talking urgently to Roan, but he ignored him, walked to the nearest display, feeling as though he were toiling up a hill.

"This is a collection of famous jewel stones, Master," Sostelle was saying. "All natural minerals, found here on Terra, and treasured by Men for their beauty and their rarity."

Roan stared down at rank on rank of glittering, faceted crystals—red, green, pale blue, violet, clear white.

"There is the Napoleon emerald," Sostelle said. "Worn by an ancient war chief. And beyond is the Buddha's Heart ruby, once the object of veneration of five billion worshipers. And there, just beyond—the Iceberg diamond, said to be the largest and finest ever found in Antarctica."

"Look, Roan," Daryl called. "These are called monies. They're made of solid natural gold, and in early times they were traded back and forth in exchange for, oh, other things," he finished vaguely. "Rather a bore, really. Come along to the next room, though. There are some fabulous things. . . ."

Roan followed, stared at looming walls decorated with objects as baroque and primitive as the crude weapons of the wild men on Aldo Cerise, others of a powerful, barbaric beauty, and still others of a glittering intricacy that his mind could not comprehend. There were more cases—miles of them, each glowing with its own soft light, each with its array of objects of metal, stone, wood, glass, fabric, synthetic.

"Look!" Daryl was poking Roan. "Those clothes were made from fibers that grew from the dirt; they scraped them clean in some way, and then worked them all together, and colored them with—with fruit juice or something. Then they sawed out pieces and looped them together with little strings. That was called sowing—"

"No, that was when they made the plants that they got the fibers from," someone interrupted. "But aren't they funny?"

Roan gazed at the display of old uniforms. Some were shapeless and faded, brown with age, curled with time, even protected as they were by the vacuum of the display cases; others, farther along, were more familiar.

"You see those long, sharp things? They used those to stick into each other," a high excited voice called. "And these odd-shaped objects made some sort of lightning and tore holes in people; there must have been a great deal of blood."

Roan stopped, staring at a tunic of brilliant blue, with narrow silvery-gray trousers, and a belt with a buckle bearing an eagle in place of a dove, and the words *Terran Space Forces*.

"It's like the ITN uniform," he said to no one. "But it was made before there was an Empire . . ."

Daryl was beside Roan, his face puckered in thought. He looked up at Roan, his eyes snapping wide.

"You!" he said in a strained voice. "I know where it was I saw your face! Look, everybody, come with me . . . !" He turned, ran off.

"What's the matter with him?" Roan growled, but he followed.

In a small room off the main hall, a crowd clustered

around a lighted case. They looked around as Roan came up, gave way, staring at him, silent now. Roan halted before the high glass panel, stared at a hazy scene, bright lit. He blinked, cleared his vision. The figure of a man stood before him, clad in a uniform like the one he had just seen, leaning against the flank of a ship of quaint, primitive design. The eyes, blue like cool fire, looked into Roan's from across the centuries. The deep red hair was hacked short, but its stubborn curl still showed. A deep, recorded voice spoke from a slot beneath the display:

"This was Vice Admiral Stuart Murdoch, as he appeared in his last solido, taken only moments before he embarked on his last, heroic mission. Admiral Murdoch is renowned as the hero of the Battle of Ceres and of the Siege of the Callistan Redoubts. He was lost in space in the year eleven thousand, four hundred and two of the Atomic Era."

"Master," Sostelle said in the silence. "It's you!"

Roan turned, looked at Daryl. "How . . . ?" he started. He put his hands on himself as though to assure himself that he was Roan Cornay, alive here and now. But Daryl and the others stared back at him as though he was himself a thing from out of the remote past, like the ancient figure in the glass case.

Roan laughed suddenly, wildly. "I wanted to know who my father was," he said. "But I never suspected he was sixteen thousand years old."

"He . . . really . . . is . . ." Daryl said, and licked at his lips. He whirled to the others. "Don't you understand? He really *did* come from Beyond, just as he said! He's returned from the dead!"

"No," a loud voice said. It was Hugh, his face raw and cut from the beating Roan had given him. "He's a dirty Lower, and he should be turned over to the dogs."

"He's returned from the dead!" Daryl screeched. "Come along! It's easy enough to prove!"

"The genetic analyzer!" someone called. "In the next hall . . ."

"Roan, this will show them all," Daryl said breathlessly. There was a strange light in his eyes. "And then—you'll tell me how it feels to be dead, and rise again!"

"You're insane, Daryl," Roan said. "You're all insane!" he shouted. "I'm the most insane of all, for being here, where I don't belong—" He broke off. "Tomorrow," he said. "Tomorrow I'll leave. With Askor and Sidis. They're my kind. I understand them. They're not pretty, but they've got the beauty of reality about them . . ."

"And you'll take me, Master?" Sostelle whispered.

"Sure, Man's best dog is his friend, eh?" Roan stumbled, almost fell. He was hardly aware of walking, Sostelle at his side, Daryl trotting ahead, under a high arch with a flame burning under it in a metal tray, on into an even bigger room that echoed with the batlike cries of the Terrans.

". . . classify persons wishing to contribute to the germinal banks," Daryl was saying. "Here in the Hall of Man, all the records were kept—"

"My genetic pattern won't be here," Roan said, almost clear-headed for the moment.

"He's afraid," Hugh said. "Will he confess his pretensions now?"

Roan looked around at gleaming equipment, towering metal panels, winking clinical lights.

"Put your hand here, Roan," Daryl urged. He indicated an opening, guided Roan's hand to it. He felt a sharp tingle for an instant, nothing more. There was a soft hum and a plastic tab extruded from a slot in the face of the genetic analyzer. Daryl snatched it, looked at it, then whirled to face the others.

"It's him! It's Stuart Murdoch, returned from beyond the crematorium!"

He didn't remember again then; not until they were in a vast room with ancient flags hanging from age-blackened rafters.

". . . minster hall," an excited voice was saying. "Over thirty thousand years old. Think of the toil, the human tears and sweat and heartache that went into building this, so long ago, to preserving it down through the ages, to bring it here—for us . . ." The voice went on, excited, rapturous.

"What's it all about?" Roan asked. "What's this old building? It looks like something on Tambool. . . ."

"It's very ancient, Master," Sostelle said. Somewhere, a bright light was flaring in the gloom.

". . . took them so many ages to create, with all its traditions and memories—and we, us! Yes, in a single night! A single hour! We can destroy it all. Thirty thousand years of human history end—now!" Roan watched as a slender man in flowing pale garments ran forward, applied the torch to the base of a hand-hewn column. Fire licked upward. In moments it had reached the faded pennants; they disappeared into smoke. Fire ran across the high peaked ceiling. Voices shouted as the crowd pushed forward. Suddenly a woman whirled madly, striking out at those around her; they fell back, yelping, and the frenzied girl tore at her garment, stripped it off, threw it at the fire. Roan saw with a dull shock that there was no hair on her body.

"Give me something sharp!" she screamed, then plunged, caught up a jagged fragment of smoking wood, scored it down the creamy white of her chest and stomach. Blood started. The woman staggered back, wailed faintly, fell, and dogs darted forward, bore her away.

"Get back!" someone was calling. The ceiling was a mass of boiling smoke and flame; each massive timber supporting the rafters blazed, crackling. Roan backed away, then turned and ran.

Behind him, the roof fell with a great thunder; a blast of scalding air struck at him, and sparks flew all around . . .

Later, he stood at the top of a broad flight of marble steps, where a group of men wheezed under the weight of a black stone statue of a man with a wide headdress and a straight-ahead gaze.

"See him, Roan?" Daryl called. "Isn't he wonderful? The labor, the hopes that went into that image. And now . . ."

The Pharaoh Horemheb went over with a resounding smash, tumbled down head over throne, pulverizing the steps as it struck them. The head flew off, struck a man standing below, who fell screaming, and a crowd closed around him like fish after a bait.

"Master, you're not well," Sostelle was saying. "Let me take you home . . . !"

"Wait. Have to see Desiranne." Roan shook his head, started down the stairs. Daryl skipped ahead, dragging a picture in a heavy frame. At the foot of the stairs, he raised it high, brought it down on the bronze figure of a girl with a water jar; it burst into a cloud of dry chips.

"The Mona Lisa," he caroled. "The only one in the world—and I destroyed it!" He spun on Roan. "Oh, Roan, doesn't it give you a wonderful feeling of power? Those old ones—the ones that conquered the universe—they treasured all this! And we have the power to do as we like with it. They made it—we finish it! Doesn't that make us their equals?"

Roan stared past him at a bigger-than-life white marble of a thick-bodied woman with her garment down around her hips. She was chipped and her arms were missing.

"Shame," Roan mumbled. "Shouldn't break . . . old things." He felt as though he were falling.

"I didn't do that one," Daryl said. "It was already broken—but I'll finish it!" He ran to the statue and pushed. It didn't budge. Daryl made a face and ran on to pull down a painting of a man with one ear missing.

"It's hot in here," Roan said aloud. The walls were sailing by, going faster and faster. He groped for support, sank down on the steps. All around, people were running like gracyls in molting time, carrying things that smashed, or broke, or were torn apart. Someone started a blaze in the center of the floor, and pictures went flying into it. The floor shook as heavy marbles toppled.

"Get a cutter," a girl screamed, "to use on the bronzes!"

"What a night!" Daryl exulted. "We did the Louvre

long ago, and the Grand Palais d'Arte, and the Imperial Gardens; we were saving this one for a special occasion—and your being here—it's just made it perfect—"

Roan got to his feet, fighting the blackness. "I can't wait any longer," he shouted over the din. "Where's Desiranne?"

"Roan, Roan! Forget her for now! There's her performance coming! There's lots of luscious sport to be had before then—"

Phrygette was there tucking back a strand of corn-yellow hair with a white arm smudged with soot.

"I'm bored," she said. "Daryl, let's get on to the performance."

"But there are still lots of things to do," he cried, dancing round her. "The books! We haven't even begun on the books—and the tapes, and the old films, and . . . and . . ."

"I'm going," Phrygette pouted. She looked at Roan. He stared back, seeing her face dancing in fire.

"Don't look at me like that," she said sharply. "You look so peculiar . . ."

Roan took a deep breath and held one part of his mind away from the whirling dizziness that enveloped him. He produced something that could be defined as a smile.

"If you were a sixteen-thousand-year throwback, you'd look peculiar, too." He seemed to be watching everything through a view screen now; Daryl looked tiny and far away, and all around the floor curved upward. A wild singing whine rang in Roan's ears. His face felt furnace-hot. "I want to see Desiranne now," he said.

"Oh, all right," Daryl gave Phrygette an icy look. "Spoilsport!"

CHAPTER ✷ TWENTY-THREE

They were in a moldy velvet and chipped gilt room lit by tiny lights glaring down from above like stars as seen in Deep Space, set in a ceiling that slanted away toward a small, bright-lit platform below. There were seats ranked beside Roan's, and more rows lower down, and others swinging in wide sweeps farther up, and still more, perched like tiny balconies just above the stage, and all of them were filled with slim-necked, soot-streaked Men and Women.

"In all that you've told me of other worlds, Roan," Daryl said in a low, vibrant voice, "there has been nothing to equal what you will see Desiranne do here tonight."

"What will she do? Play some instrument? Sing?" The thought of seeing her again made his pulse throb in his head, driving back the sickness. He remembered Stellaraire and her erotic dancing. Surely Desiranne wouldn't do anything like that . . .

"Master," Sostelle whined at Roan's side. "Please—let me bring the doctor to see you now."

"The stuff you gave me is working," Roan said. "I feel better. I'm all right."

A blue mist blew across the stage. Out of it, a little blue and silver dog emerged, singing an eerie, piercing little song in a register so high it was barely within hearing. The blue color faded, and now there were pale pastels— mauve, bluish pink, sunshine-yellow, rain-gray—swirls, clouds, blown foams. The blue dog's song ended in a tiny yelp, and behind Roan, Sostelle winced. Roan could make out another figure in the mist now, dressed in diaphanous robes, swathed from head to foot. It came forward and the scarf blew from its head. It was Desiranne and her pale hair swirled down about her shoulders.

The music was low and gentle, almost a lullaby, and Desiranne ran gracefully, girlishly about in the mists, playing. Then, by degrees, the tempo changed and a drum began to beat—an insistent, commanding beat. Roan began to be aware of Daryl's breathing beside him and he also remembered the fearful beat of the drums that night he stood frozen with fear by the high wire on Chlora, when he was with the circus.

Was that it? Was that what was making the small hairs on his arms prickle, and bringing the smell of danger and the cold sweat in his stomach? Something . . . he turned to Daryl to tell him to stop the show. Whatever it was going to be, Roan could feel it beginning to stink. Something was wrong. Something . . .

But Daryl was smiling expectantly and proudly at Desiranne.

"By the way," he said. "Did I mention that she is my daughter?"

"Your daughter?" Roan repeated dumbly. "You're not old enough," he blurted.

Daryl looked astonished. "Not old enough . . ." A strange expression crossed his face. "You mean—you're . . ." He gulped. "I remember learning once that long ago, men died like dogs, after only a moment of life. Do you mean, Roan, that you—that you . . . ?"

"Never mind."

On the stage, Desiranne had begun a slow, sensuous striptease. The music became more and more insinuating, erotic, then slowed as Desiranne removed her last wisp of garment. As she pirouetted, all pink and gold in the lights, the little silver and blue dog came mincing out onto the stage with something sharp that glittered silver where the light caught it.

It was a knife, long and leaf-thin and sharp. Desiranne dipped in her dance to pluck the stiletto from its cushion, danced away, holding it high. Then the music began to change again, and now a savage tempo took over. An animal music. It went straight to some dark, forgotten part of Roan's mind and again fear began to swell in him insistently. He came to his feet—

Desiranne stopped, stood poised; she held the scalpel-keen blade in her right hand and with great grace and sure slowness, cut off the little finger of her left hand.

A terrible cry tore itself from Roan's throat. He plunged down through the crowd, not even aware of the screams and the smash of his fists on anything that impeded him. With a leap he was on the stage, snatching the knife from Desiranne's hand as she moved to stroke it across his wrist. He caught her, looked into eyes as vacant and dead as the glassless windows of a ruined city.

"Why?" Roan screamed. "Why?" Blood ran down

Desiranne's arm. For a moment her eyes seemed to stir with returning life; then she wilted. Roan caught her up, whirled on the others who had crowded around the stage now, all shouting at once. The air reeked of blood; it was a taste in the mouth.

"Get a doctor! She'll die!"

Daryl's livid face was in front of him. He shook his fists over his head. His mouth looked loose and wet.

"Your daughter!" Roan said hoarsely, looking down at the small, gentle, beautiful face. "Your own daughter!"

"She felt nothing! She was drugged! Do you realize that her one chance for a perfect Death Performance is ruined forever? That this is all she has lived for and now she will never have it? I reared her for this, trained her myself! All these years I've kept her perfect, waiting for the one, the ideal occasion—and now—"

Roan snarled and kicked him brutally, and Daryl doubled over, mewing, coiled on the bloody floor.

"Sostelle—get a Man doctor!" Roan jumped down, ran toward the rear of the theater. Desiranne hung limp in his arms, her face as pale as chalk.

In a vast gilt room, Desiranne lay on a narrow couch of pale green silk with curved legs wrought of silver and ivory. A small crowd of eager-eyed Terrans stood by, watching. The doctor, a scrubbed-looking dog carrying a pouch, clucked and sprayed something from the pouch over Desiranne's stumped finger, looked over at Roan.

"She will survive. The tourniquet saved her from excessive bleeding. A pity; so fair she was. But, you, sir; you don't look well. Sostelle tells me—"

"Never mind me; why doesn't she wake up? Are you sure she isn't going to die?"

"She won't die. I'll see to a bud implant from self-germinal tissue, and in a year or two, with the proper stimuli, she'll be as good as new. Now I must insist, sir: Let me have a look at you."

"All right." Roan sank down in a high-backed chair; the doctor applied a smooth, cold metal object to him, muttered to himself.

"You're a sick master," he said. "Temperature over one hundred and four; blood pressure—"

"Just give me some medicine," Roan interrupted. "My head aches."

"I've heard a bit of your background, sir," the doctor said as he rummaged in his bag. "I think I see what's happened here. You've no immunity to the native diseases of Terra. And, of course, they find in you a perfect host. Now—"

"I've never been sick," Roan said, "not like this. I thought it was just the wine, but . . ." He tottered in the chair as a wave of dizziness passed over him.

"Master!" Sostelle was at Roan's side, "They are coming—Master Hugh and many others—and with them are the Enforcers. Kotschai himself—"

"Good!" Roan snarled, showing his teeth. "I need something to fight! Terrans are no good—they just fall down and cry."

"Please, sir," the doctor said sharply. "You must stand still if I'm to administer my medicants—"

"Doctor," Sostelle whimpered. "Give him something to bring back his strength. See how he faints . . ."

"Ummm, yes, there are stimulants—dangerous, mind you, but—"

"Quickly! They come! I smell the odor of human hate!"

"The scent is thick here in this room," the doctor grunted. He sprayed something cold against the inner side of Roan's elbow.

"Master, you must flee now," Sostelle took his arm.

Roan shook him off. "Bring 'em on," he yelled. "I want to crush the life out of something! I want to pay them back for what they did to Desiranne!"

"But, Master, Kotschai is strong and cruel and skilled in inflicting pain—"

"So am I," Roan shouted. Ice seemed to be pumping through his veins. The ringing in his head had receded to a distant humming. Suddenly he was light, strong, his vision keen; only his heart seemed to pound too loudly.

"Oh, Master, there are many of them," Sostelle cried. "You cannot kill them all. And you are sick. Run— quickly—while I delay them—"

"Sostelle—go and find Askor and Sidis. Get them and bring them to the ship."

"If I do as you command, Master, will you make your escape? The door is there; it leads by a narrow way to the street below."

"All right." Roan let his breath out in a hiss between his teeth. "I'll run. Just get them and send them to me— and take care of this poor girl."

"I will, Master!"

"Good-by, Sostelle. You were the best man I found on

Terra." He opened the door and stepped through into dusty gloom.

The street was not like the others Roan had seen on Terra. It was unlit, with broken pavement through which rank weeds grew. He ran, and behind him dogs yelped and called. There was a gate ahead, a stark thing of metal bars and cruel spikes. Roan recognized it from Daryl's description. Beyond it he saw the ominous darkness, smelled the filth and decay of the Lower Town. Without pausing, he leaped up, pulled himself to the top, and dropped on the other side.

Roan didn't know how many hours later it was. He had run—for miles, it seemed—through dark, twisting, ancient streets, empty of people, with the police baying at his heels. Once they cornered him in a crumbling courtyard, and he killed two of them as they closed in, then leaped up, caught a low-hanging roof's edge, and fled away across the broken slates where they could not follow.

Now he was in a street crowded with faces that were like those remembered from evil dreams—Terrans, with scars, pockmarks, disease-ravaged faces, and starvation-wracked bodies. Women with eyes like the sockets in a skull held out bony hands, quavering pleas for bread and copper; children like darting brown spiders with oversized eyes and knobby knee joints trailed him, shouting in an incomprehensible language. A vast, obese man with one eye and an odor of old sickness trailed him for two blocks, until Roan turned, snatched up a foot-long knife from a display before a tumbledown stall, and gestured with it.

There were no dogs here, only the warped, crooked people and the evil stench and the glare of unshielded lights and the sense of age and decay and bottomless misery. Roan could feel the strength going from his legs; he stumbled often, and once he fell and rested awhile on hands and knees before he could stand again, shouting to scatter the ring of glittering-eyed people who had closed in on him.

He felt a burning, terrible thirst, and went toward a smoky, liquory, loud-smelling bar. Inside it was hot, steamy, solid with noise that sawed at him like ragged knives. He sank down at a wobbly table and a green-toothed female slid into the seat beside him and elbowed him invitingly. Roan made a growling sound and she went away.

A huge, big-bellied Man was standing before him.

"What'll it be?" he growled in very bad Terran.

"Water," Roan said in a dry whisper. "Cold water."

"Water costs too," the Man said. He went away and came back with a thick, greasy tumbler, half full of grayish liquid.

"I have no money," Roan said. "Take this. . . ." He fumbled the golden clasp from his garment, tossed it on the table.

The barman picked it up, eyed it suspiciously, bit into it.

"Hey," he grunted. "That's real gold!"

"I need . . . a place to rest," Roan said. The sickness was back in full force now, washing up around him like water rising in a sinking ship. "Get me a doctor . . ."

"You sick, huh?" the Man was leaning toward him,

leering; his eyes swelled until they were as big as saucers. Roan forced his eyes shut, then opened them, fighting to hold onto consciousness.

"I know . . . where there's more . . ." He could feel his mind cutting loose from his body again, ready to float away into a tossing sea of fever fantasies. But he couldn't—not yet. He tried to get to his feet, slammed back into the chair. The glass clashed against his teeth.

"Drink up, buddy," the thick voice was saying. "Yeah, I'll get a doc fer yuh. You know where there's more, eh?"

Roan gulped; the warmish, stagnant-smelling liquid gagged him. The Man brought more water, cold this time and in a slightly cleaner glass, as though he had wiped it on his shirt.

"Look, bo, you take it easy, huh? I'm Soup the Insider. Sure, I'll fix yuh up with a room. Swell room, bed and everything. Private. Only look around good before yuh close the door; yuh can never tell what yuh might be locking yourself in with." He guffawed.

"Got to have rest," Roan managed. "Be . . . all right in the morning. Find my friends. Hope Desiranne is all right. Then get out . . . this filthy place . . ."

"You just take it easy, bub. I'll fix yuh up good. Then we'll talk about where to get more of these little knick-knacks. And you don't talk to nobody else, see?"

"Get me . . ." Roan gave up trying to talk and felt the big man's arm under his, leading him away . . .

He fought his way up from a nightmare of heat and pursuit and blood and cruelty and opened his eyes to see a spotted glare panel set in a blotched ceiling, casting a sick light on a threadbare velvet wall. An ancient, withered Man stood beside the bed, blinking down at him with eyes that were polished stones set in pockets of inflamed tissue.

"Sick, ye are, true enough, lad. Ye've got every ailment I ever heard of and six or eight I haven't, you."

Roan tried to sit up; his head barely twitched, and pain shot through it like an ax blow. He lay, waiting for the throbbing to subside. His stomach ached as though it had been stamped by booted feet, and a sickness seemed to fester through his body like sewage bubbling in a cesspool.

"Sore, hey?" the oldster cackled. "Well, it might be; ye've tossed up every meal ye've et sine ye learned to guide spoon to lip, you."

Through the wall Roan heard an angry scream and a slap. "For half a copper I don't even smile!" a female voice shrilled, and a door slammed.

"Got to get out," Roan said. He tried to throw back the rough blanket, and the blackness swirled again.

". . . him something to make him talk," the thick voice of the big man was saying.

"Whatever ye say, Soup—but it'll kill him, it."

"Just so he talks first."

Roan felt a cold touch on his arm, a sharp stab of pain.

"Where's the loot, bo?" Soup's thick voice demanded.

"Ye'll have to wait a little hour, Soup. First he'll sleep a bit, eh, to get back the strength to talk, he."

"All right; but if you let him die before he spills, I'll squeeze that scrawny neck of yours."

"No fear o' that, Soup . . ."

Time passed, like a storm of yellow dust that choked and harried and would never cease. Sometimes voices stabbed at him, and he cursed them and struck out; and again he was running, falling, and far away on the floodlit stage the knife was cutting into Desiranne's white flesh, and he fought his way toward her, but always the sea of mad faces blocked his way until he screamed and clawed his way out of the dream—

". . . tell me now, before the blasted glutton comes back, he," a scratchy voice was saying. "Then I'll give ye more nice medicine, and ye'll sleep like a whelp at a bitch's teat."

"Get . . . away . . . me . . ." Roan managed. "Got . . . go . . ."

Something sharp and painful poked his throat.

"Ah, ye felt that, then, lad? Good. Now speak once more, tell old Yagg where the pretty treasures lie. Not in Upper City, eh? For the dogs would tear a man to bits if ever he ventured there. Where, eh? Is there some house that's been missed, some buried trove—"

There was a great smash, and a bull roar.

"So! Yuh'd cheat Soup, would yuh? I'll rip your head off—"

"Now, Soup—you misjudge me, you! I was just trying to find out—for you. No harm, what?"

There was a growl and a sound of two heavy blows and a squeal. Then Soup's wide fame loomed over Roan, breathing foul breath and flecks of spittle.

"All right, give, bo! You ain't going to die and not tell Soup, not after he give yuh a place to die in!"

Roan croaked, and his hand moved feebly. "Tell . . . you

. . . later . . ." The face faded and Soup's voice mumbled, drifted off into the insistent clamor of fever images.

Light again, and sounds.

". . . didn't you send for me sooner?" a tremulous voice was complaining. "That quack Yagg like to killed him, with his poisons! He's full of disease! Look at those sores—and see the swelling here. He'll die—mark my words, he's a goner—but we can do our best . . ."

"Yuh better . . ."

Stellaraire was standing by the bed, looking down at him. Her hair was burnt off and her face was scarred and blistered.

"Come with me, Roan," she said urgently. "We'll leave this 'zoo and go so far away they'll never find us. Come . . ." Then she was running away, and Henry Dread was shooting after her, the blaster bolts echoing along the steel corridor, echoing . . .

Henry Dread holstered the gun. "Damned Gooks," he said. "But you and I, Roan: we're different. We're Terries." His face changed, became small and petulant. "I trained her," Daryl said. "What higher art form can there be than destruction? And the destruction of one's self is its highest expression . . ." Deftly, Daryl fitted a noose about his neck, hoisted himself up. His face became black and twisted and terrible. "You see?" he said pleasantly. He went on talking, and many voices chimed in, and they cheered and the dust cleared away and Iron Robert held up his arms, melted off at the elbow.

"Iron Robert born to fight, Roan," he said. "Can't fight, now. Time for Iron Robert to die." He turned and the iron door opened and he walked into the furnace. The flames leaped out of the open door, scorching Roan's face. He turned away, and rough hands pulled him back.

"Yuh can't die yet," Soup's voice said. "Yuh been laying here for two days and two nights, yelling to yourself. Now talk, damn you, or I'll choke the life out of yuh!" Hands like leather-covered stone-crushers closed on Roan's throat—

There was a terrible growling, and then a scream and suddenly the hands were gone and there were awful sounds of tearing flesh and threshing limbs and then Sostelle's face was leaning over him, and there was blood on the dog's jaws.

"Master! I came as quickly as I could!"

Roan cried out, turned away from the phantom.

"Master! It's your dog, Sostelle! And I have another with me. Look, Master . . ."

A cool hand touched Roan's forehead. There was a faint odor of a delicate perfume, almost lost in the stench of the foul room. Roan opened his eyes. Desiranne looked down at him. Her face was pale and he could see the faint blue tracing of the veins in her eyelids. But she smiled at him.

"It's all right now, Roan," she said softly. "I am with you."

"Are you . . . real?"

"As real as any of us," she said.

"Your hand . . ."

She held it up, swathed in bandages. "I'm sorry I'm no longer perfect, Roan."

The dog doctor appeared, looking concerned. He

talked, but Roan couldn't hear him for the thunder in his ears. He lay and watched Desiranne's face until she faded and dissolved in mist, and then the mist itself faded into darkness shot with lights, and the lights twinkled like distant stars, and then went out, one by one . . .

Roan was sitting up in bed. His arm, resting on the patched blanket over his knees, was so thin that his fingers met around it, and it was scarred with half-healed pockmarks. Desiranne sat by the bed, feeding him thin soup. Her face was thin and paler than ever, and her hair was cut short, held back by a simple scarf of clean cloth. Roan lifted his hand, took the spoon.

"I can do that now," he said. The spoon trembled, spilling soup; but he went on, emptied the bowl.

"I'm stronger now," he said. "I'm getting up."

"Roan, please rest a few days longer."

"No. We've got to get to the ship now, Desiranne. How long has it been? Weeks? Maybe Askor and Sidis will be there, waiting for me. We'll leave this poisoned world and never come back." He had thrown back the blanket and put his feet down on the floor. His legs were so thin that a choked laugh grunted from him.

"I look like old Targ," he said. With Desiranne's hand under his arm, he stood, feeling his senses fade in vertigo from the effort. He took a step and fell, and Desiranne cried out and then Sostelle was there, helping him back into the rags of the cot.

It was a week later. Roan sat in a chair by the window, looking out at the decayed roofs and tottering walls of

Lower Town. There was a sickly plant in a clay pot on the windowsill, and a fresh breeze brought odors of spring-time and corruption.

Sostelle came in, carrying a patched cloak.

"This is all I could get, Master."

"I told you never to call me 'Master' again," Roan snapped. "My name is Roan."

"Yes . . . Roan. Here is a garment. But please—don't go. Not yet. The dogs are about again today—"

Roan stood, ignoring the dizziness. "We're going today. Askor and Sidis are probably waiting for me, wondering what happened. They probably think I'm dead." His fingers fumbled with the chipped buttons.

"Yes, Mas— Roan." The dog helped him with the cloak. It was a faded blue, of a rough weave that scratched Roan's pale skin. Desiranne appeared at the door.

"Roan—you're so weak . . ."

"I'm all right." He forced himself to smile gently at her, to walk without staggering across to her. "It's not far," he said. "We can do it."

They went down patched stairs, ignoring the eyes that stared from half-concealment at the dog who had torn the throat out of the formidable Soup, and the pale Upper woman, and the sick madman. Out in the sun-bleached time-eroded street other faces, weather-burned and life-scarred, watched as they passed; and when one of the watchers ventured too close, Sostelle bared his fangs and they drew back.

After half an hour, Roan and his escort stopped to rest at a dry fountain with broken carvings of Men with the tails of fish. Roan looked at them, and wondered on what world they lived. He and Desiranne sat on the carved stone lip of the monument, feeling the warmth of the sun, while Sostelle paced up and down, his human-like hands hooked in his leather belt. When Roan had rested, they went on.

It was late afternoon when they reached the raised avenue that ran past the port and on to the bright towers of Upper City. Roan shaded his eyes, staring past the orderly trees and the banked flowers in the distance.

"Where is it?" he said. "I don't see the ship." There was a new sick feeling in him now, not the fever of pain and infection, but the hollow sickness of terrible loss. He scrambled up the embankment, led the way along under the gentle trees. He could see parked flyers, the flash of color of moving chariots, the tiny figures of dogs at work; but *Hell's Whore* was gone.

"Perhaps the people, sir," Sostelle said. "Master Daryl and the others; they may have moved her . . ."

"They couldn't have," Roan said in a voice that almost broke. "Only Askor and Sidis knew how to open her ports—how to lift her."

"Roan—we must go back now." Desiranne's hand was on his arm. He touched the thin fingers, looking at Sostelle.

"You knew," he said.

"Roan—I could not be sure—and how could I have told you . . .?"

"It's all right." Roan tried desperately to hold his voice firm. "At least they got away. I knew those pansies couldn't hold them."

"Perhaps one day they'll come back, Roan," Sostelle said. "Perhaps—"

"No. They're gone, back to where they belong—out there." Roan tilted his head back, looking up into the bottomless blue of the deep sky. "I sent them away myself," he said. "I betrayed them to their enemies and then turned my back on them. There's nothing for them to come back for."

CHAPTER ✳ TWENTY-FOUR

Roan sat with Desiranne and Sostelle at a small table in the bar that Soup the Insider had once owned. It was evening and the room was filled with yellow light and the last of the day's heat. In one corner, a Man with magic fingers caressed a stringed instrument that mourned for love and courage and other forgotten things. A one-eyed Man came in silently from the street, crossed to their table.

"I seen another patrol," he said accusingly. "You and yer woman and yer dog better pull out tonight."

Roan looked at him with an expression that was the absence of all expression.

"Yer calling 'em down on us," the Man said, his lips twisting with the hates that ate at him like crabs. "When the dogs get on a man's trail, they don't never quit. And long's they're in the Town, ain't nobody safe."

"They're not looking for me," Roan said. "Not after a year. I'm not that important."

"A year—ten years. It's all the same to dogs. They ain't like a man. They're trained to hunt—and that's what they're doing."

"He's right, Roan," Sostelle said. "Kotschai will never forget the man who shamed him by escaping him. Perhaps we'd best leave now, and find another place—"

"I'm not leaving," Roan said. "If they want me, let them find me." He looked at the one-eyed Man. "If you fought them—if we all fought them—we could wipe them out. There are only a few hundred of them. Then you could leave this pesthole. You could spread out into the countryside, start new villages—"

The Man shook his head. "You was lucky," he said. "You got clear of 'em. But that was because you was in Upper Town, where they wasn't expecting no trouble. When they come down here, they come in packs, with nerve guns and organization. Nobody's going to jump that kind of force. And neither are you." He straightened, showing his teeth. "You're going to get out, like I said—or you ain't going to live long."

Roan laughed at him. "Is that a threat? Is being dead worse than living in this ghetto?"

"You're going to find out pretty soon—you and your . . . friends." He swaggered away.

"Roan," Sostelle started. "We could leave by night, make our way to—"

"I'm going out." Roan stood. "I need fresh air."

"Roan—you're challenging the dogs—and the Men as well . . . ?"

Desiranne caught at his hand. "They'll see us . . ."

Roan pushed her gently back. "Not us. Just me. Let *them* beware."

"I'm going with you."

"Stay here with Sostelle," Roan said flatly. "I've hidden from them for a year. That's long enough."

As he walked away, he heard Sostelle say: "Let him go, Mistress. A Man like Roan cannot live forever as a hunted slave."

The rumor ran ahead of Roan. People stared, made mystical signs, then darted out to follow as he strode along, taking the center of the hut- and garbage-choked street. Others slipped away into decay-slimed alleyways to spread the word. The last of sunset faded and the few automatic polyarcs that still worked came on, shedding their tarnished brilliance on broken walls, cracked facades, and Roan, walking the night with his shadow striding ahead.

"They're close," someone called to Roan from a doorway. "Better run quick, Mister Fancy-talk!"

He was in a wide avenue with a center strip of hard-packed dirt where flowers had once grown. At the far end was the wide colonnaded front of a building the roof of which had fallen in. It gleamed a ghostly white in the glare from a tall pole-mounted light. Tall weeds poked up among marble slabs there, and rude huts grew like toadstools in the shadows of the chipped pediments.

A dog appeared on the broken steps, standing tall, curve-shouldered, cringe-legged, cruel-fanged, wearing the straps and sparkling medallions of the police. Roan walked toward him, and the trailing crowd fell back.

"Stop there, red-haired Man!" the dog yelped. He drew the curiously shaped gun strapped under his foreleg and pointed it at Roan. "You're under arrest."

"Run," Roan said in a strange, flat voice. "Run, or I'll kill you."

"What? Kill me? You're a fool, Red-hair. I have a gun—"

Roan broke into a run straight toward the dog and the animal crouched and fired and in the sudden shock of pain Roan felt his legs knot and cramp and he fell. The dog stalked up to him, waving back the gathering crowd.

It's only pain, Roan told himself. He rested on hands and knees. *Pain is nothing; dying without feeling his throat under your hands is the true agony . . .*

He rose to his feet in a sudden movement, and the police dog whirled, reaching for the gun, but Roan's swing caught him below his cropped ear, sent him spinning. With a growl, the dog scrambled to all fours, and Roan's foot met him under the jaw with a solid impact and the shaved body rolled aside and lay still. Roan stooped, picked up the gun, as a mutter of alarm swept across the mob.

"You see?" Roan shouted. "They're dogs—nothing more!"

"Now they'll kill you for sure!" a gaunt woman yelled. "Serve you right, too, you trouble-bringer!"

"Here they come!" another voice screeched. Two more dogs had appeared from the ruin, coming on at a relentless lope. Roan took aim and shot one; it fell, yelping and kicking out, and the other veered aside and dashed for safety. The crowd shouted now.

"But these are just ordinary dogs," the one-eyed Man had come up close to Roan. "Wait until you meet Kotschai, face to face. Then you'll learn the taste of honest fear!"

"They say he's three hundred years old," a short, clay-faced Man said. "His Masters have given him their magic medicine to make him live long, and with every passing year he's grown more wise and evil. My gran'fer remembered him—"

"He's just a dog," Roan shouted. "And you're Men!"

Across the square a squad of uniformed dogs burst into view, fanned out, halted, facing the crowd, which recoiled, leaving Roan to stand alone. Then an avenue opened through the police and an immense dog paced through. In silence he advanced across the plaza, skirted the injured dog, which was crawling painfully, whimpering. A dozen feet from Roan, he halted.

"Who dares defy Kotschai the Punisher?" he growled. He was taller than Roan, massive-bodied, with the thick, sinewy forelegs of a tiger and jaws like a timber wolf. His body had been shaved except for a ruff around the neck and his pinkish-gray hide was a maze of scars. He was dressed in straps and bangles of shiny metal decorated with enamel, and there was a harness studded with spikes of brass across his chest, and above his yellow eyes was a brass horn that seemed to be set in the bone of his brute-flat skull. His tail had been broken and badly set, and it swung nervously, as though it hurt all the time.

"How does a dog dare to challenge a Man?" Roan demanded.

"It is the order of my master." The wicked jaws grinned and a pink tongue licked black gums.

"Can you fight all of us?" Roan motioned toward the silent mob.

"They do not count," Kotschai said. "Only you. I see you have a gun, too. But my dogs have more."

"You and I don't need guns," Roan said. "We have hands and teeth for fighting."

Kotschai looked at Roan with his small, red-circled eyes. He lifted his muzzle and sniffed the air.

"Yes," the dog said. "I smell the odor of human bloodlust." He seemed to shiver. "It is not a scent I love, Master."

"Then you'd better learn how to crouch on all fours and heel on command, dog," Roan said loudly, so that everyone could hear.

"I have never learned such lessons, Master," Kotschai said.

"You haven't had a proper teacher, dog."

"That may be true." Kotschai motioned his dogs back. He unbuckled his gun harness, threw it aside.

"It is said that once Man was Terra's most deadly predator," he said. "I have wondered long how it was that the pretty creatures I call Master made the dogs their slaves. Perhaps in you I see the answer."

"Perhaps in me you see your death."

Kotschai nodded. "Perhaps. And now I must punish you, Master."

Roan tossed the gun to a Man, reached to his shoulder, ripped loose the clasp that held his garment, wrapped the ragged cloth around his left forearm.

"Now I'll instruct you in courtesy, dog," he said, and Kotschai snarled and charged.

Roan's padded arm struck into the open jaws as the

dog's bristly body slammed against him. He stumbled back, twisting aside from the horn that raked his jaw, locked his free arm around the dog's shoulders, keeping his face above the vicious chest spikes, and together Man and dog fell. Roan locked his legs around the heavy torso, and Kotschai snarled, raking with all four limbs as Roan's locked arms and legs crushed, crushed—

With a frantic effort, the dog wrenched his jaws half free of Roan's strangling forearm, lunged for a better grip with his teeth, and Roan struck with his fist, kicked free, hurled the animal from him. Kotschai scrambled to his feet, jaws agape, the stubble along his spine erect. Roan faced him, blood on his arm, teeth bared in an ancient defiance. All around, dogs and Men stood silent, gaping at the spectacle of Man pitted against beast.

The dog charged again, and Roan slipped aside, dropped on the broad back, locked ankles under the dog's belly, wrapped his arms around the thick neck, pressing his face close to the mightily muscled shoulder. Kotschai went down, rolled, and Roan held on, throttling the breath in the dog's throat. Kotschai reared high, tottering under the weight of the Man on his back, throwing his horned head from side to side, and Roan's grip loosened—

At once, the dog twisted, the great jaws snapping a hair's breadth from Roan's unprotected shoulder. Roan doubled his fist, struck a smashing blow across the dog's face, but the jaws snapped again, and this time they met hide and muscle. Roan found a grip on the corded throat, forcing the fanged head back, and he felt the locked teeth tear his flesh . . . .

The garment wrapping Roan's arm had slipped down.

It flapped in the dog's face, and the animal snapped at it, and in the instant's diversion, Roan ripped free. But even as he retreated a step the dog was on him, and again the rag-snarled fist was thrust into the yawning jaws, and again Roan fell, and now Kotschai was above him, snarling and worrying the impeding rag, struggling to find a clear thrust at Roan's throat, while Roan fought to hold the fighting body close . . .

A minute that was an eternity passed, while the two antagonists contended, chest to chest, their agonized breathing the only sound in all the wide plaza. And slowly the jaws grew closer, as Roan's grip loosened. He looked into the yellow eyes, and felt the hot, inhuman ferocity that burned an inch from his face now. And then he saw another face, above and behind that of the dog—the features set and pale, the one eye glaring—

There was a shock, and the pressure was gone. Kotschai kicked convulsively, growling; the growl became a howl, choked off. Roan thrust the two-hundred-pound body from him, got to his knees, then to his feet. Blood was running hot across his chest from the wound in his shoulder, and his breath was raw in his throat. He was aware of the Man standing before him, looking half triumphant, half afraid, and of a roar from the mob of humans, and of the dogs starting forward uncertainly, guns ready. Roan shook out his torn and bloody tunic, pulled it on.

"Thanks," Roan said, then yelled and charged the advancing dogs. He felt the wash of fire as the field of a nerve gun touched him, and then he was on the nearest dog, feeling the solid smash of his fists on hide, and then the shouting was all about him and the ragged horde leaped past him, howling out their long-pent fury. The dogs fought bravely, but as quickly as one Man fell another leaped his body to grapple his antagonist. The police had fallen back almost to the broken marble steps of the ruined building before whistles and barkings sounded from a sideway, and now more dogs arrived, long pink tongues hanging out, stub tails whipping, firing as they came; and still more Men scrambled to join the fight which had spread all across the square now.

The one-eyed Man was beside Roan. His face was bleeding from a dog bite but his single eye gleamed with life.

"I killed three of 'em!" he yelled. "Got one by the throat and choked him till he died!" He ran on.

The dogs had formed a tight phalanx, guns aimed outward to sweep the crowd, and they retreated slowly as Men rushed at them, shouting curses, leaping the bodies of the fallen, striking out with clubs, knives, fists. Now the dogs reached a narrow way, and more Men fell as the enemy retreated, leaving a trail of casualties behind them. They reached a gate and slipped through it and it clanged behind them. The Men tried to climb it, but the dogs shot them down, and they fell, all but one who hung, impaled on spearpoints.

But a wild yell was echoing along the street, across the plaza. Men and women danced, screaming their triumph. The one-eyed Man was back, seizing Roan's arm, pumping his hand.

"We beat 'em!" he was shouting at the top of his lungs.

"They'll be back!" Roan shouted. "We'll have to collect the weapons, set up a defensive position . . ."

No one was listening. Roan turned to another Man as One-eye darted away, tried to explain that the dogs had retired in good order for tactical reasons, that they would renew the assault as soon as reinforcements arrived with heavy weapons.

It was useless. The Lowers capered, all yelling at once.

Something made Roan look upward. A point of brilliant light sparkled and winked against the night sky, and Roan felt the clutch of a ghostly hand at his heart.

"A ship . . ." he said aloud, feeling his voice choke.

"Roan!"

He whirled. Sostelle was there, unruffled by the frenzy all about: "The Lady Desiranne commanded me to come . . ."

Roan clutched at him. "It's a ship!" he said hoarsely, pointing.

"Yes, Roan. We saw it from the rooftop. Oh, Roan—is it—your ship . . . ?"

A great searchlight lanced out from the port area; the finger of chalky bluish light glared on low clouds, found the ship, glinted on its side.

"No," Roan said, and the ghostly hand gripped even tighter. "It's not my ship. It's a big one—a dreadnought of the line. It's Trishinist and his plunderers of the Imperial Terran Navy."

Roan and Sostelle watched from the shelter of the causeway as the mile-long vessel suspended itself five miles over the city, like an elongated moon ablaze with lights from stem to stern. Its pressor beams were columns of pale fire bearing on smoking pits spaced at hundred yard intervals across the flower beds and glassy pavement of the landing ramps. Three smaller shapes of light had detached themselves from the mother vessel, dropping quickly toward the earth.

"They're landing about three hundred men," Roan said. "How many fighting dogs are there?"

"I don't know, Roan. Perhaps as many, perhaps more—but look there—"

From the Upper City, a flock of flyers had appeared, moving swiftly toward the port. Roan could see the crossed bones insignia of the police blazoned on the sides of the grim, gray machines. The landing craft from the ITN battleship were settling to the broad pavement now; ports cycled open; a cascade of men poured out of each, formed up in ragged columns. The police flyers closed ranks, hurtling to the attack at low altitude. Something sparkled from the prow of the first of the landing craft in line, and the lead flyer exploded into arcing fragments with a flash that lit the landscape for two miles around in dusty orange light. The other police vessels scattered, screaming away at flank speed, hugging the ground, but not before an aerial torpedo got away to burst near an ITN column, sending half a dozen men sprawling.

"The dogs are brave enough," Roan said. "But they don't know how to fight a force like Trishinist's. The ship won't fire; he'll want the city intact to loot; but the ground party will walk through them to take the city, and then they'll come on to Lower Town, and from here they'll go on to the next city, and when they're finished there'll be nothing left but ashes."

"Perhaps if the Lowers joined with the dogs—"

"No use. They're just a mob, drunk on a taste of victory."

"Why, Roan?" Sostelle whined. "What do these men seek here? Surely in the wide skies there must be worlds enough for all creatures . . ."

"They destroy for the love of it—like Daryl and his friends. Poor Terra. Her last, forlorn hope is gone now."

The landing force had advanced across the ramp to the reception buildings; a detachment broke off, and Roan saw the wink of guns as they smashed their way into the glass-walled lounge where he had met Daryl that first day, so long ago. The dogs, meanwhile, had grounded their flyers and were advancing in open order across a wide park to intercept the invaders at the causeway.

"Terra's own—her lost, wandering sons—returned to deal her her deathblow," Sostelle whispered. "In a sad world, this is the crowning sadness."

Roan was studying the advancing ITN column. Even from the distance of half a mile he could make out the hulking forms, the shambling gaits of the mongrel humans in the blue and silver uniforms. Two large men marched at the head of the column, a smaller figure between them.

Sostelle raised his nose and sniffed.

"Look there!" Roan said. "Can you see . . . ?"

"My eyes are not as keen as those of a Man, Roan; but—"

Roan was on his feet. His heart beat in his throat,

almost choking him. Then he was running, springing across a stretch of open grass, leaping up the embankment to the causeway. He heard Sostelle at his side.

"Roan—you'll be killed! Both sides will fire their guns at you—"

But Roan ran on toward the approaching ITN detachment. The leader—a huge figure in ill-fitting blues—held up a hand, halted the column, brought a short-barreled power gun around . . .

Then he threw it aside.

"Roan! Chief!" he bellowed.

"Askor! And Sidis!"

They came together and Roan seized the half-breeds' broad shoulders in a wild embrace, shouting, while Askor grinned so widely that every one of his twenty-eight teeth showed.

"Chief, we knew we'd find you," he roared out. Sidis was looming then, his steel teeth glittering in the polyarc light.

"Askor and me come in here ready to blow this dump apart if we didn't find you OK." He clapped Roan on the back with his steel hook, and Roan seized him, danced him around, while the troops standing by at the ready gaped and grinned.

"I told that lunkhead you was OK." Askor gripped Roan's arm and pounded his back with a great, horny hand.

"Gee, Boss, you look different," Sidis said. "Your hair's got gray and you got lines in your face . . . and you ain't been eating good, neither. But to the Nine Hells with it! We're together!"

Roan laughed and listened to both men talk at once, and then other crewmen were crowding forward, and Roan caught a glimpse of a once-familiar face, now thin and dirty and streaked with tears. It was Trishinist, and there was an iron collar around his neck to which a length of heavy chain was welded.

"I knew you big plug-uglies would come back," Roan said. Sostelle was by his side, his tail wagging. "Didn't I, Sostelle?" Roan demanded, blinking back an annoying film in his eyes.

"Yes, Roan," the dog said. "You knew."

"Chief, I guess maybe we better take a few minutes to straighten out these fellows coming out from the city," Askor said. The dogs were marching across the causeway now, four abreast, advancing in defense of their masters.

"Sostelle—can't you stop them?" Roan asked.

"No," the dog said, almost proudly. "The dogs will fight."

Then Askor was away, bawling orders, and Roan stood with Sidis under a tree as delicate as a lilac as the two columns met in fire and dust.

CHAPTER ✸ TWENTY-FIVE

It was an hour after dawn; in a half-shattered house at the edge of the city, the leader of the surviving dogs stood before Roan and Askor. His fur was singed and there was blood clotted at the side of his head, but he stood straight.

"My animals are overwhelmed, Masters," he said. "Only twenty-three survive, and all of those are injured. We can no longer fight."

"You put up a good scrap," Askor said approvingly. "You knocked off a couple dozen ITN's and even nailed one or two of my own boys."

"I request one hour's time to permit my dogs to clean themselves and polish their brasses before we are put to death," the dog said. "They wish to meet their end in proper fashion, and not as masterless curs."

"Huh? Who said anything about killing you? You lost, we won, that's the breaks of the game."

"But . . . now your soldiers will loot the Upper City, which we were sworn to protect."

"Forget it. You tried. Now I got other plans for you dogs. What would you say to joining up?"

"Joining . . . ?"

"The ITN," Askor explained. "I need good fighters . . ." He looked at Roan. "Sorry, Chief. I guess this last year I kind of got a habit of talking like it was *my* show."

"It is," Roan said. "You've earned it."

"If we hadn't of found *Archaeopteryx* and our old crew cruising around near Alpha Four looking for us, we never would of made it. But what about signing up the dogs, Chief? You like the idea OK?"

"Sure; they're Terrans too, aren't they?"

The dog's eyes gleamed. He straightened his back even more. "Sirs! My dogs and I accept your offer! We will fight well for Terra, sirs!" He saluted and limped away.

Sidis came up. "Boss, uh, the boys are kind of looking around a little in the city, if that's OK. They been a long time in space, and, uh . . ."

"No unnecessary killing or destruction," Roan said. "I leave it to them to decide what's necessary."

"Them poor Terries in the dump town," Askor said. "They look worse than the Geeks back in that place, Tambool, Chief. We give 'em some food and blasted down the gates so's they could help themselves to some of the stuff that's laying around in the fancy part of town. I got a idea we could sign on a few of them, too, after the fun's over."

"Yeah, Boss," Sidis said eagerly. "With a couple hundred of Trishinist's Gooks, and the dogs, and now these Terries, we got a nice-sized little navy shaping up. We could maybe even man two ships. What you got in mind for our next cruise?"

Roan shook his head. "I'm staying on Terra," he said.

Askor and Sidis stared at him.

"This world needs every Man it can get," Roan said. "The old equilibrium's been shattered—and if I leave now, leave them to their own devices—they'll die. The Lowers outnumber the Uppers a hundred to one—but they don't know how to run a world. And if the automatic machinery isn't properly tended, they'll all starve. They'll starve soon, anyway, when the system breaks down completely. But I can help. I have to try."

Askor nodded. "Yeah . . . from what I saw, there ain't much hope for these Terries on their own."

"There's still life in the old world," Roan said. "Now that the blockade is broken, the word will spread; they'll be coming, to get in on the spoils. But with a little time and luck, I can organize her defenses—enough to give her a chance."

Askor frowned. "Defenses? What about *Trixie*? There ain't many tubs in space can take her on."

"I can't ask you to stay here," Roan said. "For me, it's different. I have a wife now. And in a few months I'll have a son . . ."

Askor and Sidis looked at each other.

"Uh . . . you know, Boss, it's a funny thing," Sidis said. "I feel at home here myself." He waved a thick-fingered hand. "The air smells right, the sunlight, the trees—all that kind of stuff. I been thinking—"

"Uh, Chief," Askor broke in. "I'll be back . . ."

Roan looked after him. "I guess I'm a great disappointment to him: Married, settled down, no more raiding the spaceways . . ."

"It ain't that, Boss." Sidis snapped the top off a tall wine bottle and occupied himself with swallowing. A big Gook named Gungle appeared at the door, grinned across at Roan.

"Hey, Cap'n, what you want to do with this Terry captain we got here? Askor said bring him along from Alpha for you to roast over a slow fire if you wanted to." He tugged the chain in his hand and Trishinist stumbled into the room.

"Roan—dear lad," he babbled. "If you've a heart, surely you'll take a moment now to instruct these animals to release me—"

Gungle jerked the chain. "Talks funny, don't he, Cap'n?"

"Maybe we should find a nice deep hole to put him in," Roan said thoughtfully, studying the former officer. "But somehow the idea bores me. You may as well just shoot him."

"Roan—no! I'm far too valuable to you!"

"He's all the time talking about something he knows, Cap'n," Gungle explained. "Said you wouldn't never find out, if we was to blow a hole in him."

"Yes, Roan," Trishinist gasped. "Only set me free—with a stout vessel, of course—one of the flagship's lifeboats will serve nicely—and an adequate supply of provisions—and perhaps just a few small ingots of Terran gold to help me make a new start—and I'll tell you something that will astonish you!"

"Go ahead," Roan said.

"But first, of course, your promise—"

Gungle gave the chain a sharp tug. "Tell it," he growled.

Trishinist bleated. "Your word, Roan—"

"I guess I might as well go ahead and plug him, Cap'n," Gungle said apologetically, tugging at his pistol. "I shun't of bothered you." He turned on the cowering man.

"I'll speak," he bleated. "And throw myself on your mercy, Roan. I have faith in your sense of honor, dear lad—"

Roan yawned.

"You're a Terran!" Trishinist screeched. "Yes, of the Pure Strain—the ancient strain! There was a ship—oh, old, old, it was, Roan! Hulled in Deep Space by a rock half as big as a lifeboat, and drifting through space and centuries—until I found it. There was the body of a Man—frozen in an instant as the rock opened her decks to space. They took from his body the frozen germ cells, and at my order—*my* order, Roan! our finest technicians thawed them, and induced maturation! And then—but the rest you know . . ." He stared at Roan, his mouth hanging open, his eyes pleading.

"His name was Admiral Stuart Murdoch," Roan said. "He died sixteen thousand years ago."

"Then—you knew . . ." Trishinist's face went gray; he sagged.

"I didn't know the whole story. Tell me, Trishinist, if I let you go, will you settle down here on Terra and live a useful life?"

"Live? Life?" The former captain straightened. "Roan, I'll be a model citizen, I swear it. Oh, I'm tired, tired! of killing, and struggle, and hate! I want to rest now. I'll till a plot of soil—Terran soil—and marry a Terran woman, raise a family. I want . . . I want to be loved . . ."

"Cripes," Gungle said.

"Get out," Roan said. "And if you betray me, I'll find you, wherever you are."

"Gee, Cap'n," Gungle said disgustedly. He dropped the chain and Trishinist caught it up, darted from the room. Roan heard a yell, then the scamper of retreating feet. Askor came in, grinning.

"I figured you'd let him go, Chief. And, uh, now I got something to show you . . ." He turned, beckoned. A girl appeared in the doorway, smiling shyly. She was small, pretty, obviously Terran. She was dressed in soft-colored garments from the Gallian World, and she held a baby in her arms. Askor went to her, put a protective hand on her shoulder, led her to Roan. A fat, three-month-old face looked up at Roan, suddenly smiled a wide, half-familiar smile.

"My kid," Askor said proudly.

Roan blinked.

"Me and Cyrillia," Askor went on, grinning. "I, uh, kind of took her along when me and Sidis left here, Chief. We was in kind of a hurry, but I seen her, and . . . you know . . ."

"You took her with you?" Roan took the baby. He was solid, heavy, with the round face of a Minid and the pert nose of his mother. "Then—this means—"

"Yeah," Askor said. "I guess that proves even a Gook's got a little Earthblood, huh? I want to stay here, Chief. With you. And the rest of the boys too. You need us here. Terra needs us to start her new Navy—and ever since Roan was born—" Askor blushed.

"We named him for you, sir," Cyrillia said in a soft voice.

"Hell's hull, Chief—all the boys are tired of this ship-board life. They all want to get a nice Terry gal and settle down. We'll keep *Trixie* shipshape—we'll cruise her enough to train the green hands and keep the crew in trim . . ."

"There are plenty of ships," Roan said, through a smile that felt as large and silly as Askor's. "We can crew fifty of them if we want to, and stand off anybody that comes looking for easy pickings. And meanwhile, we'll be building, and learning, and growing. Give us a few hundred years—"

"Just give me now, Boss," Askor said, taking the baby and holding him in his huge hands. "That's more than any Gook ever had a right to hope for."

It was evening. Roan sat with Desiranne's hand in his on a grassy hillside above the city. Cyrillia, Askor, Sidis, and Sostelle were grouped around them. Below, fires winked and glimmered in a dozen places across the dark city. Faint sounds of raucous laughter, shouts, the unmelodic harmonies of drunken looters rose like the murmur of surf.

"Roan," Sostelle said. "Shouldn't you put a stop to the destruction—"

"No!" Desiranne spoke almost fiercely. "Let them destroy it! It's false, hateful, full of hideous memories! Let it all be burned clean—and then we can start new. We still have the soil and the sun; we still have Terra!"

"But the museums—the ancient things, the treasures of Terran art . . ."

"No," Cyrillia said. "The First Era of Man has ended. Let it be forgotten."

"But thirty thousand years of history; all Terra's past . . ."

"Terra's past is lost forever," Roan said. "Now she has only the future."

✳ PART II ✳
THE
NISS STORIES

BY
KEITH LAUMER

Editor's note: *The Niss appear in three other stories written by Laumer, in addition to the novel* Earthblood. *Interestingly, the four treatments of the Niss are all different. In the novel, they do not even physically resemble the Niss portrayed in the three stories below, nor is there any logic by which one story might lead to the next. The only thing the Niss really have in common, in all four stories, is that they are the great alien threat to the human race. It is as if Laumer chose to write four variations on the same theme.*

THE LONG REMEMBERED THUNDER

❋ 1 ❋

In his room at the Elsby Commercial Hotel, Tremaine opened his luggage and took out a small tool kit, used a screwdriver to remove the bottom cover plate from the telephone. He inserted a tiny aluminum cylinder, crimped wires and replaced the cover. Then he dialed a long-distance Washington number and waited half a minute for the connection.

"Fred, Tremaine here. Put the buzzer on." A thin hum sounded on the wire as the scrambler went into operation.

"Okay, can you read me all right? I'm set up in Elsby. Grammond's boys are supposed to keep me informed. Meanwhile, I'm not sitting in this damned room crouched over a dial. I'll be out and around for the rest of the afternoon."

"I want to see results," the thin voice came back over the filtered hum of the jamming device. "You spent a week with Grammond—I can't wait another. I don't mind telling you certain quarters are pressing me."

"Fred, when will you learn to sit on your news breaks until you've got some answers to go with the questions?"

"I'm an appointive official," Fred said sharply. "But never mind that. This fellow Margrave—General Margrave, Project Officer for the hyperwave program— he's been on my neck day and night. I can't say I blame him. An unauthorized transmitter interfering with a Top Secret project, progress slowing to a halt, and this Bureau—"

"Look, Fred. I was happy in the lab. Headaches, nightmares and all. Hyperwave is my baby, remember? You elected me to be a leg-man; now let me do it my way."

"I felt a technical man might succeed where a trained investigator could be misled. And since it seems to be pinpointed in your home area—"

"You don't have to justify yourself. Just don't hold out on me. I sometimes wonder if I've seen the complete files on this—"

"You've seen all the files! Now I want answers, not questions! I'm warning you, Tremaine. Get that transmitter. I need someone to hang!"

Tremaine left the hotel, walked two blocks west along Commerce Street and turned in at a yellow brick building with the words ELSBY MUNICIPAL POLICE cut in the stone lintel above the door. Inside, a heavy man with a creased face and thick gray hair looked up from behind an ancient Underwood. He studied Tremaine, shifted a toothpick to the opposite corner of his mouth.

"Don't I know you, mister?" he said. His soft voice carried a note of authority.

Tremaine took off his hat. "Sure you do, Jess. It's been a while, though."

The policeman got to his feet. "Jimmy," he said, "Jimmy Tremaine." He came to the counter and put out his hand. "How are you, Jimmy? What brings you back to the boondocks?"

"Let's go somewhere and sit down, Jess."

In a back room Tremaine said, "To everybody but you this is just a visit to the old home town. Between us, there's more."

Jess nodded. "I heard you were with the guv'ment."

"It won't take long to tell; we don't know much yet." Tremaine covered the discovery of the powerful unidentified interference on the high-security hyperwave band, the discovery that each transmission produced not one but a pattern of "fixes" on the point of origin. He passed a sheet of paper across the table. It showed a set of concentric circles, overlapped by a similar group of rings.

"I think what we're getting is an echo effect from each of these points of intersection. The rings themselves represent the diffraction pattern—"

"Hold it, Jimmy. To me it just looks like a beer ad. I'll take your word for it."

"The point is this, Jess: we think we've got it narrowed down to this section. I'm not sure of a damn thing, but I think that transmitter's near here. Now, have you got any ideas?"

"That's a tough one, Jimmy. This is where I should come up with the news that Old Man Whatchamacallit's got an attic full of gear he says is a time machine. Trouble is, folks around here haven't even taken to TV. They figure we should be content with radio, like the Lord intended."

"I didn't expect any easy answers, Jess. But I was hoping maybe you had something . . ."

"Course," said Jess, "there's always Mr. Bram . . ."

"Mr. Bram," repeated Tremaine. "Is he still around? I remember him as a hundred years old when I was a kid."

"Still just the same, Jimmy. Comes in town maybe once a week, buys his groceries and hikes back out to his place by the river."

"Well, what about him?"

"Nothing. But he's the town's mystery man. You know that. A little touched in the head."

"There were a lot of funny stories about him, I remember," Tremaine said. "I always liked him. One time he tried to teach me something; I've forgotten what. Wanted me to come out to his place and he'd teach me. I never did go. We kids used to play in the caves near his place, and sometimes he gave us apples."

"I've never seen any harm in Bram," said Jess. "But you know how this town is about foreigners, especially when they're a mite addled. Bram has blue eyes and blond hair—or did before it turned white—and he talks just like everybody else. From a distance he seems just like an ordinary American. But up close, you feel it. He's foreign, all right. But we never did know where he came from."

"How long's he lived here in Elsby?"

"Beats me, Jimmy. You remember old Aunt Tress,

used to know all about ancestors and such as that? She couldn't remember about Mr. Bram. She was kind of senile, I guess. She used to say he'd lived in that same old place out on the Concord road when she was a girl. Well, she died five years ago . . . in her seventies. He still walks in town every Wednesday . . . or he did up till yesterday, anyway."

"Oh?" Tremaine stubbed out his cigarette, lit another. "What happened then?"

"You remember Soup Gaskin? He's got a boy, name of Hull. He's Soup all over again."

"I remember Soup," Tremaine said. "He and his bunch used to come in the drug store where I worked and perch on the stools and kid around with me, and Mr. Hempleman would watch them from over back of the prescription counter and look nervous. They used to raise Cain in the other drug store . . ."

"Soup's been in the pen since then. His boy Hull's the same kind. Him and a bunch of his pals went out to Bram's place one night and set it on fire."

"What was the idea of that?"

"Dunno. Just meanness, I reckon. Not much damage done. A car was passing by and called it in. I had the whole caboodle locked up here for six hours. Then the sob sisters went to work: poor little tyke routine, high spirits, you know the line. All of 'em but Hull are back in the streets playin' with matches by now. I'm waiting for the day they'll make jail age."

"Why Bram?" Tremaine persisted. "As far as I know, he never had any dealings to speak of with anybody here in town."

"Oh hoh, you're a little young, Jimmy," Jess chuckled. "You never knew about Mr. Bram—the young Mr. Bram—and Linda Carroll."

Tremaine shook his head.

"Old Miss Carroll. School teacher here for years; guess she was retired by the time you were playing hookey. But her dad had money, and in her day she was a beauty. Too good for the fellers in these parts. I remember her ridin' by in a high-wheeled shay, when I was just a nipper. Sitting up proud and tall, with that red hair piled up high. I used to think she was some kind of princess . . ."

"What about her and Bram? A romance?"

Jess rocked his chair back on two legs, looked at the ceiling, frowning. "This would ha' been about nineteen-oh-one. I was no more'n eight years old. Miss Linda was maybe in her twenties—and that made her an old maid, in those times. The word got out she was setting her cap for Bram. He was a good-looking young feller then, over six foot, of course, broad backed, curly yellow hair—and a stranger to boot. Like I said, Linda Carroll wanted nothin' to do with the local bucks. There was a big shindy planned. Now, you know Bram was funny about any kind of socializing; never would go any place at night. But this was a Sunday afternoon and someways or other they got Bram down there; and Miss Linda made her play, right there in front of the town, practically. Just before sundown they went off together in that fancy shay. And the next day, she was home again—alone. That finished off her reputation, as far as the biddies in Elsby was concerned. It was ten years 'fore she even landed the teaching job. By that time, she was already old. And nobody was ever fool enough to mention the name Bram in front of her."

Tremaine got to his feet. "I'd appreciate it if you'd keep your ears and eyes open for anything that might build into a lead on this, Jess. Meantime, I'm just a tourist, seeing the sights."

"What about that gear of yours? Didn't you say you had some kind of detector you were going to set up?"

"I've got an oversized suitcase," Tremaine said. "I'll be setting it up in my room over at the hotel."

"When's this bootleg station supposed to broadcast again?"

"After dark. I'm working on a few ideas. It might be an infinitely repeating logarithmic sequence, based on—"

"Hold it, Jimmy. You're over my head." Jess got to his feet. "Let me know if you want anything. And by the way—"he winked broadly—"I always did know who busted Soup Gaskin's nose and took out his front teeth."

✳ 2 ✳

Back in the street, Tremaine headed south toward the Elsby Town Hall, a squat structure of brownish-red brick, crouched under yellow autumn trees at the end of Sheridan Street. Tremaine went up the steps and past heavy double doors. Ten yards along the dim corridor, a hand-lettered cardboard sign over a black-varnished door said "MUNICIPAL OFFICE OF RECORD." Tremaine opened the door and went in.

A thin man with garters above the elbow looked over his shoulder at Tremaine.

"We're closed," he said.

"I won't be a minute," Tremaine said. "Just want to check on when the Bram property changed hands last."

The man turned to Tremaine, pushed a drawer shut with his hip. "Bram? He dead?"

"Nothing like that. I just want to know when he bought the place."

The man came over to the counter, eyeing Tremaine. "He ain't going to sell, mister, if that's what you want to know."

"I want to know when he bought."

The man hesitated, closed his jaw hard. "Come back tomorrow," he said.

Tremaine put a hand on the counter, looked thoughtful. "I was hoping to save a trip." He lifted his hand and scratched the side of his jaw. A folded bill opened on the counter. The thin man's eyes darted toward it. His hand eased out, covered the bill. He grinned quickly.

"See what I can do," he said.

It was ten minutes before he beckoned Tremaine over to the table where a two-foot-square book lay open. An untrimmed fingernail indicated a line written in faded ink:

"May 19, Acreage sold, One Dollar and other G&V consid. NW Quarter Section 24, Township Elsby. Bram. (see Vol. 9 & cet.)"

"Translated, what does that mean?" said Tremaine.

"That's the ledger for 1901; means Bram bought a quarter section on the nineteenth of May. You want me to look up the deed?"

"No, thanks," Tremaine said. "That's all I needed." He turned back to the door.

"What's up, mister?" the clerk called after him. "Bram in some kind of trouble?"

"No. No trouble."

The man was looking at the book with pursed lips. "Nineteen-oh-one," he said. "I never thought of it before, but you know, old Bram must be dern near to ninety years old. Spry for that age."

"I guess you're right."

The clerk looked sideways at Tremaine. "Lots of funny stories about old Bram. Useta say his place was haunted. You know; funny noises and lights. And they used to say there was money buried out at his place."

"I've heard those stories. Just superstition, wouldn't you say?"

"Maybe so." The clerk leaned on the counter, assumed a knowing look. "There's one story that's not superstition . . ."

Tremaine waited.

"You—uh—paying anything for information?"

"Now why would I do that?" Tremaine reached for the door knob.

The clerk shrugged. "Thought I'd ask. Anyway—I can swear to this. Nobody in this town's ever seen Bram between sundown and sunup."

Untrimmed sumacs threw late-afternoon shadows on the discolored stucco façade of the Elsby Public Library. Inside, Tremaine followed a paper-dry woman of indeterminate age to a rack of yellowed newsprint.

"You'll find back to nineteen-forty here," the librarian said. "The older are there in the shelves."

"I want nineteen-oh-one, if they go back that far."

The woman darted a suspicious look at Tremaine. "You have to handle these old papers carefully."

"I'll be extremely careful." The woman sniffed, opened a drawer, leafed through it, muttering.

"What date was it you wanted?"

"Nineteen-oh-one; the week of May nineteenth."

The librarian pulled out a folded paper, placed it on the table, adjusted her glasses, squinted at the front page. "That's it," she said. "These papers keep pretty well, provided they're stored in the dark. But they're still flimsy, mind you."

"I'll remember." The woman stood by as Tremaine looked over the front page. The lead article concerned the opening of the Pan-American Exposition at Buffalo. Vice-President Roosevelt had made a speech. Tremaine leafed over, reading slowly.

On page four, under a column headed *County Notes* he saw the name Bram:

> Mr. Bram has purchased a quarter section of fine grazing land, north of town, together with a sturdy house, from J. P. Spivey of Elsby. Mr. Bram will occupy the home and will continue to graze a few head of stock. Mr. Bram, who is a newcomer to the county, has been a resident of Mrs. Stoate's Guest Home in Elsby for the past months.

"May I see some earlier issues; from about the first of the year?"

The librarian produced the papers. Tremaine turned the pages, read the heads, skimmed an article here and there. The librarian went back to her desk. An hour later, in the issues for July 7, 1900, an item caught his eye:

> A Severe Thunderstorm. Citizens of Elsby and the country were much alarmed by a violent cloudburst, accompanied by lightning and thunder, during the night of the fifth. A fire set in the pine woods north of Spivey's farm destroyed a considerable amount of timber and threatened the house before burning itself out along the river.

The librarian was at Tremaine's side. "I have to close the library now. You'll have to come back tomorrow."

Outside, the sky was sallow in the west; lights were coming on in windows along the side streets. Tremaine turned up his collar against a cold wind that had risen, started along the street toward the hotel.

A block away a black late-model sedan rounded a corner with a faint squeal of tires and gunned past him, a heavy antenna mounted forward of the left rear tail fin whipping in the slipstream. Tremaine stopped short, stared after the car.

"Damn!" he said aloud. An elderly man veered, eyeing him sharply. Tremaine set off at a run, covered the two blocks to the hotel, yanked open the door to his car, slid

into the seat, made a U-turn, and headed north after the
police car.

Two miles into the dark hills north of the Elsby city
limits, Tremaine rounded a curve. The police car was
parked on the shoulder beside the highway just ahead. He
pulled off the road ahead of it and walked back. The door
opened. A tall figure stepped out.

"What's your problem, mister?" a harsh voice drawled.

"What's the matter? Run out of signal?"

"What's it to you, mister?"

"Are you boys in touch with Grammond on the car set?"

"We could be."

"Mind if I have a word with him? My name's
Tremaine."

"Oh," said the cop, "you're the big shot from
Washington." He shifted chewing tobacco to the other
side of his jaw. "Sure, you can talk to him." He turned and
spoke to the other cop, who muttered into the mike
before handing it to Tremaine.

The heavy voice of the State Police chief crackled.
"What's your beef, Tremaine?"

"I thought you were going to keep your men away
from Elsby until I gave the word, Grammond."

"That was before I knew your Washington stuffed
shirts were holding out on me."

"It's nothing we can go to court with, Grammond. And
the job you were doing might have been influenced if I'd
told you about the Elsby angle."

Grammond cursed. "I could have put my men in the
town and taken it apart brick by brick in the time—"

"That's just what I don't want. If our bird sees cops cruising, he'll go underground."

"You've got it all figured, I see. I'm just the dumb hick you boys use for the spade work, that it?"

"Pull your lip back in. You've given me the confirmation I needed."

"Confirmation, hell! All I know is that somebody somewhere is punching out a signal. For all I know, it's forty midgets on bicycles, pedaling all over the damned state. I've got fixes in every county—"

"The smallest hyperwave transmitter Uncle Sam knows how to build weighs three tons," said Tremaine. "Bicycles are out."

Grammond snorted. "Okay, Tremaine," he said. "You're the boy with all the answers. But if you get in trouble, don't call me; call Washington."

Back in his room, Tremaine put through a call.

"It looks like Grammond's not willing to be left out in the cold, Fred. Tell him if he queers this—"

"I don't know but what he might have something," the voice came back over the filtered hum. "Suppose he smokes them out—"

"Don't go dumb on me, Fred. We're not dealing with West Virginia moonshiners."

"Don't tell me my job, Tremaine!" the voice snapped. "And don't try out your famous temper on me. I'm still in charge of this investigation."

"Sure. Just don't get stuck in some senator's hip pocket." Tremaine hung up the telephone, went to the dresser and poured two fingers of Scotch into a water glass. He tossed it down, then pulled on his coat and left the hotel.

He walked south two blocks, turned left down a twilit side street. He walked slowly, looking at the weathered frame houses. Number 89 was a once-stately three-storied mansion overgrown with untrimmed vines, its windows squares of sad yellow light. He pushed through the gate in the ancient picket fence, mounted the porch steps and pushed the button beside the door, a dark panel of cracked varnish. It was a long minute before the door opened. A tall woman with white hair and fine-boned face looked at him coolly.

"Miss Carroll," Tremaine said. "You won't remember me, but I—"

"There is nothing whatever wrong with my faculties, James," Miss Carroll said calmly. Her voice was still resonant, a deep contralto. Only a faint quaver reflected her age—close to ninety, Tremaine thought, startled.

"I'm flattered you remember me, Miss Carroll," he said.

"Come in." She led the way to a pleasant parlor set out with the furnishings of another era. She motioned Tremaine to a seat and took a straight chair across the room from him.

"You look very well, James," she said, nodding. "I'm pleased to see that you've amounted to something."

"Just another bureaucrat, I'm afraid."

"You were wise to leave Elsby. There is no future here for a young man."

"I often wondered why you didn't leave, Miss Carroll. I thought, even as a boy, that you were a woman of great ability."

"Why did you come today, James?" asked Miss Carroll.

"I . . ." Tremaine started. He looked at the old lady. "I want some information. This is an important matter. May I rely on your discretion?"

"Of course."

"How long has Mr. Bram lived in Elsby?"

Miss Carroll looked at him for a long moment. "Will what I tell you be used against him?"

"There'll be nothing done against him, Miss Carroll . . . unless it needs to be, in the national interest."

"I'm not at all sure I know what the term 'national interest' means, James. I distrust these glib phrases."

"I always liked Mr. Bram," said Tremaine. "I'm not out to hurt him."

"Mr. Bram came here when I was a young woman. I'm not certain of the year."

"What does he do for a living?"

"I have no idea."

"Why did a healthy young fellow like Bram settle out in that isolated piece of country? What's his story?"

"I'm . . . not sure that anyone truly knows Bram's story."

"You called him 'Bram', Miss Carroll. Is that his first name . . . or his last?"

"That is his only name. Just . . . Bram."

"You knew him well once, Miss Carroll. Is there anything—"

A tear rolled down Miss Carroll's faded cheek. She wiped it away impatiently.

"I'm an unfulfilled old maid, James," she said. "You must forgive me."

Tremaine stood up. "I'm sorry. Really sorry. I didn't mean to grill you, Miss Carroll. You've been very kind. I had no right . . ."

Miss Carroll shook her head. "I knew you as a boy, James. I have complete confidence in you. If anything I can tell you about Bram will be helpful to you, it is my duty to oblige you; and it may help him." She paused. Tremaine waited.

"Many years ago I was courted by Bram. One day he asked me to go with him to his house. On the way he told me a terrible and pathetic tale. He said that each night he fought a battle with evil beings, alone, in a cave beneath his house."

Miss Carroll drew a deep breath and went on. "I was torn between pity and horror. I begged him to take me back. He refused." Miss Carroll twisted her fingers together, her eyes fixed on the long past. "When we reached the house, he ran to the kitchen. He lit a lamp and threw open a concealed panel. There were stairs. He went down . . . and left me there alone.

"I waited all that night in the carriage. At dawn he emerged. He tried to speak to me but I would not listen.

"He took a locket from his neck and put it into my hand. He told me to keep it and, if ever I should need him, to press it between my fingers in a secret way . . . and he would come. I told him that until he would consent to see a doctor, I did not wish him to call. He drove me home. He never called again."

"This locket," said Tremaine, "do you still have it?"

Miss Carroll hesitated, then put her hand to her throat, lifted a silver disc on a fine golden chain. "You see what a foolish old woman I am, James."

"May I see it?"

She handed the locket to him. It was heavy, smooth. "I'd like to examine this more closely," he said. "May I take it with me?"

Miss Carroll nodded.

"There is one other thing," she said, "perhaps quite meaningless . . ."

"I'd be grateful for any lead."

"Bram fears the thunder."

✳ 3 ✳

As Tremaine walked slowly toward the lighted main street of Elsby a car pulled to a stop beside him. Jess leaned out, peered at Tremaine and asked:

"Any luck, Jimmy?"

Tremaine shook his head. "I'm getting nowhere fast. The Bram idea's a dud, I'm afraid."

"Funny thing about Bram. You know, he hasn't showed up yet. I'm getting a little worried. Want to run out there with me and take a look around?"

"Sure. Just so I'm back by full dark."

As they pulled away from the curb Jess said, "Jimmy, what's this about State Police nosing around here? I thought you were playing a lone hand from what you were saying to me."

"I thought so too, Jess. But it looks like Grammond's a

jump ahead of me. He smells headlines in this; he doesn't want to be left out."

"Well, the State cops could be mighty handy to have around. I'm wondering why you don't want 'em in. If there's some kind of spy ring working—"

"We're up against an unknown quantity. I don't know what's behind this and neither does anybody else. Maybe it's a ring of Bolsheviks . . . and maybe it's something bigger. I have the feeling we've made enough mistakes in the last few years; I don't want to see this botched."

The last pink light of sunset was fading from the clouds to the west as Jess swung the car through the open gate, pulled up under the old trees before the square-built house. The windows were dark. The two men got out, circled the house once, then mounted the steps and rapped on the door. There was a black patch of charred flooring under the window, and the paint on the wall above it was bubbled. Somewhere a cricket set up a strident chirrup, suddenly cut off. Jess leaned down, picked up an empty shotgun shell. He looked at Tremaine. "This don't look good," he said. "You suppose those fool boys . . . ?"

He tried the door. It opened. A broken hasp dangled. He turned to Tremaine. "Maybe this is more than kid stuff," he said. "You carry a gun?"

"In the car."

"Better get it."

Tremaine went to the car, dropped the pistol in his coat pocket, rejoined Jess inside the house. It was silent, deserted. In the kitchen Jess flicked the beam of his flashlight around the room. An empty plate lay on the oilcloth-covered table.

"This place is empty," he said. "Anybody'd think he'd been gone a week."

"Not a very cozy—" Tremaine broke off. A thin yelp sounded in the distance.

"I'm getting jumpy," said Jess. "Dern hounddog, I guess."

A low growl seemed to rumble distantly. "What the devil's that?" Tremaine said.

Jess shone the light on the floor. "Look here," he said. The ring of light showed a spatter of dark droplets all across the plank flood.

"That's blood, Jess . . ." Tremaine scanned the floor. It was of broad slabs, closely laid, scrubbed clean but for the dark stains.

"Maybe he cleaned a chicken. This is the kitchen."

"It's a trail." Tremaine followed the line of drops across the floor. It ended suddenly near the wall.

"What do you make of it, Jimmy?"

A wail sounded, a thin forlorn cry, trailing off into silence. Jess stared at Tremaine. "I'm too damned old to start believing in spooks," he said. "You suppose those damn-fool boys are hiding here, playing tricks?"

"I think," Tremaine said, "that we'd better go ask Hull Gaskin a few questions."

At the station Jess led Tremaine to a cell where a lanky teenage boy lounged on a steel-framed cot, blinking up at the visitor under a mop of greased hair.

"Hull, this is Mr. Tremaine," said Jess. He took out a heavy key, swung the cell door open. "He wants to talk to you."

"I ain't done nothin'," Hull said sullenly. "There ain't nothin' wrong with burnin' out a Commie, is there?"

"Bram's a Commie, is he?" Tremaine said softly. "How'd you find that out, Hull?"

"He's a foreigner, ain't he?" the youth shot back. "Besides, we heard . . ."

"What did you hear?"

"They're lookin' for the spies."

"Who's looking for spies?"

"Cops."

"Who says so?"

The boy looked directly at Tremaine for an instant, flicked his eyes to the corner of the cell. "Cops was talkin' about 'em," he said.

"Spill it, Hull," the policeman said. "Mr. Tremaine hasn't got all night."

"They parked out east of town, on 302, back of the woodlot. They called me over and asked me a bunch of questions. Said I could help 'em get them spies. Wanted to know all about any funny-actin' people around here."

"And you mentioned Bram?"

The boy darted another look at Tremaine. "They said they figured the spies was out north of town. Well, Bram's a foreigner, and he's out that way, ain't he?"

"Anything else?"

The boy looked at his feet.

"What did you shoot at, Hull?" Tremaine said. The boy looked at him sullenly.

"You know anything about the blood on the kitchen floor?"

"I don't know what you're talkin' about," Hull said. "We was out squirrel-huntin'."

"Hull, is Mr. Bram dead?"

"What you mean?" Hull blurted. "He was—"

"He was what?"

"Nothin'."

"The Chief won't like it if you hold out on him, Hull," Tremaine said. "He's bound to find out."

Jess looked at the boy. "Hull's a pretty dumb boy," he said. "But he's not that dumb. Let's have it, Hull."

The boy licked his lips. "I had Pa's 30-30, and Bovey Lay had a twelve-gauge . . ."

"What time was this?"

"Just after sunset."

"About seven-thirty, that'd be," said Jess. "That was half an hour before the fire was spotted."

"I didn't do no shootin'. It was Bovey. Old Bram jumped out at him, and he just fired off the hip. But he didn't kill him. He seen him run off . . ."

"You were on the porch when this happened. Which way did Bram go?"

"He . . . run inside."

"So then you set fire to the place. Whose bright idea was that?"

Hull sat silent. After a moment Tremaine and Jess left the cell.

"He must have gotten clear, Jimmy," said Jess. "Maybe he got scared and left town."

"Bram doesn't strike me as the kind to panic." Tremaine looked at his watch. "I've got to get on my way, Jess. I'll check with you in the morning."

Tremaine crossed the street to the Paradise Bar and Grill, pushed into the jukebox-lit interior, took a stool and ordered a Scotch and water. He sipped the drink, then sat staring into the dark reflection in the glass. The idea of a careful reconnoiter of the Elsby area was gone now, with police swarming everywhere. It was too bad about Bram. It would be interesting to know where the old man was . . . and if he was still alive. He'd always seemed normal enough in the old days: a big, solid-looking man, middle-aged, always pleasant enough, though he didn't say much. He'd tried hard, that time, to interest Tremaine in learning whatever it was . . .

Tremaine put a hand in his jacket pocket, took out Miss Carroll's locket. It was smooth, the size and shape of a wrist-watch chassis. He was fingering it meditatively when a rough hand slammed against his shoulder, half knocking him from the stool. Tremaine caught his balance, turned, looked into the scarred face of a heavy-shouldered man in a leather jacket.

"I heard you was back in town, Tremaine," the man said.

The bartender moved up. "Looky here, Gaskin, I don't want no trouble—"

"Shove it!" Gaskin squinted at Tremaine, his upper lip curled back to expose the gap in his teeth. "You tryin' to make more trouble for my boy, I hear. Been over to the jail, stickin' your nose in."

Tremaine dropped the locket in his pocket and stood up. Gaskin hitched up his pants, glanced around the room. Half a dozen early drinkers stared, wide-eyed. Gaskin squinted at Tremaine. He smelled of unwashed flannel.

"Sicked the cops onto him. The boy was out with his friends, havin' a little fun. Now there he sets in jail."

Tremaine moved aside from the stool, started past the man. Soup Gaskin grabbed his arm.

"Not so fast! I figger you owe me damages. I—"

"Damage is what you'll get," said Tremaine. He slammed a stiff left to Gaskin's ribs, drove a hard right to the jaw. Gaskin jackknifed backwards, tripped over a bar stool, fell on his back. He rolled over, got to hands and knees, shook his head.

"Git up, Soup!" someone called. "Hot dog!" offered another.

"I'm calling the police!" the bartender yelled.

"Never mind," a voice said from the door. A blue-jacketed State Trooper strolled into the room, fingers hooked into his pistol belt, the steel caps on his boot heels clicking with each step. He faced Tremaine, feet apart.

"Looks like you're disturbin' the peace, Mr. Tremaine," he said.

"You wouldn't know who put him up to it, would you?" Tremaine said.

"That's a dirty allegation," the cop grinned. "I'll have to get off a hot letter to my congressman."

Gaskin got to his feet, wiped a smear of blood across his cheek, then lunged past the cop and swung a wild right. Tremaine stepped aside, landed a solid punch on Gaskin's ear. The cop stepped back against the bar. Soup whirled, slammed out with lefts and rights. Tremaine lashed back with a straight left; Gaskin slammed against the bar, rebounded, threw a knockout right . . . and

Tremaine ducked, landed a right uppercut that sent Gaskin reeling back, bowled over a table, sent glasses flying. Tremaine stood over him.

"On your feet, jailbird," he said. "A workout is exactly what I needed."

"Okay, you've had your fun," the State cop said. "I'm taking you in, Tremainè."

Tremaine looked at him. "Sorry, copper," he said. "I don't have time right now." The cop looked startled, reached for his revolver.

"What's going on here, Jimmy?" Jess stood in the door, a huge .44 in his hand. He turned his eyes on the trooper.

"You're a little out of your jurisdiction," he said. "I think you better move on 'fore somebody steals your bicycle."

The cop eyed Jess for a long moment, then holstered his pistol and stalked out of the bar. Jess tucked his revolver into his belt, looked at Gaskin sitting on the floor, dabbing at his bleeding mouth. "What got into you, Soup?"

"I think the State boys put him up to it," Tremaine said. "They're looking for an excuse to take me out of the picture."

Jess motioned to Gaskin. "Get up, Soup. I'm lockin' you up alongside that boy of yours."

Outside, Jess said, "You got some bad enemies there, Jimmy. That's a tough break. You ought to hold onto your temper with those boys. I think maybe you ought to think about getting over the state line. I can run you to the bus station, and send your car along . . ."

"I can't leave now, Jess. I haven't even started."

✳ 4 ✳

In his room, Tremaine doctored the cut on his jaw, then opened his trunk, checked over the detector gear. The telephone rang.

"Tremaine? I've been on the telephone with Grammond. Are you out of your mind? I'm—"

"Fred," Tremaine cut in, "I thought you were going to get those state cops off my neck."

"Listen to me, Tremaine. You're called off this job as of now. Don't touch anything! You'd better stay right there in that room. In fact, that's an order!"

"Don't pick now to come apart at the seams, Fred," Tremaine snapped.

"I've ordered you off! That's all!" The phone clicked and the dial tone sounded. Tremaine dropped the receiver in its cradle, then walked to the window absently, his hand in his pocket.

He felt broken pieces and pulled out Miss Carroll's locket. It was smashed, split down the center. It must have gotten it in the tussle with Soup, Tremaine thought. It looked—

He squinted at the shattered ornament. A maze of fine wires was exposed, tiny condensers, bits of glass.

In the street below, tires screeched. Tremaine looked down. A black car was at the curb, doors sprung. Four uniformed men jumped out, headed for the door. Tremaine whirled to the phone. The desk clerk came on.

"Get me Jess—fast!"

The police chief answered.

"Jess, the word's out I'm poison. A carful of State law is at the front door. I'm going out the back. Get in their way all you can." Tremaine dropped the phone, grabbed up the suitcase and let himself out into the hall. The back stairs were dark. He stumbled, cursed, made it to the service entry. Outside, the alley was deserted.

He went to the corner, crossed the street, thrust the suitcase into the back seat of his car and slid into the driver's seat. He started up and eased away from the curb. He glanced in the mirror. There was no alarm.

It was a four-block drive to Miss Carroll's house. The housekeeper let Tremaine in.

"Oh, yes, Miss Carroll is still up," she said. "She never retires until nine. I'll tell her you're here, Mr. Tremaine."

Tremaine paced the room. On his third circuit Miss Carroll came in.

"I wouldn't have bothered you if it wasn't important," Tremaine said. "I can't explain it all now. You said once you had confidence in me. Will you come with me now? It concerns Bram . . . and maybe a lot more than just Bram."

Miss Carroll looked at him steadily. "I'll get my wrap."

On the highway Tremaine said, "Miss Carroll, we're headed for Bram's house. I take it you've heard of what happened out there?"

"No, James. I haven't stirred out of the house. What is it?"

"A gang of teen-age toughs went out last night. They had guns. One of them took a shot at Bram. And Bram's disappeared. But I don't think he's dead."

Miss Carroll gasped. "Why? Why did they do it?"

"I don't think they know themselves."

"You say . . . you believe he still lives . . ."

"He must be alive. It dawned on me a little while ago . . . a little late, I'll admit. The locket he gave you. Did you ever try it?"

"Try it? Why . . . no. I don't believe in magic, James."

"Not magic. Electronics. Years ago Bram talked to me about radio. He wanted to teach me. Now I'm here looking for a transmitter. That transmitter was busy last night. I think Bram was operating it."

There was a long silence.

"James," Miss Carroll said at last, "I don't understand."

"Neither do I, Miss Carroll. I'm still working on finding the pieces. But let me ask you: that night that Bram brought you out to his place. You say he ran to the kitchen and opened a trapdoor in the floor—"

"Did I say floor? That was an error; the panel was in the wall."

"I guess I jumped to the conclusion. Which wall?"

"He crossed the room. There was a table, with a candlestick. He went around it and pressed his hand against the wall, beside the woodbox. The panel slid aside. It was very dark within. He ducked his head, because the opening was not large, and stepped inside . . ."

"That would be the east wall . . . to the left of the back door?"

"Yes."

"Now, Miss Carroll, can you remember exactly what Bram said to you that night? Something about fighting something, wasn't it?"

"I've tried for sixty years to put it out of my mind, James. But I remember every word, I think." She was silent for a moment.

"I was beside him on the buggy seat. It was a warm evening, late in spring. I had told him that I loved him, and . . . he had responded. He said that he would have spoken long before, but that he had not dared. Now there was that which I must know.

"His life was not his own, he said. He was not . . . native to this world. He was an agent of a mighty power, and he had trailed a band of criminals . . ." She broke off. "I could not truly understand that part, James. I fear it was too incoherent. He raved of evil beings who lurked in the shadows of a cave. It was his duty to wage each night an unceasing battle with occult forces."

"What kind of battle? Were these ghosts, or demons, or what?"

"I don't know. Evil powers which would be unloosed on the world, unless he met them at the portal as the darkness fell and opposed them."

"Why didn't he get help?"

"Only he could stand against them. I knew little of abnormal psychology, but I understood the classic evidence of paranoia. I shrank from him. He sat, leaning forward, his eyes intent. I wept and begged him to take me back. He turned his face to me, and I saw the pain and anguish in his eyes. I loved him . . . and feared him. And he would not turn back. Night was falling, and the enemy awaited him."

"Then, when you got to the house . . .?"

"He had whipped up the horses, and I remember how I clung to the top braces, weeping. Then we were at the house. Without a word he jumped down and ran to the door. I followed. He lit a lamp and turned to me. From somewhere there was a wailing call, like an injured animal. He shouted something—an unintelligible cry—and ran toward the back of the house. I took up the lamp and followed. In the kitchen he went to the wall, pressed against it. The panel opened. He looked at me. His face was white.

"'In the name of the High God, Linda Carroll, I entreat you . . .'

"I screamed. And he hardened his face, and went down . . . and I screamed and screamed again . . ." Miss Carroll closed her eyes, drew a shuddering breath.

"I'm sorry to have put you through this, Miss Carroll," Tremaine said. "But I had to know."

Faintly in the distance a siren sounded. In the mirror, headlights twinkled half a mile behind. Tremaine stepped on the gas. The powerful car leaped ahead.

"Are you expecting trouble on the road, James?"

"The State police are unhappy with me, Miss Carroll. And I imagine they're not too pleased with Jess. Now they're out for blood. But I think I can outrun them."

"James," Miss Carroll said, sitting up and looking behind. "If those are police officers, shouldn't you stop?"

"I can't, Miss Carroll. I don't have time for them now. If my idea means anything, we've got to get there fast . . ."

Bram's house loomed gaunt and dark as the car whirled through the gate, ground to a stop before the porch. Tremaine jumped out, went around the car and helped Miss Carroll out. He was surprised at the firmness of her step. For a moment, in the fading light of dusk, he glimpsed her profile. *How beautiful she must have been . . .*

We haven't got a second to waste," he said. "That other car's not more than a minute behind us." He reached into the back of the car, hauled out the heavy suitcase. "I hope you remember how Bram worked that panel."

On the porch Tremaine's flashlight illuminated the broken hasp. Inside, he led the way along a dark hall, pushed into the kitchen.

"It was there," Miss Carroll said, pointing. Outside, an engine sounded on the highway, slowing, turning in. Headlights pushed a square of cold light across the kitchen wall. Tremaine jumped to the spot Miss Carroll had indicated, put the suitcase down, felt over the wall.

"Give me the light, James," Miss Carroll said calmly. "Press there." She put the spot on the wall. Tremaine leaned against it. Nothing happened. Outside, there was the thump of car doors; a muffled voice barked orders.

"Are you sure . . . ?"

"Yes. Try again, James."

Tremaine threw himself against the wall, slapped at it, searching for a hidden latch.

"A bit higher; Bram was a tall man. The panel opened below . . ."

Tremaine reached higher, pounded, pushed up, sideways—

With a click a three by four foot section of wall rolled

silently aside. Tremaine saw greased metal slides and, beyond, steps leading down.

"They are on the porch now, James," said Miss Carroll.

"The light!" Tremaine reached for it, threw a leg over the sill. He reached back, pulled the suitcase after him. "Tell them I kidnapped you, Miss Carroll. And thanks."

Miss Carroll held out her hand. "Help me, James. I hung back once before. I'll not repeat my folly."

Tremaine hesitated for an instant, then reached out, handed Miss Carroll in. Footsteps sounded in the hall. The flashlight showed Tremaine a black pushbutton bolted to a two by four stud. He pressed it. The panel slid back in place.

Tremaine flashed the light on the stairs.

"Okay, Miss Carroll," he said softly. "Let's go down."

There were fifteen steps, and at the bottom, a corridor, with curved walls of black glass, and a floor of rough boards. It went straight for twenty feet and ended at an old-fashioned five-panel wooden door. Tremaine tried the brass knob. The door opened on a room shaped from a natural cave, with water-worn walls of yellow stone, a low uneven ceiling, and a packed-earth floor. On a squat tripod in the center of the chamber rested an apparatus of black metal and glass, vaguely gunlike, aimed at the blank wall. Beside it, in an ancient wooden rocker, a man lay slumped, his shirt blood-caked, a black puddle on the floor beneath him.

"Bram!" Miss Carroll gasped. She went to him, took his hand, staring into his face.

"Is he dead?" Tremaine said tightly.

"His hands are cold . . . but there is a pulse."

A kerosene lantern stood by the door. Tremaine lit it, brought it to the chair. He took out a pocket knife, cut the coat and shirt back from Bram's wound. A shotgun blast had struck him in the side; there was a lacerated area as big as Tremaine's hand.

"It's stopped bleeding," he said. "It was just a graze at close range, I'd say." He explored further. "It got his arm too, but not as deep. And I think there are a couple of ribs broken. If he hasn't lost too much blood . . ." Tremaine pulled off his coat, spread it on the floor.

"Let's lay him out here and try to bring him around."

Lying on his back on the floor, Bram looked bigger than his six-foot-four, younger than his near-century, Tremaine thought. Miss Carroll knelt at the old man's side, chafing his hands, murmuring to him.

Abruptly a thin cry cut the air.

Tremaine whirled, startled. Miss Carroll stared, eyes wide. A low rumble sounded, swelled louder, broke into a screech, cut off.

"Those are the sounds I heard that night," Miss Carroll breathed. "I thought afterwards I had imagined them, but I remember . . . James, what does it mean?"

"Maybe it means Bram wasn't as crazy as you thought," Tremaine said.

Miss Carroll gasped sharply. "James! Look at the wall—"

Tremaine turned. Vague shadows moved across the stone, flickering, wavering.

"What the devil . . . !"

Bram moaned, stirred. Tremaine went to him. "Bram!" he said. "Wake up!"

Bram's eyes opened. For a moment he looked dazedly at Tremaine, then at Miss Carroll. Awkwardly he pushed himself to a sitting position.

"Bram . . . you must lie down," Miss Carroll said.

"Linda Carroll," Bram said. His voice was deep, husky.

"Bram, you're hurt . . ."

A mewling wail started up. Bram went rigid. "What hour is this?" he grated.

"The sun has just gone down; it's after seven—"

Bram tried to get to his feet. "Help me up," he ordered. "Curse the weakness . . ."

Tremaine got a hand under the old man's arm. "Careful, Bram," he said. "Don't start your wound bleeding again."

"To the Repellor," Bram muttered. Tremaine guided him to the rocking chair, eased him down. Bram seized the two black pistol-grips, squeezed them.

"You, young man," Bram said. "Take the circlet there; place it about my neck."

The flat-metal ring hung from a wire loop. Tremaine fitted it over Bram's head. It settled snugly over his shoulders, a flange at the back against his neck.

"Bram," Tremaine said. "What's this all about?"

"Watch the wall there. My sight grows dim. Tell me what you see."

"It looks like shadows; but what's casting them?"

"Can you discern details?"

"No. It's like somebody waggling their fingers in front of a slide projector."

"The radiation from the star is yet too harsh," Bram

muttered. "But now the node draws close. May the High Gods guide my hand!"

A howl rang out, a raw blast of sound. Bram tensed. "What do you see?" he demanded.

"The outlines are sharper. There seem to be other shapes behind the moving ones. It's like looking through a steamy window . . ." Beyond the misty surface Tremaine seemed to see a high narrow chamber, bathed in white light. In the foreground creatures like shadowy caricatures of men paced to and fro. "They're like something stamped out of alligator hide," Tremaine whispered. "When they turn and I see them edge-on, they're thin . . ."

"An effect of dimensional attenuation. They strive now to match matrices with this plane. If they succeed, this earth you know will lie at their feet."

"What are they? Where are they? That's solid rock—"

"What you see is the Niss Command Center. It lies in another world than this, but here is the multihedron of intersection. They bring their harmonic generators to bear here in the hope of establishing an aperture of focus."

"I don't understand half of what you're saying, Bram. And the rest I don't believe. But with this staring me in the face, I'll have to act as though I did."

Suddenly the wall cleared. Like a surface of molded glass the stone threw back ghostly highlights. Beyond it, the Niss technicians, seen now in sharp detail, worked busily, silently, their faces like masks of ridged red-brown leather. Directly opposite Bram's Repellor, an apparatus like an immense camera with a foot-wide silvered lens stood aimed, a black-clad Niss perched in a saddle atop it. The white light flooded the cave, threw black shadows across the floor. Bram hunched over the Repellor, face tensed in strain. A glow built in the air around the Niss machine. The alien technicians stood now, staring with tiny bright-red eyes. Long seconds passed. The black-clad Niss gestured suddenly. Another turned to a red-marked knife-switch, pulled. As suddenly as it had cleared, the wall went milky, then dulled to opacity. Bram slumped back, eyes shut, breathing hoarsely.

"Near were they then," he muttered. "I grow weak . . ."

"Let me take over," Tremaine said. "Tell me how."

"How can I tell you? You will not understand."

"Maybe I'll understand enough to get us through the night."

Bram seemed to gather himself. "Very well. This must you know . . .

"I am an agent in the service of the Great World. For centuries we have waged war against the Niss, evil beings who loot the continua. They established an Aperture here, on your Earth. We detected it, and found that a Portal could be set up here briefly. I was dispatched with a crew to counter their move—"

"You're talking gibberish," Tremaine said. "I'll pass the Great World and the continua . . . but what's an Aperture?"

"A point of material contact between the Niss world and this plane of space-time. Through it they can pump this rich planet dry of oxygen, killing it—then emerge to feed on the corpse."

"What's a Portal?"

"The Great World lies in a different harmonic series than do Earth and the Niss World. Only at vast intervals can we set up a Portal of temporary identity as the cycles mesh. We monitor the Niss emanations, and forestall them when we can, now in this plane, now in that."

"I see: denial to the enemy."

"But we were late. Already the multihedron was far advanced. A blinding squall lashed outside the river cave where the Niss had focused the Aperture, and the thunder rolled as the ionization effect was propagated in the atmosphere. I threw my force against the Niss Aperture, but could not destroy it . . . but neither could they force their entry."

"And this was sixty years ago? And they're still at it?"

"You must throw off the illusion of time! To the Niss only a few days have passed. But here—where I spend only minutes from each night in the engagement, as the patterns coincide—it has been long years."

"Why don't you bring in help? Why do you have to work alone?"

"The power required to hold the Portal in focus against the stresses of space-time is tremendous. Even then the cycle is brief. It gave us first a fleeting contact of a few seconds; it was through that that we detected the Niss activity here. The next contact was four days later, and lasted twenty-four minutes—long enough to set up the Repellor. I fought them then . . . and saw that victory was in doubt. Still, it was a fair world; I could not let it go without a struggle. A third identity was possible twenty days later; I elected to remain here until then, attempt to repel the Niss, then return home at the next contact. The Portal closed, and my crew and I settled down to the engagement.

"The next night showed us in full the hopelessness of the contest. By day, we emerged from where the Niss had focused the Aperture, and explored this land, and came to love its small warm sun, its strange blue sky, its mantle of green . . . and the small humble grass-blades. To us of an ancient world it seemed a paradise of young life. And then I ventured into the town . . . and there I saw such a maiden as the Cosmos has forgotten, such was her beauty . . .

"The twenty days passed. The Niss held their foothold—yet I had kept them back.

"The Portal reopened. I ordered my crew back. It closed. Since then, have I been alone . . ."

"Bram," Miss Carroll said. "Bram . . . you stayed when you could have escaped—and I—"

"I would that I could give you back those lost years, Linda Carroll," Bram said. "I would that we could have been together under a brighter sun than this."

"You gave up your world, to give this one a little time," Tremaine said. "And we rewarded you with a shotgun blast."

"Bram, when will the Portal open again?"

"Not in my life, Linda Carroll. Not for ten thousand years."

"Why didn't you recruit help?" Tremaine said. "You could have trained someone . . ."

"I tried, at first. But what can one do with frightened rustics? They spoke of witchcraft, and fled."

"But you can't hold out forever. Tell me how this thing works. It's time somebody gave you a break!"

✷ 5 ✷

Bram talked for half an hour, while Tremaine listened. "If I should fail," he concluded, "take my place at the Repellor. Place the circlet on your neck. When the wall clears, grip the handles and pit your mind against the Niss. Will that they do not come through. When the thunder rolls, you will know that you have failed."

"All right. I'll be ready. But let me get one thing straight: this Repellor of yours responds to thoughts, is that right? It amplifies them—"

"It serves to focus the power of the mind. But now let us make haste. Soon, I fear, will they renew the attack."

"It will be twenty minutes or so, I think," said Tremaine. "Stay where you are and get some rest."

Bram looked at him, his blue eyes grim under white brows. "What do you know of this matter, young man?"

"I think I've doped out the pattern; I've been monitoring these transmissions for weeks. My ideas seemed to prove out okay the last few nights."

"No one but I in all this world knew of the Niss attack. How could you have analyzed that which you knew not of?"

"Maybe you don't know it, Bram, but this Repellor of yours has been playing hell with our communications. Recently we developed what we thought was a Top Secret project—and you're blasting us off the air."

"This is only a small portable unit, poorly screened," Bram said. "The resonance effects are unpredictable. When one seeks to channel the power of thought—"

"Wait a minute!" Tremaine burst out.

"What is it?" Miss Carroll said, alarmed.

"Hyperwave," Tremaine said. "Instantaneous transmission. And thought. No wonder people had headaches—and nightmares! We've been broadcasting on the same band as the human mind!"

"This 'hyperwave'," Bram said. "You say it is instantaneous?"

"That's supposed to be classified information."

"Such a device is new in the Cosmos," Bram said. "Only a protoplasmic brain is known to produce a null-lag excitation state."

Tremaine frowned. "Bram, this Repellor focuses what I'll call thought waves for want of a better term. It uses an interference effect to damp out the Niss harmonic generator. What if we poured more power to the Repellor?"

"No. The power of the mind cannot be amplified—"

"I don't mean amplification; I mean an additional source. I have a hyperwave receiver here. With a little rewiring, it'll act as a transmitter. Can we tie it in?"

Bram shook his head. "Would that I were a technician," he said. "I know only what is required to operate the device."

"Let me take a look," Tremaine said. "Maybe I can figure it out."

"Take care. Without it, we fall before the Niss."

"I'll be careful." Tremaine went to the machine, examined it, tracing leads, identifying components.

"This seems clear enough," he said. "These would be powerful magnets here; they give a sort of pinch effect. And these are refracting-field coils. Simple, and brilliant. With this idea, we could beam hyperwave—"

"First let us deal with the Niss!"

"Sure." Tremaine looked at Bram. "I think I can link my apparatus to this," he said. "Okay if I try?"

"How long?"

"It shouldn't take more than fifteen minutes."

"That leaves little time."

"The cycle is tightening," Tremaine said. "I figure the next transmissions . . . or attacks . . . will come at intervals of under five minutes for several hours now; this may be the last chance."

"Then try," said Bram.

Tremaine nodded, went to the suitcase, took out tools and a heavy black box, set to work. Linda Carroll sat by Bram's side, speaking softly to him. The minutes passed.

"Okay," Tremaine said. "This unit is ready." He went to the Repellor, hesitated a moment, then turned two nuts and removed a cover.

"We're off the air," he said. "I hope my formula holds."

Bram and Miss Carroll watched silently as Tremaine worked. He strung wires, taped junctions, then flipped a switch on the hyperwave set and tuned it, his eyes on the dials of a smaller unit.

"Nineteen minutes have passed since the last attack," Bram said. "Make haste."

"I'm almost done," Tremaine said.

A sharp cry came from the wall. Tremaine jumped. "What the hell makes those sounds?"

"They are nothing—mere static. But they warn that the harmonic generators are warming." Bram struggled to his feet. "Now comes the assault."

"The shadows!" Miss Carroll cried.

Bram sank into the chair, leaned back, his face pale as wax in the faint glow from the wall. The glow grew brighter; the shadows swam into focus.

"Hurry, James," Miss Carroll said. "It comes quickly."

Bram watched through half-closed eyes. "I must man the Repellor. I . . ." He fell back in the chair, his head lolling.

"Bram!" Miss Carroll cried. Tremaine snapped the cover in place, whirled to the chair, dragged it and its occupant away from the machine, then turned, seized the grips. On the wall the Niss moved in silence, readying the attack. The black-clad figure was visible, climbing to his place. The wall cleared. Tremaine stared across at the narrow room, the gray-clad Niss. They stood now, eyes on him. One pointed. Others erected leathery crests.

Stay out, you ugly devils, Tremaine thought. *Go back, retreat, give up . . .*

Now the blue glow built in a flickering arc across the Niss machine. The technicians stood, staring across the narrow gap, tiny red eyes glittering in the narrow alien faces. Tremaine squinted against the brilliant white light from the high-vaulted Niss Command Center. The last suggestion of the sloping surface of the limestone wall was gone. Tremaine felt a draft stir; dust whirled up, clouded the air. There was an odor of iodine.

Back, Tremaine thought. *Stay back . . .*

There was a restless stir among the waiting rank of Niss. Tremaine heard the dry shuffle of horny feet against the floor, the whine of the harmonic generator. His eyes burned. As a hot gust swept around him he choked and coughed.

NO! he thought, hurling negation like a weightless bomb. *FAIL! RETREAT!*

Now the Niss moved, readying a wheeled machine, rolling it into place; Tremaine coughed rackingly, fought to draw a breath, blinking back blindness. A deep thrumming started up; grit particles stung his cheek, the backs of his hands. The Niss worked rapidly, their throat gills visibly dilated now in the unaccustomed flood of oxygen . . .

Our oxygen, Tremaine thought. *The looting has started already, and I've failed, and the people of Earth will choke and die . . .*

From what seemed an immense distance, a roll of thunder trembled at the brink of audibility, swelling.

The black-clad Niss on the alien machine half rose, erecting a black-scaled crest, exulting. Then, shockingly, his eyes fixed on Tremaine's, his trap-like mouth gaped, exposing a tongue like a scarlet snake, a cavernous pink throat set with a row of needle-like snow-white teeth. The tongue flicked out, a gesture of utter contempt.

And suddenly Tremaine was cold with deadly rage. *We have a treatment for snakes in this world*, he thought with savage intensity. *We crush 'em under our heels . . .* He pictured a writhing rattler, broken-backed, a club descending; a darting red coral snake, its venom ready, slashed in the blades of a power mower; a cottonmouth, smashed into red ruin by a shotgun blast . . .

BACK, SNAKE! he thought. *DIE! DIE!*

The thunder faded.

And atop the Niss Generator, the black-clad Niss snapped his mouth shut, crouched.

"DIE!" Tremaine shouted. "DIE!"

The Niss seemed to shrink in on himself, shivering. His crest went flaccid, twitched twice. The red eyes winked out and the Niss toppled from the machine. Tremaine coughed, gripped the handles, turned his eyes to a gray-uniformed Niss who scrambled up to replace the operator.

I SAID DIE, SNAKE!

The Niss faltered, tumbled back among his fellows, who darted about now like ants in a broached anthill. One turned red eyes on Tremaine, then scrambled for the red cut-out switch.

NO, YOU DON'T, Tremaine thought. *IT'S NOT THAT EASY, SNAKE. DIE!*

The Niss collapsed. Tremaine drew a rasping breath, blinked back tears of pain, took in a group of Niss in a glance.

Die!

They fell. The others turned to flee then, but like a scythe Tremaine's mind cut them down, left them in windrows. Hate walked naked among the Niss and left none living.

Now the machine, Tremaine thought. He fixed his

eyes on the harmonic generator. It melted into slag.
Behind it, the high panels set with jewel-like lights
blackened, crumpled into wreckage. Suddenly the air
was clean again. Tremaine breathed deep. Before him
the surface of the rock swam into view.

NO! Tremaine thought thunderously. *HOLD THAT
APERTURE OPEN!*

The rock-face shimmered, faded. Tremaine looked
into the white-lit room, at the blackened walls, the
huddled dead. *No pity*, he thought. *You would have sunk
those white teeth into soft human throats, sleeping in the
dark . . . as you've done on a hundred worlds. You're a
cancer in the cosmos. And I have the cure.*

WALLS, he thought, *COLLAPSE!*

The roof before him sagged, fell in. Debris rained
down from above, the walls tottered, went down. A cloud
of roiled dust swirled, cleared to show a sky blazing with
stars.

Dust, stay clear, Tremaine thought. *I want good air to
breathe for the work ahead*. He looked out across a landscape of rock, ghostly white in the starlight.

*LET THE ROCKS MELT AND FLOW LIKE
WATER!*

An upreared slab glowed, slumped, ran off in yellow
rivulets that were lost in the radiance of the crust as it
bubbled, belching released gasses. A wave of heat struck
Tremaine. *Let it be cool here*, he thought. *Now, Niss
world . . .*

"No!" Bram's voice shouted. "Stop, stop!"

Tremaine hesitated. He stared at the vista of volcanic
fury before him.

I could destroy it all, he thought. *And the stars in the Niss sky . . .*

"Great is the power of your hate, man of Earth," Bram cried. "But curb it now, before you destroy us all!"

"Why?" Tremaine shouted. "I can wipe out the Niss and their whole diseased universe with them, with a thought!"

"Master yourself," Bram said hoarsely. "Your rage destroys you! One of the suns you see in the Niss sky is your Sol!"

"Sol?" Tremaine said. "Then it's the Sol of a thousand years ago. Light takes time to cross a galaxy. And the earth is still here . . . so it wasn't destroyed!"

"Wise are you," Bram said. "Your race is a wonder in the Cosmos, and deadly is your hate. But you know nothing of the forces you unloose now. Past time is as mutable as the steel and rock you melted but now."

"Listen to him, James," Miss Carroll pleaded. "Please listen."

Tremaine twisted to look at her, still holding the twin grips. She looked back steadily, her head held high. Beside her, Bram's eyes were sunken deep in his lined face.

"Jess said you looked like a princess once, Miss Carroll," Tremaine said, "when you drove past with your red hair piled up high. And Bram: you were young, and you loved her. The Niss took your youth from you. You've spent your life here, fighting them, alone. And Linda Carroll waited through the years, because she loved you . . . and feared you. The Niss did that. And you want me to spare them?"

"You have mastered them," said Bram. "And you are drunk with the power in you. But the power of love is greater than the power of hate. Our love sustained us; your hate can only destroy."

Tremaine locked eyes with the old man. He drew a deep breath at last, let it out shudderingly. "All right," he said. "I guess the God complex got me." He looked back once more at the devastated landscape. "The Niss will remember this encounter, I think. They won't try Earth again."

"You've fought valiantly, James, and won," Miss Carroll said. "Now let the power go."

Tremaine turned again to look at her. "You deserve better than this, Miss Carroll," he said. "Bram, you said time is mutable. Suppose—"

"Let well enough alone," Bram said. "Let it go!"

"Once, long ago, you tried to explain this to Linda Carroll. But there was too much against it; she couldn't understand. She was afraid. And you've suffered for sixty years. Suppose those years had never been. Suppose I had come that night . . . instead of now—"

"It could never be!"

"It can if I will it!" Tremaine gripped the handles tighter. *Let this be THAT night*, he thought fiercely. *The night in 1901, when Bram's last contact failed. Let it be that night, five minutes before the portal closed. Only this machine and I remain as we are now; outside there are gas lights in the farm houses along the dirt road to Elsby, and in the town horses stand in the stables along the cinder alleys behind the houses; and President McKinley is having dinner in the White House . . .*

****

There was a sound behind Tremaine. He whirled. The ravaged scene was gone. A great disc mirror stood across the cave, intersecting the limestone wall. A man stepped through it, froze at the sight of Tremaine. He was tall, with curly blond hair, fine-chiseled features, broad shoulders.

"Fdazh ha?" he said. Then his eyes slid past Tremaine, opened still wider in astonishment. Tremaine followed the stranger's glance. A young woman, dressed in a negligee of pale silk, stood in the door, a hairbrush in her hand, her red hair flowing free to her waist. She stood rigid in shock.

Then . . .

"Mr. Bram . . . !" she gasped. "What—"

Tremaine found his voice. "Miss Carroll, don't be afraid," he said. "I'm your friend, you must believe me."

Linda Carroll turned wide eyes to him. "Who are you?" she breathed. "I was in my bedroom—"

"I can't explain. A miracle has been worked here tonight . . . on your behalf." Tremaine turned to Bram. "Look—" he started.

"What man are you?" Bram cut in in heavily accented English. "How do you come to this place?"

"Listen to me, Bram!" Tremaine snapped. "Time is mutable. You stayed here, to protect Linda Carroll—and Linda Carroll's world. You've just made that decision, right?" Tremaine went on, not waiting for a reply. "You were stuck here . . . for sixty years. Earth technology developed fast. One day a man stumbled in here, tracing down the signal from your Repellor; that was me. You showed me how to use the device . . . and with it I wiped out the Niss. And then I set the clock back for you and Linda Carroll. The Portal closes in two minutes. Don't waste time . . ."

"Mutable time?" Bram said. He went past Tremaine to Linda. "Fair lady of Earth," he said. "Do not fear . . ."

"Sir, I hardly know you," Miss Carroll said. "How did I come here, hardly clothed—"

"Take her, Bram!" Tremaine shouted. "Take her and get back through that Portal—fast." He looked at Linda Carroll. "Don't be afraid," he said. "You know you love him; go with him now, or regret it all your days."

"Will you come?" asked Bram. He held out his hand to her. Linda hesitated, then put her hand in his. Bram went with her to the mirror surface, handed her through. He looked back at Tremaine.

"I do not understand, man of Earth," he said. "But I thank you." Then he was gone.

Alone in the dim-lit grotto Tremaine let his hands fall from the grips, staggered to the rocker and sank down. He felt weak, drained of strength. His hands ached from the strain of the ordeal. How long had it lasted? Five minutes? An hour? Or had it happened at all?

But Bram and Linda Carroll were gone. He hadn't imagined that. And the Niss were defeated.

But there was still his own world to contend with. The police would be waiting, combing through the house. They would want to know what he had done with Miss Carroll. Maybe there would be a murder charge. There'd be no support from Fred and the Bureau. As for Jess, he was probably in a cell now, looking a stiff sentence in the face for obstructing justice . . .

Tremaine got to his feet, cast a last glimpse at the empty room, the outlandish shape of the Repellor, the mirrored portal. It was a temptation to step through it. But this was his world, with all its faults. Perhaps later, when his strength returned, he could try the machine again . . .

The thought appalled him. *The ashes of hate are worse than the ashes of love*, he thought. He went to the stairs, climbed them, pressed the button. Nothing happened. He pushed the panel aside by hand and stepped into the kitchen. He circled the heavy table with the candlestick, went along the hall and out onto the porch. It was almost the dawn of a fresh spring day. There was no sign of the police. He looked at the grassy lawn, the row of new-set saplings.

Strange, he thought. *I don't remember any saplings. I thought I drove in under a row of trees* . . . He squinted into the misty early morning gloom. His car was gone. That wasn't too surprising; the cops had impounded it, no doubt. He stepped down, glanced at the ground ahead. It was smooth, with a faint footpath cut through the grass. There was no mud, no sign of tire tracks—

The horizon seemed to spin suddenly. *My God!!* Tremaine thought. *I've left myself in the year* 1901 . . .!

He whirled, leaped up on the porch, slammed through the door and along the hall, scrambled through the still-open panel, bounded down the stairs and into the cave—

The Repellor was gone. Tremaine leaped forward with a cry—and under his eyes, the great mirror twinkled, winked out. The black box of the hyperwave receiver lay alone on the floor, beside the empty rocker. The light of the kerosene lamp reflected from the featureless wall.

Tremaine turned, stumbled up the steps, out into the air. The sun showed a crimson edge just peeping above distant hills.

1901, Tremaine thought. *The century has just turned. Somewhere a young fellow named Ford is getting ready to put the nation on wheels, and two boys named Wright are about to give it wings. No one ever heard of a World War, or the roaring Twenties, or Prohibition, or FDR, or the Dust Bowl, or Pearl Harbor. And Hiroshima and Nagasaki are just two cities in distant floral Japan . . .*

He walked down the path, stood by the rutted dirt road. Placid cows nuzzled damp grass in the meadow beyond it. In the distance a train hooted.

There are railroads, Tremaine thought. *But no jet planes, no radio, no movies, no automatic dish-washers. But then there's no TV, either. That makes up for a lot. And there are no police waiting to grill me, and no murder charge, and no neurotic nest of bureaucrats waiting to welcome me back . . .*

He drew a deep breath. The air was sweet. *I'm here*, he thought. *I feel the breeze on my face and the firm sod underfoot. It's real, and it's all there is now, so I might as well take it calmly. After all, a man with my education ought to be able to do well in this day and age!*

Whistling, Tremaine started the ten-mile walk into town.

THE OTHER SKY

❋ 1 ❋

It was late. The third level walkaway was deserted except for a lone Niss standing under the glare of a polyarc fifty feet ahead. Vallant hurried along, only half-listening to the voice of the newser from the tiny tri-D set he carried:

". . . perturbation in the motion of Pluto. The report from the Survey Party confirms that the ninth planet has left its orbit and is falling toward the Sun. Dr. Vetenskap, expedition head, said that no explanation can be offered for the phenomena. Calculations indicate that although Pluto will cross the orbit of the Earth in approximately forty-five years, an actual collision is unlikely; however, serious consequences could follow a close passage of the body . . ."

Vallant turned the audio up. Ahead, the immobile Niss was staring at him with small red eyes.

". . . inexplicable disappearance from Pluto of a Survey scouting vessel," the newser was saying. "The boat's crew, operating in the northern hemisphere of the uninhabited planet, had left it in order to take solar observations; the stranded men, rescued after a three-day ordeal, stated that they observed the scout to rise, apparently under full control, and ascend to extreme altitude before being lost from view. The boat was fully fueled, and capable of an extended voyage. The Patrol is on the lookout for the stolen vessel, but so far—"

As Vallant came abreast of the waiting Niss, it moved suddenly into his path, reached out a four-fingered parody of a human hand, twitched the set from his grip and with a convulsive motion, crushed it flat.

"Here, what the devil—" Vallant started. But the Niss had already tossed the ruin aside, turned away to resume its immobile stance under the glare of the light.

Vallant stared at the creature, the dusty grey-green hide, furrowed like an alligator's, the flaccid crest that drooped over one pin-point eye, the dun-colored tunic and drab leather straps that hung loosely on the lean, five-foot body.

He took a step; the Niss turned its narrow head to face him. The tiny eyes glittered like rubies.

"Why did you smash my Trideo?" Vallant said angrily.

The Niss stared for a moment longer; then it opened its mouth—a flash of snow-white in the gloom—and flicked a tongue like a scarlet worm past snake teeth in an unmistakable gesture.

Vallant doubled a fist. Instantly, the Niss flipped back the corner of its hip-length cape, exposing the butt of a pistol-like apparatus with a flared muzzle.

Vallant locked eyes with the alien; the words of the ten-times-daily public service announcement came back to him:

"Remember—it is our privilege to welcome the Niss among us as honored guests, who share their vast knowledge with us freely, to the betterment of all mankind."

The Niss stood, waiting. Vallant, fists still clenched, turned and walked away.

At the door to his apartment block Vallant took out his electro-key, pressed it in the slot. From behind him there was a tiny sound, a whistling cough. Vallant turned; a wizened face on a turkey neck peered at him.

"Ame," a voice as thin as smoke said. "Lord, boy, you look wonderful . . ." The old man came closer, stood round-shouldered, one veined hand clutching the lapels of an oddly cut coat. A few strands of wispy, colorless hair crossed the age-freckled skull. White stubble covered the sagging cheeks; the pale lines of old scars showed against the crepey skin.

"Guess you don't know me, Ame. . ."

"I can't say that I do," Vallant said. "What—"

"That's all right, Ame; no way you could, I guess . . ." The old man held out a hand that trembled like a leaf in a gentle breeze. "We served in the Navy together; we've been through a lot. But you don't know. It's been a long time . . ." The wrinkled face twisted into an unreadable expression. "Longer than you'd think."

Vallant shook his head. "You must have me confused with someone else, old-timer. I've never been in the Navy."

The old man nodded as though Vallant had agreed with him. "There's a lot you need to know about, Ame.

That's why I came. I had to, you see? Because if I didn't, why, who knows what might happen?"

"I don't—"

"Look, Ame," the old man cut in urgently, "could we go inside?" He glanced both ways along the walkaway. "Before one of those green devils shows his ugly face . . ."

Vallant looked at the old man. "You mean the Niss?"

The old eyes were bright. "That's who I mean, Ame; but don't you worry, boy; we'll take care of them—"

"That's careless talk, granddad. The Syndarch frowns on unfriendly remarks about our honored guests." Vallant opened the door. "You'd better come inside."

In Vallant's flat, the old man fumbled in his coat. "We got no time now to waste, Ame. There's things we've got to do, fast, and I need help . . ."

"If you're a former Navy man, the Society will take care of you," Vallant said.

"Not money, Ame. I've got all that I need." He took out a much-folded paper, opened it with shaking hands, handed it across to Vallant. It was a map, creased and patched, grimy and oil-splattered. The legend in the corner read:

TERRESTRIAL SPACE ARM—
POLAR PROJECTION. Sol IX
March 2212.

The old man leaned, pointing. "See this spot right here? A river cuts through the mountains—a river of liquid nitrogen. The gorge is a thousand feet deep—and the falls come thundering down out of the sky like the end of the world. That's the place, Ame. They'd kill to get it, make no mistake—and that'd be only the beginning."

"Who'd kill?"

"The sneaking, filthy Niss, boy—who else?" the old man's voice snapped with an echo of youthful authority. "They trailed me in, of course. You heard about the stolen Survey boat?"

Vallant frowned. "You mean the one that disappeared on Pluto?"

The ancient head nodded quickly. "That's right, Ame. That was me. Lucky, them coming down like they did. Otherwise, I'd have had another thirty-odd years to wait. Might not of made it. I figured to lose them but I'm getting old; not as sharp as I used to be. I killed one an hour ago. Don't know how long I've got—"

"You *killed* a Niss?"

"Not the first one, either." The old man's toothless grin was cheerful. "Now, what I have to tell you, Ame—"

"Look . . ." Vallant's voice was low. "I won't turn you in—but you can't stay here. God knows I have no use for the Niss, but killing one. . ."

The old man looked into Vallant's face, searchingly. "You *are* Amory Vallant . . . ?"

"That's right. I don't know how you know my name, but—"

"Look here, Ame. I know it's hard to understand. And I guess I wander; getting old . . ." He fumbled over his pockets, brought out a warped packet, paper-wrapped, passed it over to Vallant.

"Go ahead—take a look."

Vallant unfolded the wrappings, took out a once-glossy

tri-D photo. It showed a line of men in regulation ship suits standing against a curving wall of metal. The next was a shot of a group of boyish-faced men in identical Aerospace blue blouses, sitting at a long table, forks raised toward mouths. In another, two men stood on a stormy hillside scattered with the smoking fragments of a wrecked ship.

Vallant looked up, puzzled. "What—?"

"Look closer, Ame. Look at the faces." The old man's bony finger reached, indicated a man in a worn uniform, looking down at torn metal. He had a lean face, short-cropped sandy hair, deep-set eyes—

"Hey!" Vallant said. "That looks like me!"

"Uh-huh. In the other ones, too . . ." The old man crouched forward, watching Vallant's face as he shuffled through the pictures. There he was—standing on the bridge of a capital ship, clipboard in hand; leaning on a bar, holding a glass, an arm over the shoulders of a square-faced red-headed man; posing stiffly before a bazaar stall manned by a sullen Niss with his race's unfortunate expression of permanent guilt stamped on the grey-green features.

Vallant stared at the old man. "I've never been in the Navy—I never saw the inside of a ship of the line—I was never on the Niss world . . . !" He flipped through the remaining pictures. "Here's one where I've got gray hair and a commodore's star! How the devil did you fake these up, old-timer?"

"They're not fakes, Ame. Look there—that red-headed young fellow—do you know him?"

Vallant studied the picture. "I have a friend named

Able; Jason Able—at Unitech; we're both students there. This looks like him—only older."

The old man was nodding, grinning. "That's right, Ame. Jase Able." The grin faded abruptly. "But I didn't come here to talk about old times—"

"Is he a relative of yours?"

"Not exactly. Listen, Ame. My boat; they got it. Didn't have time to camouflage it like I planned. It's at the Granyauck Navy Yard now: I saw it yesterday. We've got to have that boat, Ame; it's the fastest model there is—you know how to handle her?"

"I guess so—I'm an Astronautics major. But hold on a minute. How do you know me? And where did you get these pictures? What's the map all about? Why did you kill a Niss—and what's this about a boat? You know the Syndarch outlawed private space travel thirty years ago . . . !"

"Hold on, Ame . . ." The old man wiped a trembling hand across his forehead. "I guess I'm going too fast—but I have to hurry. There's not time, Ame—"

"Start with the boat. Are you saying you stole it and came here from Pluto?"

"That's right, Ame. I—"

"That's impossible. Nobody could stay alive on Pluto. And anyway the Patrol or the Niss would stop any ship—"

"It's the same thing, Ame; the Syndarch is just the traitors that made peace with the Niss after the War—"

"War?"

"You don't even know about the War, do you?" The old man looked confused. "So much to tell, Ame—and no time. We've got to hurry. The War—not much of a fight to it; it was maybe thirty years ago; our ships were just starting their probes out beyond Big Jupe. The Niss hit us; rolled us up like a rug. What the Hell, we didn't have a chance; our ships were nothing but labs, experimental models, unarmed. The Niss offered a deal. Ramo took 'em up on it. The public never even knew. Now the Niss have occupied Earth for twenty-five years—"

"Occupied! But . . . they're supposed to be our honored guests—"

"That's the Syndarch line. As for why I came back, I had to, Ame. I had to tell you about Galliale and the Portal—"

"Galliale . . . ?"

"I could have stayed . . ." The old man's eyes were distant, the present forgotten. "But I couldn't chance it, Ame . . ." He seemed to pull himself together with an effort. "And anyway, I kind of missed the old life; there's no place for ship boots in fairyland."

There was a buzz from the front entry. The old man struggled to his feet, stared around the room, his lips working. "They're here already. I thought I'd thrown 'em off; I thought I was clear . . ."

"Hold on, old-timer; it's probably just a friend; sit down—"

"Any back way out of here, Ame?" The old man's eyes were desperate. From the door, the buzz sounded insistently.

"You think it's the police?"

"It's them or the Niss. I know, boy."

Vallant hesitated a moment, then went quickly to the

bedroom, into the closet, felt over the wall. A panel dropped, fell outward; a framed opening showed dark beyond it.

"I discovered this when they were doing some work on the other side; it's one advantage of cracker box construction. I phoned in a complaint, but they never fixed it. It opens into a utility room in the Municipal Admin block."

The old man hurried forward. "I'm sorry I got you into this, Ame. I won't come here again—you come to my place—the Stellar Castle on 900th—room 1196b. I been away two days now—I've got to get back. Don't tell 'em anything—and be sure you're not followed. I'll be waiting." He ducked through the opening.

From the next room, there was the sound of heavy pounding—then of splintering plastic. Vallant hastily clipped the panel back in place, turned as a thick, dark man with an egg-bald head slammed through the door-way. He wore tight cuffed black trousers and there was a bright metal servitude bracelet with a Syndarch escutcheon on his left wrist. His small, coal black eyes darted around the room.

"Where's the old man?" he rapped out in a voice like bullets hitting a plank.

"Who are you? What's the idea of smashing my door?"

"You know the penalty for aiding a traitor to the Syndarch?" The intruder went past Vallant, stared around the room.

"There's nobody here," Vallant said. "And even the Syndarch has no right to search without a warrant."

The bald man eyed Vallant.

"You telling me what rights the Syndarch's got?" He barked a short laugh, cut it off suddenly to glare coldly at Vallant.

"Watch your step. We'll be watching you now." Beyond the door, Vallant caught a glimpse of a dull Niss face.

"That reminds me," he said. "The Niss owe me a Tri-D set; one of them smashed mine today."

The beady eyes bored into him. "Yeah," the Syndarch man said. "We'll be watching you." He stepped past the smashed door.

As soon as he was gone, Vallant went to the closet and removed the panel.

✳ 2 ✳

Vallant stepped through the opening, fitted the panel back in place, felt his way past brooms and cans of cleaning compound, eased the door open, emerged into a dim-lit corridor. Lights showed behind a few doors along its shadowy length. He went toward a red exit light; a lone maintenance man shot him a sour look but said nothing. He pushed out through a rotating door onto the littered walkaway, went to a nearby lift, rode up to the fifth level, took the crosstown walkaway to the shabby section near the Gendye Tower. Here, near the center of the city, there were a few pedestrians out; a steady humming filled the air from the wheelways above. Between them, Vallant caught a glimpse of a bleary moon gleaming unnoticed in the remote sky.

It took Vallant half an hour to find the dark sideway where a dowdy plastic front adorned with a tarnished sunburst huddled between later, taller structures whose lower levels were darkened by the blight that washed about the bases of the city's towers like an overflowing sewer. Vallant stepped through a wide glass door that opened creakily before him, crossed to the dust-grimed directory, keyed the index; out-of-focus print flickered on the screen. Jason Able was registered in room 1196b.

Vallant stepped into the ancient mechanical lift; its door closed tiredly. Everything about the Stellar Castle seemed ready to sigh and give up.

On the hundred and tenth floor he stepped out, followed arrows to a warped plastic door against which dull florescent numerals gleamed faintly. He tapped; the door swung inward. He stepped inside.

It was a mean, narrow room with one crowded, dirt-glazed window, opening on an air shaft through which the bleak light of a polyarc filtered. There was a bunk bed, unmade, a wall locker with its doors ajar, its shelves empty, and beyond, a tiny toilet cubicle. A hinge-sprung suitcase lay near the bed; next to it, the single chair lay overturned. Vallant rounded the bed. The old man lay on his back on the floor. The waxy face—thin-nosed, sunken-cheeked—stared up at him with eyes as remote as a statue of Pharaoh.

Vallant touched the bony wrist; it was cool and inert as modeling clay. The packet of pictures lay scattered on the floor. Vallant felt inside the coat; the map was gone. He went to the locker; there was a covered bird-cage on its floor among curls of dust, a small leather case beside it.

He checked the suitcase; it contained worn garments of strange cut, a leather folder with six miniature medals, a few more edge-crimped photos, a toy crossbow, beautifully made, and a Browning 2mm needler.

A tiny sound brought Vallant upright; he reached for the needler, searching the gloom. From somewhere above him, a soft scraping sounded. Among the shadows under the ceiling, two tiny amber lights glinted; something small and dark moved. Vallant flipped the pistol's safety off—

A shape no bigger than a cat dropped to the bed with an almost noiseless thump.

"You are Jason's friend," a piping voice said. "Did you come to help me?"

✷ 3 ✷

It was almost man-shaped, with large eyes which threw back crimson highlights, oversized foxlike ears, a sharp nose; it wore form-fitting clothing of a dark olive color which accentuated its thin limbs and knobby joints. Dark hair grew to a widow's peak on its forehead.

"What are you?" Vallant's voice was a hoarse whisper.

"I'm Jimper." The tiny voice was like the peeping of a chick. "The Not-men came. Jason is dead; now who will help Jimper?" The little creature moved toward Vallant. There was a jaunty cap on the doll-sized head; a broken feather trailed from it.

"Who killed the old man?"

"Are you his friend?"

"Yes . . . he seemed to think so."

"There was a large man—great in the belly, and with splendid clothes, though he smelled of burning drug-weed. Two of the Not-men were with him. They struck Jason a mighty blow, and afterward they took things from his clothes. I was afraid; I hid among the rafters."

"What are you—a pet?"

The little creature stood straighter.

"I am the Ambassador of the King. I came with Jason to see the King of the Giants."

Vallant pocketed the gun. "I've been to a lot of places; I never saw anything like you before. Where did you come from?"

"My land of Galliale lies beyond the Place of Blue Ice—the world you know as Pluto."

"Pluto? Out there the atmosphere falls as snow every winter. Nothing could live there."

"Green and fair lies Galliale beyond the ice." The little figure crept closer to the foot of the bed. "Jason is dead. Now Jimper is alone. Let me stay with you, Jason's friend."

"But—I don't need a pet . . ."

"I am the Ambassador of the King!" the manikin piped. "Do not leave me alone," he added, his tiny voice no more than a cricket's chirp.

"Do you know why they killed the old man?"

"He knew of the Portal—and my land of Galliale. Long have the Not-men sought it—"

The tiny head came up suddenly; the long nose twitched. "The Not-men," the bird voice shrilled. "They come . . . !"

Vallant stepped to the door, listened. "I don't hear anything . . ."

"They come—from below. Three of them, and evil are their thoughts."

"You're a mind reader, too?"

"I feel the shapes of their intentions . . ." The tiny voice was frantic. "Flee, Jason's friend; they wish you harm . . ."

"What about you?"

"Jason made a carrying box for me—there—in the locker."

Vallant grabbed up the cage, put it on the bed; the Ambassador of the King crept inside.

"My crossbow," he called, "it lies in Jason's box; and my knapsack."

Vallant retrieved the miniature weapon and the box, handed them in to their owner.

"All right, Jimper. I'm not sure I'm not dreaming you—but I'd hate to wake up and find out I wasn't."

"Close are they now," the small voice shrilled. "They come from there . . ." He pointed along the gloomy hall-way. Vallant went in the opposite direction. He glanced back from the first cross-corridor; three Niss stepped from the elevator; he watched as they went to the room he had just left, pushed inside.

"It looks as though you know what you're talking about, Jimper," Vallant said. "Let's get away from here before the excitement begins."

✸ 4 ✸

There were a scattering of late-shift workers hurrying through the corridor when Vallant reached the secret entry to his flat. He waited until they had hustled out of sight, then opened the utility room door, stepped inside. In the cage, Jimper moaned softly.

"The Feared Men," he peeped.

Vallant stood stock-still. He put his ear against the removable panel. A heavy voice sounded from beyond it.

"How did I know he'd die so easy? I had to make him talk, didn't I?"

"Fool!" hissed a voice like gas escaping under pressure. "Little will he talk now."

"Look, your boss isn't going to blame me, is he?"

"You will die, and I with you."

"Huh? You mean—"

There was a sudden hiss, then a sound of rattling paper. "Perhaps this will save our lives," the Niss voice said. "The map . . . !"

In the cage, Jimper whined. "I fear the Not-men," he piped. "I fear the smell of hate."

Vallant raised the cage to eye level. The little creature inside blinked large, anxious eyes at him. "They found the old man's map," he said. "I left it lying in plain sight. Was it important?"

"The map?" Jimper stood, gripping the bars of the cage. "Vallant—with the map they can seek out my Land of Galliale, and fall upon us, unsuspecting! They must not have it!"

"They've already got it—and if I'd walked in the front door, they'd have had me too. I'm in trouble, Jimper. I've got to get away, hide out somewhere . . ."

"First, the map, Vallant!"

"What do you mean?"

"We must take it from them. You are a giant, like them; can you not burst in and take it from them?"

"I'm afraid heroics are out of my line, Jimper. It's too bad, but—"

"Jason died for the map, Vallant. He came to warn you, and they killed him. Will you let them take it now?"

Vallant rubbed his jaw. "I've gotten mixed up in something I don't understand. I don't know the old man; he never got around to saying why he came to see me—"

"To save a world, Vallant—perhaps a Galaxy. And now only you can help!"

"The map is that important, is it?"

"More than you could know! You must make a plan, Vallant!"

Vallant nodded. "I guess my number's up anyway; I'd never get clear of the city, with the Syndarch and the Niss after me. I might as well go down fighting." He chewed his lip. "Listen, Jimper. I want you to sneak around front, with my key. You can reach the keyhole if you climb up on the railing. When you plug it in, the buzzer will go. Then I'll move in and hit them on the flank. Maybe I can put it over. Can you do it?"

Jimper looked out through the brass bars of the bird-cage. "It is a fearsome thing to walk abroad among the giants . . ." He gripped his five-inch crossbow. "But if you ask it, Vallant, I will try."

"Good-by." Vallant put the cage on the floor, opened it. Jimper stepped out, stood looking up at the man. Briefly, Vallant described the location of his apartment entry; he handed over the electro-key.

"Be careful; there may be somebody watching the

place from outside. If you make it, give it one good blast and run like hell; I'll meet you back here. If I don't show up in ten minutes, you're on your own."

Jimper stood straight; he settled his cap on his head.

"I am the Ambassador of the King," he said. "I shall do my best, Vallant."

Vallant waited, his ear to the thin panel. The two who lay in wait inside conversed excitedly, in low tones.

"Look," the man said. "The guy's wise we're after him. He won't come back here; we've got to get the map to the Syndarch—"

"To the Uttermagnate!"

"The Syndarch's my boss—"

"He is a dirt beneath the talons of the Uttermagnate!"

Faintly, the door buzzer sounded. The voices ceased abruptly. Then:

"OK, you cover him as he comes in; I clip him back of the ear . . ."

Vallant waited a quarter of a minute; then he pushed on the panel, caught it as it leaned into the room, stepped in after it, the gun in his hand. He crossed quickly to the connecting doorway to the outer room. The man and the Niss stood across the room on either side of the entry, heads cocked alertly; the alien held a gun, the man a heavy sap.

"Don't move!" Vallant snapped.

The two whirled on him like clockwork soldiers. Vallant jumped aside, fired as the Niss burned the door frame by his ear. The Browning snarled; the alien slammed back, fell, a cluster of needles bright against the leathery hide over his heart. The man dropped the length of weighted hose, raised his hands.

"Don't shoot . . . !" he choked. Vallant went to him, lifted the map from his pocket.

"Talk fast!" Vallant snapped. "Who's the old man?"

"All I know is," the man stuttered, "the Niss boss said bring the old guy in."

"You tailed him here, but he lost you. How'd you get to him?"

"There was four teams working him. Mullo picked him up when he'd taken a hack on One Level."

"Why'd you kill him?"

"It was an accident—"

"Why'd you come back for me?"

"Once the old guy was dead, you was the only lead . . ."

"Lead to what?"

Sweat popped out on the man's veined temples. He had a narrow, horsey face, a long torso with too-short legs.

"I . . . dunno. It was something they wanted."

"You take orders from . . . those?" Vallant glanced at the dead Niss.

"I do like I'm told," the man said sullenly.

"You know any prayers?"

The man's face broke like smoke in a gust of wind. He fell to his knees, clasped his hands in a grotesque parody of adoration. He babbled. Vallant stood over him.

"I ought to kill you—for my own protection," he said. "But that's where you skunks have the advantage . . ." He hit the man hard behind the ear with the gun butt; he fell on his face. Vallant trussed him with a maroon bathrobe cord, knotted a handkerchief over his mouth, then rose, looked around at the laden book shelves, the music storage unit, the well-stocked pantry beyond.

"It was nice while it lasted," he muttered. He went to the closet, stepped through into the dark room beyond.

"Jimper!" he called. There was no answer. The cage was empty, the tiny knapsack beside it. He picked it up, stepped out into the corridor, went to the exit, out into the walkaway, turned back toward the entrance to the apartment block.

As he passed the dark mouth of a narrow service-way, a sudden thump! sounded, followed by a squeal like a rusty hinge. Vallant whirled; a giant rat lay kicking long-toed hind feet, a three-inch length of wooden dowel projecting from its chest. Beyond it lay a second, its yellow chisel-teeth closed on a shaft which had entered its mouth and emerged under its left shoulder. Vallant took a step into the alley; a foot-long rodent darted at him. He pivoted, swung a foot, sent it thudding against the wall. He saw Jimper loose a bolt from his bow, then toss the weapon aside and draw a two-inch dagger. A red-eyed rodent rushed him; he danced aside, struck—

Vallant snatched him up, aimed a kick at the predator, quickly retreated to the dim-lit walkaway.

"I'm sorry, Jimper; I forgot about the rats . . ."

"My . . . bow . . ." Jimper keened. His head drooped sideways. Vallant was suddenly aware of the lightness of the small body; there seemed to be only bones under the silken-soft garments.

"How long since you've had a meal?"

"Jason gave Jimper food . . . before he went away . . ."

"You mean you waited there two days, in the dark, without food and water?"

Jimper stirred, tried to raise his head. "Jimper is tired . . ."

The elfin face was grayish, the eyes hollow.

"You've had a rough time, partner."

Vallant walked back up the alley, recovered the crossbow. The rats were gone—even the two dead ones, dragged away by their fellows.

"I'll get you some food," Vallant said, "then maybe you can tell me what this is all about."

"Then . . . you will help Jimper?"

"I don't know, Jimper. I just killed a Niss, and gave a Syndarch man a severe headache. I'm afraid I've permanently spoiled my popularity in this area. I have a couple of hours maybe before they find them. That means I'll have to make some very hurried travel arrangements. Afterwards, we can discuss future plans—if we still have any."

✳ **5** ✳

Vallant stood in the angle of the security wall surrounding the Navy Yard, sheltered from the glare of the polyarcs. "Do you know which one it is?" he whispered.

"Well I know her, Vallant; a fleet vessel; none can match her."

"Point her out to me." He lifted the cage to a shed roof, scrambled up beside it. Over the wall-top, the lights threw back dull highlights from the tarnished hulls of three Syndarch hundred-tonners squatting in an irregular row. Beyond, half a dozen of the Syndarch's private racing stable were parked, their peeling decorative paint giving them a raffish air. Far to the right, Jimper pointed to a smaller vessel, agleam with chromalloy and enamel, glistening under the polyarcs. Men worked around it; nearby stood four armed men in the pale green of the Syndarch contract police.

"I'll have to take some chances now," Vallant said softly. "You'd better stay here; I won't be able to look out for you."

"I will look out for myself, Vallant!"

"All right, partner; but this will be risky."

"What will you do, Vallant?" Jimper's voice was a mouse's squeak, but he stood with a bold stance, looking up at Vallant.

"I'm going to waltz into Operations as though I owned a controlling interest, and see what happens. Keep your fingers crossed."

"Jimper will be near, Vallant. Good luck."

Vallant stooped, put out a hand. "Thanks, partner—and if I don't make it, good luck to you—and your land of Galliale." Jimper laid his tiny hand solemnly against Vallant's palm.

"Stout heart," he piped, "and fair hunting."

Vallant strode through the gate, walking briskly like a man intent on serious business. A Niss eyed him from a sentry box by the gate as he rounded the end of a building, went up steps, pushed through wide doors, went along a carpeted corridor and under an archway into a bright room with chart-lined walls. A fat man with a high, pink forehead loomed up from behind a counter, glanced at Vallant, let his bored gaze wander past. Vallant rapped smartly on the counter.

"A little service here, please, my man. I need a clearance order; I'm taking a boat out."

The fat man's eyes flicked back to Vallant. He plucked a plastic toothpick from a breast pocket, plied it on large, square teeth. "So who're you?" he inquired in an unoiled tenor.

"I'm the Syndarch's new pilot," Vallant said coldly. He wiped a finger across the dusty counter, examined its tip distastefully. "I trust that meets with your approval?"

There was an extended silence, broken only by the lick of the fat man's toothpick.

"Nobody never tells me nothing," he stated abruptly. He turned, plucked a paper from a desk behind him, scribbled on it, tossed it at Vallant.

"Where's old man Ramo going this time?"

Vallant looked at him sharply. "Mind your tone, my man."

The toothpick fell with a tiny clatter. The fat man's face was suddenly strained. "Hey, I din't mean nothing. I'm loyal, you bet." He indicated himself with an ink-stained thumb. "I just got kind of a haha informal way of talking."

"What was that lift-off time again?" Vallant was still looking sternly at the man.

"Plenty time yet, sir." The squeaky voice was half an octave higher. "I wasn't expecting the pilot in fer half an hour yet. I got my paper work all set early, just in case, like. All you got to do, you got to sign the flight plan." The man pointed with the blue thumb.

Vallant scribbled *Mort Furd* in the indicated space, folded his copy and tucked it away.

"About that crack," the fat man started.

"I'm giving you the benefit of the doubt," Vallant said.

Outside, Vallant walked quickly across to the low shed under the glare sign reading EQUIPMENT—STATION PERSONNEL ONLY. Inside, a small man with lined brown skin and artificial-looking black hair looked at him over a well-thumbed picto-news.

"I want to draw my gear," Vallant said briskly. "I'm taking the new boat out in a few minutes."

The little man got to his feet, held out a hand expectantly.

"Let's see that Issue Order."

"I'm running late," Vallant said. "I haven't got one."

The little man sat down and snatched up his paper. "Come back when you got one," he snapped.

"You wouldn't want to be the cause of delaying Leader Ramo's departure, would you?" Vallant looked at him pointedly.

"I do my job; no tickee no washee." The little man turned a page, appeared absorbed in his reading.

"Hey," Vallant said. The man glanced up, jaw lowered for a snappy retort. He saw the gun in Vallant's hand, froze, mouth open. Vallant plucked a length of wire from the table, tossed it to him. "Use this to tie your ankles together," he ordered. The magazine fell to the floor as the man complied. Vallant went behind him, cinched his hands with another length of stranded copper. He went along the bins, picked out a vacuum suit, pulled it on over his street clothes. He added an emergency power pack, a field communicator, emergency rations, a recycler unit.

Vallant stepped from the door—and was face to face with a heavy built Niss holding a gun like the one Vallant had first seen at the hip of the alien who had smashed his Tri-D set. The gun came up, pointed at his chest.

"Would you mind pointing that thing in some other direction?" Vallant started to edge past the alien. It hissed, jabbed the strange gun at him.

Vallant took a deep breath, wondering how fast Niss reflexes were.

"Perhaps I'd better explain," he started—

There was a sharp clatter behind the alien; the narrow head jerked around; Vallant took a step, hit the creature on the side of the head; it bounced backwards, went down hard on its back; the gun skidded away. Vallant jumped to the Niss, caught it by the harness, dragged it into the shadows of the shed. Jimper stepped into view.

"Well smote, Vallant!" he chirped.

"Your timing was perfect, partner!" Vallant looked toward the lighted ship. The ground crew was still at work, the guards lounging nearby.

"Here we go; make a wide swing. Wait until they're all admiring me, and then run for it." Vallant started across the open ramp with a long stride. A man with a clipboard strolled forward to meet him. Vallant flapped the Clearance Order at him.

"All set to lift?" he barked.

"Eh? Why, no; I haven't even run idling checks—" the man backed, keeping pace.

"Skip 'em; I'm in a hurry." Vallant brushed past, reached the access ladder, thumbed the lock control; it cycled open. A small figure bounded from shadow, leaped up, disappeared inside.

"Hey—"

"Clear the area; I'm lifting!" Vallant went up, swung through the open port, clanged it behind him, climbed up into the dim-lit control compartment, slid into the deep-padded acceleration couch, threw the shock frame in place.

"Get on the bunk, Jimper," he called. "Lie flat and hang on." He slammed switches. Pumps sprang into action; a whining built, merged with the rumble of the preheat burners. The communicator's light blinked garish red on the panel.

"You in the yacht," a harsh voice blared. "Furd, or whatever your name is—"

A Niagara of sound cut off the voice. The pressure of full emergency power crushed Vallant back in the seat. On the screen, the pattern of lights that was the port dwindled, became a smudge, then glided from view as the ship angled east, driving for Deep Space.

"We're clear, Jimper," Vallant called. "Now all we have to do is figure out where we're going . . ."

✳ **6** ✳

Mars was a huge, glaring disk of mottled pink, crumbling at the edge into blackness. It lit Jimper's face eerily as he perched on the edge of the chart table, watching the planet swing ponderously past on the screen.

"Not this world, Vallant!" Jimper piped again. "Jason came with me from the world of the Blue Ice—"

"You said your country was warm and green, Jimper; with a big orange sun. Let's be realistic: Pluto is only a few degrees above absolute zero. Your home couldn't be there!"

"You must believe Jimper, Vallant." The little creature looked appealingly across at the man. "We must go to Pluto!"

"Jimper, we need supplies, information. We'll land at Aresport, rest up, take in some of the scenery I've heard about, then see what we can find out about the old man's itinerary—"

"The Not-men will capture us!"

"Jimper, we couldn't be that important. Mars is an autonomous planet. I know commerce has been shut off for years, but the Syndarch couldn't have any influence out here—"

"Vallant—the Not-men own all the worlds! There are no Giants but those who serve them—but for those on Earth—and why they let them live, I cannot say—"

"You've got a lot of wild ideas, Jimper—"

"Look!" Jimper's finger pointed at the screen. A black point was visible, drifting across the center of the planetary disc. Vallant adjusted a control, locked a tracking beam on the vessel.

"If he holds that course, we're going to scrape paint . . . !" He keyed the communicator. "*Ariane* to Mars Tower West; I'm in my final approach pattern; request you clear the Sunday drivers out of the way."

"Pintail Red to Pintail One," a faint voice came from the speaker. "I think I've picked up our bogie; homing in on 23—268—6, sixteen kiloknots . . ."

"Pintail Red, get off the clear channel, you damned fool—" The angry voice dissolved into a blur of scrambled transmission.

"Panam Patrol—out here?" Vallant twiddled controls, frowning at the instruments. "What was that course? 23—268—6 . . ." He flipped a switch, read off the numerals which glowed on the ground glass.

"Hey, Jimper—that's us they're talking about . . . !"

A speck separated itself from the vessel on the screen, raced toward *Ariane*.

"Hang on to your hat, Jimper," Vallant called. "He means business . . ." He slammed the drive control lever full over; the ship leaped forward.

"I guess the Ares Pavilion's out, Jimper," he said between clenched teeth, "but maybe we can find a cozy little family-type hotel on Ganymede."

✸ 7 ✸

Vallant sagged over the control panel, his unshaven face hollow from the last week on short rations.

"*Ariane* to Ganymede Control," he croaked for the hundredth time. "Ganymede Control, come in . . ."

"None will answer, Vallant," Jimper piped.

"Looks like nobody home, Buddy," Vallant slumped back in the couch. "I don't understand it . . ."

"Will we go to Pluto now, Vallant?"

"You don't give up easily, do you, partner?"

Jimper sprang across, stood before Vallant, his feet planted on dial faces. "Vallant, my land of Galliale lies beyond the snows, deep among the Blue Ice mountains. You must believe Jimper!"

"We're low on rations and my fuel banks were never intended for this kind of high-G running, weeks on end. We'll have to turn back."

"Turn back to what, Vallant? The Not-men will surely slay you—and what will happen to Jimper?"

"There's nothing out there, Jimper!" Vallant waved a hand at the screen that reflected the blackness of space, the cold glitter of the distant stars. "Nothing but some big balls of ice called Uranus and Neptune, where the sun is just a bright star—"

"There is Pluto."

"So there is . . ." Vallant raised his head, looked into the small, anxious face. "Where could this nice warm place of yours be, Jimper? Underground?"

"The sky of Galliale is wide and blue, Vallant, and graced with a golden sun."

"If I headed out that way—and failed to find Galliale—that would be the end. You know that, don't you?"

"I know, Vallant. I will not lead you wrong."

"The old man said something about mountains of ice; maybe—" Vallant straightened. "Well, there's nothing to go back to. I've always had a yen to see what's out there. Let's go take a look, Jimper. Maybe there are still a few undreamed of things in Heaven and Earth—or beyond them."

✳ 8 ✳

The planet hung like a dull steel ball against the black; a brilliant highlight threw back the glinting reflection of the tiny disc that was the distant sun.

"All right, Jimper, guide me in," Vallant said hoarsely. "It all looks the same to me."

"When we are close, then I will know." Jimper's pointed nose seemed to quiver with eagerness as he stared into the screen. "Soon you will see, Vallant. Fair is my land of Galliale."

"I must be crazy to use my last few ounces of reaction mass to land on that," Vallant croaked. "But it's too late now to change my mind."

For the next hours, Vallant nursed the ship along, dropping closer to the icy world. Now plains of shattered ice-slabs stretched endlessly below, rising at intervals into jagged peaks gleaming metallically in light as eerie as an eclipse.

"There!" Jimper piped, pointing. "The Mountains of Blue Ice . . . !" Vallant saw the peaks then, rising deep blue in a saw-tooth silhouette against the unending snow.

The proximity alarm clattered. Vallant pushed himself upright, read dials, adjusted the rear screen magnification. The squarish lines of a strange vessel appeared, dancing in the center of the field. Beyond, a second ship was a tiny point of reflected light.

"We're out of luck, partner," Vallant said flatly. "They must want us pretty badly."

"Make for the mountains, Vallant!" Jimper shrilled. "We can yet escape the Not-men!"

Vallant pulled himself together, hunched over the controls. "OK, Jimper, I won't give up if you won't; but that's an almighty big rabbit you're going to have to pull out of that miniature hat!"

✷9✷

It was not a good landing. Vallant unstrapped himself, got to his feet, holding onto the couch for support. Jimper crept out from under the folded blankets that had fallen on him, straightened his cap.

"We're a couple of miles short of the mark, Jimper," Vallant said. "I'm sorry; it was the best I could do."

"Now must we hasten, Vallant; deep among the blue peaks lies Galliale; long must we climb." Jimper opened his knapsack, took out a tiny miniature of a standard vacuum suit, began pulling it on. Vallant managed a laugh.

"You came prepared, fella. I guess your friend Jason made that for you."

"Even in this suit, Jimper will be cold." The long nose seemed redder than ever. He fitted the grapefruit-sized bowl in place over his head. Vallant checked the panel. The screens were dead; the proximity indicator dial was smashed. He donned his suit hurriedly.

"They saw us crash; they'll pick a flatter spot a few miles back; that gives us a small head start." He cycled the port open; loose objects fluttered as the air whooshed from the ship; frost formed instantly on horizontal surfaces.

Standing in the open lock, Vallant looked out at a wilderness of tilted ice slabs, fantastic architectural shapes of frost, airy bridges, tunnels, chasms of blue ice.

"Jimper—are you sure—out there . . . ?"

"High among the ice peaks," Jimper's tiny voice squeaked in Vallant's helmet. "Jimper will lead you."

"Lead on, then." Vallant jumped down into the feathery drift-snow. "I'll try to follow."

The slopes were near-vertical now, polished surfaces that slanted upward, glinting darkly. The tiny arc-white sun glared between two heights that loomed overhead like cliffs. In the narrow valley between them, Vallant toiled upward, Jimper scampering ahead.

Far above a mighty river poured over a high cliff, thundering down into mist: its roar was a steady rumble underfoot.

Abruptly, Jimper's voice sounded in a shrill shout. "Vallant! Success! The Gateway lies ahead!"

Vallant struggled on another step, another, too exhausted to answer. There was a sudden heavy tremor underfoot. Jimper sprang aside. Vallant looked up; far above, a vast fragment detached from the wall, seeming to float downward with dreamlike grace, surrounded by a convoy of lesser rubble. Great chunks smashed against the cliff-sides, cascaded downward; the main mass of the avalanche shattered, dissolved into a cloud of ice crystals. At the last moment, Jimper's warning shrilling in his ears, Vallant jumped for the shelter of a crevice. A torrent of snow poured down through the sluicelike narrow, quickly rising above the level of Vallant's hiding place. His helmet rang like a bell bombarded with gravel, then damped out as the snow packed around him. Profound silence closed in.

"Vallant!" Jimper's voice came. "Are you safe?"

"I don't know . . ." Vallant struggled, moved his arms an inch. "I'm buried; no telling how deep." He scraped at the packed snow, managed to twist himself over on his face. He worked carefully then, breaking pieces away from above, thrusting them behind. He was growing rapidly weaker; his arms seemed leaden. He rested, dug, rested . . .

The harsh white star that was the sun still hung between the ice cliffs when Vallant's groping fingers broke through and he pulled himself out to lie gasping on the surface.

"Vallant—move not or you are surely lost!" Jimper piped in his ears.

He lay, sprawled, too tired even to lift his head.

"The Not-men," Jimper went on. "Oh, they are close, Vallant."

"How close?" Vallant groaned.

"Close . . . close."

"Have they seen me?"

"Not yet, I think—but if you stir—"

"I can't stay here . . ." With an effort, Vallant got to his hands and knees, then rose, tottered on, slipping and falling. Above, Jimper danced on a ledge, frantic with apprehension.

"It lies just ahead!" he shrilled. "The gateway to my land of Galliale; only a little more, Vallant! A few scant paces . . ."

Ice chips flew from before Vallant's face. For a moment he stared, not understanding—

"They have seen you, Vallant!" Jimper screamed. "They shoot; oh, for a quiver of bolts . . . !"

Vallant turned. A hundred yards below, a party of four suited figures—men or Niss—tramped upward. One raised the gun as a warning.

"Vallant—it is not far! Hasten!"

"It's no use," Vallant gasped. "You go ahead, Jimper. And I hope you find home again, up there in the ice."

"Jimper will not desert you, Vallant! Come, rise and try again!"

Vallant made a choking sound that was half sob, half groan. He got to his feet, lurched forward; ice smashed a foot away. The next shot knocked him floundering into a drift of soft snow. He found his feet, struggled upward. They were shooting to intimidate, not to kill, he told himself; they needed information—and there was no escape . . .

There was a ridge ahead; Vallant paused, gathering strength. He lunged, gained the top as a near-miss kicked a great furrow in the ice; then he was sliding down the reverse slope. A dark opening showed ahead—a patch of rock, ice-free, the mouth of a cave. He rose, ran toward it, fell, then crawled . . .

It was dark suddenly; Vallant's helmet had frosted over. He groped his way on, hearing the sharp ping! of expanding metal.

"This way!" Jimper's voice rang in his helmet. "We will yet win free, Vallant!"

"Can't go . . . farther . . ." Vallant gasped. He was down

now, lying on his face. There was a minute tugging at his arm. Through the frost melting from his face plate, he saw Jimper's tiny finger, pulling frantically at his sleeve. He got to his knees, stood, tottered on. A powerful wind seemed to buffet at him. Wind—in this airless place . . .

Without warning, a gigantic bubble soundlessly burst; that was the sensation that Vallant felt. For a moment he stood, his senses reeling; then he shook his head, looked around at the cave walls. Through the water trickling down over his helmet, he saw packed earth walls shored up by spindly logs. Far ahead, light gleamed faintly—Jimper scampered out of sight. . .

A terrific blow knocked him flat. He rolled, found himself on his back, staring toward four dark figures, silhouetted against the luminous entrance through which he had come a minute before.

"I will bring rescuers!" Jimper's voice shrilled in Vallant's helmet.

"Run!" Vallant choked. "Don't let . . . them get you, too . . ."

Faintness overtook him . . .

"Do not despair, Vallant," Jimper's voice seemed faint, far away. "Jimper will return . . ."

They stood over him, three Niss, grotesque and narrow-faced in their helmets, and one human, a whiskery, small-eyed man. Their mouths worked in a conversation inaudible to Vallant. Then one Niss made a downward motion with his hand; the man stepped forward, reached—

Suddenly, a wooden peg stood against the grey-green

fabric of his ship suit, upright in the center of his chest. A second magically appeared beside it—and a third. The man toppled, clutching . . . Behind him a Niss crouched, a flick of scarlet tongue visible against the gape of the white mouth—

A shaft stood abruptly in its throat. It fell backwards. Vallant raised his head; a troop of tiny red and green clad figures stood, setting bolts and loosing them. A Niss leaped, struck down two—then stumbled, fell, his thin chest bristling. The last Niss turned, ran from sight.

"Vallant!" Jimper's voice piped. "We are saved!"

Vallant opened his mouth to answer and darkness closed in.

✳ **10** ✳

Vallant lay on his back, feeling the gentle breeze that moved against his skin, scenting the perfumed aroma of green, growing things. Somewhere, a bird trilled a melody. He opened his eyes, looked up at a deep blue sky in which small white clouds sailed, row on row, like fairy yachts bound for some unimaginable regatta. All around were small sounds like the peeping of new-hatched chicks. He turned his head, saw a gay pavilion of red and white striped silk supported by slim poles of polished black wood topped with silver lance heads. Under it, around it, all across the vivid green of the lawnlike meadow, thronged tiny manlike figures, gaudily dressed, the males with caps and crossbows, or armed with foot-long swords, their mates in gossamer and the sparkle of tiny gems.

At the center of the gathering, in a chair like a doll's, a corpulent elf lolled in the shadow of the pavilion. He jumped as he saw Vallant's eyes upon him. He pointed, peeping excitedly in a strange, rapid tongue. A splendidly dressed warrior walked boldly toward Vallant, planted himself by his outflung hand, recited a speech.

"Sorry, Robin Goodfellow," Vallant said weakly. "I don't understand. Where's Jimper?"

The little creature before him looked about, shouted. A bedraggled fellow in muddy brown came up between two armed warriors.

"Alas, Vallant," he piped. "All is not well in my land of Galliale."

"Jimper—you look a bit on the unhappy side, considering you brought off your miracle right on schedule . . ."

"Something's awry, Vallant. There sits my King, Tweeple the Eater of One Hundred Tarts—and he knows not his Ambassador, Jimper!"

"Doesn't know you . . . ?" Vallant repeated.

"Jason warned me it would be so," Jimper wailed. "Yet I scarce believed him. None here knows faithful Jimper . . ."

"Are you sure you found the right town? Maybe since you left—"

"Does Jimper not know the place where he was born, where he lived while forty Great Suns came and went?" The manikin took out a three-inch square of yellow cloth, mopped his forehead. "No, Vallant; this is my land—but it lies in the grip of strange enchantments. True, at my call the King sent warriors who guard the cave to kill the Not-men—the Evil Giants—but they would have killed you, too, Vallant, had I not pleaded your helpless state, and swore you came as a friend. We Spril-Folk have ever feared the memory of the Evil Giants."

"Kill me?" Vallant started to laugh, then remembered the shafts bristling in the bodies of the Niss. "I've come too far to get myself killed now."

"Near you were to a longer journey still, Vallant. I know not how long the king will stay his hand."

"Where are we, Jimper? How did we get here?"

"The king's men dragged you here on a mat of reeds."

"But—how did we get out of the cave . . . ?"

"Through the Portal, Vallant—as I said, yet you would not believe!"

"I'm converted," Vallant said. "I'm here—wherever here is. But I seem to remember a job of world-saving I was supposed to do."

Jimper looked stricken. "Alas, Vallant! King Tweeple knows naught of these great matters! It was he whom Jason told of the Great Affairs beyond the Portal, and the part the Folk must play."

"So I'm out of a job?" Vallant lay for a moment, feeling the throb in his head, the ache that spread all through his shoulders and back.

"Maybe I'm dreaming," he said aloud. He made a move to sit up—

"No, Vallant! Move not, on your life!" Jimper shouted. "The King's archers stand with drawn bows if you should rise to threaten them!"

Vallant turned his head; a phalanx of tiny bowmen stood, arrows aimed, a bristling wall of foot-tall killers. Far away, beyond the green meadow, the clustered walls and towers of a miniature city clung to a hillside.

"Didn't you tell the King that I came to help him?"

"I pledged my life on it, Vallant—but he names me stranger. At last he agreed that so long as you lay sorely hurt, no harm could come to you—but take care! The King need but say the word, and you are lost, Vallant!"

"I can't lie here forever, Jimper. What if it rains?"

"They prepare a pavilion for you, Vallant—but first must we prove your friendship."

Jimper mopped his face again. Vallant stared up at the sky.

"How badly am I hurt?" Vallant moved slightly, testing his muscles. "I don't even remember being hit."

"A near-miss, meant to warn you, Vallant—but great stone chips are buried in your flesh. The King's surgeons could remove them—if he would so instruct them. Patience now, Vallant; I will treat with him again."

Vallant nodded, watched as Jimper, flanked by his guards, marched back to stand before the pudgy ruler. More piping talk ensued. Then Jimper returned, this time with two companions in crumpled conical hats.

"These are the Royal Surgeons, Vallant," he called. "They will remove the flints from your back. You have the royal leave to turn over—but take care; do not alarm them with sudden movements."

Vallant complied, groaning; he felt a touch, twisted his head to see a two-foot ladder lean against his side. A small face came into view at the top, apprehensive under a pointed hat. Vallant made what he hoped was an encouraging smile.

"Good morning, doctor," he said. "I guess you feel like a sailor getting ready to skin a whale . . ." Then he fainted.

✳ ✳ ✳ ✳

Vallant sat on a rough log bench, staring across the four-foot stockade behind which he had been fenced for three weeks now—as closely as he could estimate time, in a land where the sun stood overhead while he slept, wakened, and slept again. Now it was behind the tops of the towering poplar-like trees, and long shadows lay across the lawns under a sky of green and violet and flame. A mile away, lights glittered from a thousand tiny windows in the toy city of Galliale.

"If I could but convince the King," Jimper piped dolefully, a woebegone expression on his pinched features. "But fearful is the heart of Tweeple; not like the warrior kings of old, who slew the Evil Giants and freed the Fair Land of Galliale."

"These Evil Giants—were they the Niss?"

"Well might it be, Vallant. The legends tell that they were ugly as trolls and evil beyond the imagining of man or Spril. Ah, but those were brave days, when the Great Giants had fallen and only the Folk fought on."

"Jimper, do you suppose there's any truth in these legends of yours?"

The tiny Manikin stared. "Truth? True they be as carven stone, Vallant! True as the bolt sped from my bow! Look there!" He pointed to a gaunt stone structure rising from a twilit hill beyond the forest to the east.

"Is that a dream? But look at the stones of it! Plain it is that giants raised it once, long and long ago."

"What is it?"

"The Tower of the Forgotten; the legend tells that in it lies a treasure so precious that for it a king would give his crown; but the Thing of Fear, the Scaled One, the Dread Haik set to guard it by the Evil Giants, wards it well, pent in the walls."

"Oh, a dragon, too. I must say you have a completely equipped mythology, Jimper. What about these Great Giants—I take it they were friendly with the Spril?"

"Great were the Illimpi, Vallant, and proud were the Spril to serve them. But now they are dead, vanished all away; and yet, some say they live on, in their distant place, closed away from their faithful Folk by spells of magic, and the Scaled Haik of the Niss."

"Jimper—you don't believe in magic?"

"Do I not? Have I not seen the Cave of No Return with my own eyes—and worse, passed through it?"

"That's the tunnel we came in by, Jimper. You went through it with your friend Jason on the way out—and now you've returned."

"Ah, have I indeed, Vallant? True it is I passed through the Cave—and only my sworn fealty to my King forced me to it—but have I returned in truth? Who is there who welcomes my return?"

"I admit that's a puzzler . . ."

"Tales have I heard of others, long ago, who came from the Cave, strangers to the Tribe of Spril—and yet of our blood and customs. Always they talked of events unknown, and swore they had but ventured out into the Blue Ice—and now I am of their number; the stranger in his own land, whom no one knows."

Vallant rose, looking across toward the city. A long procession of torch bearers was filing from the city gates, winding across the dark plain toward Vallant's stockade. "It looks as though we have visitors coming, Jimper."

"Woe, Vallant! This means the King has decided your fate! Well has he wined this night—and drink was never known to temper the mercy of the King!"

"Jimper, if they're coming here to fill me full of arrows, I'm leaving!"

"Wait, Vallant. The captain of the guard is a decent fellow; I'll go to meet them. If they mean you ill, I'll . . . I'll snatch a torch and wave it thus . . ." He made circular motions above his head.

Vallant nodded. "OK, partner—but don't get yourself in trouble."

Half an hour later, the cavalcade halted before Vallant, Jimper striding beside the breast-plated captain. He ran forward.

"Mixed news, Vallant. This is the judgment of the King:—that you shall stand before him in his Hall, and show proof that you are friend to the Spril-Folk; and if you fail . . ."

"If I fail?" Vallant prompted.

"Then shall you enter the Cave of No Return, whence no man or Spril has ever come back."

The main avenue of the city of Galliale was ten feet wide, cobbled with cut stones no bigger than dice, winding steeply up between close-crowded houses, some half-timbered, others of gaily patterned masonry, with tiny shops below, gay with lights and merchandise, and open casement windows above, from which small, sharp-nosed faces thrust, staring at the looming giant who strode along, surrounded by the helmeted warriors of the King, toward the dazzling tower of light that was the Royal Palace of Tweeple the Eater of One Hundred Tarts.

"I don't understand why His Highness isn't content to let me sit out there under my canopy and smell the flowers," Vallant said to Jimper, who rode on his shoulder. "I've even volunteered to be his royal bodyguard—"

"He sees you grow well and strong, Vallant. He fears you may yet turn on the Folk as did the Evil Giants in the olden time."

"Can't you convince him I'm the good variety? I'd be handy to have around if that Niss who escaped came back, with a couple of his friends."

"Never will he return, Vallant! All who enter the Cave—"

"I know—but if he sends *me* out there in the cold, I'm likely to turn around and sneak right back in—tradition or no."

"Ah, if Jason were but here to vouch for you," Jimper piped. "Well he knew the tongue of the Spril, and wondrous the tales he told; charmed was King Tweeple, and many were the honors of Jason the Giant. But now, alas, the King knows naught of all these things."

"How did Jason happen to find Galliale?"

"He told of a great battle fought between the worlds, where Niss died like moths in the flame under the mighty weapons of the men of Earth—"

"The old man talked to me about a war; he said we lost."

"Jason's ship was hurt," Jimper went on. "He fell far, far, but at last brought the ship to ground among the Blue

Ice crags. He saw the Portal among the snows—the same in which we fought the Not-men, Vallant—and so he came to fair Galliale."

"And then he left again—"

"But not until he had tarried long and long among us, Vallant. At his wish, sentinels were posted, day and night, to watch through the Cave of No Return, which gives a fair view of the icy slopes and the plain beyond, for sight of men. Often, when he had drunk a hogshead or two of the King's best ale, he would groan, and cry aloud to know how it went with the battle of the Giants; but he knew the magic of the Cave, and so he waited. And then one day, when he had grown old and bent, the sentries gave him tidings that a strange vessel lay in view beyond the cave. Grieved was the King, and he swore that he would set his bowmen to guard the entrance to that enchanted path, that Jason the Teller of Tales might not walk down it to be seen no more; but Jason only smiled and said that go he would, asking only that an ambassador be sent with him, to treat with the Giants; and it was I, Jimper, warrior and scholar, whom the King chose."

"That was quite an honor; too bad he doesn't remember it; and I'm sorry I don't know any stories I could charm the old boy with. I haven't made much headway with the language yet."

"Long before Jason there was another Giant who came to Galliale," Jimper chirped. "No talker was he, but a mighty Giant of valor. The tale tells how he went in against the Scaled One, to prove his love to the King of those times. I heard the tale from my grandfather's father, when I was but a fingerling, when we sat in a ring under the moons and talked of olden times. And the King of those times—would have slain him—but in sign of friendship, he entered the Tower of the Forgotten, there to battle the Fanged One who guards the treasures. Then did the King know that he was friend indeed, and of the race of goodly Giants—"

"And what happened to him in the end?"

"Alas, never did he return from the Tower, Vallant—but honored was his memory!"

"That's a cheery anecdote. Well, we'll find out in a minute what Tweeple has in mind."

The procession had halted in the twenty-foot Grand Plaza before the palace gates. The warriors formed up in two ranks, flanking Vallant, bows ready. Beyond a foot-high spike-topped wall, past a courtyard of polished stones as big as dominoes, the great two-foot high entrance to the palace blazed with light. Beyond it, Vallant caught a glimpse of intricately carved paneling, tiny-patterns tapestries, and a group of Spril courtiers in splendid costumes, bowing and curtsying as the plump elf-king waddled forth to stand, hands on hips, staring up at Vallant.

He spoke in a shrill voice, waving ringed hands, pausing now and again to quaff a thimble-sized goblet offered by a tiny Spril no taller than a chipmunk.

He finished, and a servant handed him a scarlet towel to dry his pink face. Jimper, who had climbed down and taken up a position in the row of Spril beside the King, came across to Vallant.

"The king says . . ." He paused, swallowed. "That his royal will is . . ."

"Go ahead," Vallant urged, eyeing the ranks of ready bowmen. "Tell me the worst."

"To prove your friendship, Vallant—you must enter the Tower of the Forgotten, and there slay the Fanged One, the Scaled One, the Eater of Fire!"

Vallant let out a long sigh. "You had me worried there for a minute, Jimper," he said, almost gaily. "I thought I was going to provide a target for the royal artillery—"

"Jest not, Vallant!" Jimper stamped angrily. "Worse by far is the fate decreed by the King! Minded am I to tell him so—"

"Don't get yourself in hot water, Jimper; it's OK. I'm satisfied with the assignment."

"But, Vallant! No one—not even a Great Giant—can stand against the Fearsome One whom the Evil Giants set to guard the tower!"

"Will he be satisfied if I go into the Tower and come out again alive—even if I don't find the dragon?"

"Delude yourself no more, Vallant! The Scaled One waits there—"

"Still—"

"Yes, to enter the Tower is enough. But—"

"Fair enough. I may not come out dragging the body by the tail, but the legend won't survive the experience. When do I go?"

"As soon as may be . . ." Jimper shuddered, then drew himself erect. "But have no fear, Vallant; Jimper will be at your side."

Vallant smiled down at the tiny warrior. "That's a mighty brave thing to do, Jimper; I wish I could put your mind to rest about the dragon."

Jimper looked up at him, hands on hips. "And I, Vallant, wish that I could stir in you some healthful fear." He turned, strode back across the courtyard to the King, saluted, spoke briefly. A murmur ran out from the group of courtiers; then a treble cheer went up, while tiny caps whirled high. The King signaled, and white-clad servitors surged forward, setting up tables, laying out heaped platters, rolling great one-quart barrels into position.

"The King decrees a night of feasting, Vallant!" Jimper chirped, running to him. "And you too shall dine!"

Vallant watched while a platform normally used for speeches was set up and vivid rugs as fine as silk laid out on it; then he seated himself and accepted a barrel of ale, raised it in a toast to the King.

"Eat, drink, and be merry . . ." he called.

"If you can," Jimper said, mournful again, "knowing what tomorrow will bring."

✸ 11 ✸

In the fresh light of morning, Vallant strode across the emerald velveteen of the Plain of Galliale, feeling the cool air in his face, ignoring the throb in his head occasioned by last night's fifteen barrels of royal ale, watching the silhouette of the tower ahead growing larger against the dawn sky. A long sword—a man-sized duplicate of the tiny one at Jimper's belt—brought from the King's Treasury of Ancient Things for his use, swung at his side; in his hand he carried a nine-foot spear with a head of polished brass. Behind him trotted a full battalion of the Royal Guards, lances at the ready.

"I'll have to admit that King Tweeple went all-out in support of the expedition, Jimper," Vallant said. "Even if he did claim he'd never heard of your friendly Giant."

"Strange are the days when valued tales of old are unknown to the King. But no matter—pleased is he to find a champion."

"Well, I hope he's just as pleased when I come out and report that the Scaled One wasn't there after all."

Jimper looked up from where he scampered at Vallant's side. He was splendid now in a new scarlet cloak and a pink cap with a black plume. "Vallant, the Scaled One dwells in the Tower, as sure as blossoms bloom and kings die!"

Another quarter hour's walk brought Vallant and his escort through the forest of great conifers and out onto a wild-grown slope where long mounds overgrown with vines and brambles surrounded the monolithic tower at its crest. Near at hand a slab of white stone gleamed through underbrush. Vallant went close, pulled the growth away to reveal a weathered bench top.

"Hey, it looks as though someone used to live here— and a giant at that." He glanced at the tumuli, some large, some small, forming an intersecting geometric pattern that reached up to the tower's base.

"Those are the ruins of buildings and walls; this whole hilltop was built up at one time—a long time ago."

"Once those Giants whom the Spril served dwelt here," Jimper piped. "Then the Evil Giants came and slew our masters with weapons of fire; there was a great king among the Spril in those days, Vallant: Josro the Sealer of Gates. He it was who led the Folk in the war against the Ugly Ones." He looked up at the Tower. "But, alas, the Scaled One lives on to wall away the treasure of the Illimpi."

"Well, let's see if we can go finish the job, Jimper." Vallant went up past the mounded ruins. At the top he paused, looking back down the silent slope. "It must have been beautiful once, Jimper," he said. "A palace of white marble, and the view all across the valley . . ."

"Fair it was, and enchanted in its memory," Jimper said. "Long have we feared this place, but now we come to face its dreads. Lead on, Vallant; Jimper is at your side!"

A shrill trumpet note pierced the air. The troop of King's Lancers had halted. Their captain called an order; the two-foot lances swung down in a salute.

"They wait here," Jimper said. "The King will not risk them closer—and they guard our retreat, if the Scaled One should break out, which Fate forefend!"

Vallant returned the salute with a wave of his hand. "I guess if you believe in dragons, to come this far is pretty daring." He glanced down at Jimper. "That makes you a regular hero, partner."

"And what of you, Vallant! In your vast shadow Jimper walks boldly, but you go with only your lance and blade to meet the Terrible One!"

"That doesn't count; I don't really expect to meet him."

Now four warriors came forward, stumbling under the weight of a foot-long box slung from their shoulders by leather straps. They lowered it gingerly before Vallant, scampered back to the ranks.

"What's this, a medal—already?" Vallant pressed a stud on the side of the flat box; its lid popped up. Nestled in a fitted case lay a heavy electro-key of unfamiliar design. Vallant picked it up, whistled in surprise.

"Where did this come from, Jimper?"

"When long ago the Spril-Folk slew the Evil Ones, this did they find among the spoils. Long have we guarded it, until our Goodly Giants should come again."

Vallant examined the heavy key. "This is a beautiful job of microtronic engineering, Jimper. I'm beginning to wonder who these giants of yours were." He went up the last few yards of the vine-grown slope to the vast door of some smooth, dark material which loomed up in the side of the tower; the structure itself, Vallant saw, was not of stone, but of a weathered synthetic, porous and discolored with age.

"I'd give a lot to know who built this, Jimper," he said. "It must have been a highly technical people; that stuff looks like it's been there for a lot of years."

"Great were our Giants, and great was their fall. Long have we waited their return. Now it may be that you, Vallant, and Jason, are the first of those ancient ones to come back to your Galliale."

" 'Fraid not, Jimper. But we can still be friends." Vallant studied the edge of the door.

"Looks like we'll have to dig, Jimper. The dirt's packed in here, no telling how deep." Jimper unsheathed his sword, handed it to Vallant. "Use this; a nobler task could not be found for it."

Vallant set to work. Behind him, the ranks of the bowmen stood firm, watching. The unyielding surface of the door extended down six inches, a foot, two feet, before he came to its lower edge.

"We've got a job ahead, partner," he said. "I hope this snoozing dragon of yours is worth all the effort."

"For my part," Jimper said, "I hope the sound of our digging awakens him not too soon."

Two hours later, with the door cleared of the packed soil and an arc excavated to accommodate its swing, Vallant returned Jimper's sword, then took the key from the box.

"Let's hope it still works; I'd hate to try to batter my way past that . . ." He lifted the key to the slot in the door; there was a deep-seated click!, a rumble of old gears.

"It looks as though we're in business."

Vallant hammered back the heavy locking bar that secured the massive door; then, levering with his sword-blade, he swung the thick panel back, looked into a wide corridor inches deep in dust. The Captain of the Guard and four archers came up, waiting nervously to close the door as soon as Vallant was safely inside. Jimper sneezed. Vallant stooped, lifted him to his shoulder. He waved to the escort, who raised a nervous cheer, then stepped into the dust of the corridor, watched as the door slowly clanked shut behind him.

"We're in, Jimper," he said. "Now—which way to the dragon?"

Jimper fingered his crossbow, staring ahead along the dim hall. "H-he could be anywhere . . ."

"Let's take a look around." Vallant explored the length of the corridor which circled the tower against the outer wall, floundering through dust drifted deep under the loopholes high in the walls. At one point a great heap almost blocked the passage. He kicked at it, yelped; rusted metal plates showed where the covering of dust was disturbed.

"It looks like a dump for old armor," he complained, clambering over the six-foot obstruction. "Maybe this was an early junk yard . . ."

Jimper muttered fretfully. "Walk softly, Vallant . . ."

They completed the circuit, then took a stairway, mounted to a similar passage at a higher level. Everywhere the mantle of dust lay undisturbed. They found rooms, empty except for small metal objects of unfamiliar shape, half buried in dust. Once Vallant stooped, picked up a statuette of bright yellow metal.

"Look at this, Jimper," he said. "It's a human figure . . . !"

"True," Jimper agreed, squinting at the three-inch image. "No Spril form is that."

"This place must have been built by men, Jimper! Or by something so like them that the differences don't show. And yet, we've only had space travel for a couple of centuries—"

"Long have the Giants roamed the worlds, Vallant."

"Maybe—but humans have been Earth-bound until just lately. It's comforting to know that there are other creatures somewhere that look something like us—I guess."

They followed corridors, mounted stairs, prowled

through chambers large and small. Faint light from tiny apertures in the walls was the only illumination. High in the tower, they came to a final narrow flight of steps. Vallant looked up.

"Well, if he's not up here, I think we can consider the mission accomplished."

"Certain it is that somewhere lurks the Dread One," Jimper chirped. "Now l-let him b-beware!"

"That's the spirit." Vallant went up the stairs—gripping his sword now in spite of his skepticism; if there were anything alive in the tower, it would have to be here . . .

He emerged in a wide, circular room, high-vaulted, thick with dust. A lustrous cube, white, frosty-surfaced, twelve feet on a side, was mounted two feet clear of the floor at the exact center of the chamber. It seemed almost to glow in the dim room. Cautiously, Vallant circled it. The four sides were identical, unadorned, shimmering white.

Vallant let his breath out, sheathed the sword. "That's that," he said. "No dragon."

Perched on his shoulder, Jimper clutched his neck and whimpered.

"I fear this place, Vallant," he piped. "We have blundered—I know not how . . ."

"We're all right, old-timer," Vallant soothed. "Let's take a look around. Maybe we can pick up a souvenir to take back to old Tweeple—"

"Vallant, speak not with disrespect of my King!" Jimper commanded.

"Sorry." Vallant's boots went in to the ankle as he

crossed the drifted floor to the glistening polyhedron; he touched its surface; it was cool, slippery as graphite.

"Funny stuff," he said. "I wonder what it's for?"

"Vallant, let us not linger here."

Vallant turned, looked around the gloomy room. Vague shapes bulked under the dust blanket. He went to the table-like structure, blew at it, raising a cloud that made Jimper sneeze. He brushed at the array of dials and bright-colored knobs and buttons that emerged from the silt.

"It's some kind of control console, Jimper! What do you suppose it controls?"

"L-let us depart, Vallant!" Jimper squeaked. "I like not these ancient rooms!"

"I'll bet it has something to do with that . . ." Vallant nodded toward the cube. "Maybe if I push a couple of buttons—" He jabbed a finger at a large scarlet lever in the center of the panel. It clicked down decisively.

"Vallant—meddle not with these mysteries!" Jimper screeched. He crouched on Vallant's shoulder, eyes fixed on the lever.

"Nothing happened," Vallant said. "I guess it was too much to expect . . ." He paused. A draft stirred in the room; dust shifted, moving on the table top.

"Hey—" Vallant started.

Jimper huddled against his neck, moaning. Dust was flowing across the floor, drifting toward the glossy surface of the cube, whipping against it—and beyond. Vallant felt the draft increase, fluttering the fabric of his ship suit. The dust was rising up in a blinding cloud now; Vallant ducked his head, started toward the door. The wind rose to whirlwind proportions, hurling him against the wall; air was whining in through the loopholes; dust whipped and streamed, flowing to the face of the cube, which glared through the obscuring veil now with a cold white light. Vallant lunged again for the door, met a blast like a sand storm that sent him reeling, Jimper still clinging to his perch. He struggled to a sheltered angle between floor and wall, watched as the wind whirled the dust away, scouring the floor clean, exposing a litter of metallic objects. Nearby lay a finger-ring, an ornate badge, an odd shaped object that might have been a hand gun. Beyond were a scatter of polished metal bits, the size and shape of shark teeth.

Now, suddenly, the wind was lessening. The white-glaring rectangle was like an open window with a view of a noonday fog. The shrilling of the gale died. The room was still again.

"Now must we flee . . ." Jimper whistled; he flapped his cloak, settled his pink cap, edging toward the door. Vallant got to his feet, spitting dust. "Not yet, Jimper. Let's take a look at this . . ." He went close to the glowing square, stared at it, reached out a hand—

And encountered nothing.

He jerked his hand back quickly.

"Whew! That's cold!" He massaged the numbed hand. "Half a second, and it was stiff!"

Somewhere, far away, a faint, metallic clanking sounded.

"Vallant! He comes!" Jimper screeched.

"Calm down, Jimper! We're all right. It was a little thick there for a minute, but I suppose that was just some sort of equalization process. Or maybe this thing is a central cleaning device; sort of a building-sized vacuum cleaner—"

Abruptly, the panel before Vallant dimmed. Shapes whipped across it. The shadowy outlines of a room appeared, sharpened into vivid focus. Sounds came through; an electronic hum, the insistent pinging of a bell, then a clump of hurried feet.

A man appeared, stood staring across at Vallant, as through an opened doorway.

Or almost a man.

He was tall—near seven feet, and broad through the shoulders. His hair curled close to his head, glossy black as Persian lamb, and through it, the points of two short, blunt horns protruded, not quite symmetrically on either side of the nobly-rounded skull.

He spoke—staccato words in a language strange to Vallant. His voice was deep, resonant.

"Sorry, sir," Vallant got out, staring. "I'm afraid I don't understand . . ."

The horned man leaned closer. His large dark-blue eyes were fixed on Vallant's.

"*Lla*," he said.

Vallant shook his head. He tried to smile; the majestic figure before him was not one which inspired the lighter emotions. "I guess—" he started, then paused to clear his throat. "I guess we've stumbled onto something a little bigger than I expected . . ."

The horned man made an impatient gesture as Vallant paused. He repeated the word he had spoken. Vallant felt a tug at the knee of his suit.

"Vallant!" Jimper peeped. Vallant looked down. "Not now, Jimper—"

"I think—I think Jimper understand what the Great Giant means. In the ceremony of the crowning of the king, there is the phrase, *'qa ic lla'*. . . It is spoken in the old tongue, the speech of long ago; and the wise elders say those words mean 'when he speaks!' He would have you talk . . ."

The horned giant leaned toward Vallant, as though to see below the edge of the invisible plane between them. Vallant stooped, raised Jimper up chest-high. The Manikin straightened himself; then, standing on Vallant's hand, he doffed his feathered cap, bent nearly double in a deep bow.

"Ta p'ic ih sya, Illimpi," he chirped.

A remarkable change came over the horned man's face. His eyes widened; his mouth opened—then a vast smile lit his face like a floodlight.

"I' Ipliti!" he roared. He turned, did something out of sight of Vallant beyond the edge of the cube, whirled back. He spoke rapidly to Jimper. The little creature spread his hands, looking contrite.

"N'iqi," he said. *"N'iqi, Illimpi."*

The giant nodded quickly, looked keenly at Vallant.

"Lla, Vallant," he commanded.

"He knows my name . . ." Vallant gulped. "What am I supposed to talk about?"

"He is a Great Giant," Jimper peeped excitedly. "Well he knows Jimper's kind, from of old. Tell him all, Vallant—all that has befallen the race of Giants since last the Portal closed."

✳ 12 ✳

Vallant talked for five minutes, while the giant beyond the invisible barrier adjusted controls out of sight below the Portal's edge.

". . . when I came to, I was here—"

The giant nodded suddenly. "Well enough," he said clearly. Vallant stared in surprise. The horned man's lips, he noticed, did not move in synchronization with his words.

"Now," the giant said, "what world are you?"

"What . . . how . . . ?" Vallant started.

"A translating device; I am Cessus the Communicator. What world are you?"

"Well, I would have said I was on Pluto, except that . . . I couldn't be. And on the other hand, I must be . . ."

"Your language . . . A strange tongue it is; none that I have known in my days in the Nex. Best I find you on the Locator . . ." He flipped unseen levers; his eyes widened.

"Can it be?" He stared at Vallant. "A light glows on my panel that has not been lit these ten Grand Eons . . . that of Lost Galliale . . ."

Vallant nodded eagerly. "That's right—Galliale is what Jimper calls the place. But—"

"And your people; are all—as you?"

"More or less."

"None have these?" he pointed.

"Horns? No. And this isn't my home world, of course. I come from Terra—third from the sun."

"But—what of the Illimpi of Galliale?" The giant's face was taut with strain.

"Nobody lives here but Jimper's people. Right, Jimper?"

"True," Jimper spoke up. "Once the Evil Giants—foes of the Great Giants—came; but from thicket and burrow we crept, after the last Great Giant fell. We loosed our bolts to find their marks in vile green hide, then slipped away to fight again. So we dealt with them all, we bowmen, for against our secret bolts, of what avail their clumsy lightnings? The last of them fled away down the Cave of No Return, and free at last was my land of Galliale from their loathsome kind. Now long have we waited for our Giants to come back, and in their absence have we tilled and spun and kept fair the land."

"Well done, small warrior," Cessus said. He studied Vallant's face. "You are akin to us—that much is plain to see; and you dwell on the double world that lies third from the sun—so some few survivors made good their secret flight there—"

"Survivors of what?"

"Of the onslaught of those you call the Niss."

"Then—what the old man said was true? They're invaders—"

"That, and more, Vallant! They are the bringers of darkness, the all-evil, the wasters of worlds!"

"But—they haven't wasted the Earth; you hardly notice them; they're just a sort of police force—"

"They are a poison that stains the Galaxy. Long ago, they came destroying—but listen; this was the way of it:

"Ages past, we Illimpi built the Portal—this block of emptiness before which you stand—linking the star-clouds. We sent colonists into the fair new world of Galliale— adventurers, man and woman, the brave ones who never could return; and with them went the Spril-Folk, the faithful Little People.

"They thrived, and in time they built a Gate—a useful link to a sunny world they called Olantea, circling in the fifth orbit of a yellow sun twenty light-years distant. There they built cities, planted gardens that were a delight to the senses.

"Then, without warning, the Niss came to Galliale, pouring through the Gateway, armed with weapons of fire. Swift and terrible was their assault, and deadly the gasses they spread abroad, and the crawling vermin to spread their plagues. The peaceful Illimpi of Galliale battled well, and volunteers rushed through the Great Portal to their aid. But deadly were the weapons of the Niss; they carried the Tower of the Portal and some few, mad with blood lust, rushed through it, never to return. Then the Portal failed and lost was our link with our colony. The long centuries have passed, and never did we know till now how it fared with Lost Galliale."

"So the Spril finished off the Niss, after the Niss had killed the Illimpi? Nice work, Jimper. But how did you manage it?"

"Proof were we against their sickness," Jimper piped. "But no defense had they against our bows."

"If the Niss are such killers, why haven't they used their weapons on us? The story that Syndarch tells is that they're our great friends, sharing their wisdom—"

"Proof have we seen of that lie," Jimper chirped. "Deep are the plots of the Niss."

"It is the Portal they seek," Cessus said. "All who came to Galliale were lost to them—"

"Just a minute," Vallant cut in. "I'm lost. The Niss came through the Gateway from this world Olantea—but that was held by the Illimpi. The Niss must have hit them, and captured the Gateway—which I take it is some sort of matter transmitter. But why wasn't Galliale warned? And why is it none of the Galliales escaped through the Portal here, back to the home world? And how did the Gateway get shifted from Olantea to Pluto—"

Cessus was frowning in puzzlement. "Do you not know, Vallant—"

"Vallant!" Jimper cocked his head. "The Scaled One—I hear him stir!"

"It's your imagination, Jimper. We've explored the whole building, and didn't find him, remember?" He turned back to the Portal. "I—"

The horned man was looking at Jimper. "What manner of creature is this Scaled One?"

"It's just a superstition of Jimper's—" Vallant started.

"A Haik, Great Giant," Jimper shrilled. "A guardian set by the Niss when they had closed the Portal against the Illimpi, before they fared forth against the Spril, from which adventure no Niss returned—"

Cessus whirled on Vallant. "How have you restrained the beast?"

Vallant's mouth opened. "I hope you don't mean—" he began.

There was a sudden clangor as of armor clashing against stone.

"The Fanged One comes!" Jimper shrilled.

"What weapon have you," Cessus rapped out.

"Just this ham-slicer . . ." Vallant gripped the sword hilt. "But I have a feeling it's not quite what the program requires . . ."

The clatter was louder now; Jimper screeched; the horned Giant whirled to reach beyond the screen's edge—

There was a screech of tortured steel from the doorway; a hiss like an ancient steam whistle split the air. Vallant spun, stared at a vast *thing*—like a jumble of rusted fragments of armor plate, wedged in the doorway, scrabbling with legs like gleaming black cables three inches thick, armed with mirror-bright talons which raked grooves in the hard floor as though it were clay. From a head like a fang-spiked mace, white eyes with pinpoint pupils glared in insane ferocity. The Haik surged, sending chips of the door frame flying as it forced its bulk through the narrow way.

"Ye Gods!" Vallant yelled. "Jimper, why didn't you tell me this thing really existed!"

"Tell you I did, Vallant; now slay it with your sword!"

"What good is a hat pin against a man-eating rhino like that!" Vallant backed, watching as the material of the wall chipped and crumbled under the force of the Haik's thrust. His eye fell on the gunlike object on the floor. He jumped for it, caught it up, raised it and pressed the button on its side. A lance of blue flame licked out, touched the Haik's snout. The monster clashed its jaws, gained another foot.

The flame played on its cheek, dimmed abruptly, fell back to a weak yellowish glow, died with a harsh buzz. Vallant threw the weapon from him.

"Vallant!" Jimper shrieked. "The door frame! It crumbles . . . !"

"Sorry, Jimper! I guess we'll just have to round up a posse and come back after him . . . !" Vallant grabbed up the little creature, stepped to the screen—

"No, Vallant!" the horned man shouted—

"Here I come, ready or not—" Vallant closed his eyes, and stepped through the Portal.

✳ 13 ✳

There was an instant of bitter cold; then silence, a touch of cool air, an odor of almonds . . .

Vallant opened his eyes. A great, dim, vaulted hall arched high above him; far away, mighty columns loomed into shadows. Beyond one iodine-colored wall towered misty with distance, decorated in patterns of black lines set off with glittering flecks of gold and copper.

"Where is he?" Vallant blurted, staring around. "What happened to Cessus the Communicator?"

Jimper huddled against Vallant, peering up into the mists far overhead. "Lost are we now, Vallant. Nevermore will we see the spires of Galliale—nor the drab cities of your world . . ."

"He was right here—and the room behind him . . ."

"Dread are the mysteries of the Great Giants . . ." Jimper keened.

"Well," Vallant laughed shakily. "At least we left the Haik behind." He sheathed the unused sword. "I wonder who lives here." Faint echoes rolled back from the distant wall. "We're in a building of some kind; look at this floor, Jimper. Slabs the size of tennis courts. Talk about Giants . . ."

"Vallant, can we not go back? I dread the Haik less than I fear this place of echoes."

"Well . . ." Vallant studied the empty air around them. "I don't see anything that looks like a Portal. Maybe if we just feel our way . . ." He took a cautious step; Jimper wriggled down, darted ahead. He paused, puzzled, turned back—and froze, staring. Vallant whirled. At the spot where he had stood, a glossy black cable, dagger tipped, writhed in the air, three feet above the stone floor.

"The Haik!" Jimper squealed. With a deafening screech, the many-spiked head of the monster appeared, followed an instant later by its two-ton bulk, crashing thunderously through the Portal. For a moment it crouched as though confused; then at a sound from Jimper, it wheeled with murderous speed on its intended victims.

Vallant whipped out the sword. "Run, Jimper! Maybe I can slow him down for a second or two—"

Jimper snatched the crossbow from his back, fitted a six-inch quarrel in place, drew and let fly; the dart whistled past Vallant's head, glanced off the Haik's armor. The creature gaped tooth-ringed jaws, dug in its talons for the spring—

There was a sudden rush of air, a shriek of wind. From nowhere, a vast grid slammed down, struck with an impact that jarred the floor, knocked Vallant from his feet. He scrambled up, saw the grid receding as rapidly as it had come. The broken thing that had been the Haik flicked cable-legs in a last convulsion, then lay, a shattered, rusted hulk, leaking thin fluid against the stone.

"Whatever that was," Vallant said shakily, "it just missed us . . ." He looked up. Far up in the dimness, a great pale shape hung, a misty oblong, with smaller dark patches, whose outline wavered and flowed, bulging and elongating—

Then it withdrew and was gone.

"Jimper . . . !" Vallant croaked. "Did you see that . . . ?"

"I saw naught, Vallant," Jimper shrilled. "The Haik charged and then—I know not."

"It was . . ." Vallant paused to gulp. "A face . . . a huge, rubbery face, a mile long and five miles up . . . and I'd swear it was looking right at me . . . !"

"Another invasion of mind-fleas in the Hall," said a voice as clear as engraved print.

"Ill-struck, Brometa," a second voice answered. *"I hear their twittering still."*

"Vallant!" Jimper gasped. "Those there are who speak close by—and in the tongue of the Spril-folk—yet I see them not . . ."

"N-nonsense," Vallant gulped. "They're speaking English . . . But, where are they?"

"We should have plugged the hole they burrowed last time," the silent voice said. *"There, give me the whisk; I'll attend to these fleas—"*

"No!" Vallant yelled at the top of his lungs, staring upward into the formless shadows. "We're not fleas . . . !"

"Yapud! Did you hear words amid the twitterings just now?"

There was a pause; distant rumblings sounded. *"You must have imagined it, Brometa—"*

"I heard it just as you raised the whisk—"

"Don't do it!" Vallant bellowed.

"There! Surely you heard that! It rang in my mind like a light-storm."

"Yes, I do believe you're right!"

Staring upward, Vallant saw the vast cloud-face appear again, its shape changing.

"I see nothing, Yapud."

"We're friendly!" Vallant shouted. "Don't swat us!"

"These fleas have the same irritating way of projecting thought-forms out of all proportion to their size—"

"More of those hate-scorched vermin who infested the Hall last Great Cycle? Swat them at once!"

"No, this is another breed. Those others—Niss, they called themselves—what a vicious mind stink they raised before we fumigated! Hmmm. This one seems quite different, Yapud."

"Vermin are vermin! Give me the whisk—"

"Hold! Little enough I have to divert me here; let me converse awhile with these noisy fleas."

"What transpires, Vallant?" Jimper peeped. He gazed worriedly up at Vallant. "Who speaks in Jimper's head?"

"I don't know, Jimper—but it's something that thinks I'm a flea, and doesn't even know about you."

"Here, you fleas; I'll put a paper on the floor; step upon it, that I may lift you up where I can lay eyes on you."

There was a great rushing of air. A vast, white shape rushed down, blotting out the mists above. Vallant and Jimper dropped flat, clung to crevices in the floor against the rush of air that whistled past. An immense, foot-thick platform thudded to the floor fifty feet away, stretching off into the distance. The wind howled and died.

"We're supposed to climb up on that, Jimper," Vallant said. "So they can get a look at us."

"Must we?"

"I guess we'd better—if we don't want to get whisked, like the Haik."

Vallant and Jimper got to their feet, walked across to the ragged-edged, spongy mat, clambered up on it. At close range, the fibers that comprised it were clearly visible; it was like a coarse felt of pale straw.

"OK," Vallant hailed. "Lift away . . ."

They lost their balance as the platform surged up beneath them; a white light appeared, grew. Their direction of motion changed; the paper tilted sickeningly; then, with an abrupt lurch, came to rest. The glare above, like a giant sun, cast blue shadows across the white plain behind them. A mile away, two unmistakable faces loomed, block-long eyes scanning the area, their changing shapes even more alarming at closer range.

"There it is!" A shape like a vast blimp floated into view, pointing.

"Yes—and isn't that another one beside it—a hatchling, perhaps?"

"Ah, poor things; a mother and young. Always have I had a soft spot for maternity."

"Here—" Jimper started.

"Quiet," Vallant hissed. "I'd rather be a live mother than whisked."

"Size is not all," Jimper peeped indignantly.

"*Now, small ones. Perhaps you'll tell us of your tiny lives—your miniscule affairs, your petty sorrows and triumphs; and who knows? Mayhap there'll be a lesson therein for wise T'tun to ponder.*"

"How can it be that they know the speech of the Spril?" Jimper chirped.

"They don't—it's some kind of telepathy; it comes through as English, for me."

"*Here—natter not among yourselves; explain your presence—*"

"*Not so harshly, Yapud; you'll frighten the tiny things.*"

"Not so quick to fear are we!" Jimper piped. "Know that we have passed through many strange adventurings, and no enemy yet has seen our heels!"

"*Ah, this could prove diverting! Start at the beginning, bold mite; tell us all.*"

"Very well," Jimper chirped. "But at the end of my recital, hopeful I am you'll hold out aid to two poor travelers, lost far from home."

"*These fleas wish to bargain . . . ?*"

"*The offer is fair. Begin.*"

"When Jason the Giant would leave Fair Galliale to seek again his homeland," Jimper chirped, "Jimper was chosen to travel at his side . . ."

✳ 14 ✳

There was a moment of silence when Jimper, assisted at points by Vallant, had finished his account.

"*So,*" the being called Yapud said, "*the mind-fleas admit they burrowed a path through our walls—*"

"*A remarkable achievement, for such simple creatures,*" Brometa said calmly.

"*Hmph! I see nothing remarkable in the series of blundering near-disasters these fleas have managed to devise for themselves; why, even a slight exercise of intelligent effort would have aligned their environment correctly—*"

"*Yes, Yapud, I've been puzzling over that; and I think I have the answer; these tiny mites dwell in a three-dimensional space—*"

"*Spare me your allegorical apologia—*"

"*I'm being quite objective, Yapud! These entities— intelligent entities, too, mind you—are confined to a three dimensional frame of reference; obvious relationships are thus forever beyond their conceptualization.*"

Vallant and Jimper stood together, watching the vast faces change and writhe like shapes of smoke as the creatures conversed.

"Remind them of their promise, Vallant," Jimper chirped.

Vallant cleared his throat. "Ah . . . now, about our difficulty; you see—"

"*You mean,*" Yapud said, ignoring him, "*that they crawl about, cemented to a three-dimensional space, like so many Tridographs?*"

"*Precisely! As we move about, presenting various three-dimensional views to their gaze, our appearances must seem to alter quite shockingly. Of course, the concept of viewing our actual forms in the hyper-round from outside, as it were, is quite beyond them!*"

"*Poof! You're quite wrong; you've already admitted they tunneled into the Hall, which certainly required manipulation in at least four dimensions!*"

"Hmmm." Another pause. "*Ah, I see: the tunnel was punched through their space by another more advanced species; look for yourself, Yapud.*"

There was another pause. "*Well . . . yes, I see what you mean. . . . Odd. . . . Did you notice the orientation of the tunnel?*"

"*No, I hadn't—but now that you mention it, I'm beginning to see why these poor creatures have had such a time of it . . .*"

"Please, fellows, if you don't mind," Vallant broke in. "My friend and I are hoping you'll be able to help us out; you see, it's very important that we get back—"

"*That, of course, is out of the question,*" Yapud interrupted. "*We'll swat these fleas and plug the hole, and then on to other matters . . .*"

"*Not so fast, my dear Yapud. The energies required to plug the tunnel would be quite fantastic. You realize, of course, that it constitutes an infinitely repeating nexus series—*"

"All this is very interesting, I'm sure," Vallant put in, "but unfortunately, it's over our heads. Couldn't you just direct us back to our-uh-tunnel—"

"*That would do you no good; you'd end in Null space—*"

"But it leads to the Tower of the Portal—"

"*Surely you understand that since you're traversing a series of tri-valued pseudo-continua, via— Dear me, I'm afraid you won't be able to grasp the geometry*" *from your unfortunate three-dimensional viewpoint. But—"*

"Here, Brometa, you're only confusing things. Place yourself in their frame of reference, as you suggested yourself a moment ago. Now—"

"But the Portal opened from the Tower; it *has* to lead back there—" Vallant insisted.

"Tsk tsk; three-dimensional thinking. No, the tunnel was devised as a means of instantaneous travel between points apparently distant to a tri-dimensional being. Naturally, the energy displaced by such a transposition required release; thus, a non-entropic vector was established to a locus bearing a temporal relationship to the point of origin proportional to the value of C."

"Here," Vallant said desperately. "We're not getting anywhere. Could I just ask a few questions—and could you answer in three-D terms?"

"Very well. That might be simpler."

"Where are we?"

"Ummm. In the Hall of the T'tun, in the Galaxy of Andromeda—and don't say you don't understand; I plucked the concepts from your own vocabulary."

Vallant gulped. "Andromeda?"

"Correct."

"But we were on Galliale—"

"The use of the past tense is hardly correct, since the Portal you used will not be constructed for three million years—in your terms, that is."

"I'm not sure my terms are equal to the job," Vallant said weakly. "How did we happen to get into the past?"

"The velocity of light is a limiting value; any apparent

exceeding of this velocity must, of course, be compensated for. This is accomplished by the displacement of mass through quaternary space into the past to a distance equal to the time required by light to make the transit. Thus, an 'instantaneous' transit of ten light years places the traveler ten years in the subjective past, relative to the point of origin—three-dimensionally speaking."

"Ye Gods!" Vallant swallowed. "Andromeda is over a million light years from Earth; when I went through the Portal, I stepped a million years into the past?"

"A million and a half, to be precise."

"But—when the Illimpi came to Galliale through the Portal, they didn't go into the past—or did they?"

"Oh, I see; there's a further projection of the tunnel, leading . . . Brometa, how curious! The tunnel actually originates here, on the site of the Hall! Just a moment, while I scan through . . ."

"Vallant," Jimper piped, "what does it all mean?"

"I'm not sure. It seems the Illimpi started from here in Andromeda—and threw a link across to our Galaxy; then they went through, and colonized Galliale—a million and a half years in their past. When I stepped through the Portal, I dumped us another million and a half years back—three million years from Cessus—"

"And, of course," Brometa said, *"the Gateway between Galliale and Olantea will be a similar link, when it is built; it will span merely twenty light-years—"*

"Aha!" Vallant exclaimed. "So that's why no one ever comes back from the Cave of No Return, Jimper—they step twenty years into the past when they go out—and another twenty when they come back!"

"Then I came back to Galliale forty years ere I departed?" Jimper squeaked. "Small wonder King Tweeple was leaner, and knew me not . . ."

"But the Niss—the ones that poured through the Gateway into Galliale, back when the giants were killed off—"

"Twenty thousand years ago," Yapud put in.

"Huh? How do you know?" Vallant said, surprised.

"How? Why, I simply examined the data—"

"Remember," Brometa put in, *"your three-valued space places unnatural limitations on your ability to perceive reality. Three-dimensional 'time' is a purely illusory discipline—"*

"Please, no extended theoretical discourse, Brometa! I'm answering the flea's questions!"

"So twenty thousand years ago, the Niss invaded Galliale from Olantea—and dropped twenty years into their past in the process. They couldn't go back, because they'd step out into Olantea, another twenty years earlier—"

"—where they promptly expired, as is their custom when surrounded by their enemies," Yapud cut in. *"However, on Galliale, they were successful!—for a while. When they came, they blazed a path before them with disruptor beams; then they spread plagues which only the Spril survived."*

"And then the Spril wiped out the Niss, by hiding and picking them off," Vallant put in. "But . . . the Galliales should have warned the Olanteans; the invasion came from Olantea—twenty years in the future—and they were in communication with the Olantea of twenty years in the past—"

"They had no opportunity; the Niss held the Gateway. On Olantea, the Niss struck with blind ferocity from space; they descended first on the Olantean satellite; there they set up an engine with the power to shatter worlds. To save the mother world, the Olanteans launched a desperate assault. They carried the dome under which the engine had been assembled, and then, quickly, before they could be overcome, they triggered the energies buried deep in the rock. Thus died the moon of Olantea."

"What about the Niss?"

"It was a terrible defeat—but not final. The mighty detonation of the Olantean moon destroyed the equilibrium of the system; vast storms swept the planet; when they ceased, it was seen that Olantea had left its ancient orbit, and drifted now outward and ever outward. Snow covered the gardens and the fountains and the towers of Olantea; the seas froze. A winter came which never spring would follow.

"The Niss—those who remained—struck again—a last desperate bid to annihilate their enemies. They attacked Olantea, seized the Gateway to Galliale, and poured in their numbers through it, fleeing the cold that now locked Olantea in a mantle of ice. Their fate, you know."

"But—what happened to Olantea?"

"It found a new orbit at last, far from its sun. You call it Pluto."

"And the remains of the moon are the asteroids," Vallant said, awed. "But—Cessus said that we humans were related to the Illimpi . . ."

"Some few Illimpi escaped from dying Olantea to colonize the Earth. There they lived in peace for two

hundred centuries—until the first flashes of nuclear explosion summoned their remnant from Mars."

"And now they're occupying us," Vallant said. "Snooping around to find a clue to the Portal . . ."

"Bah! That would merely provide us with a plague of the evil nits!" Brometa burst out. *"That we cannot allow to come to pass. We must give aid to these inoffensive fleas, Yapud—"*

"True," Yapud agreed. *"I confess I was quite carried away, viewing the Niss onslaught and the death of a world as I did, from the three-dimensional viewpoint. I see now that even these mites have feelings of a sort—and the destruction of beauty is a crime, in any continuum!"*

"I suppose the old man—" Vallant stopped suddenly. "He came back from Galliale! That means he went there after I met him—and then came back through time, twenty years—"

"Forty years; twenty when he entered Galliale, and twenty more on his departure."

"And he knew! That's why he waited, Jimper! You said he told the King he couldn't leave until the time was right; he posted sentinels by the Gateway to watch the Valley of Blue Ice, and settled down to wait. When the Survey Team landed near the Gate, he had his chance!"

"And knowing he would emerge into his past, he brought me with him to prove that he had indeed visited Fair Galliale—"

"But who told him about the Gateway? He—"

"Vallant!" Jimper squeaked. "He came to you, spoke of old days of comradeship, and the war against the Niss. He showed you pictures—"

"Then—that means he *was* Jason—the same Jason I knew!" Vallant shook his head. "But that means I've already—I mean, *will* see him again. But how can I get three million years into the future?"

"*Yes . . . that is something of a problem*," Yapud conceded.

"Uh—I know it's asking a lot," Vallant said, "but if you could just transfer us ahead through time . . ."

"*No . . . we can scan it—as you visually scan space when you stare into your night sky—but as for traveling in substance—or transmitting three-dimensional beings—*"

"Wait—I have a thought," Brometa put in. "*You spoke of the three-dimensional framework; why not . . .*" The conversation turned to technicalities.

"Vallant," Jimper piped. "Will I ever see again the towers of Galliale?"

"We'll know in a minute; they seem to be discussing ways and means . . ."

"*. . . the whisk would be simpler,*" Yapud was saying, impatiently.

"*These Illimpi,*" Brometa said. "*It's just occurred to me that they're remote descendants of ours, Yapud! We can't allow these Niss fleas to trouble them—*"

"*Impossible!*"

"*But the relationship is quite obvious, once you examine it—*"

"*Nonsense! Next you'll be saying these fleas are our kin!*"

"*Hmmm. As to that, they appear to be ancestral to the Illimpi—*"

"*Nonsense. They are the degenerate descendants of the Illimpi who escaped from freezing Olantea to Earth—*"

"*True—but later, they crossed space via mechanical FTL drive, and colonized Andromeda; later, they recolonized the Milky Way via the Portal—*"

"Then it's quite clear!" Yapud exclaimed. "*I told you the Illimpi were no descendants of ours. They're our ancestors!*"

"Ancestors?"

"*Certainly; they will set up a Portal here, a few years from now, and use it to retransmit themselves to the Milky Way, an additional million and a half years in the past, and from there, they will reestablish a new link to Andromeda, three million years prior to now, and so on, in order to study their past—*"

"Stop!" Vallant called. "You're making my head ache! Compared to this, the business of Jason and me telling each other about the Gateway is nothing! But how can I start the ball rolling if I'm stranded here?"

"*Obviously, we can't allow that to happen,*" Brometa said. "*There's no telling what it might do to the probability stress-patterns. But as to how—*"

"*Just a minute, Brometa,*" Yapud put in. "*Place yourself in their three-valued universe for a moment; if the transit were made strictly within the parameters of their curious geometry, the aleph and gimel factors would cancel out nicely—*"

"*Why—how obvious! It should have occurred to me, Yapud!*"

"Have you thought of something?" Vallant asked anxiously.

"*Fleas, if we place you back in your native spaciotemporal coordinates, will you pledge yourselves to purge your Galaxy of Niss? We'll prepare a simple pesticide for you; an elementary excitor effect should be adequate; direct it on a Niss and the creature will blaze up nicely, without affecting other forms of energy concentration. I think a range of one light year for the hand model should do . . ."*

"I'll attend to preparing a suitable three-dimensional capsule," Yapud put in. "*Rather amusing to realize that these fleas can be confined merely by drawing a plane about them . . .*" his voice faded.

"What are you going to do?" Vallant asked nervously. "I hope you're keeping in mind that we don't live long enough for any really extended processes . . ."

"*We'll give you a—ah—ship, I think the term is. It will travel at a velocity just under that of electromagnetic radiation—and will follow a route which will require three million years for the transit to your home galaxy. Naturally, the subjective elapsed time aboard will be negligible. The duration of the voyage will be adjusted with precision so as to place you in the close vicinity of earth at the same time that you departed. We'll take a moment to encapsulate the vessel in certain stress patterns, which will render it impervious to unwelcome interference by the Niss or any others—*"

With a whoosh! of displaced air which sent Vallant and Jimper skittering across the spongy plain, a gleaming, hundred-foot hull swooped down to settle gently a hundred yards away.

"*I've taken the precaution of installing a duplicator for the production of the anti-Niss weapons,*" Yapud said. "*Just set it up in any convenient location and shovel dirt* in the hopper at the top—and stand well back from the delivery chute."

"*One other detail,*" Brometa added. "*Since the Illimpi will be our ancestors, I think we owe it to them to help all we can. If we nudge Olantea from its cold orbit and guide it back to its ancient position, fifth from the Sun, once more it will flower. There seem to be some fifty million Illimpi still there, carefully frozen in special vaults under the ice, awaiting rescue. We can time matters so that they thaw as the Earth fleas eliminate the last of the Niss.*"

"*That should be a joyous reunion. I note that the first of the new colonists will begin to cross to Galliale as soon as the Haik follows the fleas here . . .*"

"What of Jimper?" the Spril piped. "Long have I fared from the hills of fair Galliale. . ."

"Don't worry, Jimper. I'll drop you off; you'll arrive home another twenty years in your past, but I guess it can't be helped."

Jimper looked startled. "I have but remembered another fanciful tale, told to me long agone, by the father of my grandfather, when he was well gone in strong ale. He told of venturing into the Tower, and traveling far, only to return at last to Galliale . . ."

"The old boy had a tale for every occasion," Vallant said.

"You fail to grasp the implication," Jimper sighed. "For him was I named, Vallant . . ."

✳ 15 ✳

Aboard the ship, Vallant slept for a week. When he

awoke, Pluto hung silver-black in the viewpoint. He brought the vessel in over the Blue Ice Mountains, settled it by the Cave, watched as Jimper scampered to its opening, turned to wave, and disappeared within.

Nine days later, he swept past startled Niss patrols to slide into Earth's atmosphere; one alien vessel which came too near plunged out of control into the Atlantic.

Vallant landed in wooded country north of Granyauck, left the ship by night, caught a ride into the city. On the campus of the University Complex, he found the vast dormitory in which Jason Able was housed, followed numbers until he reached his room. He knocked. A tall, square-jawed red-head opened the door.

"Oh, hi, Ame," he said. "Haven't seen you for a day or so. Been on a trip?"

"I guess you could say that," Vallant said. "Pour me a beer, Jase, and I'll tell you all about it . . ."

THE SOUL BUYER

The cards fell on the baize-topped table with a soft slap, slap. The fat man with the purple-veined nose reached out a meaty hand with rings, lifted the corner of his down-card. He puckered his lips, counted off bills, tossed them in.

"Up five hundred."

Tony Adair breathed a six-inch smoke ring across the table, propelled a tiny one through the center, not watching as rubber bands snapped against rolls, bills dropped on the green drift under the shaded billiard light.

"To you, Adair," said a freckle-blotched man with red hair like an eyebrow over each ear.

Behind Adair a small man, dapper in a yellow vest and black shirt leaned forward. "Take it easy, Tony boy."

Adair reached a slim wallet from an inner pocket, laid two crisp bills on the table.

"See the five and up a thousand."

The fat man beetled small eyes in a red face. "You're playing it cold as an eight-hour corpse, mister. You got a four-card flush working against three aces and kings over on the board, and you ain't even looked."

Adair smiled gently. The fat man snorted, counted out money. "Okay, smart man. I'm calling the grand—and up a grand."

Two players cursed and folded. The freckled man cursed and added money to the pot. Adair spread two more new bills on the table.

"And up another thousand."

The color drained from the fat man's jowls. He riffled his roll. "Table stakes," he snapped. "I got six cees that say you're lying." He tossed the money in.

"I hadda mix in this," the freckled player muttered. He turned his cards face down. The fat man grinned with one side of his face, flipped over his down-card and prodded four aces into a row.

"Tough I was short," he started, reaching for the heaped bills.

"Yeah," Adair cut in. "I could have used the money." Negligently he turned his down-card up. The fat man's mouth opened.

"Jeez, a king-high straight flush," someone muttered.

The fat man's eyes were glints behind puffed lids. His hand moved toward his hip pocket. "A cold-deck artist," he grated.

"Watch the lip, lard bucket," the freckled player said. "It's your deck—and I dealt it."

Adair gathered in the money. Behind him the small man rose, buttoning his jacket.

"That's enough for tonight, Tony. We got no time for sore losers."

"Sure, Jerry," Adair drawled.

"I get no chance to win it back, huh?" the fat man snarled.

Adair considered. "We'll cut the deck," he said. "You first. Look at your card and then name your bet."

"Hey, Tony—" Jerry Pearl began.

"Okay, you named the game, smart man." The fat man riffled, passed the deck for a cut, then lifted off cards, showed a king of hearts. He glanced at Adair, bright-eyed. "My check's good, everybody knows that." He took out a checkbook and pen, scribbled, tore off the green slip.

"King bets five grand," he purred.

Adair reached, eased the top card off the deck, dropped it before the fat man, face up: a black ace. He picked up the check, looked at it, then tore it in two and dropped it on the table. He rose, a big man with coal-black eyes.

"No hard feelings, I hope," he said softly. Nobody answered.

Outside, Adair lit a thin cigar, looked up past ragged roof-lines at a lop-sided moon the color of a bruise plowing through a dark sky bright with clouds. From somewhere down the street music murmured, as faint as old memories. Beside Adair, Jerry Pearl mopped at his face with a white-monogrammed black nylon handkerchief.

"That game was good for another ten gees, Tony," he complained. "You could have strung them rubes along for another hour."

"Why?" Adair said mildly.

"Why?" Pearl raised his shoulders. "Why does any guy gamble? For the dough . . ."

"How many card players do you know who fill inside straights like they were beer glasses?"

Jerry grinned, showing crooked teeth linked by gold bridge work. "Nobody, Tony. But nobody. You got a million-dollar talent there, kid."

"Uh-huh. It's a neat trick. How do I do it, Jerry? And why?"

"Jeezus, Tony, what's the difference? You're a guy with a permanent hot fist."

"I had a pretty fair education once, Jerry. By now I might have been a big-shot engineer—but I dropped it in favor of the galloping dominoes." He spread his hands, looked at the strong tanned fingers—skillful fingers. "Win or lose, it was my hand, my brain, my eyes—against the other guy."

"Sure, Tony—"

"That's finished now. I bet—I win. It's not me doing it, Jerry. I'm like a rigged slot machine; I come up three bells every time."

"So you got lucky; why knock it? Look, we can still hit Maxies."

"Forget it, I said no more."

"Tony, you were always a guy that loved the action—"

"It was the game, Jerry—not just the money. Now—the game's dead."

"Look, Tony, when I took you on to manage—"

Adair smiled at the small man. "I need a manager like Heinz needs a pickle. I haven't lost a bet since the night that old geezer sold me the Bolita ticket . . ."

"Come on, Tony. We'll have a drink—"

Adair looked at Jerry Pearl thoughtfully. "Funny about

that ticket. The old bird headed straight for me like a Salvation Army lassie for the two-dollar window."

"I remember, Tony. A bum, a Bowery grifter. That overcoat—down to here—and smelling like a dog's bed. You only bought the ticket so he'd go breathe on somebody else."

"Uh-huh. But why did he pick me to breathe on?"

"He liked your looks, Tony."

"It was in a joint on 26th. What was the name of it?"

"I couldn't tell you, Tony—"

"Angelo's."

"Maybe. So what? Since then you've made real dough—"

"I think I'd like to talk to that old fellow, Jerry."

"Huh? Cripes, Tony, that's a couple of months ago. The town is full of pan-handlers—"

"You've got contacts. Ask around. There can't be too many hustlers in the business sporting a beard, eyes like cherry gumdrops, a nose like two fresh bullet holes in yesterday's corpse, and trailing an aroma of over-aged gorgonzola."

"Forget it, Tony. You're riding a hot streak. Don't louse it up."

"What's the matter, Jerry? Superstitious?"

"All I know is, leave it lie, Tony."

"Will you find the old boy—or shall I?"

"Okay, okay, Tony. But I ain't guaranteeing nothing . . ."

"That suits me, Jerry. I never asked life for a guarantee."

The telephone woke Tony Adair from a light doze. He

blinked at the clock on the table. Eleven A.M.—about time Jerry was reporting in . . .

"Mr. Adair?" a brisk female voice stated. "You're an acquaintance of Mr. J. Pearl?"

"That's right."

"This is the supervisor at All Saints'. There has been an accident. I'm sorry to alarm you, but your name was among—

"I'm sorry, Mr. Adair. Perhaps if you'd come down . . . ?"

"I'll be there in twenty minutes."

A plump woman in white looked up as Adair entered Jerry Pearl's room.

"Ah . . . are you . . . ?"

"That's right, Mrs. Umnnn. Leave me alone with the patient, please." Jerry Pearl's eyes fluttered as Adair swung a chair around and sat down beside the bed.

"What happened, Jerry?" he said softly.

"The . . . driver." Pearl's voice was a whisper through bandages. He moved his head from side to side, eyes closed. "His face . . ."

"Take it easy, Jerry . . ."

"Red eyes. Red eyes . . ."

A step sounded at the door. A portly man in broad grey lapels and rimless glasses blinked at Adair over pursed lips.

"How bad is he?" Adair asked.

"Who are you? You're not a physician . . . ?"

"My name's Adair—"

"Visiting hours are from two to four." The man

stepped back, inviting Adair to precede him from the room.

Adair rose, assumed a grave expression. "I should think a hundred-thousand-dollar contribution to the hospital fund ought to buy a man an answer to a civil question."

"Eh?" The portly man whipped off his glasses, cleared his throat, smiled without gaiety, replaced the glasses.

"I understand a car hit him," Adair said. "Do you know the details?"

The portly man frowned. "There are some curious aspects to the case. Mr. . . . ah . . . Pearl was in shock. He was difficult to handle, hence the sedative. Quite frankly, he was raving. He seemed to feel he'd been—ha ha—run down intentionally."

"How do you know he was not?"

"What? Why, the car crashed and the driver was at least as badly injured as this . . . Mr. Pearl."

"You've got the driver here too?"

"Why, yes. Three twenty-three, if I'm not mistaken."

Heels clicked in the corridor. A starched nurse in a tight grey permanent appeared at the door, whispered in the portly man's inclined ear.

"Eh? What's that, Miss Perch?"

The nurse nodded grimly, lips pressed tight.

Adair followed along the corridor, around a corner, past a screen, into a small room with pale green walls and curtains that fluttered at an open window. The rumpled bed was empty. A faint miasmic odor hung in the air.

"Where is he?"

"Why, doctor, I can't imagine . . . !"

"Get Leonardi up here immediately! And call Johnson in Admissions . . ."

Miss Perch hurried away. The portly man turned to Adair. "The woman's gone mad," he snapped. "My apologies, Mr. Adair. I assure you we operate a modern medical facility here, not a bedlam—"

"Some people are allergic to hospitals," Adair said. "He was not badly hurt, I take it?"

The man snorted. "Heaven knows. Miss Perch's report was incoherent."

"How do you mean?"

"I'm not at liberty to discuss case histories—" He broke off, showed Adair the painted smile, let it fall. "Grateful though we are for the endowment—"

"Don't waste any diplomacy on me, Doc. I never gave the hospital a nickel. I just queried the price of a civil answer in this pill factory."

On the ground floor Adair encountered Miss Perch. "I was most interested in your observations on the driver," he said. "Very unusual. The doctor seemed rather skeptical . . ."

Miss Perch raised her eyebrows. "In twenty-eight years no one has ever before questioned my competence—"

Adair raised a hand. "I would not dream of doubting you, Miss Perch. If you said—what was it again . . . ?"

Miss Perch set her jaw. "Body temperature fifty-two," she said. "And no pulse."

Adair drove four blocks west to the precinct station house, asked for the patrolman who had been the first on the scene.

"The Chevy was making an illegal U-turn, for my money," the cop said. "I helped get the driver out. The ambulance guys took him and that's the last I seen of him. Wow, did that guy need a bath! Even the car stinks."

"Where's the car now?"

"In the lot. I figure it for a hot car. I—"

"I'd like to take a look at it."

"You the owner?"

"I'm a friend of the pedestrian that was hurt."

"Well . . ." The cop led Adair along a dark corridor, out into a cindered car park lined with rusty hulks, some with crumpled fenders and broken glass, one with a bullet-starred windshield. He pointed to a late-model sedan with a crushed grill and a flat-tired wheel twisted out of line. Adair went across, opened the door on the passenger's side. An odor of moldy wool and long-dead fish struck his nostrils. Behind him the cop snorted. "See what I mean?"

"What have you got on the driver?"

"Like I said: the ambulance guys took him to the hospital. They won't release him without we say so."

"Prints?"

"Beats me."

"Mind if I dig around?"

"Nix, buddy. If it's a hot car . . . you know how it is."

A glint of metal caught Adair's eye. He leaned into the car, casually scooped a tiny ring of keys from the floor, dropped it in his pocket. "You'd better start checking that hot car angle," he said. "The driver left the hospital via the fire escape about half an hour ago."

✳ ✳ ✳ ✳

The lobby lights were on when Adair entered his hotel an hour later. The desk clerk called, "Oh, Mr. Adair. Will you call this number . . .?"

Adair dialed. A female voice said, "All Saints'. Oh, Mr. Adair? Doctor Pherson wants to speak to you . . ." There was a long pause, then a male voice cut in:

"Sir, I assume you're aware of the gravity of interfering in the routine of this institution?"

"What's the matter, Doc, still sore about that hundred grand I didn't give you?"

"Your impertinence is intolerable, sir! I'm warning you, I'll have the law on you—"

"Give me a break, Doc. I'm already a three-time loser on library fines—"

"Kidnapping is a considerably more serious crime than book theft, you wiseacre."

"If you think I stole your smelly patient, you're barking up the wrong fireplug."

"I'm warning you: Mr. Pearl is in serious condition. I don't know what your game is, but the consequences—"

"What's that about Pearl?" Adair cut in sharply.

"The man has probable internal injuries; I suggest you tell me his whereabouts at once—"

"You mean Jerry Pearl has left the hospital?"

"You know as well as I that you spirited him away—for what fantastic reason, I fail to imagine—"

"The last I saw of Pearl he was flat on his back in room 305—supposedly too doped up to talk. Get the police, fast. I'll check back with you in an hour."

"Key, Mr. Adair?" the clerk offered as he hung up.

Adair shook his head. "I'll be back in an hour. If the hospital calls, take a message."

It was a ten-minute drive to the blighted area of second-hand stores and sagging warehouses between which Angelo's showed a narrow façade of crumbling brown paint. A grimy window was blanked off by a green cloth shade. Through a triangular tear in one corner a dim light glowed.

Adair tried the door, stepped into the sour-smelling gloom of a long room lit by a neon beer sign behind a zinc-topped bar. A thin man with an acne-scarred face under lifeless blond hair looked up, shifted a frayed toothpick in the corner of his mouth, made a quick motion with his hands out of sight.

"We ain't open," he said flatly. Adair nudged the door shut behind him.

"Pour four ounces of the best Scotch in the house into a clean water glass," he said. He glanced around the room. There was a narrow rear door with a new Yale lock, another door with a chipped white-enameled plaque lettered TOILET, and a dozen wire-legged tables still showing the rings of yesterday's beers. The bartender poured out a four-finger jolt.

"A buck."

Adair picked up the glass, sniffed it, put it back on the bar.

"I met a man here three months ago. Long black overcoat, Smith Brothers beard, hat down over his eyes . . ."

The bartender's eyes shifted left, right . . . "So?"

"Seen him lately?"

The bartender reached for a towel, began mopping at

the bar. "You think I keep track of all the bums hustling drinks in the joint?"

"About five-three," Adair said. "Snub nose, enflamed eyes, and a breath you could saw up and nail to the wall."

"Get lost, Mac. Must be some other bar—"

"For ten you could try a plausible lie," Adair said softly. "What's got you scared, Slim?"

The bartender tilted his head toward the street door. "On your way, Jack," he growled.

"What about a man of forty-five, five-six, thin hair, wearing a black shirt, yellow vest, and a brown suit. He could have had a bandaged head."

"He could've had sideburns and a monocle. I ain't seen him."

"Thanks, pal. You've been a big help. Okay if I use the phone?"

"It's your dime, brother."

Adair dialed his hotel. "Any calls for me?"

"My, Mr. Adair, but we're popular tonight. I have a call for you on the line right now. If you'll hold on, I'll tie it in . . ."

There was a loud pop on the line. Then—

"Tony . . ." There was a sound of heavy breathing.

"Jerry! Where are you?"

"It's . . . a hotel. Around . . . the corner . . . from that joint, Angelo's . . ."

"What's going on, Jerry? What's the idea of jumping the hospital?"

"Tony . . . can you come . . . . right away . . . ?"

"Sure. Stay put. Don't go anywhere."

"And, Tony . . . don't . . . bring anybody with you . . ."

✻ ✻ ✻ ✻

A mercury vapor lamp on a tall pole shed a wan light on drab store fronts and empty pavement as Adair walked the fifty yards to the corner, and along to a sagging marquee edged with dead forty-watt bulbs. He pushed through a grease-blurred glass-paneled door into a dim, cluttered lobby full of the odor of failure and cheap cigars smoked long ago. A strip of worn red carpet led across scuffed brown linoleum to a black varnished counter with a battered goose-neck lamp and an edge-curled register anchored by a length of knotted twine. A gnome-like ancient in armbands and a warped wicker eye-shade darted a look at Adair.

"Got a telephone here?" Adair asked.

The gnome tipped his head toward a shadowy corner. Adair went to the booth, glanced in at scribbled walls, came back to the desk.

"Friend of mine made a call from here—just a couple of minutes ago. Five-six, bandaged head, brown suit with no gravy stains. Which way did he go?"

The man pushed the book toward Adair. "Clean bed cost you four dollars."

"Not tonight, pop. How about my friend?"

The old man plucked at a flaccid, veined cheek with fingers like a wooden Indian's. "I don't remember so good these days." He flicked a crafty look at Adair. "I remember better for paying guests."

"I've got a room. Where did he go?"

"Ain't no law says you got to use the room . . ."

Adair took four singles from his wallet, folded them longways, tapped them on the counter-top.

"He was nervous," the gnome said, watching the bills. "Prob'ly up to something crooked. Walked up and down, looking at a strap-watch. Then the other feller come along, and they left. Didn't make no call from here. But that was no couple of minutes ago. More like an hour."

"What did this other fellow look like?"

"Looked like some kind of foreigner. Overcoat down to here, beard, mean-looking eyes. Would not have him in the hotel." He reached for the bills suddenly. Adair moved the money out of reach. The old man stooped, came up with a sawed-off ball bat.

"You gimme my money, you chiseler," he shrilled.

"Your ball-playing days are over, pop. Did the man with the beard have a gun?"

"I'll call a cop, your chiseler—"

"Skip it. We know all about you at Headquarters."

"Huh?" The bat disappeared. "You never showed me no buzzer," he said reproachfully. "Naw, I didn't see no gun."

"Thanks." Adair dropped a single on the counter. "And by the way, better make book from another phone from now on; you're running out of wall space."

A light rain was falling in the dark street as Adair pushed through the heavy doors. Fifty feet away, a round-shouldered figure in shabby black detached itself from the gloom of an alley mouth, shuffled forward, holding up an arthritically curled hand.

"Mr. Adair," a voice like burning straw hissed.

Adair halted, eyed the broad-brimmed hat, pulled low over the wizened face, red-edged eyes, an unkempt beard.

"Mr. Adair, for you I have advice—good advice, worth a small payment, perhaps . . ."

Adair looked both ways along the street; in the bleak light from the lamp at the far corner, nothing moved.

"Maybe I could use some advice at that," he said.

"Luck good these days, eh, Mr. Adair?" The voice was a thin rasp.

"I can't complain." Adair moved casually between the bearded man and the street. The other pivoted to face him.

"A sad thing, when a man's luck turns . . ."

"You know a lot about luck, do you?"

A wheeze that might have been laughter came from the direction of the beard.

"It is enough," the thin voice went on, "perhaps to cause a man to think."

"Think about what?"

The clawed hands spread in a wide gesture. "The wisdom of . . . complacency." The bearded man edged closer. Adair caught the reek from the moldy overcoat. "But let us step out of the wind and the harsh light." The hunched shoulders twisted to indicate the dark mouth of the alley. Adair looked past the other into the opening, black and narrow.

"Don't be afraid . . ." the hunched man said.

"You're right. I hate to do business in the street. After you."

The man backed past a rank of overflowing garbage cans; Adair followed. The scarred bricks underfoot gave back an oily glistening. Thirty feet from the street, the alley ended in a brick wall. Adair's guide turned, his face dark under the wide hat.

"Now, we can deal in peace."

"Start talking," Adair challenged.

"Do I detect a note of concern in your voice, Mr. Adair? You find the surroundings . . . disturbing?"

Adair shook his head. "I was raised in dark alleys. Now where's Jerry Pearl?"

"Don't trouble your head, Mr. Adair. Just take the old peddler's advice: drift with the tides and let fortune come your way untroubled by unwholesome curiosity."

"You've put your finger on it; my unwholesome curiosity is aroused by a couple of things—"

"Much as poor Mr. Jerry Pearl's was, I fear . . ."

"Keep talking."

"You didn't know? Alas, he . . . had an accident."

Adair stepped close, caught the smaller man by the coat, pushed him back against the wall. The hat fell off, rolled away.

"I don't know who you are—or what . . ." Something crunched under Adair's hand. He choked at the odor that came in waves. "You come apart easy," he grated. "Better get gabby while you're still in one filthy piece."

The matted head twisted; angry red eyes glared up at Adair. "I laugh at pain, foolish Tony Adair! Is not your skill with dice, with cards, your incomparable knack of selecting the fleetest quadruped enough? The gift is yours alone, among the faceless masses. Take it and go in peace."

Abruptly the small man twisted, lashed out with a thin arm. Adair saw a tiny glint of glass, felt a blow, a sharp sting in his forearm. He thrust the other back, struck at the wizened face, saw the overcoated figure go down. A small silvery cylinder flopped against the left sleeve of his jacket; he jerked the hypodermic free, pulled back his sleeve, sucked at the minute wound. A pervasive, bitter taste filled his mouth. He spat, sucked again, then pressed a thumb deep into the great vein of the upper arm, leaning against the wall as a wave of vertigo rocked the pavement underfoot. From a remote distance, an ache crept along his arm. Before him the dark-coated man scrambled to his feet.

"Adair, can you hear me?"

Adair grunted. A needle-like tingling had begun in the hand, starved of blood circulation.

"Be at peace, Tony Adair," the hissing voice went on. "The drug kills slowly, first robbing the limbs of will, while keening the senses. . ." The bearded, insect-like face waggled in mock commiseration. The baleful eyes were a glint of crimson from deep sockets.

"Wealth and good fortune would have been yours, Tony Adair, but, monkey-like, curiosity gnawed at you . . ."

Adair moved his left hand, as heavy as an anvil, inside his coat, felt the cold butt of the Mauser 6.35 automatic. With an effort he curled numbing fingers, brought the gun out and up, jammed it hard into the muffling layers of the other's garments, and squeezed the trigger. The shock kicked his arm back hard against the brick wall as the figure before him lurched, rictal mouth gaping pinkly, fell in a swirl of coat-skirts, kicking lean black-bristled ankles in the muck of the alley, then lay still. Adair dropped the gun in his coat pocket, fumbled out a pen knife. The keen blade made a one-inch cut across the bluish puncture wound; crimson blood welled. He sucked hard, spat, massaging the forearm toward the wound.

He bound a handkerchief tightly above the cut, pushed away from the wall, and moved with painful slowness past the inert body toward the alley mouth.

The street glistened, empty in the night rain. Adair swayed, feeling the working of the drug. Over the pain of the numbed arm, he was aware of an unnatural sharpness of the senses: his ears caught the stealthy rustle of a rat, the tap and ping of raindrops in a thousand keys, the minute creak of masonry under the pressure of the wind. Far away, horns blew, machines whined and muttered, elevator doors clashed, music tootled and thumped. Nearer, there was the rustle of clothing, hoarse breathing. Adair slitted his eyes against the actinic glare of the street lamp's multi-colored corona, walked toward the marquee of the hotel. Ahead, door hinges screeched, shoe leather rasped on grit. Jerry Pearl stepped into view. His head jerked as he saw Adair.

"Tony boy . . ." The bandages were gone from his head. He came toward Adair, his feet clapping loud against the pavement. Adair felt the wet coat across his shoulders, hair damp against his forehead. He drew a breath and steadied himself against the wall.

"I ran into a little delay, Jerry," he said briskly. "What's up?"

"Ah . . . what kind of delay, Tony?"

"I met our friend, the numbers peddler . . ."

Jerry's eyes met Adair's—and slipped aside. "Oh, yeah? What'd he have to say, Tony?"

"I didn't pay too much attention. You're looking better, Jerry; a fast recovery."

"Ahhh, them medics; they doped me, Tony. I'm okay. Say, ah, where'd he go?"

"Who?"

"You know. The . . . uh . . . old man."

"He didn't go anywhere, Jerry. I shot him."

Jerry Pearl stared at Adair. Arcs as black as mascara marked the hollows under his eyes. "Dead . . . ?" His voice was a strained whisper.

Adair didn't answer. Pearl stepped past him, walked quickly to the alley, turned in. Adair followed, watched as Pearl knelt by the huddled figure. A matted wig had fallen away, revealing a flaccid, leathery crest. A tongue like a scarlet worm trailed from one corner of the puckered mouth.

"I guess maybe it's time for some law, Jerry," Adair said. "After the cops are through scratching their heads over this, we'll pass it along to the medical boys to pickle in a bottle of alcohol."

Pearl looked up quickly. "No. No police, Tony. This had gone too far already—"

"Uh-huh. I guess I messed things up by getting here a few minutes early. It happened I was just around the corner when you phoned. Mr. Smelly here wasn't quite ready."

"You're wrong, Tony. It's not what you think—"

"How do you know what I think, Jerry? And your Bronx dialect has slipped. Maybe you'd better tell me what it's all about."

"Tony, what do you mean . . . ?"

"You were here an hour ago casing the set-up with our pal. And I don't remember telling you which garbage can he was back of—but you went to it like a rat to cheese."

Pearl rose. "I was careless," he said slowly. "I'm sorry, Tony—but you shouldn't have killed him." He looked at Adair. "You may have killed your luck."

"Luck wouldn't interest a dead man."

"What do you mean? He only meant to talk to you— frighten you—"

"I guess he forgot to tell you; there was a change in plan."

"I see . . ." Pearl straightened his back. "I see how it must look to you, Tony—"

"Yeah. Now let's go find that copper."

"Tony . . . there are some things I have to tell you now. It would be better for you if I did not, but I can hardly expect you to trust me after . . . this."

Adair said nothing; Pearl shook his head impatiently.

"You're a stubborn fool, Adair. You have the gift of wealth in your hands; why not forget what's happened here, and just go on winning at cards?"

"Maybe I'm tired of cards, Jerry. And maybe I'm tired of being the counter in somebody else's game."

The two men stood toe to toe. "You have no conception of what you're meddling in, Tony."

"Why don't you explain it to me, Jerry?"

Pearl sighed. "Tony, I have to admire you; you're a fighter. But the forces that oppose you are— unconquerable."

"Meaning . . . you, Jerry?"

Pearl shook his head. "I've neither opposed nor helped you, Tony. I'm an observer—nothing more."

"What about this?" Adair jerked a thumb toward the corpse. "What is it? and why?"

"Merely a tool: a slave of a powerful master."

"Why the interest in me?"

"You were a thread in the pattern; someone else would have served as well."

"Maybe better; I don't take kindly to serving."

"You would have lost nothing, Tony. It was in the interest of the grand design that you prosper."

"What does this grand design have to do with brownies with B.O. peddling Bolita and handing out free advice in dark alleys?"

Pearl's face tightened. "I've told you too much already, too much for your good as well as mine."

"But not quite enough to soothe my curiosity, Jerry. Where does this leather-upholstered freak come from? And why should my luck at the track interest anyone outside of me and the Internal Revenue boys?"

"You wouldn't understand, Tony. As for the Niss, it's a native of . . . a very distant place."

"It must have some kind of quarters—probably near here, I'd say. Let's take a look at them."

Pearl considered. "If I show you the Niss headquarters, will you take it as an indication that I'm . . . not working against you?"

"I don't know. Try me."

"I don't want you to believe I was involved in a plan to kill you, Tony. I'd like you to accept the fact that I'm at least neutral. But for your own sake, I wish you'd walk away and put what you've seen out of your mind."

"Not a chance, Jerry. I'd just sit around and brood."

"Come along, then. But you won't like what you see."

Pearl led the way past dusty store fronts to a blind-eyed godown, rattled a chained hasp, stepped into darkness and the smell of moldy burlap. Adair followed, glanced around at sagging board shelving, drifted litter, a scurry of bright-eyed rats. Pearl moved suddenly. Adair pivoted, facing him. Pearl laughed softly. "Just checking your vision, Tony. Not bad, for a . . . city man."

"Just consider me one of the night people, Jerry. And don't bother testing my nerves; just lead the way."

Pearl crossed the rubbish-strewn room to a metal-covered fire door, threw a bolt, pushed the door open. He stepped through, moved his hands over the wall near the door; a section of the partition folded back. Through the narrow opening, Adair saw a red-lit passage. Pearl gestured him in. Adair stood fast.

"After you, Jerry." Pearl smiled sourly and stepped through. At once he took four quick strides, reached out and passed a hand over a metal plate set in the wall. The dusky crimson glow faded. Adair watched as Pearl's dimly glowing figure flattened itself against the wall. He listened to the other's breath sigh out, once, then stop.

Half a minute passed. Adair stood quietly, waiting. Pearl moved from the wall, stepped carefully across to the opposite side. The rustle of cloth against skin, the creak of muscles, the rasp of feet against concrete were loud to Adair's ears. Pearl's hands scraped as he moved them over the wall. Adair glanced along the rough-plastered surface, saw a small button set in a round plastic plate. He stepped forward quietly, pressed the button. A panel like the first folded back with a clatter. Pearl froze.

"Was that what you were looking for?" Adair asked.

Pearl took out a lighter, thumbed it aflame. He stared at Adair.

"I see you've made a fool of me, Tony. How the devil you can see here is beyond me . . ."

"I'm full of little surprises, Jerry. Now let's make another try at finding that Niss headquarters."

"Tony—you're not . . . another observer . . . ?"

"Just a local boy, trying to get along."

"Listen to me, Tony. This is no place for you. You were always decent to me. I don't want to see you hurt—"

"You didn't intend to lead me anywhere, did you, Jerry? This was just a gag to get me in off the street and ditch me."

"That's right. For your own good, Tony."

"Nice try. Now let's cut out the kidding and get down to business. Lead on, Jerry."

"Tony, you're meddling with forces that can destroy you as effortlessly as you'd swat a fly."

"You seem safe enough, Jerry. What's your secret?"

"Try to understand, Tony. I am the agent of a mighty power—an empire of a vastness inconceivable to you. And even I have to move with the utmost care." As Pearl spoke, his hand moved behind his back; Adair heard the rustle of fingers on the rough wall, then the clatter of static as an electric circuit closed. Far off, a bell shrilled supersonically.

"Somehow your explanation doesn't seem to simplify matters, Jerry," Adair said.

"The less you know, the safer you'll be, Tony," Pearl said smoothly. Over the background sighing of moving air, the crackle as the surrounding walls flexed under load, Adair picked out the vibration of distant footfalls.

"Why did he run you down, Jerry? Didn't you tell him you're neutral?"

"A little disagreement. I was wrong. I should have listened."

From beyond the board partition at his side, Adair caught the tiny whisper of breathing, the stealthy movement of feet. He scanned the wall, made out the hairline rim of a hinged panel. He moved forward a step, waiting . . .

The section of wall snapped aside. Through the opening a spider-lean figure in tight-fitting black leaped with a hiss, crouched, poised, rounded shoulders hunched, long arms spread. For an instant, Adair looked into pupilless red eyes in a puckered face; then the Niss sprang, hands clawed—

Adair's shot was a vivid stab of flame across the gloom, a roar in the closed tunnel. He saw a mouth like a wound gape, the flick of a crimson tongue past needle-like white teeth. Then the creature was down, bucking scorpion legs in the dust of the floor.

"It looks like Mr. Friendly was twins," he said. "Any more in the family?"

"You murderous fool!" Pearl burst out. "You'll have the horde down on us . . ."

"We'll surprise them and meet them halfway."

"That wouldn't be convenient for me." Pearl moved to step past Adair. Adair blocked his path.

"Don't attempt force with me." Jerry Pearl stared up at Adair. "Remember the car that ran me down? If you'd examine the wreck, you'd find the left front wheel nearly torn off. I did that with my hands as the wheels passed over my chest."

"I wondered about the car crashing. Funny, that explanation never occurred to me." Adair brought the gun up to cover Jerry Pearl's chest. Pearl shook his head impatiently.

"That won't help you, Tony. Don't you understand yet?"

"Sure, I understand, Jerry. You're no more human than—that thing is."

"Then stand aside."

"These steel-jacketed slugs pack a wallop. Want to bet I can't poke a hole through whatever it is you're made of?"

"I'm trying to protect you, Tony—to keep you out of this. My reflexes are twice as fast as yours. I could knock the gun from your hand before you could pull the trigger."

"Want to gamble on it, Jerry?" Adair said softly.

Pearl half-smiled. "I doubt that you'd have the cold-blooded nerve to shoot me—"

He spun, fell to his knees as the shot slammed in the narrow way. Dazedly Pearl shook his head, climbed to his feet, holding his arm close to his side. He looked at Adair warily, then laughed shortly.

"You see how easy it is to subvert a being? The threat

of pain and death—and I do your bidding. Come, then.
I'll lead you to the Niss. But I wish you'd turn back."

"It's too late to turn back now, Jerry. I was dealt into
this game; I'll play my hand out."

They were in a low, earth-floored tunnel, walled with
time-stained masonry, shored with ancient timbers that
glowed with a dim greenish light. The clay underfoot
was thickly patterned with strangely narrow footprints
with prominent heels. A rhythmic thumping sounded
monotonously at the threshold of audibility. A draft of icy
air carried a faint, foul odor.

"We're two hundred feet under the streets now," Jerry
Pearl said. "We've been lucky—but we won't get much
farther without blundering into a party of Niss."

"Maybe I can take one alive. He might even part with
some information if I find the right place to squeeze."

"You're talking like a madman. *You'll* be lucky to get
out of here alive. The main assembly area is just ahead.
Move quietly now . . ."

Adair followed, listening to the rising level of sound.
The clay underfoot gave way to a glossy dark paving,
beaded with moisture. The walls here were narrow, high,
meeting in an arch ten feet overhead. The passage
curved; ahead, a ruddy glow shone. Pearl halted. Adair
moved up beside him.

"There they are," Pearl whispered softly.

It was a domed chamber, ribbed with lime-encrusted
buttresses, floored with a glossy slime of clay, lit by
spheres of blackish-red light atop ornate stands, divided
by a murmuring streamlet of dark liquid and pervaded

by a stench of raw sewage. From the dark side tunnel Adair and Jerry Pearl watched a dozen or more black-uniformed Niss, devoid of false hair, some with long knives strapped to their sides, who prowled the cave restlessly or stood in nervous groups, hissing among themselves.

"This is the club house, eh?" Adair breathed. "A charming air of informality and bad drains."

"I think you can see that it would hardly reward you to charge in, gun blazing. They're as vicious as ferrets."

"You might find it expedient to pitch in on my side, Jerry—under the circumstances."

"I've spent a great deal of time building my position here; I'm hardly likely to throw it away now."

"They don't know the truth about you, eh, Jerry? Your disguise has them fooled—just like it did me."

"They accept me as a Terrestrial. Otherwise they'd have known better than to try to eliminate me with feeble methods."

"They almost succeeded. You were out cold when they hauled you into the hospital."

"Yes—I was stunned—but don't let it give you false ideas."

"Let's both avoid false ideas."

"Yes. Underestimating you could be dangerous—for both of us. Now come away—before we're caught here . . ."

"I think I'd like to stick around, Jerry. One of them might just wander over this way. They're as nervous as a roomful of expectant fathers."

"At least withdraw to a better position," Pearl urged. "There's a small alcove a few yards back."

Pearl moved back, indicated a side chamber eight feet square, with closed doors set in its three walls. "In here . . ."

Adair stepped in, noting a faint line of discontinuity across the floor and up the walls. At his side, Pearl moved quickly; Adair whirled—

A grill of one-inch bars slammed down an inch from his foot; beyond the barrier, Pearl dived for the cover of the corridor. Adair fired from the hip, spattered masonry chips beside Pearl's hand.

"Next one's in, Jerry!"

Pearl froze, crouched two feet from safety. "Don't shoot again, Tony! Wait until you've heard me . . . !"

"I've got five left in the clip. Better talk fast before the neighbors get here . . ."

"No. The Niss are totally deaf in our sound range without their hearing aids." Pearl straightened, eyes on the gun. "I would have come back and released you, Tony. After—"

"Do it now."

"No. You'll have to believe me, Tony. If you shoot me, you're trapped permanently. There is something I have to do—the culmination of years of work. Then I'll return for you."

"You can do better than that, Jerry."

"You asked what it was the Niss and I fell out over. It was you, Tony. They planned to kill you for your curiosity. I argued. They turned on me. I was neutral, Tony—but not any more!"

"So you're launching a vendetta against the Niss—"

"The Niss are nothing. Once they were a power in the

Galaxy; now—they're slaves—as your people will be slaves—and mine as well, in the end."

"Oh? Who's our new owner going to be?"

"A creature who manipulates the lesser breeds as man manipulates fruit-flies. That's what you're challenging, Tony—not the Niss. But no living being can stand against the Norn."

"I don't believe in bogey-men. Nobody's that tough."

"Tough? Oh, no; the Norn's no tougher physically than many another species. It can't wreak destruction even as well as you Men, with the raw violence of your H-bomb. Its power is a subtler one—against which there can be no defense."

"Keep talking—and don't make the mistake of thinking I'm too spellbound to shoot."

"The Norn's power is the power over the human soul. It offers no punishment—only reward: wealth, power, the woman of your dreams—subject only to . . . the Norn."

"The woman of my dreams wouldn't be for sale, Jerry."

"Tony, the time is running out; minutes could make the difference between abject slavery and a . . . more limited form of submission—for my race, and yours too. Let the explanations wait."

"Not a chance, Jerry. Show your cards or fold."

"What kind of man are you?" Pearl stared with agonized eyes at the gun. "After so much—to be balked by a puny human and his primitive weapon . . ."

"A Neanderthal with a stone axe could put up a pretty potent argument too, Jerry. Give."

Pearl's shoulders slumped. "Very well. Listen to me,

Tony. I'll try to make you understand. Then I'm going. You may shoot if you wish; if I wait any longer everything's lost anyway.

"The Norn lives in a different world of awareness than you or I—or the Niss. It perceives the universe as a tangled skein of lines of living force. Past, future—these are only parts of a pattern; a confused fabric of the potential and the actual.

"The Norn has the power to manipulate these strands; it lies in its den—like your spiders in their webs—and rearranges the pattern to suit its needs. By human standards, it has near-moronic intelligence. Its drives are simple: food and a nesting place. But it eats, Tony. It eats enormously—and burgeons.

"Your world was chosen as a nesting place long ago. The Norn came here as a miniscule spore; it drifted, altering the microscopic lives around it, drawing the unwary amoeba within reach. It grew—and its radius of effectiveness grew. It led beetles and mice into its den, tempting them with food and ripe females. The time came when it needed better concealment, more elaborate arrangements. It summoned a slave race—the Niss—as its attendants. Now it worked on a larger scale, diverting a workman from his duties, while the Niss slaves moved about its business; or delaying a watchman for the moments needed to allow necessary supplies to be pilfered."

"How many of these Norns are there?"

"Only one; the presence of another Norn disrupts the pattern. Now, it's entering the second phase of its life cycle. It's growing rapidly, and requires more nourishment than can be supplied by a casual herding of rat packs or stray dogs or derelicts. A massive logistical program will be necessary—soon. This will require measures that can no longer be concealed. Human servants will be recruited—in every walk of life. Nourishing the Norn will become the chief business of the planet—until the day when the planetary resources can no longer support it. Then it will spore. Its seed will be flung into space—and new worlds will be colonized from the husk of the old."

"I see. Help wanted, male, to loot planet—"

"It will take a while, Tony, the looting. Perhaps a thousand years. And the Norn can offer its servants the fulfillment of every dream of avarice that's haunted man since he crept down from the treetops."

"Why was I collecting goodies? I hadn't signed a contract."

"The Norn works blindly; it was in its interest that you prosper—for reasons buried in the pattern."

"If its workings are blind, how does it manage the payoff?"

"Picture the Norn mind, suspended in a net of awareness, surrounded by the filaments of the fabric. Its only aim is a cozy nest. Here's a line that threatens its comfort: Snap it short, or shunt it away. Here's a line that means food, security; weave that thread close and strong. The Norn smoothes away the irritation—and the slave gains its dearest wish; it becomes your servant forever."

"My heart desires a slice of this Norn."

Pearl's laugh was a humorless bark. "Could you cut that slice—knowing you were turning your back on all the treasures of the world—for yourself, and your descendants, for a thousand years?"

"Where is the Norn's nest?"

"I've said all I'm going to say, Tony. I'm going now—
and hope I'm not too late. Shoot if you must—and you'll
rot here—unless the Niss find you first." He turned and
walked away.

Adair felt over his jacket pockets for the key ring he
had palmed from the floor of the car that had run down
Jerry Pearl. The doors facing him on three sides were
featureless, tight-set in the plain wall. Half a minute's
search turned up a tiny hole at the edge of each. Adair
tried the center door; with the third key the lock snicked
open on a narrow corridor like the one he and Pearl had
followed, empty and dark to normal eyes. Adair stepped
out, followed the passage as it meandered, then turned
abruptly to open into the Niss common-room. He
watched, narrow-eyed, as the lean uniformed Niss paced
and muttered: What were they waiting for . . . ?

Adair's ears caught a sharp sound from the far side of
the chamber. The Niss ignored it. In the gloom of a dark
corner, a figure stirred. It was Pearl, unnoticed in the
shadows, leaning forward over something held in his
hands. He stooped, working quickly, then stood, faded back
out of sight. A harsh hissing cut across the background
sounds. Adair sniffed, caught a faint hint of a half-familiar
odor . . .

A Niss near the corner where Pearl had appeared
tottered suddenly, fell, kicking its legs convulsively.
Nearby, others turned to gape. One of them raised its
knife, dropped it, and fell backwards; another took two
drunken steps and pitched on its face. A hiss of alarm

spread across the room. Those Niss who had surged forward toward the fallen ones collapsed, twitching. Others sprang toward dark exits, hammered vainly on closed doors—and reeled, fell, and lay still.

Adair jumped back, sprinted for the cage he had escaped, snorting the reek of cyanide from his sensitized nostrils. He slammed the door, tried keys, swung the left-hand door wide, and moved off quickly along the tunnel, visible to him by the minute glow from the natural infra-phosphorescence of the walls. The passage branched; Adair took the right turning, working his way toward Jerry Pearl's last position. There were more branches, an intersection with a wider corridor. Adair stopped, listened; there was no sound other than the steady rustle of the air and the muffled, rhythmic thumping. He went on, reviewing in his mind the turnings of the passage. He was, he estimated, very close to the point where Jerry Pearl had tossed his canister in among the Niss. Ahead, a hairline marked a closed door. The odor of cyanide was sharp in the air.

Fifty feet farther, an interesting tunnel led sharply down. Adair studied the wet clay of the floor; in the maze of footprints, Pearl's were not discernible. He turned, started down the descending way.

It dropped in a sharp spiral, debouched into a circular room a hundred feet across. Far above, sounds whispered back from a vaulted ceiling festooned with stalagmites, from the tips of which water drops fell in a restless tattoo. A water-filled pit ten yards wide filled the center of the room. Adair took a step, his feet sinking into soft clay; then he froze. The black surface of the pool stirred; liquid mud streamed back from a great bloated form that rose up like a surfacing corpse, with a hissing sigh of released air. Two flaccid, boneless arms lay coiled like dead-white cobras across the swollen slope of a body like black jelly. Two other limbs, multi-jointed, black and shiny like the chitinous tail of a king crab, lay folded, claws parted. One twitched, moved out, groped among heaped carcasses of small animals at the edge of the pool, popped a dainty into a loose-lipped mouth bisecting an otherwise featureless head the size of a washtub.

Abruptly, the great body rippled, heaved its bulk around to face Adair. One of the boneless arms moved out, slapped mud, sent small bones flying. Then:

"Come closer, Tony Adair," called a voice like footsteps in deep mud. "Tell me of your dreams . . ."

In the muck rimming the oily pool, bristly rats the size of rabbits played among the heaped debris of the Norn's feeding, indifferent to the blind arms that groped among them.

"Come closer, Tony Adair," the Norn's voice rumbled. "Have no fear. You are more pleasing than the Niss-things: ugly creatures, and evil-smelling . . ."

Gun in hand, Adair studied the sheer walls that rose around him; the shadowy recesses of the chamber were almost totally dark, even to his drug-sharpened vision. High up among the arches of the vaulted ceiling, he caught a hint of furtive movement. Nearer at hand, there was a quick rasp of horny joints; Adair stepped back; with a snap of pincers, a chitinous limb spattered mud at his feet.

"What is your fancy?" the heavy voice droned as though unaware of the murderous blow. "The crown of a kingdom? Power of life and death . . . ?"

"Maybe I've already got it . . ." Adair raised his voice. "Come down and join the party, Jerry."

The Norn stirred in its mud-bath. The snake-like arms gathered in tidbits, feeding the great mouth. Water drops pattered in an incessant restless rain. Adair raised the gun, took aim, fired. Muck spattered beside the bulbous, eyeless head. The Norn gobbled, waving a horny arm.

"The next one will poke an eye in that head, Jerry," Adair called. "You've got sixty seconds to make it down here; and I think I ought to tell you: this gun is kind of special. I reworked the action myself. If I release the trigger, it fires—and at this range, I can hardly miss."

"You're lying . . ." Pearl's voice echoed from above.

"Want to bet, Jerry?" Adair laughed softly. "No, you can't risk it, can you? Now get a move on."

Pearl moved into view on a platform twenty feet above.

"I'll summon the Niss," he said hoarsely. "If you've harmed the Norn, they'll tear you to living shreds."

"A good thought, Jerry—but I was watching from the wings when you gassed them all."

Pearl groaned. "Hold your fire, for God's sake, Tony; I'm coming down."

Standing before Adair, Pearl took an elaborate, long-barreled weapon from his pocket, tossed it aside.

"All right, Tony, you hold the initiative. But listen to me: I was sent here to find the Norn's weakness. It has none. There's a saying: *The Universe was created for the pleasure of the Norn.* I understand that now. It satisfies its enormous greed by feeding the lesser greeds of others. I wanted to make myself indispensable—to earn for my race the role of useful servants. It would have been better than death—"

"Would it?"

"You haven't seen a world in the last phases of the Norn lifecycle: the remaining populace, toiling like madmen to feed the immense maw that sprawls over continents, sea-bottoms, fills every cave and crevice. Then the final frenzy as the Norn, maddened by hunger, devours its slaves, then in convulsions that rive continents, spores—"

"And you wanted to MC the show, eh? What could it pay you that would make it worthwhile?"

"While I lived, every whim satisfied, every impulse indulged. Fame, glory, happiness, riches—for a thousand years. And if I could resist—then someone else would serve in my place. There's no escape, once the Norn chooses a nest-world."

"I could end that right now—with one bullet. It looks soft enough."

Pearl choked. "Throw the gun away, you fool! You don't know what you're saying. We can reach some agreement—" He moved toward Adair.

"Don't try any slick moves, Jerry. I'm full of some swell stuff the Niss slipped into my arm. I can practically hear your brains working."

"Tony . . ." Pearl's voice was shaken. "I understand now. You've been injected with *Mus*. No wonder you can see in the dark. You're dying, Tony; did you know that?

But of course you do. That's why you're willing to threaten the Norn."

"Tony Adair," the Norn burbled. "I offer you a world—the wealth of all its mines, its fairest shes as slaves—and more: I pledge you life eternal . . ."

Pearl half sobbed, half laughed. "Life eternal—to a man who'll be dead in half an hour." He shook himself. "The only creature in the Universe who could be immune to the Norn's bribe—and I brought you here myself."

"Life eternal," Adair said. "I have to admit, that's quite an offer. If I wasn't already a dead man—could it do it?"

Pearl stared at Adair. "It can do anything, Tony— anything that serves its own survival."

"Yes, quite an offer," Adair repeated. "But still a little too stingy."

"What do you mean, Tony? What do you want?"

"I want it all . . ."

I don't understand, Tony." Sweat glistened on Pearl's face. "You blundered into this—"

"Your ideas about the natives die slow, don't they, Jerry? All right, we've wasted enough time. Let's get moving. Go back into the room where you left the Niss breathing cyanide. Bring me one of their knives."

"What are you going to do?"

"I'll show you when you get back."

Adair waited, holding the gun. The Norn fed restlessly, muttering of gold and emeralds. Pearl returned carrying a two foot weighted blade.

"The part that's talking does not even know what the rest is doing, does it, Jerry?" Adair asked.

"It's almost mindless. It picks concepts from the minds around it and mouths them like a parrot—whatever it senses will please. It's blind, lying in its web of Psi, plucking at the strands of the fabric that only it can see—"

"Deaf, too. Move in closer, Jerry. Just out of reach of the arms."

"Tony—I have to know what you're planning."

"You say you have fast reflexes, Jerry. I want you to entice it to strike. When it does—cut off its arm."

"Are you mad—"

"Do as I say, or I'll put a bullet through the head."

"Wait, Tony. I . . . I'll do as you say . . ." Pearl edged closer to the multi-ton creature sunk in its wallow. With a sudden surge, a white arm lashed out—and in a motion too quick to follow, Pearl whipped the machete down—

With a bellow, the Norn coiled back the wounded member, churning the pool to a brown froth—and a two-foot section of severed tentacle lay twitching in the muck.

"Rake it over here," Adair snapped. With the knife, Pearl dragged the pale flesh back. It writhed, flopped, then began to contract on itself. The raw, yellowish flesh of the cut end puckered, drew in.

"It acts as though it were alive—"

In the pool, the violent activity ceased abruptly. The armored members went slack, sprawled out, claws lax. The boneless arms sagged. The wide mouth gaped, regurgitated a gallon or two of lumpy fluid. Then the head, with a sigh like gas escaping from a swamp, sank from sight, lifeless limbs trailing.

"It's . . . dead." Pearl turned on Adair, a wild look in his eyes.

"But this isn't." Adair nodded toward the severed tentacle tip. It had formed itself into a rough sphere now. A lump grew on the upper surface; four buds bulged lower down on the ten-inch globe of brownish jelly. Two buds burst and thin grey crab-legs poked forth. The other buds elongated, formed tiny pink fingers that coiled and probed the air. A slit formed in the dorsal bulge, opened.

"I will give you riches, Tony Adair," a tiny voice piped. "I will make you happy . . ."

"It was a guess," Adair said. "You told me how it propagated parthenogenetically when the parent dies. You also said there could be only one Norn to a world. Since nature favors the young at the expense of the old, it figured."

"Do you realize what this means, Tony? We can control the Norn, keep its growth within bounds—"

"We'll install it in a fancy private sewer with the kind of atmosphere it craves, and feed it plenty of raw meat. All it wants is food and a nest that smells like home. That's where it has it all over us, with our complicated desires. And it will attend to our needs—"

"Tony—have you forgotten—"

"What did you call that stuff? *Mus*? Don't let it bother you, Jerry. I bled most of it out of my system; I just got enough to put a fine edge on my night vision."

There was a pause. "Why don't you shoot me now, Tony? How do you know I won't wait my chance to kill you and take it all?"

"You need me, Jerry. I could kill the Norn if I had to; you couldn't. Kill me, and in the next breath you'll be back on your knees, begging it for favors. You haven't got what it takes to run the bluff."

There was a harsh laugh from Pearl. "You're right. You're willing to risk it all—to gain it all. And I'm not."

"There's another reason, too, Jerry. I need you. I've got a yen to see this galaxy you keep talking about; you've got the contacts . . ."

"Yes, you'll have the stars, Tony," said the being who had been Jerry Pearl. "The Norn made one fatal error. It tackled a race greedier than its own."

✴PART III✴
STORIES

BY
ROSEL GEORGE BROWN

SAVE YOUR CONFEDERATE MONEY, BOYS

It was not, of course, the sort of thing that happens to the ordinary person.

But then Grandfather Mayberry was not the ordinary person, even to begin with. When Walter—I don't think it's respectful to refer to your grandfather as Walter, either, but we were never allowed to call him anything else. He was frequently referred to in the family as Yankee Walter, but no one ever said it to his face. It happened that his mother, great-grandfather's first wife, was from Massachusetts and because of this everyone always thought of Walter as being a little bit *different*. I think maybe this might account for a lot of Walter's peculiarities. I mean when people expect you to be a little peculiar all the time—well, as Walter's descendant I can understand how he felt. Whenever anyone mentions something like Protointegrationist somebody looks a little guiltily over at me as though I caused the second secession and whoever mentions it in front of me is being tactless.

I was only a child then.

And I remember thinking it was awful to secede and not have anybody care. I mean to have big industry just move away and to get poorer and poorer and have to pick the cotton yourself.

And wrap it in tissue paper and sell it to the tourists for ten cents a boll—Confederate money.

But look at it this way. Your Confederate money's worth something now. And why?

Well, when Walter announced that he had no intention of dying, I was immensely relieved. If Walter said he wasn't going to die that winter, he wasn't going to. So I had Mama spray on the tightest corset I could stand and took off for my year of Precollege with a light heart and a twenty-inch waist.

I didn't really expect to be able to pass the college boards, even with Precollege. And if I did, I wouldn't have been able to go to college. It was all the family could do to send the boys. But Mama didn't want anyone to say her girls weren't educated, so we all went to Precollege and gracefully flunked the college boards.

It was that summer—after my two semesters of Precollege—that I brought the Price boy back with me, Jerry Price. I ended up not marrying him, of course. He really wouldn't have done at all, but boy, could he court!

Well, I was all watery-eyed and pink-skinned over Jerry then and I knew the family would just love him and I sort of hoped he'd stay more than just two or three days. I mean if he could find a summer job maybe he could stay until September 15, which was the date for the college boards. The thing was, would Jerry like the family?

"The one I really want you to meet," I told him, feeling a little uneasy about it, "is my grandfather. Walter."

"You call him Walter?"

"Yes. Er . . . he's a real character. You know . . . The thing is, though, he's almost bedridden."

"*Bedridden*? You mean rocking chair ridden."

"No. Bedridden. I know it sounds unusual, but my grandfather Mayberry refused to take his chloresterol pills. Or antichloresterol pills, or whatever it is. He said they weren't Natural. And now it's too late. He's ruined his arteries."

"It takes a real character to do something like that."

I didn't like Jerry's tone of voice, but I couldn't help but agree with it. Maybe Walter wasn't a character. Maybe he was just stupid.

"The thing is," I said, because the postbellum buggy was almost there, "that the extra cot is in his room and you'll have to sleep there. I mean I'm sure you'll find Walter an interesting character."

"Sure," Jerry said.

Surely, I thought, Jerry will not disapprove of the bottle under Walter's pillow or his swearing or his insulting—but then even Walter wouldn't be able to find anything insulting to say about Jerry.

The house looked silent and empty when we drove up. Cousin Dickie helped me out of the buggy and held out his hand. I didn't put anything in it so he drove off in a huff and left a whirlwind of dust for us to track into the house.

I swang open the screen door and yelled, "Yoo-hoo!" But I could hear it echo way to the kitchen without striking anything soft.

"Must be out showing the end of the season tourists around," I said. "The trains are all local here and they never run on time so nobody knew just when we'd be in. I mean, if they'd known, they'd certainly all be here to welcome you."

"Sure," Jerry said.

Really, I thought, they could have left somebody. It all seemed such an anticlimax.

"Well," I said, "there's still Walter. You'll want to bring your bags up, anyway."

Halfway up the stairs I stopped. I could hear water splashing and a quavery voice singing, "Don't Sit Under the Apple Tree."

Oh, Lord, I thought. He's gone and gotten drunk in the bath tub again and there's no one to get him out.

Jerry looked at me with raised eyebrows.

"Grandfather Mayberry," I explained, "remembers all the old World War songs. He likes to just splash in the bathtub and just sing and sing. Isn't it wonderful!" I finished up as enthusiastically as I could.

"Sure," Jerry said. "My grandfather," he added, "makes a hobby of taking school kids out on hikes. You know."

"Sure," I said. I decided then and there I'd rather let Walter drown than send Jerry in there to get him out of the tub.

Just then the screen door slammed and Mama said, "Yoo-hoo! Annabelle! Is your young man with you?"

"Yes!" I called, hissing on the *s*. Mama's phraseology is always so irritating. I wasn't at all sure Jerry wanted to be referred to as "my young man."

"Be right down!" I added. "Jerry," I said, "you just put

your things in there and come on down when you're ready."

What I wanted was a moment alone with Mama and I got it.

"Someone has got to do something about Walter," I whispered. "He's there in the bath tub again and singing and you *know* he's dr . . ."

"Don't you dare," Mama cried, "say that. Your grandfather Mayberry is perfectly all right and he'll get out of the tub when he's ready."

"Mama, at a time like this you cannot close your eyes to ugly reality. You know Walter can't get out of the tub by himself and none of the men are here and pretty soon he'll start yelling and then Jerry will have to go hoist him out. Call up cousin Jefferson. *Please!*"

"Now, dear," Mama began soothingly, "I haven't written you about it, but Walter has had the most amazing . . ."

There was a hoarse screech and Jerry came barreling down the steps with his cuff ruffles untaped and one boot off.

He grabbed Mama with one hand and me with the other. "Get out of the house!" he cried. "We'll lock it in and get it when the rest of the men get back."

Mama removed his hand firmly.

"Your grandfather Mayberry," she told me, "is out of the bath."

"There is an alligator up there!" Jerry cried, still trying to herd us out.

"Is *this* your young man?" Mama asked in a tone which she never used with the tourist trade.

"Yes," I answered. "Mama, if Jerry sees an alligator . . ."

"Please make yourself at home, Mr. Price," Mama said with a severe look at his hanging cuffs. "Since we no longer have servants you'll have to excuse me while I get supper started."

We hadn't had servants for as far back as I could remember.

"Look, Annabelle," Jerry began, whispering nervously and looking like he'd gotten off on the wrong floor of a hospital. "I don't want to insult your . . ."

It was at that moment that I found out what the word galumphing means, because Walter came galumphing down the stairs.

In all justice to Jerry, I could see how a mistake might have been made.

"Hello, Annabelle," Walter said, as though he'd just seen me last morning. "Your boyfriend's got no guts."

"And you," I said furiously, "have no manners. Walter, how *can* you come out in front of company looking like this?"

"Can't look any other way, chick," he said. "Hormones."

"I'm going to be a freshman in pre-med next year," Jerry said, "and I've never heard of a hormone with those kinds of side effects."

"Cap," Walter said, "you've got an awful lot of ignorance to lose."

"*Annabelle!*" It was time for me to see to the biscuits and set the table.

"Make yourself at home, Jerry," I said, feeling sure this was not the way things were at *his* home.

The kitchen was unnaturally cool. Furthermore, it didn't smell like anything at all.

The air was clear.

"Mama!" I cried. "We've got an atomic stove!"

It was built into the side wall. The old wood stove was still there, of course, for the tourists. But the tin chimney was gone and the lids were clean and the cracked one had been replaced.

Mama smiled and pressed a button. The wall panel slid back and inside were eight dinners, neatly set on plates and plain raw.

"All I have to do," Mama said, "is press a button and the food is cooked and the plates come out just warm."

"You had a good crop of tourists?"

"No. Your grandfather Mayberry provided this for us."

"You know Walter can't even provide himself with cigars."

Mama bit at her upper lip with her lower teeth, a sign that I will never learn to be tactful. "Walter has built up quite a little business. At first we thought of it as just a hobby but now it's growing into—well, it looks as though we may find ourselves carrying on the tourist trade as a sort of hobby."

"Whatever kind of business can Walter have got into?" A horrible thought struck me. "Not Yankee wines?"

"*Dear!* It's a . . . um . . . mail order business."

"There's something you're trying not to tell me. But if you don't, Walter will. And he'll make it sound even worse than it is."

"Dear, your grandfather Mayberry is handling the

distribution of Swamp Water Youth Restorative for the entire Confederacy."

"Sw . . . !" I simply collapsed into hysterics. It was such an absurd thing and Mama said it so primly.

"Oh, Mama!" I finally managed. "That's plain disgraceful. We didn't need an atomic stove that bad. And oh, he'll tell Jerry! I'd better go get him right now."

"It is not disgraceful. Swamp Water Youth Restorative actually does restore youth."

"Is that those hormones Walter was talking about? Is that what makes him look so peculiar?"

"I don't know that he looks peculiar. It is simply the next stage after old age. People look different at different stages. You should have seen yourself when you were one day old."

"Oh, all right. I don't know why you have to remember these things and bring them up all the time. Let's put it this way. Walter has changed since I was home for the Christmas holidays."

"Yes, and I just explained it. The Youth Restorative contains hormones which, as I understand it, cause changes in the basic structure of the cells of the human body. DNA or RNA or something like that. Women are not expected to understand these things, Annabelle."

"That's your excuse for things you don't want to understand. But I've seen Walter so I know this Youth Restorative does something. Where on earth did he get this stuff? Surely it isn't plain old water from the swamps."

"No. It's from—dear, didn't you all hear any rumors over at Precollege?"

"We hear all kinds of rumors."

"Well, this thing is big. It involves the whole Confederacy and there's more to it than just Walter's mail order business. Is that the men coming in?"

It was either them or a herd of elephants. Every time Brother walks in the house the chandeliers sway. And there would be Uncle Gary and . . .

"Set the table, Annabelle!"

I got out the good silver, because of Jerry, but not the crystal, which makes me nervous.

Everyone was a little stiff during dinner. I think this was partly due to the fact that while the rest of us had chicken and mashed potatoes, Walter had a string of raw fish. And the more everyone tried not to notice it, the more he chuckled.

I could have just *died*.

After dinner we cleared the dishes and I found out we had a dishwasher-stacker-disposal unit that even ground up the bones and sloshed the leavings in a bucket for the hogs.

Mama and I left the men to smoke in the dining room while we went out to smoke on the gallery. There's nothing sillier than this segregated after dinner smoking, particularly as this is the time when all the interesting things get said. I know, because once when I was ten I hid in the china cabinet, and boy, what I didn't hear!

The stars were flung all over the sky and just blazing away and I had to sit there through two cigarettes fending off Mama's questions about Jerry. Finally she said, "I do wish your father were alive," which meant she gave up.

"Now where did Walter get this Youth Restorative?" I asked.

"Ah, that," she said with a sigh. "You know, Annabelle, you couldn't have picked a worse time to bring a guest home. Particularly one we know almost nothing about. I've written Ada Sue in Jackson to find out what the Prices are like, but I haven't heard from her yet and Jerry's in there listening to all that talk and I'm not sure that Walter will remember to be discreet."

"If there's anything Walter's good at, it's being indiscreet. You still haven't answered my question."

Mama sighed again and got that dignified look on her face that she uses when she says things she doesn't want people to laugh at. "The Swamp Water," she said, "comes from the planet Venus."

At that moment Jerry walked out, flipped a cigarette into the petunias, took my elbow and guided me out for a walk in the starlight.

"I'll bring her back alive."

I knew without looking that Mama smiled and then went frowning into the house.

A little down the road, near the Leaning Pine Tree, I stumbled over a rock and came out of my daze.

"Jerry," I said, "my mother is stark, raving mad. There's a plain bad streak in the family." I shuddered. Who'd be next?

Jerry laughed. "Don't you know what's happened?"

"No. And if somebody doesn't explain it to me pretty soon I'll lose what little remains of my mind."

"The Venusians have landed," Jerry said, "in a swamp around Bayou Teche. They landed, in fact, in a bayou that runs behind your great Aunt Felicie's house. You *have* a great Aunt Felicie?"

"Great aunt by marriage. Aunt Felicie is nine hundred years old and she insists on living by herself out there with the alligators. Every Christmas she comes in with a great big pot of gumbo. Otherwise, we never see her."

"Well, your great Aunt Felicie took to the Venusians and the Venusians took to your great Aunt Felicie."

"I suppose Walter told you all this and I suppose you swallowed it hook, line and sinker. But will you please explain why nobody's heard about the Venusian landing?"

Jerry shrugged. "Apparently Felicie tried. She wired the president of the Confederacy. She wired her state representative. She even wired the Union government and several top Union scientists. When no one came she apologized to the Venusian representatives and wrote a letter to Grandfather Walter."

"Did the Venusians learn English from her?"

"No. They learned Cajun from her."

I giggled. It all sounded so exactly like Aunt Felicie.

"Do I see a nice piney bank up there?" Jerry asked, pointing to the bluff beyond the old Carey place.

"You do. Here, hold my hand and I'll take you around the back way. You can't get there from the road."

I led Jerry around the dark, crumbling house, which looked like a place where no one had lived but many had died. We crossed a queasy little bridge with stars laughing in the creek beneath.

"What did Aunt Felicie say in her letter to Walter?" I asked when I had gotten Jerry across the creek safely and on to an overgrown path that no one could have found but me.

"She said the Venusians wanted to know what sort of

present the people of the Confederacy would most appreciate. And of course Walter, being badly in need of rejuvenation himself, suggested a Rejuvenator."

"The Venusians didn't know he and Aunt Felicie are both half crazy?"

"They're not so crazy. Let me finish. The Venusians thought this was a perfectly good idea, and they whipped one up."

"*Really*, Jerry."

"You said you wanted to hear. You're the one that wants to waste all this starlight talking."

"I mean it's hard to believe the Venusians just happened to have a recipe for human Rejuvenation with them. Particularly since I assume they're not human."

"Not human the same way we are. But they do have one useful area of scientific knowledge under control. And that's virology. The study of viruses."

"Given time," I said, "I could have figured out what virology is."

"You're not being a good listener," Jerry said. We sat down and watched the fireflies across the road, and there was something lovely and comforting about the darkness and the stars and the little surprise glowings of the lightning bugs.

"What does virology have to do with Swamp Water Youth Restorer?" I asked, dropping pebbles off the edge of the bluff.

"Just this. The Venusians had increased their own life span enormously through the use of viruses."

"I thought Walter said it was hormones."

"He does think so. But from what he says, I think it's

all done with viruses. This is a guess. I gather they have a virus that goes in and replaces the template of the living cell. The template is the pattern from which new cells are formed. And if you change the template, a different cell is formed. Now maybe for themselves, they can rejuvenate without changing their appearance a great deal.

"But you can figure out what happened. Working with viruses with which they were familiar, they found one which alters cellular patterns but not to the extent of causing shock or death. But it was, after all, a Venusian virus, and the effect is—well, rather amphibious. You see how Walter looks."

"I don't know," I said, "but what I'd rather look like Aunt Felicie and die at a reasonable age than end up like Walter."

"If you think Walter minds, you're wrong."

"Oh, I know. Walter's enjoying the living soul out of all this."

"At the rate the mail order business is going, everyone may soon be just exactly like Walter."

"Jerry, I get the oddest picture of the old guard UDC sprouting tails and swarming down en masse to Bayou Lafourche. In all humanity, somebody ought to go and warn the alligators."

Well, Jerry left in a huff the next day and at the time I thought it must have been because of something I'd done—or more likely what I'd not done—the night before.

But the next week we got a frantic telegram from Aunt Felicie. Apparently Jerry had gone North and convinced somebody about the Venusians, because Aunt Felicie's house was running over with Union scientists. Well, this would get Jerry into a good Eastern medical school.

Of course, nobody told him *not* to do this, but he should have asked us about it beforehand. It sounded like he was selling out to the Yankees.

Even so. The Venusians are on our side, because that's where the nice, warm swamps are. Not to speak of Aunt Felicie, who has a way with people when she tries.

No doubt the Union scientists learn many useful things from the Venusians. But Walter has an exclusive franchise on the Swamp Water Youth Restorative.

And the swamps are a paradise for rich old post-senescents, which is nice for the poor old natives. Not to speak of the poor young natives.

The latest thing is, of course, top secret. But since cousin Jefferson is in the senate I know all about it and I think it's a grand idea. Watch for the Annexation of Venus.

FLOWER ARRANGEMENT

Later on, I couldn't remember quite why I did it. I was sitting there in my usual condition of vague awareness, wishing Barbara's voice would stop grating away because there was a man who was going to talk to us about St. Augustine grass, and I was hoping he'd say what to do for the brown spots in my lawn.

"Oh, come on, girls," Barbara was saying. "We *ought* to enter the Federated Gardens show. Last year we won third prize."

What Barbara wanted, of course, was for us to urge her to do the Arrangement. She was the only one of us with any talent, and to be fair, Barbara is a real maestro.

Every year we each make a Dried Arrangement and Barbara comes along and says, "Um!" and presses her lips together and waves her hand over your weedy-looking mess and pokes sticks in and out of the starfoam and, *presto*, you have a beautiful Arrangement to keep in your living room until the next Dried Arrangements meeting.

Every year I take it home and everyone says, "Oh, isn't that beautiful! Did you make it?" And of course I had been rather pretending I had made it, only if somebody asked me about it directly, I had to say, "No, Barbara James made it." I frequently wished I had the courage to rush out of the Dried Arrangements meeting before she got to me and set my weedy, wispy Arrangement on the buffet and leave it there.

Needless to say, I do not have this kind of courage.

Only as Barbara got to the part where she says, "O.K. Any volunteers?" something popped inside of me and I shot my hand up and said, "I'd be glad to have a try at it."

Barbara's mouth quirked a little, because she knew perfectly well what kind of Arrangements I make, and because she had probably already decided exactly what sort of Arrangement the Eastbank Garden Group was going to enter in the Federated Gardens show.

But she said, "That's fine, Sally Jo. You're to use camellias in it somewhere. I think you'd do best with a simple fan Arrangement. I'll mail you their rules book, and if you'd like any—er—advice, why, I'd be glad to help."

That was it, of course. She wasn't going to let it be my Arrangement at all.

I didn't even hear what the man said about St. Augustine grass. All the time I was thinking, thinking, thinking. Was there *any* kind of Arrangement I could make that Barbara couldn't do better? Something really different, so that when I looked at it, I wouldn't have to picture Barbara pressing her lips together?

It was about eleven o'clock at night when I got home, and of course Ronald was asleep, but I just couldn't bear this by myself.

"Ronald!" I cried in a loud whisper so as not to wake Tommy. "Do you *know* what I've done!"

Ronald snuffled irritably, then sat up with a jerk and grabbed me by the shoulders.

"You ran over somebody!"

"No. I volunteered to make the flower Arrangement for the Federated Gardens show!"

Ronald mumbled blasphemies and sank back into his pillow.

"Darling, please stay awake. You see, the thing is, I'm actually going to do this. Only there's the matter of Barbara. Now, if I can only find something—come to think of it, there's the Hogarth Curve. Barbara can do fans or Japanese things or crescents, but the one thing Barbara has never won a prize on is the Hogarth Curve. It tends to droop, you see. Darling . . ."

But he was asleep.

For a wild moment I even considered waking up Tommy, just to have someone to talk to.

The wild moment passed and I eyed the telephone. But there isn't anyone you can call up at eleven o'clock at night and say, "About the Hogarth Curve—"

I crossed my arms over my chest and slipped my feet out of my shoes so I could stride up and down the house quietly. Naturally I couldn't think of anything. I never can when I try.

But it hit me the next day. I was putting some appliqué on a pot holder for the bazaar in January—I loathe appliqué—and there it was!

The Hogarth Curve wouldn't do, because while Barbara wasn't really successful with that kind of

Arrangement, she could look at it and immediately see what was wrong. But the Hogarth Curve isn't the only line in the world. Lines reminded me of math, and math reminded me of that *Mathematics for Morons* book Ronald brought home in one of his numerous unsuccessful attempts to improve my thinking ability.

I stuck my finger with a needle, hissed at the stab, held the pot holder carefully away so as not to get blood on it. Appliqué, ha!

There was *something* in that book I wanted to remember. Some really interesting line. I grabbed the book and started down the index. B. I was sure it began with a B. No. Moebius Strip. That was it.

Feverishly, I flipped the pages back to find out what it was that was so interesting about the Moebius Strip, and whether it could be done with an aspidistra leaf soaked in glycerin.

"Brring!" went the alarm clock, which I always reset in the morning to tell me to go get Tommy.

"Damn, damn, damn," I said, glancing hastily around at the part on Moebius Strips. There were other interesting-looking lines, but I just had a feeling the Moebius one was right.

Walking into the kindergarten, I peered around for Tommy.

"Everything all right?" Miss Potter asked.

"Um? Oh." I guess I had a glazed look in my eyes. "Come to think of it, I've been pondering it all morning and I haven't told anybody yet. I'm going to make the Arrangement for the Federated Gardens show."

"How nice! You could make a real family project out of it!" Miss Potter said with her usual misplaced enthusiasm. "Tommy *loves* to make things!"

"I know."

Tommy talked all the way home, but I didn't hear a word he said.

"Make yourself a peanut butter sandwich," I said when I pushed open the back door.

"Boys my age need a good hot lunch."

"My mother used to have to *force* me to eat a good hot lunch. I'd have liked nothing better than to come home and make myself a peanut butter sandwich."

Tommy gave me his accusatory look.

"Oh, all *right*," I said.

After lunch, we went out in the garage where I have my lab—ferns being pressed between newspapers, cattails hanging up to dry, my bucket of things in glycerin.

"What I need," I mused, "is the biggest aspidistra in the world."

I found a really nice one. Brownish, of course, but with a reddish streak and hints of deep green in it. And best of all, a light stripe right down the middle.

"This," I said, "is going to be the very soul of our flower arrangement."

"What's a soul?"

"A soul . . ." The telephone rang. I am not always this fortunate.

"I wanted to let you know," Barbara said, "that I've got the perfect container for your Arrangement. A pale blue cloisonné bowl. Oval. Just the thing for a fan Arrangement."

"I'm not making a fan Arrangement."

"No? Well, I think it would do very nicely for one of the Japanese Arrangements."

"I'm not using Japanese lines," I said.

There was a silence. Then, "You're *not* going to try a Hogarth Curve!"

"No. It's not the sort of thing you can describe, Barbara. You'll just have to see it. When I'm ready."

"I can come by any evening." Fortunately, Barbara works. "Suppose I come by this evening and bring you the bowl?"

"I already have a base," I lied. "I'll call you when I have the Arrangement in shape."

"I didn't mean to interfere."

"It isn't that. It's that the thing is—gestating. I need to *feel* it for a while."

"Of course," Barbara said, as though I had just told her I was calling in a medium.

A base. Really, I didn't want any base at all. I needed something that was nothing.

The pastry board was too big.

But I have a lovely chopping board, oblong, just the right size. I scrubbed the onion and garlic smell out of it as best I could and stuck on a piece of starfoam with floral clay.

Now the Moebius Strip.

"*Tommy!*"

His eyes were wide and puzzled. He didn't know what he'd done.

"*Why* did you tear Mama's aspidistra leaf into strips?" A whole bunch of them, meeting at the stem.

"It's prettier that way."

I could see what he meant. There was something festive-looking about it. Like streamers tied to a stick.

"Let's try it like it is," Tommy said.

He picks up these insidious cooperative suggestions from Miss Potter, and he has me in the midst of family projects before I'm aware of what's going on.

"Well, I guess it wouldn't hurt to try. Hand me a piece of that green wire."

I gathered the ends of the streamers together, carefully half-looped them and wired them to the bottom of the stem, so that the stem was part of the curve, too. They were pliable, but not limp or crackly, from the glycerin. My idea was to make a Dried Arrangement and then wire in some camellias at the last minute.

If I had been a purist, I would have left the Arrangement the way it was, with just the one leaf. Tommy and I, however, at not purists.

"Go out into the garage and get me six dried okra pods off the shelf," I said. "I am a fairy godmother."

"Which ones is the okra?" Tommy asked.

"The stripy ones."

Tommy was back in a flash. "What are you going to turn them into?"

"A handsome young Dried Arrangement."

"Can I stick some in?"

"One."

I wired them all and put in five, their slight crescents all curving in the same direction. Tommy put the sixth one in, curving, of course, in the wrong direction.

Still, you know, it didn't look bad.

"Now," I said, "we need something behind it. For a background. Something pale. Go into the garage," I commanded, waving my magic floral wire, "and get me four ferns. They're between the sheets of newspaper."

It's obvious what's wrong with all this. You should *never* use an even number of things in a flower arrangement. It's gauche and bourgeois and almost as bad as serving iced sherry.

Just as I was really getting started, Ronald came in demanding dinner.

"How am I ever going to get my Arrangement made if people keep interrupting?" I said, because I was knee-deep in weeds and it was infuriating to have to stop. "Don't you and Tommy ever think of anything but food?"

"Sally *Jo!*"

I opened cans of this and that, like the ladies on television. Ronald and Tommy ate morosely and of *course* the Tylers dropped by after dinner and Marcelle said, "What is *that?*" And I said, "Oh, it isn't finished yet," and Tommy said, "*I* helped," and Marcelle said, "That's awfully clever of Tommy to help make something. But tell me, dear, have you ever wondered about his subconscious?"

No, I hadn't, but it was *my* subconscious, and after that I kept wondering, Why is my subconscious like a Moebius Strip? The best answer I could come up with was that it's because it has a half-twist in it.

But the next morning I got the fern in exactly right, balancing the five okra pods with three large ferns and the wrong-way one with a small fern. The aspidistra showed up beautifully against the fragile dried road fern.

Then, of course, Tommy and Ronald revolted against my Creative Period, each in his own way. Tommy fell down and split his lip wide open, requiring stitches, and Ronald came down with the flu, requiring continuous bed care.

I'd rather be locked up with two live octopi.

And then Marcelle called and said the pot holders *had* to be done by the next week, so every time I had an odd moment I had to sit down and work on that wretched appliqué.

"I'll resign!" I screamed one day, hurling a half-appliquéd pot holder across the room. "Do you know that I still have the bias binding to sew on? And, Ronald, they're *round*."

"For God's *sake*, resign! I've never heard of making pot holders for a garden club, anyway."

"It's for our bazaar. And I can't resign before the show. I wouldn't be able to make the Arrangement."

"Which would suit me just fine," Ronald said. "Where's my pipe?"

"Did you look on your pipe rack?"

"There's a tube of toothpaste on my pipe rack."

"Then your pipe's in the medicine cabinet."

By the time Tommy was back in school and Ronald was back at work, I had *one* day to finish my Arrangement in.

Barbara, of course, had been calling every night "to find out how everybody is," and hinting for me to let her take over. Somewhere, probably out of sheer irritation, I found the strength of mind to refuse her.

"But you'll need my Pink Perfections," Barbara said. "After all, it's a camellia show."

"Couldn't you meet me before the show? I'm going over at eight o'clock and Ronald's going to drop Tommy off at school for me. The show doesn't start until nine. You could stop by on the way to work."

"I'll be there *at* eight o'clock," Barbara said. "How many Pink Perfections do you want me to bring? Three? Five?"

"Four," I said, and hung up before she could even gasp.

I worked most of the night. I filled in the curve of the Moebius Strip with some soft, sort of thistle down things. I covered the starfoam with curly moss and left the rest of the chopping board bare. I worked in the mindless way that produces the best effect.

The alarm went off at six. I hopped out of bed and darted about the chilly house to get my family clothed and fed and out. I was more excited than I ought to have been over a flower show. I'd stuck my neck out too far, refusing to let Barbara help. And using a totally unorthodox Arrangement. And furthermore—you don't ordinarily think of Flower Arranging as a vice, but it was something nasty in me that made me volunteer to do it, and to exclude Barbara, who after all needs to make Flower Arrangements because she doesn't have any children. And if one is going to have a vice at all, and neglect home and family and friends, one ought to be able to say, "There, at least I got a prize."

I broke the eggs into a bowl and got the bacon started. Then I popped into the living room and turned the light on for a quick look at my Moebius Strip. There was something not quite right about it. For one thing, it no longer looked like a Moebius Strip. On the other hand, it didn't look *not* like a Moebius Strip.

The bacon started complaining and I went to separate the pieces and at this point Tommy woke up and informed me that he was wet, as is his tendency on cold mornings. Then Ron said he couldn't find his cuff links and the cat started yowling to come in and I didn't have time to think about anything at all.

Until I started in to get my flower Arrangement to bring to the John D. Ransom auditorium, where the show was going to be. Then Tommy said, "I fixed it for you." And so he had. It looked Moebius, only more so.

Barbara was waiting for me just inside the door, her arms wrapped around herself, doing a little two-step to warm up. The auditorium was like a vault and the heating system was just getting started, with random, thunderous shrieks.

"Why, Sally *Jo!*" Barbara cried, stopping in mid-two-step. "It's *interesting*."

I carried the Arrangement over to the niche marked EASTBANK GARDEN GROUP. ARRANGEMENT BY SALLY JO WARNER. I set it down carefully, though Barbara says an Arrangement should always be so tight you can turn it upside down and shake it.

Interesting! I had a moment of wild triumph and then I was a little ashamed of myself. Barbara was generous enough to like it.

"However," Barbara said, pressing her lips together

and making me feel normal again, "where are we going to put the Pink Perfections?"

Barbara opened the shallow box with four camellias in it. They were, of course, perfect and spotless and exactly alike. I can understand how Barbara manages to discipline her house and her dog and her husband, but I have never figured out how anyone can discipline flowers.

"The camellias? Oh, yes, the camellias . . ."

There was a baffled bellow from Ronald. He was trying to get Tommy's snowsuit off. I ran over before the zipper or Tommy could get jammed. The instant I had the snowsuit off, there was a wail from Tommy. "She ruined my Flower Arrangement!"

My heart sank. "No, no, dear," I said, hurrying after him to where Barbara was, but he was right. There were bits of weed and fluff piled up on the floor and a gleam of joy in Barbara's eyes, and there was nothing left of the fascinating shape Tommy and I had made. "See?" I went on. "It's beautiful. It's a perfect Hogarth Curve." It was. It didn't droop at all. And Barbara had made the Arrangement.

"There was something funny in there," Barbara said. "I thought it must be Tommy's, so I saved it."

"It's my inside-out balloon," Tommy said, his chin quivering, "and she turned it back right-side in!"

It was Tommy's multi-colored balloon, and it really didn't look much like a balloon any more, though it was still blown up. "How did your balloon get in there?"

"I put it in," Tommy said, "to make the Arrangement more rounder. It's the roundest thing I ever made." Tears were gathering in his eyes.

"Now, dear, I don't know why I didn't see it."

"I put it in after you made it. Then I blew it up and tied it and poked in the end. It was the roundest thing in the whole world!"

"But it's still tied! See? So nobody could have turned it right-side out. It looks the same on both sides."

"No, it don't. The other side got magnetic paint on it. That's why the balloon got ripples in it."

Ron had been standing around looking impatient and he said, "Tommy, there's no such thing as magnetic paint."

"There is, too," Tommy said. "I made it."

"How did you make it?"

"You mix up silver paint like you use for Christmas Arrangements and you add that silver glitter that you sprinkle and then you add all the old magnets you have around and you stir it good."

"How many old magnets?" I asked.

"Lots and lots and lots."

"Then what?"

"Then you turn the balloon inside out and blow it up and pinch the end with a clothes pin and paint it and then when it's dry you let the air out."

"And just why do you do all this?" Ron asked.

That was a silly question and Tommy didn't bother to answer it.

"What about the magnets?" I asked.

"You bury them in the back yard."

"Oh. And do metal things stick on the magnetic paint?"

"Well—hair does, if you brush it first."

"*Metal* things."

"I *think* they do. A teeny bit. But now it's all on the wrong side and it's ruined."

"I have to get to work," Ron said.

"Here, catch." I tossed the balloon to Tommy.

It stayed up in the middle of the air.

"See?" Tommy said. "It's no good no more."

We all stood staring, in a state of shock.

"It's a funny shape," Ron said finally. "Those puckers sort of go *in* and if you follow that striated band . . . if you follow . . ."

I was trying to follow it with my eyes, too.

". . . you get vertigo," Ron finished, looking off in another direction.

"Yes, you do," I said. "Well, we can't just leave it here. Tommy, would you like to take it to show Miss Potter?"

"Miss Potter, hell!" Ron exclaimed. "There's something extraordinary about this. I'm going to take it down to work with me and let the boys at the lab have a look at it. I've never seen anything that just stayed in mid-air like that. You notice it doesn't seem to float, as it would if it contained a gas, and . . ."

But I was busy apologizing to Barbara for Tommy's manners and assuring her the Hogarth Curve was beautiful.

I pinned the left-over camellia in my hair, because I felt I deserved something, and Ron said he'd drop Tommy and me off at kindergarten.

"Isn't it marvelous," I asked Ron as I wiped off the windshield, because Tommy kept huffing on it, "to have a son who's an important scientist before the age of six?"

"Now don't be getting delusions of grandeur about him," Ron said. "Whatever you and he made was purely accidental."

"That goes to show what *you* know about the scientific method. I was making a Moebius Arrangement and Tommy was making the roundest thing in the whole world, and when you're working on something and something *else* happens, something scientifically important, it's called—I can't remember what it's called, but it's a perfectly good word beginning with R. Or maybe L."

"Serendipity. But you and Tommy . . . Never mind."

Later on in the morning Ron called to tell me to go see a man named Craddock over at the lab, and I'd have to go by myself because Ron was busy, and I said, "All right," but it wasn't all right. The thought of going to that strange place to talk to important men was terrifying.

I opened my closet and looked unhappily through my inappropriate house dresses and equally inappropriate party dresses. I finally decided on my black skirt, dark gray sweater and white cotton blouse, which I hoped would give the impression of a businesslike outfit.

On the way down on the streetcar, I found a woman staring at me and I realized I had been practicing my facial expression. It was the one where I hang a cigarette out of the side of my mouth, narrow my eyes to a slit, and say, "I'm Warner. You Craddock?"

What actually happened was that an office boy said, "What are you so nervous about, lady?" and brought me through a maze of forbidding-looking chambers and deposited me on a bench facing a back that was, presumably, Craddock's.

I sat there trying to decide whether to address him or just wait, when he turned, looked at me, and jumped two feet.

"I didn't know anyone was there," he explained, and since he was the one who had acted a little silly, I felt much better about him immediately.

"I'm sorry," I said. "I was just sitting here trying to decide . . ." That wouldn't do. "My name's Warner," I said, omitting the facial expression.

"Dr. Warner?"

"Sally *Jo* Warner."

"And you discovered this new—force field?"

"If you mean the right-side-inside-out balloon," I answered, "yes. With my son. Thomas." I decided that if he was going to be a scientist, we should stop calling him Tommy.

Craddock was one of those thin, pale, freckled-all-over people with eyes the color of the rims of his horn-rimmed glasses and he wore the same general expression of stubborn intentness that Tommy has. And I could sense in his expression the same scorn for me that Tommy so frequently has.

"I'd like to discuss this with your son," he said.

Of course. *I* couldn't be expected to say anything sensible.

"Thomas has school in the mornings," I said.

"Ah? Um. Which school?"

"Miss Nicholls."

"Miss—"

"It's a small private school. Kindergarten through third grade."

"A third-grade child did this?"

"No. Kindergarten. And I was not without influence in this discovery. I went to Grey Rock Junior College."

"Um. Sciences?"

"Yes."

"I mean what sciences?"

"We learned all the sciences in one course. Chemistry, biology, physics and—well, I'd have to look in the book to remember the others."

"Never mind," Craddock said, a shudder going through his slight, clattery frame. "Just tell me how you did this." He nodded at the balloon, which was encased in a glass box with a tube sort of thing leading into it.

"Well, first you take an aspidistra leaf . . ." I began, and went on from there. Craddock wrote it all down, though he kept saying, "I just don't see how the balloon fits into all this," and finally I said, "*Now* we get to the balloon. And the magnetic paint."

"Where did you get the magnetic paint?"

"My colleague made it."

Craddock was awfully picayunish about details. "How *much* silver paint? How much is 'the rest of a pack of glitter'?" Then he was disturbed because lots and lots and lots of magnets is eight.

When I got to the part where Barbara made a Hogarth Curve out of my Moebius Strip, I asked him for a cigarette because I was still upset over it.

"I know how you feel," Craddock said, being agreeable

for the first time. "I don't think it's right to make a Hogarth Curve out of a Moebius Strip, either. I wouldn't even think it was possible."

"Well, that's all," I said, and Craddock grabbed my cigarette before I dropped it into what looked like an empty dish. "I have to rush off and pick up my colleague at kindergarten."

On the way to Miss Nicholls, my mind was afire with ambition. Tommy would appear on TV. Everyone would forget about the time Tommy smeared Miss Potter's chair with mucilage right before she sat down. He'd be offered scholarships to MIT. He'd dictate articles for scientific journals and I'd write them up.

And if anyone ever made remarks about my thinking ability again, I'd just say, "*My* method produces results."

About two o'clock that afternoon, Craddock called and bawled, "The force field is leaking! Another hour and it'll all be gone!"

"Stop sounding as though it's my fault," I said.

"Sorry. I'm just anxious."

"Why don't you catch the drippings in a pot or something?"

"We tried to. But you should see the cloud chamber."

I said, "I'm sure the cloud chamber is very interesting," because it was none of his business if I didn't know what a cloud chamber was.

"The lines just wiggle and disappear into another dimension. I don't know how else to describe it."

"What's making it leak?"

"There's something unusual in the nuclei of the atoms. They're decaying."

"Tommy blew up the balloon," I said, and wondered if he had cavities, though of course it was a different kind of decay. Still, the thought made me a little nervous.

"We're getting photographs of everything," Craddock went on, "but what's worrying us is that we haven't been able to duplicate the—uh—experiment."

"I'll bet you didn't soak the aspidistra in glycerin. You couldn't have. There hasn't been time."

"Glycerin wouldn't have anything to do with it. For that matter, neither would the aspidistra."

"Plants," I informed him, "even dried ones, have all sorts of influence. If you put a bouquet of roses in a room, the whole room and all the furniture is a different shape."

"That's your subjective reason. It's because you like roses."

"There! That proves my point! Why does the lamb love Mary so?"

Craddock choked a little. "Mrs. Warner . . . all right, why *does* the lamb love Mary so?"

"They learn things like this at Miss Nicholls," I pointed out. "The answer is, 'Mary loves the lamb, you know.' People like roses because roses like people. Which means roses have something *you* don't know about."

"All *right*, there *are* things I don't know. The first thing I don't know is how to carry on an intelligible conversation with you. But let's skip everything except what I called you for. Will you and your colleague please make another of those balloon affairs?"

"I doubt if it can be done."

"Why? If there are any materials you need, I can certainly—"

"It isn't that. It's—well, whatever we do, it's going to be a little bit different. And I don't know if Tommy can find where he buried the magnets. But I'll try."

But before I went shouting around for Tommy, I called Barbara, because something had occurred to me while I was talking to Craddock and it was only decent to tell Barbara.

"What time," I asked, "do the judges come around tonight?"

"About seven-thirty," Barbara said.

"I'm sorry, but you ought to know. We're not going to win."

"What?"

"Your Hogarth Curve," I said, thinking of the leaking balloon, "is going to droop at three o'clock," and left the explanation for later.

I found Tommy in the back yard, deeply involved with sticks and bits of string and old nails.

I knew immediately and sadly what he was doing.

It was too bad Tommy wasn't going to be a famous scientist before the age of six, but that was mostly just a joke. And it was too bad the Eastbank Garden Group wasn't going to win a prize in the Federated Gardens Show, but it was no longer my Arrangement, anyway, and Barbara's always winning other prizes for us. And it was too bad Craddock wasn't going to have his force field, but he hadn't been very nice about the whole thing.

No, the real tragedy was that Tommy was going to be

bitterly unhappy about something I had absolutely no control over.

I called Craddock and tried to explain to him why Tommy would never in the world get interested in making another Moebius Strip thing. And there's no way to *make* a child create something, any more than you can make him eat.

"You see," I told Craddock, who was sputtering helplessly on the other end of the line, "he's already made the roundest thing in the whole world. I mean, things *tend* to be round, and all you have to do is follow a tendency. But now he's working on something else and he'll keep at it and won't think about anything else and it's going to be tragic when he finds out it just can't be done."

"And what is he trying to do?" Craddock managed to say.

"He's trying to make the squarest thing in the whole world."

FRUITING BODY

No one who has wondered what the Giaconda is smiling about has not also wondered what the *Francesa arthura* is thinking about. We are not so unsophisticated as to attempt to answer either of these questions. But we feel that some account of the life of the author (or Arthur, as his name happens to be) of the *Francesa arthura* might, despite the protestations of the current generation of critics, prove illuminating. (We are afraid, because the aforesaid critics are so sharp of tooth, to say just how.)

Arthur Kelsing collected fungi and women. He occasionally fed the former (not the poisonous variety) to the latter, and frequently wished he could feed the latter (the poisonous variety) to the former.

But civilization is not so ordered. Is not, as Arthur frequently ruminated, either coherent or logical.

But rather (Arthur's father had been absent and he was reared by a hard-pressed mother who gave the impression of being domineering) civilization seemed to have been cooked up in that intuitive and irritating

fashion in which women go about things. And Arthur
could only hope that there was some agreeable end in
view. Because when women go about doing something in
their vague, unreasonable way, they insist they *are* doing
something and if you just wait and mind your own
business, they'll show you what it is when it's finished.

Arthur's wife had been, for instance, a woman. (This
was the real reason why he divorced her.) And the first
thing she did was hide all his left socks. All but about
three at a time.

"I don't know where they are," she'd say. "But by the
time you get back to the three you wore first, you'll have
those pairs matching again and isn't that really all that
matters? They *should* be rotated, so as to make them wear
longer, and this just forces you to do something you
should be doing anyhow."

"I don't like to be forced," Arthur said. You can see
immediately that there was a broad principle involved,
not just a matter of the socks. "It's childish of you to hide
my left socks, and you're to get them out right now."

"I told you, I don't *know* where they are."

"You're supposed to wash all the socks at once and put
away matching pairs."

"You're not supposed to do anything of the kind,"
Patty had snapped, unrolling a wad of hair from a brush
curler and rolling it the other way with her fingers. "You
don't understand laundry. You wash white socks with the
towels and colored cotton ones with the blouses and
woolen-type socks with my skirts and nylon socks with my
underwear. And some of them get tangled up so you don't
see them and you discover the extra one later and save it

to wash next time you wash the things it goes with. You can't put one sock in the washing machine by itself. Really," Patty had said, turning from the mirror, her curl vibrating, "I can't go on loving you passionately if you put on your underwear and socks and shirt and tie and just stand around in your bare legs. Men look nice with bare chests but *not* bare legs. Why can't you put your pants on first?"

"Because the crease . . . never mind," Arthur had answered, clenching his eyelids and then wondering whether he should tell her right then that she had just ruined their marriage.

It wasn't just that, either, or the socks. It was fungi, too. She kept filching his best specimens for her dried-flower arrangements.

Anyway, if Arthur Kelsing were now a bachelor, and a confirmed one, you can see there were good reasons for it. And if he were also a confirmed fungus collector, there were good reasons for that, too.

And if he were able to combine his hobbies, there were good reasons for that, too. He found, in fact, a certain similarity, a certain sympathetic magic that took place between certain women and certain fungi.

Most men, all perhaps, are familiar with at least some of the properties of women. Many however, are not similarly familiar with properties of fungi.

Arthur was lucky. As a child he had grown up in a small town in the south and was given to wandering the countryside where he could steal watermelons and cow bells and what not. And one day, when he was about twelve, he found some interesting looking mushrooms growing out of a . . . well, not everybody would have eaten them, but Arthur had eaten mushrooms before and besides, if they *were* toadstools he'd get sick and it would serve his mother right. (Don't eat that kind of thing, she'd said. It might be toadstools. As if it were *her* business what he ate or didn't eat.) So he broke them carefully, so as to leave the cow patty intact, washed them in the nearest creek and rushed home so he could be sick in a public place.

Only he didn't get sick. He had the most fascinating hallucinations you can imagine—no, you can't imagine them unless you've tried it. (The mushrooms, he discovered later, were of the genus *Panaeolus*. Anybody can pluck them off of cow patties after a rain and after all, what do you think fertilizer is?)

It was not long after—to be specific it was during a Halloween hay ride—that he discovered women. This particular woman was thirteen years old and as different from his mother as certain *Panaeoli* are from canned button mushrooms (*Agaricus campestris*). So Arthur naturally assumed that just as there are different kinds of fungi, so there are different kinds of women.

Arthur had to have his stomach pumped out six times (one of them after he should have known better) before he learned to be really careful about the toxins in mushrooms.

It only took one marriage to make him cautious about women. But there were other disillusionments that might have discouraged a man of less passion. (Or would perhaps have led a more generous man to compromise.

But had Arthur been a better person, he would have been much less interesting.)

But to get back to Flora (the unfortunate name of the thirteen-year-old woman), while Flora had her attractions, when you came right down to it, her only *real* attraction was that she was willing. And Arthur soon wanted more from life than he got from Flora and the chance variety of *Panaeolus*. Which brought him to his first experiment.

But meanwhile Arthur had undergone a complete change that delighted his teachers and his poor old mother (who was actually quite a pretty woman of thirty-five and so discreet her employer never regretted taking her on as his mistress also.) Arthur became a junior scientist, a child genius. It is true that he still lagged in English and social science, but he could definitely no longer be classified as a big lout. He even stopped stealing watermelons. He stole mushrooms. He spent hours pouring over heavy books full of diagrams and long words. He was engrossed in studies of botany and anatomy.

Some attributed this remarkable change to the fact that he was beginning to grow up (which was true) and others, particularly his mother, to the influence of little Flora (which was also true.)

But what Arthur had done was to begin his search for the Silver Chalice. He had, so early, perceived if only dimly his ideal. And he glowed with a knightly glow.

Women and fungi; you may think, are not the way.

They are not perhaps *your* way. But they are *a* way.

For his experiment, Flora was not it by a long shot, and his lower south variety of *Panaeolus* was not it, though the differential was less. So he tried a combination of the two. (He had to powder it and put it in her drink. She drank but she didn't eat mushrooms, especially after he had described the effects. A girl doesn't have to eat mushrooms, she'd said, to have a good time.)

So that Flora became, briefly, the girl of his dreams— he and Flora both dreaming mushroom dreams, Flora merging with the dream girl produced by *Panaeolus*.

But there were difficulties.

For one thing, the dosage was wrong. As a big lout, Arthur had been able to tolerate more than Flora, and he had neglected to take this into account when preparing his Instant Dreams powder. His main objective had been to put in plenty.

For another—*most* important and key to Arthur's entire future—the dream girl, the girl produced by the hallucinations of *Panaeolus*, was not quite right. She had a squint. This was due not to Arthur's mind, which was perfect in its way, but to the type of mushroom he was using. Now, there have been men, romantic poets particularly, who admire a little—sometimes a lot—of grotesquerie in women. (Try some of the French Decadents.) But Arthur had a classical soul, Classical and Romantic being used here in the technical sense. Anything macabre or perverted one sees in him is being read into his character by the beholder. It was amazing, later, how many dirty-minded people . . .

O, and Flora. Unfortunately (or to be honest, fortunately) she died. It was blamed not on Arthur, but on Flora's mother, who had neglected to tell her, so everyone said, not to eat toadstools.

It was thus that Arthur learned to experiment on small animals first, and thus that he began to be a real scientist. Arthur was quick to perceive that he might have got himself in a whole lot of trouble and he never made the same mistake again.

He made other mistakes instead.

Patty, for instance.

"Patty," he'd said, "you're everything I've dreamed of." But oddly enough, she wasn't. He just happened to fall in love with her when he was twenty-four, for no reason at all. (Actually there was a reason. Patty had his mother's mannerism of talking with her eyebrows, but Arthur never consciously realized this. He didn't know that what he'd missed was having a strong woman around the house.)

It was a fine, beautiful, normal love and very boring.

Certain varieties of *Amanita* he was working on, on the other hand . . .

Arthur by the age of forty, though he was not as affluent as some mushroom farmers, was very goodlooking—tall and wide built but thin enough to look emotional—and yet slightly cruel of mouth and cynical of voice, so that women could see there was a lot beneath the surface.

Arthur also had a curl in the front of his dark hair which, late at night, fell over his forehead in an unconsciously engaging way. Arthur didn't exactly set the curl, but he did sort of comb through it with hair oil and wind it over his finger.

So that he usually managed to have his friends in at home—all his friends were beautiful girls and for them he had made his apartment slightly exotic. They took well to hallucination parties for two and mushrooms are cheaper than gin and don't leave a hangover.

Everyone can't do this, you understand. The women have to be weighed, for instance, to be sure of proper dosage. They must be free of certain diseases—heart ailments and respiratory disorders, etc.—and only an expert with Arthur's additional intuitive perception could know which fungus goes with which girl.

Arthur became, as the years went by, something of an artist in this line and eventually came to be much sought after by society matrons.

But he was a man of principle, and a seeker of the Silver Chalice, and he never Did It for Money.

Besides, he had a thriving mushroom farm in Pennsylvania. He had a good foreman and there really isn't a great deal one needs to do for mushrooms except go pick them at the right time. Arthur had no taste for button mushrooms, himself.

Arthur had been working on a variety of *Lepiota* which looked very promising. Indeed, he'd been neglecting his women for several weeks and hadn't the least desire to do anything but hover over his spores.

But just to deny the faint suspicion that occasionally came over him that he was getting middle-aged and peculiar, he accepted an invitation to Betty Rankin's cocktail party. If you are single long enough, you become an eligible bachelor, and if you refrain from being excessively unpleasant about not having got "caught" (or caught again), you get invited to everything there are extra women at.

Arthur, let us add, did not have the "I was smart"

complex with which most bachelors ward off implied charges of homosexuality, frigidity and unacceptability to women. He *knew* he was attractive to women, he *knew* what he wanted and hadn't got yet, and he didn't have to be defensive (or offensive, as I'm afraid we frequently become).

"I just don't seem to be lucky in love," he'd say from under his curl, and women just loved it.

And there, across the room, he saw her.

Never in dreams, never in imaginings—but he knew her when he saw her.

She had ash-blond hair and heavy, straight-brown eyebrows and deep-grey eyes and a rounded body with apparently neither bones nor fat in it. Glaucous and firm fleshed were the words that came to Arthur's mind. A head shining like *Agaricus campester* (Gris.). Her age might have been anywhere (with good care) from twenty-five to forty.

She was dressed in a simple black sheath and a frilly white apron.

She was the maid.

Now, Arthur Kelsing was no callow youth and he knew better than to try to make love to the maid at a cocktail party. He quietly got her name and address from Betty Rankin, and became intimate with the extra debutante at the party, as he was expected to do, and watched Frances out of the corner of his eye.

The debutante was nervous and excited and hadn't wanted to make her debut in the first place (it was her mother's idea) and always broke out in pimples before parties. Let us put it to Arthur's credit that she had a good time not only at that party but also at subsequent ones, where the air of being used to older men gave her a sophistication that eventually led to her marriage to the heir of a brass manufacturer's fortune.

Arthur went home that evening and looked at himself in the mirror, seeing in amazement that having found Frances made him look no different.

Frances. Frances Griffith was her name.

But Arthur went on looking at himself, inside and out, and felt for the first time inadequate.

He was ashamed, for instance, of his curl. It was mannered, it was artificial. She would see through it. He wet his comb and combed it out.

He looked less handsome, but more real.

I'm Me, he thought. It would be foolishness to try to offer her anything else.

Except the mushrooms.

Yes, that would be the one really original thing, the one thing Arthur alone could offer.

The proper mushroom.

He stayed up all night, leafing through his notebooks, thinking there must be some he had forgotten, though he knew them all by heart.

There were none, of course. Except a variety of *Strophergia* he had whose spores he was momentarily expecting to germinate. He strode over and turned on the mic lamp in the damp, cold little room which was his laboratory. Nothing yet. It chilled him a little, as it always did, to see in what wretched circumstances his dreams must incubate. He checked the temperature and humidity and switched off the light.

There had been the *Collybia* in Nicaragua, of course. Arthur had been in a cautious phase then, having recently been poisoned with a *Boletus laricis*, but they had stayed in his mind and he had a feeling . . .

Arthur paced his apartment, scratching his hand across his emerging beard, blowing faint whistles of air through his teeth.

He was possessed with excitement, both physical and metaphysical.

Because it shows something, that Frances should exist at all. That she should answer, down to the smallest detail, a description which he had not known was in his mind. But which *must* have been there all along. Otherwise he would not have recognized her so immediately and so intensely.

And so, therefore, must the mushroom exist, whose dream would be the dream Frances. So that she would have two existences, one in reality and one in unreality, each as real as the other and together constituting Arthur's ideal. And thus making a solid link between the inside of Arthur's mind (which he sometimes worried about) and the outside world (whose existence he was sometimes unsure of).

There was not a thing wrong with either Arthur's theories or his conclusions.

The only thing he had not consciously noticed was that what Frances really looked like—blond and alabaster of skin and boneless and fatless of body—was an *Amanita solitaria*.

But it is certainly not fair to go poking uninvited into Arthur's unconscious, and one has no reason to link this up with later events. And if Robert Burns' love could be like a red, red rose, why should anyone find it queer that Arthur's love was like a white, white mushroom? (Except that Arthur didn't make the connection.)

Arthur knew he needed a warm shower and a nap, having had no sleep at all and not being young enough not to show it. But sleep was out of the question and a warm shower did not seem the thing at the moment.

So he had a cold shower and shaved and drank a cup of coffee improved with brandy and went to see Frances.

Even if she weren't home, he could begin to become familiar with her natural habitat.

The street Betty Rankin had written down was respectable enough at the south end. But Frances lived at the north end.

And as Arthur watched for the 900 block, he began to feel a little unsettled inside. For this was almost a slum. Rows of houses, once splendid, now rooming houses bursting at the seams with the poor, the derelict, the hopeless, and somewhere in there a few families about to climb out of it all.

But where, in all that, a place for Frances?

Griffith. He looked for cards at the entrance, but there was nothing to betray the inhabitants of 902 Elm Street. Children spilled across his feet, babies in drooping diapers bumping down the steps, headed for the curb.

"I'm looking for Miss Frances Griffith," he asked an older child, who should have been in school.

The boy leered, asked for a cigarette, led the way through a hall that reeked of stale people, up two flights of stairs, stopped before a peeling, dark green door and yelled, "Francie!" at the top of his voice.

Then he held out two fingers for another cigarette and left.

Arthur didn't smoke but he always carried cigarettes and a lighter. Women loved this kind of foresight. Arthur was irritated when he discovered he'd done this for Frances. It was part of the charm he'd been accumulating for several decades and he didn't intend to use it on Frances. He wanted to strip himself bare for her.

He stood sweating nervously before that unpropitious looking door, forcing himself *not* to think of charming things to say to Frances.

He wanted to be unprepared. But he needn't have worried.

Frances opened the door. She was brilliantly glaucous in a negligee with a striate margin and she opened the door only far enough to extrude a dark, heavy man dressed in striped coveralls and a mechanic's cap.

It was Frances who began the conversation.

"Next," she said.

Arthur married her anyway. That is, in spite of her and her family's objections. They felt she had quite a career in front of her (as indeed she would have) and nobody could see any advantages in Arthur.

She was, however, easily led and subject to drugs and Arthur managed the legalities with no trouble. The reason he married her was so he could keep her locked in his apartment. This was absolutely necessary as she had a strong tendency to wander off toward any man that went by, and her old boy friends were always trying to look her up.

And what he planned to do in no way impaired her

domestic abilities, as she only had two domestic abilities, the other one being a talent for standing around holding trays of *hors d'oeuvres*. There was a maid to do the housework.

Still, there was no denying the initial disappointment that came to Arthur when he found her conversation was limited to "Yeah," and "who cares" and "not on your life." He could overlook her morals, but the stupidity was more difficult.

There remained the hope, for a while, that she was educable. But there were insurmountable difficulties. For one thing, she was very nearsighted. This gave her eyes a distant, enchanted quality, but it also enabled her to say with truth she couldn't see the letters on the page. "Not on your life," she said when faced with a book. Also she was completely intractable. "So you want me to look at the pictures," she'd say, not looking. Mostly she slept and changed clothes. She didn't even spend much time putting on make up, because she didn't need it.

What she was, Arthur soon realized, was a pale reflection of a reality that existed in a hallucination he had not yet had. She was, in another sense, a shadow in the cave. And further Arthur (who never hesitated to mix his literary allusions) began to feel like the Lady of Shallot. He was half sick of shadows and he was ready to look down to Camelot. Only he didn't expect any curse to come upon him (any more than Plato would; it took a Romantic to think up that part.)

You see, Arthur, in searching for simple ideals, the perfect woman, the perfect hallucinogenic mushroom, inadvertently stumbled on the secret of the universe, which had eluded scientists and philosophers all these centuries. The secret of the universe is that the world isn't real. This was indisputably proved by Frances, whose unreality was unquestionable. Obviously no Deity, no *élan vital* would create something like the objective Frances. On the other hand, one has to account for her, and this is best done by assuming that Arthur is God (it grates at first, but see how well it works out). Thus he can recognize this odd manifestation of Frances as a corner of reality sticking into this swirling dream of matter which we have all agreed to call "reality."

Which leaves Arthur to explore the actual reality which he has already created but from which he had been diverted by things like being born and living and what not.

That is what mushrooms are for.

And Arthur was the only person in the world who combined expert botanical knowledge with a native talent for understanding and absorbing hallucinogenic mushrooms. Talent plus hard work, that's what makes an outstanding artist, such as Arthur, or God.

The *Stropharia* Arthur had been working on when he met Frances wouldn't do at all. It was not even hallucinogenic, though he had crossed it with a strain of *Psilocybe mexicana*.

He had therefore to fly to Patagonia for the *Boletus* and when he got back Frances was gone. Fortunately, she didn't have enough sense to go far, and he found her back at 902 Elm St. and had to stand in line for an hour outside her door, so as not to make a public scene.

"Get lost," she told him, when his turn came. But he

then and there fed her the Boletus and then was in a fever to get home and try the new mushroom himself.

He'd been right. This was It.

Now, this might have been the end of the story, except that the objective Frances continued to be so much trouble when the effects of the Boletus wore off.

And furthermore she became less and less attractive, by herself.

Having achieved so much, Arthur had a brilliant idea, to perfect Frances.

Why should not Frances and her mushroom become symbiotic on each other, as in the case of lichen, especially since they had a natural affinity?

Why not, as a matter of fact, grow this Boletus inside of Frances, thereby rendering her permanently happy, her chemistry improved by the exudations of the fungus, and the fungus in turn nourished by Frances' body (or even, perhaps, her mind?)

This did not seem as impossible as it may at first sound to the layman, or even to the scientist. Bacteria, which grow inside of people, are fungi. Mushrooms are fungi. Both reproduce sexually, which means they can be bred for certain characteristics. (It has only recently been observed that bacteria reproduce sexually, but they have actually been doing it all along.)

There is much that is not understood about the relationships or possible relationships between fungi and people, since medicine and mycology are two different specialties, and physicians and mycologists do not always agree about what is a fungus.

Arthur therefore had a field pretty much uncluttered

by previous experimentation and since he knew exactly what he wanted to do, he could go pretty much in a straight line.

(It is a curious psychological fact that Arthur did not spend any time wondering what Frances' vision was under hallucination. He merely assumed, as he was God, that it was the same as his. Herself, improved.)

It took Arthur a year to breed *Frances Arthuriensis*, which will not be found in the C. M. I. for obvious reasons.

During this time it had been necessary for Arthur to make a few changes in his way of life. There were Frances' ex-boy friends who were a constant nuisance. Arthur had no compunction about giving Frances drugs, but he couldn't well keep her asleep twenty-four hours a day and he didn't want to over use anything from his mushroom pharmacy. The chemistry of hallucinogenic mushrooms is ill understood, even by Arthur, and he did not want to take a chance on building up possible toxic reactions, or causing possible neurological changes, until he had the *Frances Arthuriensis* ready.

So he bought a cabin in the Ozarks. He had it equipped with all the modern conveniences except a paved road (it was necessary to bump over a pasture and up a wooded slope to get to it. Only his little foreign car could weave between the trees, and even so, one had to know which trees). He hired two idiot boys from one of the neighboring farms, two miles away, and bought a razor back hog, planning to indulge an old dream of raising truffles, which ordinarily are impossible to grow in America. (This is worthy of mention because it shows that

Arthur was not a monomaniac. It is true that his zeal in regard to Frances implies a perhaps unusual degree of uxoriousness. But he maintained other interests, too.)

Once installed, Arthur proceeded with the breeding of *Francesa arthura* with almost daily success. He crossed the Patagonian Boletus with a more temperate North Carolina Boletus and with the help of air conditioning, at first achieved a mushroom that could survive an Arkansas summer. (A generation of mushrooms requires several days.) He then crossed it with a small Daedalea from Cade's Cove. Meanwhile he was working upward with the largest *E. coli* he could find and filaments of myxomycete plasmodium.

At the end of a year Arthur managed to mate a microscopic mushroom with a new parasitic slime mold. Applied to the skin of a shaved cat (there were those later who thought the most loathsome thing Arthur ever did was to shave a cat) it showed itself soon in fairy rings. This sounds delightful, but actually it is ring worm. The cat died, of course, not having Frances' chemical make up. But the important thing was that the *Francesa arthura* lived.

It is not to be supposed that Arthur meant to give Frances a bad case of ring worm. Whether it would make a pleasant symbiosis for Frances or not, it would certainly be aesthetically unpleasing.

No, *Francesa arthura* was for internal use only, and as Arthur was too humane to give it to Frances without testing it, he fed it to one of the idiot farm boys.

The effect was noticeable the very next day. The boy became alert, his mouth no longer drooped open, he no longer slept half the day. In fact, Arthur learned upon questioning him, he had stopped sleeping altogether. It should be noted that the boy's intelligence did not at any time increase, but he certainly looked better. It was almost as though there were a little switch in him that had been pushed from "slow" to "fast."

As it happened, the boy was dead six months later, but it must be remembered that *Francesa arthura* was not *his* mushroom, but Frances', and also that nature had fashioned him perhaps to live slow for many years, and who is to say he was not happier living fast for a few months?

Anyhow, Arthur meanwhile decided that *Francesa arthura* was ready for Frances, and Frances was ready (indeed, long overdue) for *Francesa arthura*.

Her neural tone improved almost immediately and she presented a problem Arthur had not planned on, though he knew from the farm boy. She no longer slept. Never. But at the same time, she grew to resemble more closely the Frances of his hallucinogenic dream. Her movements became more fluid and graceful. She began to enjoy long walks in the woods. She listened and smiled as he explained his interests to her. (The fascinating varieties of fungi housed in cow patties, for instance, and the interesting habits of lichen.) There was never the least reason to think she understood or cared, but she had learned how to listen, which is a mannerism, not an intellectual attainment.

Furthermore, she displayed, for the first time, a marked affection for Arthur. He no longer felt he was the object of her passion solely because he kept everybody else locked out. Now she followed him around, she took his word as law, she obeyed his every whim, even to the extent of doing simple housework.

Within a week, Arthur felt secure enough to sleep soundly at night without locking Frances in her cage, though he had to warn her severely about going for long walks in the woods, moon or no moon.

"Stay close to the house," he'd say, and she did. He sometimes waked at night and saw her out of the window, white and beautiful under the moon, just standing there enjoying the wind in her hair.

If Arthur thought he was God, he soon had Frances to back him up. And as she drew closer to him she became, in a sense, more distant from the world. She grew more spiritual, more distant in the eyes, whiter, even almost luminous.

The initial alertness supplied by *Francesa arthura* began to change a little. She did not droop in languor, but she became more inward, supplying something to *Francesa arthura* as it was supplying her with its intoxicants.

Soon she gave up her long walks, her dancing about the house. She did nothing, but it was a different sort of nothing from what she had done before. It was a happy, purposeful nothing.

She just stood around outside, mostly.

She . . . vegetated.

One morning, several days after Frances stopped eating, Arthur found her leaning against a tree, sending rhizomorphs into it.

He was horrified.

He cut them off. (It was not painful as they were naturally vegetative rhizomorphs.)

He brought her inside, forced her to eat, increased the nitrogen in her diet. "You've got to fight back," he said. "It's a symbiote, not a parasite."

But Frances wasn't interested in fighting back. She ate, as Arthur instructed her to, and for a while there were no more rhizomorphs. The rhizomorphs became merely something to remember about, not to fear.

Until this matter of fate came up. Fate has little literary validity, but is very important in life.

Arthur got sick.

It was only pneumonia, which nobody gets very excited about any more, but it necessitated Arthur's being in the hospital for two days and there was absolutely nothing he could do about Frances except instruct her to eat regularly. After the two days, the doctor insisted on two more, and you know you can't leave without a release.

Arthur drove back, expertly jockeying his little foreign car through the trees, and he had the feeling you always have when you know something awful has happened. "In five minutes I'll be laughing at myself," he said, and tried to laugh without having to wait the five minutes.

He rounded a stand of trees and saw her, a yard or two from the cabin's clearing, sitting by a rotten tree stump, her arm resting on the stump, her beautiful white head resting on her arm.

"Frances!" he cried and bumped the car to a stop beside her.

She smiled at him dreamily, recognizing him faintly somewhere beyond the grey smoke of her eyes.

"No!" he cried, because she seemed so immobile,

despite the fact that she drew her legs under her a little and moved her head.

"You didn't eat?" he asked.

She roused a little, took a breath, so that he noticed she hadn't *been* breathing. That was what had made her look so immobile. "I wasn't hungry," she said.

"But I *told* you."

"I forgot," she said, and stopped breathing, smiling to herself.

Arthur began to pull at the rotten wood and found it threaded with rhizomorphs.

"Bring me a drink of water," Frances said, as Arthur went into the house after his knife. "It hasn't rained since I started rooting."

"Mushrooms don't root," Arthur said, and this added to his irritation, because he had explained to her a thousand times that a rhizomorph is not a tree root.

"You've got to learn to be more self-sufficient," Arthur said as he cut away at the thousand tiny tendrils that extended through her pores and into the rotten wood. Frances held the glass in her hand and drank the water.

She ate two coddled eggs he gave her after he brought her in and cleaned her up. (It had been dusty out there, and there were insects and what not.) But she threw them right up. She did a little better with the consommé and Arthur let it go at that.

"It's a matter of habit," he told her. "We'll start working up to solid food again tomorrow."

He had missed her badly those four days, and held her close to him while he slept. She still didn't sleep, but he had given her stern instructions not to get up and wander during the night.

He waked the next morning with a jetstream of sunshine in his face and a heaviness of Frances' head on his right shoulder. He felt weak and convalescent. He'd done too much, after spending four days in a hospital bed.

He leaned up and Frances' gaze shifted from the window to his face and she smiled with her coral mouth. "I'm attached to you," she said.

"Yes, but you're hurting my shoulder." And as he went to turn over he saw what she meant.

She *was* attached to him.

He got his knife again, an awkward procedure as Frances was attached at his shoulder and hip, but it wasn't as easy as hacking away at a rotten log.

It didn't hurt when he cut the hyphae, but blood began seeping out and it soon became evident that it was *his* blood.

And for the first time he felt a wave of disgust for his wife. "You're a parasite," he said. "You're no better than anybody else. At least most of them are willing to settle for money."

It was then that Arthur decided to divorce his wife.

You will wonder, perhaps, why Arthur did not simply murder her. That is safe only in stories. Murder is illegal, and particularly unsafe among married couples, where the motive is obvious.

But divorce takes a long time and there had to be an immediate separation.

Arthur therefore called a doctor (partly to do this

minor surgery safely, partly to serve as a witness that his wife had become a dangerous parasite).

Dr. Beeker had never (Good Heavens!) seen a case of this kind before and recommended (strongly!) that the two of them be brought immediately to a hospital to have the separation made.

But Arthur said No, it might be dangerous to wait, his wife had been acting very peculiar and he didn't know what she had that he might catch and furthermore he had just been ill himself and was feeling weak from loss of blood. (Though, indeed, she wasn't stealing his blood, only the nutrients from it.)

"I don't know," Dr. Beeker said, slicing unhappily at the rhizomorphs with a scalpel, "what effect this is going to have on Mrs. Kelsing. I really feel she should be seen by a specialist. Ah . . . well, tropical diseases, maybe."

"A botanist," Arthur suggested. "My wife needs a good going over by a competent botanist, and although we will be separated, I intend to pay for it."

But by the time Dr. Beeker had given Arthur a coagulant and an antibiotic and written a prescription, Frances had slipped out and attached herself to the tree stump again.

Dr. Beeker could not bring himself to cut her rhizomorphs again.

Arthur drove into Fayetteville, had a botanist and the police sent out to his cabin, and consulted a lawyer.

As it turned out Frances was considered non compos (or non compost, as a cartoonist later put it). But Arthur had to retain the lawyer in any case, because the botanist became suspicious and called in a mycologist and the general conclusion was that Frances was not a natural phenomenon and Arthur in fact was accused of attempted murder.

Arthur's lawyer was pleased no end as there were fascinating legal problems involved, one of which was that the Frances upon whom the attempted murder had allegedly been perpetrated could not be produced. She did not exist. (Not any more.) On the other hand, a most important element of the crime of murder was missing. No evidence of a dead body of Frances could be produced. The D.A., being in his right mind, would not accept the charge. As Arthur had figured, there were no existing statutes covering the situation. Or at least none except one most people had forgotten about.

By the time the scientists had finished their studies, Frances' condition had proceeded to the state that it was not safe to separate her from the stump and indeed, she had no desire to do anything except be watered during dry seasons.

Eventually Frances became one of the eighth wonders of the world (it has been years, of course, since she has moved or spoken) and considerably enriched the state of Arkansas via the tourist trade, including a large number of artists, poets, philosophers, sociologists, anthropologists and general aesthetes. And she remains—perhaps will remain forever—happy and famous and beautiful.

Whereas Arthur, who made all this possible, was convicted by the people of Arkansas under an old witchcraft law. It was the final ignominy for Arthur, that his life's work should be dismissed by the people of Arkansas as witchcraft.

And so he died, despised, misunderstood, a figure of tragic irony, but returning, we hope, to the reality from which he sprang, the eternal hallucination.

VISITING PROFESSOR

"There's a new twenty-second century man coming in tomorrow," my husband said through a mouthful of dried Martian furz. "God! Do we have to have this damn furz for breakfast *every* day?"

"Furz is the *only* food that provides everything you need for nutrition. *Everything.* Scientists say you could live entirely on furz and be perfectly healthy. Healthier, as a matter of fact. For only ten credits a year. And you get all that food value with only two hundred calories a meal. Think of it!"

"I'll be damned if I'll think of it. I get paid to think about Domestic Architecture from 1875 to 1890, not about Martian furz."

"*Paid!* Is that what you call that flimsy, half-starved credit guarantee the University sends you every month? If we ever have a baby we'll have to live on furz three times a day."

"Baby!" William paled, pushed away his bowl of furz and lighted a cigarette. "I just bought you an electric zither. What do you want with a . . ."

"Never mind," I said darkly. "Just be glad your daddy didn't buy your mama an electric zither."

"Now what do you mean by that?" William snapped, because he is always the one to start arguments. "You always say something obscure when I'm hungry and it activates my digestive juices. That's how ulcers get started. The hydrochloric acid or whatever it is starts digesting the stomach."

"That's ridiculous! In the first place I wasn't talking to your digestive juices. And in the second place you've just had a nice, big bowl of furz."

"It *wasn't* nice. It leaves you feeling guilty because you want to eat something else and you know you don't need to. And when you feel guilty your large intestine contracts and that leads to . . ."

"William, I *won't* be made responsible for your digestive tract. The doctor said you were in perfect health and marriage has done wonders for you."

William grinned. "I like you, anyway, furz and all." He reached for his lecture notes and stood up to leave.

"*Love* me, William," I reminded him. "Understatement is all very effective when you're lecturing on nineteenth-century history. But not when you're making love to your wife."

"I don't have time to make love to you," William said, glancing at the chronometer set in his thumbnail. "I have an eight o'clock class."

"That isn't what I meant. Oh, William, you're absolutely impossible. But go ahead and ask him to dinner tomorrow night."

"Who?" William asked, kissing me goodbye.

"The twenty-second century man, you idiot. You were going to ask me to have him to dinner before you got off on the furz."

"Oh, yes. Fine." William jumped on the conveyor belt that led to the Faculty Building.

"Tell him six o'clock!" I shouted.

"Right. Six o'clock."

"Is he married?" I screamed for William was going off fast.

"Either that or living in sin!" William screamed back at me.

Which is why there was always a delightful suspicion attached to the Jrobs. Four square blocks of Ivy Leave faculty heard William's quip.

Five minutes later dear old Mrs. Blake, Mrs. Romantic Poetry Blake, came dithering over bearing a jar of those dreadful creech preserves you were too polite to throw away.

"I thought you might like a jar of my creech preserves," she said with dignity. Then she threw restraint to the winds. "*Who's* living in sin, my dear? Isn't it fascinating?"

"The Jrobs," I answered thoughtlessly, because my mind was full of other things. Thank God he was married. That meant I could have a soufflé. Bachelors are too undependable for soufflés and timbales aren't nearly as impressive. Venusian grilch cheese soufflé with a soupcon of saffron. Green peas. Popped potatoes. But were the Teenie vacuums dependable? The last batch didn't pop right and I'd have to go all the way into town to get Acme Frozen Vacuums and even so . . .

Mrs. Blake's conversation was beginning to create static in my train of thought.

"Quite like Percy Bysshe and Mary," she was rattling on. "Or even George Gordon, Lord B. Though I must say I think Byron was something of a cad. I mean about the little girl in the convent. Though if you can write such lovely poetry and look like Manfred . . . Does Mr. Jrob look like Manfred?"

"Manfred?" I asked, frowning. I didn't like the gist of the conversation at all.

"My dear, I didn't mean to be superior. You're late nineteenth century architecture, so of course you wouldn't know. Manfred. Dark, gloomy, handsome, romantic."

"What about Manfred?" I asked, deciding we couldn't have cheese for dessert if we were having cheese soufflé for the entrée.

"Mr. Jrob. The one that's living in sin. Does he look like Manfred?"

"Mr. and Mrs. Jrob aren't living in sin," I answered, horrified. "He's coming in from the twenty-second century to occupy the Future chair at the University."

"But you *said* they were living in sin," Mrs. Blake insisted, working her eyebrows.

"My husband was just having his little joke. I'm sure they're perfectly respectable people and after all they'll be friends of ours."

"Of course," Mrs. Blake said, smiling with delight. "We must take up for our friends, mustn't we? And now I've got to fly. I promised a jar of creech preserves to Norma. She's just out of the hospital, poor thing, and I've always said there's nothing like creech preserves for a hysterectomy."

Had the Jrobs been different, I might have gone about the neighborhood clearing up after Mrs. Blake's rumor. As it was, I maintained an enigmatic smile practically during the entire stay of the Jrobs at Ivy Leave. And I must say, I don't envy the Cheshire cat. Because it's a strain on the facial muscles.

But the Jrobs deserved everything they got. More, in fact, but tempers tend to get flabby in an intellectual atmosphere.

The Jrobs were in the midst of an argument as they arrived at our modest inflated bubble.

"Ivy *Leave!*" she was sputtering. "I thought you said Ivy *League.*"

"Now, now, Beta. Remember this is mid twenty-first century, not mid-twentieth century. Don't you ever read anything? Ivy Leave is . . ."

"Come on in," William said heartily, before they had a chance to toe the button.

I took both index fingers and pulled my mouth into a smile. How dare she use such a nasty tone about Ivy Leave? Before she even saw a pay check.

"How quaint!" Mrs. Jrob remarked when she was in the door. "Amazing what you've done with that old claka crate."

"I don't know what a crate is," I said, "but that's our new Young Professional Pined Finish Family Cabinet."

"Notice her middle low coastal accent, Beta," Mr. Jrob said, extending a hand that might easily have held a peanut. "It's charming, isn't it?"

"It has a hairy sort of charm," Mrs. Jrob agreed nastily. I soon discovered that "hairy" was their general word of abuse. It was easy to see why. Both the Jrobs were completely hairless, except for an obviously dyed blonde fringe around Mrs. Jrob's dome.

"Mash yourself up a hunk of furniture," I said much more cheerfully than I felt, "and make yourselves at home. What would you like to drink, Mrs. Jrob?"

"Mead?" she asked. It was obviously an unusual physical effort for her to shape her chair.

"Beta!" Mr. Jrob said reprovingly. "Mid-twentieth century America, remember? Try to seem like a part of the native atmosphere."

"Port? Claret cup? Grog?"

Mr. Jrob cleared his throat in embarrassment. "Martini," he said. "We would be delighted to have a martini."

"What's a martini?" I asked. "I'd be glad to make it if . . ."

William laughed. "Nice try, J. Only you're a little off your century too. The latest respectable drink is a Suspicion."

"Fine! Fine!" Mr. Jrob said. He was never quite as offensive as his wife.

"What's in a Suspicion?" she asked nervously. "I remember the time you came back from a field trip with a canteen full of kumiss. I've got my capillaries to think of, you know."

"Dear, I got that from Marco Polo."

"I don't care if you got it from Willy Mays. It did something to my capillaries."

"The Suspicion," William said, "is pretty harmless. It's straight French Vermouth with just a suspicion of gin in it and a clove of garlic. Some people put a sprinkling of nutmeg on the top, or a little . . ." He stopped, because of the expression on Mrs. Jrob's face. "You don't *have* to have the nutmeg."

"Hideous," Mrs. Jrob shuddered. "Absolutely hairy."

"Beta!"

"Oh, all right. But just give me a plain Vermouth."

William went back to make the drinks and left me unprotected.

"Have you found a place to live yet?" I asked Mrs. Jrob conversationally.

"We *bought* a place to live. Fortunately," she added, looking around my living room which is really, quite nice.

"A bubble?"

"Of course not. Synthetic slabs supported by electronic beams. They wouldn't let me bring my robot, of course, and there won't be enough power for my matter converter, so there'll be a lot of wastage. But I suppose you get used to primitive conditions after a while."

"You're so brave," I murmured. "Where are you going to put your house?"

"Hasn't your husband told you? He offered us your back yard. From his description it ought to just fit."

"Just fit!" On my peonies.

I asked William to take a look at the soufflé. If I'd looked at it it would have fallen.

After dinner we played some primitive middle low American music on the tape recorder and I was just feeling vengeful enough to bring out my electric zither when the footbell tinkled.

Mrs. Blake fluttered in, wearing her second best grey voile peplum and a surprised smile.

"Oh, excuse me, my dear, I had no *idea* you had company. Dr. Blake has a class tonight, you know, and I just thought I'd pop over to tell you about Norma's hys . . . oh, my, men present. My dear, they took everything out. *Everything.* Well, I'll just run . . ."

"No, indeed," I assured her. "Do sit down and talk. The men don't pay any attention to us anyway." I waved toward the company. "Meet Mr. and Mrs. Jrob from the twenty-second century."

Mrs. Blake peered nearsightedly at Mr. Jrob, donned her antique pince-nez, and took it off with a very disappointed expression.

"Tell me, Mr. Jrob, do you write poetry?"

I couldn't help it. I giggled.

"Poetry?"

"You know. 'The isles of Greece, the isles of Greece, where burning Sappho loved and sung . . .' That sort of thing."

"I most certainly do *not*."

"What a hairy thought," Mrs. Jrob sniffed. "'The aisles of grease.' It reminds me of your faculty lunch room."

"Well, I just thought, in the circumstances . . . I mean, from what William suggested . . . oh, well, everyone can't write poetry," Mrs. Blake explained lamely.

The men went back to their deep discussion of late twentieth-century advertising semantics, which left Mrs. Blake a clear field on Norma's hysterectomy.

"Hairiest thing I ever heard of," was Mrs. Jrob's comment.

Mrs. Blake left early, apologizing herself out of the

door. But she whispered in my ear before she left, "Manfred, *indeed!*"

At first, Mr. and Mrs. Jrob were the center of much delighted attention. Mostly Mrs. Jrob, because she was home all day. For blocks around wives homed in on what came to be referred to as "the love nest." Mrs. Jrob was given to understand that at Ivy Leave faculty wives were Broad-minded. Uninhibited. Not concerned with the unimportant Legal Technicalities of social existence. Godwin was mentioned frequently. Rousseau. Françoise Sagan.

But Mrs. Blake's rumor, for which I am in no way responsible, soon bore bitter fruit. Creech, I should say.

It was William who, by pure chance, mentioned it. He's given to mentioning things when faced with a bowl of furz in the morning. Which is one good reason for serving furz.

"Too bad about Jrob," he said.

"What's too bad?"

"Nobody can take over his classes."

"You mean he's leaving?" I cried delightedly, wondering if the peonies would grow up again from the roots.

"May have to. It seems they've been living in sin."

"Oh, but that's just a rumor Mrs. Blake started. Anyway, so what? It's perked up the whole neighborhood."

"It perked up the board of administrators, too. It seems word got down to the undergraduate level. That's why J's classes were so large. He lectures like a billy goat. And one of those undergraduates is a pasty-faced little freshman who just happens to be old B.D.'s grandson. So word got back to B.D. and President Grayson said he had that expression on his face he gets when he's decided to leave his money to Harvard."

"Harvard! But all there is there is . . ."

"I know. But you know the tradition. Businessmen think there is an exclusive section of the Hereafter reserved for people who leave their money to Harvard."

"Let's not discuss B.D. Get back to Jrob. What did President Grayson tell him?"

"As I get the story, Jrob says to the Pres, 'What do you mean, *legally* married?' And it turns out he really is living in sin, only it isn't a sin in the twenty-second century and furthermore he refuses to *get* married as he says that would make him lose face and ruin his social life when he goes back home on vacations."

"So he's going to be fired?"

"Asked to resign because of cultural lag."

"My, but this is going to be fun!" I sighed happily. Because William knows all about Architecture from 1875 to 1890, but I know all about college professors. And I knew the upheaval to come would furnish conversational material for years.

The sociology department was up in arms immediately. It was the first Cause we'd had since Integration. Professor Insfree grew a beard and two female teaching fellows shaved their heads.

The psychology department followed. Musty old tomes, predating the Organization Man and the growth of suburban morality, were routed out of the basement in the library. The *libido* came into its own again.

"We're lost. We're all lost," several members of the

English Department were heard to remark with tragic joy. Fitzgerald and Hemingway enjoyed a brief revival.

The Jrob dilemma sifted down to the student level. A group of sophomores began to wear brown chitons and glare at everybody. *Blast*, the student organ of Ivy Leave, began to publish articles advocating free thought, though apparently the only thing students considered worth thinking about freely were other students of the opposite sex.

Above all, the roar "Academic Freedom!" echoed from one end of the campus to another.

There was even a pantie raid interpreted, for some obscure reason, as a gesture for academic freedom.

Bulletins began to appear on the campus. As fast as the signs were torn down they came back up.

"All the world loves a lover except the Administration."

"Were Pericles and Aspasia married?"

"Don't let them make you do it, Professor Jrob!"

"Up with academic freedom."

"Down with the administration."

It was gratifying, I thought, the way faculty and students alike rallied around the injured Jrobs. I didn't like them, but it occurred to me I could do a little rallying myself and I popped in to see Mrs. Jrob one morning to offer aid and encouragement.

"They won't *dare* fire your . . . er . . . Mr. Jrob now," I told her. "The entire faculty would resign in protest. They might even go back to Harvard."

"Lord! I'll be glad to get out of this hairy place," was her only comment.

It was for the principle of the thing, not for Mrs. Jrob, that I marched through the History Building with the other wives, bearing my placard. "The Faculty Wives Accept Mrs. Jrob."

Thus Mrs. Jrob managed to be a tremendous social success, though she refused to join the Garden Club or the Sewing Club and her only comment on the Wives' Tea, which was compulsory, was "Hairy."

Though all did not end well, because of certain unexpected events, President Grayson was shouted down and the Jrobs were asked to stay. President Grayson made one last stand. He came into his office one morning and through his window zinged a dagger with a note attached. It bit into the wall and quivered. President Grayson summoned the maintenance department without a moment's hesitation and the note was removed. It read, "What does Ivy Leave stand for, anyway?"

For some reason this epistle enraged President Grayson beyond endurance. He called a meeting of the entire student body and faculty. The wives, janitors and assorted news reporters came too.

"This note!" he cried waving it in the air, "sent anonymously, reads, 'What does Ivy Leave stand for, anyway?' Well, I can tell you one thing it does *not* stand for. Free Love!"

"Boo. Hiss."

President Grayson was not making the impression he intended. He couldn't understand why the issue was not as clear to everyone else as it was to him.

"All right," he said, several times because there was a group singing, for no apparent reason, "La Marseillaise."

"All right. Even the freshmen here are not children. I'll put it to you in its crudest terms. Do you want your University to stand for fornication?"

There was a shocked silence.

"Well, do you?"

The shouting began.

"Yes!" from the sophomores.

"No!" from the seniors.

"Define your terms!" from the faculty.

"Allons, enfants de la patrie . . ." from an assorted group.

In the end, of course, he lost. Well, not in the *end*.

It was at the Insfree's cocktail party that the turning point came. We had a jolly time that fall, because of the prevalent notion that a party for the Jrobs was a declaration for academic freedom. The Jrobs, unfortunately, did not like to go out to parties because Mrs. Jrob felt other people's houses weren't properly filtered, and she had her lungs to consider.

They appeared, however, at the Insfrees. And to everyone's consternation they were accompanied by a bald headed little boy of about ten. The little boy bore an evil grin and he kept glancing slyly at Mrs. Jrob. There was a heavy collar around his neck and Mrs. Jrob held the rope firmly, for he had a tendency to buck.

"Not broken in yet," I heard her explain as she passed her hostess, taking the sanitary precaution of not shaking the extended hand.

Mrs. Blake was all shook up. "Mr. Jrob," she said, or rather asked, "I didn't know you had a child!"

"That's not my child," Mr. Jrob answered, as though

the thought were, indeed, a hairy one. "I don't even know his name."

"Omicron," Mrs. Jrob said. "I've told you a thousand times."

"Poor, dear child," Mrs. Blake murmured, stooping to commiserate with him.

"Watch out!" Mrs. Jrob shouted. Too late.

"He's used to robots," Mr. Jrob explained. "I suppose he doesn't understand yet that it's all right to bite robots but it's not all right to bite people. Why *I* should be saddled with this child I don't know."

"It certainly isn't *my* fault," Mrs. Jrob said petulantly, smoothing her blond fringe with a shapeless hand. "How he got out of the Personality Adjustment Center I don't know. Much less how he got here. I'm going to sue them for negligence. I sent them the boy and they were supposed to return me the man. If *this* is the man—well, all I can say is, he takes after his daddy."

"No wonder he bites," said Professor Graham, of psychology. "All that pent up hostility. You mean you actually put him in an institution for the duration of the academic year?"

"No, indeed," Mrs. Jrob replied. "He's been in it since he was six. Before that he was in the Tot's Pleasure Dome. I know my responsibilities. Ordinarily he's perfectly happy there and I bore him to tears. I don't know what got into him."

"You mean he's never known what a home is?"

"Not *my* home. What kind of a home do you think it would be with a child around? I take him out to the zoo on Sunday afternoons."

"Poor little thing." Mrs. Blake was practically sobbing. "Why don't you let me take him home with me. Just this evening. So he can get to bed at a reasonable hour. And find out what a *real* home is like." Considering her mangled wrist, Mrs. Blake was the heroine of the evening.

Mrs. Jrob handed Mrs. Blake the end of the rope. "Go ahead. It's *your* home."

As Professor Graham remarked to me, despite his recent article, *Libido Revisited*, there's something a little sordid about it. The libido is all very well, but not with a *child* around.

Dr. Blake was similarly incensed. "He doesn't even write poetry. Now that I think about it, what excuse *does* he have?"

Professor Insfree retired to the back of the house and returned with his beard shaved off. It was a symbol to all of us.

Omicron was back in no time. He rushed in panting, his eyes wild, and handed the end of the rope to his mother. "Get me out of this hairy century," he screamed.

"What happened?" Mrs. Jrob asked.

"She tried to poison me!" Omicron grabbed at his throat dramatically. "I can still taste it. The old hag shoved poison in my mouth."

"Creech preserves," I guessed brilliantly. "They're perfectly harmless, Mrs. Jrob. They may taste a little odd to your son." As a matter of fact, they taste a little odd to everyone.

"Mrs. Blake let you come back here alone? Nobody held your rope?"

"*Held* it? She tried to take my collar off." Omicron

shuddered. "Threatened my entire sense of security. And would the other kids get a laugh out of it if I showed up without my collar. What would I have to take off at graduation? I had to freeze her."

Professor Blake fixed Omicron with a furious gaze. "What have you done to my wife, you unnatural child?"

"*Give* me that Freeze Gun," Mrs. Jrob said with tight lips.

"Aw, Mama . . ."

"*Give* it to me or I'll leave you here."

"Aw . . ." He handed it over.

"The question is," Professor Blake blazed, "*what* did he do to my wife?"

"Froze her."

"Is she . . . is she . . . ?" He had a horrible thought.

"Not literally. You people are so hairy. She'll be immobilized for twenty-four hours."

"I'll sue," Professor Blake shouted as he stormed out.

"You needn't bother. We won't be here. I'm taking Omicron back."

"Not a bad idea," several people remarked.

And so, in the end, Mr. Jrob resigned from the Future Chair because of cultural lag, and everybody was reasonably happy.

Except me. Because I found something out just as the Jrobs were leaving.

"Well, I guess I won't be seeing you again," I remarked happily as they stood on their pile of synthetic boards waiting for Translation.

"Not exactly," Mrs. Jrob answered.

"What do you mean, not exactly?"

"You died when I was a baby, Grandma."

Which is why I am so interested in the electric zither.

CAR POOL

"Happy birthday to *you*," we all sang, except Gail, of course, who was still screaming, though not as loud.

"Well, now," I said jovially, glancing nervously about at the other air traffic, "what else can we all sing?" The singing seemed to be working nicely. They had stopped swatting each other with their lunch boxes and my experienced ear told me Gail was by this time forcing herself to scream. This should be the prelude to giving up and enjoying herself.

"*Boing* down in Texas in eighteen-ninety," Billy began, "Davy, *Davy* Eisenhower . . ."

"A-B-*C*-*D*-E—" sang Jacob.

"Dere was a little 'elicopter red and blue," Meli chirped, "Flew along de airways—"

The rest came through unidentifiably.

"Ba-ba-ba," said a faint voice. Gail had given up. I longed for ears in the back of my head because victory was mine and all I needed to do was reinforce it with a little friendly conversation.

"Yes, dear?" I asked her encouragingly.

"Ba-ba-ba," was all I could make out.

"Yes, indeed. That Gail *likes* to go to Playplace."

"Ba-ba-ba!" A little irritable. She was trying to say something important. "*Ba-ba-ba!*"

I signaled for an emergency hover, turned around and presented my ear.

"Me eat de crus' of de toas'," Gail said. She beamed.

I beamed.

We managed to reach Playplace without incident, except for a man who called me an obscenity. The children and I, however, called him a great, big alligator head and on the whole, I think, we won. After all, how can a man possibly be right when faced with a woman and eight tiny children?

I herded the children through the Germ Detection Booth and Gail was returned to me with an incipient streptococcus infection.

"Couldn't you give her the shot here?" I asked. "I've *just* got her in a good mood, and if I have to turn around and take her back home . . . and besides, her mother works. There won't be anyone there."

"Verne, dear, we can't risk giving the shot until the child is perfectly adjusted to Playplace. You see, she'd connect the pain of the shot with coming to school and then she might never adjust." Mrs. Baden managed to give me her entire attention and hold a two-and-a-half-year-old child on one shoulder and greet each entering child and break up a fight between two ill-matched four-year-olds, all at the same time.

"Me stay at school," Gail said resolutely.

There was a scream from the other side of the booth. That was Billy's best friend. I waited for the other scream. That was Billy.

"Normal aggression," Mrs. Baden said with a smile.

I picked up Gail. Act first, talk later.

"Oh, *there* she is," Mrs. Baden said, taking my elbow with what could only be a third hand.

Having heard we'd have a Hiserean child in Billy's group, I managed not to look surprised.

"Mrs. His-tara, this is Verne Barrat. Her Billy will be in Hi-nin's group."

I was immediately frozen with indecision. Should I shake hands? Merely smile? Nod? Her hands looked wavery and boneless. I might injure them inadvertently.

I settled on a really good smile, all the way back to my bridge. "I am so delighted to meet you," I said. I felt as though the good will of the entire World Conference rested on my shoulders.

Her face lighted up with the most sincere look of pleasure I've ever seen. "I am glad to furnish you this delight," she said, with a good deal of lisping over the dentals, because Hisereans have fore-shortened teeth. She embraced me wholeheartedly and gave me a scaly kiss on the cheek.

My first thought was that I was a success and my second thought was, Oh, God, what'll happen when Billy gets hold of little Hi-nin? Hisereans, as I understood it, simply didn't have this "normal aggression." Indeed, I sometimes have trouble believing it's really normal.

"I was thinking," Mrs. Baden said, putting down the two-and-a-half-year-old and plucking a venturesome little girl in Human Fly Shoes from the side of the building, "that you all might enjoy having Hi-nin in your car pool."

"Oh, we'd love to," I said eagerly. "We've got five mamas and eight children already, of course, but I'm sure everyone—"

"It would trouble you!" Mrs. His-tara exclaimed. Her eye stalks retracted and tears poured down her cheeks. "I do not want to be of difficulty," she said.

Since she had no apparent handkerchief and wore some sort of permanent-looking native dress, I tore a square out of my paper morning dress for her.

"You are too good!" she sobbed, fresh tears pouring out.

"No, no. I already tore out two for the children. I always get my skirts longer in cold weather because children are so careless about carrying—"

"Then we'll consider the car pool settled?" Mrs. Baden asked, coming in tactfully.

"Naturally," I said, mentally shredding my previous sentence. "We would feel so honored to have Hi-nin—"

"Do not *think* of putting yourself out. We do not have a helicopter, of course, but Hi-nin and I can so easily walk."

I was rapidly becoming unable to think of anything at all because Gail was trying to use me for a merry-go-round and I kept switching her from hand to hand and I could hear her beginning to build up the ba-bas.

"My car pool," I said, "would be terribly sad to think of Hi-nin walking."

"You would?"

"*Terribly.*"

"In such a case—if it will give you pleasure for me to accept?"

"It would," I said fervently, holding Gail under one arm as she was beginning to kick.

And on the way home all the second thoughts began.

I would be glad to have Hi-nin in the car pool. Four of the other mamas were like me, amazed that anyone was willing to put up with her child all the way to and from Playplace. I could count on them to cooperate. But Gail's mama . . . I'd gone to Western State Preparation for Living with Regina Raymond Crowley.

I landed on the Crowley home and tooted for five minutes before I remembered that Regina was at work.

"*Ma*-ma!" Gail began.

"Wouldn't you like to come to Verne's house," I asked, "and we can call up your mama?"

"No." Well, I asked, didn't I?

I was carrying Gail down the steps from my roof when I bumped unexpectedly into Clay.

"What is that!" he exclaimed, and Gail became again flying blonde hair and kicking feet.

"Regina's child," I said. "What are you doing home?"

"Accountant sent me back. Twenty-five and a half hours is the maximum this week. Good thing, too. I've got a headache." He eyed Gail meaningfully. She was obviously not the sort of thing the doctor orders for a headache.

"I can't help it, honey," I said, sitting down on a step to tear another handkerchief square from my skirt. "I'm going to call Regina at work now."

"Don't you have a chairman to take care of things like that?"

"I am the chairman," I said proudly.

"Why in heaven's name did you let yourself get roped into something like that?"

"I was *selected* by Mrs. Baden!"

"Obscenity," said Clay. It is his privilege, of course, to use this word.

The arty little store where Regina works has a telephane as well as a telephone, and in color, at that. So I could see Regina in full color, taking her own good time about switching on the sound. She switched on as a sort of afterthought and tilted her nose at me. I don't suppose she can really tilt her nose up and down, but she always gives that impression.

"Gail has an incipient streptococcus infection," I said. "They sent her home."

"*Ma*-ma!" Gail cried.

"Why didn't they give her a shot there? That's what they did with my niece last year."

I explained why not.

Regina sighed resignedly. "Verne, people can talk you into anything. There are times when you have to be firm. I work, girl. That's why I put Gail in Playplace. I can't leave here until twelve o'clock."

"But what'll I do with Gail?"

"Take her back. Or you keep her until I get home. Sorry, Verne, but you got yourself into this."

I switched off, furious.

Then I remembered Hi-nin. I couldn't be furious. I was going to have to get Regina's cooperation.

I picked up Gail and went into the bedroom. "I do not

dislike Regina Crowley," I wrote with black crayola on a piece of note paper. I stuck it into a crevice of my mirror and gave Gail my bare-shoulder decorations to play with while I concentrated on thinking up reasons why I should not dislike Regina Crowley.

"I do," Clay said, sneaking up so quietly I jumped two feet.

"So do I," I said, gazing wearily at my note. "But I have to have her in a good mood. You see, there's this Hiserean child and since I'm chairman of the car pool, I have to—"

"*Don't* tell me about it," Clay said. "My advice to you is get elephantiasis of your steering foot and give the whole thing up now." He glanced meaningfully at Gail, who couldn't possibly be bothering him. She was playing quietly on the floor, pulling the suction disks off my jewelry and sticking them on her legs.

When I finally got Gail home, she sped into her mother's arms and I couldn't help being a little irritated because I had been practically swinging from the ceiling dust controls to ingratiate myself, and her mama just said, "Oh, hi," and Gail was satisfied.

"By the way," I said, watching Regina hang up her dark blue hand-woven jacket, "you wouldn't mind picking up an extra child tomorrow, would you?"

"Mind! Certainly I mind. I've got as much as I can do with my job and Gail and eight children in the heli already."

"It's a Hiserean child," I said. "The mother is so lovely, Regina. She didn't want us to go to any trouble."

"That's fine. Because I'm not going to go to any trouble."

I put my fists behind my back. "Of course I understand, Regina. I think it's remarkable that you manage to do so much. And keep up with your art things as you do. But don't you think it would be an interesting experience to have a Hiserean child in the pool?"

Regina pulled off her hand-woven wrap-skirt and I was shocked to see she wore a real boudoir slip to work.

"Everybody to their own interesting experiences," she said, laughing at me. This was obviously one of her triple-level remarks.

"De gustibus," I said, to show I know a few arty things myself, "non disputandum est."

"You have such moments, Verne! Have you ever seen a Hiserean child?"

"I saw one today."

"Well."

"Well?"

"De gustibus, as you said. You know the other children will eat it alive, don't you? *Your* child will. Now Gail . . ."

It's true that Gail never kicks anyone small enough to kick back. It's also true that Billy bites.

I unclenched my fists and stretched up with a deep breath so as to relax my stomach and improve my posture.

"Hiserean children," I pointed out, "are going to have to be adjusted to our society. As I understand it, they're here to stay. Their sun blew up behind them and personally I think we're lucky they happened to drift here."

"I don't see why it's so lucky. I wish we'd gotten one

of the ships full of scientific information. Or their top scientists. Or artists, for that matter. All *we* got were plain people. If you like to call them people."

"They're at least educated people with good sense. And we've got their ship to take apart and learn things from. And their books and, after all, some music and their gestural art. I should think you artists would find that real avant garde."

"Just hearing you say it like that is enough to kill Hiserean art."

"Regina, I know you think I'm a prig, but that isn't the point. And if it matters to you, I'm *not* a prig."

"Do you wear boudoir slips?" Regina was biting a real smile.

"No, I don't. But I'd like to."

"Then why don't you?"

"Because I put one on once and I thought I looked absolutely devastating and you know what my husband said?"

"I won't try to guess Clay's bon mot."

"He said, 'What did you put that on for?'"

Regina laughed until she popped a snap on her paper house dress. "But seriously," she said finally, "if he didn't know, why didn't you tell him?"

"That's not the point. The point is I am not the boudoir-slip type. My unmentionables are unmentionable for esthetic reasons only."

Regina laughed again. "Really, Verne, you're not half bad when you try."

"If you honestly think I'm not half bad, could you do it

just as a favor to me? Pick up Hi-nin when you have the car pool?"

"The Hiserean child? No."

"Please, Regina. I'd do it *for* you except that the children would notice and it would get back to Mrs. His-tara. If there's anything I could do for you in return—"

"What could you possibly do?"

"I don't know. But I *can't* go back and tell that dear creature our car pool doesn't want her."

"*Stop* looking so intense. That's what keeps you from being the boudoir-slip type. You always look as though you're going out to break up a saloon or campaign for better Public Child Protection. The boudoir slip requires a languorous expression."

"Phooey to looking languorous. And phooey to boudoir slips. I'd wear diapers to nursery school if you'd change your mind about taking along Hi-nin."

"Would you wear a boudoir slip?"

"I—hell, yes."

"And nothing else?"

"Only my various means of support. And my respectability."

Regina laughed her tiger-on-the-third-Christian laugh. "What I want to find out," she said, "is how you manage that respectability bit."

It dawned on me while I was grinding the pepper for Clay's salad that Regina had explained herself. All of a sudden I saw straight through her and I wondered why I hadn't seen it before. Regina *envied* me.

Now on the face of it, that seemed unlikely. But it

occurred to me that Regina's parents had been the poor but honest and uneducated sort that simply are never asked to chaperone school parties. And the fact is that they were not what Regina thought of as respectable, though it never occurred to anyone but her that it mattered. And since all her culture was acquired after the age of thirteen, she felt it didn't fit properly and that's why she went out of her way to be arty-arty.

Whereas I took for granted all the things Regina had learned so painstakingly, and this in turn was what made me so irritatingly respectable.

As Regina had suggested, perhaps it *is* the expression on one's face that makes the difference.

"Hey!" a cop yelled, pulling up as close to us as his rotors would allow. "What the hell?"

"I beg your pardon," I said frigidly. It is very frigid in November if you are out in a helicopter dressed only in a boudoir slip.

"Look de bleesemans!" Gail cried.

"He might shoot everybody!" Billy warned.

Meli began to cry loudly. "He might *choot! Ma*-ma!"

"Pardon me, madam," the cop said, and beat a hasty retreat.

When we landed on Hi-nin's roof, Mrs. His-tara came up with him. She looked at me sympathetically. "You are perhaps molting, beloved friend?" Her large eyes retracted and filled with tears. "Such a season!"

"No—no, dear. Just—getting a little fresh air."

I put Hi-nin on the front seat with me. He gave me a big-eyed, toothless smile and sat down in perfect quiet, except for the soft, almost sea sound of his breathing.

It was during one of those brief and infrequent silences we have that I noticed something was amiss. No sea sound.

I looked around to find Billy's hands around Hi-nin's throat.

"Billy!" I screamed.

"Aw!" he said, and let go.

Hi-nin began to breathe again in a violent, choked way.

"Billy," I said, wondering if I could keep myself from simply throwing my son out of the helicopter, "Billy . . ."

"It is nothing, nice mama," Hi-nin said, still choking.

"Billy." I didn't trust myself to speak any further. I reached around and spanked him until my hand was sore. "If you *ever* do that again—"

"*Waa!*" Billy bawled. I'm sure he could be heard quite plainly by the men building the new astronomical station on the Moon.

I put Hi-nin on my lap and kept him there. "That's just Billy's way of making friends," I whispered to him.

Under Billy's leadership, several other children began to cry, and all in all it was not a well-integrated, love-sharing group that I lifted down from the heli at Playplace.

"The children always sense it, don't they," Mrs. Baden said with her gentle smile, "when we don't feel comfortable about a situation?"

"*Comfortable!*" I cried. It seemed to me the day had become blazing hot and I didn't remember what I was dressed in until I tried to take off my jacket. "My son is an inhuman monster. He tried to—to—" I could feel a big sob coming on.

"Bite?" Mrs. Baden supplied helpfully.

"Strangle," I managed to blurt out.

"We'll be especially considerate of Billy today," Mrs. Baden said. "He'll be feeling guilty and he senses your discomfort about his aggression."

"*Senses* it! I all but tore him limb from limb! That dear little Hiserean child—"

"I do not want to be of difficulty," Hi-nin said, tears pouring out of those great, big eyes.

Tears were pouring out of my small blue eyes by this time and Mr. Grantham, who brings a set of grandchildren, came by and patted my shoulder.

"Chin up!" he said. "Eyes front!"

Then he looked at his hand and my recently patted shoulder.

"Oh, excuse me," he said. "Would you like to borrow my jacket?"

I shook my head, acutely aware, suddenly, that Mr. Grantham is not a doddering old grandfather but a young and handsome man. And all he thought about my bare shoulder was that it ought to be covered.

"You just run along," Mrs. Baden said. "We'll let Billy strangle the pneumatic dog and everything will be just fine. Oh, and dear—I don't know whether you've noticed it—you don't have on a dress."

I went home and sat in front of the mirror feeling miserable in several different directions. If Regina Raymond Crowley appeared in public dressed only in a boudoir slip, people would think all sorts of wicked things. When I appeared in public in a boudoir slip, everybody thought I was just a little absentminded.

This, I thought, is a hell of a thing to worry about. And then I thought, Oh, phooey. If even I think I'm respectable, what can I expect other people to think?

I took down the note on the mirror about Regina. No wonder I didn't like her! I turned the paper over and wrote "Phooey to me!" with my eyebrow pencil.

I was still regarding the note and trying to argue myself into a better mood when Clay came tramping down from work at three o'clock.

"Why are you sitting around in a boudoir slip?" he asked.

"You're a double-dyed louse and a great, big alligator head," I told him.

"Don't mention it," he said. "Where's Billy?"

"Taking his nap. Tell me the truth, Clay. The absolute truth."

Clay looked at me suspiciously. "I'd planned on a little golf this afternoon."

"This won't take a minute. I don't ask you things like this all the time, now do I?"

"I still don't know what you're talking about."

I took a deep breath. "Clay, is there anything about me, anything at all, that is not respectable?"

"There is *not*," he said.

"Well—I guess that's all there is to it," I sighed. I pulled off my boudoir slip and got a neat paper one out of the slot. "Anyway," I said bravely, "boudoir slips have to be laundered."

Clay looked at me curiously for a moment and then said, "This looks like a good afternoon to go play golf."

"Do you think there's anything not respectable about Regina Crowley?"

"There is *everything* not respectable about Regina Crowley," Clay said vehemently.

"You see?"

"Frankly, no."

"Well, do you think her husband uses that tone of voice when he says, 'There is *everything* respectable about Verne Barrat?'"

"I don't know why he should say that at all."

"She might ask him."

"Darling, you're mad as a hatter," Clay said, kissing me good-by.

"Do you really think so?"

"Of course not," Clay roared as he tramped up the steps to the heli.

About nine o'clock the next morning I heard a heli landing on the roof and I thought, Now who? There was much tooting, and when I went up, Regina practically threw Hi-nin at me.

"I told you so," she snapped at me. Her face was burning red and she wasn't bothering to tilt her nose.

"What happened? Why did you bring him back to *me?*"

"His hand," she said, and took off.

Hand? He was holding one hand over the other. No! I grabbed his hands to see what it was.

One hand had obviously been bitten off at the wrist. He was holding the wound with the tentacles of his other little boneless hand. There was very little blood.

"It is as nothing," he said, but when I cradled him in my arms, I could feel him shaking all over.

"It will grow back," he said.

Would it?

I took him in the heli and held him while I drove. I could feel him trying to stop himself from shaking, but he couldn't.

"Does it hurt very much?" I asked.

"The pain is small," he said. "It is the fear. The fear is terrible. I am unable to swallow it."

I was unable to swallow it, too.

"The hand," said Mrs. His-tara without concern, "will grow back. But the things within my son . . ." She, too, began to tremble involuntarily.

"Billy," I began, feeling the blood come through my lower lip, "Billy and I are . . ." It was too inadequate to say it.

"It was not Billy," Hi-nin said without rancor. "It was Gail."

"Gail! Gail doesn't bite!" But she had, and I broke down and plain cried.

"Do not trouble yourself," said Mrs. His-tara. "My son receives from this a wound that does not heal. On Hiserea he would be forever sick, you understand. On your world, where everyone is born with this open wound, it will be his protection. So Mrs. Baden warned me and I think she is wise."

As soon as I got home, I called up Regina. She looked

pale and lifeless against the gaudy, irresponsible objects in the art shop.

"It wasn't my fault," she said quickly. "I can't drive and watch the children at the same time. I told you the children would eat . . ." She stopped, and for the first time I saw Regina really horrified with herself.

"Nobody said it was your fault. But don't you think you could have taken Hi-nin home yourself? To show Mrs. His-tara that—I don't know what it would show."

It reminded me, somehow, of the time Regina stepped on a lizard and left it in great pain, pulling itself along by its tiny front paws, and I had said, "Regina, you can't leave that poor thing suffering," and she had said, "Well, I didn't step on it on purpose," and I had said, "Somebody's got to kill it now," and she had said, "I've got a class." I could still feel the crunch of it under my foot as its tiny life went out.

"Sorry, Verne," she said, "you got yourself into this," and hung up.

That night Regina called me. "Can you give blood?" she asked.

"Yes," I said. "If I stuff myself, I can get the scales up to a hundred and ten pounds."

"What type?"

"B. Rh positive."

"Thought you told me that once. Gail is in the hospital. They have to replace every drop of blood in her body. She may die anyhow."

I thought of the little fluff and squeak that was Gail. I eat de crus' of de toas'.

"What's the matter with her?" I asked fearfully.

"That damn Hiserean child is *poison*. Gail had a little cut inside her mouth from where she fell off the slide at school."

"I'll be at the hospital in ten minutes," I said, and hung up shakily. "Dinner is set for seven-thirty," I told Clay and Billy, and rushed out.

The first person I saw at the hospital was not Regina. It was Mrs. His-tara.

"How did you know?" I asked. Her integument was dull now and there were patches of scales rubbed off. Her eyes were almost not visible.

"Mrs. Crowley called me," she said. "In any case I would have been here. There is in Hi-nin also of poison. There remains for him only the Return Home. We must rejoice for him."

The smile she brought forth was more than I could bear.

"Gail's germs were poison to him?"

"Oh, no. He poisons himself. It is an ancient hormone, from the early days of our race when we had what your Mrs. Baden so wisely calls aggression. It is dormant in us since before the accounting of our history. An adult Hiserean, perhaps, could fight his emotions and cure himself. Hi-nin has no weapons—so your physicians have explained it to me, from our scientific books. How can I doubt that they are right?"

How could I doubt it, either? It would be, I thought, rather like a massive overdose of adrenalin. Psychogenic, of course, but what help was it to know that? Would there be some organ in Hi-nin a surgeon could remove? Like the adrenals in humans, perhaps?

Of course not. If they could have, they would have.

I hurried on to find the room where Gail was. She was not pale, as I had expected, but pink-cheeked and bright-eyed. They were probably putting in more blood than they were taking out. There were two of the other mamas from our car pool, waiting their turns.

Regina was sitting by the bed, her face ugly and swollen from crying.

"She looks just fine!" I exclaimed.

"Only in the last fifteen minutes," she said. "When I called you, she was like ice. Her eyes didn't move."

"We're lucky with Gail. Did you know about Hi-nin?"

"The little animal!" she said. "He's the one that did it."

"He didn't do anything, Regina, and you know it."

"He shouldn't have been in the car pool. He shouldn't be with human children at all."

"He's going to die," I said quickly, before she had time to say things she'd have nightmares about later on.

"Sorry," Regina said, because we were all looking at her and because her child was pink and beautiful and healthy while Hi-nin . . .

"Regina," I said, "what did you do after it happened?"

"*Do!* It scared the hell out of me—that creature shaking all over and Gail screaming. At first I didn't know what had happened. Then I saw that *thing* flopping around on the front seat and I screamed and threw it out of the window. And then I noticed Hi-nin's wrist, or whatever you call it. I said, 'Oh, God, I *knew* you'd get us in trouble!' But the creature didn't say anything. He just sat there. And I let the other children off and brought Hi-nin to you because I didn't want to get involved with that Mrs. Baden."

"And Gail?"

"She seemed all right. She just climbed in the back with the other children and pretty soon they were all laughing."

"And all that time little Hi-nin . . . Regina, didn't you even pat him or hold him or kiss it for him or anything?"

"*Kiss* it!"

At that moment Mrs. His-tara came in, with Mrs. Baden and a doctor behind her. I should have known. Mrs. Baden didn't leave people to fight battles alone.

Mrs. His-tara looked at Mrs. Baden, but Mrs. Baden only nodded and smiled encouragingly at her.

The doctor was gently pulling the needle out of Gail's vein. The room was silent. Even Gail sat large-eyed and solemn.

"Mrs. Crowley," Mrs. His-tara began, obviously dragging each word up with great effort, "would it be accurate to tell my son that Gail has received no hurt from him? We must, you see, prepare him for the Return Home."

Regina looked around at us and at Gail. She hadn't dared let herself look at Mrs. His-tara yet.

"Doctor!" Regina called suddenly. "Look at Gail's mouth!"

Even from where I was, I could see it. A scaly growth along both lips.

"That's a temporary effect of the serum," the doctor said. "We tried an antitoxin before we decided to change the blood. It is nothing to worry about."

"Oh."

"Mrs. Crowley," Mrs. His-tara began again, "it is much to ask, but at such a moment, much is required. If you could come yourself, and if Gail could endure to be carried . . ."

But Gail did, indeed, look queer, and she stretched out her arms not to her mother but to Mrs. His-tara.

"The tides," Mrs. His-tara said, "have cast us up a miracle."

She gathered Gail into the boneless cradle of her curved arms.

Regina took her sunglasses out of her purse and hid her eyes. "Mind your own damned business," she told Mrs. Baden and me.

"It *is* our damned business," I whispered to Mrs. Baden, and she held my arm as we followed Regina down the hall.

Mrs. His-tara threaded her way through a cordon of other Hisereans who must have been flown in for the occasion. I couldn't see the children, but I could hear them.

"Him cold!" said Gail. "Him scared!"

"He's scared of you," Regina said. "We're sorry, Gail. Tell him we're sorry. We didn't understand."

Gail laughed. A loud and healthy laugh.

"Gail sorry," she said. "Me thought you was to eat."

There was a small sound. I thought it was from Hi-nin and I held Mrs. Baden's hand as though it were my only link to a sane world.

"Dat a joke," Gail said. "Hi-nin 'posed to laugh!"

Then there was a silence and Regina started to say

something but Mrs. His-tara whispered, "Please! It is a thought between the children."

Then there was a small, quiet laugh from Hi-nin. "In truth," he said with that oh, so familiar lisp, "it is funny."

"Me don't do it again," Gail said, solemn now.

When I got home it was so late that the stars were sliding down the sky and I just knew Clay wouldn't have thought to turn the parking lights on. But he had.

Furthermore, he was still up.

"Were you worried?" I asked delightedly.

"No. Regina called a couple of hours ago."

"*Regina?*"

"She said she was concerned about the expression on your face."

Clay handed me a present, all wrapped in gold stickum with an electronic butterfly bouncing airily around on it.

I peeled the paper off carefully, to save it for Billy, and set the butterfly on the sticky side.

Inside the box was a gorgeous blue fluffy affair of no apparent utility.

"Oh, *Clay*!" I gasped. "I can't wear anything like *this*!" I slipped out of my paper clothes and the gown slithered around me.

Hastily, I pulled the pins out of my hair, brushed it back and smeared on some lipstick.

"I look silly," I said. "I'm all the wrong type." My little crayola note was still stuck in the mirror. Phooey to me. "You're laughing at me."

"I'm not. You don't really look respectable at all, Verne."

I ran into the dining area. "Regina told you about the boudoir slip!"

I heard Clay stumble over a chair in the dark.

"Obscenity!" he said. "All right, she did. So what? I think you look like a call girl."

I ran into the living room and hid behind the sofa. "Do you really, truly think so?"

"Absolutely!" Another chair clattered and Clay toed the living room lights. "Ah!" he said. "I've got you cornered. You look like a chorus girl. You look like an easy pickup. You look like a dirty little—"

"Stop," I cried, "while you're still winning!"

AND A TOOTH

They went a little further than maybe they had to.

It was all a result of the accident.

I wasn't *in* the accident, you understand. Everyone thinks that was it, but it wasn't. All this was . . . well, the damage from within. Emotionally shattering, I guess.

The only thing odd you'll notice about me is the drooping eyelid. The left eyelid. I notice it tends to bother people a little at first. They don't want to look straight at me. Maybe they think I mind. But I don't. It's a little thing and sometimes I think it even makes my dull, old face a little more interesting. You see, I'm really past the age when . . . but I'm not starting very logically.

I am not, perhaps, the most interesting person in the world. Age forty-five, I.Q. 110, five feet four inches tall weighing a hundred and fifty pounds. Widow with no children. (They were all killed in the accident and I'd stayed home to get the bills paid and write a letter or two. If I'd known they were going to get killed I'd have gone, too. It's odd, but I find myself regretting that most of all.)

❋ ❋ ❋ ❋

She's a fool, you know. She's all tied up in the past and she thinks she's real virtuous devoting herself to the memory of my husband and children like that. So they're gone. Too bad. I'm not. There's a thing or two she didn't learn in those 45 years—old, fat thing! I don't like to eat and *I'm* slim. Only I can't get out of here.

O, and my name is Margaret Tilden—Meggie. You'll be wondering why I think a story about me would be interesting. Well, for one thing, the psychiatrist told me I shouldn't just assume I'm dull. (But housewife, age forty-five, doesn't it sound dull?) I haven't been psychoanalyzed, you understand. If I had been, they don't say anything but Uh and Ah, I understand.

It was the experiment, that's what I thought you might find interesting. It was partly chance and circumstance that it happened to me, I guess.

It just happened that when I heard about the accident I went into a coma. I've never had any mental illness before, you understand, but this was a terrible shock. Anyway, I had to be brought to the hospital. And I just happened to drop into the lap of an experimental project they had going on.

I don't even remember the treatment, I was that far gone. What I *do* remember is coming to and feeling—not sad, not shocked, not grieving for my dead. Something much worse. I felt unreal. I had to look at my arms and legs and try to believe it was *me*. And remember the past and feel that it happened to *me*.

Maybe I can't make you understand what this kind of feeling is. As though I were an appliance that had been turned off. And I kept searching around in my mind for the right thought, the right button to press to make me go on again. (Does this sound very silly?)

I knew that what waited for me was hopeless, helpless grief. And you might wonder why I should go seeking that when I could lie in a comfortable bed feeling nothing, nothing at all.

Let me point out that even "comfortable" bed meant nothing to me. Nothing, nothing, nothing. How can I describe the awful nothingness of nothing?

Actually, I'm glad they're dead. There. I said it and why not? I get sick of all the hypocrisy in the world. The only difference between me and everybody else is that I don't mind admitting I'm no plaster saint. And I don't mind admitting that all my life I've felt as though I had a pillow stuffed over my face every time I tried to open my mouth.

It was Her, of course. *Her* mealy mouth could open any time it wanted to. And all that time *she* was happy— or she pretended to be happy. That's all very well, but what about *me?*

Me, me, me!

How does the genie feel when it gets out of the bottle?

Well, I'm not all the way out of the bottle yet. Genies are powerful, you know, but they've got to trick their way out of the bottle. A trick. That's what I need.

Where do I start?

But you see I couldn't find the right thought, the right button to press, and I *wouldn't* be able to because what I had developed was schizophrenia. You'll be thinking I had a split personality. No, that isn't really what schizophrenia means. Dr. Blumenthal (the psychiatrist) explained it to me but I couldn't possibly remember all that. I *do* know I had a serious mental illness and it even brought a change of life, which I guess I was due for anyway. So I had those physical symptoms plus my psychiatric symptoms.

So you can see where I jumped at a chance to have all my problems solved by an operation. And to do something useful for science at the same time—I felt so *useless*. My life was all for Henry and the children and now . . .

Of course they explained the operation wasn't fool-proof and the results couldn't be predicted with any degree of accuracy. I went into it knowing it wasn't quite safe.

And in fact, not quite . . . human.

She's always trying to dramatize herself. I say, a fact's a fact and what does it mean, Human? Like the French say about sex, if it can be done, it's normal. It wasn't done fairly, of course. She got the right eye, which is the best one.

As soon as I heard about the operation I jumped at the chance. I didn't realize the most important part of it would be a side effect. But I saw a chance to become world famous—and it sounds like money to be world famous. Interviews on TV, articles in magazines—and hell, these scientists pull down a big salary. Why not charge them for the privilege of examining me? They do things for money. I do things for the glory of Science. Does that sound fair to you?

That Dr. Blumenthal, he has a greasy face and little rat eyes. He wants the money *and* the glory and he won't let me do a damn thing. He says he isn't ready to publish his results yet and that he doesn't want garish publicity.

His results! What does he think I am, a paramecium?

Actually (this isn't making it very interesting, but I want to tell the truth) the only effect of the operation I can swear to is that my left eyelid droops. For a while I had trouble seeing out of one eye, but to tell the truth my vision seems as good as it always was by now.

Dr. Blumenthal tells me I can control the muscles in my left eyelid, though I cannot have the vision of the eye. Well, I'm not really much concerned about it.

Of course my head was shaved and my hair is still quite short—about two inches long now, but I believe I'll keep it short. I think it looks rather nice this way. There's just a thin scar and I have thick hair.

I'm very glad I had it done. Somehow I feel much freer and *better*. And I'm sure I enjoy all the attention I get from the doctors and everybody.

But Dr. Blumenthal! Such a lovely, kind man and really quite good looking. It's amazing he's remained a bachelor all these years. I don't mean . . . what I mean is, I've heard women always fall in love with their psychiatrist. He's not my *psychiatrist* of course. I mean you'd hardly call this a psychoanalysis. But I think he understands that part, too.

I could have laughed. In fact, I *did* laugh, but then all the laughing I did had to be to myself. The operation, Dr. Blumenthal said, would serve not only the function it was supposed to serve, but it would also, merely by the fact of having the operation, serve to alleviate the strong guilt feelings and the death wish he said I harbored in some part of my mind.

Guilt feelings? What good would it have done anybody if I'd gotten killed, too? And besides, Henry had it coming to him and who can blame me for wishing he was dead.

Over and over.

Once for each child.

If they thought *I* was neurotic they should have seen Henry—the prissy louse. If you can imagine anybody being prissy and lascivious at the same time. Prissy with me and lascivious with other women.

You see, what he did was periodically start a love affair. And it wouldn't work. I mean, he *couldn't*. So he'd come home and prove his manhood by getting *me* pregnant. You see? You see what I went through.

All three times, that was how it happened.

And those were the only three times. Those other women, they at least had the satisfaction of laughing at him. *She* wouldn't even let me do that.

And Dr. Blumenthal says I *subconsciously* wished they were all dead.

Dear Dr. Blumenthal has suggested a lobotomy. On the half of my brain I don't use, of course. He says he doesn't want to keep me in the hospital forever and I'll want to go out and live a normal life.

Does it sound odd to talk about living a normal life with half your brain gone? Well, it would have to me, too. But the brain isn't like an arm or a leg. When a part of the brain is gone, other parts can take over the lost functions and actually people don't come near using all of their brain when they have it (as most people do). And what they did with me was the culmination of a long series of operations starting with monkeys. They didn't just cut my brain in half. They separated out the part of my mind which was causing me trouble and instead of just cutting the connections to it, they connected it up with one of my eyes. This was the part of the operation that was experimental, and that I had to volunteer for. In fact, I had to insist on it. I *wanted* it done, because I could see the scientific value of doing something like this with a human being instead of with just monkeys. I pointed out that it would even be unethical to kill off part of my mind without giving it a *chance* to see if it could function by itself. Why should I have any more right to exist than *it*? But my most telling point was that I was the perfect subject. I have no dependents, I had no previous history of mental disease and in spite of the fact that I was in the grip of an emotional disorder, I think I was perfectly capable intellectually of deciding of my own free will that I wanted to volunteer.

Does it sound like something unethical was done? No, no. There are a number of operations for mental disorder and this was done primarily as a curative measure. Very successful it was, too. Or will be, after the lobotomy. You see, I have these periods of blankness . . .

Yes, I will be glad to have the lobotomy and be out of this stuffy room, though I certainly wouldn't want Dr. Blumenthal to cut his experiment short just for that reason.

I mean, I *do* have his visits to look forward to and it means so much to have a strong man to lean on since I've lost Henry. And I can't help thinking I mean more to him than just another patient. Though of course it's purely Platonic. I'm sure. Even though he did do something unusual. It was when we were discussing what I'll do after my lobotomy. I was saying how hard it was to go back and try to take up my life again, and he reached out and held my hand!

I had what I thought was to be my last check up with the surgeon. Questions, questions, questions. I didn't answer one of them. I expect to get paid, I said, for every question I answer from now on. *That* shut him up, I can tell you.

Then I did something stupid. I threatened to expose the surgeon and Dr. Blumenthal and everybody else. I didn't mean it, of course. But they all act so damn *superior*. I told them I was going to say they tricked me into the operation. Of course I had signed a release. . . . They scare easy, these doctors.

They tossed me in a locked room for "observation."

I wasn't thinking fast enough. I haven't had time. I've gone and showed my hand. I didn't realize soon enough—this is all too new—but my best bet would have been to lie low. Just not to *exist* until I was out of reach of the damn doctors. That Dr. Blumenthal, he uses forceps on your mind.

But they can't any of them read inside of my mind.

And I'm getting an idea or two.

While I practice holding up my right eyelid. I've got to *learn* to do it, because She's got the involuntary control of it.

So today he came in while I was practicing. When I heard the door click I quick dropped my *left* eyelid— which meant I couldn't see too well, but all I had to do was sit there and talk. And act sweet.

That's not hard to do. I can always tell from his questions what he wants me to answer. You learn that from having a husband. All those years of being a housewife— that was experience, of a kind. Henry took advantage of her. She *knew* about those other women. But she wouldn't admit, even to herself, that she knew.

I don't mind admitting it. And I don't mind admitting that the male species owes me a lot of revenge. I hate them all. And Him. That Doctor Blumenthal.

Not her, though. I know how she'd think and act.

So that's how I acted, only I added a little of my own. I reached out and took his hand, for comfort. I know this surprised him, but it didn't displease him. I know these men! You see, I'm (we're) his creation and he's proud of us on his own behalf. But human emotions don't separate themselves out so easily, and after all I'm a woman and he's a man and some of it spills over.

He talked a lot to me about *her*, meaning me, really, only he didn't know it. He's so easily fooled! He's wondering if I'm disturbed by living in the same skull with her. And he thinks she's (I'm) unbalanced!

Normal, he says. She's normal and I'm not. As if he's the one who decides what's normal and what's not.

So he talks calmly of murdering me.

But of course it would be unbalanced of me to think of murdering *him*.

Now is that fair?

✳ ✳ ✳ ✳

The lobotomy is set for Friday and I must say, Dr. Blumenthal was as usual right. It is necessary that it be done, and be done soon. The periods of blankness are getting longer and longer and I always wake up to find myself so *tired*. What could I be doing when I'm not there to see?

And this depression I've been having. It's partly the onset of grief, now that I have my emotions back. At first I was so glad to feel *real* again that I was glad just to be able to cry. But now I guess the reaction is setting in and I'm beginning to think of the long, grey years ahead with no one for me to care for.

If I could only be of use to somebody!

It's the most exhilarating feeling! I even dance up and down the room when no one is here. Everything I do seems to succeed. O, that operation was a lucky thing.

It's the first time in my life I've ever felt really free, really happy, able to do exactly what I want to do.

And O, boy, do I have plans!

Plans, plans, plans.

First, I found I could control that drooping eyelid. Then I found I could fool Dr. Blumenthal into thinking I was *her*. Then—and this was the most important part of all—I found I could take control whenever I wanted to.

She has the strongest half, but she doesn't use her power so it doesn't do her any good. She forces herself to be self-effacing. Uses her strength to overcome herself, if you can imagine it. And *I'm* supposed to be the one with a psychosis!

I've asked Dr. Blumenthal to do me a favor. I want to go for a nice ride up through Blue Mountain and back one afternoon before the lobotomy. Since that's only two days, and they'll be doing things to me Thursday afternoon, I guess it'll be tomorrow.

It was the eyelid.

I didn't like it, I tell you.

No, of course that didn't have anything to do with what I did. As a psychiatrist, I don't have likes and dislikes.

Now is not the time to explain all that. I'm upset, naturally. You'll just want to know what happened. That won't be easy to tell without going into the background of the patient.

No, of course I don't ordinarily go picnicking on Blue Mountain with one of my mental patients. The one I took was *not* a mental patient. She was perfectly normal. A charming woman with a very strong ego.

The eyelid? You're suggesting that I threw her against the rock because I was annoyed at her drooping eyelid? No, no. Legally, no, though subconsciously. . . . Legally, I was defending myself. It was self-defense.

I *did* call for help. But meanwhile I had to do something to keep from falling off the mountain. I'd like to see *you* gauge your shove when you're about to fall off a hundred foot drop and you have half a second to make plans in.

And there's an insane eye staring at you. The wrong eye.

You don't understand the strength of the insane. The fact that she's smaller than me has little to do with the situation. In the first place she caught me completely unawares. I didn't even know we were near a drop. There were a group of rocks in the way of the view. And in the second place, her strength was operating at full capacity.

Please. As her physician I insist on riding in the ambulance. I really see no need for me to have to defend myself, but if you must question me, at least don't take me away from my patient.

No, I won't be doing the medical treatment. I imagine it's a concussion but there is no way to know how serious it is until we get to the hospital. I want to be with her when she regains consciousness.

There would be no cause for alarm.

You see, as I pushed her back, to prevent myself being thrown over the edge of the cliff, her reactions when falling against the rock were involuntary. And since the desirable half of her personality is basically the stronger, that's the part which would have taken over and involuntarily protected itself by injuring the less desirable half of her mind. This may sound abstruse to you, but I assure you it's psychologically sound.

Indeed, this whole thing may turn out to be fortunate and certainly it will be interesting in the extreme to see . . .

No, of course I do not think of my patients as guinea pigs. I mean fortunate for the *patient*. You can't possibly understand.

Yes, I know I have spoken of her as both sane and insane. Let me ask you to believe that it is an utterly unique situation. Not what you probably think of as a "split personality." You will notice, if she regains consciousness, that it will be the right eye that opens, because that is her dominant side. The other half of the brain is not Meggie. It is not sane. It is . . . it is to be put out of operation by surgery that has already been scheduled. That's why I say it may turn out to be for the best that . . .

You may question her, but I warn you that she will remember nothing of what has happened. If you insist, you can remain with me to see that I do not attempt to intimidate her—this is ridiculous—and when I (of if you prefer, the attending physician at the hospital) feel it is perfectly safe, you are welcome to question her alone.

I have not the least hesitation. She is perfectly sane, her answers will be perfectly honest.

There!

O, no, Meggie, you mustn't . . .

Yes, I know she talks reasonably, but it isn't *her*. Look, she's got both eyes open. You certainly can't believe an insane person.

I *know* I said she was sane. But see, she's got both eyes open and she can't see out of the right one. It's her word against mine and surely you can't . . . it'll be easy to make tests on her vision.

But that has everything to do with it, which eye she can see out of. I've got my notes to prove it. I can review the whole case . . .

Meggie, you signed a release. There's no ethical question . . . no, you were never kept prisoner. I really . . . see, she's lapsed into unconsciousness again.

And look, that one staring, blind eye. It's dead. You see what's happened. Surely you see. She killed it. She killed my Meggie and now she's left alive. It wasn't the blow of being pushed against the rock. All that did was stun her so she could . . .

Can't you see it? That one dead eye?

I'm not doing anything to her. I'm just closing it. It's dead.

Get your hands off me! All right, I'll leave it alone. I don't know how you can stand to look at it.

What? No, Meggie. You're not going to get away with it. I know you can talk in a reasonable fashion. So can most schizophrenics.

But you're mad. You're stark, simply mad and I know it.

No, there can be no panel of psychiatrists. My results are unique and dependent on a comparison of the dead Meggie . . . now the tests would be invalid.

Of course as a psychiatrist I don't make moral judgments. But this is different.

No, indeed you won't give me a sedative, *dear* Dr. Blumenthal. This is healthy, wholesome laughter and I've been collecting it for twenty years.

Don't you understand what happened? And you a psychiatrist! Who do you think felt guilty? Who had a death wish? Who was glad, instinctively, to be a martyr?

O, you *fool*.

You were going to prove your manhood by creating a new Margaret Tilden, weren't you? And you didn't know I was tired of being a testing ground? You're really no better than Henry.

O, you couldn't know, how good my laughter is.

Because this time *I* win. I'm out of the bottle and I'll

tell you something else. I'm just beginning to see out of the right eye. Just a feeling of light, so far. See, I close my left eye and I still see light, like a sensitive spot.

See, she's unconscious again. You've got to believe me . . . maybe she'll die.

Yes, I see it moving. But it's wide open. Maybe the other half of her mind isn't completely . . . yes, it's looking at me, but I can't make out what expression.

Meggie! Hang on. I'm here.

Look, she's beginning to smile. Thank God! If only she can emerge, for a moment.

Meggie, can you try to tell these men . . . tell them what we were trying to do. Tell them.

Look, it's crying, that one eye. She *couldn't* think I deliberately pushed her against . . . Meggie, just relax then, and we'll talk later. It's all a misunderstanding . . .

It's gone. The expression. The smile. Meggie!

That eye, staring so! Can't you see? Can't you!

No. I don't suppose you can.

The Following is an excerpt from:

A RISING THUNDER

A NEW HONOR HARRINGTON NOVEL

DAVID WEBER

Available from Baen Books
March 2012
Hard Cover

Chapter One

"Get your goddamned ships the hell out of *my* space!"

The burly, dark-haired man on Commander Pang Yau-pau's com was red-faced and snarling, and Pang took a firm a grip on his own temper.

"I'm afraid that's not possible, Commodore Chalker," he replied as courteously as the circumstances permitted. "My orders are to protect Manticoran vessels passing through this terminus on their way home to Manticoran space."

"I don't give a *damn* about your 'orders,' Commander!" Commodore Jeremy Chalker spat back. His six destroyers were 2.4 million kilometers—eight light-seconds—from Pang's cruiser, and one might have thought it would be difficult to maintain a properly infuriated conversation over such a distance, especially with the delays light-speed transmissions built into its exchanges. Chalker seemed able to manage it quite handily, however. "You're in violation of my star system's sovereignty, you've evicted Solarian Astro Control personnel from their duty stations, and I want your ass *gone!*"

"Sir, it's not my intention to violate anyone's sovereignty," Pang replied, choosing to let the rather thornier question of the Solly traffic controllers lie. "My sole interest at this time is the protection of the Star Empire's merchant vessels."

Sixteen more seconds ticked past, and then—

"Shut your mouth, return control of this terminus to the personnel whose control stations you've illegally seized, and turn your ass around *now*, or I will by *God* open fire on the next fucking Manty freighter I see!"

Pang Yau-pau's normally mild brown eyes hardened, and he inhaled deeply.

"Skipper," a quiet voice said.

The single word couldn't have been more respectful, yet it was edged with warning, and Pang hit the mute button and glanced at the smaller screen deployed from the base of his command chair. Lieutenant Commander Myra Sadowski, his executive officer looked back at him from it.

"I know he's a pain in the ass," she continued in that same quiet voice, "but we're supposed to do this without making any more waves than we have to. If you hand this guy his head the way you want to—the way he *deserves*, for that matter—I think it would probably come under the heading of at least a ripple or two."

Myra, Pang reflected, had a point. There was, however, a time and a place for everything. For that matter, the Admiralty hadn't sent Pang and HMS *Onyx* to the Nolan

Terminus to let someone like Jeremy Chalker make that sort of threat.

No, they didn't, another corner of the commander's brain told him. *At the same time, I don't suppose it's too hard to understand why he's so pissed off. Not that it makes me like him any better.*

At the moment, *Onyx,* her sister ship *Smilodon,* the *Roland*-class destroyer *Tornado* and the much older destroyer *Othello* were over six hundred and fifty light-years from the Manticore Binary System and barely *two* hundred light-years from the Sol System. It was not a particularly huge force to have wandering around so deep in increasingly hostile territory, as Pang was only too well aware. In fact, Nolan was a protectorate system of the Solarian League, and Chalker was an SLN officer, the senior Frontier Fleet officer present. He looked old for his rank, which suggested a certain lack of familial connections within the SLN, although he must have at least some influence to have ended up with the Nolan command. The system's proximity to the Nolan Terminus of the Nolan-Katharina Hyper Bridge was what had brought it to the Office of Frontier Security's attention a hundred-odd T-years ago, and the local OFS and Frontier Fleet officers had been raking off a comfortable percentage of the terminus user fees ever since. Judging from the reaction of the SLN captain who'd commanded the OFS-installed terminus traffic control staff when Pang ordered him to turn his control stations over to Manticoran personnel, another chunk of those fees had probably been finding its way into his pockets, as well. Precious little of that revenue had ended up in Nolan itself, at any rate.

Well, at least this time we can be pretty confident we're not hurting some innocent third-party star system's revenue stream, he thought. *And it's not like we're planning to* keep *the terminus…Öjust now, anyway. We'll give it back to them when I'm sure we've gotten all our ships safely through it. And if someone like Chalker takes one in the bank account in the meantime, I'm sure I'll be able to live with my regret somehow.*

Of course, Pang never doubted that the rest of the Solarian League Navy was going to be just as infuriated as Chalker by Manticore's "arrogance" in seizing control of Solarian-claimed termini even temporarily. What was going to happen when Lacoö^n Two kicked in hardly bore thinking upon, although anyone who really thought *not* executing Lacoö^n Two was going to make one bit of difference to the Sollies was probably smoking things he shouldn't.

"I'm not the one making the waves," he told Sadowski out loud, then glanced across *Onyx*'s command deck at Lieutenant Commander Jack Frazier, his tactical officer.

"I hope we're not going to have any business for *you*, Guns," he said. "If we do, I want to hold the damage to a minimum."

"You're thinking in terms of something more like what Admiral Gold Peak did at New Tuscany than what she did at Spindle, Sir?"

"Exactly." Pang smiled thinly. "Do you have Chalker's flagship IDed?"

"Yes, Sir." Frazier nodded with an answering smile. "I do. By the strangest coincidence, I've just this minute discovered that I've got her IDed, dialed in, and locked up, as a matter of fact."

"Good."

Pang paused a moment longer, taking an additional few seconds to make sure he had his own temper under control, then un-muted his audio pickup.

"Commodore Chalker," he said in a hard, flat voice quite different from the courteous one he'd employed so far, "allow me to point out two things to you. First, this terminus is, in fact, not in Nolan's territorial space. Unless my astrogation is badly off, it's five light-hours from Nolan, which puts it just a bit outside the twelve-minute limit. The Solarian League's claim to its possession rests solely on the SLN's supposed power to control the space about it. And, second, in regard to that supposed power, I respectfully suggest you consider the actual balance of force which obtains at this moment. Based on that balance, I submit that it would be unwise to issue such threats against Manticoran shipping...Öand even less wise to carry them out."

"Well piss on you, *Commander!* You and the rest of your 'Star Empire' may think you can throw your weight around any way you like, but there's a cold dawn coming, and it's going to get here sooner than you think!"

"I have my orders, Commodore," Pang responded in that same flat voice, "and I don't intend to debate the question of who's responsible for the current state of tension between the Star Empire and the Solarian League. I fully intend to return control of this terminus to the League—and, obviously, to restore your personnel to their stations—as soon as I've satisfied myself, as my orders require, that all Manticoran merchant vessels in this vicinity have been given the opportunity to return to Manticoran space through it. I regret"—neither his tone nor his expression was, in fact, particularly regretful— "any inconvenience this may cause for you or any other Solarian personnel or citizens. I *do*, however, intend to carry out *all* of my orders, and one of those orders is to use whatever level of force is necessary to protect Manticoran merchant shipping anywhere. And 'anywhere,' Commodore Chalker, includes Solarian space. So if you intend to fire on Manticoran freighters, why don't you just start with the ones right here under my protection? Go ahead—be my guest. But before you do, Admiral, I suggest you recall the Royal Navy's position where the protection of merchant shipping is concerned."

He sat waiting, watching his com for the sixteen seconds his words took to reach Chalker and for the signal to come back. Precisely on schedule, Chalker's face turned even darker.

"And what the fuck does *that* mean?" the Solarian snarled.

"It means my tactical officer has your flagship identified," Pang said, and his smile was a razor.

For another sixteen seconds, Chalker glared out of Pang's display. Then, abruptly, his facial muscles went absolutely rigid, as if some magic wand had turned his face to stone. He stayed that way for several seconds, then shook himself.

"Are you *threatening* me?" he demanded incredulously.

"Yes," Pang said simply. "I am."

Chalker stared at him, and Pang wondered what else the other man could have expected to happen.

"You think you can come waltzing into Solarian space and *threaten* Solarian citizens? Tell a *Solarian* warship you'll *open fire* on it?" Chalker said sixteen seconds later.

"It's not my wish to threaten anyone, Admiral. It is my intention to carry out my orders and to deal with any threat to the merchant shipping for which I'm responsible, and you've just announced your intention to fire on unarmed merchant vessels. Should you do so, I will fire on *you*, and I suggest you recall what happened to Admiral Byng at New Tuscany. If you actually intend to attack after doing that, go ahead and let's get it over with. Otherwise, Sir, I have rather more important matters which require my attention. Good day."

He punched the stud that cut the connection and sat back in his command chair, wondering if Chalker was furious enough—or stupid enough—to accept his challenge. If the Solly officer did anything of the sort, it would be the last mistake he ever made. There was no question about that in Pang's mind, although he was a bit less certain about the potential consequences for the future career of one Pang Yau-pau.

Better to be hung for a hexapuma than a housecat, he thought. *And it's not like I could've found some kind of magic formula to keep the jerk happy, no matter what I did! At least this way if he's stupid enough to pull the trigger, it won't be because he didn't know exactly how I'd respond.*

He watched his tactical repeater, waiting to see what Chalker would do. *Onyx* and *Smilodon* were both

Saganami-Cs, armed with Mark 16 multidrive missiles and mounting eight grasers in each broadside. At the moment, SLNS *Lancelot*, Chalker's antiquated *Rampart*-class destroyer flagship and her consorts were far outside the effective range of their own pathetic energy armament, and the situation was almost worse when it came to missiles. The Sollies *were* within their missiles' powered engagement range of Pang's command, but *Lancelot* was barely twenty percent *Onyx*'s size, with proportionately weaker sidewalls and a broadside of only five lasers and a matching number of missile tubes. If Chalker was foolish enough to carry out his threat, he could undoubtedly kill any merchant ship he fired upon. *Lancelot*'s chance of getting a laser head through *Onyx*'s antimissile defenses, on the other hand, much less burning through the cruiser's sidewalls, ranged from precious little to non-existent.

Good thing Chalker wasn't on station when we arrived, though, I suppose, Pang thought. *God knows what he'd've done if he'd been inside energy range when we transited the terminus! And when you come right down to it, it's a good thing he's such a loudmouthed idiot, too. It was only a matter of time until one of the incoming Solly merchies diverted to Nolan to let someone know what was going on out here. If the jackass had been willing to keep his mouth shut until he managed to get into energy range, this situation could've turned even stickier. In fact, it could have gone straight to hell in a handbasket if someone stupid enough to pull the trigger had managed to get that close before he did it.*

Without a clear demonstration of hostile intent, it

would have been extraordinarily difficult for Pang to justify actually opening fire on units of the SLN. He would have had little choice—legally, at least—but to allow Chalker to approach all the way to the terminus threshold, and that could have turned really nasty. Fortunately, Chalker had been unable to keep his mouth shut, and his open threat to fire on Manticoran merchant ships constituted plenty of justification for Pang to give him the Josef Byng treatment if he kept on closing.

Thank you, Commodore Chalker, he thought sardonically.

As a matter of fact, although Pang Yau-pau wasn't prepared to admit it to anyone, even Sadowski, he was only too aware of his own crushing responsibilities and the sheer vastness of the Solarian League. Nor was he going to admit how welcome he'd actually found Chalker's bellicosity under the circumstances. Any officer who commanded a Queen's starship knew sooner or later he was going to find himself out on a limb somewhere where he'd have to put his own judgment on the line, yet at this particular moment Commander Pang and his small command had crawled out to the end of a very, very long limb, indeed.

They were a mere three wormhole transits away from the Manticore Binary System, but it certainly didn't *feel* that way. The Dionigi System was only ninety-six light years from Manticore, but it was connected to the Katharina System, over seven hundred and thirty light-years away, by the Dionigi-Katharina Hyper Bridge. And the Nolan-Katharina Bridge, in turn, was one of the longest ever surveyed, at nine hundred and fifteen light-years. Even allowing for the normal hyper-space leg between Manticore and Dionigi, he could be home in less than two weeks, instead of the eighty days or so it would have taken his warships to get there on a direct voyage.

It would have taken a ship with a commercial-grade hyper generator and particle screening better than *seven months* to make the same trip through hyper, however, as opposed to only thirty days via Dionigi, which rather graphically demonstrated the time savings the wormhole networks made possible for interstellar commerce. And that, in turn, explained the sheer economic value of that same network . . . and Manticore's commanding position within it.

Which explains why the Sollies back in Old Chicago are going to be at least as pissed off as Chalker, Pang reflected grimly. *They've been mad enough for years about the size of our merchant marine, the way we dominate their carrying trade. Now they're about to find out just how bad it really is. Once we get all of our shipping out of Solly space, they're really going to be hurting, and we'll have done it by simply calling our own freighters home, without using a single commerce-raider or privateer. But when Lacoö^n Two activates and we start closing down as much as we can of the entire network, it's going to get even worse. They don't begin to have the hulls to take up the slack even if all the termini stayed open; with the termini closed, with every ton of cargo having to spend four or five times as long in transit, to boot . . .*

On the face of it, it was ridiculous, and Pang would be surprised if as much as five percent of the total Solarian population had a clue—yet—about just how vulnerable the League really was or how bad it was actually going to get. Something the size of the Solarian League's internal economy? With literally hundreds of star systems, system populations running into the tens of billions, and the mightiest industrial capacity in the history of mankind? That sort of Titan couldn't possibly be brought to its knees by a "Star Empire" which consisted of no more than a couple of dozen inhabited planets!

But it could, if its pigmy opponent happened to control the bulk of the shipping which carried that economy's lifeblood. And especially if the pigmy in question was also in a position to shut down its arterial system, force its remaining shipping to rely solely on capillary action to keep itself fed. Even if Solarian shipyards got themselves fully mobilized and built enough ships to replace every single Manticoran hull pulled out of the League's trade, it *still* wouldn't be enough to maintain the shipping routes without the termini.

Of course, it's not going to do our *economy any favors, either*, Pang told himself. *Not an insignificant point, especially after the Yawata Strike*.

He wondered if the Star Empire's continued possession of the termini would be a big enough economic crowbar to pry a few Solarian star systems free of the League's control. If the bait of access was trolled in front of system economies crippled or severely damaged by the termination of cargo service, would those systems switch allegiance—openly or unofficially—to Manticore instead of the League? He could think of quite a few in the Verge who'd do it in a second if they thought they could get away with it. For that matter, he could think of at least a handful of Shell systems that would probably jump at the chance.

Well, I guess time will tell on that one. And there's another good reason for us to make sure we're *the ones who control the hyper bridges, isn't there? As long as we do, no one can launch naval strikes through them at us . . . and we* can *launch naval strikes through them at the League.*

Attacking well defended wormhole termini along the bridges between them was a losing proposition, but the tactical flexibility the network as a whole would confer upon light, fast Manticoran commerce-raiders would be devastating. For all intents and purposes, the Star Empire, for all its physical distance from the Sol System and the League's other core systems, would actually be inside the Sollies' communications loop. The League's limited domestic merchant marine would find itself under attack almost everywhere, whereas the Manticoran merchant marine would continue to travel via the termini, completely immune to attack between the star systems they linked.

No wonder Chalker was so livid. He might be so stupid he couldn't visualize the next step, couldn't see Lacoön Two coming, but he obviously did grasp the Manticoran mobility advantage which had brought Pang's squadron to Nolan. He might not have reasoned it out yet. Solarian arrogance might have blinded him to the possibility that Manticore might actually conduct *offensive* operations against the omnipotent League instead of huddling defensively in a frightened corner somewhere. But the mere presence of Pang's ships this deep into the Solarian space would have been enough to push his blood pressure dangerously high, and Pang suspected that deep down inside, whether Chalker consciously realized it or not, the Solarian officer probably *was* aware of the implications of Manticoran mobility.

He glanced at the date-time display in the corner of the master plot. Over ten minutes since he'd bidden Chalker good day, he noticed. If the Solly had been infuriated—and stupid—enough to do anything hasty, he'd probably have already done it. The fact that he hadn't (yet) didn't mean stupidity and arrogance wouldn't eventually over-power common sense and self-preservation, but it seemed unlikely.

"Unlikely" wasn't exactly the same as "no way in hell," Pang reminded himself. All the same, it was time to let his people get a little rest . . . and it probably wouldn't hurt for him to display his own imperturbability, either. Confidence started at the top, after all, and he looked back down at his link to AuxCon.

"I think Commodore Chalker may have seen the error of his ways, Myra," he told Lieutenant Commander Sadowski. "We'll stand the squadron down to Readiness Two."

"Aye, aye, Sir," she acknowledged.

Readiness State Two, also known as "General Quarters," was one step short of Battle Stations. Engineering and life-support systems would be fully manned, as would CIC, although Auxiliary Control would be reduced to a skeleton watch. The ship would maintain a full passive sensor watch, augmented by the remote

FTL platforms they'd deployed as soon as they arrived, and the tactical department would be fully manned. Passive defenses would be active and enabled under computer control; electronic warfare systems and active sensors would be manned and available, although not emitting; and *Onyx*'s offensive weapons would be partially manned by their on-mount crews. Readiness Two was intended to be maintained for lengthy periods of time, so it included provision for rotating personnel in order to maintain sufficient crew at their duty stations while allowing the members of the ship's company to rest in turn. Which still wouldn't prevent it from exhausting Pang's people if they had to keep it up indefinitely.

"Let Percy take AuxCon while you head back over to the Bridge to relieve me," he continued to Sadowski. Lieutenant the Honorable Percival Quentin-Massengale, *Onyx*'s assistant tactical officer, was the senior of Sadowski's officers in Auxiliary Control. "We'll pull *Smilodon* and the tin-cans back and let *Onyx* take point for the first twelve hours, or until our friend Chalker decides to take himself elsewhere. After that, *Smilodon* can have the duty for the next twelve hours. We'll let the cruisers swap off while the destroyers watch our backs."

And while we keep Othello *out of harm's way*, he added silently to himself. Unlike her more youthful consort, *Tornado*, the elderly destroyer *wasn't* armed with Mark 16s, and Pang had already decided to keep her as far to the rear as he could.

"Run a continually updated firing solution on him, Guns," the commander said out loud to Lieutenant Commander Frazier. "And have CIC keep a close eye on his emissions. Any sign of active targeting systems, and I want to hear about it."

"Aye, aye, Skipper."

Jack Frazier was normally a cheerful sort, fond of practical jokes and pranks, but no trace of his usual humor colored his response.

"Good." Pang nodded curtly, then looked back down at Sadowski. "You heard, Myra?"

"Yes, Sir."

"Well, I figure you already know this, but to make it official, if it should happen that Chalker is stupid enough to actually fire on us or one of the merchies, you're authorized to return fire immediately. And if that happens, I want him taken completely out. Clear?"

"I acknowledge your authorization to return fire if we're fired upon, Sir," Sadowski said a bit more formally, and Pang nodded again, then stood and looked back to Frazier.

"You have the deck until the XO gets here, Guns, and the same authorization applies to you," he said. "I'll be in my day cabin catching up on my paperwork."

PRAISE FOR
LOIS McMASTER BUJOLD

What the critics say:

The Warrior's Apprentice: "Now here's a fun romp through the spaceways—not so much a space opera as space ballet... It has all the 'right stuff.' A lot of thought and thoughtfulness stand behind the all-too-human characters. Enjoy this one, and look forward to the next."   —Dean Lambe, *SF Reviews*

"The pace is breathless, the characterization thoughtful and emotionally powerful, and the author's narrative technique and command of language compelling. Highly recommended." —*Booklist*

Brothers in Arms: "...she gives it a genuine depth of character, while reveling in the wild turnings of her tale... Bujold is as audacious as her favorite hero, and as brilliantly (if sneakily) successful."   —*Locus*

"Miles Vorkosigan is such a great character that I'll read anything Lois wants to write about him... a book to re-read on cold rainy days."   —Robert Coulson, *Comics Buyers Guide*

Borders of Infinity: "Bujold's series hero Miles Vokosigan may be a lord by birth and an admiral by rank, but a bone disease that has left him hobbled and in frequent pain has sensitized him to the suffering of outcasts in her very hierarchical era.... Playing off of Miles's reserve and cleverness, Bujold draws outrageous and outlandish foils to color her high-minded adventures."   —*Publishers Weekly*

Falling Free: "In *Falling Free* Lois McMaster Bujold has written her fourth straight superb novel.... How to break down a talent like Bujold's into analyzable components? Best not to try. Best to say: 'Read, or you will be missing something extraordinary.'"
          —Roland Green, *Chicago Sun-Times*

The Vor Game: "The chronicles of Miles Vokosigan are far too witty to be literary junk food, but they rouse the kind of craving that makes popcorn magically vanish during a double feature."   —Faren Miller, *Locus*

MORE PRAISE FOR
LOIS McMASTER BUJOLD

What the readers say:

"My copy of *Shards of Honor* is falling apart I've reread it so often…. I'll read whatever you write. You've certainly proved yourself a grand storyteller.
—Lisa Kolbe, Colorado Springs, CO

"I experience the stories of Miles Vorkosigan as almost viscerally uplifting… But certainly, even the weightiest theme would have less impact than a cinder on snow were it not for a rousing good story, and good story-telling with it. This is the second thing I want to thank you for… I suppose if you boiled down all I've said to its simplest expression, it would be that I immensely enjoy and admire your work. I submit that, as literature, your work raises the overall level of the science fiction genre, and spiritually, you work cannot avoid positively influencing all who read it."
—Glen Stonebreaker, Gaithersburg, MD

"'The Mountains of Mourning' [in *Borders of Infinity*] was one of the best-crafted, and simply best, works I'd ever read. When I finished it, I immediately turned back to the beginning and read it again, and I can't remember the last time I did that."
—Betsy Bizot, Lisle, IL

"I can only hope that you will continue to write, so that I can continue to read (and of course buy) your books, for they make me laugh and cry and think … rare indeed."
—Steven Knott, Major, USAF

What do you say?

Cordelia's Honor
pb • 0-671-57828-6 • $7.99
Contains *Shards of Honor* and Hugo-award winner *Barrayar* in one volume.

Young Miles
trade pb • 0-671-87782-8 • $17.00
pb • 0-7434-3616-4 • $7.99
Contains *The Warrior's Apprentice*, Hugo-award winner *The Vor Game*, and Hugo-award winner "The Mountains of Mourning" in one volume.

Cetaganda
0-671-87744-5 • $7.99

Miles, Mystery and Mayhem
pb • 0-7434-3618-0 • $7.99
Contains *Cetaganda*, *Ethan of Athos* and "Labyrinth" in one volume.

Brothers in Arms
pb • 1-4165-5544-7 • $7.99

Miles Errant
trade pb • 0-7434-3558-3 • $15.00
Contains "The Borders of Infinity," *Brothers in Arms* and *Mirror Dance* in one volume.

Mirror Dance
pb • 0-671-87646-5 • $7.99

Memory
pb • 0-671-87845-X • $7.99

Miles in Love
hc • 1-4165-5522-6 • $19.00
trade pb • 1-4165-5547-1 • $14.00
Contains *Komarr, A Civil Campaign* and "A Winterfair Gift" in one volume.

Komarr
hc • 0-671-87877-8 • $22.00
pb • 0-671-57808-1 • $7.99

A Civil Campaign
hc • 0-671-57827-8 • $24.00
pb • 0-671-57885-5 • $7.99

Miles, Mutants & Microbes
hc • 1-4165-2141-0 • $18.00
pb • 1-4165-5600-1 • $7.99
Contains *Falling Free* "Labyrinth", and *Diplomatic Immunity* in one volume.

Diplomatic Immunity
hc • 0-7434-3533-8 • $25.00
pb • 0-7434-3612-1 • $7.99

Cryoburn
hc • 978-1-4391-3394-1 • $25.00

Falling Free
pb • 1-4165-5546-3 • $7.99

Mission of Honor　　　hc • 978-1-4391-3361-3 • $27.00
　　　　　　　　　　　　　pb • 978-1-4391-3451-1 • $7.99

The unstoppable juggernaut of the mighty Solarian League is on a collision course with Manticore, and billions of casualties may be just over the horizon. But Manticore's enemies may not have thought of everything—if everything Honor Harrington loves is going down to destruction, it won't be going alone.

HONORVERSE VOLUMES:

Crown of Slaves (with Eric Flint)　　pb • 0-7434-9899-2 • $7.99
Torch of Freedom (with Eric Flint)　hc • 1-4391-3305-0 • $26.00
　　　　　　　　　　　　　　　　　　pb • 978-1-4391-3408-5 • $8.99

Sent on a mission to keep Erewhon from breaking with Manticore, the Star Kingdom's most able agent and the Queen's niece may not even be able to escape with their lives....

The Shadow of Saganami　　hc • 0-7434-8852-0 • $26.00
　　　　　　　　　　　　　　　pb • 1-4165-0929-1 • $7.99
Storm from the Shadows　　hc • 1-4165-9147-8 • $27.00
　　　　　　　　　　　　　　　pb • 1-4391-3354-9 • $8.99

A new generation of officers, trained by Honor Harrington, are ready to hit the front lines as war erupts again.

A Beautiful Friendship　　hc • 978-1-4516-3747-2 • $18.99
"A stellar introduction to a new YA science-fiction series."
—*Booklist* starred review

ANTHOLOGIES EDITED BY DAVID WEBER:

More Than Honor　　　　　pb • 0-671-87857-3 • $7.99
Worlds of Honor　　　　　　pb • 0-671-57855-3 • $7.99
Changer of Worlds　　　　　pb • 0-7434-3520-6 • $7.99
The Service of the Sword　　pb • 0-7434-8836-9 • $7.99
In Fire Forged　　　　　　　hc • 978-1-4391-3414-6 • $26.00